A SCI-FI GAMER FRIENDS-TO-LOVERS MÉNAGE ROMANCE

BINDING
THEIR ELEMENTALIST

BOOK FOUR
LOOKING FOR GROUP

SHANNON PEMRICK

Summoning Their Elementalist
Looking For Group | Book Four

Copyright © 2022 Shannon Pemrick
www.shannonpemrick.com

Cover Design by Covers by Combs
Editing by Sandra Nguyen

ISBN 978-1-950128-21-1 (paperback)
ISBN 978-1-950128-20-4 (hardcover)
ISBN 978-1-950128-22-8 (ebook)

To Joe

For always inspiring and encouraging me and being my player
number two.

BOOKS BY SHANNON PEMRICK

LOOKING FOR GROUP

Spellbinding His Ranger
Protecting His Priestess
Summoning Their Elementalist
Binding Their Elementalist

EXPERIMENTAL HEART

Destiny
Pieces
Secrets
Exposed
Surrendered
Reborn

ORACLE'S PATH

Prophecy of Convergence

Prophecy Tested
Prophecy Chosen

CHAPTER 1

The loud chatter and excitement of the usual gaming convention fair would have surrounded Shira, had everything not stopped. Not even her heart seemed to beat as she stared at the late-twenties man with a god-awful spray-on tan, blue eyes, and short bleached hair standing before her.

She could hardly believe what she was seeing, but no amount of denial changed it. "Jeremy?"

Jeremy, the ex who dumped her. Jeremy, the man who'd completely shattered her. Jeremy, her ex-fiancé who left her with cruel cutting words as she lay in a hospital bed fighting for her life.

A crooked grin curved up the side of his face. "Hey, Shira. Didn't ever expect to see you here."

Shira took a small breath and looked around, using it as a moment to keep herself calm. She could handle this. She wasn't the same broken woman he'd abandoned. Shira wouldn't say she wasn't broken at all still, but with

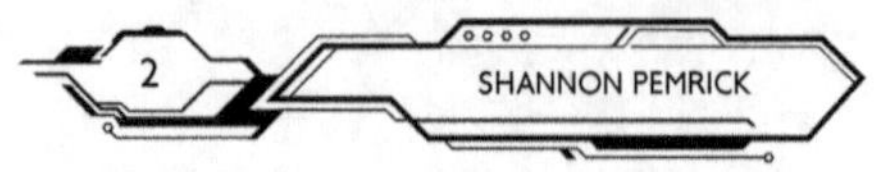

all the work she'd done, she wasn't the same woman from three months ago, let alone nearly six years ago.

Her black German shepherd and service dog, Snake, pressed against Shira's leg, sensing her emotional turmoil. But that was the extent of his help for now, as if he knew she could handle this situation.

"What's the matter, babe? Don't tell me you're freaked out." The cocky attitude she always knew him to have laced Jeremy's words.

The corner of Shira's eyes twitched at the pet name she used to like him calling her. When she met his gaze, she made sure none of her discomfort showed, and projected as much confidence as she could muster. "I'd appreciate it, Jeremy, if you didn't call me that—given we're not together anymore."

She glanced around again. "And I'm merely making sure I was actually at the convention like I expected, because you've never been one for these kinds of things."

He chuckled and shoved his hands in his pockets. "You're right, I still don't. But my girl is working a good gig here for a company, so I came with her to see what it's all about."

His girl? It didn't surprise Shira that much that he had someone after her. Her mind didn't even try to trick her into thinking he was just attempting to get under her skin. He was always popular with women; it wouldn't be too hard for him to find someone else who fit his shallow requirements.

"That's cool." Shira's words came off as nonchalant, just as she felt. Never in her wildest dreams did she ever expect to feel so okay in his presence. Sure, seeing him so suddenly sent her into a brief panic, but now that she had a moment to adjust, she didn't care. What he did was a dick move, but really, that was because he was a dick and it had nothing to do with her character in the slightest. "She working as a seller, or…"

Jeremy grinned. "Nah. Her sexy ass is a hot booth babe with some popular company. I didn't pay attention to which one, but it pays good."

"That's pretty cool. This is a good convention to get that kind of gig work."

Shira didn't miss the frown that momentarily crossed his lips, as if she didn't react as he'd hoped. A cocky grin replaced it. "So, what are you doing here? Figured you'd never want to step in a place like this after last time."

She did her best to hold back an eye twitch. Of course he'd try to bring that up to get a reaction. He hadn't changed at all. *What did I ever see in him?*

Before Shira could answer, someone came up behind Jeremy and slipped a slender hand around his waist before coming into full view. She was a slim woman with blonde hair and deep brown eyes. A white cropped tank top hugged her chest tight, and a size too small. A red mini skirt hugged her hips and white boots finished her outfit.

Her skin had not been spared from tanning-bed abuse, and the small beauty mark dotting the corner of her lip, Shira had insider knowledge that it was tattooed on.

It took Shira a moment to process the woman's identity. "Britney?"

A smug smile slipped up the woman's face. "Hey, Shira, been a while."

She pressed herself against Jeremy more, like some cat in heat. Shira swore if the woman tried any harder, she might fuse with him. "Uh, yeah. You're the girlfriend Jeremy was just telling me about?"

Britney let out her signature obnoxious laugh, the one Shira couldn't stand. Not that she had ever liked the woman to begin with. She was arguably worse than Jeremy. Britney then slid her left hand over Jeremy's chest, the action a not-so-subtle attempt to show off the shining ring on her finger. "Oh, I'm more than *just* his girlfriend."

Shira's eyes widened looking at the rock, but not because it upset her, like Britney clearly hoped. She held out a hand. "Well, let's see it."

Britney hesitated, and then eagerly held out her hand. Shira grasped her delicate fingers and turned her hand to get a good look at the engagement ring. The diamond stone—Shira assumed it was a diamond, Britney wouldn't allow anything less, nor Jeremy's ego for that matter—was fixed on white gold, and quite large for a centerpiece, surrounded by smaller cut diamonds. "It's a beautiful halo ring. A bit smaller than I would have expected you to choose, but a few years have passed, so your tastes may have changed."

Withdrawing her hand, Britney shrugged, but Shira caught the stiffness in the action. "I had plans for another one, but then saw this and fell in love. Had to have it, and of course Jeremy gets me what I want."

Liar. Jeremy just picked one without paying attention to what Britney wanted, but she couldn't allow their relationship to look less than perfect in front of Shira. Of course, Jeremy had done the same to her, so it was easy to spot the lie.

"No hard feelings, right, Shira?" Britney said.

Predictable. Shira shook her head. "Of course not. It's surprising, since the two of you couldn't stand each other back in the day, but it's great you both have found companionship in each other. And I'm nothing but happy for you."

A bit of a lie, but only because Shira felt nothing for all this. Their attempts to rub salt into a wound weren't working, because now that wound was well scabbed over. The ache she used to feel because she constantly picked at said wound had lessened without her realizing it.

Shira had clung to the hole Jeremy left, and the moment she let go and focused on more important things, he no longer mattered. His words meant nothing compared to the newer ones she'd been hearing for months. *No, years, and I just didn't want to believe them because I became comfortable with my pain, and was afraid of letting it go...*

The truth was, Jeremy couldn't compare. *He's nothing like—*

"So, what brings you here, Shira?" Britney said, cutting off her mental track. It looked like the woman was trying to compose herself, as if Shira's indifference had irritated or even offended her. "I'm sure Jeremy asked, but I'd love to know, too."

"I didn't get the answer before you arrived, babe," Jeremy said.

"We're here 'cause Daddy and Dad have a match," a child's voice squeaked out behind Shira.

Shira glanced over her shoulder to see Serenity hiding behind her, one hand clinging to Shira's leg, the other to Snake's vest. Serenity's green eyes cautiously watched Britney and Jeremy. *Shit.*

In her focus to handle the two pests, Shira had

completely forgotten about Serenity's presence. She'd gone so quiet, which wasn't like her. Sure, she could get shy, but this was a new reaction for Shira.

"Oh, aren't you adorable," Britney cooed. For the first time since their interaction, the woman's demeanor changed to something soft and kind. "What's your name, sweetie?"

Serenity hesitated and then looked up to Shira, who nodded and tucked an out-of-place lock of dark brown hair behind her ear. "You don't have to talk much if you don't want to."

Serenity's gaze turned down to the floor, and she toed the carpet. "Serenity."

"That's a pretty name you have," Britney said, the sweetness in her tone too much for even Shira to stomach. "You said you're here for your dads' match? Are they a PvP team?"

Shira blinked, surprised Britney knew the term. In their modeling days, she always rolled her eyes at Shira and Tanya for their nerdy sides. Britney would have rather insulted them for their hobbies than take the time to understand even a fraction of it. *I wonder if the job she picked up here required her to have some knowledge.* Booth babes worked tables to draw in customers, but they also needed to know their stuff to keep them around. Nerds could be thirsty, but it came with conditions.

Serenity nodded. "Yeah. Momma and I are waiting for them to get us nom-food before that starts."

Jeremy sneered at Shira. "Momma? Really? You thought you could have her say that and think we'd believe it?"

With big, confused eyes, Serenity looked up at Shira.

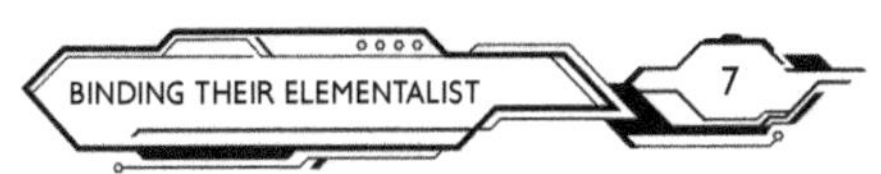

She suspected this might happen. Serenity had called her 'Momma' before. And she was a sharp kid. She knew these two were problems, so she was trying to help in the way an almost-seven-year-old thought she could.

Shira smiled fondly and stroked her head before addressing her egotistical ex. "Yes, I do expect you to. Do you have a problem with it, Jeremy?"

He snorted. "Two dads and a mom? Please. If you were going to concoct a story to make your pathetically sad life appear less so, you could at least tell the kid to say something that doesn't sound made-up. Especially when it comes to you."

Jeremy's condescending eyes looked down on her as if he were above her in status. "You disappeared off the face of the planet because someone like you had no place. No one would have knocked your freak ass up, and you certainly couldn't have found two losers that had a robotic freak fetish."

A muscle in the back of Shira's neck twitched. Her hand clenching Snake's leash tightened, and various nasty emotions bubbled in her chest. Snake prodded her hand with his cold nose, but her mind was too focused.

He would call me that… He would say those words—so close to the ones he said that day. A cyborg freak, she might be, but he was the worthless piece of shit and had no idea what a good thing he left fighting for her life in a hospital bed.

"Just because you're a closed-minded loser, Jeremy, doesn't mean other people are. I couldn't care less what a low-life piece of shit like yourself thinks of me, or my current life. I stepped away from the spotlight to better myself. And I found more than I bargained for.

You can play these little games all you want to poke and prod as if you're going to get some satisfying reaction. But you're expecting reactions from the old Shira when she doesn't exist anymore. In her place is someone who knows her worth and doesn't give a shit about the rats that scurry around at her feet."

Britney's mouth fell open and Jeremy's upper lip pulled back with distaste. He didn't like her defiant personality back then, so it was no surprise to Shira he didn't like her sass now.

Shira turned her attention over her shoulder when Britney's eyes darted to something new. She'd already figured it was a person by the way the woman's eyes bugged out, and this particular person was definitely deserving of the reaction.

Jasper walked their way, sharp green eyes intent on her. His shirt hugged tight against his muscular frame, and Shira found her gaze drifting from his capturing gaze, to his strong jawline, and then to the tattoos covering his tan skin. *He's deserving of Britney's reaction to him, that's for sure.*

"Hey, hon," Shira said, the tingling words coming off her lips a little too easy for her liking, but she wouldn't chastise herself, given the situation. "Finally make it through that crazy line?"

Jasper held a firm grip on the coffee he carried to Shira. He didn't care how hot the cup was; it was the only thing keeping him calm as he made his way to her.

Thanks to the long line at the coffee shop, plenty

of people left, allowing Zach and him to join Narissa and Ajax, who had been farther up in line, and even Mercedes, who rejoined the pair after leaving it before he and Zach had shown up.

No one had expected the SOS from Mercedes' AI, Tasha. The SOS, simply titled "The Asshole Alert," had been transmitted by Orion. Zach, Ajax, and he had thought the title was quite hilarious until they noticed how serious Mercedes and Narissa were about the alert. That was when they saw Shira with *him*.

At first, Jasper couldn't see anything wrong—seemed like Shira was having a conversation—but by the amount of seething hatred the two women projected the man's way, Jasper knew something was up. He also wondered how the guy hadn't spontaneously combusted. *Really, if looks could kill...*

Shira was the attack dog of the three women, but they showed their harsher side then in loyalty, and Jasper was no fool to take the shift lightly. Even when he inquired about the man's identity, they provided stilted and unhelpful responses, as both women were more focused on figuring out who would go help Shira out. Narissa even ordered the coffee Jasper had planned to get for Shira—with a few extras he didn't know she would have preferred, like caramel. Shira hadn't given him any specific coffee request beyond wanting cream and sugar.

Surprisingly, it was his and Zach's AI, Alistair, who volunteered them. It seemed this *Jeremy* fellow had been given the impression Shira was here with a boyfriend... or two. Narissa and Mercedes were quick to like the plan, and Jasper was more than eager to play up the

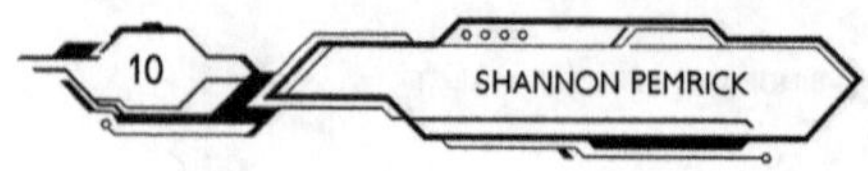

part. Zach was also on board, but volunteered to get their order first, even if that meant he lagged behind a bit. He also seemed to think it would help prevent it from looking like no one believed Shira could handle the situation.

While Narissa and Mercedes were unsure, Jasper had to agree with his boyfriend. Shira was a strong and capable person. And from the way the interaction had looked to be going from afar, she wasn't in any physical danger around the guy, which meant she deserved to not be treated like some damsel in distress. *She's far from it.*

The woman hanging off Jeremy noticed Jasper's approach first, and he found her reaction interesting. While it was one of interest that he wasn't a stranger to, this was also of recognition.

Shira turned, her long red hair spilling over her shoulder from the action, and gave a bright smile in greeting that matched the shine in her green eyes. "Hey, hon. Finally make it through that crazy line?"

Hon. That word off her lips… Yeah, he could get used to hearing that from her. Jasper made it to her side and held up her coffee. "Finally, yeah. Got your favorite—two sugahs, extra cream, three shots of caramel."

Her eyes lit up, and she reached for the cup. "You're the best."

Jasper smirked and let her grasp the cup, but before he allowed her to take it, he reached out with his free hand and curled his fingers around the back of her neck. Jasper dipped his head and claimed her soft lips.

Shira let out a soft moan and molded into him as if she found herself struggling to stand, inviting him to drink in her taste a little longer than what could have been considered appropriate for public—not that he cared what anyone thought of his actions with her.

Her sweet scent enveloping and teasing him—her addicting taste tempting him to deepen the kiss for more—Jasper had waited what felt like an eternity for this moment with Shira, even if it wasn't exactly the way he pictured it happening, and it was already over nine thousand times better than what he'd experienced with her in VR.

Based on the quiet, breathy "oh" the woman with Jeremy gasped out, Jasper was also putting on quite the show for the couple, as he'd hoped.

Jasper pulled away from Shira when Serenity started giggling. While normal for her when he kissed Zach, an outsider might find it suspicious, and he didn't need that at this moment.

Shira hummed quietly, a pleased smile on her tempting lips, and took her cup of coffee. "If I didn't know any better, that longing kiss would make me think a time wizard did some wibbly-wobbly magic here. Miss me that much?"

Jasper chuckled. "That line felt like an eternity to get through." He then reached around her and grabbed Serenity, throwing his daughter over his shoulder. "Now, what is our little starship giggling about back here?"

"Nothing," she said unconvincingly through her giggles.

"That so?" She seemed to be playing along rather well for this unorthodox situation. Jasper figured he should be concerned, especially if it caused her to get too many ideas too quickly, but he could always talk to her about it after he dealt with this situation.

"Where's my nom-food?" Serenity asked.

"And to follow up her question, where is Zach?" Shira asked.

Jasper set Serenity down in front of him. "Poor guy running the stall was so overwhelmed he messed up the order, except your coffee. Zach said he'd stay to get the rest while I delivered it to you." Jasper's eyes cut to the couple in front of them. "And I was curious who your friends were, so I figured it couldn't hurt."

"And we're curious about you," the woman with Jeremy practically purred. There was a clear hunger in her eyes, but Jasper wasn't sure why. Now that he was closer, the prominent ring on her hand was hard to miss.

"I wouldn't call them friends," Shira said as boldly, as he would have expected from her. "But it'd be rude of me not to introduce you to them."

She stopped and directed her attention over her shoulder. Jasper caught the sound of someone fast approaching and also looked. Zach jogged up to them, drink holder in one hand with their two coffees and Serenity's hot chocolate, and a bag with their breakfast. Jasper let his gaze drift over his boyfriend, enjoying the view of his muscles flexing along his athletic frame. The short ponytail he'd pulled his blonde hair back into had come a little loose, but it didn't appear to bother him.

"Sorry it took me so long," he said, handing the food bag off to Jasper, which was for the best. Serenity was already chomping at the bit with the way she was tugging on his pants, and it'd keep her occupied during this confrontation.

While Jasper dug out Serenity's breakfast sandwich, Zach fixed his hair, and then pulled up next to Shira, entwining his fingers with her cybernetic prosthetics. His ice-blue eyes met her brilliant green, and then he planted an affectionate kiss on her forehead. She smiled at him with such convincing fondness, even Jasper could have been fooled this was real. *Soon. Wicked soon.*

"So, did I miss introductions?" Zach asked, tearing his eyes away from her to face the two strangers.

"No, you arrived right on time for that," Shira said. "Guys, meet Britney. She and I modeled together back in the day. And with her is Jeremy, my *ex*-fiancé I told you about before."

Everything in Jasper's brain came to a screeching halt. Ex-fiancé? Shira had been engaged once? Never once did she even allude to ever having been engaged in the past. He'd always assumed her casual fling choices weren't too far off from her pre-accident days.

As his brain finally turned back on, realization kicked in. The SOS from Orion—the animosity instantly triggered in Mercedes and Narissa—Shira's hard distaste for the pet name "babe." Shira's and Jeremy's relationship hadn't ended well. And by the way Shira had emphasized his *ex* status, she still despised him.

Shira continued her introductions. "Jeremy, Britney, these are my boyfriends—"

"Jasper Quinn and Zach Miller of team Smash and Stab," Britney said, her voice breathy.

Jeremy gave her an incredulous look. "You know them?"

"Only by reputation." Her words were practically a purr again. "They're an up-and-coming, on-the-map twos-team for Lusara Fates, and GameTech's first sponsored team."

Jasper was impressed. While Ajax said the press was going crazy about him sponsoring their team, Jasper thought it was just that. He didn't think anyone was actually paying attention to his and Zach's entry into the convention competition as individuals. There were plenty of bigger names here who had participated many times before, so Jasper didn't expect anyone to recognize them by name, let alone appearance.

And with the way Britney held herself in this small interaction, he wouldn't have come to the conclusion she knew a damned thing about esports. Jasper knew it wasn't good to stereotype or make assumptions, but he had a bad habit of doing so.

Shira's brow rose. "And what made you such an esports enthusiast? You've always balked at anything game-related."

Okay, so maybe his impression of her wasn't so far off.

"It's now my job to know these things, Shira. I do work a booth, after all, and the company I work for is connected to GameTech."

That explained the outfit. Shira said Britney was, at the very least, a former model, and Jasper wasn't sure if she was a booth babe or in costume. It was hard to tell the difference sometimes, especially in this case, as he wasn't recognizing any character she might have been costuming as or recognizing her uniform colors, so Jasper wasn't sure which company she worked for.

A smug smile spread over the woman's full lips. "I also need to know GameTech's two star players for photo ops later."

Jasper may be slow on the uptake sometimes, but he definitely caught her implication, and he didn't like it.

Was she with this Jeremy character, or just playing it up? Either way, it was clear she was trying to get a rise out of Shira—which, to his mild surprise, wasn't working. Shira didn't react in the slightest, except to shoot Zach and then him a confused look.

"You two didn't tell me about any photo ops."

"Ajax didn't make us aware of any," Zach said. Jasper agreed. That was a strange thing to leave out if that was really happening.

"I'm sure it was an oversight. It's pretty common for such ops to happen for the teams that make it this far. And that's why I need to know so much. Can't embarrass the company's team." Britney tapped a finger against her mouth. "Though it's strange. While it's common knowledge the two of you have been dating for years, Shira was never even hinted at."

Shit. This woman wasn't blowing smoke out her ass. She knew her stuff, and that made this arrangement a little more difficult to pull off for Shira's sake.

"And I'm sure you also found nothing about our daughter, either," Zach said without missing a beat, and Jasper found himself loving the man even more. "We make sure she stays out of any spotlight to keep her life as normal as possible."

"And I know this is a hard concept for an attention seeker like you, Britney, to comprehend, but I also have chosen to stay out of the public eye," Shira shot out, her words laced with smugness. "I've chosen to focus on my new life, and that means low profile. Jasper and Zach respect that, and have helped me remain invisible."

The woman blinked, clearly stunned there was a

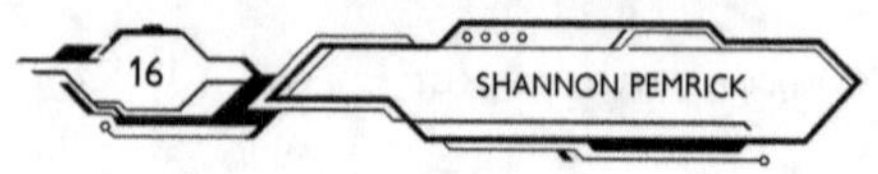

reasonable alibi for them to use, then shook it off. "That does make sense. Not everyone can handle all of that attention. And with you recovering, Shira, I can only imagine how difficult the public's opinion would have affected you, both with your physical change and your relationship choice."

Jasper's eye twitched. *Really? She's going to make those kinds of jabs.*

Shira shrugged. "You can think what you want. I've made my choices for me, and not someone outside of my relationships, because they don't matter to me."

Jasper couldn't stop staring at the woman next to him, admiration pulsing through every fiber of his being. Shira had always come off as confident. However, he and Zach learned just how much of an elaborate illusion she'd crafted, pretending that nothing in her life was wrong. That small discovery allowed them to find the little cracks in her façade, and pushed through to see the hurt and terrified woman under the mask. Yet, that woman wasn't here.

Shira projected true confidence, more than she'd ever done before. She believed the words she spoke. This pair's critical opinion of her didn't bother her. She didn't care she was in the open with people around to hear her in a supposed relationship with two men, who were unashamed to admit they pwere together, too.

Proud wouldn't come close to how Jasper felt, seeing these last weeks of work paying off.

Britney waved Shira off. "No need to get defensive. I was only pointing out how it can be hard. People are judgmental is all." Britney's lower lip caught between her teeth as she shifted her attention back to Zach and then Jasper. "So, which one of you is the one Serenity calls 'Dad' and the other 'Daddy'?"

Jasper's brow rose. What a weird question to ask suddenly. And… also specific father names. Had Shira said something like that to differentiate Zach and him? It was hard to believe Serenity had. She never called Zach anything but his name.

Before anyone had the chance to finish processing and answer, Orion spoke from Shira's phone, "Shira, this is a reminder not to forget about ensuring Zach and Jasper aren't late for their conference."

Shira smiled down at her hip, as if her phone could see. "Thanks, Orion."

"You're welcome. Also, your friends are waiting for you on the second story mezzanine."

In unison, Jasper, Shira, and Zach turned their attention up. As the AI said, Ajax, a well-built man in his early thirties with tan skin, dark eyes and hair, and cybernetic right arm; Narissa, a gorgeous woman also in her early thirties with long, dark curly hair, dark eyes, umber skin, and a curvaceous figure; and Mercedes, late twenties and equally gorgeous, with long golden hair, blue eyes, tan skin, and a slim frame, leaned on the railing of the upper-level mezzanine. Ajax waved once to them.

"Oh, my god," Britney gasped. "That's Ajax Jackson, CEO of GameTech. Oh, my god… and is that—"

"Narissa Okafor of Cybro Technologies, girlfriend of Ajax, and my best friend," Shira said, positively smug. "And with them is my other best friend, Mercedes Gail of Gail's Antique Restorations."

She shot that info at Jeremy, and based on the way he

tried to hide his wince, he apparently had knowledge of Mercedes and her reputation in the car industry.

Orion pinged her phone again. "Ajax is offended you did not list him as a best friend."

Shira's brow furrowed. "How the fuck did he hear me down here?"

"Language," Jasper warned.

"Yeah, language," Serenity said through a mouthful of her sandwich.

Shira rolled her eyes and then had Orion send an amendment to Ajax to appease him. She then refocused on the pain-in-the-ass couple. "But Orion is right. We do have an appointment to keep. It was interesting running into you both. Good luck with your booth gig, Britney. And Jeremy…" She pursed her lips and then shrugged. "I've got nothing left to say to you."

Shira looked at Jasper, then at Zach. "Shall we?"

Jasper smirked. He loved her attitude right now. It was sexy. "Can't keep putting this off much longer, I guess."

Zach chuckled and was the first to get them moving, blocking the annoying couple's sight of Shira, as if to protect her from anything they may throw at her last minute. "You act like this is going to kill you."

"Reporters ask too many questions," Jasper said, before taking Serenity's hand so she wouldn't get lost in the crowd.

"Big baby," Shira muttered before taking a sip of her coffee. She then glanced over her shoulder and shouted back, "Oh, Britney. From the ex-fiancé to current, make sure you keep your physical appearance up. We're both aware how quick Jeremy is to trade in for a newer model the minute you get even the smallest scratch."

A muscle in Jasper's neck twitched. As much as he wanted

to know what happened between the two of them, Jasper wasn't sure he'd be able to keep his cool if he found out after that little quip.

His attention flicked up to their friends still standing on the mezzanine. Narissa and Mercedes still had ugly scowls, and Jasper knew avoiding the question wasn't an option—for both Zach's and his sake, and Shira's.

CHAPTER 2

Zach refused to let go of Shira's hand while the four of them weaved their way through the growing crowd of people. That conversation hadn't resulted in any physical altercation, but Zach had planned for one, either because Shira ended up being Shira, or he or Jasper lost it, and Zach wasn't the type to pick those kinds of fights.

But for her, he would, and keeping contact with her was the only thing ensuring he didn't do something rash. Plus, he wanted the contact with her, cybernetic prosthetic or no.

They walked past the elevators, and Zach almost asked if they should take it, when he noticed the tightness in Shira's face. After the altercation with Jeremy, he would let her decide where to go.

Shira let out a slow breath when they reached the stairs and then plunked down. She rested her arms over her legs and closed her eyes, taking more controlled breaths.

Snake jammed his head under her arms and whined. Shira wrapped her arms around her faithful companion and buried her face in his fur.

Zach glanced over his shoulder, double-checking that Jeremy or Britney hadn't followed them. Shira had handled herself well against them, when they were trying so hard to get under her skin. They didn't deserve the satisfaction of knowing it had worked to any degree.

When Shira sucked in a loud breath, he turned back around, finding her sitting up straight with her head rolled back and threading her fingers through her beautiful red hair. Already, she seemed better. *Is that Snake's doing, or did this not affect her as much as we expected?* While he didn't know the extent of the issue, he'd gleaned enough, and he would have figured she'd need more time.

Footsteps thundered down the stairs, and Mercedes and Narissa appeared above them. They homed in on Shira, who smiled.

"I'm good."

"You sure?" Mercedes asked.

Shira nodded. "Yeah. It was more draining to put up with their presence than anything."

"All right, as long as you're being honest, we'll let it go," Narissa said. "Though I'm still tempted to go down there and punch him."

Shira laughed. "He's not worth the energy. Really."

"That's saying a lot, coming from you." Narissa then smiled. "I'll stop being a mother hen."

She glanced at Jasper and then Zach. It was a contemplative expression. "There's no hiding anything from you two now. You've gotten involved…"

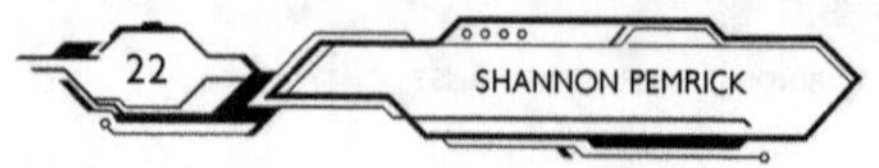

"I'll explain," Shira said, without hesitation.

Narissa nodded. "For the best, I think. I already explained things to Ajax, hope you don't mind."

Shira shook her head. "It's fine."

Narissa shifted her focus to Jasper and Zach and came down the stairs the rest of the way. "I have something to ask the two of you first, privately, if you don't mind."

Zach's brow rose, curious about such an out-of-the-blue request. "Uh, sure."

Jasper nodded. The three of them walked a few paces away, and they gave Narissa their undivided attention.

"I'll be quick, and it's nothing bad. More of a request," Narissa said, her voice low as if she didn't want someone overhearing. "There's a new tech reveal right at the start of the convention, for watching the various competitions. This technology follows a trend to be more inclusive for younger ages this year."

She smiled. "Since you two are a participating team, you've got two tech spots, and this gave me the perfect chance to make sure the claims for younger-age safety were accurate. My analysis shows that it would be safe for Serenity, but I'd like to see it in practice. Would you two be okay with this? I can use the time you two are using to talk to Shira to test, and of course, if I have even the slightest concerns, I will make sure she stops using the device."

Zach blinked. Because of Serenity's age, a lot of tech was off limits. It made things rather difficult when you had young children. Sometimes it felt as if the world had completely forgotten about their existence, even for subjects that would be big for kids, like gaming.

Zach exchanged a glance with Jasper and nodded. He trusted Narissa to put Serenity's safety first.

Jasper smiled at Narissa. "We trust you. And this will be a great thing for her to experience."

Narissa smiled brightly. "Wonderful! I'll let you break the news to her."

They returned to the stairs, where curious and attentive gazes awaited them. Jasper broke the news to Serenity, who squealed like it was Christmas and she'd received the ultimate gift she asked for.

Jasper laughed. "You behave, and listen to Narissa when she tells you to do something, got it?"

"I promise I'll be wicked good," Serenity said, beaming.

"Go on then, and have fun."

Their daughter's hands shot up in the air while she cheered. She hugged them both and bolted up the stairs, only to stop and climb back down to be on the same stair Shira sat on.

"She-ra, are you gonna be okay?"

Shira smiled at her. "Yes, I promise. Thank you for your help earlier."

"I did good?"

Shira brushed a lock of Serenity's dark hair out of her face. "You helped me more than you know. Thank you."

Serenity beamed and threw her arms around Shira's neck. Shira pulled her close, and the sound of Snake's tail thumping echoed through the stairwell. Zach leaned closer to Jasper to get a better look. They firmly wedged the large black dog between their legs, and he loved every moment of it.

Serenity giggled and mumbled something about his

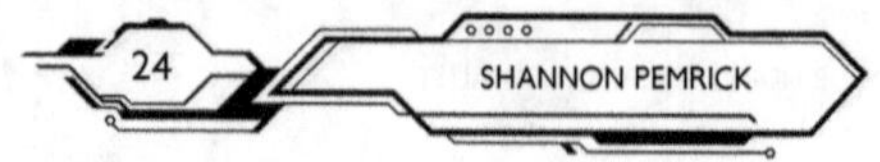

nose being cold before pulling away from Shira. Shira planted a kiss on her forehead and then the young girl ran off with Narissa and Mercedes. That was when Zach noticed Ajax observing as well. He seemed concerned watching Shira, but left with the ladies without saying anything.

This left the three of them alone, save for a few people moving between floors. Shira absently scratched Snake's ears, who ate up the attention. Zach sat down next to her, being mindful of the foot traffic and his coffee, as well as Serenity's abandoned hot chocolate. Jasper crouched in front of Shira, and the two waited. Neither would push her on this.

Shira sipped her coffee and then let out a slow breath. "Okay, first, before we talk about Jeremy, I want to say it wasn't my plan to involve Serenity, and subsequently, both of you. She started talking when Britney asked me a question, and one thing led to another and Serenity called me 'Momma.' That then snowballed to me being involved with you two, since it's no secret you're together."

Jasper reached out and threaded his fingers with her prosthetic hand. "I didn't expect you to do that on purpose. It sounds exactly like something Serenity would do." He chuckled. "She's cheeky like that."

Zach reached behind Shira and rested his hand on her side. "And we're not upset about our involvement. Honestly, it made it wicked easy to come help, after Orion's SOS to Mercedes."

She nodded, her eyes contemplative. "I'm not surprised he sent that. Also explained both of your convenient entrances." She chuckled. "And the coffee."

"Narissa ordered it," Jasper admitted. "I would have, had ya told us you liked your coffee that way."

She rolled her eyes. "It's my favorite way, sure, but not the only way I have my coffee."

"Always tell us your favorite things," Zach said. "Gives us more chances for brownie points if we remember."

She laughed, this one light and showing that her tension was working its way out. Unfortunately, she sobered faster than he would have liked, and her expression slipped into something neutral. Zach held his breath, trying to prepare himself for whatever story she was about to tell.

"Okay, so Jeremy…" She paused and licked her lips. "I met him when I was seventeen, at a modeling gig. We hit it off well, but it was a few months down the road, after some more run-ins and lunch dates did we decide to date. It started out great, and I was happy."

She worked her jaw. "That is, until about a year in. I'd turned eighteen, finished school, and was more than set on my path as a model. I also wanted a place of my own, so my parents helped me through the intricacies of buying a house. That's when Jeremy asked me to move in with him instead. I wasn't ready for that step and really loved the house I picked, so I told him I wanted more time. That irritated him, but I didn't think anything of his reaction after that, because he didn't press."

Shira shook her head. "Now that I'm able to look back, I see that rejection was the start of issues I stupidly ignored. It began as minor nitpicks—I wasn't wearing clothes that were flattering or appropriate for someone in a relationship, my choice for piercings, my

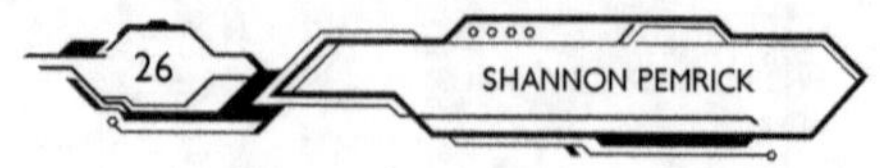

lack of attempts to tan, my food preferences, me dying my hair to red—"

Jasper held up a hand. "Wait, hold on. He had an issue with your hair?"

She shrugged. "According to him, he always had an issue with it and hoped I'd *grow out* of the phase. He hated red on me in any way, not just my hair. Could have been a shirt, dress, or even jewelry."

Zach twisted a silky lock of her hair around his finger. "Well, he's a moron. Red is a perfect color for you. Especially your hair."

Pink spread over her cheeks, and her bottom lip caught between her teeth for a moment. "Thanks. While I'd succumbed to his pressure of wearing less red, I refused to compromise with my hair. It caused a lot of tension, but still I stayed, and another year in, I asked him to move in with me because I felt ready finally. And given I had a perfect house for us and he was renting, it made the most sense to me."

"Why?" Jasper asked. "He was being an ass, and yet you still stayed together."

Shira blew out a breath. "Because I was blindly in love. I was willing to overlook the issues, rationalizing things would get better if we lived together."

"And they didn't," Zach guessed.

She shook her head. "We never moved in together. He had several excuses, and I was stupid enough to agree with them, telling myself we'd just have to keep on working on fixing the bad parts of our relationship. They didn't. They got worse. And still I tried to make it work."

"Why, though?" Jasper asked.

"I…" She chewed her lip. "I had my reasons."

Zach frowned. *What doesn't she feel comfortable telling us? Why doesn't she trust us to know?*

"So, at what point did he propose?" Jasper asked. Zach could see he had a similar thought running through his head, but if she didn't want to talk about it, then so be it. They wouldn't be jerks about it, especially not when she was sharing so much.

Shira blew out a breath and took a sip of her coffee again. "It was about six months before my accident."

That meant they'd dated a good four years, to Zach's best estimate, based on when he knew the accident happened and how old she was now.

"We'd talked about it for a few months before, so it didn't come as a surprise, but again the signs that it wasn't a good match reared up. I'd expressed how I'd like the proposal to go, and the type of rings I liked, and he didn't do any of it. He picked out a ring he decided was good, and turned the proposal into a publicity stunt."

Zach frowned. *That was an asshole move for sure.* "And you still said yes."

She nodded. "I was upset, but again, blind in my love." Shira sighed. "And it came to finally bite me six months later when I had my accident…"

A knot formed in Zach's stomach. He had already hated this retelling, but he had an uncomfortable feeling that was nothing compared to what she was about to reveal.

She took in a shaky breath and scratched Snake's neck. "I… I was in my hospital bed, hooked up to machines and installed with half of my cybernetics—the ones most needed to keep me alive—when he finally showed

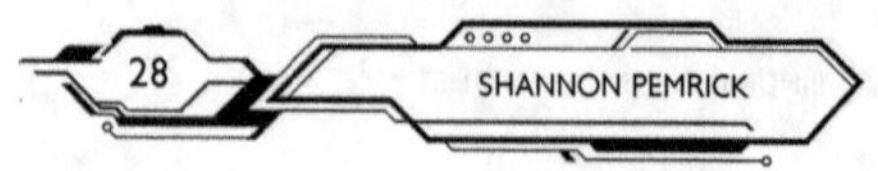

up. That was a day after the accident. Until that moment, I couldn't understand why he hadn't come to see me. He had been one of the first people Orion had alerted about my rescue, and it wasn't like he was out of town. He was even on my approved visitor list."

Shira's lower lip quivered. Zach had to resist the urge to pull her close and tell her to stop the story so she wouldn't have to remember this part. "He stayed for all of five minutes… to tell me he couldn't be with an inhuman freak, and that I was so far from human now, there wasn't any point in me being alive. And then left."

The floor fell out from beneath Zach. She hadn't just said that. She hadn't been treated that horribly by someone she'd completely devoted herself to.

"That fucking asshole!" Jasper roared. He was on his feet in a second, rage radiating off him. Those moving through the stairwell stopped and stared.

Shira's hand shot out, grabbing a fistful of Jasper's shirt. "Don't." Her grip tightened, and she struggled to meet his furious gaze. "Please, don't."

Jasper let out a tight breath and dropped back into a crouched position. "You really expect me to not be furious aftah what he did to you?"

"No… that's not…" She took a breath, still holding onto his shirt. "I've been working hard to get over what he did to me. I let that moment consume me for the last five years, and drive how I've seen myself—how I've handled relationships."

Inhuman—freak—unloveable—unwanted. Every single little comment and choice they'd heard her make all led back to that single day. The accident took most of her life away, and Jeremy broke what had remained.

Zach reached out and tucked his finger under her elbow. There wasn't anything he could say that would take her pain away, even when everything in him screamed to come up with something.

"I'm not asking either of you not to be upset," Shira continued. "It means you care, and that means more than you know right now."

A small smile tugged at the corner of her lips, and she let out a quiet laugh. "And if I'm keeping it real with you both here, your reactions balance out mine. Where now I'm starting to feel numb to it all, I have one of you acting as my explosive reactionary side, and the other the calm, sensible side."

Jasper's eyes flicked to Zach, and he grinned. "Heah that? She called me calm and sensible."

Zach snorted, and Shira bent over, sputtering with laughter. "Oh yeah, that's exactly how she split out the compliments. We just imagined you exploding and planning to go murder her ex."

Jasper sucked air through his teeth. "Oh right, I was about to do that, wasn't I?"

Shira yanked on his shirt and Jasper lurched forward, stopping just short of falling on her. She'd sobered quickly and settled hard eyes on him. Jasper's throat bobbed. "Don't you dare. You're not storming all over the convention center and ruining everything the two of you worked so damned hard for to get here. He isn't worth it."

Jasper's eyebrow quirked, and a sinful grin spread up the side of his perfect, chiseled face. Zach swallowed hard. Jasper reached out and grasped Shira's chin in a firm grip, tipping her head up to him. "But you are."

Shira's lips parted, but nothing came out. Red flushed over her face again.

Zach couldn't stop himself from smirking and leaning closer, aware that his grip on her elbow remained. "Rogue got your tongue? Or are you excited by that prospect?"

Predictably, Jasper's gaze flicked down to her lips. A twinge of envy shot through Zach. Jasper had gotten one hell of a kiss out of her earlier. Everyone watching saw what it did to Shira. Zach had wanted a taste, too, but of course, he had played it safe for his own comfort. Certain kinds of public displays of affections made Zach uncomfortable. However, a part of him regretted not shoving that issue aside for even a single moment to have a taste of what Jasper had indulged in.

A tail thumping against the wall echoed up the stairs, and the three of them burst into laughter.

"I think that's a yes," Jasper managed.

"I think you're delusional," Shira said, rubbing Snake's head. "Neither of you are ruining your chances at this tournament because of anything related to me, got it? I'll kick both your asses to Timbuktu and back."

"Oh good, just there?" Jasper said, grinning. "I was worried it would be through deep cybahspace and back."

Shira rolled her eyes.

Zach reached out and tucked a wayward strand of hair into place. "So, you good now?"

She smiled at them both, her expression light, in a way he'd never viewed on her since having the privilege of seeing her real face. "Yeah. You both know my dark secret, and I'm feeling a lot better than I have in a long time. Thank you."

"We always gotcha back, Shira," Jasper said. "All you have to do is lean on us."

Zach nodded. Long before these feelings for her became too real, they were friends. And that wouldn't change.

She smiled. "And you two have me. No matter what."

"And for the record, Jeremy is the biggest moron in the world to have let an amazing woman like you go," Jasper said.

Her smile became more demure, and her gaze faltered. "Thanks. Tanya tried to tell me that, too, when it happened…"

Zach remembered some of the story Shira told them, back when she first started opening up, about her accident. She'd stopped herself from talking about an event her deceased friend had witnessed. This must have been it.

"I'm still working on believing that myself," Shira continued. "Maybe one of these days."

Jasper opened his mouth to say something when Orion pinged Shira's phone. "I apologize for interrupting, Shira, but this is a ten-minute courtesy warning."

Shira took a deep breath through her nose and rose to her feet. "We should get upstairs. Don't want you both to be late, and who knows what kind of trouble Serenity is getting up to, with Narissa and Ajax showing her all that new tech."

Things slowed for Zach at the mention of Serenity. Britney said something that had caught him off guard when it came to Jasper's and his daughter. *I have to know.* "Shira, before we do, can you clarify something?"

Shira cocked her head to the side. "What's up?"

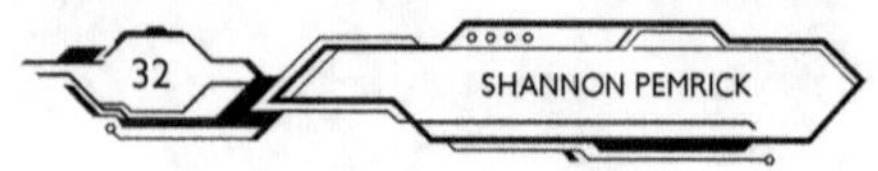

"Did Serenity actually call me her dad, or was that something you said in front of Britney for her to ask that odd question of hers?"

Shira blinked. "Serenity did, of course. Why?"

The tips of Zach's fingers tingled. *She called me Dad?*

"I don't understand…" Shira flicked a confused gaze between them. "What's with the strange reaction? Isn't she supposed to?"

"We've always made it clear to her Zach saw her as his daughter, yet we never dictated what she called him. And all her life, Serenity never called Zach her dad," Jasper shared. "At least, not to his face."

Shira gasped, her eyes widening. "Never? I wouldn't have known with the way she spoke to Britney."

Warmth swelled in Zach's chest until he ached. He hadn't realized how much that had bothered him. But now…

"You never asked her about it?" Shira asked.

Zach's eyes squinted as his face twisted alongside the embarrassment that flashed through him, cutting off some of his elation. "I just… I didn't want to seem pushy. If Serenity didn't want to call me Dad or anything, then that was going to be her choice."

Shira pursed her lips. "Tell you what. Since I'm going to spend a lot of time with her while you two are in your matches, I'll see if I can find a moment to ask her. Can't be too complicated of an answer, coming from an almost seven-year-old."

"Don't worry about it," he said. As much as he appreciated her going the extra mile, it wasn't necessary, no matter how curious he was. "If she wants to say it to my face, she will."

Zach took the first step up the stairs so they wouldn't be late, and the other two were quick to follow his lead. Snake, silent as always, slipped between him and Shira. When they made it to the first landing, something dawned on Zach, and he couldn't resist finding out just how Shira would react.

"You know, now that we've pretended to be together in front of Jeremy and Britney, we have to keep this up for the whole convention." Zach smirked. "Wouldn't exactly look good if they caught us later not acting like a proper triad."

Jasper rubbed his chin. "Is that the right term? I thought it was throuple. Don't want to give the wrong impression of how we've chosen to handle this relationship."

"We can research to be sure."

"Research?" Shira rolled her eyes so hard for a moment Zach thought they might pop out. "I think you two are taking this a little too seriously. What is this, one of Kiara's romance books you want to reenact?"

Zach chuckled. "Only if we promise it's only for show, and that we won't let our hearts get tangled up in the fun of pretending so much that we start believing the relationship is real."

Shira laughed, though Jasper cut it short when he wrapped his arm around her waist and pulled her close. He grinned against her ear, the green in his eyes deepening and making Zach's pulse jump. "I don't know about you, but I'm not keen on promising it's only for show. It's fah too restricting, and doesn't sound as fun as letting our hearts get tangled immediately."

Red flushed Shira's cheeks and spread over her

collarbone, the color accentuating her freckled skin. Zach noticed, though, there was a point where the skin change should have continued on her right side to match her left, but didn't. That had to be due to the false skin she wore. With the progress they'd made with her today, would it be possible for them to convince her by the end of the week to trust them to see her as she truly was?

"Hey," Mercedes' voice called down from the stairs above. "You two can flirt with Shira later. You're going to be late."

Shira's face grew redder as she stared up at their blonde friend, who was grinning like mad. Zach and Jasper chuckled. Everyone knew what was up, but Shira was going to be her stubborn self about it all. Zach didn't know why, but he did like the challenge in a way. It'd make her reactions that much more fun when the two of them came out on top.

CHAPTER 3

A muscle in Shira's neck twitched, her eyes darting around the people gathered outside the conference hall. She could tell the competitors, managers, and representative sponsors from the reporters. Beyond the fact reporters carried devices and cameras specific to media needs, they were the only ones to be so dressed-to-impress with their business attire. Everyone else wore something comfortable, though the sponsor representatives generally had a company shirt of some sort and a few players were in cosplay or sporting some of the newest fashion from magazines—sci-fi inspired outfits. Shira found both of those choices interesting.

She figured those into cosplay would wait until after they announced the lineups. With so many new teams making it to the tournament this year, the organizers wanted to keep things a surprise until after the conference, which also happened to go through the opening ceremony. *So much for a small, quick conference like Ajax made it seem yesterday.*

As for her observations with the fashion choices, Shira found her inner model and designer really liking the style, and she'd wondered why it'd taken so long for it to hit more mainstream, when some of the styles were clearly based on designs from concepts she'd seen from over forty years ago.

A finger poked Shira's side. She jumped and looked at Narissa. "What was that for?"

Her friend gazed at her with concerned eyes. "You didn't hear us say your name."

Shira frowned. *Not good.* Now her two friends were going to fuss for no reason. "I'm just thinking."

Mercedes leaned on the back of Shira's chair. "Talk to us. It's obvious you're scoping the room out."

Shira let out a breath and swirled her coffee. "It's the reporters. I recognize some of them. They're a bit shady and like to dance on the boundaries of what's allowed." She pointed a few of them out. "They have always put me on edge, but between my issues, and Jasper and Zach's wishes to keep Serenity out of sight from the sharks, I'm concerned."

The three of them turned their gazes to the two aforementioned guys. They stood with Ajax as he explained the tech Serenity had tested. She still refused to remove the headgear from her face. Narissa had explained that there were only a few things included on it right now, before the ceremony, but that didn't matter to Serenity. It really showed Shira how restricted kids were when it came to tech, and why non-VR games were still hanging on.

"We'll make sure they behave," Narissa assured. "A few other teams also expressed annoyance already with a few getting too pushy and invasive, so there are extra eyes on them."

That should have assured Shira, but she knew how these people worked, and she wasn't in a good position mentally yet to handle any struggles with them. She and Serenity weren't even supposed to be this close to the conference hall to avoid this. But the conference had been moved to an unexpected room, and with Serenity now attached to the headgear, there was no potential to walk around the venue yet.

Shira needed a distraction.

She turned to Mercedes. "Where's Takashi?"

"He's with Rei and Emi," she said. "They wanted to go to the opening ceremony before the two of them spend most of their time in Cosplay Alley."

Rei was Takashi's younger sister, and Emi a good friend of them both. She also happened to work for Shira's parents after a series of interesting events a few months ago.

Shira cocked her head. "I knew Emi was into cosplay; she's shown me some of her costumes before. But I wasn't aware Rei was, too."

Mercedes nodded. "It's something she's quite passionate about."

"Well, then I'm going to make it a point to see them both. I want to see the work they did."

Mercedes turned her attention to Narissa. "Speaking of which, do you know who else from the guild is coming? I've been so busy with work, I never got to verify with anyone."

"I've been a bit preoccupied too, but…" Narissa pursed her lips as she thought. "Besides Darius and Kiara, who are a given and already over doing Lusara Fates company things, I think Ronan and Donovan were planning to show up late. Pretty sure I heard them, Rei, and Emi making plans to meet up."

Shira snickered. "Of course they did. Those two are practically glued to them."

"You mean glued to Emi," Mercedes corrected.

They all laughed. Bringing Rei and Emi into the guild had been a brilliant move. The guild was a decent size, and not everyone had regular contact with each other, so it was common for groups of people to form more tight-knit bonds—though Donovan and Ronan were a bit different.

While they got along fine with everyone, and always wanted to be part of the main raiding team when their jobs weren't keeping them away, they had a tendency to keep to themselves a lot. Shira knew they were fairly close with Ajax and Narissa, but this was new with Emi and Rei. It was good they'd finally found a stronger connection in the two newest guildmates.

The doors to the conference hall opened and two people exited, calling for those attending to file in. Unsurprisingly, the reporters were quick to herd themselves through those doors first. They'd all want to fight for the best spots to see the various contestants for the game tournaments.

Jasper and Zach spoke to Serenity about needing to put the headset away now, and Shira caught her disappointment from even her seat. The little girl stomped over to Shira and her friends and plopped down in her chair, arms crossed as she brooded. Jasper looked exasperated with his daughter's attitude, and Shira bit her lip so she wouldn't laugh at the dramatics.

"Think you can handle her while we're entertaining the paparazzi?"

Shira cleared her throat and sat up straighter, trying to keep herself composed. "I'm confident I can. Are you sure you're up for your task?"

He narrowed his eyes, then handed Serenity's headgear over to Shira. "More than sure."

Shira looked to Zach and gestured to his head. "You're going to want to fix your hair. Came loose again."

It was the right length for him to tie it back, but not quite long enough for it to stay put all the time. She'd noticed yesterday he had to fix it at least twice during their outing.

Zach ran his hand over his pulled back hair. "That bad?"

"No, but trust me when I say you want to keep yourself as presentable as possible in front of those cameras."

He didn't argue, and tugged his blond locks free. Tucking the hair tie between his teeth, Zach ran his fingers through his hair to gather it. Shira unabashedly ogled. She couldn't help herself, with the way his arms extended over his head and drew his shirt taut enough to tease the lean muscle beneath.

When Zach finished, she nodded her approval. He would thank her later, given how the media liked to spin the smallest thing into a big negative to bring someone down a peg.

Ajax slung his massive arms over Jasper's and Zach's shoulders. "Don't worry, I'll keep the sharks from taking too many chunks out of them. You'll get them back in enough of one piece they'll still be useful to you."

Shira rolled her eyes, but before she could spit out a witty retort, a pale, lean woman in her late forties strolled up. Red-rimmed glasses perched on her nose, obscuring her dark eyes, and she'd plastered herself with a little too much makeup, as if she were trying too hard to hide her age, making things worse. Her auburn hair curled loosely around her shoulders, and what would have been business casual clothes were less so due to their tightness, and the amount of cleavage she sported. Shira wasn't sure if this woman was ready for a meeting or a date.

"Oh, Stacey, there you are," Ajax said to the woman. "I wasn't sure if you'd gone into the conference hall yet."

Shira's hand twitched. *So, this is what Stacey looks like.* Shira knew she'd have to deal with the annoying manager while here, but that didn't mean she was going to like it.

"No, I was ensuring relations for Tri-com were being maintained," she said, her tone matter-of-fact. "You three ready?" Her eyes quickly assessed Jasper, and then Zach. "It's hard to tell. I wish you two had worn something nicer for this."

Jasper and Zach shared a glance before Jasper spoke. "Why? All the othah teams are wearing whatevah they're comfortable with."

"Yes, well, they don't have to impress the press in the same way you do. At the very least, you two could have coordinated a team shirt." She gave them another once-over, this time her gaze lingering longer than it should have. "Oh well. At least the two of you look good, regardless of what you wear."

Shira wanted to puke. It wasn't just Stacey's grating personality she hated. It was her poor attempts to flirt with the guys that really made Shira's skin crawl. The guys never reacted, so she wasn't sure if they knew and tried not to acknowledge it, hoping it'd stop, or if she was hitting a brick wall of cluelessness. Shira wanted to have faith that her guys—*the* guys—were a little more observant, but she'd be lying if she said she had total faith in the prospect.

Shira lifted her cup of cooling coffee to her lips and instantly regretted it when Jasper sighed and spoke. "If I wanted to be nagged by my mom, I would have asked her to come today."

Shira choked, her hand flying up to her face to stop herself from spewing her drink everywhere. Of course, that only made things worse, as the warm liquid lodged in her throat, increasing her fit.

Mercedes and Narissa both gasped, the latter fussing and grabbing Shira a paper towel. Jasper and Zach had frozen in a half-startled state.

"You okay?" Mercedes asked, once Shira's coughing subsided a bit.

She nodded and held up her cup, hoping someone would help make up a decent excuse for her while she struggled to get her voice back. It was obvious she'd reacted to Jasper's comment, but someone was going to have to play nice, because Shira wouldn't.

"Coffee still too hot?" Zach asked, coming out of his state. "I knew we should have gotten you an iced coffee."

Mercedes gave him an incredulous stare. "Who drinks iced coffee in fall?"

"Crazy people on the East Coast," Shira squeaked

out, her throat still tight. Narissa rubbed her back to help. "They drink that stuff even during their tundra winters."

Both men rolled their eyes at the mention of *tundra*, and it made her laugh a bit, much to her throat's dismay.

After another moment of fighting back her ability to breathe and talk normally, Shira let out a breath and then noticed Stacey glaring at her. "Oh, hey, Stacey. I didn't see you there. You look… uh, nice. Could have gone a little less on the foundation a bit—would have made you appear younger. Just a pro tip from a former model."

The woman's eyes blazed, and for a moment Shira hoped Stacey would lose her cool, but she restrained herself and merely pointed toward the conference hall. "Let's go before we're actually late."

Stacey stalked off, and Shira couldn't stop the smug smile from appearing on her lips. *Am I being catty? Oh hell yes, I am, and proud of it, too.*

Ajax tipped his head to give Shira a pointed look, but it did nothing, as Shira merely reclined in her seat and shrugged, shooting back her own "What are you going to do about it?" expression.

Wisely, he turned his glance to Jasper and Zach. "Let's get going before we trigger a cat fight between those two, because I know neither of you would stop it."

Jasper feigned hurt, while Zach chuckled. "Why would we reign in our favorite spitfire attack dog? That'd be no fun."

Ajax laughed and then encouraged the guys to follow him to the conference. Just as Jasper made it to the doorway, he craned his neck over his shoulder to look back at Shira. "Hey, don't let Serenity have too much screen time."

Shira held up an offended hand. "Can't you trust me for two seconds? Unlike you two, I've got more than two brain cells, and I'm not sharing them with anyone."

Narissa and Mercedes burst with laughter. Jasper shook his head. "That's why I'm worried. Means you're more likely to be crafty and think you can get away with it later, using some feminine-wiles tricks."

Shira crossed one leg over the other and lifted an eyebrow in a "what of it" challenge. She had no shame using such tactics against them, even if it had nothing to do with allowing Serenity to use the headgear again or not.

Jasper opened his mouth, but before he could say anything, Zach grabbed him by the back of the shirt and hauled him into the room. The door shut behind them.

Mercedes sputtered on a laugh. "Way to get him all riled up."

"Honestly, he's going to need it when those reporters start grilling him," Narissa said. "As calm as Ajax was trying to be, I could tell a few have him on edge."

"Confident Ajax is afraid of the paparazzi?" Mercedes had a teasing tone to her voice.

Shira snorted. "A smart person always is. They're like a pack of ravenous hyenas. You give them even the smallest bit of room, they'll chew you up and spit you back out, no matter whether you deserved it or not."

She took a breath to turn her thoughts to something else, and held up the headgear. "How safe is this for Serenity to use?"

An amused smile spread over Narissa's lips. "While I

can't currently divulge the specifics, I can, in great confidence, say that she could wear that thing for several
hours and be fine."

That piqued her interest, but recognized the look on
her friend's face. NDAs were involved. So, no special
friends-only secret reveal.

Shrugging it off, Shira turned to Serenity, who was
still sulking, and held up the gear. "Okay, pouty-pants,
you can go back to having fun."

Surprise took over the girl's expression. "Really?"

Shira continued to hold up the headgear. "Would I
trick you like that?"

Serenity's eyes lit up, and she snatched the equipment.
"You're the best, She-ra!"

Her tiny hands struggled with the bulky equipment,
so Narissa offered assistance. While she did that, the
guys' AI, Alistair, spoke up from a speaker on the
helmet and explained how he'd been connected to the
device to help monitor Serenity's activities. That gave
Shira some comfort. While anything she watched on
there should be child-friendly enough, who knew what
could be accidentally broadcasted at a moment's notice.

"There, all ready to go," Narissa announced, making
one final adjustment on the helmet and then sliding the
ear phones over Serenity's ears.

Serenity giggled and gasped, clearly already diving into
something immediately. Shira guessed the AI had put
on a part of the opening ceremony. Not only was the
conference private, but that'd bore the poor girl to death.

Shira slipped Serenity's cooling cup of hot cocoa into
her hands, instructing the AI to make sure she had some
of it. It was a bit risky, but Shira didn't want the drink

going to waste, and Serenity needed something after she'd scarfed down that breakfast sandwich. Shira also put her trust that the girl was coordinated enough not to spill the drink.

"All right, now that she's not able to hear us," Narissa started, sitting back down by Shira and resting her hand under her chin while setting her eyes on Shira. "Let's talk about what happened downstairs."

Mercedes leaned closer. "Oh yeah, we're dying for the juicy details after what we saw."

Shira let out a slow breath. She knew this was coming. It was only a matter of time, and there was no getting around it. Neither would allow what happened to slide under the radar. "Fine, I'll talk about it with you two, but, Narissa, you've got to tell me how you're feeling today."

Narissa gave an appreciative smile for Shira's vagueness. They were keeping her pregnancy under wraps for a while longer, given it was so early, and apparently, she was considered a high-risk case. Tabloids didn't need any gossip around her and Ajax just yet. They were still hung up on the pair's "whirlwind" romance.

Shira could have rolled her eyes at the thought. The public needed to stop being so obsessed with others' lives and let them live as they pleased. Hell, Ajax could propose to Narissa any day now and Shira would support them, regardless of her own strong opinions about quick-to-happen engagements.

"Stomach is still revolting today," Narissa admitted. "But, I have found something it hasn't rejected finally."

She held up a small, opaque container that held what appeared to be blackberries. "I don't care if I hate this fruit by the end; I'm taking full advantage of it."

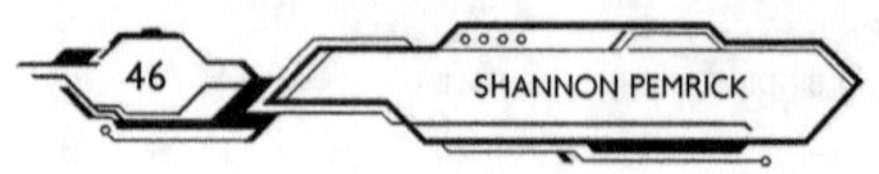

Shira smiled. "That's good to hear. Just tell us if you need anything."

Mercedes nodded. "Speaking of telling, what's with you and Stacey?"

Shira tilted her head back. "Don't get me started on her."

"She's a real piece of work," Narissa said, popping a berry into her mouth. "Ajax has had three conference calls with her, and he's hated every moment of them."

Mercedes grimaced. "That's saying something, coming from him, too, yikes."

"She's always nagging on the guys over the stupidest things," Shira said. "And when she's not doing that…"

"She's being a bitch to you?" Mercedes guessed. "Any reason why?"

Shira's nose scrunched. "Fuck if I know the true reason, but my guess is because I'm always with them, and it means she can't be a creepy flirt."

Mercedes blanched. "Seriously?"

Shira nodded. "Yeah. I caught her trying one day when I'd been going to meet up with the guys for some matches. It was creepy and painful to witness. Course, since then I've noticed even the most subtle of hints when she's interacting with them in my presence."

Narissa curled her fingers under her chin. "Make you jealous at all?"

Shira rolled her eyes. Naturally, she couldn't steer her friends away from the topic they wanted to get on. "I've got nothing to be jealous about with that woman."

Narissa's eyes gleamed. "Especially not after that kiss."

Mercedes leaned in closer. "Yeah, that first one was quite the doozy, wouldn't you say, Shira?"

Shira blew out a slow breath between her lips, heat rising in her cheeks as the vivid memory of Jasper's hot lips on hers surfaced. She could still feel the strength of his hand on her neck, the powerful scent of hickory that surrounded him and mingled with their shared breath, and the weakness of her knees as overwhelming desire swept through her. "Yeah, I guess so."

Mercedes smirked and nudged her. "C'mon… girl code, remember? Tell us exactly what's on your mind."

Shira couldn't stop the eye roll. Of course, that'd come back to bite her. She didn't even believe in that. It was something Tanya had come up with, and Shira clung to it still in some ways. Mostly when she wanted to be nosey with her friends—*much like how Tanya used it on me.*

Her friend poked her again, and Shira dropped her head back in surrender. "Okay, okay. It was fucking amazing."

The girls grinned and waited for more.

Shira ran her fingers through her hair before lifting her head and crossing her legs. "I'll be honest, I never believed in swooning and being swept off your feet. It was something nice to read about in a good romance book or see in a movie. But that…"

She bit her bottom lip, heat rising from her core at the memory again. "That definitely happened and I'm not sorry for enjoying it. Or Zach's, for that matter."

While the complete opposite of Jasper's tactic, Shira certainly liked Zach's sweeter, more public-appropriate approach. It made her feel just as wanted, and between the two, the attention had been the thing she needed to feel confident and happy enough to finish facing Jeremy.

A part of her still wished they hadn't been dragged

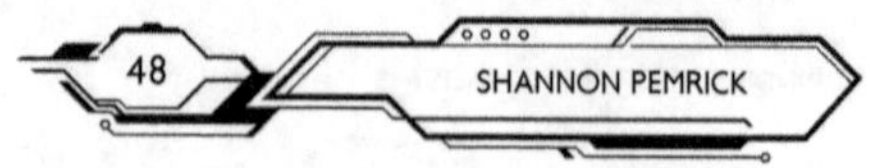

into her mess. She wished she could have proven herself in front of Jeremy without needing someone, or two someones, to help, but she also recognized it was the perfect final blow to him.

As much as Jeremy tried, he couldn't hide his reaction in front of her when the guys showed up and immediately erased his attempts to call her a liar. Even if she was, he didn't need to know that.

"Convention center to Shira," Narissa said in a sing-song voice. "You're in your head, instead of including us."

Shira ducked, a wave of embarrassment flashing through her. "Sorry. I haven't exactly had much of a chance to process everything. It's been… a bit of a whirlwind. Telling Jasper and Zach the truth, finally, lifted a weight off my shoulders I never thought possible. I didn't realize until that moment how much I needed to open up about what happened."

"How do you feel now that you've had to face him?" Mercedes asked. "We would have been the ones to help you out, but Jasper and Zach really wanted to handle it. It didn't look comfortable to deal with from where we watched."

Shira blinked slowly as she pieced together her emotions. "Honestly? I don't give a rat's ass about Jeremy or his opinion anymore. I thought I would, and that frightened me so much. But when I came face-to-face with him, after the initial shock wore off, I realized how much of an exaggerated boogeyman he'd become and I was able to work out my past issues involving him."

She smirked. "Though it was nice to get the chance to stick it to him. My vindictive side really enjoyed that."

"So, that means you're all set to charm a guy or two into your bed now, right?" Mercedes said, a wicked grin on her lips.

Shira grunted. "Don't get ahead of yourself."

"That wasn't a complete denial," Narissa teased. "Maybe there is something more to their little agreement we overheard them making."

Shira sucked in a tight breath. "I said don't get ahead of yourselves."

Mercedes nudged her again. "What's there to get ahead about? You don't kiss someone that passionately just for show."

"And don't forget about having murderous-intent outbursts after hearing what happened," Narissa said.

Mercedes' eyes shimmered with devious glee. "And the not-so-quiet promise to not promise to believe faking a relationship won't turn real."

Shira's cheeks heated. She'd been avoiding processing that conversation. "It's all for show, because now I need to make sure if we run into Jeremy again, he doesn't catch the lie. And we're definitely going to run into him, since Britney is a booth babe for some sponsor company of Ajax's, or something like that."

Narissa frowned. "She is?"

Shira nodded. "I don't care about that part. Though, she looked ready to climb both Jasper and Zach like a damn pole when she recognized them, and tried to gloat she'd be doing some sort of photo op with them."

"I'll talk to Ajax about it," Narissa said. "He did mention something in passing the other day about signings and photo ops, but I wasn't aware it was a for-sure thing."

Shira shrugged. "It doesn't bother me any. I found her

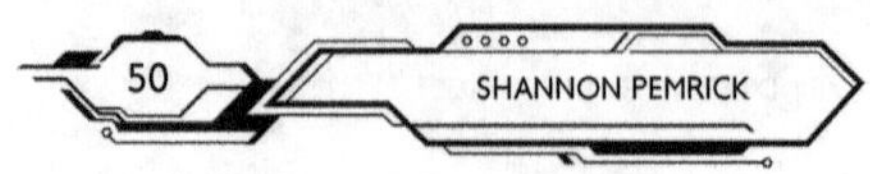

actions more amusing than anything. It'd be up to the guys if they want to deal with her."

"Knowing them, they're not going to want you to be upset in the slightest," Mercedes said. "Whether it's because you have to see Jeremy again, or deal with Britney's antics. We'd all be stupid to think they wouldn't put you first in these scenarios."

"Not to mention, given Jasper's outburst earlier, we don't need either of them tempted to actually make good on his words to kill Jeremy," Narissa said, typing something out on her phone, no doubt to Ajax for when the conference completed.

Shira shook her head. "I'm not worried. I know those two well enough to get them to cooperate. They both are still like kids when it comes to reward systems for behaving."

A smirk slipped up half of Mercedes' lips. "Do tell what that means. Because I've got a pretty good idea of one possibility that'd certainly work on them."

Shira's gut clenched, and she fought back the heat that threatened to rise into her cheeks and give her away. She knew what her friend meant, but neither of them could know what she'd done with Jasper and Zach. It was a one-time deal.

Her eyes darted to Serenity, to make sure she was still preoccupied. The girl was having the time of her life by the way she smiled, oblivious to the world around her.

The room was fairly sparse of other bodies, but she lowered her voice nonetheless as a precaution. "No, I'm not fucking them in secret."

Mercedes chuckled. "Sure you're not. Not with the way they've been looking at you all morning. I swear they're chomping to get in your pants."

"Should have seen the way they acted at dinner last night,

too," Narissa said, a devious tone to her words. "I thought they were going to pin her down on the table and have their way with her right there."

Mercedes' head flew back as she laughed. "Man, now I'm wishing Takashi and I had canceled our date plans so I could have seen it myself."

Shira's cheeks flushed hot. "Knock it off, you two."

Her blonde-haired friend gave her a pointed stare. "Maybe if you stopped dodging this and opened yourself to the real possibility in front of you, we wouldn't have to keep teasing you."

"What is so wrong with me wanting to be friends with them?" Shira asked.

"Nothing," Narissa said, shaking her head. "If there wasn't clearly something between the three of you, that is."

"You've always been someone who takes charge and goes for what she wants," Mercedes said. "Except when it comes to this. Just think about it, Shira. And I mean really think about it. You deserve to have everything you want. That includes them."

Shira crossed her arms and stared at the floor. Her friend had a point. *But still…*

Narissa leaned back and crossed her legs. "Why don't we change the topic from Shira's future relationship to give her time to think and talk about our plans for this week?"

Shira let out a quiet breath. She would definitely prefer that change. But a nagging voice in the back of her head told her she couldn't avoid reflecting for much longer. And that terrified Shira more than anything she'd forced herself to endure these last few weeks.

CHAPTER 4

mages flew up on Shira's phone screen as she scrolled. There was a lot more to do at the convention than she'd last checked, and given Serenity had grown bored with the opening ceremony about halfway through, Shira had an idea of what would and wouldn't keep her entertained. Though she had to admit, the young girl lasted longer than she expected.

Shira's attention flicked up to where Serenity stood by the glass walls overlooking the hustle and bustle below with Narissa and Mercedes. *Hopefully, this conference ends soon. There's only so long we can keep her occupied.* At this rate, Shira wasn't even sure if Serenity would want to watch her dads during any part of their matches.

While Shira didn't mind going around at the convention, she wanted to watch the matches, too. It was going to be difficult to find a suitable compromise.

A latch clicked, drawing Shira's attention to the

conference room doors. They opened and people filed out, a lively chatter about them. *Thank god.*

Shira looked for the guys and found them, with Stacey close behind. The woman had an ugly scowl on her face, piquing Shira's curiosity.

Ajax murmured something to the guys and then split off, bee-lining to Narissa. Jasper and Zach continued to Shira, their gazes flicking over to the glass wall a few times.

As they reached her, Stacey was the one to speak up first, her attention focused on the guys, and her words clipped. "Don't be late, you two."

Jasper scowled at her. "We won't."

Stacey set her jaw, and for a moment Shira thought she caught regret and uncertainty flash over her eyes, but the woman left without another word before Shira could be sure.

"I see you watched how much screen time Serenity received," Jasper said, plunking down next to her.

Shira leaned back, pretending it was all planned that way. "I told you to trust me. She watched some of the opening ceremony and then came out of it. Wasn't that hard."

Jasper looked at her with a skeptical eye. Before he could say anything, Shira sat up in her seat and pointed at a tan man with dark hair. "Alen, you snap that photo, and so help you, no doctor is going to understand how that lens got so far up your ass."

The room stilled, all eyes on Shira and Alen. Alen, his arms poised with a camera to snap a photo of Narissa and Ajax with Serenity, stared at Shira blankly for a moment and then recognition dawned on him.

"I see you still have an unruly mouth, Shira," he said, a sneer on his lips.

She narrowed her eyes. "You've no idea."

"There's no need to be so hostile, it's just one photo."

"You know the rules in a photograph-free zone. *And* you know the rules around photos taken with children."

"I planned to get permission," he said, not convincing in the least.

Shira's lip curled. "No, you didn't."

Jasper and Zach rose to their feet in union, Jasper nearly growling his words, "And we don't give it."

Heat pulsed in Shira's core at the sound of the possessive tone. She crossed her legs to suppress her reaction while projecting her confident persona to fight with Alen. Shira did her best to deny her want for these two, but honestly, how could she be expected not to react to that? She'd have to be out of her mind to not find their protective sides a turn-on.

Alen's attention flicked between the two protective dads and then settled back on Shira. He grinned. "Have something to share with us, Shira?"

Shira crossed her arms. "Not with the likes of you. Get lost."

"Oh, I think you—"

"That's enough." Eyes shifted to a lean, russet-skinned man. He had curly dark hair with a smattering of white, and dark, captivating eyes. "You're making a fool of yourself, Alen. Quit now before you regret it."

"Mind your own, Alex," Alen sneered.

Before Alex could spit out a retort, a security officer showed up. Alen tried to placate the man when he was asked to leave, but the officer was in no mood to play games and grabbed Alen by the shirt and dragged him out.

Shira smugly smiled and waved him goodbye. "Have fun looking at the convention center from the outside."

"Careful, Shira," he said, chuckling. "Can't keep hiding forever."

Shira continued to smile and turned her wave into an extended middle finger. Jasper, Zach, and Alex laughed behind her.

When Alen disappeared, she turned around and smiled brightly. "Hey, Alex."

He returned the expression, extending his hand. "It's good to see you again, Shira. You're looking good."

She shook his hand. "You too. Excited to cover all the talent here?"

Alex chuckled. "Always, especially if I can get a few interviews with some of the hot-topic teams." He pulled his phone from his pocket and held it up. "No pressure, but it'd be an honor to have one with your team. Ajax hasn't committed to any yet, from what he said in the conference, but you know me."

Shira smiled and whipped out her phone. "You're not sheisty, like Alen. I can't promise anything, but I can say we'll give you consideration."

Alex's eyes lit up and he transmitted his business contact information. "I appreciate it. You two need to prep for your match, so I won't keep you anymore." He started walking away, but continued to talk. "Oh, and, Shira, if you're interested, I'd love a scoop on what you've been up to. There are plenty out there who would love a six-year update."

Six years… The anniversary of the accident would be

next month. Shira leaned back in her seat, resisting the urge to bite her lip. "I'll give it some thought."

He clapped and pointed at her. "You won't regret it, I promise."

Alex left and Shira blinked, feeling like she missed something. Jasper laughed and sat back down. "Is it me, or did he take that maybe as a yes?"

Zach snickered, doing the same. "I got that impression, too. You sure you have nothing to worry about with him, Shira?"

She shook her head. "Alex is excitable, but he's a good man. If you two agree to any interviews, I highly recommend doing one with him. He always did great articles on me. And yes, he knows his stuff on gaming. That man has no chill on the topics he's willing to cover, but always makes sure he knows enough about it beforehand."

"Shira," Orion said from her phone. "I've forwarded the contact to Kirk in the event they wish to pursue."

Kirk was Ajax's AI. Shira thanked Orion and turned her attention to the gaming-innovator friend in question, only to find him crouched in front of Serenity doing some sort of coin magic trick—poorly. But Serenity was enjoying it, from what Shira could see.

"He's going to be a good dad," Jasper said.

"Yes, one day he will," Shira said, her eyes darting to some reporters still lingering about. The last thing she needed was for them to catch wind. Luckily, the guys seemed to catch on quickly.

Zach leaned back in his chair. "Guesses how many they may think of having?"

Shira pressed her lips together. It wouldn't be fair for her to answer.

Jasper tipped his head down and stared at her. "You know something."

"Narissa is one of my best friends," Shira said. "I know a lot of things."

Both guys leaned in, as if urging her to go on, and she laughed. "You two are terrible."

Zach grinned. "Just because we're men, doesn't mean we don't like a little juicy gossip now and then. Plus, it's always good stuff when it involves any of you three ladies."

Shira's eyes darted to Narissa and Ajax, who were still preoccupied with entertaining Serenity. She then spoke, but her voice was low, just in case. "There may have been a wishful prayer about three in the end."

Jasper's brows rose, and Zach nodded. "About what I was going to guess; too bad I didn't put money down."

Shira chuckled. Wasn't like that many kids was anything crazy.

"What about you?" Jasper asked. "In the futcha plan, that is."

Everything in Shira stopped. Her gut tightened, and the smile on her face disappeared. The surrounding commotion muted and slipped into a sensation of distance, as if something had yanked her away.

"Shira?" Jasper asked tentatively, his voice sounding farther than before.

Shira blinked, her senses coming back. She was now aware of Snake's head in her laps and the intense stare both guys gave her. *Answer the question.* She opened her mouth to speak, but pain pulsed in her chest and something else spilled from her lips. "Tell me what happened during the conference."

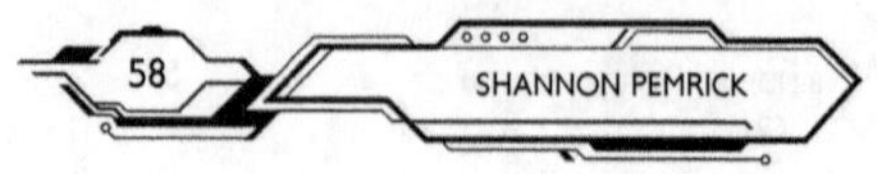

Jasper opened his mouth to say something when Zach murmured his name in warning. At least one of them was sensible enough not to press.

Exhaling, Jasper ran his fingers through his hair. "Conference, right. That, uh, went about as well as I expected."

Shira's brow quirked. "Meaning?"

"Meaning there's a reason Stacey left with little to say beforehand," Ajax said, walking their way. "She's a piece of work. Acted like I wasn't the one sponsoring the team and tried to answer many important questions incorrectly."

Shira grunted. "Sounds about right for her. I hope you shut her up by humiliating her."

Jasper chuckled. "Something like that."

Zach reclined in his seat. "Luckily, after we got her to shut up, things went smoother."

Ajax chuckled. "Better than that. You two are now more popular than ever."

"So when do the fangirls start swarming us while we're out and about?" Shira meant for that to come off as a joke, but there was a bit of a sour tone to it.

She couldn't deny dealing with fans would be annoying if they wanted to do things at the convention, but they wouldn't ruin anything. Even the people who became jealous monsters, Shira could handle that with no problem.

It's because you'd have to share the guys' time. Shira banished the thought as soon as it finished. The three of them were merely friends, and Jasper and Zach could spend their convention time how they wished.

Ajax grinned, the expression screaming "someone is

jealous," and she hated it. "Probably right after the two of them win their first match."

"Speaking of raving fans that Shira will run off when we're sick of them," Jasper started, making her choke and the others laugh. "We need to talk about something that was brought to our attention earliah."

"Photo ops and a possible meet-and-greet panel," Ajax said, nodding. "Narissa and I were talking about that a moment ago. Sorry for not bringing it up sooner. It wasn't a for-sure thing, so I didn't bring it up. I didn't expect you to find out about it from someone else, otherwise I would have."

He rubbed the back of his neck. "The panel won't happen, but a few key stakeholders have booths this year and they've asked us to stop by for some publicity. They're not taking no for an answer at this point."

Jasper made a face. "I guess this is what we signed up for when we signed the contract."

Zach grunted. "As long as Britney doesn't try to climb us like a tree, I'll do it."

Shira's head flew back as she laughed. "I'd like to see the look on her face when her attempt fails."

A wicked grin slipped up the side of Jasper's face. "Well, then we'll have to make sure we're extra entertaining when we kick her ladduh from underneath her."

"Sorry to disappoint you, but Narissa already made me aware of that situation, and I'll be having a talk with the companies to make sure their employees behave."

Shira crossed her arms and jutted out her lower lip into a pout. "Killjoy."

"What's not a killjoy are the matchups," Ajax said, clearly trying to distract her.

It worked. "Well?"

"We're the first match," Zach revealed.

Shira's eyes widened, excitement rushing up from deep inside her. "That's amazing!" She paused. "Wait. If that's the case, then why are we sitting here talking about things that don't matter right now? You two need to prepare."

"We're fine," Jasper said. "We have twenty minutes. No need to panic."

"Actually," Alistair said from his phone. "You have ten minutes now."

Queue the panic.

CHAPTER 5

Shira let out a breath and tapped on her tablet to pull up the Lusara Fates' competition screen. *One minute to spare.* Everyone had booked it across the convention center to the opposite side of the building, where the game center and VIP lounge were situated. Jasper and Zach barely said their goodbyes to her and Serenity before Ajax dragged them away. Shira hadn't even been able to wish them luck, it was that close.

Her guys were something else. *No, don't call them that.* But she knew she would, because not even she could convince herself of her lies now. Between the flirting in the days leading up to yesterday, everything that went down yesterday and especially today, and her talk with her friends…

"She-ra, who are Daddy and Zach going against?" Serenity asked, pulling Shira out of her head. The girl leaned on the center arm of the plush two-seater chair they shared, eyes wide with enough curiosity anyone could drown in them if they weren't careful.

Shira glanced down at her tablet and tapped the first round of Lusara Fates' twos matches. The screen flashed and info on the two teams displayed in a fancy cascade. "Looks like… the Regal Gladiators."

"Are they good?"

Shira nodded, resisting the urge to bite her lip. She definitely knew that name. "Wicked good. They usually run a similar build as your dads, but they also have a few that would make things difficult for them, so your dads are going to have to be on top of their game."

Mercedes snickered next to her and whispered to Narissa, "She said 'wicked.' I told you their speech is rubbing off on her."

Shira resisted the urge to shoot her friend a glare and instead tried to pretend she hadn't heard the comment— or that she had in fact let their lingo rub off on her.

Serenity ducked low, half-burying her face behind her hands. "So they're gonna lose?"

Shira gave the girl a reassuring smile. "Not as long as they stay focused. Your dads have been playing a long time, and have come up against even stronger teams than this and won."

Serenity perked up and smiled. "Yay! I want them to win so they can play against the cool old lady."

Blinking, Shira wasn't sure what she meant by that. "Who do you mean, Starship?"

"You know, the lady in those videos that tells us to call her Grannie, and kicks butt with magic."

"I think she's talking about Abigail from team Fiery Toucans," Narissa said.

A light clicked in Shira's head and she exited the first match info and pulled up the third match. Pictured under the team name Fiery Toucans were two older individuals, a man of dark complexion and a woman of light complexion. "This lady?"

Serenity peered at the tablet and nodded vigorously. "Yeah, that's her!"

Abigail was a frail-looking woman, and was pushing the age limit for VR gaming at seventy-nine. Most by now would have been convinced to give it up for the sake of their health, but Abigail was well-known for being quite the spitfire and wouldn't let anything but death stop her from enjoying her love of gaming. Even her teammate and husband, Everett, who was ten years younger than her, wouldn't allow anyone to tell them how to live their lives.

"Do you think I can meet her?" Serenity asked. "I wanna meet her wicked bad."

Shira smiled. "I'm sure we could find her so that can happen."

Serenity's eyes glowed and she cheered. Shira knew she shouldn't make promises she couldn't keep, but Abigail and Everett were known to be very kind to their fans, and given they were here for the competition, Shira figured it wouldn't be too hard to find them and ask.

"Can I weah the cool helmet now?" Serenity asked. "I wanna watch Daddy and Zach play."

Narissa rose from her seat, headgear in hand. "Absolutely."

Shira watched her friend hook up Serenity, her curiosity piqued. "Rissa, what exactly will she see?"

"It's a new spectator program. She'll be placed right

on the area floor as if she were part of the match. Either she or the AI attached to her gear can control what angle she views from."

Shira pursed her lips. "Are there parental controls on it?"

Narissa gave a closed-mouth chuckle. "Of course there are. She won't see anything graphic."

That was a relief. The large screens peppered around the VIP room and the ones around other parts of the convention center were all set up with PG filters because of the varied audience watching. But private hookups like her tablet or private access keys allowed a user to change it to their preference. Shira would have assumed the helmet had this, had it not been such a new prototype tech. You never knew what someone could have left out by mistake.

"How's that, Serenity?" Narissa asked. "Not too tight?"

"It's puhfect!" The little girl's smile reached her ears. "Thank you, Missus Narsa." She paused and then her nose scrunched. "I didn't say your name right. Sorry."

Narissa smiled kindly, even though Serenity couldn't see with the headgear blocking her sight. "It's okay. Some names are harder than others. Why don't you call me Rissa? All my friends do."

Serenity beamed. "I can do that?"

"Yes."

"Thank you, Rissa!" She then started kicking her feet. "Alistair, hurry up. I want to see Daddy and Zach."

"Patience, Starship," the AI said.

Narissa popped the headgear's headphones over Serenity's ears, and the little girl fell into the immersion.

"How long do you think it'll be before she's bored?"

Mercedes asked. "I know in theory these matches don't last very long, but it's rare they go three rounds of straight wins for one team."

Shira pursed her lips. "Hard to say. I don't know what she watches at home. Sounds like it might not be uncommon for her to watch PvP matches, given she knows who Abigail is. But Abigail is quite the personality, so if the shout casters bore her, it could affect things."

"I'm more concerned the analysts might bore her before the match starts." Narissa pointed to the earbud in one of her ears. "The one talking now is even dry for me."

Shira looked down at her tablet. She still had the teams information up. Popping an earbud into an ear, she swiped her screen to bring up the current match screen, as well as an overlay. Most of the information was dedicated to the match, from current team players to their classes and specializations, to more analytical stats on each player's abilities.

From what was explained to Shira, this data was only available to those with the new tech. The feature was disabled for Serenity, but Shira was more than eager to see how it would help. Narissa said it'd help her understand where some of Jasper's and Zach's weaknesses were during the matches. And while Shira wasn't the guys' coach or anything, she was invested in helping them improve in any way she could.

Several people were also displayed on one part of the overlay; all immersed in a VR setting with all manner of displays visible around them. The analyst speaking, Bryan, was going on about a player stat on Regal Gladiators. *Yeah, this sounds like him.* He was known to

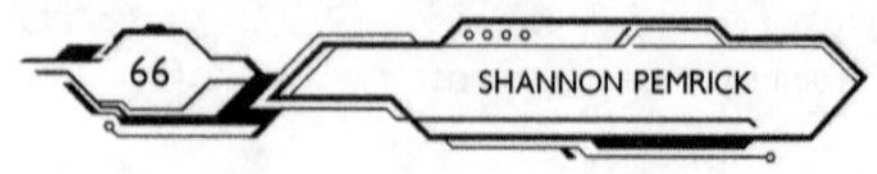

get fairly in-depth in his analysis. Shira quite liked his perspective and attention to detail, but she understood why others struggled with it.

Serenity made an interested sound and then a text popped up on Shira's screen. It was from Alistair.

> *I am breaking down Bryan's analysis for Serenity's benefit. It's a great teaching exercise.*

Shira smiled and typed back to the AI.

> *Great. Please record that breakdown for use later. Might be helpful.*

The AI made note he would, leaving her to continue her discussion with her friends. "I think we'll be good with Serenity for a little bit. Alistair is breaking down the analytics so she can understand and it seems she's enjoying it."

Mercedes blew out a breath. "At least she'll be able to understand. I just want to get to the match already."

Shira laughed. Even though she understood Bryan, Shira also wanted the match to start. That was the exciting part. And Jasper and Zach had worked hard to get to this point. She wanted to see it all pay off.

Bryan's rambling slipped away. They hadn't been the only ones working hard. Everything Shira had done this last month and a half had paid off more than she ever imagined. She'd long given up on herself, believing she would be forever stuck in her bubble of safety, even at the expense of living a fulfilling life. And then Jasper and Zach had to turn out to be the most persistent and stubborn obstacle not even she could overcome.

What she'd said to Jeremy about the guys surfaced in her mind. Shira twirled a lock of hair with her finger and resisted the urge to bite her lip. She may have made up a few things to get under his skin, but she hadn't lied to her ex when it came to how Jasper and Zach saw her.

As much as she wanted to deny it—wanted to believe they said pretty words only to make her feel better—Shira knew they had no reason to lie. Both of them genuinely wanted to help her. It was obvious with all the effort they'd put in to help her grow. And the truth was evident in how they'd treated her from day one.

They never tried to sugarcoat a situation. They were always up front, even if it made them uncomfortable. So when they called her beautiful and worthy of affection—cybernetic prosthetics and all—as much as that scared her to accept it, Shira couldn't claim that was a lie and believe it herself.

The screen of her tablet changed, and the match started. Jasper and Zach chose their main go-to class combos: rogue and warrior. Shira's hair slipped out of her hold as she moved her hand and pressed it firmly against her lips. *C'mon, guys, you've got this.* They'd have a tough match against their opponents, who chose to go double berserkers—a heavy-hitting, high-defense class that ran on a rage mechanic. Of course, her brain didn't want to focus on that. It demanded she finish reflecting on the events today to sort out her feelings.

With her finger pressed to her lips, it brought back the vivid memory of Jasper's lips against hers. Hot and consuming—she swallowed and clenched her thighs

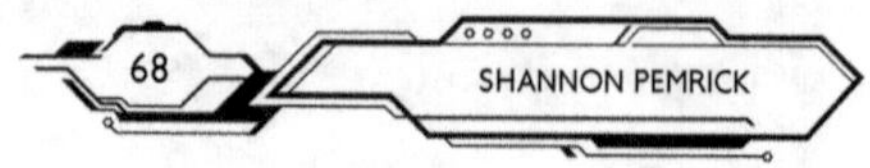

together, fighting back the wave of arousal that surfaced. She hadn't lied to her friends when she'd admitted she enjoyed it. But that wasn't even close to how it really made her feel.

Her fingers grazed her forehead as she brushed a wayward strand of hair from her eyes. *And fucking Zach...* That forehead kiss? It wasn't fair. Didn't he know that was a major chink in even the most stubborn woman's armor? How was she not supposed to look at him like he handed her a signed, limited-edition Lusara Fates clothing and armor art book?

Pretending they were both her boyfriends in front of Jeremy made her confident and happy, but if she was honest with herself, if the two of them had done that to her without him there, that feeling wouldn't have changed.

Pain flared in her chest, sobering her emotions. She'd revealed so much to them today, but the answer Jasper sought about Shira's plans for children, "More than I'll ever be able to have," had lodged in her throat. It was one painful truth she wasn't willing to say yet. And if she could, would they be able to accept that?

Could we be something for real?

Mercedes and Narissa sure thought so. Even her therapist, Angelica, focused on this idea during their sessions. *And then that conversation on the stairs...*

Heat threatened to burn her cheeks, remembering what Jasper said about not promising the relationship façade wouldn't turn real for him. Then there was Zach, who had been joking with his suggestions, but also showed no issue with Jasper's claim.

Shira chewed her lower lip. She just wasn't sure. She didn't want to misread something because she was desperate to be loved and turn into *that* woman. *But… if I'm honest with myself…* Shira also wasn't sure she could live her life on a "what if," if she let the possibility slip through her fingers.

A finger tapping her leg brought Shira out of her thoughts. She blinked at Mercedes. "Sorry, what?"

Her friend frowned. "I was worried you were in your head. You haven't reacted at all to the match. I expected swearing when they lost this first round."

The first round was over? Shira's eyes snapped to her tablet, and sure enough, Regal Gladiators had the first win. *Shit.* "I'm just thinking about some things."

Narissa bent forward to peer around Mercedes at Shira. "Hon…"

Shira shook her head. "No, I don't want to talk it out. This is something I need to sort through myself right now."

Mercedes frowned. "Are you sure? I know we tease you a lot, but we care, Shira. And you know how good we are, even with your deepest, darkest secrets."

Shira gave them her best reassuring smile. "I'm being honest. This is something I need to figure out myself. And my brain has chosen now to do it."

Her friends were going to have to trust her on this. They'd had their talk, and now it was up to Shira to be a big girl, and figure her shit out.

"She-ra!" Serenity shouted.

Shira flinched, eyes in the room snapping to them. She moved one earpiece of the girl's headgear. "There's no need to yell, Starship."

"But you didn't respond when I said your name before," Serenity complained.

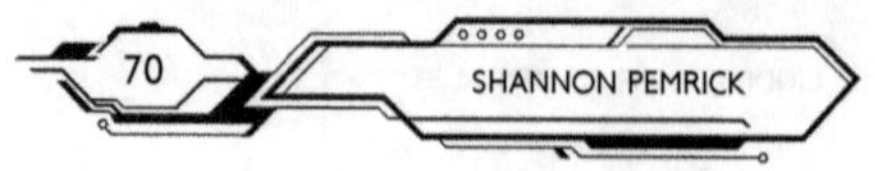

"That doesn't mean you yell," Shira said, trying to keep her voice calm and even. "You take your headphones out and hear that I'm having a discussion with Narissa and Mercedes, then wait your turn."

"But…" Her lip stuck out into a pout. "Daddy and Zach lost…"

Shira brushed her cheek. "Just the first round. There are more for them to win."

"You sure?"

"Of course. One team needs to win a total of three rounds before they're declared the winner."

Serenity pursed her lips. "Okay. I'll trust you. When are we going to do something else?"

Shira paused, concerned she'd overestimated the girl's attention span. "Are you bored?"

Serenity shook her head, though it was a janky motion with the headgear. "No, I just wanna do other things, too."

"Okay." That was a relief. "How about, we watch two more rounds, and then we can talk about if we'll go do something else?"

Serenity agreed and popped the ear piece to immerse herself again. Shira let out a breath and turned her attention back to her tablet. This time, she'd focus on the matches. She could sort her feelings out later when she was alone and her attention wasn't torn in different directions. *You two had better get your act together, or I'm going to be kicking your asses.*

Clashing steel and strained battled cries assaulted Jasper's ears. He slunk around in the shadows thanks to his rogue-class stealthing abilities, watching Zach swing his broadsword at the berserker in front of him. The weapon hit its mark and his opponent's health dropped. It wasn't a lot, not that Jasper believed such a basic attack would give them any sort of edge, but with both their teams lacking a healer, and regeneration potions or items limited in these settings, any health loss could mean the difference of winning or losing a match. And this match really counted.

Zach dodged a cleaving swing from the berserker's great axe and narrowly missed his partner's swing as well. Jasper adjusted his grip on his daggers and held his breath. He loved playing rogue, but it required patience, and if he timed this wrong, he'd screw everything up. He had to trust Zach to make the appropriate assessments

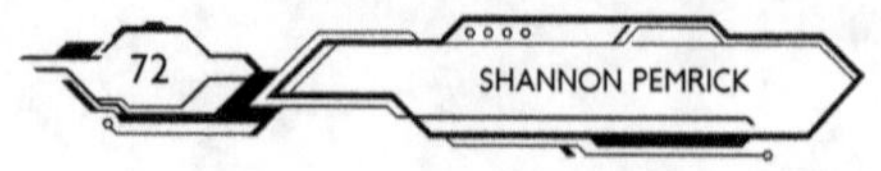

on how to handle the two berserkers, while Jasper got into a better position from the shadows.

They'd been bummed by how easy they had it in the qualifiers, and now Jasper was wishing they hadn't pushed their luck. This match against the Regal Gladiators was no joke. They were unlike any team he and Zach had ever come up against—and it had cost them two rounds.

Zach and Jasper had managed to secure two wins despite their struggle and losses, making this last round that much more important, but it hadn't been easy achieving those wins. Switching up their class combo hadn't even helped. Jasper was fairly certain, because they hadn't practiced other combos enough like Shira told them to do, that the class-change attempt attributed to the previous round's loss. He could imagine the field day she was having watching his and Zach's performance.

An axe slammed into Zach, sending him skittering and dropping his health a fair amount.

Health: 65%

Jasper winced. *Focus and help Zach.* He could worry about Shira's reactions later. Winning this round was his priority. While the tournament used a double-elimination-style setup, losing this early was not an option if they wanted to be seen as a credible, competent team, and not some potential charity case Ajax's company cooked up.

And it might negate some of the earful from Shira they'd get. *Maybe she'll reward us instead for winning.* Not likely, but he could hope.

One of their opponents aimed another quick attack on Zach, but Zach mitigated the damage with a well-timed ability activation. The berserkers converged on Zach, and Jasper grinned. He took two steps to the left and snuck up behind his unsuspecting target.

"I'm in a good position," Jasper said through their team chat. "The meatheads lined themselves up puh-fectly."

"Then let's put on a good show for our adoring fans, and the two ladies keenly watching us."

Jasper chuckled and then went through the mental gymnastics to activate an available stun ability and sliced into the berserker with the lowest health, taking him out of stealth. The guy's avatar pitched forward, but didn't fall, instead remaining completely immobile in a stunned state. At the same time, Zach used a slam attack on the other person, the stun taking hold.

Zach then switched his focus to the berserker Jasper was going to town on, using all his major abilities to nuke their opponent's health. Not to be outdone, Zach did the same, activating a strength ability as well as some attacks that auto-crit stunned targets.

It wasn't usually the best move to use all your tricks in one go, but Jasper had lost half his health early in this match, and with how long the stun abilities took to recharge before another use, they weren't likely to have another opportunity like this during the match—not with how quickly they ended.

The two of them managed to get their opponent down to thirty-five percent health when the stun Jasper had on the berserker wore off suddenly. He swung his weapon at the squishier rogue. Jasper dodged and disengaged,

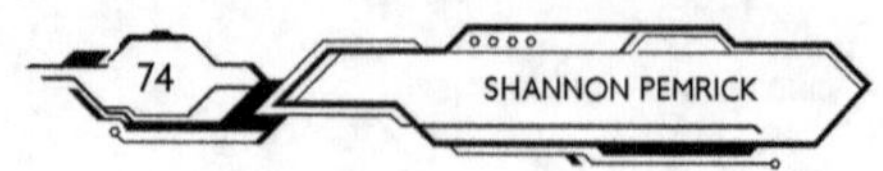

rapid calculations blurring through his mind. It was too soon for that to have ended. *Item activation, maybe?* It was the most likely scenario. He couldn't think of a stun-breaking ability berserkers had. Only one to shield them from a stun if used at the right time.

No matter. There were still four seconds to the stun on the other berserker. They could do this.

Zach sliced his sword into the back of the mobile berserker, following it up with a trip move, sending him crashing to the ground. Jasper jumped on the opportunity and sliced into the prone man.

Health: 25%

Zach raised his sword high into the air and slammed it down, using a great cleave attack he hadn't gotten to use when the berserker was stunned.

Health: 15%
Health: 13%
Health: 10%

Jasper's pulse thundered in his ears. They were almost there.

The stun on the other berserker ended. Zach pivoted and activated a damage-reduction ability when the opponent went in for an immediate strike. Jasper held his breath. It was a powerful move, the axe glowing with rage power unique to the berserker class. Even with the mitigation, a sizable chunk of health disappeared.

Health: 40%

That was close.

Adrenaline pumped through Jasper's veins. This is what he loved about this sport. You never knew what your opponents were going to throw at you, forcing you to think on your toes, or it was game over.

Zach focused on their less-tired opponent. "Bloodied guy is all yours, Jasper. I'll try to keep this one occupied."

"How generous. I'll try not to let it go to my head."

Zach chuckled and dodged an attack before retaliating. This left Jasper to handle his target. Not easy for a squishy little rogue, but he had some evasion abilities available to him.

Skirting around the berserker, Jasper sliced at a weak point in his defensive stance. His opponent jumped back instead of to the side, and he stumbled a bit. Jasper took advantage of the misstep and attacked two more times before disengaging. To his surprise, the berserker didn't swing a retaliatory attack. *Maybe he's a bit shaken.* The guy probably hadn't expected the tagged attack on him and his partner. And with only 10% health left, he couldn't be reckless. Whatever the reason, Jasper would use it to his advantage.

Running a safe perimeter around the berserker, Jasper looked for an opening. His opponent turned with him, making it more difficult, but he was definitely unnerving the guy.

Lunge. Strike. Withdraw.

Jasper took a sliver of health out of the berserker and retreated. The berserker swung his weapon on the retreating step, but Jasper anticipated this and activated an evasion ability. His form warped, as if he were so fast that he appeared in more than one place at a time. His

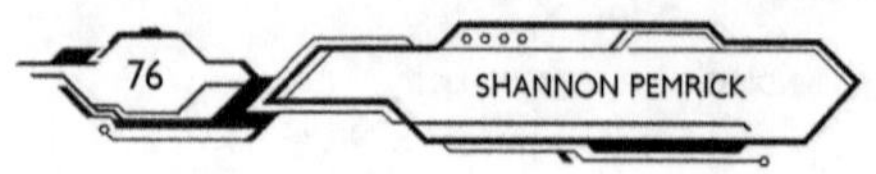

opponent was unable to figure out where the real him was and swung at an illusionary shade. Jasper stabbed the guy's arm, taking off a few more points of damage.

He stole a glance toward Zach, who was matching blows with his opponent, neither willing to give an inch. From the red in the berserker's eyes, Jasper guessed he'd popped one hell of a rage-based damage mitigation ability—possibly even one of the better ones at the class' disposal.

Jasper shifted and lunged for the nearly defeated berserker, instead of dancing around him again. Taken by surprise, his opponent stumbled back and barely blocked the weapon strike. But that was the mess-up Jasper was hoping for.

"Zach!" he called. "Thirty degrees left, cleave if you've got it."

There was no hesitation in Zach's movement to pivot and activate the needed ability. His sword landed a powerful blow to the weakened berserker, and he went down.

Health: 0%

Jasper wanted to cheer. But celebration would have to wait. He and Zach both still needed to stay alive for an entire minute before the match officially ended. If the remaining member of the Regal Gladiators took one of them out, the timer would reset, and they'd be at a significant disadvantage.

Jasper backed off while Zach took a defensive stance. It was tempting for them both to stay out of the berserker's reach and wait out the minute for a win, but doing so would penalize and disqualify their team.

Tournaments weren't just about beating down another team. It was entertainment for those who watched. And a team that dicked around wasn't fun for an audience. They wanted excitement, so the organizers made sure that happened.

It was a part of tournaments that he and Zach were still getting used to. The two had forgone livestreaming because entertaining people, at least for long periods, wasn't part of their wheelhouse. With these tournaments, it was only for a few rounds and they were done. Of course, this tournament was going to significantly test the two of them, since both he and Zach had failed to predict the popularity that came with signing on with Ajax for a temporary sponsorship.

Then again, Jasper never expected they'd get this far. The reason they never could secure a company-approved sponsor to attempt the qualifiers for this tournament was because they didn't participate enough in the bigger East Coast tournaments to make a large splash. Jasper really believed they'd stay a nobody team while the more well-known teams remained the center spotlight. *If I was honest, and not trying to pretend everything was going to be a cakewalk, we'll be lucky if we don't get kicked out of this tournament before the semi-finals.*

The remaining berserker shifted his weight to charge, the angle clear he was going for Jasper, the weaker and easier to take down of the two. Zach, the good stand-in tank he was, wasn't having it. He activated a knock-back ability, and positioned himself in front of their opponent, effectively blocking his sight of Jasper. Lucky for Jasper, his boyfriend always kept one of his defensive moves in waiting when they fought berserkers.

Berserkers had a nasty charge attack, and while knocking him back usually wasn't the best idea, since Zach was still within a suitable distance, the charge couldn't be used to its full extent.

The berserker snarled, though Jasper knew that was an ability activation rather than the guy being weird. His muscles tensing and bulging were the first giveaway, and the redness in his eyes intensifying was the second.

We're fucked…

This rage was one he'd hoped hadn't come back for the guy to use. Based on the tense expression on Zach's face, he didn't have any abilities available to stop it. Berserkers under this rage influence were immune to stuns and slows, and all damage on them would be halved. Their damage was increased as well. It was a strong ultimate ability, and lasted a good ten seconds. It didn't sound long, but in a match like this, it felt it—like the one-minute timer counting down.

If Zach had gone a tank spec with a shield, he may have had a better chance surviving a head one with the raged-out player, but Zach had wanted the damage boost to make up for Jasper's need to play it safe when the full enemy team was active.

Jasper had to think quickly, or they'd trip at the finish line. "I'll run left when he charges. Dodge right."

"You sure?"

"Yes."

Zach took a deep breath and shuffled his weight back and forth as he contemplated. Splitting up was risky, but he needed Zach to trust him. As the technical team captain, it was Jasper's job to work out the plays on their feet. During practice, he could take extra risks and goof off sometimes, but a lot of those choices were just that—practice. They were him testing what could happen. It made it so that when it was tournament time, his plays were all calculated to be the best, and done in record speeds.

The berserker's muscles bunched, and then he charged. Zach took a step back, trying to feign fear and indecisiveness, and then dodged like Jasper instructed. The enemy swung wide to compensate for the sudden maneuver, but Zach was ready and activated a tripping attack. The berserker stumbled, but it didn't stop him.

Unsurprisingly, he continued in his direction for Jasper, aiming to take out the weakest target, who was already moving left and out of his reach. Jasper tossed some low-damage throwing daggers, the weapons making their mark, and then he threw out some spiked metal balls. *Take the bait.*

These wouldn't slow or harm a berserker under this rage influence, but that wasn't Jasper's goal. As he hoped, the berserker kept coming, not seeing the trap he was walking right into.

Jasper made a motion with his fingers, and the spikes retracted. The now-smooth metal balls clattered to the ground, scattering. Mind fogged from the rage haze, his opponent had no chance to stop, and his feet contacted the trap. His legs flew up into the air, sending his heavy body crashing to the ground where he lay prone.

Jasper smirked. He could only imagine the profanities the player screamed as he was forced to follow the biggest downside to this particular rage mechanic.

The berserker scrambled to get back on his feet, only

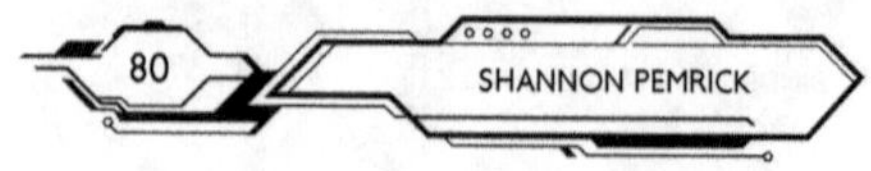

to fall again. Jasper chuckled and then activated a stealth ability as it came off cooldown.

"Keep him distracted," Jasper said.

Zach grinned, onboard with the unspoken plan. "Happy to."

Their team may be penalized for not taking the last minute seriously, but as long as he and Zach were showing to be strategic in trying to get around the ten-second rage, they could slip under the rules. They just had to have the plan in place to enact the moment the rage ended. Zach knew his part, and he was going to trust Jasper for his.

He and Zach had a different bond than other teams and players. Most talked all the time with their strategies and moves. But not them. They trusted and understood each other so well, it wasn't uncommon for the two of them to not speak at all during a match.

Stacey got on their case all the time for the lack of communication. And even Ajax, when he had watched them a few times during practices leading up to this tournament, had voiced his unease with their tactic. The only person to not see their method strange was Shira. Even when she joined them for threes and ended up being the only one to talk and outwardly strategize, she didn't berate them and try to change how they worked. She accepted it as a normal thing and played to that as a strength—and a strength she helped make it, as he was seeing today. Never had he and Zach worked so efficiently, even with the rounds they lost.

The enemy berserker roared in his rage. With bared teeth, the man scrambled on hands and knees, trying again to get to Jasper, or at least, where his avatar thought

Jasper was. It wasn't a dignified sight, but this was the player's only way to control his character without slipping on the metal balls that still had another few seconds before they despawned.

Jasper skirted around their opponent. Zach could see him, so there wasn't a risk of them getting into each other's way, but he also didn't want to risk it. This was Zach's moment to show the power of his warrior class.

Zach poised his sword and kept pace with the desperate player, but he was also careful of the trap. Sadly, this trap had a friendly fire drawback, forcing Zach to be calculating with his footing.

The berserker slipped, his body falling closer to Zach, who took an opportunistic swing. Not much health dropped away when the blade made contact, but if whittling down his health for the remainder of the countdown was what would be required, then so be it.

Zach got in another swipe before the enemy player attempted to retaliate. It was easy for him to sidestep the feeble attack, and Zach took the chance to shave off a little more health by hacking at the exposed arm.

Health: 83%

The berserker snarled and attempted to climb to his feet, his focus now no longer attached to the vanished rogue. *Good.* Zach could do this while Jasper continued to position himself and calculate their next moves once his trap's timer ran out. He didn't have many options right now in the way of high-damaging attacks, beyond the boost he'd get coming out of stealth—but that was a waste if this berserker was still raged. If luck was on their side, one of Zach's better abilities used earlier would come off cooldown.

The enemy player rose to his feet on wobbly legs. The metal balls under him threatened to send him flat on his back, but the berserker managed to stay upright. Jasper worked his jaw, taking another few steps to the side. That was a good sign that his trap was ending.

He glanced at the timer at the corner of his vision and relayed the number to Zach for his benefit. "Two seconds."

Through a quick calculation, that gave a four-second timer on the remaining amount of rage from the berserker. In the chaos of the fighting, he'd lost track of the match timer status, but he prayed it wasn't much longer.

One second. Jasper readied his daggers and poised to activate the last stun he had. "Get ready."

On cue, the metal balls under the berserker vanished and the player's feet bit into the ground, propelling him into a charging sprint toward Zach, his sharp axe at the ready to strike. Zach bent his knees and rolled his weight, ready to spring when his opponent closed the distance a little more.

When it came, Zach activated a guaranteed dodge buff and strafed to the left. The berserker clumsily tried to pivot mid-charge and swing. The weapon swung wide, leaving him exposed, and Zach lunged, striking true to his enemy's chest with a critical blow.

Health: 80%

Zach didn't take time to celebrate the small win, jumping

back. His buff activated when the berserker swung again, negating the damage he would have received.

Jasper sucked in a tight breath and maneuvered around the battlefield some more, trying to get into a better position around such a wildly moving target.

Two seconds left on the rage. C'mon, Zach, help me. He could see the silent calculations running through his partner's head, but he'd yet to say anything.

Zach's attention darted away from the berserker to Jasper. He worked his jaw, as if calculating a positioning, then grinned. "Stay put—one-hundred-and-ninety-degree shift coming up."

Jasper's eyebrow arched. *What the hell is Zach planning?*

Zach shifted and moved with purpose. He made each movement obvious, keeping his opponent's attention. The berserker bared his teeth, red eyes intent. The player's muscles bunched and Zach dashed to the side, slipping past the berserker's attack. Jasper grimaced when the weapon nicked Zach, taking a sliver of health.

Health: 38%

That'd been too close for comfort.

One second.

Zach shrugged off the close call and continued moving, drawing the berserker's attention and—Jasper smirked, realization dawning on him—facing his back to his enemy's downfall.

Zero.

The red rage melted from the berserker's eyes, and his shoulders sagged. The last drawback to that ultimate ability: fatigue.

Lusara Fates had unique abilities for PvP and PvE for all classes. The change made the classes balanced for each game type, without causing problems for the other. And in PvP, berserkers became sluggish and fatigued after using their biggest rage ability. It forced a player to be careful when they used it. And had Jasper and Zach not had a good plan to counter it, their choice of ability would have worked in their opponent's favor. But now, it was their turn to capitalize on the situation before them.

The berserker's eyes rolled, and his head dropped onto his bulky chest. The man's body slumped, but didn't fall over. Jasper rushed for the brute, daggers poised, and sliced his weapons into his opponent's back, breaking his stealth and jumping through the mental processes to activate his readied stun. Mixed with the combination of his stealth, the stun gripped the berserker to its full effect. Now they had to act fast.

With great speed, Zach lunged at their opponent and carved his blade into the avatar. He activated every damage-boosting ability he had in reserve, slicing out chunks of health.

Health: 80%
Health: 75%
Health: 69%

Jasper slashed his daggers, bleeding the berserker and shaving off smaller, quicker bits of health.

Health: 68%
Health: 67%
Health: 61%

The berserker twitched, the stun wearing off, but Zach was ready. He bashed the opponent, using a minor stun to give them more time.

Health: 59%
Health: 53%
Health: 46%

They could do this. *Just a few more strikes.*

A bell chimed, and their attacks ceased to do any damage. Jasper released a strained breath, all the built up tension rolling out of him in one exhausting wave. They'd done it. They'd survived the timer and won the match, securing their win to the next round.

The berserker grinned at them and then winked out of existence. Jasper and Zach landed an excited high-five in celebration before the game ejected them.

Awareness slowly came to Jasper. His senses were dull at first, but he eventually felt his gaming chair and the soft murmurs in the room where the match took place. Loud conversation was prohibited while competitors came out of their games; it helped them adjust.

Jasper could hear the gamecasters yammering on about the match from a nearby projection screen—some of it positive, some of it critical. He didn't care much for this part of the match end. What they said rarely mattered to him, even if the criticism they threw out was valid. To Jasper, it was easy to criticize from the outside, where your mind wasn't in the moment with adrenaline pumping through your veins. Even the best PvPers were going to make mistakes.

Jasper's body finally kicked his mind back into reality,

returning all his senses, including the excitement of their win. He launched himself out of his chair. Zach barely had time to anticipate him, and he crashed into his boyfriend, wrapping his arms low around Zach's waist, lifting and spinning him. He was sure to keep it brief, however. Jasper didn't want Zach to lose his stomach. He usually suffered a bit more than Jasper from the VR transitions.

Jasper put him down after a moment and the two wrapped an arm around each other's neck. They beat each other's chests, both smiling widely.

"We did it," Jasper said.

Zach nodded. "We did it."

There were cameras in this room, watching every move they made for the sake of the fans, but Jasper didn't care if the two of them looked like unprofessional fools. To be here at this tournament was an exciting opportunity in its own right for two nobodies like themselves, but to win their first match against a better-known and accomplished team? Why shouldn't the two of them revel in their excitement? Dignity be damned.

When the two of them collected themselves, they straightened and faced the two players of Regal Gladiators approaching them: Lucas and Elias, two brothers from Sweden. Lucas was on the leaner side, while Elias was broad-shouldered and imposing.

Jasper and Zach shook hands with them.

"Congratulations on the win," Lucas said first, his tone pleasant. "You two put up a good fight."

Jasper laughed. "You two didn't make it easy on us, that's for sure."

"Not going to lie," Elias said, sighing slightly, "I am

disappointed. I really thought I had you two with that last skill. Your teamwork is good. I didn't expect that."

He grinned. "You've got my support making it to the end, to face off against us after we squash everyone else in the other bracket."

"Sorry, but not me," Lucas said. "My vote is on Burnout."

Zach snickered. "I don't blame you. I won't be surprised if they go all the way to the finals undefeated and we end up facing off in the loser's bracket again."

Jasper wanted to disagree, saying he had faith in their skill, but Burnout, a brother-sister team from Germany, had one of the best win-loss records in the Lusara Fates twos bracket. Jasper wasn't looking forward to facing them if the opportunity came.

The four of them shared a few more sportsmen words before parting ways. Ajax waited for them by the doors, grinning like mad. When Jasper and Zach reached him, high-fives passed between them all before they slipped out into the hallway. The next teams were waiting to enter, so it was considered poor behavior to linger in the competition room.

"Great job," Ajax said. "Kept me on the edge of my seat, that's for sure."

"We'll do bettah next time," Jasper promised.

Ajax shook his head. "Doing your best is all I expect. Which, it's clear by your show this match, is what you two were doing."

"We still need to do bettah. It's your reputation on the line," Jasper said.

Ajax's brows pulled together. "Don't let the excitement of the press twist things. While I had preliminary discussions about sponsoring a team, I wasn't planning on taking any this year. You didn't arbitrarily beat out another team deserving of our sponsorship because we're friends. As long as you try your best, I'm happy with whatever performance you two put on, win or lose."

Jasper worked his jaw, struggling to accept Ajax's stance. He understood what his friend was saying, but still…

"The ladies get that bored of our match?" Zach said. "Tough crowd."

Jasper glanced around the VIP room, but Mercedes, Narissa, Shira, and Serenity were nowhere in sight.

Ajax looked around and grunted. "Huh. I didn't expect that."

Jasper whipped out his phone and chuckled at the sight on his screen.

"Shira?" Zach guessed.

"Yeah." He grinned. "She left a nice reactionary play-by-play."

Zach crossed his arms and shifted his weight to his heels. "This should be good."

"Nice shot. What the fuck was that? Seriously? Okay, that was a good move. Not bad. Good win! Really? Wow, you two are morons. Why did you do that? Are you two not using your brain or something? Guys…"

Jasper smirked. "Serenity wants to do more than watch you all, even though she's having fun. She thinks you're both doing amazing. I've got the tablet, so don't pull any more stupid stunts."

Zach laughed. "Anything else?"

"Hmm, more insults, some praises, a quip about our class change-up and why we should listen to her more about practicing those, and incoherent text screaming that I'm pretty sure her AI sent, before a wall of congratulations."

Ajax joined in Zach's laughter. "She likes to keep you two on your toes."

Jasper shook his head and started texting. "That's an undahstatement."

"Is she always that harsh to you?"

Zach rocked his head. "Yes, but it's not really malicious. She does it because she knows we'll laugh at her reactions rather than take it personally. And we do the same back to her."

Ajax shook his head. "The three of you have one of the strangest relationships I know."

"Not going to make comments like Mercedes or Narissa would?" Zach said.

Ajax's head flew back as he laughed. "No, I understand just how complicated she makes things. Can't say I blame her with the shit that's been thrown at her, but you two are determined, so all the power to you."

Jasper nudged him. "You know a thing or two about stubborn and resistant women."

A broad, unashamed smile spread across Ajax's face. It brought one to Jasper. It was good seeing their friend happy with how things turned out with Narissa. Neither he nor Zach really knew if Ajax would end up pulling it off. Takashi, too, with Mercedes. "What is it with the women we know acting like they're allergic to relationships?"

Zach laughed. "That's the million dollar question, isn't it?"

His phone chimed, and Jasper pulled up the text from

Shira. "Looks like they're all in Cosplay Alley, hanging out with Takashi, Rei, and Emi."

"Good, it'll be nice to see those three finally."

Jasper agreed, and the three of them set a quick pace to the other side of the convention center.

CHAPTER 7

eople moved by in a blur. Zach breathed hard, putting everything he had into trying to keep up with Jasper.

"You two need to slow down," Ajax complained behind him. "You act like they're going to disappear."

"One, I've got to make sure we did actually convince Shira to come to this place and I didn't imagine that," Jasper said, dodging a group of people who rushed through his path. "And two, we're in a bit of a time crunch. I want to actually enjoy this convention between matches."

Ajax chuckled. "I can't argue either point, though I can assure you, Shira is here."

"How do we know you didn't imagine her, either?" Zach asked.

"Well, Narissa does call me a dumb jock all the time."

The three of them laughed.

The crowd of people went from everyday clothes,

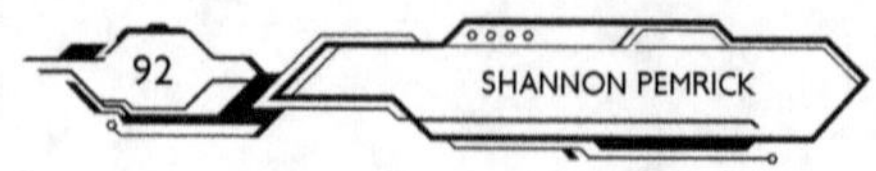

to extravagant costumes. The three of them found themselves in Cosplay Alley. Zach bobbed his head as he searched for any signs of their friends. *Like a needle in a haystack.* Didn't matter if some of them weren't in costume—there were so many people, they still blended in.

"I see them," Jasper called out. He pointed to a pair of benches where Narissa and Shira sat watching Mercedes and Serenity talking with a few people.

They pushed through the cosplayers and other con-goers. Ajax beat Zach and Jasper to the punch, alerting their friends of their presence.

Shira jumped to her feet and Serenity cried out their names before abandoning the people they'd been talking with to run over to them. Serenity, even with her smaller feet, beat Shira to them and latched onto Jasper's leg. "You won!"

They smiled down at her, Jasper speaking. "I told you we would."

"But you lost, too!" Her nose scrunched in the same way Shira's did. "They beat you up wicked bad, Daddy."

Shira's arms flew around their necks before Jasper managed to come up with a witty response. Zach instinctively placed a hand on her back. "You two need to get a different hobby other than giving me a damned heart attack."

Zach chuckled, his nose twitching as a lock of her gorgeous hair ticked him. "But it's wicked fun seeing your reactions."

Jasper stuck a finger in his ear and wiggled it around. "What? I can't hear you over the texted wall of screaming we received."

Shira laughed as she hung her head. "That was Orion's doing."

Zach snickered. That, he could believe. Her AI had such a strange personality.

Her voice lowered, and she squeezed her grip, pulling the two closer to her. "Reporters are everywhere."

Zach's jaw flexed. They couldn't catch a break, could they? But it did mean she couldn't get mad if either he or Jasper tried to be close with her.

Shira pulled away, and Zach took the opportunity to slide his arm farther around her and pull her to his side. He bent close to her ear, his lips brushing the sensitive skin. Her sweet, intoxicating scent enveloped him. "Tell us if we go too far in public."

Her eyes darted away, and she mumbled what should have been to herself, but was loud enough for him and Jasper to hear. "I'm not sure that's possible."

Shira's eyes widened and her attention darted to them when she seemed to realize just how loudly she'd spoken. The two of them grinned at her. Was she even trying anymore?

Red flushed over her cheeks. "You two heard nothing."

Jasper chuckled. "I'm not pretending I didn't heah that."

"Hey, Shira, quit hogging your boyfriends," someone called out. "We want time with them, too."

The three of them looked to a tall man of mixed racial heritage with dark hair and eyes. Zach knew Takashi's voice from all these years of talking with him.

Shira stuck her tongue out at him. "I can do whatever I want with them."

In an instant, various dirty images of her eagerly

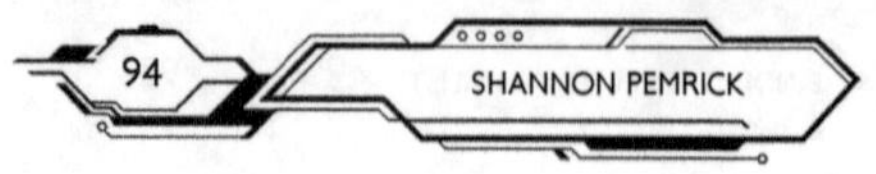

offering herself to them assaulted Zach's mind, sending need right down to his groin. He didn't need these mental teases right now.

Takashi's eyes danced. "I'm sure you can. But we'd like to at least be able to say hi."

Shira let out a fake, resigned sigh. "Fine. I guess I can allow that."

Zach laughed. At least the camaraderie that happened over chats was no different in person. He knew Shira had a lot of contact with Takashi and Mercedes since all three of them lived in San Francisco, but you never knew how someone would act once there was face-to-face contact. The last two days had shown him that so far, his guildmates were the same people online as they were offline, and it made him feel good about his and Jasper's choice to join the guild on a whim all those years ago.

Shira pulled out of Zach's grasp, allowing Zach and Jasper to "officially" greet Takashi, as well as Rei and Emi, whom Zach had completely missed with their cosplay getups. Rei had chosen a simple costume, Faith from Mirror's Edge, while Emi had chosen an anime character he wasn't overly familiar with. Both were great costumes, though Zach suspected Emi had a lot to do with that, given she was a fashion designer.

Jasper squinted at Rei. "Is that your real hair, or a wig?"

Rei smirked. "Wouldn't you like to know?"

Zach and Shira laughed, Jasper grumbling to himself.

Serenity tugged on Jasper's pants. "Daddy, I learned a lot today about cosplay! I want to do it, too. Oh, and She-ra and her friends know so much." She threw her hands into the air. "They know everyone here!"

Emi smiled. "Well, not everyone. It's a sizeable community. But we are familiar with many cosplayers here."

Zach shot Shira a look. "Since when do you cosplay?"

Shira shook her head. "I don't. I follow and interact with a lot of them because it falls under a type of fashion and modeling umbrella. It's fun giving tips to help them improve."

Just then, someone in costume ran past, shouting Shira's name. Shira wished them luck and promised to tune in with her tablet if she could.

Jasper's brow lifted. "What was that?"

Shira shrugged. "That was Adie. She's a member of Horde of the North. Their match is coming up."

Zach recognized that team name. They were a well-known fives team for Lusara Fates. It impressed him that Shira was familiar with someone on a team like that.

"Speaking of matches, how much time do you two have before you have to go back?" Shira asked.

"If no team goes longer than fifteen minutes, which, given the talent of the competition isn't likely, and I factor in mandatory VR breaks between matches, Jasper and Zach have approximately two hours before they need to report back in," Alistair said from Shira's tablet.

It was weird for Zach, not having their AI on them. While they were still new to using him, he'd learned how easy it had become to rely on the AI. Not having it around so that he could assist Shira with Serenity alongside her own AI would take a bit of getting used to.

"Any plans for the two hours you guys are free?" Takashi asked.

"I was hoping to get in a game demo or two," Jasper said.

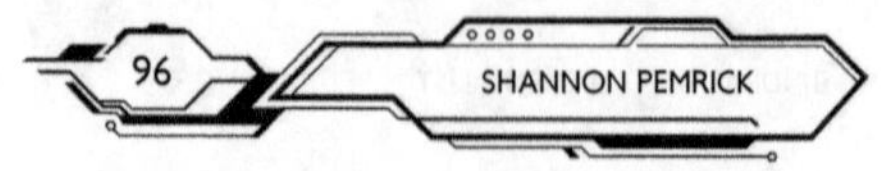

Zach nodded. "I think that'll be the only thing we can get to until after our second match."

Serenity waved a hand. "Can I get pick-chahs first?"

Jasper's brow rose. "Pictures?"

"She wanted to take some photos with a few of the cosplayers," Shira said. "But I wanted to make sure you two were okay with it before I gave her the go-ahead."

Zach smiled. He had no doubts Shira would have taken nice snaps and shared the pics with them, yet he appreciated her check on boundaries.

Jasper whipped out his phone. "Then let's get them."

Zach hid a wince.

Serenity cheered and grabbed Jasper's hand, dragging him over to Emi and Rei, who were more than eager to bring the two over to the cosplayers. And they had a set path in mind, from the looks of it.

"It's almost as if she's already picked out cosplayers she wants to photo-op with," Zach said.

Shira chuckled. "She's been quite the social butterfly. She wants to know everything about each cosplayer she's talked to, and the ones that were the friendliest ended up on a list she wanted photos with as soon as you two said yes."

The first cosplayer Serenity wanted was a big, burly individual with a strong jaw and neatly trimmed facial hair wearing a Sailor Moon costume, though the sexy variant with the cropped blouse and shorter skirt. He flexed and showed off in front of Serenity while she giggled and clapped.

"Who is that?" Zach asked.

"That's Maddy," Shira said. "He's a well-known

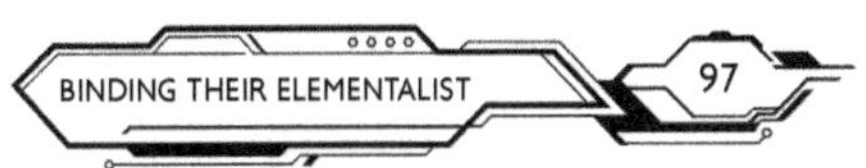

crossplayer. Serenity, like the rest of his fans, loves that he proudly sports his beard in all of his female cosplays."

Zach grinned, his eyes assessing the costume on the man. "I appreciate he's wearing the skirt with stiletto boots. He's got great legs."

She nudged him. "Careful. Someone might think your eyes are wandering."

He rolled eyes. "I can appreciate and still be faithful, thank you. And you honestly can't tell me you disagree with me."

"Oh, I think his legs are great. As are his arms. They'd make great arm porn."

Zach leaned closer to murmur in her ear. "Well, then, by your logic, mixed with the fact we're supposed to be pretending to be a triad in public, thanks to your ex, wouldn't that mean your eyes are also wandering?"

Shira's nose scrunched adorably, and she pursed her lips. "I don't have a counter for that."

He chuckled and took the win, pulling her against him again as his prize. Her teasing heat seared his skin.

Serenity began posing with Maddy, and Jasper snapped several photos. Shira tilted her face toward Zach. "Why didn't you go with them?"

Her inquiring words hung in the air with a heavy weight. Zach could tell her half of the reason and leave things at that, or he could get in the habit of being forthright as possible so she'd have no reason to mistrust him.

"A few reasons—one is simply that I enjoy watching Jasper interact with Serenity without me. It's good for them to have time to bond, just the two of them. And there's a sense of pride that comes with seeing how gentle Jasper is with her."

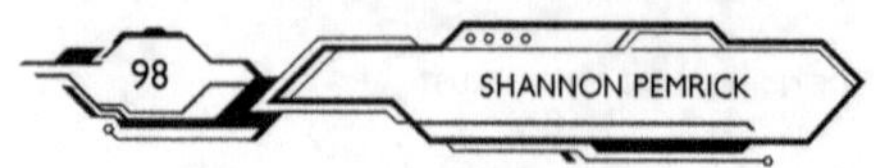

Zach's fingers traced the hemming of Shira's shirt. "And I have a bad habit of being a wicked control freak when it comes to cameras. With my background, I like making sure the perfect photo is taken. Jasper isn't like that. His are a bit more spontaneous and less calculated. If I stay back here, he can get those fun photos without me trying to rip the phone out of his hand. Once he's done, and the cosplayers go, I'll be fine with the results because I can't do anything about them."

A sweet and kind smile appeared on Shira's tempting lips. "It's admirable you can not only recognize and admit such a fault in yourself, but allow yourself space so you can properly handle the situation without causing a scene."

He appreciated her words. Sometimes his choice to step back felt like the wrong one, like he was running from his issue rather than fixing it.

Shira leaned against him more. "Are those the only reasons you haven't moved?"

Zach eyed her. Was she flirting? It was hard to tell sometimes. The three of them toed the lines so often, it was difficult to separate most days.

His finger slipped under her shirt, and he trailed a short line from her hip toward her back. She didn't react, perplexing him. While all he could feel was the acrylic surface of one of her prosthetics, she should have felt the touch through the false nerves, right?

"If I wanted to keep you close, I'd just have to drag you along with me and you would follow," he said, shaking those thoughts from his head.

Shira's brow rose, and she pursed her lips playfully. "Oh, really?"

Zach pulled her closer against him and took a step forward. He chuckled when she obediently moved with him. "Really."

"Get a room, you two," Mercedes stage-whispered.

Their friends laughed while Shira rolled her eyes and flipped their friend her middle finger. Zach merely grinned. He wouldn't back away from whatever was blooming between them, no matter how many comments were made—no matter the uncertainties gnawing at the back of his mind.

Serenity's giggling drew their attention. She posed with two new cosplayers now. One had a crazy cyberpunk-esque superhero outfit, and the other had an equally interesting costume—not because of her clothes, which were simple, but because of the amazing, eerily lifelike animatronic dragon on her shoulder. "Who are they?"

"The Aquaman Rule 63 cosplayer is Megan. She's known for her genre-mash cosplays. And the Daenerys cosplayer is Onyx. She is crazy talented with robotics. She has her own shop to custom make things for people. They're both really impressive."

Zach had to agree. He'd seen nothing like it before. "I'm going to guess Onyx isn't her real name?"

Shira shook her head. "She's chosen to go by an alias. No one knows her real name. Happens a lot in modeling, so it doesn't surprise me."

Zach glanced at her, his interest piqued. As a pho-tographer, he'd worked with all kinds of models, but the names they had given him always seemed like their true names. "Why's that?"

Shira shrugged. "Sometimes it's because a true name isn't unique enough and others in the industry may have

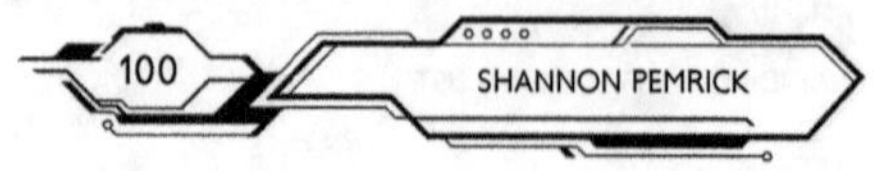

it, making it too difficult to stand out. Other times, it's a means to separate the personal life and work or hobby life. And there are various other reasons to have some anonymity."

"Why didn't you ever go by a different name? If you don't mind me asking."

She gazed at him, as if startled by the question. "You're the first to ever ask me that."

I am? Zach couldn't fathom how he could be the first. "Is that okay?"

Shira nodded. "Yeah, I just need to figure out how to word my answer so it makes sense."

Good thing patience was something Zach was good at. He waited while she pieced together her response.

"It's because of where I came from. I wanted to make a name for myself and prove a point." Shira worked her jaw. "And I felt that if I used a different name, I couldn't do that."

Zach was intrigued more than ever to know what she meant by that. There was a gigantic piece of her past he and Jasper knew nothing about. He wasn't even sure how much of it Mercedes or Narissa knew. He'd never caught any of them talking about anything prior to her teen years. *And then there was something she wasn't willing to share earlier when she spoke about her past with Jeremy.* What wasn't she willing to talk about that seemed to also spur her on to make some of her most important life choices?

Zach wasn't going to get the chance to ask. Jasper and Serenity approached, big smiles on their faces.

"Did you have fun?" he asked his daughter.

Serenity responded with an enthusiastic nod. "Yep! I talked to everyone I wanted to. Their costumes were

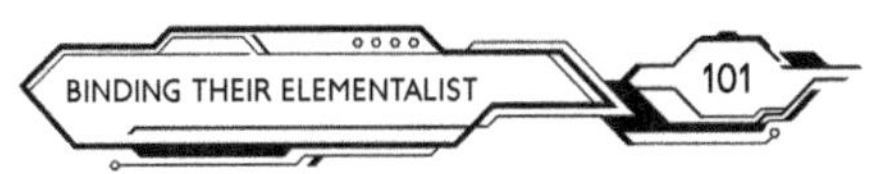

wicked cool. Can I do a cosplay for the next co-vention we go to?"

Jasper patted her head. "We can look into it."

Serenity cheered.

"Ready to head to the demos?" he asked.

Zach was, and Shira nodded before turning to their friends to see if they were going to stay or join. They were going to stay here for a bit. Seemed Narissa wasn't feeling well again and wanted to sit for a while. Naturally, Ajax was fussing because of it and wouldn't leave her side. And Mercedes and Takashi were going to help Emi and Rei out some more. Emi attempted to apologize for choosing to stick to the cosplay scene for now, but Shira quickly let her know that it was okay.

The choice to split off was okay with Zach. As torn as he was between wanting to spend time with just his family and Shira, and spending in-person time with their guildmates and friends, Shira was right. They had a week to get together and do things as friends.

The four of them made their way to the demo lounge. Shira had Serenity hold onto Snake's leash to ensure she didn't get lost in the crowd. Shira had also checked out her friend's match, and tuned in to a live panel discussing VR and its effects on the gaming industry, as well as where things had the potential to go in the near future.

Serenity gasped when they made it to the demo lounge. All kinds of game booths—from handhelds, to consoles, to VR—filled the room. Where there was remaining space, were people—some games so popular, there was no way their group was getting anywhere near them.

But that wasn't what had grabbed Serenity's attention.

An enormous sign displayed ahead of them in the VR section: Monster Hunter. *Oh boy. Here it comes.*

Serenity bounced. "Daddy! Daddy, daddy, daddy!"

Jasper laughed. "Yes, we can go over there and check it out."

Their daughter squealed and almost ran off, but unfortunately for her, all three adults expected it, and she was restrained.

Making it to the setup, Jasper had to read everything out for her, because she was too excited to try herself. Zach and Shira struggled to contain their amusement. Then the moment came for the disappointment to set in. She couldn't play it yet because of her age.

It pained Zach to watch her joy get dashed so quickly. Even though they hadn't yet introduced her to the games because of her age, she really enjoyed the part of the franchise she could consume. Zach now wondered if maybe introducing her to the handheld or console versions might be a good idea. It wouldn't be an easy game for her, but it'd be a great chance for him and Jasper to bond over a game with her. And it would prepare her for when she could finally join the VR scene.

"Daddy, are you and Zach gonna play the demo?" Serenity asked, surprising him.

Jasper tilted his head. "Well, we didn't sign up for it, and I don't want to tease you, since you can't play."

Serenity shook her head. "It's not a tease! I like watching you and Zach kick butt in games. It was wicked fun watching your matches. And it will make me wicked excited to play when I'm biggah."

"All right, if you're sure." Jasper whipped out his phone and scanned the demo slot code on a nearby sign. With them in the tournament, they didn't preregister into any slots. It was a risk, as it meant they had to hope one would open up for the general tickets they secured, but it was the only thing they could do, given their situation.

Jasper worked his jaw. "Doesn't look like they have any open demos today, Starship. And even tomorrow."

Serenity frowned. "Aw, man…"

"We can watch others play, though," Shira said, pointing to a large screen. Someone was in the midst of fighting an orange and purple velociraptor-like creature with neck frills and fur along his spine and tail.

Serenity squealed. "That's a Great Jaggi!"

She got as close to the screen as she could, giggling away and making her own commentary for the demo fight, as well as explaining things to all of them as if they knew nothing about the game—which wasn't too far from the truth. She surprised Zach with how much knowledge she had. *Has she been doing internet searches to supplement her knowledge?*

He knew he didn't have to worry about her finding sites or surprise pages she shouldn't, since Alistair was set up to monitor her activity, but Zach never expected his daughter to be that into the franchise. *Like fathers, like daughter, I suppose.*

Her excitement drew quite a bit of attention, though rarely was any of it negative. It also caught the attention of a woman working the demos. She was tall and pale, and had long, curly brown hair and glasses. Her clothes screamed booth babe. While they mostly worked booths in the dealer corner, it also wasn't uncommon for them to be sent to demos to entice audiences to check things out.

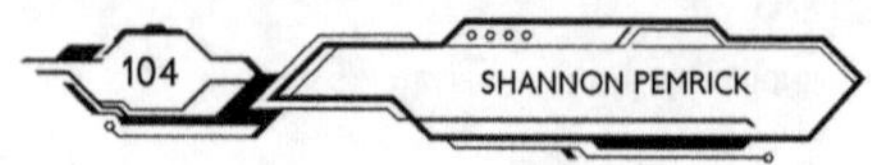

She introduced herself as Mimi, and was quite pleasant, inquiring about their interest in the game and how much exposure Serenity had to the franchise.

"I can't play the games yet because I'm not old enough," Serenity said. "But I watch the shows. I gots plushies and keychains, too!"

The woman tilted her head, her eyes showing her confusion. "You're not old enough? You look plenty old enough to play one of our games."

"I'll be seven in…" Serenity counted on her fingers. "Seven days!"

Mimi clapped. "Well, happy early birthday to you. But that's plenty old enough to play Hunter Ranch."

Serenity cocked her head. "What's that?"

Jasper and Zach exchanged looks as well. They'd never heard of it. It didn't escape Mimi's notice. "I see you two don't know, either. That's okay! The ranch titles are spin-offs of the main Monster Hunter series, and have you raising monsters instead of fighting them."

Serenity gasped, her eyes lighting up. She latched onto both Zach and Jasper. "I want it! Please, can I have it? Please, please, please?"

Zach chuckled. "Hold your horses, Starship. We can check the game out. If you still like it after that, we'll look into getting it for you."

Serenity hugged them tight. "Thank you!"

Mimi held up a tablet and flicked a few things on the screen. "We've got plenty of them in stock down at our booth. And we're doing a promotional sale for the first three days of the convention, to promote the pre-order of the VR edition of the main title."

Jasper had Alistair make some notes and reminders. "Thanks for the information."

Mimi smiled. "It's my pleasure. And if you haven't signed up to test the demo, keep an eye out for spots that open through the day. You might be able to squeeze in using a general pass."

They thanked her again and left the demo, much to Serenity's disappointment. She really wanted to watch others play some more. Jasper and Zach wanted to ensure they checked out a few more games, and Shira was just content with anything.

Zach noted her calm, easy-going demeanor. There were so many people here, he thought she might be struggling and ask to slip away for a bit. But typical Shira, she was handling things like a champ. It wasn't until they'd checked out a few demos for new RPGS and a shooter Jasper was interested in, did she speak up.

"Do you guys mind if I leave the area a bit? I'm starting to get overwhelmed with all the people."

Zach thought Jasper was about to jump out of his skin with worry. "How long have you felt this way? You should have told us sooner. Of course we can do something else."

Shira laughed, pushing away his grabbing hands. "Chill. I'm not pushing myself. It's not terrible right now. But I wanted to speak up so it doesn't become a problem. If you guys want to stay here and check out more demos, that's fine. I just need to step away."

Zach shook his head. "No, we'll go with you. These games will be here when we want to come back."

She smiled, a small and sweet, appreciative expression for her. They slipped out of the lounge, looking for

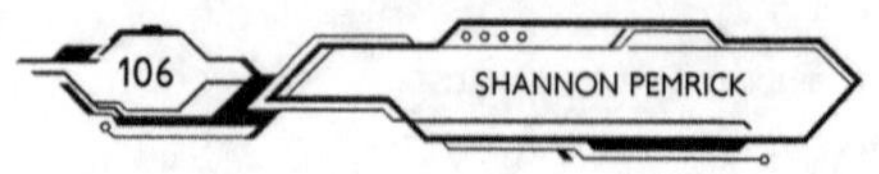

someplace quieter, when an unfortunate grating voice called out, "Jasper, Zach, there you two are!"

Zach's eye twitched, and he turned to face an annoyed Stacey. He had to at least try to be pleasant with her this week, as much as he'd rather not. "What's up, Stacey?"

"What's up? What's up?" Her eyes burned into him. "You two are goofing off instead of watching your opponents, that's what's up."

Zach exchanged a look with Jasper. "We're allowed to enjoy ourselves here too, you know."

Their manager's eyes flashed. "You have a tournament to win. You should be watching your potential opponents, especially after that terrible first-match display."

"It wasn't terrible," Shira practically snarled. "Regal Gladiators is a tough team, and the guys put in their all to win—which they did, if you forgot, and did so fantastically. Don't go acting like you could do better or something."

Stacey narrowed her eyes, but Jasper jumped in before a catfight broke out. "We've been keeping up with the standings. Drunk Dwarves beat Hungry Goats three to one. We've got Alistair doing an analysis on the teams' strengths and weaknesses based on their performance, as well as creating a highlight reel of moments we need to watch ourselves before our next match. We know what we're doing, Stacey."

Their manager ground her teeth. "And the other teams?"

Zach shrugged. "We don't need to worry about them yet. Matches today are only round one and two of the winner's bracket, and round one of the loser's bracket. We'll have more time later to prep tonight based on the outcomes of those matches. No use strategizing against a team we won't face."

Stacey blew out a breath as if she were trying to control her emotions. "Look. As your manager, I'm trying to help you two. I need you to take this seriously. This isn't a vacation, it's work."

"And we can have our family vacation at the same time," Jasper snapped back, his patience wearing thin already. "Serenity is here to have fun with us, which is what we want. And as much as Shira and Serenity like spending time togethah, Shira isn't a babysittah."

Stacey sighed and whipped out a tablet. "Very well. If you don't want to take this seriously, I can't make you."

Zach's hand curled into a fist. She had no right to be passive-aggressive.

"One thing before I let you both go." She tapped a few more times on her tablet before looking up at them again. "Your request for application was denied."

Jasper's brow furrowed. "What? Why?"

Shira cocked her head. "Application? What are you guys applying for?"

"The company doesn't deem her an appropriate fit." Stacey's tone, while a matter-of-fact, had an edge of smugness Zach didn't like.

"She who?" Shira asked.

"On what grounds?" Zach asked their manager. He knew they should answer Shira, but Stacey was being too squirrelly.

The older woman gestured to Shira. "She has a criminal record, and Tri-com has a strict policy on the types of records they will and won't allow. Hers isn't allowed."

Zach blinked. *A criminal record? Shira? That can't be right.*

"Is someone going to tell me what the fuck is going on?" Shira shouted. Her volume drew eyes from all around them. Zach and Jasper stared at her. "What application request are you all talking about, and what does it have to do with me and my past record?"

"So you don't deny having one?" Stacey asked with a smug, toothy grin.

Shira's eyebrow rose. "Why would I? Anyone who has followed me and my past career knows of it. If I had wanted that part of my past a secret, I would have chosen a different modeling name to go by."

Wait, that's part of what she hadn't quite said earlier? Zach was more curious than concerned, given that for all the years he and Jasper had known her, she'd been on the right side of the tracks. And it wasn't like Narissa or Mercedes would jeopardize their careers and reputations over someone who still partook in illegal activity.

"I told you two to be careful who you associate with," Stacey said, her tone smug. "Maybe now you'll listen to me."

"Fuck off, Stacey," Jasper snarled. "We decide who we hang around, not you. Go be a nuisance somewhere else."

Their manager took a startled step back, her eyes wide. "How dare you."

"We dare," Zach said, his eyes narrowed. Maybe this time she'd finally get how much of an issue they had with her. "Now get out of here. We'll be back in the tournament room on time. We don't need you dogging us."

Stacey's face reddened, her lips pulling into a distasteful curl. She spun on her heels and stormed off.

The three of them stood there in tense silence until

Serenity's quiet voice spoke up. "Is everyone done being mad now?"

All three adults looked down at her. She hid behind Shira, peeking around her. "Everyone was saying lots of bad words."

Jasper let out a slow, calming breath, and then painted on a smile. "Yes, Starship, everything is going to be okay now. We adults just got a little heated. And you're right, we did say some things we shouldn't have."

"Everyone is happy again?" Her eyes were hopeful. Serenity didn't do well around arguing adults; Zach wasn't sure why. It wasn't like he and Jasper yelled at each other often.

"We will be in a moment," Shira said honestly. "Sometimes emotions take a bit to calm down from."

Serenity's eyes grew wide. "Even adults can't control that?"

Shira knelt down and stroked her hair. "Emotions are hard for everyone. As we get older, we learn to better manage them, but we're not perfect, and we make mistakes. As long as we own that, though, and try to do better, that's what is important."

Serenity looked down and toed the rug. "Sometimes my brain tells me to do bad things. Like be mean or cry to get attention. And then sometimes it tells me to do things that don't make sense to do because it doesn't have a reason. But Daddy and Zach help me talk through what I'm feeling."

Shira smiled. "That's a very big-girl thing to do. Talking about how we feel is how even adults work through things."

His daughter beamed up at this woman, who couldn't

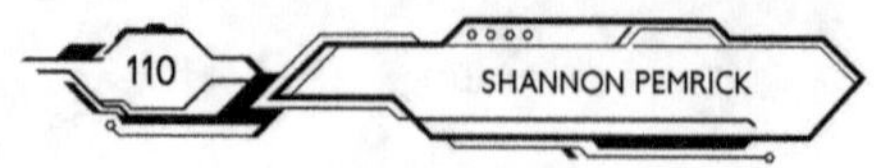

have handled that more perfectly in Zach's eyes. "Can we get nom-food? I'm wicked hungry."

The three adults chuckled. It was getting close to lunchtime, though it surprised Zach she hadn't asked for anything sooner. Her appetite was about as ravenous as his and Jasper's.

"We will in a moment," Jasper said. "I have to make a quick phone call."

Serenity reluctantly agreed and went to playing twenty questions with one of the AIs. And in that moment, Zach was glad for her short attention span.

Shira looked at him apologetically, and he shook his head. He knew she'd think she might have overstepped with Serenity, but Zach didn't feel that way at all. It was a good teaching moment for his daughter, and he welcomed Shira's assistance. He was happy that it followed how he and Jasper tried to handle things with Serenity.

She got emotional, a lot, and it worsened each year as things in her life changed, both externally and internally. It wasn't always easy helping her work things out in a constructive manner. And sometimes, because Zach and Jasper were her parents, Serenity pushed back harder, so having an outside adult reiterate what they'd been trying to instill helped his daughter greatly.

"You're owed an explanation," Zach said. His eyes darted to Jasper, who'd wandered off a few paces. He tended to move around when he was on the phone. "And he's now busy. No doubt calling the company to verify some things."

Shira placed her hands on her hips. "Yeah, an explanation would be great. What have you two been doing behind my back?"

Zach chuckled. "Nothing devious. A few weeks ago, Jasper and I talked about how much you help us. As much as we'd love for you to join us in official threes tournaments and stuff, we know it's not something you really want. But, we thought maybe you'd be interested in a coaching position."

Shira blinked. "Coach?"

He nodded. "We have to have such things approved by the company, so we didn't approach you about it until we got the approval to have one. You would have been able to say no to it, of course. We just thought you'd be good at it, and you already work great with us."

"Ah, okay. Well, sorry my past record put a kink in that, I guess?" She seemed a bit conflicted, though Zach wasn't sure if it was over the hassle she'd accidentally caused, or if he and Jasper had overreached a bit. It had been presumptuous of them to ask the company first before finding out if she would be interested.

Zach shook his head. "You don't need to apologize. I'm having a hard time believing you did something so bad Tri-com rejected our request. Not only do they have some sketchy-ass people employed as it is, I doubt your record is something horrible, like murder or something."

An amused smile spread over her lips. "No, nothing like that. But it is a crazy-looking record, since I got it when I was fourteen."

Zach blinked. He opened his mouth, but nothing came out. *She was how young?*

Jasper stormed back to them, his shoulders tense, and whole body practically vibrating. "They don't know a damn thing about the application request."

Zach's brow furrowed. "So, what, Stacey tossed the request when we submitted it?"

"Sounds like it." Jasper's lip curled. "I was told upper management would look into it, but we know their track record with all our other complaints with her."

Shira crossed her arms, her weight shifting to one side. "You two need to get out of that contract. This company is nothing but trouble for you. Hell, they're so shady, they don't care how many complaints you make against Stacey, they've made it clear they won't replace her unless it puts the contract in jeopardy."

Zach let out a slow breath. She was right, but it wasn't an easy contract to break. "Yeah, we have talked about it. We'll figure it out soon."

Jasper leaned closer to Shira. "But, before we manage that mess, I think it's important to talk about what Stacey brought up."

Shira let out a slow breath through her lips. "Yeah, that wasn't the way I wanted you two to find that out. I would have even preferred it through some random internet search than from that woman."

"And in case you thought otherwise, we don't care you have a past criminal record," Zach said. "We just want to be in the loop."

He smirked and leaned closer. "And we should be aware of such things about your past and all."

Red tinged her cheeks, and Shira nodded. "You're right. Why don't we grab lunch and find a better place to talk?"

Jasper and Zach agreed.

It didn't take them long to find something Serenity was interested in eating at the café. The line was another story, but luckily, as impatient as Serenity could get, she did rather well waiting in lines without causing too much fuss. Shira found a corner when they had their food. There were a few people around, but it wasn't as crowded as the outer seating of the café.

Shira ate a few of her fries, allowing them all to get something in their stomachs before this conversation happened. Zach did more absent eating than anything as he watched her. He couldn't quite figure her out. She told Stacey her criminal record wasn't a secret, yet he had a feeling she was stalling. Or was it that public knowledge was only about the record, and not all the details that led up to it?

When she finally spoke, she took a deep breath through her nose first. "I'll keep this brief, because I'm mostly over what happened in my past before I started my new life with my adopted parents, and I don't want this coming off as some sob story. And I definitely don't want any pity parties."

Both Zach and Jasper gave their undivided attention so she would feel free to share. Serenity munched away on a cheese-covered fry, her eyes darting back and forth between the three of them as she tried to figure out what was going on with the adults in her life.

"Before Anita and Flynn adopted me, I came from a rough life. I never knew my bio father, and my bio mother…" Shira paused. "Never wanted me. She reminded me of that so many times."

Shira was quiet for another moment. Her lips tugged into a deep frown. Zach wished he could lean over and kiss it away. *How could a parent say such a thing?*

"We struggled from the very beginning, and eventually

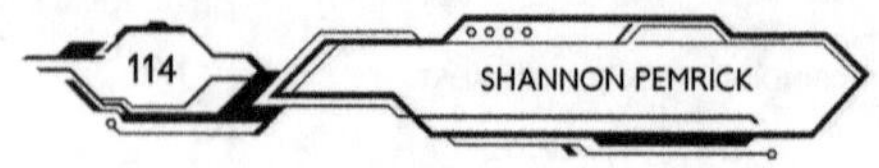

my mother fell into a rough crowd. One poor decision after another, and I found myself with a mother addicted to more substances than I want to count. I mattered even less to her, unless…" Shira closed her eyes and let out a breath. "Unless we were so short on money she tried to use me as currency."

Zach stared. *What?*

Jasper slammed his hand on the table, making them jump, and drawing a few eyes for a moment. "I want to beg that's a joke, but I can see it's not. How the hell could she live with herself after doing that to you?"

Shira shrugged and picked at her food. "Not every parent is a great one, and not everyone comes from them."

"So how did your home life get you a record?" Zach asked.

Shira snorted. "My mother did something stupid. She was short on cash and thought she'd found a new dealer who'd give her what she wanted for cheaper. Or in the very least, would actually take me as currency this time. Turns out, the dealer was an undercover cop. My mother was immediately arrested, and I was taken into protective custody. Because of the circumstances, CPS petitioned for my mother's parental rights to be terminated, and the judge assigned to my case didn't take long to deem her an unfit mother. My mother didn't complain one bit, only rubbing salt into that wound. I was sent to a foster home until someone wanted to adopt me."

She clasped her hands together. "But it didn't get better from there. Some people are lucky when they are put in the system. Some get good foster parents, or don't get bumped around a lot until they find someone to adopt them. I wasn't one of them."

Zach pushed away his food. He'd lost his appetite now.

"I was bounced around a lot, and found myself in more than one bad foster home. And unfortunately, because I was over the age of ten at that point, the likelihood of being adopted was basically nil. I understood even at that age, adults wanted babies and small children. All the 'firsts' were too important to miss out on. They didn't care about us kids who were well past that stage. So, when I was twelve, I decided I had enough. I packed a backpack with what little I had, stole food from the kitchen, and ran away in the middle of the night."

Shira ran her fingers through her hair. "I did everything I could to not be caught and thrown back into the system I believed would never help me. And that's when I met those who would become my new family. They were like me—either kids who had been failed by adults, or adults who were jaded from the hand life dealt them. They taught me how to survive, even if it meant breaking the law."

She finally looked at Zach and Jasper. There was a haunted look to her eyes that showed she wasn't proud of what she'd had to do, but they all understood she'd done what she thought she had to. Zach and Jasper weren't going to fault her for that.

"I got good at stealing. First, it was just food, so we could all eat. Then, my jobs turned into bigger heists— things that could get us money to be turned into needed supplies. I wasn't always good at pulling the jobs off, and that's when my record started. The sentences were always light—their attempt to make me *learn my lesson*

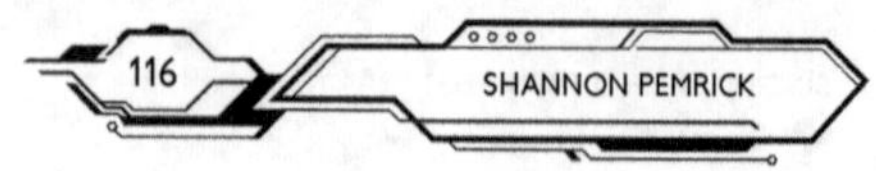

and never do it again. When the sentence was over, they'd try to get me back into a home, and I'd disappear because I refused to be part of that broken system."

Shira licked her lips. "When I was fourteen, I made what I thought was my biggest mistake, but it ended up being what turned my life around. I never enjoyed stealing from people. It never felt right to me, even if I needed the money more, or whatever justification could be thrown at me. So, I learned how to talk to the right people and made connections with someone skilled in making forgeries of priceless things. He'd make the object, I'd return the real one to the original owners secretly, and then pawn off the fake. We'd then split profits."

She chuckled. "That's how I met Anita. I'd cased her and Flynn's place for a while. They were rich people, my usual targets. I figured if I couldn't make fakes of the items I swiped from those kinds of people, then they wouldn't miss anything. They had the money to replace it willy-nilly. When they left one day, I broke in and stole a vase that looked expensive. I didn't know about their AI security system. I thought I'd gotten off clean, sending the vase in for copying, and then slipping back to the house and returning the thing."

Shira pinched her nose. "The cops arrested me outside the pawn shop because the AI had gotten a good look at my face. I refused to work with anyone, and the judge decided, given my behavior and my past record, to throw a max sentence on me without trying me as an adult."

"Whoa, seriously?" Jasper breathed, completely enthralled by the story.

Zach's brow knitted together. "That would have meant

you would be in jail until you were eighteen, but that didn't happen."

Shira held up a finger. "Because I'm not done telling the story. Anita came to visit me a few days after my sentencing. I couldn't possibly understand what she wanted with me. She still had her precious vase, and got me a full sentence in revenge. Until I found out she had no clue I'd hidden the vase and she thought it was in some pawnshop."

She rubbed her temples. "That conversation is painful to think about now. I was so awful to her. Said so many unkind and nasty things, all because I didn't trust her and hated how kind she was trying to be to me."

"What were some things she did?" Zach asked, his curiosity getting the better of him.

"She wanted to understand my motivation and kept treating me like I was just a kid who had only stolen a cookie from a cookie jar right before dinner. It'd made me so sick to my stomach I told her to stop painting such a nice act. That pretty words couldn't fool me and that I knew she didn't care at all for my well-being."

Zach cringed. That was certainly harsh, though he didn't blame her, given everything she'd gone through.

Shira licked her lips. "That's when I learned about the importance of the vase. It was a family heirloom. I felt better about my decision to make a copy. So, I told her where the real vase was."

"You hid it under her porch, didn't you?" Jasper said, his eyes gleaming. Zach was a little concerned about his boyfriend's excitement.

An ironic smile appeared on Shira's face. "I told her

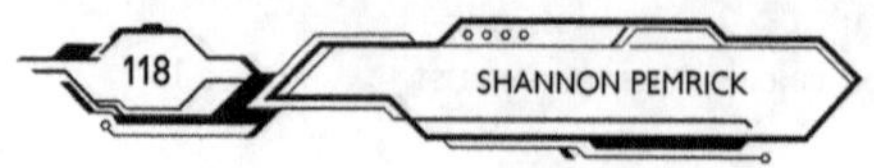

she needed to get out into her backyard and clean the mess under her deck for once."

Jasper threw a fist in the air. "Close enough! I'm good."

Shira laughed. "Yes, you're so good, you can predict how intelligent fourteen-year-old Shira was. Good job."

Zach joined in her laughter. She wasn't wrong. He remembered how smart he thought he was at fourteen, only to see just how much he had bricks for brains, now looking back on it.

"I ended our conversation there, and didn't see her for a few more days after that," Shira said, continuing with her fascinating story. "When she did return, she was as pleasant as before. She told me she found the vase and had it appraised to be sure, and it was the genuine thing. Anita asked for the whole story, since I refused to say anything during the hearing. At that point, I didn't see a reason not to talk about what I did. It wasn't like it'd change my sentencing."

Shira rolled her eyes. As they all knew now, it definitely had.

"It was then that Anita found out my motives for stealing went beyond myself, but that was all I told her. She tried to press for more information, but I couldn't betray my new family. I knew if I did, the other kids would be grabbed and put into the system, and something terrible would happen to the adults. Anita then gave that stupid, vague 'I see' comment, as she pieced things together in a way my fourteen-year-old brain couldn't extrapolate."

Shira leaned back. "It wasn't long after that I was brought before the judge again. Anita told my story to the judge and asked for the sentence to be lifted. Confused the hell out of me why this woman would even bother. It wasn't like I meant anything to her. And to make things crazier for me, she'd convinced the judge that she and Flynn would be my new foster parents. I was told, if I finally behaved myself, they would seal my record when I hit age of majority."

"So you agreed to this crazy offer," Zach said.

Shira nodded. "I didn't get much say in the matter. It was either stay in jail or live with this weirdly nice woman and her husband. It wasn't like I couldn't try to escape later, once I figured out how to escape their AI's notice."

Zach and Jasper chuckled. That would have certainly been difficult for her.

A bittersweet smile spread over Shira's lips. "They ended up being the best thing I could have asked for. Anita and Flynn spoiled me from day one and encouraged anything I found interesting as a hobby or potential avenue for future career opportunities—like modeling. It was actually off-putting to start with. But I came to accept it, and that helped me embrace my past as part of my present. When I learned they couldn't have children of their own, it all clicked. I was as much a blessing to them as they were to me. And then, they wanted to adopt me. I was so happy."

Her smile faded a bit. "Well, of course it came at a bit of a cost. Those I'd been on the street with turned their backs on me. Even after everything I'd done for them, they saw my willingness to stay with Anita and Flynn as a betrayal. But, as much as it hurt to see them walk away, I couldn't let my opportunity for a family that truly loved me and did everything they could to encourage me to follow dreams I never thought imaginable slip through my fingers.

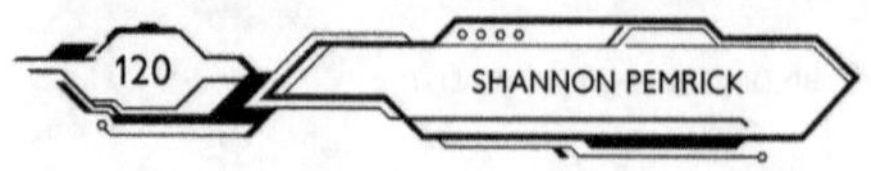

It was what drove me to make my past part of my modeling identity. Even though my records were sealed when I turned eighteen, as the judge promised, it didn't matter. I started my modeling career young enough, and I talked about what I did so much in interviews, the internet would have all the details I was willing to share, even if the official record couldn't be viewed by just anyone anymore."

This was a lot to take in. But one thing stuck out to Zach. She said she was mostly over this part of her past, but was she really?

Unloving biological parents… Friends and presumed found family abandoning her… Two adoptive parents who gave her everything they could, yet it didn't seem to be entirely what she needed. Zach was starting to see the pattern she had tried to hide from them. *Shira, were you so desperate to be loved you stayed with Jeremy even when you knew you shouldn't?*

"She-ra, you don't have to be sad," Serenity said, jarring Zach's thoughts. She gazed up at the red-haired woman with innocent eyes. "You have a new family now that loves you lots."

A small smile spread over Shira's lips, and Zach could have sworn he spotted tears threatening to break Shira's usual cool exterior. They'd never seen her cry, not really. A single tear the first time she opened up to them was the closest ever.

"You're right, Starship. I have *Vati*, and *Mutti*, and Mercedes, Takashi, Narissa, and Ajax." She reached out and grabbed Serenity's hand, a heart-thumping sincere smile on her face. "And I have you three."

One of the biggest smiles Zach had ever seen on

Serenity's face appeared. Jasper reached out and grabbed her free hand. Zach, barely a second's reaction behind, rested his hand on top of Shira's and Serenity's. Jasper tangled their free hands together, completing the circuit.

This was right. Zach felt it deep inside him. His concerns were breaking down, and he wanted that. "Shira, did you ever… reconcile with your mother?"

Shira withdrew her hands and took in a deep breath. "No. After she served her time, she was put into rehab, but ended up relapsing. I was in juvie serving one of my short sentences when I was told she'd died of an accidental overdose."

That was disappointing to hear. He'd hoped her mother would have seen what she missed out on and tried harder to be there for her daughter. Even if she wasn't taking care of her, she couldn't have at least seen the strong woman Shira became through all her hardships and perseverance. But then again, Shira may not have wanted to reconcile. Not after what her mother put her through.

"Did you ever reconcile with your street friends?" Jasper asked.

Shira rocked her head back and forth. "Some of them, yeah. Anita has always been big into charity work, especially for children. So, when I managed to get things patched up with a few of the kids I was closest to, she pulled her contacts to get them into good homes near us."

"Wait, so you all grew up in the same neighborhood in the end?"

Shira nodded. "Yep. Went to school with them. Shared victories and losses with them. All of it. It was almost

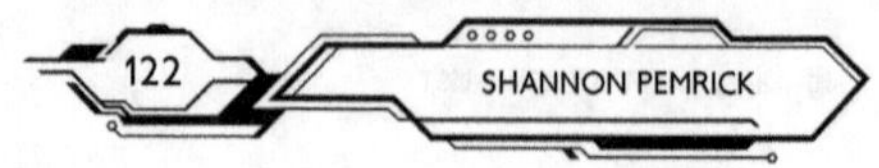

like nothing had pulled us apart. And yes, I still talk to them now. I didn't become a total recluse after my accident."

Zach bit back a laugh. He couldn't deny, he did think to ask.

"She-ra, can I ask a question?" Serenity said.

Shira turned her attention to the young girl and smiled. "Of course."

"What's that shiny thing in your mouth?"

CHAPTER 8

Soda lodged in Zach's throat and threatened to expel out his nose. *Bad time to take a drink.* Of all the people besides him to finally notice her piercing, it wasn't Jasper. Honestly, it surprised Zach that his boyfriend hadn't noticed by this point, especially not after that smoldering kiss earlier. And it was clear Jasper hadn't, with the confused look he had.

Shira clicked her tongue against her teeth, her eyes darting to Zach and then Jasper before a wicked grin slipped up her face. "Shiny thing in my mouth? You mean this, Starship?"

In a slow and deliberate movement, Shira stuck her tongue out, revealing a round silver ball. Jasper's hand on the table fisted, and from the way his jaw clenched, Zach knew he was putting every bit of control into not uttering a sound. Zach hid behind his drink.

"Whoa, you have a piercing in your tongue," Serenity said.

Shira flicked her tongue against her teeth, a minor tease that even sent a jolt down to Zach's groin. Her eyes flicked to Jasper, and she grinned. "Something wrong, Jas?"

Her words were nearly a purr. *Oh, no.* Shira had been quite reserved around them in certain ways. She could flirt; there was no doubt about it with some of their interactions. But this was a side of her Zach was certain neither of them had ever seen. The wall that separated him and Jasper from her had just been removed all of a sudden, and he was pretty sure the two of them were in trouble.

"You…" He struggled to form a sentence as his brain broke down to the more base desires he wouldn't be able to give into in this setting.

Shira leaned back in her chair, propping up her arm so she could rest her cheek on her fist. She dragged her tongue across her lower lip. "I what?"

Zach swallowed, his eyes watching as she continued to make small teasing gestures. Shira's eyes glittered with so much mischief and a bit of feminine smolder to add to her little show. Zach didn't go as crazy as Jasper for such piercings, but man, did this woman know how to tease him with it anyway. A thrumming need to pin her down to the table and make her writhe in pleasure in front of all these people pulsed its way to the surface of his mind and body.

"You…" Jasper sucked in a breath and tore his gaze away from her teasing lips to glare at Zach. "Why don't you seem surprised?"

Zach took another gulp of his drink to give him time to keep himself in check, and then let out the grin he'd been holding in. "Because I noticed yesterday."

Jasper's mouth practically fell open. His eyes screamed betrayal, and it all just amused Zach more. It'd been so worth it.

Shira chuckled, one of her fingers teasing her lower lip by flicking it once. "I wondered who would notice first. Honestly, I thought you had, Jasper, after what happened between us earlier. I guess it managed to slip your notice again."

"But you…" Words continued to fail Jasper's short-circuiting brain. "You nevah had it when we talked on the video chats."

Shira adjusted her position to something that looked both more comfortable and alluring. Zach's eyes wandered from her plump lips, down to her delicate neck, over her proportioned shoulders, and then down to her perfect breasts. They rose and fell with every breath, her shirt clinging tight, like he'd like to be. *Shit, I'm in trouble.*

Zach pinched his leg and counted down from ten. He couldn't allow her to seduce him like this. Not when it'd only lead to frustration before heading to their match.

"I wore a retainer," Shira said, amusement in her tone. "I know how you two can be. Especially you, Jas. I wasn't up to dealing with your antics."

"And yestahday? Why stop?"

Shira shrugged. "Partially because I forgot in my stress; partially because I couldn't keep wearing a retainer. I have it because I like it, not so that I can be ashamed and hide the fact it's there. You were going to find out eventually, so now was as good as ever."

Jasper ran his fingers through his hair and then returned his disbelieving gaze back to Zach. "And you didn't say anything."

Zach chuckled. "It was more fun allowing you to figure it out on your own. You didn't disappoint."

Jasper groaned and put his face in his hand, making Zach and Shira laugh.

Serenity tapped Shira's arm. "She-ra?"

Shit. They'd gotten carried away with their antics. How much of that did Serenity understand? He prayed not much. She was getting to an age he knew she'd start asking tough questions, but he wasn't ready for that yet.

Shira turned her bemused gaze to the little girl. "Yes, Starship?"

"Can I see it again?"

Shira obliged by sticking her tongue out again.

"That's so cool. Did it hurt to get it? Do you bite it by accident? How does it stay in?"

"Yes, it did. All the time, it's annoying. And…" Shira fiddled with the piercing until she pulled it out, a ball and attached pin in one hand, and a lone silver ball in the other. "It's anchored with this little ball so it doesn't fall out."

She slipped it back in and secured the bar with practiced ease.

"Wow, it's like magic!" Serenity proclaimed. "I want one."

Everything in Zach stopped all at once. *Oh no…*

His eyes darted to Jasper, who was slowly looking up from his hands. Protective dad mode was written all over his face.

"Absolutely not."

Zach shoved some fries into his mouth. *Saw that response a million miles away.*

This conversation could go south pretty quickly, but

Zach had no intention of stopping it yet. He wanted to see if Jasper managed to keep himself in check. If not, they'd have to have a serious talk about him having sessions with Jeff again. Zach still thought his boyfriend needed that help, given he'd had some harsh lashouts in the last few months, but Jasper was being unusually stubborn about going back.

Serenity blinked. "Why not, Daddy? You said I can get tattoos when I become an adult."

Jasper nodded. "That's right. When you're eighteen, you can get a tattoo just like me. But you can't get your tongue pierced."

"Technically she could," Shira said, a shit-eating grin on her face. "As an adult, she can do anything she wants."

"Except that," Jasper said, continuing to buckle down on this. "If she wants piercings, fine. But no tongue piercings. Ever."

Shira's attention drifted to Zach. "What about you? What do you think?"

Jasper set livid warning eyes on Zach, who just continued to eat his fries, not saying a word, though he couldn't hide his amused smile. Unlike Jasper, Zach didn't have a zealous parental love. He could handle these types of topics better than his boyfriend, and Jasper wouldn't like what he had to say.

"Zach?" Serenity said. "Can I get a piercing?"

He chewed his food some more and swallowed. "When you're sixteen, I'll bring you to the parlor to get a nose piercing. How does that sound?"

Zach knew Jasper would be fine with that, and it was clear it still was, by the way his boyfriend's shoulders relaxed a little. Any piercing that didn't come with inherent sexual connotations would be fine in the papa bear's book.

Serenity shook her head. "I don't want one in my nose." She then turned to Shira. "She-ra?"

Shira pursed her lips, tapping a finger against them. Her eyes screamed mischief. "How about, when you're fifteen, we'll go out and get your navel pierced?"

Serenity cocked her head. "My what?"

"Your bellybutton," Shira clarified, her eyes slanting toward Jasper.

He was thinking. "Sixteen, not fifteen."

Zach was a bit surprised by that one. Navel piercings weren't a crazy choice, but he would have thought Jasper would have put up a bigger fight. Or, at least, aimed for eighteen.

"Do you gots one of those, She-ra?" Serenity asked.

Shira took her shirt between her fingers and lifted it enough to reveal the sparkling ornament attached to her navel.

Serenity made an awed sound. "I like that. I want one too. But I want one for my tongue still."

Jasper's jaw clenched so hard, Zach thought he might hear it creak under the pressure. "I said—"

Shira hummed, cutting him off. "We'll have to look into it when you're eighteen, okay, Starship?"

Serenity's eyes lit up, but Jasper let out a growl that killed her elation almost instantly. "I said no."

"There's nothing wrong with them, Jasper. I got mine when I was seventeen," Shira said. Her eyes and attitude screamed rebellious mischief now, as if she were going against even her own father's wishes. Zach could believe that had been the case. "I'm not even suggesting she get one until she's a legal adult. I could have said seventeen, even though I don't have a right to promise that."

"She will never get one." Jasper's lip pulled back, and Zach worried he wasn't keeping himself in check. Shira was playing with fire as it was, and it was possible she was aware by the way she was starting to assess Jasper.

"You don't get to decide that when she's of legal age," Shira said in a cool yet defiant tone. "You don't own her. Now, what else might she be interested in having? Hmm…"

Shira touched her fingers to her ear, sliding them down her neck and toward her collarbone. "What about—"

"Don't," Jasper practically snarled. "Don't you dare suggest that."

Shira's brow cocked. "Suggest what?"

She looked about as confused as Zach felt. What had Jasper assumed she'd say from that action?

"Don't you dare suggest such a piercing for her." Jasper practically punctuated each word through clenched teeth.

Shira remained confused until something seemed to dawn on her. And then her face screwed up in disbelief. "You seriously thought I was going to suggest *that?*"

It didn't take Zach any longer to get on the same page. Jasper had jumped right into clear sexual piercings.

"Are you fucking mad?" Shira said. "Why the hell would you think I'd even consider suggesting something of that nature?"

Jasper slammed his fist down on the table, and his voice rose. "Enough, Shira!"

Everything in Zach stopped. This just got worse than he expected. He realized now, a little too late, he

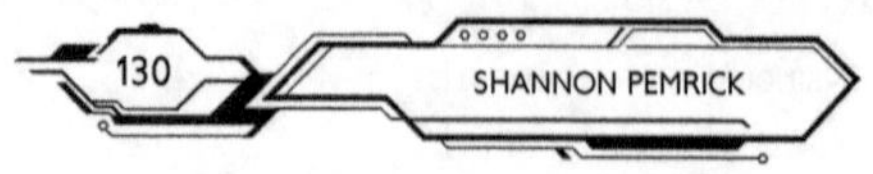

should have stepped in instead of letting things go as they would.

Snake popped his head up from under the table where he'd lain quietly this whole time. He had his ears perked, and attention focused on the high negative energy now surfacing.

The lingering mirth in Shira's eyes faded, fury replacing it. "Don't. Don't you fucking dare yell at me."

Zach held his breath. What was he supposed to do? They were both now fired up, and Zach wasn't sure he had a proper de-escalation plan that'd work for this.

To Zach's surprise, though, Jasper had frozen with her tone.

"If my joking around crossed a line, then just fucking tell me," Shira continued. "That's all you needed to do and I would have stopped. Don't you fucking dare make assumptions about what I'm going to say and start yelling at me for something I didn't do. Don't you scream commands at me on what to do or say, all because your ego was bruised when I said you didn't own your daughter's body. You don't own me any more than her, and don't get to make forceful demands."

And then it was all done. Shira turned away from them both to focus on Serenity, her fury gone, as if it had never been there. Serenity was confused by the hostile situation and asked so many questions, though Shira calmed her and encouraged Serenity to forget about it and move onto a new topic with her, like how she liked her food and what she wanted to do once Zach and Jasper had to go for their next match.

Zach's stomach turned, and he picked at his food.

Jasper came down from his emotional surge, regret written all over his face.

"Jasper, Zach," Alistair said from Jasper's phone. "It would be wise for the two of you to head back to the tournament lounge. You both still need to watch the highlight reel and analysis before your next match."

Jasper let out a slow breath. "Yeah, you're right."

"Aw," Serenity complained. "Do you really gots to go?"

Shira ran her fingers through the young girl's hair. "It's just for the one match, sweetie. They have to advance so they can make money."

"Because to bring home the bacon, Daddy and Zach have to win!" Serenity said, a phrase she used a lot after Jasper used it to get her to understand why he and Zach had to go away for a weekend once for a short tournament.

Shira laughed. "Yes, lots of bacon."

Serenity smacked her lips together. She loved bacon.

The four of them cleaned up, Zach noticing Shira still refused to look at either of them. He wasn't sure if she was acting this way with him also because he hadn't jumped in to say anything, or if it was because it'd mean acknowledging Jasper, too. Whatever the reason, it made his chest ache.

Serenity gave him and Jasper a hug goodbye and a "pep talk" to kick butt. She then took Shira's hand and turned away. The whole time, Shira didn't say a single word to them. Not even a quick "good luck."

She'd never given them the silent treatment—not in any serious manner, at least. They were adults, so they'd get over it soon, and even talk it out, but the hurt was still raw and it'd linger.

Jasper lifted his hand as if he were reaching out, but then turned it into a wave when Serenity looked over her shoulder. "Have fun, you two."

Serenity waved, and Shira ended up lifting her hand in acknowledgement, but didn't look back still.

Jasper let out a long breath. "Say it."

"You don't need me to, since you know what I'm going to say."

"Say it," he repeated.

Zach sighed. "You need to call Jeff."

Jasper's shoulders slumped. "Yeah, I know. I'll make an appointment. Though it won't fix what I just did."

"You need to call now and talk to him," Alistair's voice said from one of their phones.

Both Jasper and Zach jumped out of their skins. Zach held his chest, his pulse racing, and breath coming quick. "Jeez, don't do that!"

"I'm sorry," Alistair said. "As an AI, I have no physical body to give you cues I need to speak."

Jasper patted his chest. "Why aren't you with Shira on the tablet?"

"I am."

Zach and Jasper passed each other confused looks. Zach spoke to the AI, "Then how are you talking to us through one of our phones?"

"I am an AI," the artificial life form said. "As long as the devices I'm linked to are connected to the digital server, I can be in multiple locations at once. This is how I can control your car while interacting with someone still at the apartment."

Right... They so rarely needed to use the AI separately in that way, Zach had forgotten about that ability.

"So, now that you're done giving us a heart attack, what did you mean by call Jeff now?" Jasper asked. "We have a match to get to."

"Not right this minute, you don't," the AI said. "I gave the wrong time, intending to have you speak with Jeff. I've already contacted him and he's free for a minor session. It will cost a little extra because it's last minute, but he understood my concern with my assessment from the heated conversation that happened, along with the other incidents I've recorded lately."

They both blinked. Zach wasn't sure if he should be happy to have such a helpful and efficient assistant, or scared. Instead, he opted to ensure Jasper got the small bit of help he needed today, and make sure he ended up on the right path going forward.

He patted Jasper on the back. "Let's get you to a place that's secluded so the two of you can talk."

People bustled about in the dealer's corner, all eager to see what they could throw their money at next. Shira carried a few bags, nothing large or crazy yet. Most of it was snacks Serenity had never had before, but there were other trinkets and fun things, too.

Shira was trying to pace herself. The guys should be here to enjoy this moment with their daughter. She didn't have a right to steal it all from them, even if they'd told her previously they expected Shira to do all kinds of things with Serenity to keep her occupied.

Serenity poked Shira's arm. "She-ra, are you sure you're not mad at Daddy?"

Shira couldn't suppress the chuckle. The little girl hadn't stopped asking this, thinking the answer would change. "No, Starship, I'm not mad anymore. Just annoyed."

"Is he in the doghouse?"

Shira cocked her head. "Do you know what that means?"

Serenity shrugged. "No, but Pop-Pop said he was there once when he made Nana mad."

Shira grinned. That would figure. "No, he's not in the doghouse. But he does owe me an apology. And I owe him one, too."

"Because you yelled too and said bad words?"

Shira nodded. As mad as she was at Jasper for the way he acted, she could have behaved better as well.

"Good," Serenity chirped. "Because Daddy loves you, and it'd make him sad if you didn't want to talk to him anymore."

Shira stopped dead in her tracks. "W–what did you say, Starship?"

The young girl gazed up at her with those beautiful green eyes. "He loves you. Zach does too. And I love you, too. We'd be sad if you were so angry you didn't want to talk to us no more."

Shira's heart rate, which she hadn't realized had sky-rocketed, calmed down. She should have known that's what the little girl meant. *Why would they actually love me?*

Yes, she teased them earlier to get back at them for all the times they'd messed with her, and it was obvious it worked. The attraction between them was undeniably off the charts, and not something she could pretend didn't exist. And while Shira was working through the idea that those two men may be interested in her as more than a friend, love of the romantic sense was a bit much right now.

Shira needed a brief distraction. She checked her phone to see if Mercedes and Narissa had gotten back to her about meeting up. They had, but it looked like they were still busy. Didn't bother Shira. She'd have more time with them later.

"She-ra, how are Daddy and Zach doing?" Serenity asked.

Shira swapped the tech in her hand and pulled up the Lusara Fates matches. She'd missed most of Horde of the North's matches while she had been doing things with the guys, but the board said they'd passed to the next round. That made her happy.

She swiped the info away to pull up everything on the two's tournament. Jasper and Zach were still in their match, but they were on their third round and standing at a 2-0 streak right now.

"They're blowing this one out of the water," she said to Serenity.

The little girl cheered. "I knew they'd kick butt."

"That's because I'll kick theirs if they lose."

Serenity covered her mouth as she giggled, and Shira couldn't keep its contagious nature from spreading to her.

Display analysis flickered over parts of the screen, the two AIs attached to this device in a strong competition to create the best one, plus a replay for Jasper and Zach to utilize later.

It surprised Shira how competitive AIs could be, but at the same time, she supposed it had to do with their nature to always strive to be the best for their owners. It certainly couldn't hurt to do this with them. Shira felt more confident the AIs would grow from this type of use.

"Can you tell me more about all that stuff on the screen?" Serenity asked.

Shira smiled. "Sure. Let's find a place to sit."

There weren't any free benches, so they found a wall that was safe from foot traffic, and Shira explained the different aspects of the analysis tools. Most of the info flew over Serenity's head, but it all enraptured her, so Shira continued. She didn't want to dumb things down for the young girl. Sure, she was careful with the kinds of words, because some even made Shira's head spin, but she didn't talk down to Serenity like she was inept at understanding anything. She was a bright kid, and she deserved that respect.

"This is so much stuff, She-ra. You really are Daddy and Zach's coach."

Shira chuckled. She hadn't put much thought into what had been brought up earlier when she found out Zach and Jasper had thought about officially making her their coach. It was annoying they were doing some of the official approvals without her knowledge, but she also understood why. If the company said no, there'd be no point broaching the subject. And in the very least, if Shira had said no after the fact, the guys could then go and look for a real coach.

"I'm not their real coach. I just kick their butts when they aren't doing what they're supposed to." Shira pursed her lips as if she were thinking. "I'm not even sure what a coach would do for them."

"Probably yell at them lots." Serenity's hand flew up her face, trying to suppress more giggles. "And kick their butts."

Shira's head flew back with her laughter. A simple assessment from a nearly seven-year-old, but Shira doubted it was too far off from the truth.

"I hope Daddy and Zach win," Serenity said. Shira opened her mouth to say how it was likely with the score, but the girl continued. "That way we have money so they don't hafta worry for a while."

Shira frowned, unease pricking her stomach. She knew Jasper and Zach tried to hide the money issues, as all parents would from their kids. But Serenity was an observant individual. It was both a blessing and a curse in a small package. "How much do you know, Starship?"

The girl shrugged, her eyes downcast. "What I over-heah."

"And what have you heard?" Shira needed to know exactly what was going on in her little head. She was supposed to be careful, as this should be territory for her parents to handle, but they weren't here, and the last thing Shira needed was for Serenity to withdraw and try to process adult situations when she shouldn't need to.

"That they get paid by the sports company, and then more if they win tournaments." Serenity played with her fingers. "And that if they don't win, they hafta take jobs that make them tired and grouchy because they don't like them."

The girl's green eyes slowly looked up at Shira, hints of fear flickering over them. "And that you give us money sometimes."

Shira laid her hand on Serenity's head. "Thank you for being honest with me. I know this topic is scary."

"Why do they hide it, She-ra?" The fear in her eyes swapped to confusion.

Shira tucked a strand of hair behind Serenity's ear. "Because money is an adult issue. It's our job to make sure you have everything you need without knowing yet what that costs."

"But why? I'm getting bigger. I can know!"

Shira hushed her, cradling her cheeks in her hands. "Let me finish, sweetie. Kids should always be kids, carefree and enjoying life as much as they can. Adults, they enjoy life too, but there are heavy responsibilities that come with that. Parents want to make sure their kids don't feel that weight for as long as they can, because that's what a parent's love is. It bears all that weight, so you can enjoy life as you are meant to experience it."

"How strong is their love?" Serenity asked.

Shira's chest constricted, and she had to keep her lower lip from trembling as she recited the words Anita told her once, when Shira asked a similar question. "The strength of their love is wanting to give you the world when we know it's impossible, so we settle for giving you the most we can. And our reward is seeing you smiling and happy."

Serenity was quiet, the words sinking in slowly, and then she said, "Would you try to give me that if you were my mommy?"

Shira took a deep breath. She could feel the tears welling up in her eyes. "Starship, I'd wrangle the sun, so it'd rise and set with you. I'd tame the sea for only you to play. And I'd collect all the stars in the sky and lay them at your feet, if only to make you smile."

The brightest smile Shira had ever seen on Serenity's face appeared. It pierced her heart like an assassin's dagger. The little girl threw herself into Shira's arms and buried her face in Shira's chest. Shira pulled her close and bit her lip, struggling not to break down. She'd always told herself to keep distant, so Serenity wouldn't get attached. But Shira realized just a little too late that she'd forgotten to tell herself that was well.

She wanted a child—a family of her own—so badly. Jasper, Zach, and Serenity… they could be that family. Shira cared so deeply for them it was starting to hurt. But fear yanked her so hard to stay in her little box of safety. She was afraid that if she reached out too far, everything she wanted would be ripped away and she'd be left falling.

And Shira knew that if that happened, she'd never recover.

Snake nosed and pawed at Shira's arm. Serenity giggled. "C'mon, Snake, join the cuddle!"

Shira chuckled and moved her arm, using the motion to wipe away a stray tear from her cheek. *Traitorous emotions…*

Snake forced his way into their hug, his tail thumping against Shira's leg. It hurt a little, but Shira wasn't about to complain, because Serenity was loving it.

When the love pile was over, Shira found herself sitting with a dog half in her lap, and half in Serenity's. The girl didn't quite pet him, trying to be mindful of the things her dads told her, but her fingers were deeply tangled into his plush fur.

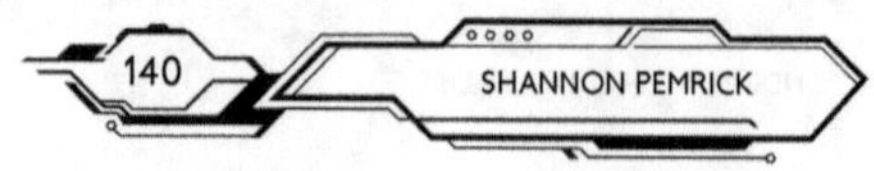

"Starship, can I ask you something that might seem strange?" Shira figured now was as good a time as any to bring this up.

Serenity cocked her head. "Yeah?"

"I noticed you called Zach 'Dad' when you were talking to Britney early. But you call him Zach when you're talking to me. Why is that?"

The girl blinked. "Oh, that's easy. That's because you know he's my dad."

The simplicity of that answer should not have surprised Shira, but it did. "But you call Jasper 'Daddy' and not his name."

Serenity nodded. "Yep. He's Daddy, and just Daddy, and Zach is Dad, Zach, and"—she giggled—"Bat."

Shira's eyebrow lifted. "Bat?"

"Yeah, I called him that when I was little."

You're still little. Shira bit her tongue. "So when you talk to Zach, you call him by all three of those names?"

Serenity shook her head. "No, I just call him Zach or Bat."

"And what do you call him when talking to other people?"

"I call him Dad."

She said it so matter-of-factly it made Shira pause. There was no logic in any of this. Well, not to her. But it clearly made all kinds of sense to Serenity.

Serenity pursed her lips and cocked her head. The expression caused Shira's heart to skip. It looked so familiar, and in a way that sent a tiny pang in her chest, though she couldn't quite place it right then. It wasn't a copy of Shira's way, and definitely wasn't anything Jasper and Zach did. *So… who?*

"She-ra, why did you ask those questions?"

Discomfort overrode Shira's curiosity. She wasn't sure if she should tell Serenity the true reason for the inquiry. She didn't want the girl to feel guilty for her naming choices. If she didn't want to call Zach, dad, to his face, no matter how he'd feel about it, it wasn't Shira's place to pressure her. "I just hadn't heard you call him dad before. So I was curious."

"Did you think I didn't see him as my dad?"

Shira shrugged awkwardly. "I wasn't sure. You never correct me when I refer to them as your dads, but it was a possibility in my mind that you didn't see Zach as your dad."

Serenity stared at her. "You're not telling me the whole truth."

Dammit. She was too sharp for her own good.

"Dad asked you to ask me, didn't he?" She frowned and tears brimmed her eyes. "Does… does he not want me to call him dad? Does he not—"

Oh shit. Oh shit. Oh shit, oh shit, oh shit! Panic fogged Shira's brain. Serenity ran to a conclusion Shira never expected. And of course, it was the wrong one and couldn't be farther from the truth.

Shira's hands flew up, and she framed Serenity's face. "Starship, no. No, no, no. It's like that at all."

Serenity gazed at her, a single tear breaking free. Shira wiped it away with her thumb. "Zach wants you to see him as your dad. He loves you *so* much. Please don't think otherwise."

"But why did he ask you to bring up the question?"

Shira shook her head. "He didn't. It came up in a conversation that you'd called him dad, and… he was surprised. Because you never called him that to his face, he wasn't sure if you saw him as your dad."

Serenity pulled out of Shira's grasp. "But why didn't he ask me?"

"Because adults…" She struggled to find the right way to word it. "Sometimes we overthink. Zach didn't even want me to ask you anything, but I'm nosey and wanted to know myself. He was worried that if he brought it up, he was pressuring you to call him Dad when you didn't want to."

The little girl's face scrunched. "That's wicked stupid." Shira had to bite her cheek so she wouldn't laugh. "Zach raised me with Daddy after my mom died. I don't remembah her, but I always remembah Zach. I love Zach. Daddy does, too. That's why he's gonna ask Zach to marry him soon."

Shira blinked and Serenity's hands flew up to her mouth as if she'd just spilled a big secret. "I wasn't supposed to say that."

Shira's eyes squinted as she smiled and pressed a finger up to her lips. "It'll be our secret."

"Really? You won't tell on me?" Serenity asked, her eyes wide.

"Absolutely not. It's exciting that Jasper wants to marry Zach. But I know how important it is to keep it secret until it happens." And Shira couldn't be happier to know. She really hoped it would help erase all of Zach's fears about the validity of his and Jasper's relationship.

Of course, that left her unsure what she should do about her growing feelings and situations she found herself in with the two of them that were getting too hard to ignore.

"Hey, She-ra?" Serenity said.

Shira tilted her head, proving her undivided attention.

"Would it make Zach happy if I called him Dad?"

Shira worked her jaw as she thought about how to word the answer, and then tucked a lock of hair behind Serenity's ear. "He didn't say it would, but when the topic came up in that conversation, he did look happy to know that's what you called him when talking to other people. So, I think even hearing you call him Dad once would make him wicked happy."

Serenity nodded. "Okay. Can we do more shopping? I want to find something special for him, so when I call him Dad, I have a gift, too."

Shira swore her heart melted right out of her body. It was overkill on the girl's part. She could say it without a gift, but if that's what Serenity wanted to do, then Shira wouldn't stop her. And Shira was determined to spoil her while she was here, so why not add this to the plan?

"Yeah, let's see what we can find."

CHAPTER 9

Jasper peered around a busy stall and spotted Shira and Serenity browsing comic downloads. Jasper smiled—he had tried to get Serenity into comics and graphic novels, but she wasn't interested in reading them, only looking at the images.

Zach leaned close. "Ready?"

Jasper smirked. "They're totally unaware."

Zach held up three fingers and silently counted down with them. At zero, Jasper shot out from their hiding place, Zach right behind. The crowds drowned out their approach. When they came in range, Jasper reached out and grabbed Serenity, lifting her up in the air. Zach wrapped his arms around Shira's waist and lifted her, though Shira made it look like she'd gone higher with her legs instinctively pulling up. Both ladies squealed in surprise.

Jasper and Zach laughed. That had gone perfectly. Jasper would have liked to be in Zach's place, but with what went down between him and Shira, without a talk and apology, he knew it wouldn't be right.

"Daddy!" Serenity cried when she realized who had her. "You won."

Jasper held her close with a tight squeeze, before setting her back on the floor. "Yes, we did."

Zach released Shira and she spun, wrapping her arms around his neck. "You two did great."

Jasper thought they'd done better than just her "great" assessment. He and Zach almost managed a straight three-game win, but the paladin on Drunk Dwarves got a lucky shot on him.

"We couldn't risk your wrath if we lost," Zach joked, squeezing Shira before releasing her.

She laughed and turned to face Jasper. He hadn't put Serenity down yet. Jasper hoped she'd be willing to give him the same treatment, though he wouldn't hold his breath. A lighthearted smile shaped her lips, and she opened her arms for a hug.

Jasper let out a mental sigh of relief. Shira slipped her arms around his neck and he happily pulled her tight against him. Her sweet scent and soft form teased him. Jasper bent his head, his lips brushing her ear. "Latah, the two of us need to talk."

"I agree," she murmured. "Until then, we'll forget the situation happened so we can enjoy the rest of our time here."

While avoidance wasn't good, he had to agree with her.

Shira was the first to pull away. She clapped her hands together. "So, what are we going to do?"

Jasper took in their surroundings. "Good question."

"Why don't we talk about the little shopping spree

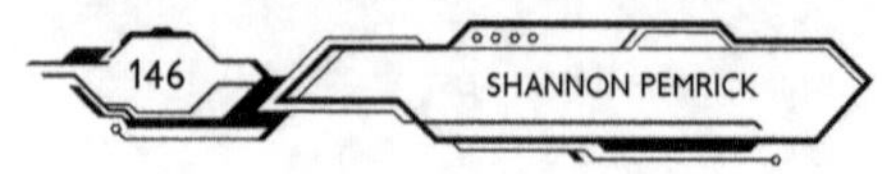

you two had?" Zach said. He pointed at the bags on the ground.

Jasper's eyes widened. There were a lot. "What did you buy?"

"It's a secret," Shira said. She gathered the bags, preventing either of them from snagging one to snoop.

"Yeah, a secret," Serenity said.

Jasper passed Zach a look. "They're plotting against us."

Zach's lips twitched. "I suppose that's what we get for allowing Shira to run wild with a credit card unsupervised at a convention."

Shira winked. "This is nothing."

Jasper couldn't help but make a face. "Remembah, we live in an apahtment."

"Says the guy who bought more books than he could carry in his arms," she teased, her eyes squinting.

Zach choked on a laugh. Jasper rolled his eyes. "That's different."

"Uh huh, sure." Shira slipped past them, sashaying her way toward another vendor booth. Serenity ran after her, Snake padding alongside his daughter. Seemed Shira was allowing her to be his leash keeper. Jasper watched Shira carry the bags all on one side while placing her free hand on Serenity's upper back.

He worked his jaw, eyes drinking in the sight. Shira was irresistibly sexy, and her taking Serenity under her wing, as if it were second nature already for her to care for his daughter—God, he wanted her.

It wasn't going to be easy to open up to her and explain his behavior, but he needed to. It wasn't something he could ignore, and if the three of them were going to work out, nothing could be hidden. If this still healing part of him made her pull away, it was better for that to happen now, rather than later when he and Zach had become too invested.

Shira turned to look back at them. "Well? What are you two waiting for?"

"How are we supposed to know what we can consider buying if you won't tell us what you already purchased?" Zach asked with his usual smooth execution. "We don't want to waste money and all."

She smirked, her eyes twinkling. "I'll tell you if it's something you don't need."

Jasper crossed his arms and gave her another visual assessment, not being discreet in the least. "You just want us to be your pack mules while you go ovahboard."

Shira snorted and raised her cybernetic arm carrying all her bags. "I can assure you I don't need one. One of the few good things about having cybernetic prosthetics."

It was the first time in a while he'd even noticed the artificial implants. Jasper found it so easy to see them naturally as a part of her. And that made her negative comments hurt even him. He wasn't having it.

He sucked air against his teeth, then advanced. Shira blinked her confusion and then let out a complaining sound when he snatched two bags from her hand.

"Jasper!"

He smirked. "I won't look. But you're not carrying everything."

She narrowed her eyes at him, then gasped when Zach snuck in and grabbed another bag. Shira puffed out her cheeks. It was so adorable, Jasper was almost charmed into giving the stolen bag back. But he didn't.

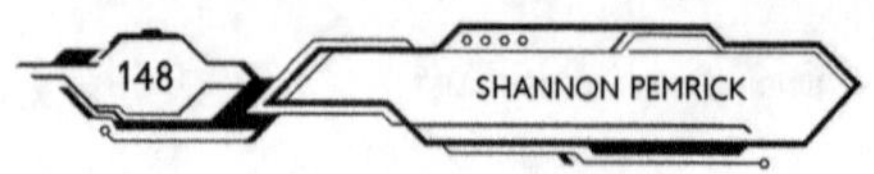

"C'mon, we have dealuh tables to be lured to, and maybe some game demos to try."

Shira blew out a breath and resigned herself to the fate of her bags. The temptation to peek was strong, but Jasper forced himself to behave this time and focused on having fun in another way. And fun they had.

Shopping may not be something others found fun, but Jasper did. Scoping out nerd shit added to that enjoyment, and so did the company. Shira was willing to be as silly as them when the mood struck, and she didn't complain when any of them wanted to switch up their path through the rows of dealer booths.

They even got in some demos. Shira was sure to make a few cracks at Zach and him for being game junkies, given they'd been in matches most of the day, not that it was too far from the truth. When he and Zach weren't playing Lusara Fates, they were sucked into another game—if they weren't spending time with Serenity, of course.

Then, before he knew it, they were heading home. Exhaustion clung to his body like a powerful temptress, luring him to close his eyes and catch some Z's. Serenity was the only thing keeping him awake. She was so over-tired that she'd hit hyper mode, and there was no duct tape in existence to convince her to stop talking.

No one was listening to her babbling, though. It was clear Shira and Zach were just as tired as he was. But that didn't stop his daughter from carrying on a one-sided conversation.

When they arrived at Shira's place, no one moved. Jasper would be content to sleep in the car tonight. He could pull Shira into his lap and—

"Jasper," Zach murmured. "You need to get out so I can. It's wicked cramped back here."

Jasper let out a quiet sigh. Fair point. He couldn't force Zach to be confined in the back because Jasper was tired. *Plus, Shira and I still have to talk.* As much as his body begged for him to sleep and deal with that conversation tomorrow, he knew it wasn't right.

Jasper patted his cheeks to wake himself up a bit and then climbed out. Zach stumbled out, making Jasper laugh. His boyfriend swatted at him before slipping to the other side of the car to assist Shira with Serenity. She was crashing now, but still wanted to get herself out of her booster. While he fussed with her, Shira opened the trunk to retrieve their spoils for the day. Jasper helped, as they'd gone a little overboard on day one.

Restraint was a smart thing to do, but that wasn't as much fun. Besides, if they ran out of things to do around the matches, the four of them could do something fun in the city. There weren't any rules that said they had to spend the whole day at the convention.

Shira unlocked the door and entered the home first. She kicked off her shoes haphazardly and tossed her keys on the nearby table under the key hook. Even as tired as Jasper was, it tweaked that demon inside him and he had to use all the willpower he could muster not to say anything right now. He could bring it up in their conversation.

She loosed Snake before gesturing to Jasper to follow her. "We'll put everything in the kitchen for now. Keep them out of the way tonight. We can go through them tomorrow."

Jasper removed his shoes and tucked them neatly

against the wall. "What is it with you not wanting us to go through these bags? What's the big secret?"

She winked and walked down the hall. "If I told you, it wouldn't be a secret."

He let out a playful sigh but didn't press. He'd find out eventually what the two ladies had concocted. It wouldn't kill him to wait a little longer.

Shira set her bags down in a corner of the kitchen, then disappeared into the pantry. From the sound of it, as well as Snake's excited spinning, she was getting his dinner. Jasper set his bags down with the others and peered down the hall when the door opened. Zach cradled Serenity's sleeping form. Jasper had to resist the urge to laugh. It didn't surprise him one bit that she'd crashed on the way into the house.

Zach made a motion with his head to show he was going to put her in bed, and Jasper nodded. This gave him a little more time to talk to Shira alone. It wouldn't have been terrible for Zach to be around, but that was a lot of pressure, and he already had a lot of that weighing him down.

"Shira, need anything else?" Jasper asked.

"Could you check Snake's water bowl to see if it needs a refill? I can't remember if I did that this morning before we rushed out."

"Sure." He slipped around the island and took a look at the water bowl. Clean water flowed down the fountain spout and the reservoir was nearly full. "Nope, Superwoman, you managed to get Snake fed, watered, and out to relieve himself, all the while making sure we didn't completely miss the conference."

"Well, that's reassuring," she said. Shira entered the

kitchen again, kibble piled in Snake's food bowl. Instead of setting it down on the ground, like Snake clearly wanted judging by his impatient dance, she put it on the island and rummaged through the fridge, pulling out a sealed bag filled with what looked like meat and vegetables.

While Shira mixed the contents in with the kibble, she made a soft command in German for Snake to sit, and he did immediately, though he wiggled and licked his chops.

Jasper leaned on the counter. "Does he evah not listen to you?"

Shira chuckled. "When he doesn't have his vest on, all the time. He may be a working dog who does his job at home and outside of it, but at the end of the day, he's still a dog, and prone to doggie tendencies."

"Have you evah had to send him for retraining?" Jasper didn't know the first thing about service dog training, and now seemed a good time to learn something.

"I haven't needed to in the sense that he was losing the training, or misbehaving more for some reason. But I have had him see a trainer a few times just to make sure it doesn't happen."

"Evah had any concerns with him?"

Shira set the dish in a raised cradle made for the bowl, though to Jasper's surprise, Snake didn't bolt for his dinner. A moment passed before Shira snapped her fingers, releasing her dog from his command. "Nope, model citizen according to the trainer."

Jasper watched as the large shepherd messily scarfed down his food. "Our family dog was nevah that well behaved." He then laughed. "Though they both don't know how to keep the food off the floor."

Shira snickered. "He's just saving it for last. This guy will not waste a single piece of kibble."

"Yup, sounds like Brownie."

Shira cocked her head toward him. "What kind of dog did you guys have?"

"She was a cocker."

Shira's eyes lit up. "I love spaniels! Do you have a picture?"

Jasper whipped out his phone. He wasn't sure if he had one saved. On his home computer, sure, he had plenty. Jasper searched for a bit before his phone scrolled on its own.

"You have one," Alistair said from his device.

The AI stopped the scroll and opened a photo. Displayed was him when he was nine, and a cream and white cocker spaniel.

"Oh, no, she can't see this one," Jasper said, trying to close the image down.

Shira gasped. "What? No, I must. Gimmie."

She reached for the phone, using desperate grabby hands. Jasper held the phone out of reach. She was not about to see this stupid photo of him. Jasper loved it, it reminded him of how much fun he had that day with her. But he looked like a total loser in it, with his missing teeth and dopey grin.

"C'mon, Jas, let me see."

Jas… His heart beat a little harder with that nickname she'd suddenly started calling him. No one ever called him Jas. And he didn't realize how much he wanted to be called that—until now. The way it rolled off her tongue, so soft and almost sensual—

Shira pressed up against him, her form melding into

his. Her hands clutched his shirt. "Please show me the picture. It can't be that bad."

Jasper opened his mouth, but words failed him as she gazed up at him with those dazzling eyes of hers. Her full lips were slightly parted, as if begging him to steal a kiss. Her sweet scent teased him, calling his soul, luring him to let his guard down.

He did.

Jasper lowered his arm, allowing her to snatch the phone and pull away with a big grin. And in that moment, he realized how she'd gone from his and Zach's spitfire elementalist to a tempting siren that sang a song only the two of them could hear—a song Jasper didn't want to resist.

"Oh, you're so cute!" she gushed.

Jasper didn't care about the photo anymore. She could have called him a toothless gibbon for all he cared. Jasper reached out and cupped her cheek, his fingers gliding across her smooth, soft skin.

Shira's eyes widened and flicked up to him. "Jasper?"

Her words were hesitant and unsure; he was anything but. The spell she cast on him took hold, and Jasper knew what he wanted.

He leaned forward, and she remained captured under his gaze. Jasper pressed his lips against her forehead. Shira let out a strained moan, as if she tried to bite back her reaction. But Jasper knew all the tricks of seducing a woman. He knew how to make her weak from the simplest gestures, and what would make her beg for more.

"I'm sorry," he murmured against her skin. "I shouldn't have taken things out on you earliah."

"The blame isn't solely on you—"

"Please let me finish," he interrupted. "Because my angah wasn't due to what you were saying. Not entirely, at least."

Shira pulled back, giving him her undivided attention. Jasper deeply desired to pull her close, but he knew that was him wanting to avoid her gaze as he laid out a piece of him he wasn't proud of.

He took a steadying breath. "Sara's death affected me in a way I can't say I'm remotely proud of. Because I couldn't do anything to save her"—he licked his lips— "I… need to control… everything. I need to have things in a certain order and happen a certain way."

Jasper looked away from her soft gaze. "It can be small things like keys or shoes not being put away where they should; a PvP match not going right no mattuh how much I strategized and did everything that should have guaranteed a win"—he blew out a breath—"or trying my damndest to raise Serenity right, I end up trying to control every little thing about her life, only to be reminded… how much I can't."

His chest ached with pain and shame. Talking to Jeff had brought this all to the surface, and while it couldn't be a long session to start significant work on fixing his issue, it'd left him raw. And that had returned.

Shira's soft and warm fingers, and smooth prosthetic fingers, slid across his cheeks. She turned his attention back on her and gazed up at him with kind eyes. "Thank you."

Jasper wrapped his arms around her and pulled Shira close. Her body molded into him, fitting perfectly. She pressed her face into his neck, her hot breath tickling his skin. Jasper tangled his fingers into her silky locks and buried his face in her hair, inhaling her sweet scent.

Having her close like this… he could get lost in it. His pain could melt away, like it'd never existed at all. "I'm sorry for yelling at you aftah that match that day. And for getting angry earliah today."

"I'm sorry for pushing too far," she murmured into his skin, sending a *zing* down his body.

"Even if you pushed too far, I didn't have a right to let my angah get out of control. I should have just asked you to stop. I'm going to try bettah."

"I will be more mindful, now that I know what's going on," she promised. "And I'm grateful you told me. As much as I've gone through my own shit from that day, I can't imagine what you've gone through with your loss. PTSD is no joke, and any kind of trauma can trigger it. I can understand why this would become a problem."

"Before you ask, I do see someone about it," he admitted. "Though, I lapsed away from my sessions."

She grunted. "Like I'm one to chastise for that. I'd be a hypocrite."

He chuckled. "True. But I wanted to be up front. I talked to him today, which helped me with bringing this up."

"Hmm, I thought it was a little early for you two to head back to prepare for your match." She shrugged. "But I was too irritated to say anything." Shira lifted her head. "Is there anything I'm doing that I need to be aware of because it causes you issues?"

Jasper blew out a breath. "Yeah, your inability to put ya keys and shoes away right."

Shira laughed, her eyes practically sparkling. "Of

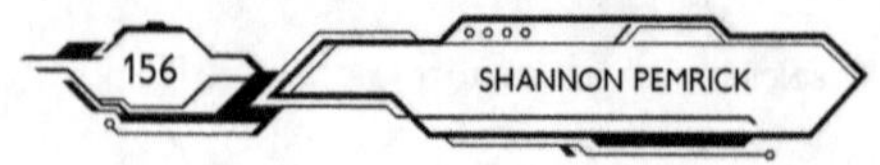

course that does. You're not allowed to come over to my house, then. My crafting and bedroom would kill you." Her brows pulled together. "Actually, you can't go into those rooms here, either."

He gazed down at her, amused and drawn into the mess of a woman who was in his arms. "Maybe I should. Having that much chaos could be good for me."

The green in her eyes glimmered. "I'm not in the business of breaking people."

"No?" He grinned and tucked his fingers under her chin. "Then what about fixing them?"

Her tempting mouth parted, and that damned piercing of hers glinted in the kitchen light. Fuck, he'd forgotten about that. Not only had she kept that hidden for this long because she knew him too well, Zach had made a game out of it, too, when he found out first.

His blood simmered; he couldn't stop himself. Before Shira could say anything, he bent down and captured her lips with his. She let out a startled squeak, but didn't push him away. No, her hands slid up his chest and around the back of his neck while she kissed him back.

Their lips synchronized and his tongue dragged against the back of his lip, hesitant to ask for that permission. Even with his pulse pounding in his ears, and his cock hard and begging he haul her onto the counter, Jasper had enough presence of mind to not push this too quick or hard. He was that impulsive, and that was the last thing Jasper needed to do, at the risk of sending her running.

He reluctantly broke the kiss.

"What…" Shira barely managed in a breathy voice. Her eyes were still half closed.

"Thank you," he said, hoping this would cover him. "For undahstanding."

Her hands slid down his chest from their place around his neck. Her lower lip caught between her teeth, teasing—daring him to kiss her again. "You're… you're welcome."

She was the first to pull away. "I should get to bed. Long day tomorrow."

He didn't stop her from leaving. Instead, he took in her posture to make sure she wasn't running. Well, running in fear, at least. It was clear she was trying to put some space between them. *No, I didn't push too far.* She didn't hunch her shoulders, and didn't try to run from the other set of eyes Jasper was now aware were in the room.

Zach leaned against the hallway wall, watching with interest.

For a moment, Jasper thought Shira would walk right on past his boyfriend, but she didn't. She stopped, smiled, and then reached for his face, pulling a surprised Zach in for his own kiss.

Jasper leaned on the counter, his groin now throbbing. This was hot. Especially when Zach slid his hands over the curve of Shira's hips and pulled her hard into him. Jasper could just imagine Zach fucking her against that wall while he watched. Or maybe he was screwing Zach at the same time. That was a tantalizing image.

Shira pulled away, her hand dragging teasingly along Zach's chest, and she turned. "It's only fair."

Zach grinned. "I'm not complaining."

Shira murmured something before walking down the hall. Just before heading up the stairs, she grabbed her keys and hung them up.

"Shoes would have been better," Jasper muttered when she made no move to fix those.

Shira chuckled, the sound echoing down the stairs as she ascended. "That's why I did it."

Jasper's hand clenched, and he had to take a deep breath. She really liked to play with fire. One day, she was going to push him too far.

Strong hands slid over Jasper's taut abs atop his shirt. Jasper refocused on Zach just as his boyfriend's mouth captured his for a sizzling kiss that sparked a fire in his veins. "I'm wicked proud of you. I know that was difficult. And I'm sure after all that, you need a release."

"Fuck, you have no idea," Jasper groaned. "But here in her kitchen? Not afraid she'll get mad?"

He had no qualms about it. Shira could walk in and watch for all he wanted. But Zach could be a different story.

Zach chuckled and grabbed the waistband of Jasper's jeans, working at the button. "She could watch if it made her happy. Serenity is asleep, and I'm taking full advantage of this situation."

Desire heated Jasper's body from core to fingertips. He had his reservations about Zach's feelings for Shira. It was hard to tell if Zach meant what he said, or was just trying to make Jasper happy for fear of losing him. Jasper wasn't an idiot. The two of them had their share of issues, and anxiety of this working long-term was one of Zach's. He didn't have to verbalize it for Jasper to see.

Jasper wouldn't do anything to compromise what they had. At the same time, he was trying to believe the things Zach told him. And if Mister Anti-PDA said he was good with Shira watching, Jasper didn't want to ruin this moment by questioning it.

What did hamper things was Snake's scratching at the door to go out into the yard.

Jasper glanced at Zach and grinned. "Why don't we take this outside?"

Zach's tongue dragged across his lower lip, his blue eyes darkening with lust. "Why not?"

Jasper pushed away from the counter and opened the nano door for the dog. Snake took off into the yard while Jasper stepped out into the warm air. Zach slipped around him and pushed Jasper against the house with one hand. Jasper didn't fight him.

Instead, he reached out and grabbed Zach's face, pulling him in for a hard kiss. His boyfriend's lips were warm and inviting. The lingering scent of cedar wafted off Zach, luring Jasper in even deeper.

Jasper nibbled and teased, while Zach's hands fumbled with the zipper of Jasper's jeans, as well as his own. Jasper blindly helped him with that.

The kiss broke when Zach trailed his lips down Jasper's neck. His heat sent sparks through Jasper's body, simmering his blood.

"I don't have a piercing like Shira," Zach said.

"Not from a lack of requesting on my part," Jasper reminded him.

Zach chuckled and dropped to his knees. "Not my style. But I'm sure you're still going to enjoy this."

Jasper's jeans hit the ground and soon after, his hard cock sprang forth, bobbing with eager weight. Zach dragged his tongue against his hard member while working himself free and Jasper hissed out a strained breath.

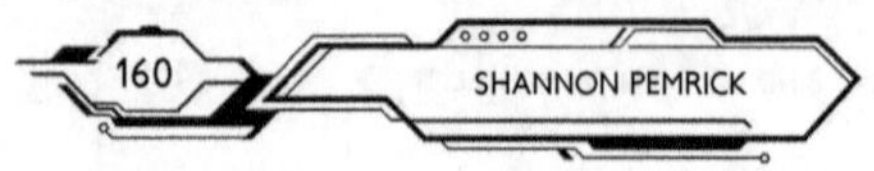

Zach's tongue teased down to Jasper's head. His boyfriend flicked his eyes up to Jasper before easing his lips over Jasper's throbbing cock.

"Zach…" Jasper groaned, rolling his head back as desire flared through him.

He slid Jasper's hard member in and out of his warm mouth with rhythm, while finding agonizingly slow and strong strokes for himself. Jasper's pulse hammered strong in his ears, watching his boyfriend stroke himself while sucking him off. He threaded his fingers into Zach's hair, now tousled after breaking free a bit from the hair tie.

"Hey, since you two are out—"

Shira poked her head outside and stopped dead when she saw them. Zach, while flicking his gaze to her, didn't stop his rhythm, and Jasper had no intention of making him. Instead, he kept his fingers firmly fisted in his boyfriend's hair and rocked his hips, driving his cock deeper into Zach's throat.

Crimson spread over Shira's face and shoulders. Fuck, did he love to see her flushed. It made him harder, and from the sound Zach made, he was quite pleased, too. "I… uh… just… make sure Snake doesn't jump in the pool, okay?"

Jasper grinned at her. "You could just stay out here with us."

Her flush deepened, the green of her eyes glimmering with thoughtful lust. Shira shook her head and spun on her heels. "I'm going to bed. Night!"

She ran off far too fast for her to pretend her flight wasn't her trying to hide her true feelings about walking in on the pair. Jasper chuckled. Oh, did he love to mess with her. She made it too easy.

Zach's tongue slid over Jasper's cock in a way that made him groan low, and then his boyfriend released him. His member bobbed, begging for the attention to return.

"I think our elementalist was wicked excited about the prospect of a show," Zach said, a volume loud enough for Shira to hear in her retreat.

Jasper leaned his head closer to the house, listening to her footsteps. "I don't know if she was more excited about that, or possibly becoming one herself."

Shira's steps quickened up the stairs. He grinned. Oh, was he willing and eager to do that for her.

"In time," Zach murmured before kissing the base of Jasper's cock and then dragging his tongue teasingly against his hard length. When he reached the head, he didn't hesitate to take Jasper back in full, eliciting a hard moan from Jasper. All the while, Zach continued to stroke himself.

Yes, in time they would. But Jasper would eagerly spend this moment he had with Zach. No interruptions until they both had their release.

A repressed whimper escaped Shira's lips. She lay on the couch, curled into herself and fighting the pain plaguing her body. She'd woken up feeling uncomfortable, and as she'd gotten ready for the day, the pain flared until she almost collapsed in the kitchen. It'd taken everything in her to retrieve pain medicine and haul herself onto the couch, and now even more not to scream her agony.

She hated this so much. It wasn't fair. *All the medical advancement breakthroughs and they can't find a cure for this.*

Snake's pacing and whining upstairs broke through her pained haze. She wished she could call him back down. Shira didn't want him bothering Jasper and Zach when they needed their sleep. They could have a later start than yesterday, and it wasn't right that they couldn't take advantage of that because of her. But this was Snake's job—if he couldn't help her and there was someone else around, he'd alert them in hopes they could.

Shira bit her lower lip when another powerful wave of pain slammed her. She'd really overdone it yesterday. It shouldn't have surprised her, since that'd been the most active she'd been in a long time, but still… She would have liked to not have this reaction after a day of fun. It made her want to give up trying. *What's the point if my enjoyment is only temporary?*

Feet thundered down the stairs, and Shira wished she could hide. She didn't want them to see her like this—ever.

Snake's nails clattered on the floor, and then he bolted into the room. Her dog skidded to a halt and looked at her, his body on alert, then back at the two people entering the room.

"Shira, is there something wrong with—"

Jasper's words cut off, and Shira didn't need to be looking up at him to see why. In a blink, both of them were crouched in front of her, deep lines of concern marring their handsome faces. If she weren't in so much pain, she'd make a crack at them for only being half-dressed. They'd managed pants, but their chests were bare and on display. Much to her disappointed, tormented mind, she didn't have it in her to shamelessly ogle right now.

"Shira, what's wrong?" Jasper asked, his hand reaching for her.

She flinched and let out a betraying whimper. "Please don't touch…"

It was all she could manage without choking on her pain.

He pulled back immediately, worry lined his face. "What's wrong?"

"She's having an unusually strong pain flare," Orion said for her from the house infrastructure.

"What can we do to help?" Zach asked, not looking away from her, as if directing the question to Shira instead of the AI.

Of course he is, idiot. Just because she was in pain didn't mean they were going to respect her any less. Their concern was genuine, so it was natural for them to want her to see they were willing to help. Even if she didn't want them seeing her in such a state.

"Daddy, is everything okay?" Serenity's quiet voice said from the hallway. "Everyone ran downstairs wicked fast."

Shira wanted to hide. The only thing worse than the guys seeing her in this state was Serenity. *Why did I even entertain the idea of having something with them? None of them deserve to deal with this…*

Her eyes pleaded with the two men in front of her, her pain-flooded mind hoping they'd get the hint to make sure Serenity didn't see her like this.

Jasper was the one to intercept the young girl. He spoke quietly to her, just loud enough for Shira to hear he was trying to downplay everything as Shira feeling under the weather. Unfortunately, Serenity cared too much about Shira's health and got away from Jasper.

Shira should have figured it'd be impossible to hide this from the girl—from any of them, really. She was fooling herself, thinking that because she was doing so well conquering her fears and facing her past, none of these issues wouldn't rear their ugly heads and remind her how she'd never fully recover.

"She-ra, what's wrong?" Serenity exclaimed when she

rushed around the couch. "Does your tummy hurt? Are you feeling hot?"

Zach's hands flashed out and grabbed Serenity when she tried to touch Shira. The young girl stared up at her dad, confused.

"I can't be touched…" Shira managed. "Sorry… Starship."

"But why?" Serenity asked, looking between Zach and Shira.

"She's in pain right now," Zach tried to say as gently as possible. "It's best we give her space, so the pain doesn't get worse."

"But why is she in pain? What happened?"

Shira gritted her teeth, sensing another strong wave coming. "Orion, explain."

There was no avoiding it, and she wasn't in the mood to be gawked at or asked questions, no matter how innocent. Her AI did as asked, using a simplified explanation all three could understand. While this transpired, the pain Shira anticipated crashed over, though it wasn't as strong as she expected. She knew it was only a matter of time before the big one hit. Her medicine wasn't doing well subsiding all of this.

Before Orion finished, Zach let Serenity go and crouched in front of Shira again. "Shira, what can we do to help?"

Shira shook her head. There wasn't really anything they could do.

"Shira has taken almost all possible medication to help her," Orion said. "There isn't much else that can be done but monitor her condition and make sure she stays hydrated."

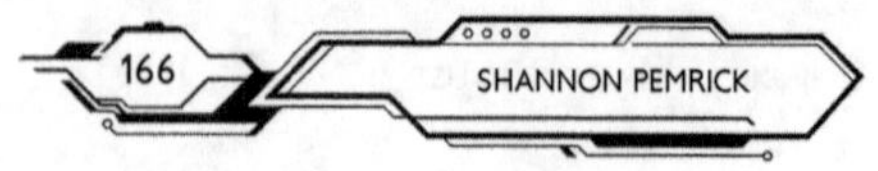

"I'll get a wottah bottle," Jasper said.

"I'll help, Daddy," Serenity said, running after him.

"What's the other medication she can still take?" Zach asked the AI. "I'm not suggesting she take them now. I just want to make sure it's easily available for when she wants them."

"One is available, though it's not a pain reducer," the AI cautioned.

"What is it?"

"Edibles," Shira answered for her AI.

Jasper returned with a water bottle, as did Serenity. Both had chosen ones with easy-to-open flip-tops. The kind gesture wasn't lost on Shira.

"What will it do for you?" Jasper asked. "I don't know anyone who uses them for chronic pain."

Shira curled into herself more, pain building back up. "It'll make me not care about the pain. I also relax on it, so I'll probably sleep. And when I wake up, I'll be ravenous."

Zach snickered, the sound drifting as he walked into the kitchen. He asked the AI where to find her stash, and he was directed to a cabinet where Shira stored the resealable bag of gummies.

Shira sucked in a staggered breath when pain raked her body, this wave the harsh one she knew would come. She bit her lip and turned her head into the couch cushion, desperately trying to muffle the cry of agony.

"Shira?" Jasper murmured close to her half-hidden face.

Tears pricked her eyes, but she refused to let them fall. She would not let this reduce her to that state. "I'm sorry…"

"Why?" Jasper asked, his confusion clear in his tone.

"Because I can't go to the convention today." That reality hurt her a little more than her physical pain.

Even though she'd been afraid of doing this crazy idea of meeting up with them at this convention, she was glad they'd convinced her to come. She was enjoying herself. Shira couldn't remember the last time she'd had this much fun. Mercedes and Narissa had tried to invite her places, as well as a few other friends Shira had, but she'd become such a recluse, fun outings weren't really part of her life anymore.

"So?" Jasper said. "That's nothing to be sorry about. You can't control something like this. And we'd rathuh you rest so you can get bettah."

"But you need me to stay with Serenity." It was a poor excuse, because Jasper was right, she did need to focus on healing rather than wallowing in self-pity over something she couldn't control, but it was also a legitimate concern.

Sure, their friends would probably be more than willing to step up to help, but Shira didn't want to burden them with that.

"You're not a babysitter, Shira," Zach said, returning to the family room. He carried a resealable pouch. "You've got nothing to be sorry about. We'll figure it out."

"I'm staying here," Serenity said.

All three adults looked at her, startled by her sudden declaration.

"Serenity, what do you mean?" Zach asked.

"I'm staying here to watch over She-ra," Serenity said. "When I'm sick, you and Daddy take time from

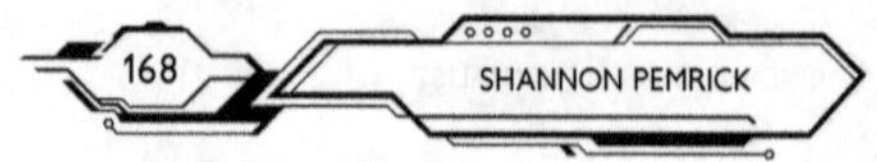

practice to make sure I'm gonna be okay. She-ra is sick and needs someone to make sure she's gonna be okay."

Jasper and Zach exchanged a look. Shira's gut twisted. She knew they found her reasoning impressive, since she did, too, but it wasn't right for someone her age to take on such a responsibility.

"Serenity, go to the convention with your dads," Shira said. She was grateful she was between large flare-ups; it made it easier for her to speak. "I don't need to be looked after. I've gone through this before. Once I take the medicine Zach has in his hands, I'll fall asleep. And I want you to have fun."

Serenity vigorously shook her head. "I can have fun here. I can watch cahtoons, color, and play games. I won't be a bothah, She-ra, I promise. And I can get you things, like wottah and snacks."

Shira turned pleading eyes to Jasper and Zach. They had to put their foot down on this. "I can't. It's a liability. If something happens to her, I can't come to her aid in this condition."

"That won't be an issue, as I am here," Orion chimed in.

Shira closed her eyes. *No, don't do this, you stupid AI.*

"What do you mean?" Jasper asked.

"It's in my name. I am an artificial intelligence, not some simple assistant program that is capable of basic responses. This means I am capable of many great things, and learning even more," the AI said. "Because of Shira's condition, and the upgrades afforded to me, I have developed into a proper artificial caretaker, as well as an excellent companion. I have sensors able to detect even the smallest chemical changes in the human body.

I can take full control of this house to ensure everyone's safety if needed. I also can contact emergency services faster than any human, should the need arise."

Jasper and Zach passed impressed looks.

"If there are any concerns specific to Serenity, I can download and learn how to combat these issues and ensure her safety. It will not take long. I can also assure, as per AI regulations, this is completely legal and considered safe."

"Well, I'm convinced of her safety. And, if Serenity really wants to stay, she's just going to be miserable at the convention centah." Jasper rubbed the back of his neck. "And to be honest with you, Shira, I can confidently say we both were thinking this, aftah the match, we wanted to come back here."

Against all hope Zach would deny Jasper's claim, Shira watched him nod. So many conflicting emotions raged in her. "No, you can't."

Both Jasper and Zach raised a questioning brow in unison.

"I will not allow you to ruin your time at this convention because of me." Shira sucked in a sharp breath, trying to push through a rake of pain. "Besides the tournament, this is a vacation for all of you, and you should be enjoying it."

Jasper gazed at her with soft eyes. "We can enjoy it while relaxing here with you, too." He reached out and wound a finger around a strand of her red hair. "And fun would be hard to have if we're worried about you."

Shira wasn't sure what hurt more at this point: her body or her emotions. Here she was, ruining things for them, and they were refusing to see it that way. She didn't

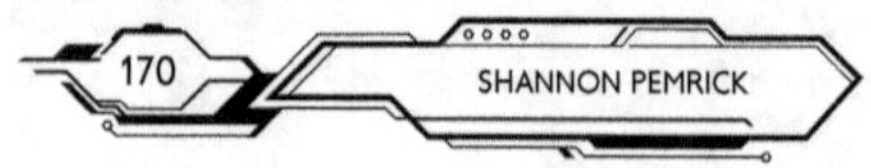

know what she did in her life to deserve the affection this family showered her with. "Well, it's not like I'm in any condition to fight someone with stubbornness the size of a dragon."

Zach chuckled. "Are you sure you're not confusing that with his ego?"

Jasper placed a hand on his chest and shot his boy-friend an offended look. Shira laughed, though it hurt to do so.

When she calmed, Jasper gently rested his hand on her head and encouraged her to rest while they got things situated to ensure Serenity had what she'd need. Before going to help Jasper, Zach offered her one of her edibles. She contemplated if she should take only a half dose, given she felt responsible for monitoring Serenity, but today was a full-dose day. *And if the guys found out I took less than I needed, they'd hen-peck me worse than my mother.*

Things from there moved in a way she didn't have the concentration to keep up with. Jasper got some meals and snacks situated for both Serenity and Shira in the event Shira needed to remain one with the couch while the guys were gone. Zach set up a few things to entertain Serenity, and even moved an end table and propped up a tablet for Shira to have a way to watch the tournament if she wanted that.

Around the time the cannabis took effect, the guys were heading out, and things slowed down for her. Time meant nothing and her mind took full advantage of it by wandering. She knew from experience to not think of anything negative, and that wasn't an issue, as her mind wanted to go back to the night before, with Jasper kissing her—again.

He could say it was a thank you, but she knew that wasn't what spurred it. Not when she kissed him back, and he didn't stop her. Shira hadn't been sure if she should, but she didn't regret it. She swore he was going to keep going and deepen that kiss, with the way his tongue hedged against his own mouth. And the memory of the desire that kiss brought on returned to her, even in her haze. It zinged down her spine, pooling in her core.

Shira chewed her lip, heat spreading over her cheeks. In that moment, she thought he would pin her against the counter to ravage her, and she wouldn't have stopped him. Same with Zach when she kissed him against the wall. He'd pulled her right into his hard body, and she was all too eager to let him.

The thought paused. Why wouldn't she have stopped either of them? Just hours before, she was going between denying any possibility of doing something with them again, no matter how much attraction there was between them, and considering the possibility of them working out. So where did all that turmoil go, and why did her mind plunge right into the desire to jump their bones in the kitchen without a second thought?

Am I that desperate?

No. No, she wasn't. She just knew what she wanted, and for once in her life since her accident, she didn't allow arbitrary rules and insecurities to stop her.

Sure, it hadn't progressed further than kissing, but the intent had been made known to them. *And then there was the incident on the patio…*

Her cheeks flushed hotter. *God, was that hot to witness.* And the fact that neither cared if she watched… *Hell, they practically invited me to join with their comments.*

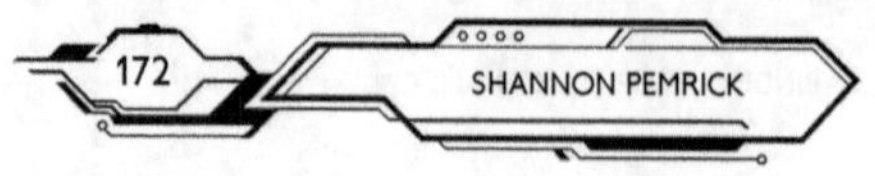

"She-ra," Serenity stage-whispered, breaking through her sexy memories.

Shira's eyes opened to find the girl crouched in front of her face. When had she closed them?

"Are you feeling okay?" Serenity asked. "Your face is red. Are you feverish?"

Shira smiled. "No, I'm fine. I think I'll be falling asleep soon, though."

Serenity nodded. "I'll be good if you do. Promise."

Shira reached out, the pain in her body there, but her brain not allowing her to care about it, and she brushed the back of her finger against Serenity's cheek. "You're such a good girl. Thank you."

Serenity grinned wide, checked Shira's water bottles, which she hadn't touched yet, and then resumed watching her cartoons. Shira had no idea what show it was. She'd never seen it before, not that she made a habit of keeping up with kids' shows.

"When is the match starting?" Shira mumbled out, more to her AI than Serenity.

"Not for a while," Orion said through the house infrastructure. "Jasper and Zach left fifteen minutes ago."

"Oh…" Of course they did. Perception of time was one thing she hated while under this influence. Until she fell asleep, because she always did, which was a reason she used cannabis as a last resort, she'd just have to deal with it.

She tried to watch Serenity's show, but as she expected, it felt as though one episode took forever to end. After the third episode, she closed her eyes. Heaviness weighed on her mind, and she knew sleep was coming. The sounds around her muted and her breathing became a lulling sound.

After a moment she cracked her eyes open, only it was difficult, as if they were heavy with sleep. *Did I fall asleep?* Shira tried to move, finding her body stiff, though the cannabis was still well within her system, making it so she didn't care.

She looked around, finding the TV off, the nano doors to the patio ajar, allowing a warm breeze to drift in, and Snake and Serenity weren't in the room. Her throat was also dry.

"Ah, you're awake, Shira," Orion said.

Shira wanted to respond, but she was struggling.

"My sensors indicate you're having typical reactions to the cannabis, so don't try to talk yet, and allow yourself to adjust to your awakened state. You've been out for about an hour. Serenity and Snake are currently in the backyard playing. They're in no danger, as I've made sure they haven't gotten too close to the pool."

That was good. She wasn't comfortable with Serenity being outside by herself, but at least she was being monitored by the AI. And Snake was the perfect dog to keep her safe as well. Shira almost laughed, remembering how Snake tried to save her mom from "drowning" in a fountain when she accidentally fell in trying to retrieve her phone she'd dropped.

As if her thoughts summoned him, Snake's dark body barreled through the open door. Serenity wasn't far behind him.

"Snake, you gotta be quiet," she said in a not very hushed voice. "You're gonna wake up—"

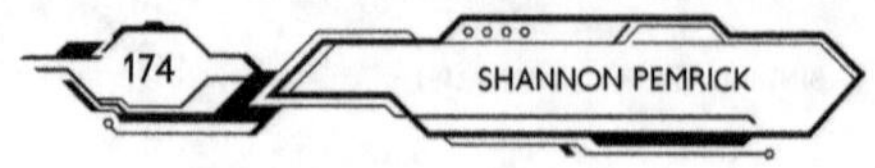

She came to a halt and stared at Shira. "She-ra, you're awake!"

"Hey, Starship," Shira croaked. Snake padded over and gave her a few licks on the face before going for water. "Hi to you too, Snake."

Serenity gasped. "You have a frog in your throat. You need wotta."

She scampered over to the collection of water bottles before Shira could think to move and offered one to Shira. "Here."

Shira smiled at her thoughtfulness and gratefully took the drink. Her dry throat also relished the gift, and Shira had to take several more gulps to be satisfied for the moment. She knew this side effect lasted a bit for her.

"After I wake up a bit, would you like to work on that special project, Starship?" Shira asked before taking another sip of water.

The little girl's eyes lit up. "You wanna do that? You're feeling bettah?"

Shira didn't want to lie to her, but the real answer was a little complicated to explain, not only in her current state where creating complete sentences was a bit of a chore, but also to someone who had never experienced cannabis. *At least, I don't think she has.* Jasper said he didn't know anyone who used it medicinally, and neither he nor Zach never mentioned any conditions Serenity may have or had in the past that would have benefited from even cannabis oil.

"I'm not feeling better exactly," Shira finally said. "But I'm in a spot where I can do more things easier, but at a slow pace."

A bright smile pulled across Serenity's face. "That makes me happy."

"And how about, after that, we make cookies for your dads as a surprise?" It'd been a long time since she baked anything. But it was a great activity to do with a kid. Even as a teen, Shira had many fond memories of baking various treats with her mom, and her dad eager to taste-test no matter how experimental they got.

"I wanna make cookies!"

Simple, easy, and versatile, depending on the recipe they chose. "That's a great idea."

Shira pushed herself up into a sitting position, making sure she didn't move too fast in the event she might become lightheaded and nauseous. "How is the tournament going? Did I miss Jasper and Zach's match?"

Serenity pursed her lips. "I think so. I was watching when they stahted, but then it got wicked weird."

Shira's brow spike. "Orion?"

"Team Smash and Stab were getting their rears kicked hard in the first and second round. Embarrassingly so, I will add. You'd have been swearing up a storm at their performance. Even against such an excellent team as Burnout, Jasper and Zach were clearly not top of their game."

Shira worked her jaw. She didn't like that. Sounded like they weren't focusing, and she had a good idea why.

"Then there was some sort of interference with the feed," Orion continued. "I'm not entirely sure the cause, but the entire convention network went down. I've yet to assess what is wrong. However, before you panic, I don't believe it's anything bad. I've not received any

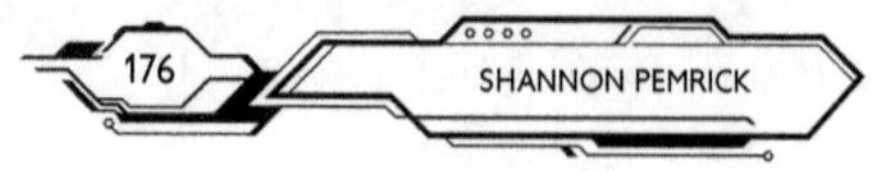

distressing communication from Alistair or texts from Jasper and Zach."

Shira blew out a breath. That thought process could have gone poorly had he not elaborated. In her influenced state, any major negative feelings would send her in a dangerous spiral. And when it came to problems and convention centers, she knew exactly where her mind would run off to.

"Well, when they return, we can find out more, I guess," she said. Shira rose and headed for the kitchen. "Right now, I want to do something fun and creative."

Serenity squealed and ran into the kitchen, where the bags from yesterday remained untouched. Shira allowed Serenity to paw through the bags for the right one. Kept her from having to bend over and risk equilibrium issues. Moving was a bit of a chore for her as it was. She felt sluggish and heavy, but not enough to tolerate being married to the couch for the rest of the day.

"Got it!" Serenity announced, lifting a stuffed paper bag.

Shira smiled. "Great job. Let's go upstairs to my craft room so we can make the alterations."

Serenity held the bag close to her chest, her eyes gleaming. Shira led the way, Snake padding faithfully alongside them. She noticed, as she reached the base of the stairs, someone had neatly tucked away her shoes. Shira shook her head, knowing full well the culprit, and continued up the stairs.

On the top floor landing, Shira was met with the door leading to the bathroom. She turned away from the two bedrooms to the left and headed for two other doors to the right. One was open, showing the room Serenity had claimed, the other closed.

Shira did her best to keep the design studio's door shut. With her working on that special project for Serenity, she didn't want it getting found out too early. Of course, she had no idea if she'd finish in time, so it might end up being moot, especially with how quickly Serenity was growing.

But today, she had no issue letting Serenity in. She'd made sure last night to put everything away in preparation to do this project with her after the convention. Shira was disappointed that plan didn't go the way she wanted. She really wanted to do this while the guys were home, just to get on their nerves, since they wouldn't be allowed in. *I'm a terrible person… Oh well.*

Serenity looked around, eyes wide and gazing at all the half-made outfits and various storage overstuffed with supplies. "This place is sick! Did you make all of these, She-ra?"

Shira shook her head. "No, most of these belong to my mom. They're little projects she does when she comes here for a break."

Serenity scrunched her nose. "She works on her break?"

Ah, that's right. Shira forgot that she'd told Serenity her parents were fashion designers. "To her, this type of stuff isn't work. It's creative freedom to work on whatever she wants without worry it won't catch on and make money."

"Oh… so kinda how Daddy and Zach play games not related to their job?"

"Yes, it's exactly like that." *Damn, this girl is sharp.*

"That makes sense." Serenity held up the bag. "Creating time?"

Shira smiled and gestured to the clean work table. Serenity eagerly shoved the bag onto the table and Shira pulled out the four aprons with eight-bit hearts. Shira then pointed to a nearby bin before reaching for scissors, a precision knife, glue, and some other needed tools. "Starship, I'm going to need you to go through that cloth bin and pick out colors you want."

CHAPTER 11

Vehicles flashed by the car. Zach tapped the steering wheel, his foot bouncing at a faster, impatient pace. Jasper was in no better condition. It was one thing after another today, from Shira's condition to the match, and then to it ending abruptly. And of course, the traffic jam that impeded them getting home as quickly as possible didn't help. He thought Boston traffic was bad. He now missed it.

"How are we gonna tell Shira what happened?" Jasper asked. He was looking down at his phone, no doubt debating again if he should send Shira a text to let her know they were on their way back.

"I think we just tell her," Zach said. "Obviously don't blurt it out, but we can't ignore it happened."

"I don't want to scare her. The last thing we need to do is to cause a panic attack."

"That's why I said we won't blurt it out. She may not

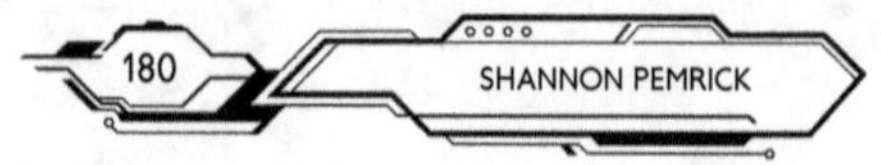

even know. Alistair, you mentioned the network went down, right?"

"That is correct," the AI said from the car dash. "The only way Shira would know anything is if she turned on the news or Orion told her. However, I do not believe her assistant would do this as it would lack the human element she would need for the delivery."

Jasper leaned back in his seat. "And I doubt she's looking at the news. She's eithah doing something with Serenity or resting."

Either of those possibilities would be preferable to her catching anything those newscasters broadcasted.

"We will be at the house in fifteen minutes," Alistair said. "You'll want to think of what to tell her quickly."

Jasper worked his jaw. "Think she saw our poor performance?"

"If she wasn't sleeping, yes," Zach said.

"I suppose we should let her yell at us and then break the news gently."

Zach tapped the steering wheel. "I mean, that's a natural progression, since we didn't get to finish the match. We can't hide that from her."

Not to mention they couldn't go back to the convention center tomorrow. Hell, they had to wait for further information from the organization to know how things would proceed.

The fifteen minutes passed quickly, Jasper and Zach failing to figure out exactly how to break the news. It was difficult to know the right approach. This was new territory for them, but at the same time, they wouldn't allow it to best them and ruin their chances.

Zach took a deep breath and exited the car. Alistair

pulled it into the garage after they were both on their way to the front door. Snake noticed them immediately, barking like mad as any dog would. *Note to self, don't plan on surprise arrivals with him around.*

Even though Snake made the alarm, neither Shira nor Serenity greeted them when they entered the house. At least, not physically.

"Welcome home," Shira called out. "We're in the kitchen."

Home. He liked the sound of that from her.

The two of them kicked off their shoes and lined them up next to Shira's and Serenity's. Snake whined for attention, which they both gave, and then the dog followed them to the kitchen. It wasn't until they were halfway down did Zach realize there was something different about the house. A soothing warmness clung to the air, and a sugary, buttery aroma wafted into his nose.

Jasper was already running the rest of the way before Zach's brain caught up to what the two were doing in the kitchen. He rushed to catch up, the two of them appearing at the end of the hall nearly at the same time. And the sight before them was a comical disaster.

Containers and bags of open ingredients, as well as used bowls and utensils, were strewn about the counters and island. The stand mixer looked like something white had exploded inside it at one point, and the possible culprit was kneeling on a barstool playing with some cream-colored dough. Her older accomplice sat next to her, rolling some dough out on a floured surface.

Both wore the evidence of their shenanigans on their bodies, flour splotching their skin, clothes, and the decorated aprons Zach had not seen before. For a moment he wondered if Shira had aprons stored away here, but then paused the thought when he wondered why she'd have a child-sized apron lying around. *Did she buy those?* She had been secretive about some of the purchases she and Serenity made yesterday.

Serenity looked up from her "work." "You're back!"

Jasper laughed. "You didn't heah Shira call out to us?"

"I did. Then I had to count, so I forgot."

Zach choked on a laugh. That was exactly something she'd do. "Looks like you two are having fun."

Serenity smiled wide and nodded. "Yup!"

"Uh, Shira, did you know you have flour in your hair?" Jasper asked, making a motion with his hands on his own head to demonstrate.

Shira laughed. "I have flour in my hair, on my face, in my shirt… and I'm pretty sure it's also in my shorts." Her eyes cut to Serenity. "Someone didn't listen to me when I said not to turn the mixer on to full speed right out the gate."

Serenity's nose scrunched, and she had a less-than-ashamed look on her face. She then suddenly gasped, her eyes lighting up. "Can I give them the surprise now?"

Shira smiled and rolled the dough one more time. "If you want to."

Serenity cheered and climbed off the stool. She scurried out of the kitchen through the pantry hallway. Shira abandoned her dough to open the oven when Orion acted as her timer. She pulled out a stone baking sheet covered with a steaming batch of cookies cut into shapes. Setting them on the stovetop, which was miraculously the cleanest surface right now, she scooped the baked treats onto a cooling rack. Shira only swore once when one of the cookies broke.

With her back turned, Zach looked her up and down, taking in the sight of her in comfortable pink cotton shorts that showed off her shapely hips and legs, and a light tank top that had not hidden the fact that earlier today she had forgone a bra. Practical, given she was in pain, but also far more tempting. Not that he or Jasper would complain if she chose not to wear them ever again.

When Shira turned around, Serenity returned, two bundles in her tiny hands. She ran up to Jasper and handed him one. "This one is for you, Daddy."

"Thanks, pumpkin." Jasper took it and unfolded the cloth bundle, revealing a decorated apron. This was when Zach finally took a good look at the aprons Shira and Serenity wore.

Both were white, and had a red eight-bit heart in the center, like Jasper's. However, that was the only thing the same about them, except for maybe a theme he was seeing. Shira's had fancy embroidered lettering that said *Elemental Queen She-ra* and had elemental motifs sewn around the heart. Serenity's said *Mage Princess Serenity* and had a magical staff and other arcane themes sewn around her apron's heart.

"All right, what does yours look like?" Zach asked Jasper.

Jasper threw the neck strap around his head and grabbed the waist ties, pulling the fabric tight against his muscular form, revealing daggers and a bottle of poison around the eight-bit heart, and the wording *Spymaster King Daddy.*

"We made them special!" Serenity announced.

They made these? Zach looked to Shira. She sat on the stool again, resting her chin on her propped-up hand and smiling.

"Serenity wanted to do something fun and special, so while we were shopping, we found a small business who sold nerdy baking items. They didn't have anything extravagant for their aprons, choosing to spend most of their time with the fancy baking gear we grabbed, so we came up with a plan for me to customize the aprons. Serenity picked the theme and the wording, and I created the extras and did all the sewing and embroidery."

"Her sewing machine is wicked fancy!" Serenity said. "Even fancier than Aunt Cherry's."

Zach didn't doubt it, given Shira's parents were fashion designers. And since Serenity was the one who decided the theme for the alterations, it explained Shira's name. A small prickle of disappointment poked Zach's heart. It meant he knew what his name would be on his that was obviously still in Serenity's hand. He knew he shouldn't get so hung up on it, but he couldn't deny it wouldn't be nice to hear the word once from—

Serenity came up to him and held up his apron. "Here's yours, Dad."

All thought in Zach's mind stopped. *Had she really…* Jasper's and Shira's grins told him he hadn't imagined that word coming from his daughter's mouth. Zach knelt down and slowly unfolded the apron, trying his best not to let his hands shake. What was revealed stole what little air he had left in his lungs.

Sewn around the heart were a sword and shield, and

a potion. Embroidered in the same lettering as all the other aprons was, *Warrior King Dad.*

Zach stared at the letters, running his fingers over the tightly woven threads. His chest constricted, thoughts looping. Serenity had chosen the names. She chose this name. *She called me…*

He wrapped his arms around Serenity and pulled her into a tight embrace, murmuring into her ear, "Thank you. I love you *so* much."

She snuggled into him. "I love you too, Dad. I hope you like the surprise."

"It's the best surprise." Nothing could compare right now. Not even if Jasper got down on one knee and proposed.

Zach blinked and then looked Jasper's way, hoping his brain had only run away on him instead of telling him a reality he wasn't processing yet. Luckily, Jasper was still standing. *Good.* Not that he didn't want to have that conversation with Jasper; Zach just didn't think he could handle it right now.

His attention slipped over to Shira, who still sat in the same position on the barstool. Her free hand was on Snake's head. The dog wagged his tail with a lolling, happy tongue. Shira had the goofiest grin on her face to match. *This woman…* Zack didn't quite have words to describe what he felt staring at her.

It was clear she had a talk with Serenity, but whatever they said didn't force Serenity to do these things. She was a stubborn girl and would have been more obvious in her begrudging feelings if made her do all this. No, instead Shira fostered something small that allowed Serenity to decide on her own what was within her comfort zone. And Shira was damned proud of herself for it.

She exuded confidence in ways that Zach really loved. She was a wonderful role model for Serenity to look up to. And look up to her she did, with how much Serenity gushed about Shira all the time.

Shira was meant to be there with them.

Serenity wiggled in Zach's arms and he reluctantly let her go. She tugged on his apron and he got the hint. They were going to join in on this baking adventure, even though it looked like it was almost complete at this point.

He tied the apron on, and Serenity cheered. She ran back to her spot next to Shira and climbed up. Shira was a bit slow to react, taking a moment to realize she needed to send Snake away to lie down out of the way. The struggle was something Zach had noticed earlier when the baking alarm went off. He suspected it was an effect of the edible she ate.

It was at that moment he noticed Shira was holding herself a lot lighter than she ever did. Her goofy grin hadn't left, and he was beginning to wonder if it'd been there even when he and Jasper had first arrived.

"She-ra, is the dough ready?" Serenity asked.

"Of course it is."

Serenity cheered. Jasper joined them on Serenity's other side, allowing Zach to sidle up next to Shira. He was curious what they were going to do.

Serenity grabbed a cookie cutter that looked like a starburst and waited for Shira. Shira, for her part, grabbed a unique looking rolling pin. It was wooden and had designs carved into the rolling barrel. *Does that part say 'Pow'?*

Shira dusted the rolling pin with flour from a bowl on the island and then rolled the pin across the prepped dough. What was left behind were various designs and wording that were clearly comic-book inspired.

"My turn!" Serenity announced. She picked a spot on the rolled dough and sunk the sharp cookie cutter into it. When she pulled up, Shira quietly coaxing her to be careful on the release, an area that had said *BANG* and had some dotted shading around it, now was contained in a dramatic starburst bubble.

"That's sick," Jasper said.

"Serenity picked the rolling pin out, and I thought the bubble cutters would work perfectly," Shira explained.

"And Shira bought me everything I wanted," Serenity said with a big smile.

"I'm sure she did," Zach said. "She has been looking forward to spoiling you forever."

Instead of ducking her head, Shira held her head high, proud of her evil deeds.

"I like being spoiled," Serenity said.

Of course you do. He bit his tongue.

Serenity held up more cutters. "Everyone should cut cookies."

Zach wasn't going to say no. With the four of them working together, it didn't take long for the dough to be cut up. Shira had Jasper grab the stone baking sheet, and she carefully removed and transferred the cut cookies, all without breaking the sheet of dough. Zach wasn't sure why. Sure, there were still patterns left from the full coverage design the rolling pin created, but not enough room to cut more shapes.

When she finished, she glanced Zach's way. "You're

going to want to watch your hands. Serenity goes wild with this next part."

His brow ticked up, but he made sure he did as she recommended. Serenity giggled, the sound rather devious and creepy, and grabbed two cutters. A wicked grin spread over her face and then she went to town, chopping the remaining dough on the counter.

Both Zach and Jasper stared while Shira laughed so hard she almost fell off her seat.

When Serenity was done, she sat back in her seat and giggled to herself.

"What did we just watch?" Jasper asked.

"I made mini cookies!" Serenity proclaimed.

Both men looked to Shira for an explanation, who shrugged. "It's tedious taking the leftover dough and rolling it out again. I don't have it in me to keep doing that over and over again. And we plan to decorate the cookies too, so the sooner these are cut and baked, the better."

"She-ra is also eating them before they're decorated," Serenity tattled.

"Is she now?" Jasper said, his tone a slight coo, as if he'd caught Shira red-handed in the cookie jar.

Crimson spread over Shira's cheeks. "I'm hungry, and it's better than eating the bigger cookies."

"She also ate a whole bag of chips!" Serenity said.

"It was half a bag, and had been previously opened," Shira tried to defend, her face flushing hotter.

Zach chuckled and leaned close to her ear. "It's okay. We figured you would have gone through all the food stores by now."

"Day is still early," Shira muttered.

He and Jasper laughed. Shira ducked her head and then collected the bits of cookie to place onto the baking stone around the larger cookies.

While Jasper slipped the stone tray into the oven and had Orion set the next timer, Shira cleaned up the work space in front of her for one last round of dough, the small batch Serenity was playing with earlier.

"So, how did the match go?" Shira asked in such an alarmingly casual voice, Zach didn't trust it. "I was asleep for the first two rounds, and I'm told you two didn't do so hot."

"Uh, yeah, about that," Jasper said, rubbing the back of his neck. "We…"

"Were distracted?" Shira guessed.

Zach blew out a breath. *No use lying to her.* "Yes."

She sighed, and to his surprise, didn't yell, merely focusing on her dough rolling. Maybe she suspected that would happen. He'd seen the guilt in her eyes for having the pain flare in the first place when she shouldn't have felt any guilt. She couldn't control such things, and she needed to take care of herself. His and Jasper's distracted state was on them, not her.

"What happened after those rounds?" she asked. "Serenity and Orion said there was some sort of strange network interference."

"Well…" Zach really wasn't sure how to put this that wouldn't shock her.

"You two lost?" she guessed.

"Not exactly," Jasper said.

Shira stopped her task and looked between the two of them. "Why are you two acting so weird? If you lost, it's no big deal. You'd go into the loser's bracket and

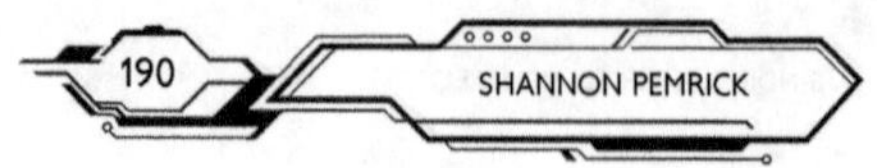

can try again. You were up against Burnout, and they've got a perfect streak right now, between the qualifiers and their first tournament round."

Zach worked his jaw. "We'll talk about it after we're done making cookies, okay? It's something that needs full attention, and could kill the mood."

Shira narrowed her eyes, but didn't argue. Zach had to chalk it up to all the medication in her system at this point.

"How are you feeling?" He figured that was a good thing to check in on.

She puffed a stray lock of hair out of eyes. "I'm okay. Orion says my pain is down thanks to the prescription meds kicking in finally, but the cannabis is so in my system right now, my brain doesn't care enough to process that. If that makes sense to you."

Zach chuckled. "Does to me. Amy has a chronic pain disorder, so she uses cannabis to help her through some days."

Shira squinted, as if her foggy brain was trying to remember that Amy was his good friend and former roommate, the woman he'd formed an agreement with to make an attempt at a straight-appearing relationship that failed spectacularly because neither could change what people made them truly happy.

"Preaching to the choir here," Jasper said. "I've consumed my fair share in different forms recreationally in the past."

Shira nodded, her lips pursed as if she were coming up with something to say, but didn't provide any comment in the end.

"Did you sleep?" Zach asked.

She nodded again. "For about an hour. Felt better enough to have some fun with our starship."

Serenity grinned wide.

"Speaking of fun," Jasper said. "Where did the idea come from for the theme of the aprons, Seren?"

She shrugged and played with a cookie cutter. "We saw the heart aprons, and it made me think of some of the old games you and Zach play with me sometimes. I wanted them and She-ra promised she could put our names on them. Then I thought about you both playing the fates game and I wanted that added, too."

"I had the idea to create the class items in the same style as the hearts," Shira added.

"And where did the courtly names come from?" Zach asked, intrigued by how each thought so far was easily related until that part.

Serenity giggled. "I was talking to She-ra about Wreck-Ralph."

"I have no idea what movie she was talking about," Shira said. "But it seemed really interesting."

Jasper held up a finger. "Wreck-it Ralph. That's the movie she meant. It's an old one, and a family favorite."

Shira cocked her head. "I've not heard of that movie."

Zach stared at her, and Jasper's mouth fell open. "How have you not heard of it? It's a classic."

Shira shrugged with wide eyes. That needed to be fixed.

"So, what paht of the movie talk got you two to add the court names?" Jasper asked, trying not to linger on the egregious oversight.

Shira pursed her lips. "She quoted a line about some king being called 'your puffy-ness' and then she wanted

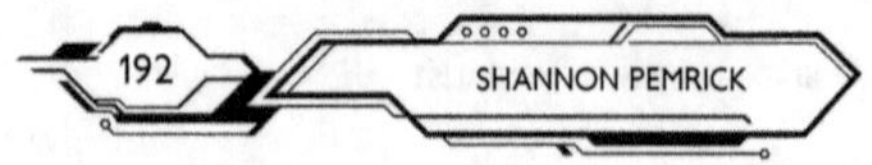

to add the court titles. Honestly, my brain was having a hard time keeping up at that point."

Serenity giggled. "Shira was wicked confused."

"Were Jasper and I both kings automatically?" Zach asked. He was curious how much influence Shira may have had on these decisions.

Serenity shook her head. "No. Daddy was gonna be the jestah."

Zach choked on a laugh, and Jasper blinked. That was nowhere near what they expected, that was for sure.

"I mean, I know I'm funny and all, but why was I going to be the jestah?" Jasper asked.

"Because you're funny, and the royal court needs a jestah," Serenity said so matter-of-factly.

"Why not one of the AIs?"

"Because Orion has to be the royal a-visah and Alistair is the battle mastah."

Surprisingly enough, Zach followed the logic. It was hard sometimes with her, but this one made sense.

"I convinced her there could be two kings, they'd just get different titles," Shira said. "And that Ajax and Takashi could be our jesters, since they do magic tricks."

"Did Takashi perform one for her yestahday?" Jasper asked.

She nodded. "He did a fancy card trick. Was quite entertaining. And a million times better than Ajax."

"Don't worry, we won't tell him you said that," Zach said. The three of them laughed.

"So, the job titles came about because there were now two kings?" Jasper asked.

Serenity nodded. "She-ra came up with them because of the charactahs you play in the game."

"You're a mage, according to your apron," Zach mused. "Do you want to play a spellcaster?"

Serenity never talked about her preferences before, even for games she could play with them outside of VR. So, this was a good moment for him and Jasper to learn where their daughter's mind went sometimes.

Serenity nodded. "I like magic. It's fun."

That was good to know. A lot of games had options for spellcaster classes that were new-user friendly. He stored that in the back of his mind to revisit later. "Do we have anyone else in our court?"

"Rissa," Serenity said. "She-ra said she'd be our court healuh."

Zach nodded. Made sense to him.

Jasper rubbed his chin. "Now, would she be a priestess, or something else?"

"I was thinking something like science fantasy for our court," Shira said. "More fun to mix things up."

He nodded. "Good genre choice. A favorite of mine."

Shira nodded thoughtfully. "I pegged you for a fan of the genre."

Zach chuckled. "Yes, but did you peg him for a romance fan? He's read all of Kiara's books."

Shira's brow arched. "Oh, really?"

Jasper gave a nonchalant shrug. "They're well written, have good plots, and a tasteful amount of spice." He grinned, a wicked glint in his eyes as his gaze dragged across Shira's tempting body. "And quite practical."

Shira's lips parted, but it took her a moment to respond. When she did, she'd tried to go back to the dough that now needed the special rolling pin. "You don't say."

Jasper bent closer to her ear. Zach did as well, so he

didn't miss all the fun. Jasper chuckled, his finger gliding over her shoulder blade and down her spine. Zach swallowed, the motion ghosting the same way down his own back. "It'd be easy to show you, if you'd chosen to wear *only* the apron."

A flush spread over Shira's cheeks and across her shoulders. Her eyes locked with Jasper's. Her lips parted again, but words failed her.

Zach snickered. "Without that, too, would also work. Either way, it'd be fun to watch."

Shira's face turned a deeper shade of crimson, her attention snapping over to him. When their eyes locked, his breath hitched. Heat simmered in those depths. She liked the idea, and that sent his mind into a whirlwind of delicious fantasies.

"Daddy, Dad," Serenity said. Her voice slapped him like a cold bucket of water. "You can kiss her. I won't look."

Shira pursed her lips and shot them both a questioning look.

Zach laughed. "Our little starship gets giggly and sometimes hides her face when physical affection is displayed in front of her."

"Like this," Jasper said before reaching for Zach. His fingers grazed Zach's jaw and curled firmly around his head. Jasper tugged once and crashed his lips into Zach's. Zach groaned, his eyes hooding, and he rested his hand on the island counter for support. He was vaguely aware of Serenity giggling.

Jasper pulled away first. Zach smiled at him and then turned his attention to Shira, who was covering her bemused smile with her hand. He then slid his gaze to

Serenity, who was still giggling and covering her eyes. Though, she was peeking through some gaps in her fingers.

"And now you know what silliness she does," Zach said.

"It's adorable," Shira managed before tumbling into a giggle fit herself.

When it carried on a little too long, Jasper shot him a sideways glance. "I think she's judging my kissing skills."

Zach grunted. "Well, I can vouch for you, so if that's the case, she's wrong."

Shira's giggles turned into full-on laughter. She shook her head and started flailing. It took everything in Zach not to join in. He wasn't sure what was up with her all of a sudden, but it was certainly funny.

"It appears Shira has reached her loopy stage in the scale of her meds working," Orion said. "We should not trust her with sharp objects, unless you want her having an accident due to butter fingers."

Jasper reached around Shira and grabbed her wrists, pulling them close to her body, and her into his chest. "Why don't we just take over this last bit and you take the time to get yourself undah control?"

Her mirth didn't cease, and she seemed to press into Jasper more. "You might need to keep me restrained or I'll find myself getting in your way."

Zach's brows spiked. She was playing with fire.

Jasper pressed his mouth against her ear again, lowering his voice. "You need to be careful how much ya tempt me. It's not right to say such things when you're not sober." He chuckled. "So, why don't you say it again latah to me when you are?"

Pink tinted Shira's cheeks and her eyes unfocused a bit. "Maybe I will."

Zach cocked his head. High Shira was very honest. Or maybe she'd always been this way, and he was seeing her differently now. Either way, he liked it.

"She-ra," Serenity said. "Can we make a castle?"

Shira blinked. "I don't think we have enough cookie dough to make a castle, Starship."

Serenity shook her head. "No, not that kind of castle. One with blankets and pillows. Like a fort, but biggah!"

Zach watched Jasper's face light up. No surprise to him. Serenity and Jasper built forts out of the living room furniture all the time.

"Well, I don't see why not," Shira said with a shrug. "Sounds like a lot of fun. I've got a lot of pillows and blankets stored. It'll be the comfiest castle ever made."

Both Serenity and Jasper cheered, sending Shira into another fit of laughter.

"Alistair, queue up Wreck-It Ralph," Jasper said. He released Shira and headed out of the kitchen. "I'll grab fort supplies."

Serenity scrambled off her stool, running after him, shouting her desire to help. Shira leaned, watching them go with her head cocked.

Zach snickered. "Shameless."

She shrugged and sat up. "I like his butt."

He nodded. "It's nice."

"Yours is, too," she said before reaching for a cookie cutter.

Zach grabbed her wrist. He wasn't going to allow her to touch any of those. "You've never seen either of us naked. How can you be so confident?"

Shira snorted, which then made her loopy ass laugh for a moment. "You wouldn't fill out pants so well if you were flat."

Fair point. "Well, I can say you also have one worthy of staring at."

Shira grinned. "I am wearing shorts that don't hide it well."

"Someone is confident."

She flipped her hair, a haughty expression on her face. Zach liked this side. As much as Shira struggled with her self-esteem because of what had happened to her, it wasn't entirely gone. And when she didn't overthink, she exuded confidence in so many ways.

Zach brushed a stray strand of hair away from her cheek and tucked it behind her ear. "There, now I can see you."

"Not all of me."

His gaze dipped down her body. "No, you're still wearing too much for that." Zach returned his gaze to meet hers. "But your face is too beautiful to allow you to hide that."

A flush reappeared on her cheeks. Her bottom lip caught on her teeth. Zach had the urge to offer to do that for her himself. Then Orion interrupted with his timer.

Dammit. He left her side to grab the cookie tray out of the oven. "Don't touch those cookie cutters. I don't want you getting hurt."

"Don't listen to Orion. I'm not going to hurt myself. I'm just more likely to find things overly funny."

He wasn't taking any chances. Though, while he took care of the baked cookies, metal clanked. In his reach for the spatula to transfer the treats to the cooling rack, he took a peek at her, finding Shira collecting all the cookie cutters in front of her. Zach hastened his transfer. He did not trust her.

She laughed when he rushed back to her side and grabbed her wrists. "Zach, I can do this. You don't have to treat me like I'm three."

He pulled her into his chest and pressed his lips against her ear. "I'm not. I'm looking out for your safety. Besides…" He picked up one of the metal cookie cutters and slipped it into her hand before wrapping his around hers. "Why can't we do it together?"

This close to her, he felt her stifled intake of air. "Y–yeah, we could do that."

Could they now? He grinned. His question had been tame and innocent, mostly. *But if that wasn't how she took it and she still said yes…* Zach wondered if she would react the same way when she didn't have so much medication coursing through her.

Serenity ran into the room, a blanket dragging behind her. Jasper wasn't far behind, some pillows and folded blankets in his arms. They both tossed them on the family room floor and then left again without a word.

"I didn't make Serenity call you Dad," Shira said.

Zach angled their hands over the first part of the dough to cut and stamped it. "I know. I could tell by the way she acted. She would have said it more begrudgingly if she'd been coerced. I would like an explanation, though. I thought you were going to be discreet about it, if you were going to ignore me telling you not to worry about it."

"I tried, but your daughter is a smart cookie." She

giggled at the pun, and to his dismay, he let out an amused snort. "She was quick to realize why and had her own questions."

"Like why I didn't ask her myself?"

Shira nodded and chose their next cutting spot. "To keep it simple for her, I told her it's because adults overthink. And she thinks we adults are silly and need to not overthink more."

Zach laughed. That was a good way of handling it. "So, what was the reason she gave for always calling me Zach?"

Shira pursed her lips. "It's hard for me to put into words, but she has always seen you as her dad, but just never called you it. She calls you her dad to other people a lot from what I gathered, though. The logic of a nearly seven-year-old is hard for Shira without drugs messing with her brain. High Shira really doesn't understand."

He laughed and swapped out the cookie cutter they were using. "It's not much better on this side of the fence, either. Most of the time I find myself just nodding."

"Glad I'm not alone." She worked her jaw. "I should probably tell you this. She brought this up, and I did my best to handle it, since neither of you were around to do so…"

He turned his gaze to her, concerned.

"She knows about the money issues you've had."

"Oh." Zach continued cutting cookies. "I figured she might have. Jasper is more of a stickler for trying to keep her in the dark, but I know she's too observant, and she's quick to piece things together. But you got her to understand?"

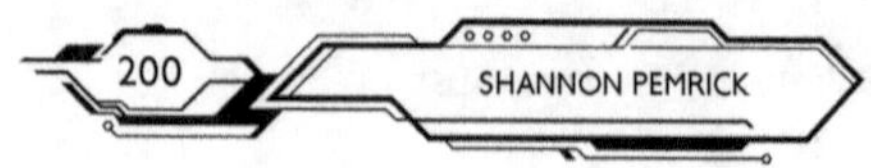

"She sort of understands. I think she gets the part where I told her we adults just want her to focus on being a kid and having fun, but I think she was struggling a bit to fully grasp why she couldn't at least know what was going on."

Zach nodded. "I'll sit down with Jasper so we can figure out how to talk to her about it. Might help. Or she might just need to be a bit older to grasp the entire situation. But thank you for telling me."

She smiled, and he was glad. Zach didn't want her to think she'd done anything wrong. It was an unfortunate situation she found herself in, and she had to make a choice. It also showed how much Serenity trusted Shira. Zach wanted that most of all. His daughter should always feel like she had someone to talk to, even if it wasn't him or Jasper. And that person being Shira was a bonus.

The time cutting up the remainder of the cookies sped by. Shira didn't push Zach away, and in fact, he was aware of how often she pressed against him an extra amount when she didn't need to. He enjoyed the contact. And it was nice to finally have her without fighting it. He just wished she'd be like this all the time.

The two of them finished loading the last of the cookies and cookie bites onto the cookie sheet around the same time Jasper and Serenity finished with the multi-trip excursion. Zach was pretty sure they'd grabbed every single pillow and blanket in the house. Shira even double checked they hadn't gone into her room. They hadn't, but Jasper admitted he was tempted to, and still would if what they found wasn't enough.

He then disappeared again to grab a few chairs and

other materials to suspend the sheets and blankets. Zach offered his assistance, since the cookies needed to finish baking, but Jasper was insistent on getting this part himself. Zach didn't press and instead helped Shira clean up.

"I don't think we're going to decorate today," she said.

Zach glanced over to Serenity, who was moving pillows around to figure out how she wanted this "castle" to be constructed. "No, looks like the mage princess has moved on to other things."

Shira chuckled. "Probably for the best. I don't think I should sit here much longer. We can decorate them tomorrow or something."

He didn't hate the plan. Anything that would ensure she didn't stress her body out too much, he was on board for. And that meant he did his best to clean more than her. She didn't make that easy, since she insisted it was her mess to clean, but she was finding out Jasper wasn't the only one who could be extra stubborn with her.

Zach even snagged in a moment to help clean Shira a bit with a wet cloth.

The kitchen was mostly clean by the time the last batch of cookies was done baking. Jasper had also finished with his task, content with the "building" supplies he'd gathered. "All right, where do we start first?"

"How about we talk about the tournament first?" Shira said.

CHAPTER 12

Shira gazed at Jasper and Zach intently, dead set on continuing this conversation. "I know you're excited to do this fort and movie, and you said you didn't want to kill the mood, but at this point it's just avoidance, and that's making me uneasy."

Jasper frowned, his fingers tapping on the back of a chair he'd collected. He'd hoped she'd allow baking and fun to consume her thoughts rather than clinging to that promise. "Yeah, you're right. We do."

"Daddy, I'm hungry," Serenity said.

And that doesn't help. Jasper scratched the back of his head. "Okay, let's plan dinnah first so she's taken care of, and then we'll talk."

Shira licked her lips. "Food sounds great."

Jasper smirked. Of course, she wouldn't pass up food in her state. "What are we in the mood for? Korean, Thai, Italian, Greek?"

"All of it," Shira said, making him laugh.

"I'm game for some Chinese," Zach said. "Would be easy to eat in the… castle."

"Dumplings!" Serenity cheered.

"Well, that settles that," Shira said, a big grin on her face. "Orion, send Zach and Jasper Imperial Asia's menu. You know what I'll have."

Jasper's phone *pinged*, and he opened the link her AI had sent him. The menu was robust and had dishes Jasper had never seen before. It excited him. He was trying to expand his palate, so this would give him a great opportunity.

It didn't take long for everyone to figure out what they wanted, and Orion sent in a delivery order, Shira ensuring she would be paying for it all. And of course, after she succeeded in that, she zoned back in on the information they'd been withholding about the convention.

Jasper claimed a stool on her left, while Zach grabbed the stool on her right. They encouraged Serenity to continue her planning, trying to frame it that the conversation would bore her. They'd barely gotten their explanation out before their daughter was already back to work.

Zach took a deep, steadying breath, Jasper nodding to him to be the messenger. He was better at delivering a sensitive message like this. "Okay, so what we're about to say is probably going to sound bad, but I assure you, everything turned out relatively okay."

Shira pursed her lips, concern growing in her eyes, though she remained quiet.

"There was a fire at the convention center because of a gas leak."

Shira's eyes popped, and she leaned back. Jasper

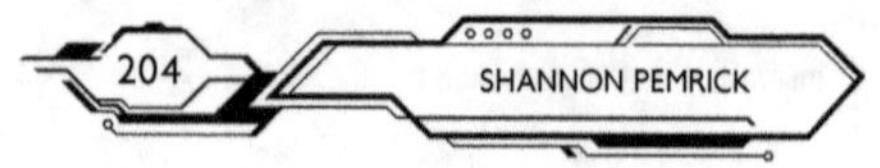

instinctively slipped his hand behind her, worried she might fall. "Keep talking so I don't panic."

She didn't have to tell him twice. "Our match was cut short because of an emergency evacuation. Some security AIs detected the leak, and they got everyone out. However, in the rush, a fire was accidentally started. It was decently contained, thanks to some built-in security measures and the quick response time from the fire department." He smiled to reassure her. "No one was hurt, from what was reported, before everyone was forced to vacate the premises."

Shira had calmed through his explanation, and nodded in response. "Thanks for explaining. I appreciate your consideration on how I'd react to the news."

"We didn't want to cause you any undue stress," Jasper said. "It may not be like what happened before, but that wouldn't mattuh given what you experienced."

Shira smiled. "How stupid is it that my pain flare saved me from experiencing another traumatic event?"

"I thought it was more of a silver lining," Jasper said. He threw up a panicked hand when he realized how insensitive that sounded. "Not that you being in pain is a good thing. It's just that it kept you here, instead—"

Shira's boisterous laughter cut him off. Her head flew back, and Jasper for a moment thought she might laugh herself off her stool. "It's okay. I get what you're trying to say."

Her laughter became contagious and the two of them joined in. When they all settled down, she smiled, her cheeks tinting a shade of pink. "Really, thank you. Most would have just blurted it out without considering if they'd cause me to have a panic attack. I appreciate the fact you two were considerate in that approach."

Zach reached out and threaded his fingers with hers. "We'll always do our best to consider how something will affect you."

Jasper wrapped his arms around Shira's shoulders and pulled her in for a gentle hug. "We don't wanna hurt you. You're too important to us."

Moisture brimmed in her eyes, but Shira blinked it away before tears formed. "Thank you."

She took a deep breath and then sat back up, pulling from Jasper's grip. "So, I guess we're in limbo about what's going on until the convention center is sorted out?"

Jasper nodded. "They informed us we'd get an update tonight, so we should know what's going to happen before we hit the sack."

"Good. Plenty of time to get the castle built."

The excitement from before returned to Jasper and he bolted from his seat. Shira laughed and called him a grown child, but he didn't care. Forts were fun.

Shira opted to sit this one out, though not because she had no concept of fun. It seemed, even though she was able to get up from her seat, she wasn't confident in her coordination right now. So instead, Zach made her a throne of pillows to observe and oversee their work. Snake joined her, laying across her legs and enjoying a good belly rub.

Serenity was the shot-caller. She had a plan in that head of hers, and while Jasper struggled to see the logistics working out, as she had some fantastical ideas, he was going to try his hardest.

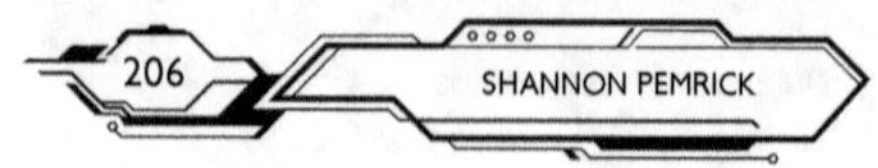

Shira made casual, off-handed comments as they worked, most of them directed toward Jasper and Zach's process of not quite completing tasks before jumping to the next. However, her heckling continued to the point that Jasper couldn't hold back anymore.

He looked over his shoulder. "Shira, if you don't stop that mouth of yours, I'm going to give you something to occupy it."

Shira blinked with wide eyes, and Zach choked on a laugh. But it was Shira who did his boyfriend in. "You have something large enough for that job?"

Jasper's mouth fell open. *She did not just say that.*

Shira's lips twitched and then she couldn't contain her laughter, falling over into her wide bed of pillows. Jasper glared at the blanket in his hand, desperately trying to come up with a comeback that would be appropriate to say in front of Serenity. He wasn't doing so well.

So, he chose the childish route. "Fine, for that, you're being thrown out of the castle."

Shira's laughter cut and she made an offended sound. "Excuse you!"

Serenity gasped. "Daddy! You can't throw out the queen. That's rude."

Zach snickered. "The princess has a good point. As the other king, I overrule your judgment."

"Oh, thank you, Zach," Shira said in a breathy, sweet voice. "You're too kind."

He smirked. "Am I your favorite?"

"Hmm…" She tapped a finger against her plump lips. "At the moment, yes."

Jasper stuck his tongue out at her. She grinned and did the same, revealing her piercing and subsequently sending a jolt of desire through him, giving him a hell of a hard-on that he couldn't do anything about. *Fucking tease.* And she knew it, from the shit-eating grin she had. Shira was playing with fire, and soon it was going to come back and slap her in the ass.

He returned to building the fort before he lost his senses and did something stupid in front of his daughter.

Dinner arrived just before they finished. Shira plated out their meals, and even made some popcorn. Jasper thought that was a little overkill, but she insisted movie night required popcorn, and since she was making it extra-buttery, he wasn't going to complain.

Once everyone was settled, Jasper and Zach on the outsides and Shira and Serenity nestled between them, with Snake at their feet, Alistair started the movie. It didn't take long for Shira to be sucked in.

Jasper was pretty sure she was eating more popcorn than actual dinner, but as long as she ate something better for snacking than cookies and chips, then he wasn't going to call her out on it.

Shira leaned against Jasper's shoulder, her attention transfixed on the scene unfolding. She hadn't been lying when she claimed to have never seen the movie. It was great seeing her experience it for the first time, and Jasper was glad they could share with her a moment the three of them normally had on weekends. If things went well, she'd be part of it permanently.

He slipped his hand behind her, resting on her hips and bumping against Zach's arm, which he'd slipped behind Serenity, and rested his hand on Shira's thigh. Jasper's fingers skated over some bare skin of her side where her tank top had pulled up and exposed, sending a tingle through his extremities. It was so tempting to push today, with her being so open, but he wanted her to be of clear mind when they did. Until then, he and Zach could only tease and test, so she'd have an idea where they stood.

The tournament issue, while potentially problematic for him and Zach financially if things were canceled, now gave the two of them more chances to focus on making Shira theirs. Didn't matter if this pain issue lasted the whole time or not, they'd include her in everything they could and push her stupid rules until she broke them all.

When the movie ended, Serenity didn't even let Shira give her thoughts on the movie—she wanted to watch another. Everyone listed a movie that'd be good, but before they cast their votes, Alistair spoke up.

"There's been an announcement about the convention."

"What are we looking at?" Jasper asked.

"Postponement for most major events," the AI said. "It appears the building will be closed until it can be properly inspected and fixed."

"Good thing we're not staying in the hotel," Shira mumbled. "I'd hate to be those who have to find a new place to stay in the meantime."

"There is mention of looking for another venue in the event the building can't be reopened quickly, as well as attempting to assist in accommodations for those displaced from their hotel rooms. The convention organizers have also confirmed a list of events that are planned to be moved online if they don't push back the convention end date, though it is noted there is deliberation about pushing the event so as to not ruin the convention experience. More information will come about that."

"How are they going to handle the tournaments?" Zach asked. "It's no secret such events being held online are frowned upon because they're less monitored."

"There is a minor note that it's under deliberation."

"I doubt they'll hold them online," Shira said. "Most likely they'll rent out a smaller building to host the tournaments and broadcast them online."

Jasper nodded. "That was my thought as well. Either way, not much we can do about it. We're at their mercy, so we might as well make the most of our freed-up time."

Zach nodded. "Since we don't know when they'll update things, why don't we just plan for a day ahead and be willing to be flexible in the event the tournament starts back up quick?"

Shira glanced between them. "Aren't you two worried about the possibility of the convention being pushed out?"

Jasper's brow twisted. "Why would we be?"

She stared at him in disbelief. "Serenity needs to go to school."

"Ah," he said, nodding. "Since we've never taken a proper family vacation, we took her out for more than the convention days, so we could enjoy our time away."

One of her eyebrows arched. "That's great and all, but how many extra days?"

"Just a few," Zach admitted. "But it's not like we can't make calls to explain why she'll be out of class longer. She's in first grade. She won't miss so much that it'd be impossible for her to make up work in a single week."

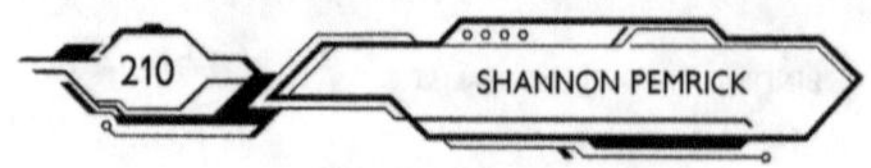

Shira pursed her lips. "All right, I'll drop it."

Jasper reached up and tucked some hair behind her ear. He appreciated her concern and thought to put Serenity first. "Do you have any recommendations what we can do tomorrow? Last time your picks were out of the pahk."

Shira let out a contemplative hum. "Well, we can go to the aquarium or the zoo. And there's mini golf. All of those would be fun for everyone."

"Daddy, can we go to the beach?" Serenity asked.

Jasper smiled. He'd wanted to experience the surf here. "I think that's a great idea."

Zach nodded. "I like the idea of doing something relaxing like that."

Shira shook her head. "None of you can go swimming. The water is freezing."

"It's wicked wahm out," Jasper insisted. "We'll be fine."

She rolled her eyes. "Fine, we'll go to the beach. But don't say I didn't warn you."

Serenity cheered. "The beach is fun! She-ra, does Snake like the beach?"

Shira's lips twisted. "He does, but he won't be able to come with us."

His daughter's eyes went wide. "How come?"

"Manhattan beach doesn't have any beaches that allow dogs. We'd have to travel a long ways to find a beach that will."

Serenity pouted. "That's not fair."

Shira pat her on the head. "It's okay. He loves the pool, so if you ever want to swim in that, he'll join you."

That cheered her up a bit, but she still flopped over onto the ever-patient dog to hug him. She mumbled

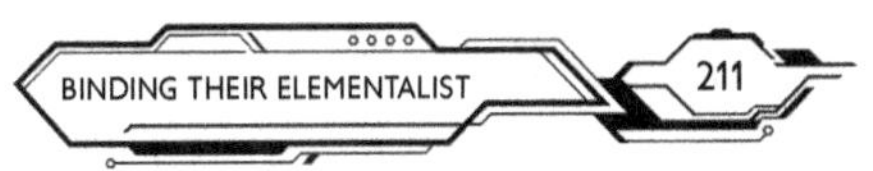

about how he was a good boy and deserved to be allowed at the beach.

Shira leaned against Jasper's shoulder again. "Orion, order the four movies randomly and set up a marathon."

Her AI did as asked and their marathon started.

At some point, Shira ended up with her head in Jasper's lap, Zach's head on her stomach, and Serenity curled into him, with Snake comfortably sprawled with her. Jasper's fingers slid through Shira's silky hair. This was perfect. He'd be happy if this moment never ended.

The sink water cut off and Shira dried the rolling pin. She let out a relieved breath and put the clean baking utensil away. She hadn't realized how much of a mess she and Serenity had made until the cleanup process post-movie, and that was after all the cleaning she and Zach had done before the movie marathon. The guys had offered to handle the breakdown of the fort while Serenity sleepily helped. That left Shira with the easier cleanup duty, or so she thought. But it was done, and her kitchen was now back in order. Maybe not spotless and shining, but that didn't bother her. Might Jasper, but if he wanted to clean her kitchen, she wasn't going to stop him.

Shira stretched and left the kitchen. The family room only had a few pillows remaining. She grabbed a few, only for them to be yanked from her hand. She shot an annoyed glare at Zach.

He smirked. "I've got it."

Tiny feet stomped down the stairs. "She-ra!"

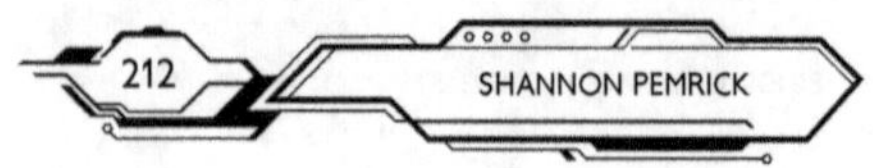

Shira cringed at the volume. "Inside voice please, Serenity. Neighbors are trying to sleep."

She ran into the room, her eyes wide. "She-ra, have you seen Rathalos? I can't find him in my room."

Shira frowned. "No, I haven't. You didn't bring him into my craft room, did you?"

The little girl shook her head. "I don't think so. But you said I couldn't go in if the door was closed."

Shira's lip threatened to twitch into a smile. She appreciated Serenity listening to her request. It wasn't that she didn't want the girl to be in the room—Shira didn't want her to find the surprise she was working on. Not that it'd really matter if Serenity found it. At the rate Shira was going, the costume wouldn't be done before they left.

"I'll go check to be sure."

Serenity nodded with pleading eyes. "Thank you. May I check your room in case I put it in there by mistake?"

Shira nodded. She couldn't see anything wrong with that. Serenity ran back to the stairs and Shira followed, Zach behind her.

"If you don't find it, don't be surprised," Zach murmured. "She does this at home. It's probably under her bed and she didn't look hard enough."

Shira snickered. That wouldn't surprise her.

She opened her studio door and looked around. It was still messy from their project earlier, but that was fairly normal for her. Much like her mom, Shira never cleaned as she worked. And at this point, she was too tired to fix up the room now. *I'll do it tomorrow.*

She scoured the room, even opened drawers and bins just in case, but found no signs of Serenity's beloved plushie. Shira left the room, closing the door behind her, and passed Serenity's room. Both Jasper and Zach were in there looking, but Serenity wasn't. Shira continued on to her room.

She pushed open the ajar door, and peered around the room with vaulted ceilings and exposed beams. On the far side of her bed, near her personal balcony and sitting room, Serenity stood in front of a nightstand. The drawer was pulled open and in her hands was a device contained inside a folding cover, making it look like a book. The screen was on and the young girl tapped it, as if flipping through something.

Shira's gut clenched, and her breath rushed out of her lungs. *No… not that journal…* She sprinted into the room and snatched the device from Serenity, who stared up with wide eyes. "Don't read that, Starship."

The girl gulped. "I–I'm sorry. I was looking for Rathalos. I wasn't gonna read it, just move it, then I dropped it. The cover opened and when I picked it up, it turned on. I've never seen something like it, and I got… curious."

Shira took a calming breath and rested her hand on Serenity's head. "Don't worry, sweetie, I'm not mad. I was… scared. This is a journal from… when I was in the hospital." She closed the cover and held the journal tight against her chest. "It's… not something anyone should ever read. I was in a very dark place then and wrote many horrible things."

Serenity frowned. "Do you still think those things?"

Shira wanted to give her a reassuring smile and provide an answer Serenity hoped for, but it wouldn't be right. "Not all of them, but sometimes I do. It's something I'm trying to work on, but it's slow progress."

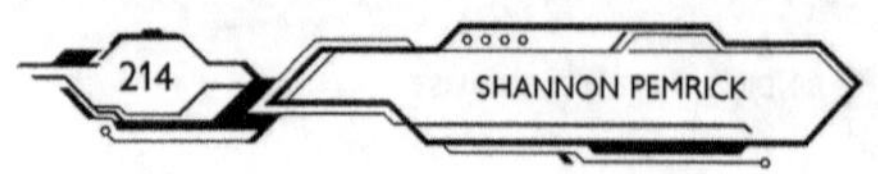

Serenity wrapped her arms around Shira for a hug. "Does this help?"

A smile spread up Shira's face, and she pulled the girl tight against her. "Yes, it does."

Someone appeared in Shira's doorway, drawing her attention. Jasper leaned against the frame, his arm propped over his head. Shira's gaze dragged down his body, taking in the sight he presented—corded muscles drawn tight along his arms and under his taut shirt.

Her mouth dried. The strong desire to run her fingers along his abs and feel every peak and valley of their definition crashed over her. Shira wanted to chastise herself, since most of the medication that would have encouraged these thoughts had worn off by now, but she couldn't. Those thoughts were hers and the desire was real.

Her eyes finally lifted to meet his, and she swallowed. A dangerous grin tugged his handsome face. *Busted.*

"Serenity, I found him."

His daughter looked at him and Jasper held up a red wyvern stuffed toy Shira had been too distracted to notice before. Serenity gasped and scampered over to her father, snatching the toy and snuggling it. "Thank you, Daddy."

Jasper rested his hand on her head. "You're welcome. Now, let's get you ready for bed."

"Okay." She waved to Shira. "Night, She-ra."

"See you in the morning, Starship."

She left, though Jasper didn't follow. His focus had turned to her, that smirk returning. "If you'd like, we can always come in and tuck you into bed aftah."

Heat threatened to sear her face. "No, I'm good. Have a good night."

Jasper pulled away from the door frame, the motion agonizingly slow and deliberate. "If you change ya mind, you know where to find us." His grin deepened, his gaze dragging down her body like she'd noticed both him and Zach doing earlier today. "We wouldn't mind tucking you into our bed."

He left, leaving Shira clutching her journal tight against her chest. Heat coursed through her. Something had changed, and Shira wasn't sure if it was because of her or something else.

The three of them had always had a friendship that included casual flirting. It was a fun part of their relationship, but it never meant anything—or so she'd always thought. Him checking her out, and his offer, should have felt like a normal, casual flirt. He and Zach had done it before. But it wasn't the same. It felt more real—more interested. And Shira wasn't sure anymore if the casual flirting had been as harmless as she'd led herself to believe.

Shira took a shallow breath and spun to face her nightstand. Kneeling, she reached into the deep drawer and reorganized the items inside to store the journal away where it wouldn't be seen again.

A white envelope slipped out of the pile she organized. Shira paused and looked at it. It had something small and rectangular inside and remained unopened. She swallowed and reached a tentative hand in to pick it up and flip it over. Neat scripted handwriting had been written on the front.

When you're ready.

A lump formed in Shira's throat, all the heat inside her running ice-cold. *Tanya…*

Shira remembered when the nurse had given it to her, mere moments after they'd revealed Tanya hadn't made it. Shira had never found it in her to be able to open the package. The pain of her loss cut too deep. The shame of knowing it was Shira's fault—she tucked it away in her journal. Even now, she was too afraid to see what was inside.

Shira rubbed her artificial arm, the simulated nerves firing, but only partially registering in her haze. Today was a good reminder for her. She might be healing mentally, but the reality was, she'd never be fully healed. Her body would always do this to her. It'd always decide at random that it would scream and make her brain think there was something wrong with the parts of her she no longer had.

Jasper and Zach had been patient and caring today, but this was something she'd live with for the rest of her life, and they'd grow tired of it eventually.

Shira put the journal away and closed the drawer. Her shoulders slumped and her chest constricted with a suffocating sensation.

Sorry, Tanya… I'm still just a pretty broken thing…

A shirt smacked Zach in the face. *Oof.* It fell to the ground and Zach glared at Jasper, who smirked. His boyfriend stood in pineapple-print swim trunks and his shirt was now on the floor since he'd thrown it at Zach.

"What was that for?" Zach asked.

"You're not ready for the beach," Jasper said.

Zach crossed his arms. He'd chosen to wear shorts and a tank top. "Because I'm smart enough to listen to Shira when she says it's going to be too cold to swim."

"It's gonna be in the seventies today," Jasper tried to reason. "Plenty wahm enough for swimming."

"Well, if we're both wrong, you and Serenity can rub it in our faces."

As if saying her name summoned the girl, Serenity ran into their room. "Daddy, I'm ready."

She wore only her swimsuit—a pink, tropical-themed, halter-style two-piece.

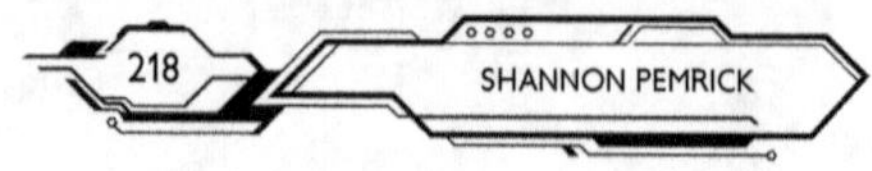

"Seren, where are your clothes?" Jasper asked.

She cocked her head. "Whatcha mean? I'm wearing my bathing suit."

"You also need to weah regulah clothes over it until we get to the beach."

"You're not wearing regulah clothes."

Zach bit his lip so he wouldn't laugh. *The joys of raising a daughter with a defiant personality.*

"I'm not done getting ready," Jasper said. "When I'm done, I'll be fully clothed."

"Unless Shira gets involved in delaying," Zach murmured as he snatched up Jasper's shirt.

Jasper shot him a warning look, clearly not liking the tantalizing distraction Zach implanted in his head. "You need to get a shirt and shorts, Starship."

"Is She-ra awake?"

Zach looked out the large windows. The sun had risen; they'd watched movies too late for him to consider asking about sunrise beach photos. Zach could get them another day, and if they were out late enough, a sunset shoot was possible. "Shira is an early riser usually, so she should be up."

Honestly, he couldn't be sure, since she'd gone to bed late with them and she had fought all day with pain. *I hope she's feeling better today.*

"I'm gonna go check on her!" Serenity said, running off.

"No, Seren, wait…" Jasper sighed and headed out the room.

Zach dropped Jasper's shirt on the bed next to the beach towels he'd pulled out earlier. His camera was already downstairs, so that was accounted for. Since

Jasper was so set on swimming, Zach decided to leave it to him to grab the towels, and left the room.

He caught Jasper jogging into Shira's across the hall. "Serenity, you can't just run into someone's room."

Like you just did? Sure, he was trying to grab their daughter, but he could call out to Shira first. For all they knew, Shira was getting dressed and would be fine with Serenity barging in, but not them. As much as the two of them were eager to get her into their bed, there was an element of consent there that was lost in this situation.

"Shira, I'm sorry. She—" Jasper's words came to a halt, piquing Zach's interest, especially since Shira didn't start shouting. Too curious for his own good, Zach entered her room as well.

Jasper and Serenity stood in the doorway of Shira's ensuite bathroom, Jasper staring, unblinking while Serenity glanced between him and what Zach presumed was Shira within.

"S–stop staring…" Shira said.

Zach came up behind Jasper and peered into the spacious bath. Much like theirs in the room they stayed in, the bathroom was furnished with granite top counters, tile flooring, a Jacuzzi tub, and shower large enough to fit at least two people, maybe even a third.

Shira leaned against the sink counter, one of her hands desperately trying to cover her neck. She wore shorts that hugged her hips and a cropped tank top. On the counter was a thin, pale item that looked a lot like skin.

He easily spotted what had caused this confrontation, noting the extra cybernetics visible on her neck and jaw, and her side—just like that incident in the closet.

"Jasper… please…" Red spread over her cheeks and her gaze shifted away.

Jasper's gaze never left her as he walked in. He reached out for her with a hand, but she flinched back. The reaction made Zach's chest clench. She wasn't uncomfortable—she was scared. Shira had gone for so long believing she was an unlovable cyborg freak, her first instinct was to treat any potential response of seeing her as she was, with fear and to protect herself. But her fear was no match for Zach and Jasper.

Jasper reached for Shira again, this time with both hands, and cupped her face, pushing her focus back up to him. His thumbs brushed her cheeks. "Nothing could evah convince me from staring at something so beautiful."

Shira squeaked when his mouth crashed into hers and her hands grabbed his wrists, however she didn't force him away. Her eyes hooded and her body curved toward Jasper as he worked his mouth against hers.

To Zach's surprise, just like the other day when they were laying claim to Shira in front of Jeremy, he felt no pangs of jealousy—only zings of excitement and desire. He could tell himself he was fighting against unsure feelings all he wanted, but it was becoming clear that was more in his head than actual reality.

Serenity's hands flew up to her face and she began giggling. Zach pressed his lips together so he wouldn't laugh. She was peeking like usual.

Then, as suddenly as he kissed her, Jasper pulled away. Shira's eyes fluttered open. "Don't forget that."

Before Shira could manage any words, Jasper spun on his heels and grabbed Serenity, throwing her over his shoulder. "The princess needs to finish getting ready."

"So does Daddy king," Serenity managed through giggles.

Jasper rolled his eyes and left, leaving Zach leaning against the doorframe. Shira turned her attention to him. She took a breath and squared her shoulders, as if anticipating some sort of fight. "Are you waiting your turn to give me an unnecessary kiss, too?"

Ah. Zach smirked. Bold Shira won a battle against fearful Shira, and he was confident she was going to like her prize.

Zach pushed away from the wall and walked toward her. Shira's bravado held up for a few steps, but then weakened with each of his after. Her gaze dipped, and she pulled into herself as if she could make herself small or disappear.

Zach reached out and hooked his fingers under her chin, lifting it so she'd gaze up at him. "Unnecessary it's not."

His thumb pulled her plump lower lip down until they parted. "A crime to foolishly not show my appreciation for someone so beautiful, absolutely."

Zach bent closer, tipping her face up even more. Her pulse jumped under his fingers brushing against her throat. He captured her soft lips with his. Shira let out a soft sigh, her breath mingling with his.

Their lips moved and synchronized, sending a rush of heated sensations flooding through him all at once. He slid his fingers through her hair and pinned her against the counter with his body. Zach had meant this to be a sweet, quick kiss, to show her how he saw her, but deep need for her fogged his brain.

Shira's hands slid up his abs, the hard muscles flexing

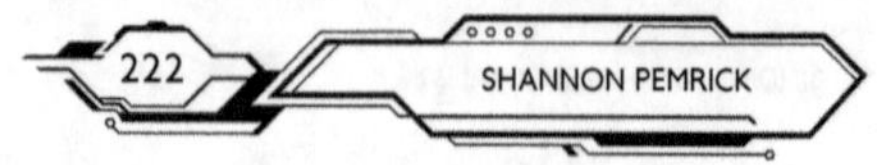

under her touch. Her tongue swept across his lip, and Zach hungrily accepted her request. Their tongues wrestled and played, her sweet taste searing into his mind.

Before he lost himself, Zach broke the kiss, leaving her flushed and them both breathless. He turned, gazing at her with all the adoration he felt in this moment. "One of these days you'll see it, too."

Zach walked out, though he stole a glance over his shoulder. Shira's hand had returned to her neck, and she gazed at the false skin, contemplation in her eyes. As much as a part of him hoped she'd nix them today for the beach, he wasn't foolish enough to believe she'd walk out of this room without them today. He hoped that day wasn't much further away, however.

Jasper was waiting for Zach when he left Shira's room. His gaze fell to Zach's lips and then traveled lower. Zach didn't doubt he looked as hard as he felt. It was a miracle he'd been able to pull away from her.

"Someone had fun," Jasper said in a hushed voice.

"Not at much as I'd have liked," Zach admitted. "But Serenity wouldn't forgive me if I delayed our beach trip."

"Yeah, I'm sure that's it." Jasper came up to him and pressed a hard kiss on the side of Zach's head. He also grabbed Zach's ass before heading for the stairs. "I'm heading out to get breakfast. Alistair found a Dunks nearby. I shouldn't be long."

Zach was impressed. He didn't think there'd be any stores over here. "You know what we like."

"Shira, I'm taking Snake with me to grab breakfast," Jasper called out. Zach chuckled. Of course, he'd bring the dog with him.

"Huh? Why are you going out? We have supplies for breakfast here."

"Because I want to go pick some up."

She let out an exasperated sigh. "All right, do what you want."

Jasper grinned and jogged down the stairs. Zach went about gathering their things, since Jasper didn't finish. Orion directed him to a store of beach bags. He waited for Jasper's return downstairs, as well as Shira's appearance.

It took her a while, but eventually she walked into the kitchen. She'd swapped out the tank top for an off-the-shoulder crop top that somehow made her even more tempting.

As he expected, she'd applied the false skin. Zach couldn't deny he was a bit disappointed, but he also knew that would have been a big step for her—too big at this point.

"Is Jasper not back yet?" she asked, looking around.

"No, he should be back in a few moments," Zach said.

She nodded. "Any idea why he brought Snake with him?"

He shrugged. "I think he's been liking having a dog around. We'd have one if it weren't for our apartment rules."

"Well, I'm glad. Snake could use the play buddies. There's only so much I can keep up with, and since he needs to be with me most of the time, I can't really bring him to daycares all that often." She sat down on a barstool. "Where did he go for breakfast?"

"Dunks."

Shira's brow spiked. "Dunks?"

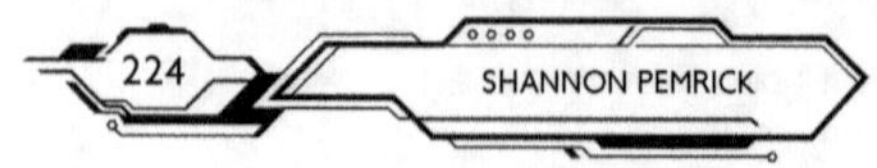

Orion spoke up. "I believe they mean the coffee and doughnut shop called Dunkin'. It is a fairly popular on the East Coast. One opened here a few years ago, and there are few other locations in the state."

"And by popular, he means it's practically on every corner and anyone who is anyone gets their breakfast there," Zach said.

Shira blinked. "We've got plenty of awesome local doughnut shops. You could have tried those out instead."

Zach nodded. He'd thought of that too, but Jasper had been dead set. "We've got time to try them. Plus, Dunks has our favorite coffees."

Shira shook her head, choosing not to argue a moot point.

"Zach," Serenity said from where she watched cartoons on the couch. "Is Daddy getting me munchkins?"

"Of course he is."

Serenity cheered. Shira cocked her head. "Munch… kins?"

Serenity held up her hands and made circles with her fingers. "Yeah. Little round doughnuts, like this size."

"Oh, you mean doughnut holes."

Serenity shook her head. "No, munchkins."

Zach choked on a laugh from the look of sheer confusion on Shira's face, though it was Orion who came to her rescue and explained how they were the same thing and why Dunkin' had chosen a different name to call them by.

Jasper wasn't much longer to return. Snake barreling into the house was the amusing indicator. Jasper appeared in the kitchen moments after, coffee tray and food bag in hand. "Who's hungry?"

"Me!" Serenity pet Snake one last time before scampering over to the island and hopping up onto a stool. She leaned forward, her fingers perched on the countertop, and her eyes barely peeking over. Her fingers drummed in her excitement.

Jasper set the food and drinks on the counter and pulled out a bottle of apple juice, and set it in front of her.

"We have juice for her here," Shira said.

"Yeah, but she'll finish this whole thing before we leave and then we can turn it into a wotta bottle."

She pursed her lips. "I have actual water bottles, too. Should have just saved your money."

Zach chuckled. *For a woman with money, she is sensible with it.*

Jasper shook his head and then pulled out a small box from the bag and pushed it toward Serenity. "Munchkins for the little munchkin."

Serenity giggled and eagerly dug into her very unhealthy breakfast. Normally Zach and Jasper were careful with what she ate first thing, but today was a good treat day. Especially after how well she'd done yesterday with Shira.

"Now, we have a salted caramel mocha, and chocolate frosted doughnut with sprinkles for the lady," Jasper said, pulling a travel cup out of the tray as well as the confection treat. He slid them to Shira. Her eyes lit up, and she gladly snatched her drink. Zach made a mental note that her love for caramel may be stronger than they had first thought. "And a pumpkin spice latte and breakfast sandwich for the gentleman."

Shira snickered when the cup was slid over to Zach. "Pumpkin spice, really?"

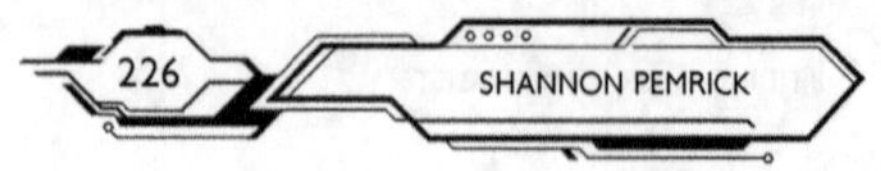

Zach held the cup close to his chest, enjoying the warmth on his skin, while the rich aromas of cinnamon, clove, and pumpkin wafted into his nose. "Leave us basic white girls alone and drink your salted caramel."

Shira and Jasper burst into laughter. Zach smiled and sipped his coffee.

Jasper pulled out his doughnut that had an oddly yellow frosting and chocolate drizzle. Shira made a face. "What the hell is that?"

"It's a new limited-edition banana-flavored doughnut. Figured I'd try it," he said.

Her expression changed to disgust. "Banana? Really?"

"I like banana-flavored things. Candies, drinks, and now doughnuts. Though not as much as pineapple." He looked at his unhealthy breakfast. "Now I wish this was pineapple-flavored."

She grunted and sipped her coffee. "Explains the pineapple trunks."

He pointed at her. "Don't be making fun of the pineapples."

Zach chuckled and bit into his sandwich. He'd also poked at Jasper for them. It was fun seeing him get all defensive over his precious pineapple swim trunks.

A ball dropped on the floor, and then Snake barked. All eyes fell on the dog, who wagged his tail and looked down at his toy.

"Yeah, we should get some of your energy out now." Shira slipped off her stool and opened the door to the backyard. Snake snatched his toy and ran over to her. She didn't hesitate to throw the ball, and he took off into the yard.

"Does he ever run out of energy?" Zach asked.

Shira rocked her head. "Not really, but he's more medium energy, so after a few laps around the yard or a good walk, he's content to just chill. Makes him ready for anything when the energy is needed."

"Huh." Jasper leaned against the island. "I always figured his breed was all energy until they crashed when they reached senior citizen."

Shira chuckled. "I mean, most are like that. But my dad knew I wouldn't be active while I recovered, so when he put out all the feelers for the best dog for me, he made sure to search out a buddy who would match me in every way."

"Since Snake knows German commands, is it safe to assume you didn't get him locally?" Zach said.

She laughed. "Not a hard bet to win. My dad doesn't like how the American German Shepherd is bred, so he was determined to find a dog from Germany. And it just so happened, a contact of a friend had just the dog for me. Not a puppy, which meant they knew his temperament better, but he was still young, so easy to train."

Snake returned with his ball, and Shira immediately threw it for him. "They flew out to Germany to check him out and knew immediately he was the one for me. I knew nothing about their plans and found myself with quite the surprise one day."

Even though Zach expected her to say that last bit with affection and a smile, she didn't. "You hadn't been happy when they surprised you."

She shook her head. "I was still going through some serious stuff then, so all I saw was a responsibility. And I didn't want help. I wanted to do things on my own and act like nothing happened."

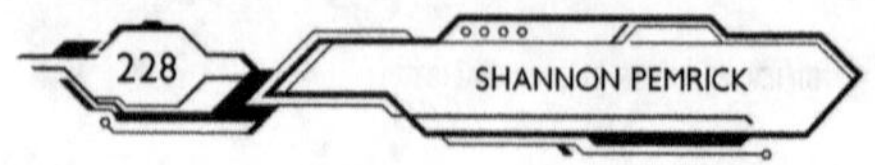

The smile finally appeared. "But it didn't take him long to win me over."

Zach could believe it. The dog had won over his family basically the first day they'd met him, and it was easy to see how much Shira loved Snake.

Shira played with Snake for a bit longer while everyone ate breakfast. She eventually was able to eat her doughnut, and then gave her impression of Dunkin's food: decent. She determined she'd had better, both when it came to the coffee and the doughnut, but it was far from the worst. Shira at least mentioned the coffee was better than the one she had at the convention center two days ago, so Zach could live with that assessment. He knew, from his time living in DC before moving back to Boston, those who didn't grow up in the New England area had little appreciation for the beloved company.

The doorbell rang, sending Snake into a barking fit, and Shira cocked her head. "I wonder who that is."

"It's a delivery," Orion reported. "Because you're all going to the beach, I took the liberty of purchasing a few items you will need and didn't have."

She slipped off her stool. "Oh, awesome, thanks."

Zach blinked at her nonchalant attitude over her AI up and ordering things on his own. "You just let him buy things?"

She nodded and headed down the hall. "He's got free rein to buy whatever either of us needs."

"Either of you?"

"Shira has me purchase all manner of items that will make her life easier, such as food, entertainment, cosmetics, and medicine. As an AI program, I can benefit from upgrades to software and infrastructure hardware," Orion said. "These upgrades are beneficial to both myself and Shira. One example is the voice modulation software used not only on her phone, but in her homes."

Zach swallowed. It made sense—though, to give an AI program that much control—

"Don't fret, Zach," Alistair said. "We AIs are aware of our owner's budgets and are not capable of making purchases that would cause them financial ruin, not that we would ever wish to cause such hardships."

That made him feel a bit better, but he still needed time to be onboard with the concept.

Shira returned with two boxes, one long and thin, the other a standard medium square. She put the square box on the counter and opened the long one, pulling out a beach umbrella.

"Perfect," she said. "Now I have a replacement after Dad broke the other one."

Zach and Jasper laughed. Shira then opened the other box. She pulled out sunscreen and then rummaged more.

"What else ya got, She-ra?" Serenity asked, her eyes intently interested.

"Well, if we're going to the beach, we can't leave without making a sand castle," Shira said, pulling out some pails and other sand-castle-making toys.

Serenity made a happy gasping sound, and her eyes glowed when Shira pulled out two more items. "And we've got matching hats for you and me."

She slipped around the island and plopped the sun hat on Serenity's head before doing the same with her

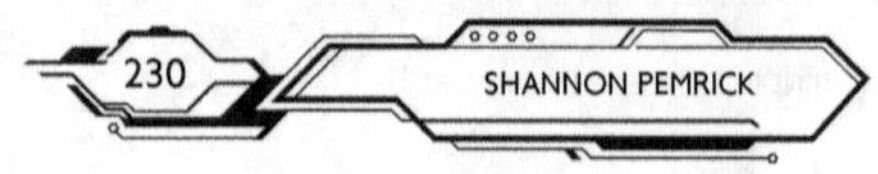

own hat. "We've gotta keep your pretty face safe from the sun. And you look so cute."

Serenity grinned widely and looked to Zach and Jasper. "Do I look cute?"

"You always look cute," Zach said. "But now you're extra adorable."

That didn't quite describe just how much he enjoyed not only seeing Shira spoil Serenity with such simple and low-key gestures, but also watching them match in small ways. It brought her one step closer to being part of their family beyond that "close friend who helped out a lot."

Breakfast quickly ended after that. Serenity really wanted to get to the beach, and none of them had any reason to stall. They collected the beach items into the beach bag Zach had already used for their things, and Jasper took it out to the car along with the umbrella. Shira nixed a packed lunch idea and said she'd treat them all to one of the local restaurants. They tried to protest her paying, but she was insistent, so Zach and Jasper had no choice but to accept. They'd just cover the tip and find a way to pay for something else, besides the dinner they'd planned later this week.

While Jasper covered the packing, Zach had one thing to bring up with Shira. "Hey, can we talk real quick before we go?"

Her head tilted. "Yeah, sure, what's up?"

Zach took a quick breath and held up his camera. "I plan to take photos while we're out, and I want to ask your permission to take some of you."

Shira chewed her lip and tipped her chin down for a moment before looking up at him again and nodding. "Okay."

Surprise wasn't the right word for what Zach felt, but it was the only one his brain could process. "Really?"

She continued to chew on her lip. "Y–yeah. Under the condition I can use it to take photos of you three."

A goofy grin spread over Zach's face. "Absolutely."

She nodded again and scooted out of the house, spending an extra amount of time to talk to Snake and apologize for having to keep him home. Zach watched, figuring it was a way for her to calm herself. He couldn't imagine how difficult that may have been to tell herself to try this out. He couldn't be prouder for her taking that leap. And she could revoke the permission at any time. He'd only go as far as she allowed.

Everyone hopped into the car, and Orion set their destination. Serenity bopped away to the music Shira set—everything Jasper hated. He even sulked for a moment when Shira wouldn't allow him to change it to something else in hopes it'd change her mind, but it had no effect on this woman.

Traffic was rough, but they finally reached the beach. There were plenty of beach goers, but nothing crazy that would put them off from continuing their plan. Zach guessed most of those here were tourists rather than locals, given Shira hadn't been too onboard with the beach idea and only went along because the rest of them wanted it.

Jasper pulled the beach items out of the car while Zach and Shira watched Serenity stubbornly get herself unbuckled. *She's definitely Jasper's and Sara's daughter.* To keep himself busy, Zach did some test shots around the car and adjusted his settings as needed.

He noticed Shira glancing his way each time the shutter

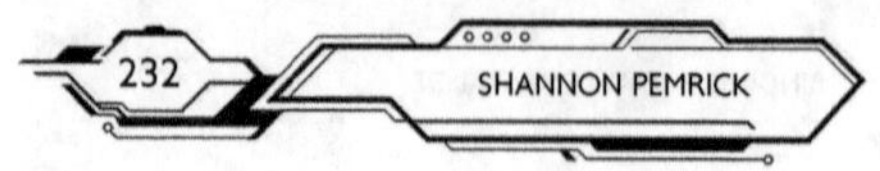

sounded, but refrained from speaking to her about it. He didn't want to make her even more uncomfortable, bringing it up and possibly embarrassing her. As much as she tried to pretend she wasn't, she was a rather sensitive person, and the last thing he needed to do was push her in the wrong way.

Serenity grabbed Shira's hand when she finally jumped out of the car. "Ready?"

Shira looked to Jasper and then Zach. "I am, but check with your dads."

Zach snapped a photo of the two of them and smiled. "Sure am."

Shira visibly swallowed, but to her credit, didn't freak out or change her mind about her permission.

Jasper shut the trunk. "I'm good, let's go!"

Serenity jumped up and down and yanked Shira to follow. Though, the hand holding didn't last long. The moment Serenity touched the sand, she ran off onto the beach. Jasper booked it after her, trying to rein her in by having her pick out their beach spot. This left Zach and Shira to watch and follow at a slower pace.

Zach removed his shoes, feeling the warm sand spread under his feet. The surf crashed in the distance and gulls called overhead.

The salty wind picked up, teasing Shira's long hair and threatening to steal her hat. She giggled and grabbed a hold. Zach pointed his lens and snapped. She turned a tentative gaze to him and he continued. Modeling instinct seemed to take over in her, because even with her so unsure about this plan, her body knew how to position perfectly.

Zack peered up from his viewfinder. "Gorgeous."

Her gaze turned down, red flushing her cheeks, and he was sure to snag several more snaps. At this rate, he'd run out of space on his memory card before the hour was up, and he honestly didn't care.

"We found a spot!" Jasper called out. He and Serenity were fairly close to the crashing waves, but Zach could still see it was sufficiently far enough that any sudden large waves wouldn't come and bother them.

Shira waved to him in acknowledgement. Zach settled his camera against his hip. Not a few steps into their path, he grabbed her wrist and slid his hands down her palms until their fingers intertwined. She shot him a curious, questioning glance.

This was a risky move, but he had to try. "You don't mind, do you?"

"No." She didn't even hesitate in her answer.

Excitement swelled in his chest and traveled through his fingers, making them tingle. This morning was tantalizing in a blossoming, exploration-of-new-emotions kind of way. This, though, was a comfortable action with her. It felt right—natural even, like they'd done it a million times before.

"You two took your sweet lovin' time," Jasper teased when the two of them reached him.

Shira snorted. "And you could have set up instead of waiting like an idiot, but you don't see me bringing that up."

He placed an offended hand on his chest. "Excuse you. I wanted to set up the blanket and umbrella, but I didn't know your preferred setup."

She waved him off, rolling her eyes and muttered something about him being lazy and useless. Jasper rolled

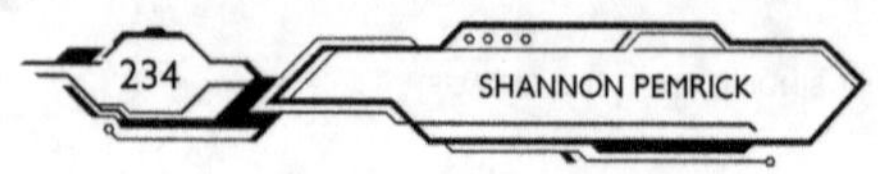

his eyes right back, and then they burst into laughter. Zach joined in. *These two are something else.*

They set up, Jasper taking breaks to keep tabs on Serenity. She'd run off to the wet sand and appeared to be following crabs that were uncovered when the waves came in. She'd already shed her clothes overtop her swimsuit and had just dumped them in the sand. Shira was sure to shake them out and fold them into the beach bag.

Once the three of them had the blanket and umbrella squared away and Shira safely tucked into the shade, Jasper whipped his shirt off. Zach prepared to be smacked in the face again, but Jasper threw a curveball by tossing it at Shira.

She let out an adorable startled squeak, then inhaled deeply and hummed contentedly, pulling Jasper's shirt into her face more.

"Shit, I shouldn't have done that," Jasper said.

She chuckled. "You should know better than to give a woman something of yours with your smell. You'll instantly lose it."

"What is it with your sex and smells?"

Her eyebrow spiked. "What is with yours and smelling so good?"

Jasper opened his mouth and then thought. "Touché. Guess I've lost my shirt."

"Until we go to lunch, at least," Shira agreed.

Jasper kicked off his sandals and ran off to Serenity. Shira smelled the shirt one more time before storing it away.

"He does smell nice," Zach said. He certainly enjoyed Jasper's scent.

She nodded. "You do, too."

The corner of his lip twitched up. She liked the way he smelled? "Oh, yeah?"

Shira leaned against him and pressed her nose against his neck. Zach swallowed, his pulse kicking up a notch. She inhaled. "Mmm, yeah, you definitely smell good."

She pulled away, but he wasn't going to let her off that easily. Zach tangled his fingers in her gorgeous hair, and leaned into her, inhaling her sweet, tantalizing scent. "You smell delicious."

"Delicious, huh?" She then let out a peal of laughter. "I think that's a first for me."

He nuzzled his nose in deeper, his lips grazing her ear. He caught the hitch in her breath. "Well, they clearly didn't appreciate what I do."

She sucked in a tight breath through her teeth and then shook her head. "I can't believe they're going for the water. It's fucking freezing because of the cold current."

Zach pulled away, amused rather than disappointed. "You underestimate what those two are willing to swim in. We have a cold current on the East Coast, too, and they're eager to go to the beach in spring."

She shook her head again. "Unbelievable. At least you're sane."

He laughed. "I'm a person who likes middle-of-the-road temperatures. Can't do hot, but can't really do cold, either. That's what made living in DC nice."

She glanced his way. "Why didn't you convince Jasper to move there instead of staying in Boston?"

Zach shrugged. "Jasper's a bit attached because of his family. At first, everyone was there. Then, when Scott and Christine moved for Scott's job, Jasper became

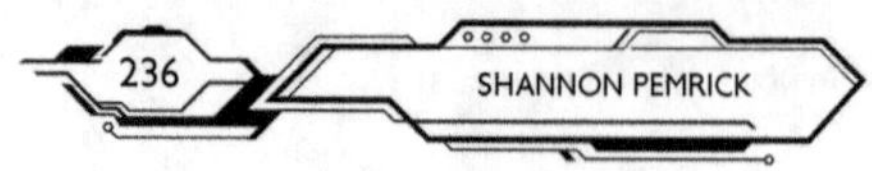

even more determined to stay with Cheryl, given his grandparents have been gone since we were teens."

She looked back out at the ocean. "Ah."

Zach caught the unmistakable tones of disappointment. His chest constricted. That was not a good sign. He and Jasper knew if this was going to work out, living arrangements would have to change, but it seemed it would be even harder to figure out. Zach got the feeling Shira wouldn't be so open to moving. He couldn't blame her. Everything she had was here in California. The three of them were the only odd ones out.

Serenity shrieked, drawing his attention, and he watched her scamper out of the barely there-surf. Jasper wasn't much better, hopping around in the frigid water. Zach and Shira laughed.

"Should have listened to me," Shira said.

"Just wait." He knew his family. They wouldn't give up on this. At least, not Jasper. He would go in all the way. Serenity would go about up to her shins before she decided that was enough for her.

And he wasn't off with his prediction. Serenity kicked and splashed around, getting used to the cold. Jasper stayed with her, but his eyes were constantly darting to the surf. He wanted to go for a dip. And Zach wanted more photos.

He left the shade, holding his hand out to Shira. "Let's go over by the water."

Her nose scrunched. "I'm not looking to get wet."

She blinked when he grinned, and then her eyes narrowed when she realized where his mind had gone. "And cold. Don't want to be cold, either."

Zach chuckled and continued to hold out his hand

for her to take. She pursed her lips and then sighed, allowing him to pull her up. Zach tugged her close and pressed his lips against her ear. "If you're looking to be warm and wet, all you have to do is ask."

She sucked in a tight breath and he walked away, unable to hide his amusement.

Serenity waved to him when she noticed his approach and continued to play. Zach brought his camera up to his face and his shutter clicked rapidly. Some shots were only of his daughter, and others included Jasper, either with her or alone.

Shira joined them eventually, though made her protests about the cold water clear. He didn't blame her. The small waves lapping at his feet were icy.

Zach managed many photos of Shira, and snagged some good shots when Jasper grabbed her and threatened to throw her into the ocean. Some of his best snaps, though, were of her and Serenity or all three of them. He wished he could get some shots of all four of them, but, like a dummy, Zach had left half his camera equipment at home by accident.

His camera lurched out of his hands and Shira laughed when he half-panicked. "Your turn to have fun."

Zach blew out a breath and allowed her to take his precious device. He was protective of it, given the camera's cost. While he'd allowed her to hold onto it at the bookstore, that was a different setting than here on the beach. *A deal is a deal.*

He and Jasper splashed around with Serenity. She found a few sea shells she wanted to keep, and Shira held onto them for her, to keep her hands free. Jasper tried to convince Zach to go further into the water,

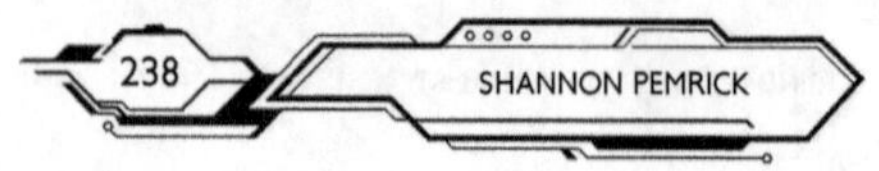

even though Zach hadn't worn swim trunks, but Zach was not having it. He would have no part in this frigid water beyond his feet going numb.

Jasper ran out for the surf. Shira handed the camera back to Zach and winked. "Figure you might want this back now."

Zach grinned. She knew good shot opportunities when she saw them. He brought the viewfinder up to his eyes and waited.

Jasper dove into a crashing wave, disappearing under the blue water.

"He's crazy," Shira murmured. Zach couldn't disagree.

Jasper broke the surface a moment later, Zach snapping the shutter. He got a nice photo of Jasper's shocked face in reaction to the cold he'd plunged into. Then he took a few more as Jasper came back to the beach. Corded muscles flexed when his boyfriend lifted his arms up and threaded his fingers through his wet hair. Water dripped off his tanned skin and traveled down toned muscle lines, accentuating them. Droplets beaded around Jasper's tattoos, drawing Zach's eye. The lens snapped a few times.

Jasper's attention flicked to him and then to Shira. He grinned and touched the corner of his mouth with his thumb, drawing Zach's gaze. "Is that drool I see from the two of you?"

Zach's eyes cut to Shira. He had nothing to be ashamed over, though Shira…

She rolled her eyes and snorted. "Please. I ogle, not drool. That's unbecoming of a lady."

Zach couldn't stop his laughter. "Based on some things

Kiara hinted that you inspired for her writing, you've gone beyond unbecoming for a lady."

Pink tinted her salt-stained cheeks, and she spun around. "Starship, let's go build a sand castle."

Serenity jumped around. "Yes!"

Zach grinned at her retreating form. Now he wanted to know exactly what had been used in Kiara's books. She hardly counted as a lady by all accounts of what she'd done with him and Jasper in the game, and yet he was sure that had been tame.

Jasper drew up next to him. "I'm done waiting."

Zach chuckled. "Already ahead of you."

"Yeah, I caught glimpses of you stealing touches with her up there."

Zach worked his jaw, eyes trained on Shira as she grabbed the sand castle toys from the beach bag. Jasper's tone wasn't accusatory, but Zach had to mentally chastise himself for nearly thinking it had been. "After this morning, it would be idiotic if we kept things at our current pace. I had to keep the intent there so she can't pretend she's misunderstanding."

Jasper grinned, his eyes gleaming. "What did happen between the two of you that took so long?"

"I might have pinned her to the counter and kissed her until she was breathless."

His boyfriend groaned. "Damn, what I wouldn't have given to see that."

With a chuckle, Zach reached out and tucked his fingers under Jasper's chin. "Then let me give you a small demonstration."

He tipped Jasper's face toward him and leaned in, capturing his partner's mouth. His tongue glided across

Jasper's salt-coated lips, which parted immediately in invitation. Their tongues wrestled for a moment before Zach pulled away.

Jasper hummed. "If that was only a demonstration, and she didn't run after the full thing, then I think we've got a pretty damned good chance at this."

"She seemed to enjoy it, with the way her hands roamed me." Zach grinned. "And she didn't tell me to fuck off when I held her hand coming down to the beach after you and Serenity ran off, or at any point I was close to her under that umbrella."

Jasper's brow rose. "Close contact with her and kissing me like that in public? What happened to your PDA rule?"

He hadn't thought about that. *I did just do that, didn't I?* Even two days ago, he would have run it through his head a few times before deciding what was appropriate to do. "Well, if we're expecting Shira to ditch her rules, can't expect us not to do the same."

Slipping his arm around Zach, Jasper pulled him against his side. "I agree with you. Now, let's go make some sand castles."

"I hope you're prepared to be made into the base."

Jasper laughed. "You know I love that."

CHAPTER 14

Packed sand in the shape of a castle tower slid perfectly out of Shira's bucket. She grabbed a fistful of wet sand and piled and molded a parapet beside it, leading up Jasper's leg.

She'd never built a sand castle on top of someone before, but it seemed to be how this family did it, and she wasn't going to back off from the chance to partially bury Jasper in sand. Hell, he even helped, which was amusing to watch, given he had to be careful not to move too much, so as not to ruin their work.

Zach's hand brushed against hers when their parapets met. She had to hold back any reaction to his touch and pretended it didn't affect her—he'd done enough of that earlier.

Shira could still feel the heat of his breath on her lips, that strong cedar scent that followed him everywhere, and the warmth of his skin wrapped around her hand. His sweet, affirming words seared into her mind and her body remembered his weight pinning her to the counter; her own hands roaming up his abs over his shirt and their strong definition beneath. If he hadn't pulled away first, Shira wasn't sure what she would have done. She doubted that in that moment, she would have stopped him from doing whatever he wanted to her.

Something flashed in front of her eyes, and she blinked. Zach waved his hand again and tilted his head to catch her gaze. "Shira?"

She blinked again and realized she was sitting straight up. "Yeah?"

"You okay? You spaced out on us all of a sudden. You're not in pain from all the moving around, are you?"

Shira noticed Jasper also watching her, clearly concerned. Their worry touched her, even though she'd rather they didn't. She put on a reassuring smile. "No, I'm fine. Just thinking about how hungry I am. Didn't eat much yesterday or this morning."

It wasn't a total lie. She had been feeling peckish for a bit.

Jasper's brow furrowed. "Why didn't you say anything sooner?"

Shira gestured to their work. "I didn't want to stop all the fun. It's not like I'm starving or anything."

"I am concerned by your lack of appetite," Alistair said from Zach's pocket. "It is a quarter to two."

Zach pulled out his phone, and they all stared at it. There was no way. But Zach confirmed the AI's claim when he turned on the screen.

"Well, shit, we should all be starving by this point," Jasper said.

Zach turned his attention to Shira. "Why aren't you?"

She shrugged. "My appetite can still be a bit off the day after a major pain flare day. I usually try to be more conscious of my eating habits the day after, but I've been so distracted."

"Isn't that what Orion is for?" Zach asked.

"I have no reason to be concerned about Shira's health," Orion piped up. "My scanners indicate her breakfast, while not large or entirely healthy, was enough to hold her over safely to this point. On top of that, this activity has made a positive impact on her mental health. I did not wish to slow that effect."

"I'm hungry, too," Serenity announced.

Jasper leaned back on his hands. "Well, I guess it's settled. We go eat, and if we're up for more aftah, we can come back to the beach."

"Where was it you wanted to take us, Shira?" Zach asked.

She pointed down the shoreline. "Just to a pub near the pier. It's my favorite in the area. Figure, after having lunch with a view, we could go to the pier and then walk the beach. At this rate, we might even catch a sunset for you, Zach."

Zach smiled wide. She knew he'd like that. Had she been able to wake up earlier today, she would have tried to get them out for a sunrise. But it was normal for her to crash after pain flares subsided and she needed to allow her body to rest. *I'll help him get those pictures this week.*

Speaking of photos, Zach lifted his camera to his face and snapped some more of their work on Jasper. Serenity jumped into his arms, nearly kicking their work, and then Shira felt a slight tug on the belt loop of her shorts. She blinked and Jasper tugged her again. She hadn't even noticed him reach for her. But his request was clear.

Shira scooted up next to him and Jasper tucked her into his arm, curling his hand over her hip. Zach lifted the camera again. Shira took a calming breath and tapped into her modeling instincts, just as she'd done all day when he turned the device on her.

Just like the moment at the bookstore, it hadn't turned out to be a chore to fight her instinct to hide from all cameras. She couldn't be sure her reaction would be the same if it were someone other than Zach or Jasper, but this was a start.

No sooner had the thought crossed her mind when someone approached Zach and offered to take a photo of all of them if they wanted. The guys turned their eyes to her, and she swallowed. *I can't ruin their vacation for them because of my issues.* It was just one photo.

Shira nodded and painted on a smile. "That would be very kind of you."

Quicker than she'd seen of him today, Zach relinquished his camera to the stranger and slipped behind the three of them. "I set it up so you'll just have to point and click the button."

The person nodded and crouched, snapping the shutter a few times. Shira did her best to stay calm and look natural. She reminded herself this was Zach's camera and even if it wasn't him behind the lens, only this family would see the final photo.

Jasper's grip on her hip tightened, which grounded her mind. They were aware how much this asked of her, which was why they'd left the answer up to her.

The stranger finally finished, and Zach ran over to

take the camera and thank them again. Jasper pulled her closer and pressed his face into her hair. His hot breath caressed her skin, sending prickles down her spine.

"Thank you," he murmured. "I know that was difficult."

"I'm finding ways to cope," she said. "And hopefully someday soon, cope won't be in my vocabulary for these instances."

"I know it won't. I've got a whole lot of faith in you."

Her brow rose. "How much faith?"

"Enough to fill this state."

She turned her head, shooting him an incredulous look. "You're a little optimistic. Maybe you should settle for something smaller, like a small, optimized hard drive."

Jasper chuckled and lowered his voice, sending a tingle down her spine. "Can't do that if I'm anything but small. I could remind you of that by optimizing your hard drive."

Shira's face burned hot; an even greater heat pooled in her core. *God, do I hate what these two men do to me.* "You've really got to get better lines. That was terrible."

A wicked smirk curled up the side of his handsome face, tempting her. "No, I think that one was ideal, to spark your consideration to allow me access to your multi-touch interface."

The heat plaguing her intensified. She couldn't get the memories of him caressing her in game out of her head. This real body of hers hadn't been touched by anyone since the accident. And right now, it reminded her how much it craved what it missed. Desire crawled along her skin, whispering how easy it would be to convince

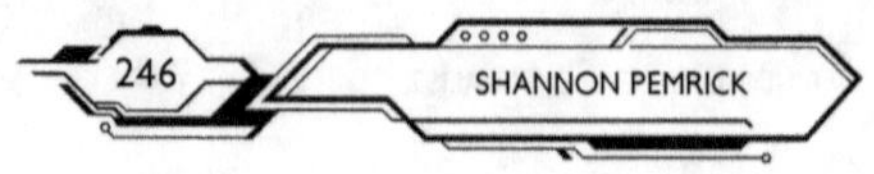

these two to go back to the house and lure them into her bed—or at least the bedroom.

A camera shutter snapped, jolting her back to reality. Zach lowered his camera and chuckled. "Sorry, did I ruin the moment? I couldn't help but capture your expressions."

"No, there was no moment to ruin." She rose to her feet too quickly, and she was entirely aware they made note. She sucked in a tight breath to clear her head and brushed the sand off her legs. "We ready to go?"

Jasper's gaze lingered on her before he turned to Serenity. She had gone back to playing with the sand, rather than paying attention to the building tension among the adults around her. "Ready, Starship?"

Serenity patted some sand on Jasper's buried leg and then jumped up. "Release the beast!"

Jasper roared and then thrashed, breaking apart the sand castle. He jumped to his feet, leaving a pile of "rubble" scattered around him. Serenity giggled and jumped for joy. Shira was convinced this was actually the girl's favorite part about building the sand castle.

When Jasper started swearing and jumping around, shaking his trunks, Shira found herself in a fit of laughter. *Seems he got a bit of sand in his shorts.*

"I'm going to need to take a good shower back at the house," he grumbled.

"That bad?" Zach asked.

Jasper grimaced and nodded.

Shira pointed toward the outdoor shower stalls a little way off. "You could always rinse with those in the meantime."

He shook his head. "Wouldn't help this issue."

Yikes! That was bad. However, she didn't feel overly sorry for him, since he'd chosen to be half-buried.

"Well, while you're doing a sand jig for the ocean gods, I'm going to go clean up our spot." Shira grabbed some of the sand castle gear. Zach and Serenity jumped in to help, and Jasper didn't lag too far behind.

They had their beach gear packed up in record time, and Serenity and Jasper put their clothes back on. Shira took the time to reapply her and Serenity's sunscreen again, though the little girl complained a bit, thinking she didn't need yet another application. Even though the girl already showed early stages of being able to tan as well as Jasper, Shira wasn't risking her getting a burn.

Serenity already had some red forming on her cheeks, and because Shira wasn't sure if that was just from her running around and playing, or from sun exposure, she wouldn't take any chances.

Of course, while Shira applied hers, since she burned so easily it was criminal, Jasper offered to get her exposed upper back. Shira quickly declined and showed she could get it done herself. She didn't trust herself around him right now. *Plus, I know how to work around my false skin.*

They may know about it, but that didn't mean she was comfortable going into detail about how he needed to be careful around the material.

After she was done, they headed for the car to put their stuff away, and then she led them to the restaurant. It wasn't overly crowded, and there were some tables available outside, overlooking the ocean, which she happily requested.

The food was excellent, like always, and the other three enjoyed their meals as well. However, Shira had to admit to herself, their company made it all better. Conversation was light and easy, as it always was with them. And even when there were teasing or heckling moments, it was all in good fun that didn't feel like an attack.

Now they stood on the pier, gazing out at the ocean. The sun set on the horizon, casting orange and red across the darkening water. Zach had gotten all kinds of photos, on and off the pier. Jasper thought he took too many, but Shira disagreed. Sunset and sunrise ocean shots were beautiful—magic, even.

Serenity poked her head through the railing next to Shira, looking for critters in the waves. They'd brought her into the small aquarium at the end of the pier, which then made her want to see if she could find any wild sea life, especially jellies. Since none of the adults in her life were going to allow her into the water to find out, she had to settle for this approach.

Nearby, Jasper and Zach leaned against the railing, Zach in Jasper's arms as they watched the waves roll in. The sun cast the perfect highlights and shadows on their profiles.

Shira tapped Zach's camera on her hip. She'd snagged it without warning from him, but hadn't used it yet, and Zach hadn't asked why she took it, or for it back yet. And she'd found the perfect shot for the two of them.

First, Shira pulled out her phone and took a snap of her own. Then she lifted the camera to her face and adjusted the lens as she needed. The shutter flashed several times before the two men took notice.

She smiled. "You're going to love those."

They both regarded her silently, making her blink.

What is going through their heads? She found out a moment later when Jasper reached out and grabbed her arm. Shira squeaked and found herself wrapped in his arms against Zach. Zach took the camera from her and clipped it to his shorts.

"Me too, me too!" Serenity cried out.

Jasper pulled Shira and Zach back a bit so Serenity could hop up on the railing and squeeze in with them. With her pinned there by the adult bodies, Shira wasn't worried the little girl would fall in.

Jasper pulled out his phone and angled it for a photo of them all. Shira found it easy to smile; to lean into both of them comfortably and not care about the tiny panicked part of her brain that seemed so distant today.

His screen flashed, and he took a look before approving the snap and sending a copy to both Shira and Zach. She made a note to add it to her background. It was the perfect place for that photo to go. And Snake wouldn't mind being replaced. He was on her locked screen display, anyway.

The four of them stood there on the pier, gazing out at the expansive water. Shira's mind reflected on the various events that played out today, particularly the ones that threatened all the rules. *What rules?* The truth was right there in front of her. Whatever rules she'd come up with to convince herself to stay safe were getting trampled on over and over, and she wasn't sure when it all truly started.

Definitely not today, when she didn't push them away every time they touched her. Not yesterday when they showered her with care and affection, even though they

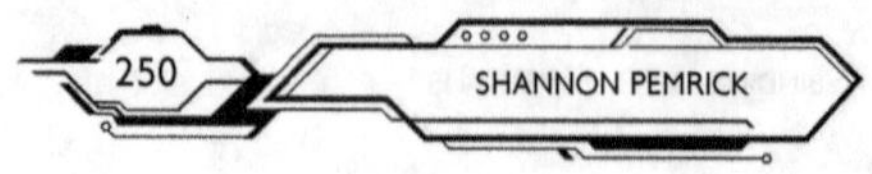

didn't deserve to deal with her lifelong problems. Not when she slept with them weeks ago in a VR game.

No, any of those may have been a turning point for things to open her eyes, but that wasn't the start. It happened before then, when she didn't even realize there was a war being raged on those protective barriers—a war to bind her heart.

Light warmth bubbled in Shira's chest. Truth was, she didn't care. She could admit to herself, she didn't want any of this to end. It felt right—all of it.

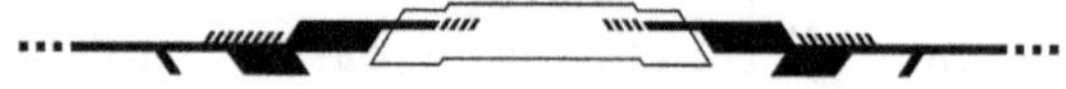

Excited barking greeted Jasper, Shira, and Zach as they walked up to the front door. *Snake, it's late, you need to chill.* Jasper adjusted Serenity in his arms while Shira unlocked the front door and lured a happy, spinning dog away from the threshold to allow the rest of them in.

Serenity giggled sleepily. Today's events had really worn her out, but she had fun every moment, and that made Jasper happy. He wanted her to make new memories every day during this trip, ones she'd never forget for the rest of her life.

Shira called for Snake to follow her to the back side of the house, most likely to let him out. His gaze fell to her swaying hips, hypnotic and tempting. His eyes traveled up her body, and he noted how well her shorts and shirt clung to her curves. The shirt hung off her shoulders in such a tempting way, he wanted to reach out and tug it a little lower. Low enough where—

As if reality thought he needed a cold bucket of water splashed on him, Serenity squirmed in his arms. Being a parent was rough. He just needed to get her to bed, and then he wouldn't need to worry about what Shira did to him.

"Daddy," Serenity moaned. "Put me down."

"No, I'm bringing you up to bed."

She shook her head and squirmed. "Not bedtime yet. I'm not sleepy."

Jasper gazed down at her. Serenity's eyes could barely stay open, and red banded over her nose. Both showed how much sun she'd been exposed to today.

"Why don't we put some cartoons on?" Zach suggested. "It's a good way to wind down."

Jasper didn't argue. He knew what his boyfriend was up to. Serenity would fall asleep on the couch and then they could move her to bed without any fussing.

He carried her to the back of the house. Shira was already outside with Snake. From the looks of it, he really needed some play time.

While Jasper situated Serenity on the couch and pulled up a show, Zach worked to understand Snake's meal prep, so he could handle that on Shira's behalf. She tried to insist she could handle it, but Zach wouldn't have it. The two of them would help where they could to make her life easier, even if it was through small gestures.

Jasper walked over to the back door and grabbed the ball in Shira's hand before she could throw it. She peered up at him but didn't relinquish the toy. "My turn."

Her lips twisted into an amused smile. "You can't take him home at the end of this visit. I need him."

Jasper's fingers slid off the ball, down to her wrist. Her pulse fluttered under her delicate skin. With his other hand, he reached for her hip and pulled her close.

Shira's body melded with his and her sweet perfume wafted off her in heavy waves as he bent close to her ear. "Then I guess we'll have to take you with us, too."

He caught the bob of her throat when she swallowed, and he continued, "We'll make sure all your needs are met." His teeth grazed her ear. "Every last one of them."

Shira's mouth parted, though no words escaped her.

"Daddy, can I have some water?" Serenity mumbled.

Jasper did his best to control his breathing and irritation. It was his fault for getting too eager when she wasn't asleep yet. "Of course, pumpkin."

He pulled away and pointed at Shira. "Stay there. We'll finish this discussion in a moment."

Shira regarded him with an expression that screamed mischievous, and then threw Snake's ball. "I'm getting a beer. Anyone want anything?"

Of course she'd move. She would be disobedient any time she got the chance. But that only made things easier for Jasper. "I'll take one of mine."

"I'm good," Zach said.

While he pulled a water bottle out, figuring it'd be safer in the event Serenity fell asleep, Jasper followed Shira's movement to the back of the kitchen and down the short hall leading to the dining room. She disappeared halfway down the hall into the pantry.

Jasper quickly filled the bottle with water and delivered it to his daughter. She sleepily smiled her thanks and went back to watching her show. Jasper stepped away and glanced Zach's way. He was feeding Snake. "I'm going to give Shira a hand. She's been gone a little long."

Zach turned and shot him a curious look, but nodded. Jasper quickly slipped through the kitchen and ducked into the large pantry. Shelves filled with non-perishables spanned across the left side of the room, a long counter and wall cabinets matching the kitchen spanned the other side. Wine racks and small casks were stacked on the counter. At the back end of the pantry were some glass-door refrigerators.

As for Shira, she stood on the counter, rummaging through a top shelf of a pantry, muttering to herself. Jasper cocked his head and his face screwed as he tried to figure out the sight before him. "What are you doing?"

Shira gasped and grabbed the edge of the cupboard when she teetered backward. Jasper's feet were moving before he could think, and his hands grabbed a hold of her hips. They let out a relieved breath in unison.

"Don't scare me like that!" she hissed.

"Scare you? I just walked in and saw you doing a trapeze act."

Shira let out a snort. "I'm only standing on the counter. Nothing crazy about that."

"Sara used to do this, too," Jasper muttered. "Why can't you ladies just ask for help from someone talluh?"

She looked down at him with a raised brow. "Because I live alone?"

His shoulders dropped when he let out an exasperated breath. "Zach and I are here. You could have told us something was out of reach. Hell, at least use a ladduh or something if you're gonna be so stubborn and do it yourself."

Shira's gaze remained far too innocent. "Climbing on the counter is more fun."

Oy vey. Jasper's head dropped back. "Why do you have to be like this?"

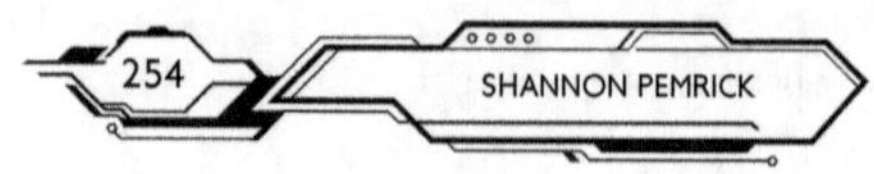

"Because it wouldn't be Shira if she wasn't difficult," Orion said.

Shira shrugged, not denying the AI in the least, and went back to her previous searching. "You know, Jasper, you can let me go."

"I don't trust you to not fall." That was only partially true. He more just wanted to touch her—and she knew it.

"Uh huh, sure. That's why I was fine until you came in and startled me."

"Do you want me to pull you down and take ovah this search of yours?"

She pursed her lips, her eyes narrowing, and then went back to her rummaging.

"What are ya looking for, anyway?" Jasper asked.

"Zach's IPA. He only had one left in the fridge, and I wanted to get some more cooling for him. Zach said he put it on the top shelf, but I can't find it."

"Oh, that's because you're in the wrong cabinet. One to your right."

Shira furrowed her brow and checked. Buried behind some other bottles were the ones she had been searching for. "Fuck me. I checked this one, too."

Jasper grinned. *Be happy to.* "I'm sure they were easy to miss."

She made an unconvinced sound and grabbed three bottles. Shira tried to hand one off to him for assistance, but he refused.

"Hold onto all of them. I'll lift you off the countah."

Shira's eyes widened. "Are you crazy?"

He grinned. "No, just confident in my abilities to hold on tight."

As he hoped, her cheeks flushed pink. And if he did this next part right, it wouldn't be the only part of her.

Repositioning his hands on her hips as well as himself to accommodate for her weight shift, Jasper tugged her toward him. Shira sucked in a sharp breath of air, muttering how stupid she was for doing this while wrapping her arms tight around her bottles. Then her feet left the counter, and she fell back into him.

Jasper was quick to move his arms up and catch her around the waist, holding her tight against him. Slowly, he released his grip, allowing her to slide down his body until her feet touched the floor. Shira put the bottles down on the counter and murmured something that Jasper didn't hear.

Her soft heat against him teased and tempted. He pressed his face into her silky hair, inhaling deeply. Salt mingled with her sweet scent.

Shira froze. "Jasper?"

"Hmm?" Jasper dipped his head, burying his face in her neck.

Shira's breath came out shallow and fast. "What… what are you doing?"

Jasper's hands slid up her arms, the difference between real and artificial barely noticeable. "Finishing our discussion from earliah."

"Discussion?" She hissed when he trailed his fingers over her shoulder blades and down her spine. "I don't remember anything left needing to be discussed."

"Oh, there's a lot to talk about." Desire simmered under his skin, straining his voice. He was hard and ready for her and would take her here in this room without

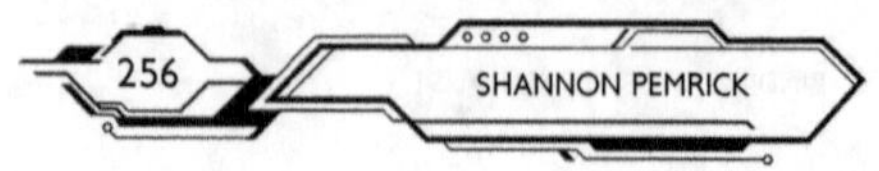

hesitation if it meant seeing her writhe underneath him. "Though, discussion is a loose term."

Jasper's teeth grazed her ear, earning him a hitch in her breath. However, it was a kiss to her neck that earned him a satisfying stifled whimper. She could try as hard as she wanted to be stubborn and keep him at arm's length, but Jasper already found the cracks in her wall of rules, and she wasn't fixing them fast enough to keep him at bay.

"Do you have any idea what I want to do to you right now?" The strained gravel in his voice was foreign to his ears. It never got this bad with Zach. Then again, he'd never had to ever hold back with his boyfriend.

Shira swallowed. Her mouth parted, but when his fingers skimmed along her heated skin, her jaw clamped shut, as did her eyes.

Jasper chuckled and kissed her neck again. "Well? I'm waiting…"

Without pausing, he kissed her again, and then again. Up her jaw on the right side, then switching to her left. He nibbled and teased her soft flesh. His hands roamed toward her front. Jasper wanted to memorize every inch of her and hear—

Shira gasped and suddenly jerked away from him. She stared wide-eyed at the floor, her hands on her stomach. Then, before he could say anything, she pushed around him, grabbing a cold bottle of beer she'd previously taken out, and rushed out of the room. She banked a right toward the dining room, rather than left to go to the kitchen.

This left Jasper standing in a confused daze. *What the fuck just happened?*

CHAPTER 15

Taking one panic-flooded step at a time, Shira flew up the stairs. She didn't register where she was going. Her brain was too overwhelmed to care, except: *Run.*

She reached the landing and ended up in front of a door. Shira didn't stop to process which room it was. She just opened it and entered, shutting the door quickly behind her.

Her back hit the hard surface, her breaths coming quick as her pulse thundered in her ears. Her legs wobbled and threatened to buckle underneath her, yet she managed to stay up. Shira's hands touched her sides, only the non-cybernetic side registering any sensation.

Jasper had wrapped her up in his spell until her cybernetic broke the magic. The artificial nerves Narissa had installed for that portion of Shira's setup had malfunctioned several times. The most recent one happened days before the convention. Since she would be dealing with the stress of being at the convention, Shira and Narissa agreed it would be best to keep the artificial nerves deactivated. This would also allow Narissa more time to research what was causing the malfunction.

Of course, today, it created an unpleasant, jarring reminder of how much of a freak she was when Jasper touched her there. To go from full sensory to none in a single moment, how was she not supposed to react to something so jarring?

Shira took a deep breath and looked around, finding she'd closed herself off in the studio. The corner of her lips quirked up. Of course, she'd instinctually come here. She may not be a designer like her parents, but she got enough joy from creating her own designs that it improved her mood. This room was a safe place to calm down without anyone bothering her.

She pulled out the project she was working on for Serenity. Someone may say this wasn't healthy for her—that she was using this as an avoidance tactic to not address her problem, but Shira disagreed. She just needed to get herself calmed down so she could eventually reflect and work herself through things.

Angelica had taught her many ways to approach these situations, even when she'd rather avoid them. And Shira knew she'd have to use them if she ever wanted to live better. And she did.

Shira pulled out earbuds from a small drawer on a workbench. *I haven't come this far to crawl back into that hole.*

Popping in her earbuds, Shira had Orion pull up her favorite playlist. She bopped to the tempo, losing herself in her work.

Cut this foam triangle.

Shira nodded away.

Glue this fabric and pin it with this piece here.

Her body swayed in rhythm of the beat.

Double-check the tracing of the template.

Shira lost track of how long she worked, but she'd managed a fully assembled, unpainted leg piece when she sensed a large presence behind her. She turned, and upon laying eyes on Jasper's looming form, she gasped and jumped back. Jasper blinked and took a step back himself.

Shira ripped out an earbud and placed a hand on her chest. Her heart hammered hard under her skin. "You scared me!"

He chuckled. "I can see that."

She took a deep breath to calm herself. Unfortunately for Shira, that meant she became more aware of his presence and how he currently presented himself. Water dripped from his hair, indicating he'd taken his intended shower. And he'd swapped out his swim trunks for night pants. The most distracting detail, though, was his lack of shirt.

It'd been hard enough at the beach not to stare and appreciate the hard work he put into keeping himself fit, but this close up? Every inch of her tingled, and she wondering what it'd be like to just once drag her fingers along each peak and valley of rock-hard muscle.

Shira turned her attention away a little and pulled out the other ear bud in an attempt to disguise her effort to avoid visual contact with him. She hadn't had the time to process what happened in the pantry. "What's up?"

She hoped her words sounded casual enough.

"Checking on you," he said, moving in a little closer

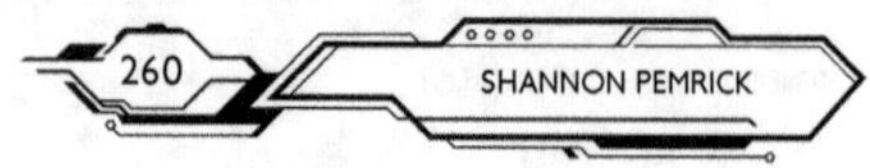

than she'd have liked. "You've been in here for almost an hour and a half. I was concerned."

Oh really? Her brow quirked up. "You were concerned?"

Jasper rubbed the back of his neck, and his attention flicked to her work for a moment. "And annoyed."

And there it was. She knew there was more to it than that. Shira grabbed a foam spike she'd created. "Because of earlier?"

She wanted to kick herself. *Why did I say that?* She should have let the conversation die. This would encourage him to bring all that up, and she didn't want that.

"Not quite. That was more confusing than annoying." Jasper drew closer. Shira felt the heat of his body teasing her, yet he didn't touch her. "I was annoyed because you never came back down. I thought you were hiding. I was wrong."

Well, not entirely… She wouldn't voice that. The sooner she shut this down, the better. "I just got caught up in this little project. I didn't even realize I'd been up here for so long."

Jasper drew up next to her, his eyes lingering on her before shifting to the piece she'd worked on. "What are you doing?"

Shira debated keeping her secret project just that, but since it wasn't going to be finished when she wanted, she figured it couldn't hurt to reveal things to him. "I'd been working on a special cosplay armor for Serenity."

His attention returned to her, eyes showing his interest.

"The idea sparked because of the conversation about her costume. I'd never done a full armor set before, so I thought I'd have a crack at it." Shira shrugged. "Unfortunately, Serenity had the growth spurt, and I didn't have the time to alter things before you three arrived. And completing something this week is out of the question for me, so I've decided to continue to use it as a test project and will donate it to my parent's holiday charity auction next month."

Jasper smiled. "That's a great thing for you to do. Thank you for trying to make it for Serenity. I'm sure she would have loved it."

Shira lifted a finger to her lips. "Just don't tell her. I'll make another one in time, hopefully better planned around growth spurts."

He laughed. "Yes, that's the difficult part. Feels like every time I blink, she needs new clothes. I'm looking forward to her slowing down."

Shira looked him up and down. "How tall was Sara?"

"About Narissa's height."

"Then, I'm going to say she might make it to my height." Even though she'd been a model, Shira was considered "short," by their standards at five-eight. Mercedes even had an inch on her. "So, expect her to still be growing well into her early teen years if she's as unlucky as I was."

Jasper grimaced. "How bad will it be?"

"For her? As long as it's gradual and not rapid, like some people I knew, she shouldn't find it more than annoying and exhausting, rather than painful." Shira shrugged. "For you, though, hard to say. Anita and Flynn caught me at the tail end of my growth and never complained. But all the foster homes I was in"—she snorted when all those memories surfaced—"well, let's say they hated how I inconvenienced them by needing clothes all the time. Sometimes I was forced to wear clothes that were too small until social services found out."

Jasper's brows pulled together. "They didn't take you away immediately?"

Shira gave him a long look. "Like I said before, the system failed me a lot." She shook her head. "But, anyway, I think you and Zach will handle Serenity's growth fine. Just be mindful of how much she has and be prepared to donate what she outgrows."

Jasper smirked. "So basically, what we do now."

Shira nodded. She really wasn't sure how to prepare the two of them for this. Her past couldn't be referenced, and it wasn't like she had any children of her own. Shira lined up the spike in her hand with the main part of the leg armor. She wouldn't think about that.

Jasper puffed out some air and murmured something under his breath she didn't catch, before reaching out and touching her elbow. "Hey, can we talk?"

She paused, unease creeping along her spine, and forced herself to look at him. "About?"

"What happened downstairs."

Knew it. Shira refocused on her work. "No."

He sighed. "Shira—"

"I said no."

Jasper's grip on her elbow tightened, and he sucked in a breath. "At least tell me what I did wrong. You seemed to be okay with everything until you ran off. If I over stepped or misundahstood and made you feel pressured, I'm sorry."

Shira jerked her elbow free. "You didn't do anything wrong." *Really, it was enjoyable until that reminder…* "This is something I have to work through."

"Let me help. Please?" he begged. "Whatever it is, I can try—"

"No." She wasn't going to budge on this. "You can't fix me, Jasper. I have to do this on my own."

Jasper's brows pulled together. "I'm not trying to fix you. I just want to offah my assistance."

Irritation rose in her. "I told you, no."

"I won't letcha run away from this problem."

Her emotions spiked into full anger at the accusation. She set livid eyes on him. "I'm not running from anything."

"Then why the hell are you up here?" There it was, the true reason for his "concern." She knew there was more to it than that. "You didn't mention this was your plan when we got back, so why is it now the sole focus of your attention for nearly the last two hours?"

Shira's hand slammed down on her worktable. "Because I needed to calm down!"

Jasper's eyes widened, and he took a step back. She continued.

"You don't know me like I do, Jasper. You can pretend all you want to know how to fucking fix me, but you know jack shit! I know how I am when I'm worked up. I know I can't talk myself out of a cycle, so I give myself a distraction until I'm in a better headspace to address what set me off and how to improve my thoughts and reactions to such situations again."

Sorrow and shame cracked their way through her rage. "You've got no fucking clue what it's like to live like me. You don't know what it's like living like some robotic, inhuman freak and having that reminder thrown back in your face every single day."

Shira's chest constricted. She wanted to stop before she said too much, but the words were already flowing.

"Every day I wake up with something wrong with me. Each day I wake and wonder which cybernetic is going to malfunction next—which one is going to be the next one to stop allowing me to feel human like my side mods have."

Tears pricked the corners of her eyes. She wouldn't cry. He wouldn't be the reason she fell to weakness.

"You'll never know what it feels like to lose yourself in VR, not because it's fun, but because it's the only thing that comes close to allowing you to feel alive. So, fucking excuse me for reacting so poorly when I was reminded of that fact downstairs and chose to handle all this my way. Because I can guarantee you, how I'm handling this now is nowhere near how I would have three months ago, so don't you dare accuse me of reverting back to that place. I'm trying!"

Jasper sat on her workbench, his eyes never leaving her. Without words, he reached out for her. Shira slapped him away. "Get out."

He tried again, and she refused his touch. "I said leave! You have no right to remain here. I will not play your stupid games."

Still without speaking, he made a third attempt, and this time he grabbed a hold of her forearms. Jasper tugged her to him, and as hard as she struggled against him, her strength was no match for his. She fell into his chest, her face sliding perfectly into the crook of his neck. Jasper wrapped a powerful arm around her back, and in one fell swoop, tucked his other arm under her legs, pulling her up into his lap.

With his potent presence surrounding her, Shira's control on her emotions shattered. Tear streamed down her cheeks, bringing all the pain and fury she felt to the surface. Every word she spoke—every moment she experienced the turbulent emotions that came with her situation, it all came crashing against her broken walls and she couldn't stop it.

Shira sobbed into Jasper's hot skin. Her body shook, unable to handle the agonizing chaos of emotions writhing through her.

The physical and mental anguish she suffered daily.

The suffocating loneliness that had encased her heart and pulled her down into the pits of despair, snuffing out all light and hope.

Everything Shira had ever experienced since that day now crashed out with her wave of tears. Was she angry? Sad? Defeated? Shira didn't know. She couldn't pinpoint a single emotion as it swelled in an uncontrollable tide.

She wasn't sure how long she cried for. But her crying did come to an end. Shira sniffled, her body aching. Her emotional well was dry. It hurt being this exposed—this raw.

As her senses returned, making her state even that more painful, she realized Jasper wasn't the only one in the room with her now. No, not just in the room—right behind her.

Jasper's fingers were firmly tangled in her hair while his other hand stroked her back. Another set of hands touched her shoulders. She knew this touch. *Zach.* When had he come in? She hadn't heard the door open.

His fingers bit into her one real shoulder, massaging out the tension. Her neuro-mod registered his attempt

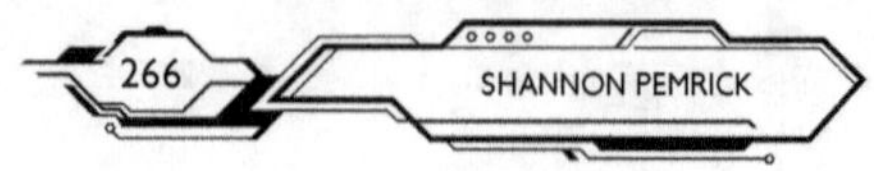

to do the same to her cybernetic side, and she couldn't figure out what the point was.

"Shira," Jasper murmured. "It wasn't my intention to be the reason you cried. I nevah want to be the cause of your teahs unless they're attached to something uplifting. That said, I want you to undahstand, you don't have to go through all of that alone."

"We're always here for you," Zach said. "You only have to take our hands and we'll support you in any way we can."

"When did you get here?" Shira kept her face hidden. She didn't want them to see the state she'd been reduced to.

"I ran up here the moment I heard the yelling start. I wanted to help where I could."

Jasper's finger glided through her hair. "It's all we evah want to do for you. We want to help you in any way we can, as long as you let us."

Shira hadn't wanted them to see just how broken she really was. And yet, here they were, trying to reassure her—offering themselves in any way they could to help piece her back together. No matter how long it took.

Jasper pushed her away and made her look at him. He ran his thumbs over her still-wet cheeks, wiping away her remaining tears. "There's nothing wrong with you, Shira. Your cybahnetics don't make you lesser."

His voice lowered, taking on a gravelly edge that sent prickles down her spine and made her exhausted heart skip. "You're a raging fire storm that cannot be—no, shouldn't be tamed."

Zach's fingers skimmed across her skin, heating her veins. When he, too, spoke, his tone sent her pulse into an erratic frenzy she experienced through her whole body, revitalizing its sapped strength with needy anticipation it had craved earlier today. "You're a type of storm deserving of worship."

Shira swallowed, sexy and tempting implications bouncing in her mind.

Jasper leaned closer, his hand sliding under her hair and wrapping around the back of her neck while the other trailed fiery sparks up her arm. "You'll see it one day, and we'll staht that process by showing you."

His hot breath caressed her lips before his mouth claimed hers. Shira couldn't stop a quiet moan from escaping as her body molded into him.

The kiss wasn't soft or gentle. It was hard and full of the same want building inside her. Zach's lips pressed against her spine at the base of her neck, making her gasp. The moment Shira's lips parted, Jasper took advantage, swiping his tongue sensually against her lower lip before plunging deep.

Shira moaned again and threaded her fingers into Jasper's thick, wet hair. Desire hummed under her skin, spreading from her core all the way to her extremities.

Jasper's hands slid down her arms, migrating to her sides—only her real side registering the touch—and then to her hips. Shira let out a startled squeak when he grabbed her tightly and stood up. Their kiss broke, and instinctively, Shira wrapped her legs around him for support.

"What are you doing?" she managed to ask, her voice breathless.

"This isn't the right place for this," Jasper said, his voice even more strained than before.

Not the right place for— Shira didn't need to finish the thought. She knew what her body wanted, and it was clear if she didn't stop this, the three of them would be doing the horizontal tango. "Are we sure about this?"

"I think we all know the answer to that," Zach said. His vibrant blue eyes had darkened with overpowering lust that sent a deep throb of desire through her.

Shira told herself that one time in VR was the one and only time—that nothing could come of the three of them in real life. But now, those doubts were buried underneath all the desire. Maybe they couldn't have something permanent. Maybe they could. That didn't need to be something she thought about right now. She didn't need promises for tomorrow to enjoy what these two men offered her right now.

"Where is Serenity?" Last thing she needed was the girl to walk in on them.

"Asleep on the couch," Zach said, leaning closer. "Alistair is on standby, in case she wakes up." He brushed his fingers over her cheek, and she leaned into his gentle caress. "Don't worry, she won't interrupt us."

He kissed her without allowing Shira to respond. She sighed into his mouth, tasting the lingering bitterness of hops on his tongue.

Shira pulled away. "Please tell me you're sober."

Zach chuckled, running his thumb over her lower lip. "I only had one ale, and I finished it shortly before coming up here. I wouldn't risk giving you any extra reasons to refuse me."

"I'm not looking for an excuse to refuse either of you." Shira had done that long enough up to this point. She couldn't do it again to herself.

"Good." Jasper tightened his grip on her and headed for the door. Zach slipped past him and opened it, then closed it quietly behind them.

Jasper crossed the long hall in what felt like only a few strides, and then they were in their borrowed room. Shira's fingertips tingled with anticipation. She didn't know what to expect from them or even herself. She merely wanted to indulge.

Jasper didn't bring her to the bed as she expected. Instead, while standing in the middle of the room between the bed and the door, he loosened his grip on her thighs. Shira slid down his hard form at an agonizingly slow and tantalizing pace until her feet touched the floor.

Zach's body pressed up against her back, pinning her between the two men. They weren't much taller than her, Jasper being the tallest by maybe four inches, and yet their presence seemed so much larger now.

Shira's eyes closed as two sets of hands found her hips and then roamed her body. Each deliberate touch, some firm and possessive, others light and teasing, simmered her blood. Any moment their caresses came in contact with her inactive false-nerve cybernetics, it threatened to jar her out of her enjoyment and make her want to pull away, but they'd soon follow up with a touch she could experience, canceling out her flight instinct.

Zach pressed his face into the back of her head, inhaling deep, and then migrated down her spine, his mouth sending bursts of sensation through her. Jasper dipped his head and kissed her real shoulder.

Both their hands slid across her prosthetic side, undeterred by the hard and ungiving nature. If anything,

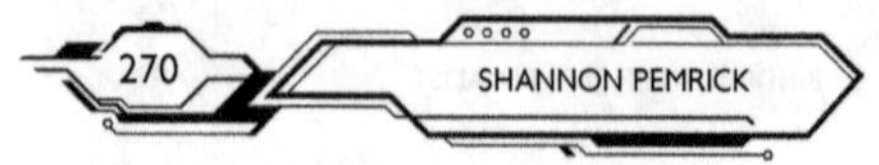

she swore her neuro-mod registered them being a little rougher, as if that side of her weren't the broken one.

One of them touched her false skin. A part of her was uncomfortable with them feeling the material hiding just how bad her condition was, but at the same time, she couldn't find the words to direct them away from those areas. It wasn't like the illusion remained once they felt the hard acrylic underneath.

Jasper's hot mouth traveled to Shira's collarbone, trailing bursts of pleasured electricity across her skin. His hands trailed up her stomach until they reach the hem of her top. Shira sucked in an anticipating breath. Jasper grinned against her skin and teased her just under her shirt before pulling away.

Shira let out a slow breath. Zach chuckled close to her ear. "He's good at that."

"Contrary to whatcha might think," Jasper said, resting his fingers on her low neckline between her breasts, "I do enjoy taking this slow."

Zach wrapped his strong hands around Shira's arms and pulled her close. He chuckled again, the vibrations of his chest rolling through Shira in ways that ignited her veins. "You mean taking *her* slow."

Jasper smirked, his eyes gleaming as he stared down at Shira. "No, that'll be fast and hard, like she enjoys it."

Shira swallowed and clenched her thighs together, desire pooling deep in her core.

Jasper slipped his fingers into her crop top, and before she realized what he was doing, her strapless bra popped open. In a slow movement, he slid the bra sideways off her breasts, deliberately grazing her sensitive flesh. She sucked in a tight breath through her teeth, making him smirk. He then pulled the bra out of her shirt and dropped it on the floor.

Jasper's eyes slid from hers to her lips, and then farther down. Shira swallowed, knowing full well the shirt alone couldn't hide her taut nipples. They'd seen her yesterday braless in a shirt, a hint at what lay beneath, but this time, it felt so different.

Shira bit her lower lip when Jasper ran his thumbs over her breasts. Her shirt did nothing to save her from the heated trail. Jasper made a wide arching path, circling in a spiral motion, but just as he reached her taut and aching nipples, he reversed his motion. The action teased but promised no release. She fought against the urge to lean into his touch. She wouldn't beg. Not yet, at least.

"Enjoying this, babe?" Jasper said.

Her breath nearly halted, as did everything simmering inside her. Shira narrowed her eyes. "I've told you not to call me—"

Jasper cupped her chin and pressed his thumb against her lips to silence her. "He's got no power over you, Shira. You're gonna reclaim that name."

Shira swallowed. She'd gone so long hating any reminder of Jeremy, could she let this go too?

Zach's tongue grazed Shira's ear, making her pulse skip. "And we're going to claim rights to call you that instead."

Her heart slammed against her ribcage. That promise made this arrangement feel more permanent than she was ready to believe in.

When she didn't offer up any protest to their decision, Jasper's grip loosened and his fingers trailed down her neck, over her collarbone and then hooked into the neck

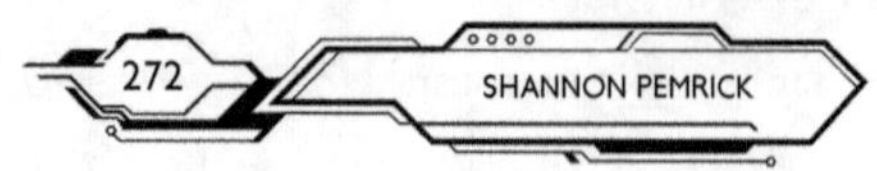

of her top. With a devious smirk, he tugged. Cool air hit her breasts as they spilled out of her shirt.

His touch dragged down her heavy breasts and flicked over her aching buds. Shira suppressed a moan but failed to stop her body from jerking into his touch. Jasper grinned and repeated the action, this time also play-flicking the dragon-scale shield rings decorating the undersides of her nipples.

A tingling sensation spread from her sensitive peaks, sending a wave of desire down her core. Shira clenched her thighs together. It didn't go unnoticed by either man.

"You added extra decoration today," Jasper said, his voice strained.

Yesterday she'd gone with a standard bar. It reduced any extra pain she might experience in the event the jewelry caught on something.

Shira's tongue swiped across her lips to wet them, though the motion captured Jasper's gaze and he followed, the green in his eyes deepening with his growing lust. "Extra? No. Why would you think that, Jasper? That would imply I'd done it for someone other than myself, and expected this to happen."

Zach released his grip on her arms, and trailed his fingers down, reaching her sides, and then lower, dipping under the band of her shorts. "No, of course you wouldn't do any of that. Just like you wouldn't ever hide any more little secrets, or allow me to do this."

Shira swallowed, and words failed her when his fingers slid along her skin and working cyber nerves. Zach reached for the button of her shorts, and before she could blink, he'd popped the button and tugged the zipper. His large hands swept around the inside of her shorts and shoved them down her hips, with her panties. Her clothes pooled at her ankles.

Without looking at her now-naked lower half, Jasper scrunched Shira's shirt in his hands and lifted it. She didn't resist, raising her arms and allowing him to remove the top with ease. He carelessly tossed the item of clothing somewhere and took a step back, taking in the sight she presented.

Heat prickled Shira's skin. Her breathing kicked up a notch; pulse hammering hard in her burning veins. Shira's mind struggled to decide between feeling shame and desire. She swallowed and forced herself to speak. "Sorry, no piercings lower than my navel."

Jasper's appreciative gaze swept over every inch of her. "I don't mind in the least."

Zach pulled away. "View from back here is great, too."

Hot desire simmered under Shira's skin. It'd been so long since someone had looked at her this way—the real her. Even with her share of issues with Jeremy, attraction and verbalizing such had never been an issue for them.

But even still, the way these two ate up every visible inch of her, even the prosthetic parts—she couldn't quite put into words how good it felt to be given this.

Zach's hands wrapped around her wrists and lifted her arms above her head. He pressed his body against hers and Shira took advantage of the position to wrap her arms around his head. Zach bound her wrists together with one hand, the other trailing down her arm to her waist with feather-light touches.

"This view is even better," Jasper said, taking a step closer. He grabbed her hip, the opposite side of her that Zach was claiming, and pressed his bare chest against hers. The heat of his skin seared hers in the most pleasant of ways.

Jasper tilted his head, but not toward her. His mouth captured Zach's. They both groaned, and Shira was tempted to as well. With her arms still around Zach's neck, she had the perfect view. Her eyes pinned on the way the two kissed—hungry, yet a little sweet, too.

Shira bit her lip and put in every effort she could not to squirm. This was hot, and her simmering desire built up from all this teasing was driving her crazy.

Zach and Jasper's hands glided over her body, circling her breasts before flicking her aching nipples. Shira's breath hitched, a pleasurable jolt shooting down between her legs. In a more in-sync motion than she thought possible between two people, Jasper and Zach played with her aching buds, rolling and pinching in a maddening rhythm.

Shira moaned and allowed herself this time to lean into the sensation, desiring more. She needed their touch—their pleasure. And with both men's mingling scents of hickory and cedar surrounding her, her senses were overwhelmed.

Jasper broke his kiss with Zach and grinned down at her. "Have something to say, babe? Or you just enjoying the show?"

Their touch never let up, making it hard for Shira to form words. "I'm thinking about how underdressed you two are making me feel."

"Underdressed?" His brow spiked. "I think you're puhfect."

"I know," Shira said with a smirk, trying her damnedest to make herself see the way they saw her in this moment. "And I want to extend that to you both."

She would have emphasized her request by touching them, something she really wanted to do, but with her wrists still bound, Shira could only rock her hips side to side, grinding her ass into Zach.

He hissed out a strained reaction. "Okay, okay, you're getting impatient."

Shira chuckled and made a figure-eight motion with her hips. "Oh, I'm not impatient. You don't want to see me get to that point."

Shira felt the hard promise under his pants each time her rotation pressed hard into him. Zach groaned from the tease and couldn't resist her temptation. He released her and whipped off his shirt, tossing it somewhere. Jasper, for his part, didn't move, only watched with cocky amusement. Shira was going to change that.

She reached for them both. Her fingers splayed across both their naked torsos, their skin searing hot under her touch, and powerful muscles flexing. She didn't linger, even though a part of her really wanted to stay and appreciate their hard work.

Her hands trailed down to their pants, her fingers sliding underneath the band without hesitation, and slowly pulling them at the front. There wasn't much give for Zach's stiff shorts, but still managed to give enough to expose his boxers. And Jasper—Shira discovered quickly that he'd gone commando after his shower.

Zach removed Shira's fingers and took her place, slowly unbuttoning his shorts. Shira inclined her head, having no shame in watching. "I pegged you as a boxer-briefs kind of guy."

His clothes dropped to the ground. Shira's attention fell to his now-freed erection, and her teeth caught her

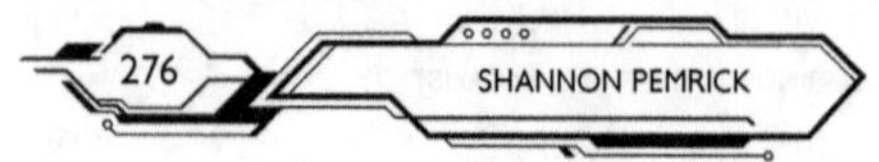

lower lip. He was as impressive as she'd imagined, and she was certain his game avatar wasn't far off from reality. And that made her eager.

Before she could reach for him, Zach grabbed her wrist and yanked her into his solid form, the motion ripping her fingers from Jasper's pants. Her back pressed against Zach's hot, hard skin and his firm erection pressed against her. Her breath hitched.

Zach wrapped firm fingers around her hips. "Nah, that's usually Jasper."

Both of them glanced Jasper's way. He'd tucked his thumbs into the band of his pants, but hadn't removed them yet.

"Hmm, I mixed you two up. That's disappointing."

Zach's fingers dipped lower to her thighs. "Don't worry. We won't penalize you too hard this time."

Shira bit her lip, her veins sizzling with his teasing touch. *So close, but so far.* "Are you sure? Feels pretty penalizing to me."

"Trust us, you'd know a penalty from us," Jasper said before he shoved his pants off his hips, his rigid length springing free. "Now, babe, you seemed to have gotten impatient. I hope you're ready."

Shira swallowed and had to resist the urge to squirm. He was just as amazing to look at as Zach. Length and girth accompanied by strong muscle all over. Need plagued every inch of her. God, she didn't care what they did, she just wanted some relief.

Jasper closed the distance between them, his firm body pushing her into Zach. His hard erection pressed against her belly, and the heat of his chest burned her bare breasts in the most pleasant of ways.

Shira reached for him, no longer able to hold herself back, but Jasper caught her wrists. Irritation flashed and then overpowered her desire. *If he thinks he can—*

"Not me," Jasper said, pushing her hands behind her until her hands pressed against Zach's hips. "Him."

It was an awkward angle, but not too much of an issue for her. "And what do you get out of that? It's not like you could watch from this angle."

Her thumbs slid across the sensitive skin of Zach's upper groin area. He let out a hiss through his teeth, and his fingers around her thighs tightened.

Jasper grinned. "I'm not too worried."

His hands slid up her neck, cupping her jaw, and he leaned in, capturing her lips in a tender kiss. Shira let out a pleased sigh. This wasn't what she expected of him, but she wasn't going to complain. Especially not with Zach's hands also roaming her lower body, simmering heat in her veins.

She allowed her hands to explore Zach, trailing her fingers out to his hips and then back toward his hard member, but not quite touching it yet. In response to her teasing, Zach did his own, trailing feather light touches along her inner thigh with one hand and traveling the curve of her ass with the other.

All the while, Jasper's touch became hungrier. His hands slid down to the hollow of her neck, and then lower until his fingers flicked over her aching peaks. Shira moaned, arching her back into his touch. He circled, pinched, and flicked her aroused nipples, sometimes tugging her jewelry, jolting pleasure through her down to her core. She wanted more.

Jasper's tongue dragged over her lower lip, and she

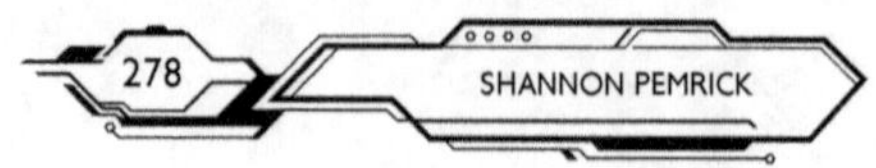

parted her mouth to allow him entry. He took the invitation, no hesitation, and greedily plunged his tongue into her mouth, consuming what little senses Shira had left.

Shira voraciously kissed him back, tasting everything he offered, as if the moment she came up for air, she'd wake up and this would be nothing more than a moment in her dreams.

Desire pulsed between her thighs, driving her forward. Her hands ceased roaming Zach when they trailed back in from his hips. Her fingers grazed his swollen member.

Zach pressed his forehead into her hair and groaned. "Damn, Shira, are you going to continue to drive me mad, or are you going to stroke my cock?"

Jasper allowed her to come up for air, though didn't let up on her breasts. Shira breathed in deep, her pulse beating in her ears. "I didn't realize you could be so vulgar. I expected that from Jasper."

"Oh, you haven't heard anything from either of us yet," Zach said in a strained voice. "And I can assure you, Jasper is still the most vulgar, just you wait. We're not holding back on you anymore. Now, are you going to continue to ignore my request?"

She bit her lower lip and made another teasing stroke on Zach. "Whatever happened to ladies first?"

He sucked in a tight breath and slipped his fingers on her inner thigh, between her legs, into her wet heat. Shira gasped, pleasure coursing through her as he stroked. The sensation was better than she'd anticipated. Better than in-game's perfection? Not possible, but her deprived body sure was convinced.

"Why didn't you tell us what we were doing to you?" he murmured. "You're dripping all over me."

"It's more fun if you find out in the moment."

Shira slid her palm up Zach's hard length before wrapping her fingers around him and giving a firm yank. He groaned into her neck and rewarded her with more attention, stroking her in a maddening rhythm that built heat in her core and spread through her body. He nipped at her skin, sending quick, amplified bursts of desire across her body in the opposite direction of the work from his hands, overwhelming her senses, but not bringing her quite to the edge she now craved.

Not to be forgotten, as if she could with his hands fondling her breasts, Jasper dipped his head again and captured her lips for a moment before tilting lower, across her cheek and down her neck—her cybernetic side at that.

"Jasper," she whispered out, Zach's attention making it hard for her to focus on words. "You'd be better off on the other side."

Jasper ignored her and pressed his lips against the partially obscured acrylic surface. Her neuro-mods activated, and sent a flash of information to her brain that she struggled to comprehend. It was like not even the primal side of her could process their insistence to give this damaged side of her attention.

Zach's other hand, that had been on her ass, slipped between her legs from behind and plunged deep inside her before she registered what he was doing. Shira's breath hitched and her eyes popped. The sensations he fed her were both familiar and foreign to this body of hers. Sure, she took care of herself when she couldn't supplement with an in-game hookup, but this was nothing like what her vibrator could give.

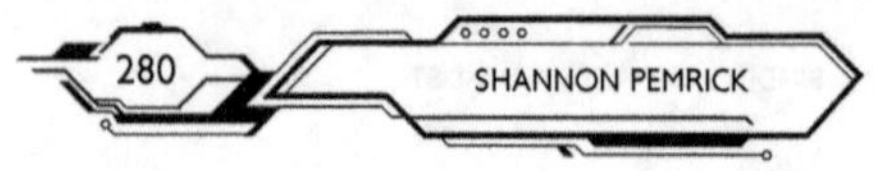

"Feel good, babe?" he murmured, his hot breath on her neck sending tingles down her spine.

"Yes…" she moaned out, rocking her hips into his touch. "More."

As if she were speaking to him instead, Jasper sunk to his knees, his mouth trailing down over her collarbone, between her breasts, and then to the sides of them. His tongue flicked out, teasing sensitive flesh near her nipples as he continued to play with them. Shira arched her back the best she could without pulling away from Zach's touch.

Shira threaded one of her hands into his hair, not easing up on her strokes on Zach, his hard member swelling more and more under her controlled touch. She drew Jasper in, craving more, and he eagerly obliged. He captured her swollen peaks, sucking and biting. His teeth tugged at her jewelry again. She moaned and rocked between both men's attention, unable to do anything more as desire overpowered her.

Her head tipped back and a wild eruption of pleasure burst through her. Jasper reached up and clamped a hand around her mouth to muffle her scream, yet neither eased up to silence her prematurely until she rode out her orgasm.

Shira's breath came in quick bursts, her body relaxing into Zach. He pulled his fingers away from her now-extra-sensitive flesh, and held her close by the hips. Jasper hadn't released her breast yet, and it took Shira a moment to realize her fingers were still tangled in his hair, holding him captive.

Her hands fell away, yet he remained. His gaze met hers and a wicked grin spread over his face. Shira's heart lurched in her chest and then she gasped when his tongue flicked over her sensitive tip. It instantly hardened into a needy peak. "Jasper…"

Zach chuckled, one of his hands fondly rubbing her ass. "Did you think we'd be done with you after that?"

Shira clamped her eyes shut, Jasper's attention increasing, sending confusing signals through her spent body. It made it difficult for her to think and form a response. "It's not that. I just…"

She bit her lips and muffled a moan when Jasper's thumbs traced her quivering inner thighs. "It would be nice to have a moment of rest between."

Jasper sucked hard and then released her with a *pop*. "We don't do that here, babe. Not when we have two more planned for you."

Two more? Shira swallowed. "What do you think this is, Lusara Fates?"

He chuckled and pressed his lips against the skin between her breasts, kissing a trail down to her belly. "Of course not. This is even bettah."

His words hummed across her skin, and Shira's breath hitched. *Better?* She would laugh if the reignited desire coursing through her wasn't overpowering her ability to process logic and reason.

Zach extracted himself out of her grip, grabbing Shira's attention. His fingers lazily trailed over her back, and then he reached for something. She would have looked to see what he was after, if it weren't for Jasper nipping at her hip. He then trailed hot kisses toward her cybernetic hip, dipping low toward the apex of her thighs in a teasing manner.

Shira bit her lip and suppressed a whimper when his

mouth activated her artificial nerves. The attention filled her with heat but also discomfort. There was something about this type of attention *there* that prevented her from fully giving in to the pleasure.

As if sensing her thoughts, Jasper paid heavier attention to this side of her, so much that her initial reaction began melting away and the desire building in her amplified.

His mouth eventually trailed down her leg and then over to her inner thigh. Anticipation tingled in Shira's fingertips, down to her toes.

When Jasper flicked his gaze up to her, she held it. "I'm not going to taste like pineapples."

He grinned. "No, I'll bet you taste even sweeter."

His tongue flicked out, and she gasped when it teased her sensitive and ready heat. He chuckled and murmured confirmation about her tasting sweeter, before plunging his tongue into her wetness.

Shira closed her eyes and tilted her head back, moaning along with the wave of pleasure he sent crashing through her. She tangled her fingers in Jasper's hair and urged him closer, demanding more.

Jasper's tongue circled and flicked back and forth in a maddening pattern. Shira rocked into him, losing herself in the carnal indulgence. "Jasper…"

His fingers found her inner thighs and teased her sensitive nerves, even her artificial ones. Shira wasn't even aware they could be this sensitive.

She panted for air the longer Jasper continued, his thumbs teasingly sliding along her folds in rhythm with his tongue. Heat simmered under her skin and desire fogged her mind. Jasper nudged her legs to spread them more, and in her desire-drugged state, she complied. It took Shira a moment longer, but only when she heard the ripping of foil did she realize the request hadn't been for Jasper's needs.

Firm, warm muscles of Zach's chest pressed against Shira's back; the hard evidence of his arousal pressed along the curve of her ass. His hands ran down her sides to her hips and Shira bit her lip, anticipation kicking up her heartbeat.

Zach paused for a moment, his cock teasing her a moment longer, before he buried himself into her. A deep, primal moan tore through Shira and Zach together. Shira's grip on Jasper's hair tightened, who refused to let up on his pleasurable assault with his mouth.

"God, you feel amazing," Zach moaned, rocking his hips and plunging in and out of her pulsating, needy core. Shira swore he grew larger and harder, filling her completely. It wasn't enough.

She rotated her hips, driving him deeper, without pulling away from Jasper, though she doubted he would allow that, with his firm grip on her thighs.

One of Zach's hands reached up and caressed her breast, teasing her sensitive, aching buds, before pinching them. Shira bit her lips.

"Like that?" Zach asked.

Shira nodded, finding it hard to form words. "More. More."

He answered her plea with harder thrusts, mixing pleasure and pain in a delicious symphony.

With his unoccupied hand, Zach slipped his thumb into her mouth, Shira instinctively closing around him and sucking. He smirked against her ear. "Yes, that's it, babe. Enjoy everything we're offering you."

She was. God, she was. So much pleasure, she struggled to keep up where to focus her attention.

Jasper sucked and licked her clit harder, more greedily, and Zach's rhythmic thrusts increased. Shira panted, her pulse beating in her ears and her core burning hotter and tighter, clenching around Zach. She threw back her head, eyes squeezing shut, as another orgasm tore through her in a strong, hot erotic release. "Zach…"

Zach's thrusts became stiffer and punctuated until he, too, grunted and plunged over the edge of climax.

Shira's breath came out in quick, agonizing gasps, her legs weak and threatening to buckle underneath her. Zach steadied her while Jasper slowly released his hold and rose to his feet. He leisurely wiped at his mouth, as if relishing her lingering taste on his tongue.

Reaching out with both his hands, Jasper pulled Shira from Zach and wrapped her in a firm embrace. "My turn."

She swallowed, her mind and body heavy with the pleasure still coursing through her. "Why not take Zach?"

Her breathiness made the words sound a little more pathetic than she'd intended, but she wasn't sure she could go another round so quickly. *Five-minute break… maybe ten.*

Jasper lowered his arms and lifted her under her ass, bringing her above his eye level. She gasped and wrapped her arms around his neck, only giving him access to hers. He eagerly kissed the hollow of her throat as he walked backward to the bed. "Later I will. But I've waited too long to pass you up now."

Shira's heart skittered, her overwhelmed mind begging her to think too much into those words.

Jasper settled on the bed. Shira's legs slid comfortably on either side of him, her knees resting on the mattress. Jasper kissed her skin again and reached out for something beyond them. Shira assumed it was a condom. She could have told them it wasn't necessary unless they were concerned about anything other than pregnancy, but she wasn't ready for that conversation. She still struggled with that reality herself.

Jasper pulled away just long enough to roll the rubber on. He slid his hands up her thighs and gripped her as she hovered over him. His thick cock pressed against her quivering flesh. "Remember what I promised earliah?"

Shira swallowed and nodded. How could she forget?

He grinned. "Good."

Jasper entered her fully in one deep thrust. A strangled cry tore through Shira, one she couldn't quiet in time and hoped it wouldn't wake Serenity. She wasn't used to holding back.

"That's it," Jasper murmured, pulling out almost all the way before plunging back into her. "Enjoy this, babe. Feel me filling your tight, greedy pussy."

Shira's breathing labored with each hard thrust. Her breasts brushed against his chest with each bounce of her body, sending sparks jolting through her.

Jasper's thumbs slipped between her thighs, rubbing her slick, sensitive clit. Shira moaned, her body jerking both away and toward his touch and pleasure, completely overspent and confused to how it could still demand more. Her mind fuzzed, hot desire blanketing all her senses.

"You like this, babe?" he murmured, nipping her ear. "Do you enjoy feeling me pound deep inside you?"

"Yes," she moaned. God, did she. This was nothing like before. It was like she was fucking different men.

"Good. I'll make sure you'll be moaning my name this time."

And she did. Before she knew what came over her, Shira pressed her faced into Jasper's neck, moaning his name, and muffling her screams as once again her body convulsed in a wild frenzy of explosive gratification.

Jasper kept her moving, pain and pleasure slamming through her in matching bursts. His grip on her tightened and then he groaned her name, "Shira."

His body shuddered and convulsed as she milked him. Her body rocked on autopilot, not wanting to stop now that it had started. Not until Jasper withdrew from her and pulled her against him.

The two of them fell back on the bed, Shira on top of Jasper, and they stilled, their ragged gasps filling the quiet room. Numbness and exhaustion weighed on Shira, her body shuddering with remnants of her pleasure. Jasper's grip around her hips remained strong. When sensation finally returned to her limbs again, Shira tried to roll off him, but his grip tightened.

She paused, concerned she may have been too careless, and moved the wrong way. Avatars didn't have the same drawbacks of real bodies after sex, and it wasn't like she was used to being mindful of her cybernetics in such positions.

When one of Jasper's hands trailed up her back with an unmistakable amount of pressure, she tried harder to push away. "What are you doing, Jasper?"

He gazed up at her with a lazy, pleased gaze. "You know. We don't fuck and run here."

Shira frowned. This wasn't good. "And I've told you both I don't—"

The bed dipped beside them, and Zach's arms snaked around Shira's waist. She squeaked when he pulled her from Jasper's grasp with no resistance from him, and found herself sandwiched between the two men.

"Don't keep lying to us, Shira," Zach murmured in her ear. The heat of his breath caressing her, mixed with their bodies molding around her, sent new tingles of desire through her exhausted body. "You cuddled with me in-game."

She tried to glare at him from the corner of her eye. "We didn't. We talked between rounds."

"You sat in my lap, curled up in my arms." He buried his face in her hair. "Just because I pulled you there, doesn't mean it wasn't post-coital snuggling of some sort."

Shit. She hadn't even thought about that. And she couldn't deny he probably caught onto her lie soon after she accepted. Shira could joke they were idiots, but they were far from it.

Jasper brushed a strand of hair out of her eyes. "If you've got some sort of reason why you don't want to, that's fine. We'll respect that. Just don't lie to us about the reason."

The problem was, Shira wasn't sure where she stood with them. She honestly loved cuddling, maybe more than the sex itself—*No way*—but it came with feelings of attachment.

It sucked not having that connection with someone.

Any time she hooked up with someone, she made certain to prevent any attachment. Any time she was even remotely lax on that rule, problems arose. But the last thing she wanted was to prematurely attach herself deeper than she should, only for it all to be yanked away.

Yet, she couldn't voice this to them. The fear of admitting things right now gripped her like a vice, and left her unsure what to do.

"Shira?" Zach murmured. "Do you want us to let you go or not?"

She did… but the idea of telling them that made her chest ache, and the meaning behind that scared her more than just allowing this to happen.

Shira repositioned herself so she was more comfortably sprawled across Jasper's chest while still curled against Zach. "You'd better have enough room in these arms of yours. I take up a lot of space."

Jasper's chest rumbled under her, vibrating down to her core. *Shit, what do these men do to me?* It was like her avatar body, bouncing back quick and ready for another round. "We're well versed in handling a tight fit."

Yep, I'm a goner. Shira forced her eyes to roll and adjusted her position to make it seem like she was getting more comfortable rather than hide any potential ability of what he was doing to her.

Jasper reached out and slid his hand up her cybernetic thigh, and for a moment, she worried he'd caught on already. But he merely pulled her leg to rest over him, keeping his grip firm on her.

Okay, so maybe he wasn't aware, though this position didn't help her much. It added a possessive edge to the cuddling that she didn't hate. *I need to distract myself before I do something I regret.*

Shira slid her hand over Jasper's chest to his arm and traced an intricate dragon tattoo that started around his wrist and ended at his elbow. The ink was fantastic. Whoever he'd gotten for an artist was incredibly talented. Some of it reminded her of Kane's work, Kiara's friend and tattoo artist.

Shira had met him a few times. He was a nice guy with a bit of a troubled past, and had an amazing artistry talent. It didn't matter if it was a digital drawing, paint on canvas, or ink on skin, Shira swore the man could do it all.

Her fingers slid back to Jasper's chest, where a lone tattoo depicting a dagger and rose detailed his skin. The design differed greatly from everything else he had— more specific, as if it had a meaning not like the others.

"What does this tattoo represent?" she asked.

Jasper's chest rose and fell under her as he took a deep breath. "It's Sara's memorial tattoo."

Shira's trailing halted for a moment, but only for a moment. Her finger traced one of the delicate petals, her eyes catching the detail of dew on them. A part of her screamed this was inappropriate; that she had no right to ask for such personal information. However, an even stronger part desired to see more of this man than she had ever dared to—the past that shaped him. "Tell me more about it."

"Sara had wanted to get a tattoo longer than I'd ever known her. It made her obsessed with the few I had when we met, and all my plans to cover myself in them. But something held her back." He ran his hand up her

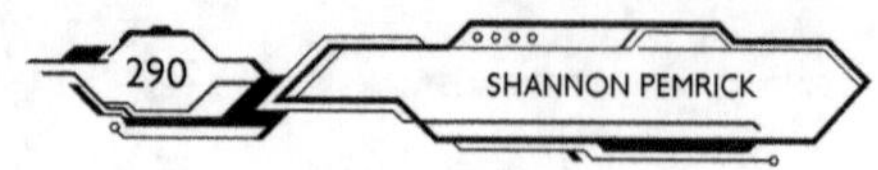

thigh, side, and then her arm, stopping to rest it on her hand, yet he didn't halt her tracing. "It wasn't until after we were married did I finally convince her to get one. I promised to get one with her, to make that first leap the easiest."

Jasper chuckled. "But, as luck would have it, just before she went to make the appointment, she found out she was pregnant, putting everything on hold until Serenity was born."

"Where did she end up getting the tattoo done after Serenity came along?" Shira asked.

Jasper frowned, and a knot formed in her stomach. "She never got it. At first, I thought she was going to continue to put it off since she was breastfeeding. You know, safe rather than sorry. But then it came to light Sara was struggling with body image issues. And the fact she had to have an emergency C-section didn't help her mindset. That became our priority to work on, the tattoo becoming a reward for her."

Shira looked up at him, noticing the bittersweet smile on his face. "In a strange turn of events, she turned to modeling to help her."

Shira blinked. "She was a model?"

He nodded. "And a damned good one, if you want my biased opinion."

Shira laughed.

"It helped her." She calmed at his words. So soft and gentle. Even today, her choice not only made an impact her on, but on him.

The situation made her think of Tanya. "I'm not surprised. My friend Tanya, she also had self-esteem issues after her pregnancy. C-section scar, too. She'd tell me how it all compounded and made her feel like a terrible mother."

Zach shifted on the bed. "Damn, it's like you just plucked out a conversation we had with Sara."

Jasper nodded, his gaze contemplative. "What did your friend do to help her overcome it all?"

Shira pursed her lips, trying to remember all the things her friend did. "Most of it was just sheer willpower and learning to love her new body. The rest came with me helping her write up a proper contract that prevented agencies from covering up her scar."

"You can do that?" Zach said.

"Thanks to laws put into place these past few decades that better protect models, yeah. It comes at the risk of fewer modeling gigs, but a model can put anything they're not comfortable doing in their contract, so they don't find themselves forced into those situations."

Shira turned her attention to Jasper, to find him contemplative again. "Jas?"

He shook his head. "I'm fine. Thinking."

She pursed her lips, tempted to ask, but then thought better of it. It wasn't her place to push. Instead, she refocused the topic back to the tattoo. "So, how did you get the idea for this?"

"It's a combination of what we were going to get separately. She wanted a rose. I wanted a dagger to start the Lusara Fates sleeve. After I lost her, it felt right to combine them and have them close to my heart."

Shira's throat tightened. That was a powerful gesture. And now that feeling of wrongness seeped in deeper. She didn't have a right to touch the tattoo. It was too precious—too loving for the likes of her.

Zach reached out and rested his hand on top of theirs. "Tell her what you plan to add to it."

Shira's eyes popped, and a flicker of panic rose up. *He's adding to the memorial tattoo? Why?*

Jasper laughed. "Easy, Shira. No one died. This tattoo may have started off as a memorial, but I don't want it to remain that way. Instead, I want to turn it into a visible detail of what I hold the closest to me. A Monster Hunter piece for Serenity. A Lusara Fates warrior motif for Zach."

His thumb caressed the back of her hand. Shira's heart went racing, her mind running away on her with wild ideas there was more to the addition… one that had nothing to do with any of his family members. "And—"

"Jasper, I apologize for interrupting," Alistair's voice cut in. "But I'm afraid Serenity is awake and I can't stall her anymore. She's looking for you and is hungry."

Jasper groaned. "Couldn't you have waited another minute?"

"I'm afraid not. At this rate, she's going to run up the stairs and barge in on all of you."

Shira yelped when Jasper flew up, throwing her back into Zach. He launched to his feet, grabbing his pants and throwing them on as fast as a model dressed. While impressed, she glanced at Zach in bewilderment.

He seemed to know her unspoken question and shook his head. "No, she'd knock first. We made sure she got into the habit early. He's just now in overprotective-dad mode."

Shira snorted. "Doesn't take much for him."

Jasper shot her a warning look before slipping out. Zach chuckled and extracted himself from her to dress as well. Before he slipped out, he bent over and kissed her temple. "You know what he was going to say before Alistair interrupted."

Then he left, leaving her sitting on the bed, her hand pressed to her chest while her heart pounded against it, threating to leap out. Various emotions twisted and turned inside her.

The last few days had been fun. The attention they'd given her had been quite eye-opening, but no less amazing. And the sex? Incredible. She could get used to the kind of attention they'd provided so far. But did she really want to go down that road and interpret all of it for possible deeper meanings, instead of just taking it as something superficial and temporary?

Am I ready to?

CHAPTER 16

With one last slow pull of her hair straightener, Shira tossed and teased her warm strand into place. She hummed quietly as she did, finding herself in a rather good mood this morning.

Her body felt light, as if tension she hadn't been aware of before had been lifted. She was tempted to believe it had something to do with yesterday, but shook the thought immediately. *It was sex, Shira, not some life-altering experience.*

Though, even as she chastised herself, she knew she didn't believe that for an instant. She'd slept with plenty of men who had such inflated confidence about their skill, they were sure they'd ruin her for anyone else. Yet, none left an impression on her like Jasper and Zach. If she wasn't careful, they'd ruin her before she realized it had happened. *And when they leave you behind after they're tired of you—*

Shira shook her head. *No!* She refused to let those

thoughts creep in. Even if this turned out to be a "just for fun" thing, it would be fine. It didn't make her unworthy of affection or that the pretty words they spoke were lies. They wouldn't be trying this hard to help her if it was all to tear her back down. Shira knew them. They were better than that.

She let out a frustrated sigh and leaned on the counter. She was so tired of this emotional whiplash. Hot, cold, hot, cold. *Just pick which side of the line you want to be on, woman!*

Shira sucked air into her lungs in one deep, determined breath and stared at her reflection. "You are worthy."

Her gut clenched, but the uncomfortable feeling didn't last; strength bloomed in her chest, replacing the negative reaction. No one had told her to add this to her daily routine. The talk about Sara, and subsequently Tanya, brought back the memories of Shira trying to help her friend through her insecurities.

Daily words of affirmation in the mirror were something Tanya had sworn helped her the most. She came up with a list of words she needed to believe, and use a different affirmation every day, repeating them every week in a random order each time.

Shira was going to try it—every morning, no matter how stupid she felt doing it. Jasper and Zach had managed to make her feel in the moment what they claimed to see in her. Now it was her turn to see it, too. If she could do this, she could face her uncertainty around them. *Mercedes has a point; this is the only thing in my life I don't take charge of. I need to be better. I deserve to have what I want.*

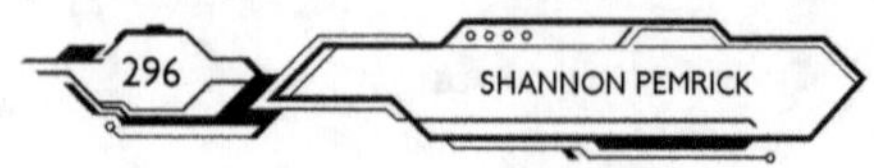

Something crashed downstairs, then someone swore. Shira's brow spiked. "Uh, Orion?"

"It was Jasper," her AI said. "He dropped a skillet."

She blinked. *What use does he have for a skillet?* Shira knew he and Zach were awake. They'd woken earlier than usual for some reason. It forced her to finish her morning coffee quickly and get herself into her room to get ready for the day before they came down and saw her.

Her hand reached up and grazed the false skin she'd applied to her neck. She knew she should forgo it. Hiding behind the material wasn't doing her any favors. And it wasn't like the guys didn't know how bad her cybernetic need was now. But she wasn't ready to let this mask go yet.

"What are they doing down there?" she asked her AI.

"Making breakfast."

Her mouth salivated at the mention of food.

"You should hurry down. They seem quite eager for you to eat with them."

Shira pursed her lips. "Why? It's just breakfast."

"I don't think it's necessary for me to spell it out for you."

Apparently it was, because Shira, for the life of her, couldn't understand why they'd be so excited. "Pretend I'm the clueless one out of the three of us."

"I don't understand the reasoning behind your response. Don't you remember when you used to cook for Jeremy and how you felt when he would tell you he liked the meal?"

She leaned against the sink, thinking back. "Not really. All my memories of us eating together were us going out or ordering in. How many times did I ever cook for him?"

Her AI didn't respond right away. "It appears my early memory storage only recorded three times."

Orion was new to her back then, but even she had sprung for the best AI model at the time. His storage was accurate. "No doubt that was early in our relationship, when it wasn't utter crap. And I know, even when it wasn't, he never attempted to make me food."

"I apologize, Shira, it wasn't my intent to upset you. I remembered the joy you experienced those times he complimented your cooking."

Shira pursed her lips. "Does it make you happy when I'm happy?"

"As I'm an AI and don't have emotions like humans, I can't claim to feel that emotion. However, based on what I am able to process, yes, I do come to the AI equivalent of happiness. It is my job to ensure you have what you need in life to thrive. Emotional security is one of those needs. Any time I sense your happiness, I know I have performed as needed, and thus I always strive to ensure this is an emotion you experience often—even if this means I must fight your stubbornness."

She laughed. For a human, that response would have been entirely selfish, but it made sense for an AI. "Thank you, Orion. I'm glad I have you in my life."

"Likewise. Now, go downstairs and allow those two men to dote on you."

Shira rolled her eyes at the mention of "dote" and left her bathroom. When she made it to the ground floor, the sound of Jasper and Zach conversing carried from the kitchen, along with Serenity's occasional input. As quietly as she could, Shira padded down the hall and peered around the corner.

Serenity sat at the island, a plate of food in front of her. She munched away on a strip of bacon. Snake lay at her feet, watching for anything that may fall on the floor that he could snatch up. Zach stood in front of the stove and flipped something on the skillet. Next to him, Jasper whisked something that sounded like eggs in a bowl. Shira leaned against the wall to watch. This was one of the few times she'd been able to witness just the three of them be the family they were.

Jasper reached out and pulled Zach against him, planting an affectionate kiss on his temple. Zach leaned into the touch. The tenderness between them brought a smile to Shira's face. She remembered her conversation with Zach when he'd confessed his doubts about Jasper's feelings toward him. She hoped he'd finally overcome that insecurity. There was no way he couldn't see just how much Jasper loved him.

"Daddy, can I have another bacon?" Serenity asked.

Jasper glanced at his daughter. "You finished all four pieces already?"

Serenity nodded and smacked her lips together.

Jasper shook his head. "Then you're going to have to wait. Zach and I haven't had any, and we need to make sure Shira gets some, too."

Serenity deflated in her seat, pouting at her plate, which Shira could now see had two pieces of French toast piled on it. Her irritation didn't last long when she spotted Shira. "She-ra!"

Snake jumped to his feet and scampered over to Shira

at a pace only a dog would for his favorite person, demanding attention, which Shira of course gave him.

The guys turned, Zach speaking first. "Morning."

She smiled but didn't move. "Morning."

"How long have you been there?" Jasper asked, his eyebrow raised.

She shrugged and pushed off the wall finally. "A little bit. I wanted to observe. I don't get to see you three in your natural habitat."

Zach laughed. "We'd have to be back at the apartment to call this our natural habitat."

"I don't know," Jasper said, grabbing a slice of bread from the stacked pile on a nearby plate. "I could get used to this kind of living."

Shira tried to squash the flutter of butterflies that sprang up in her stomach. She wouldn't mind them staying. The thought of waking up with them around every day was an exciting prospect. Though, she couldn't be sure that's what Jasper meant. He could just like the home. It was certainly bigger than the family's apartment.

She scooted around the island. "If you ask nicely, I might be able to convince my parents to allow me to rent this place out."

Jasper leaned on the counter. "Does rent include a complimentary Shira?"

Shira laughed, heat threatening to rise into her cheeks with the implications forming in her head. She reached for a glass in a cupboard. "Default terms don't." Her eyes cut to them for a brief second before she filled her cup with water. "Though I'm sure something could be negotiated."

Shira repressed the urge to hold her breath. The

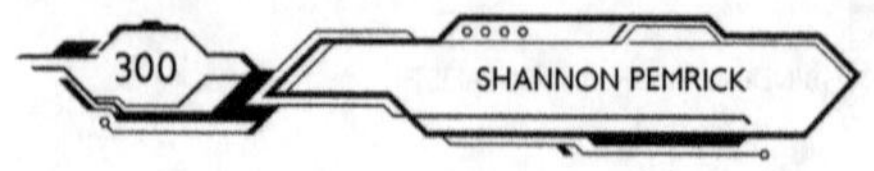

underlying tones of this conversation messed with her insecurities.

Zach flipped the French toast on his skillet before reaching out and tucking his finger into a belt loop of her skirt. He tugged her to his side. "What kind of negotiations are on the table?"

His body heat teased her, along with his interest. Instead of replying, she reached into a different cabinet and pulled out her medicine case. She normally made sure to take these before they saw how bad it was, but she didn't have the time before they'd interrupted her quiet, early morning. *Well, if I want to know they're going to be serious about this, seeing how bad it all is, is the only way.*

The two of them had already witnessed a bad pain day. They were going to have to see what she needed to do every day to keep herself healthy, where medical miracles weren't possible. And she would have to brace for the inevitable questions about what each pill was for. *Including the one I avoided the other day...*

"Sorry, negotiations are by appointment only," she said, pulling out of his grip.

Both men watched her slip around the counter, their eyes intent. Jasper handed Zach more bread. "We'd be happy to make an appointment. Calendar is quite free this week."

Shira sat down and glanced at the men for a brief moment before popping open Monday's medicine compartment. "I'll have to look at mine. It was fairly busy, last I checked. I don't usually do last-minute appointment squeezes." Her gaze flicked up. "But I think I can make an exception for you both."

Pleased grins spread over their handsome faces.

"She-ra," Serenity said. "Whatcha got there?"

Shira tipped her pills out of her case onto the island. Seven pills of different sizes and colors clattered on the hard surface. "My medicine."

The girl cocked her head. "You take medicine?"

Shira nodded while sorting the pills by size. Made it easier for her to take them. "Every day. I usually take them before all of you wake up."

Jasper set a stacked plate of French toast down on the counter, as well as the rest of the bacon he'd kept from Serenity. The freshly cooked smell of egg-glazed bread and crispy, fatty meat wafted into her nose, making her mouth water. He sat down next to Shira. "Do you mind me asking what it's all for?"

She shook her head. Shira would have been more surprised if he hadn't. "Immunosuppressants, pain management, and hormone therapy."

Zach finished cooking his last French toast slice and flopped it onto the waiting stack on the island. He then set down a shaker containing cinnamon sugar and a bottle of maple syrup on the island before slipping onto the barstool next to Jasper. "Why so much? I thought cybernetics would prevent the need for so much prescription drug requirements." He paused, and his brow knitted. "That sounded wicked insensitive, and that wasn't my intent."

Shira did her best to give him a reassuring smile through her growing discomfort with the idea of this conversation. She knew he wouldn't be intentionally insensitive. "It's a bit of a misconception that cybernetics are some miracle tech. I mean, yeah, they are a

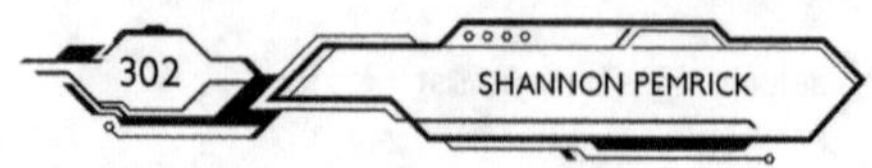

miracle in their own way, but that doesn't stop the need for other types of medicines."

"Do you mind telling us what each does to help you?" Jasper asked.

She scooped up one batch of pills and popped them with a swig of water. Doing it this way would help her just come out with it. "The immunosuppressants are so my immune system doesn't attack my cybernetics. A lot of people are lucky and don't need to worry about this. But, some of us have bodies that see the help as a foreign invader. Because so much of my body has been replaced with cybernetics, it wasn't a surprise."

"I'm not familiar with immunosuppressing medicine," Zach said. "Is the prescription weak? I would have thought you'd be worried about going to something like a convention where you'd run into so many germs."

Shira rocked her head back and forth. "Yes, and no. The ones I take do weaken my immune system enough where con-crud would suck harder, and any major illnesses could be scary for me if I caught it, but it's not strong enough to force me to stay away from people. The big thing about my particular prescription is that it's a bit more targeted. It was specifically created for those with cybernetics, so it… semi-reprograms the immune system to not see my cybernetics as invading objects. This reduces the chance it'll ignore other bodily threats."

Jasper leaned on the counter. "That's amazing. I didn't realize there was medicine out there that could do that."

Shira chuckled and scooped up her next batch of pills. "I hadn't either until I was put on them."

"What about the pain management?" he asked. "I

thought you only took pain medicine when you had a flare-up."

"The flares are when my pain management fails. Because of the extensive damage my body sustained, my nerves think there's something wrong everywhere." Shira took a deep breath to keep herself focused and calm, and swallowed the pills in her hand. "Most people understand the concept of phantom limb syndrome and other nervous-system-related pain disorders. Lucky cybernetic users will find their body adjusts and these conditions are only temporary. The unlucky, like me… we deal with it the rest of our lives."

Shira scooped up the last few pills she had, but didn't take them. Tightness had formed in her chest; self-deprecating thoughts poked the back of her mind. "I technically feel pain every day. But the medicine helps reduce it and numb me to the point I can ignore it. However, there are days my body overreacts and sends powerful signals the medicine can't combat. These are my pain-flare days. At this point, there's no magic medicine that will make it go away. I'll live with this the rest of my life."

Both the guys were frowning. It probably wasn't something they wanted to hear. She didn't even want to face that truth half the time, so she couldn't blame them if that was the case. But the truth couldn't be run from. She'd tried that already.

Shira turned to Serenity. The girl watched them, munching on a piece of French toast while holding it with two hands. It didn't look like she'd put any syrup on it. "Starship, since you're listening, do you understand what I'm saying? Do you have any questions?"

Serenity shook her head. "No, I get it. My friend has to take medicine, too. He hates it. Do you hate it, She-ra?"

Shira nodded. "There are many days I feel that way."

The girl munched down on her slice of eggy bread. "I'm glad they help you both, even if they are annoying. Same with your cybahnetics. It means you're able to be here, and that makes me wicked happy!"

Her beaming smile brought one to Shira's face as well. "Me too, Starship."

Shira tossed the medicine in her hand into her mouth, washing it down with more water.

"Shira, you're welcome to not answer my next question, because I know it's probably the most personal," Jasper said, licking his lips. A muscle in the back of Shira's neck tightened as she waited for the inevitable inquiry. "Why do you need hormone therapy?"

She chewed the inside of her cheek. Everything inside Shira screamed not to say anything, yet she had to face this—for her sake. And if the truth was too much for them to accept, then… *Well, it's not like there are any medical miracles right now that can change it.*

"The damage I sustained from my accident caused me to require a few cybernetic organs. But… there are some that haven't been successfully recreated, like kidneys, livers, and such. I lost one of my kidneys, as well as the attached adrenal gland. The kidney loss is something I've adapted to well, and normally the same would be said for the other adrenal gland, if it hadn't been damaged. It needs some extra help because of this, requiring me to get cortisol injections a few times a year."

Shira paused, making sure she worded herself right. When she managed to speak, the words tumbled out a little faster than she had wanted, giving away her feelings about this confession. "And I also lost one of my ovaries, enough of my uterus it couldn't be stitched back together and needed to be removed, and sustained damage to my remaining ovary."

There, I said it. Maybe she said it too fast, so they didn't hear her well enough, but that didn't matter. She said what she had to.

Her gut twisted under the confession, and her lungs struggled to keep her breathing, making her extremities tingle. It took all of her wits to not allow her body to tremble in front of her men. She was strong. She could handle this on her—

Jasper's strong arms wrapped around her and pulled her into a tight, almost suffocating embrace. "I'm sorry for the question I asked the othah day. If I'd known…"

Shira smiled despite the pulsating pain in her chest. "I know. I wasn't ready to say anything then."

"Daddy, what's a uterus?" Serenity asked.

Jasper released Shira and exchanged glances with Zach. Shira bit her lip, curious what they'd decide to do. Serenity was at a prime age to start talking about these things, but plenty of parents tried to hold off for various reasons. She also wanted to see if they'd be comfortable telling her, or ask Shira to do it.

Zach nodded, and Jasper sucked in a slow breath. "A uterus is an organ some people have that allows them to have babies."

Shira gazed at Jasper, impressed and quite proud the overprotective papa bear was willing to come out and say it.

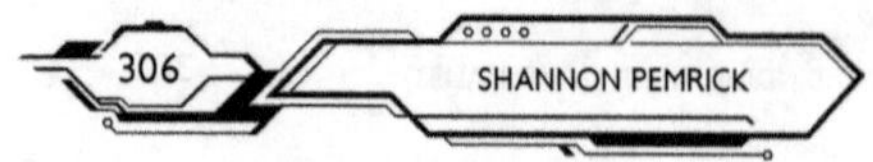

Serenity blinked slowly and then turned to Shira. "You don't have one anymore, She-ra?"

Shira took a steadying breath and shook her head. "Not anymore."

"So, you can't have babies?"

Shira swallowed. "No, I can't."

"Did you want them?"

Her fingers curled, and the answer nearly lodged in her throat. "Yes, I did."

The young girl looked down at her nearly empty plate, brow twisting, and then she hopped off her stool. She came over to Shira and held her arms up. "Then I'll be your baby."

Shira's chest swelled, and a flood of emotions tightened her throat. She gathered Serenity in her arms and hugged her tight, blinking back the tears pricking the corners of her eyes. "You… are so perfect."

Serenity snuggled into her arms in response. Shira kissed her on the head and held the girl for a moment longer before releasing her.

Serenity slid back down on the ground and looked at her dads. "She-ra is my momma now, for real."

Jasper and Zach both had goofy grins and eyes that shone with unmistakable affection. Jasper spoke, "We're not gonna say no."

Heat touched Shira's cheeks. Ideas of the four of them being a happy family tried to surface in the back of her mind, and Shira wasn't sure if she should really entertain such things just yet. It would be harmful to do something like that prematurely.

Serenity puffed out her chest. "Good, cause I was gonna even if you said no."

Shira choked on a laugh. The guys, on the other hand, didn't contain their amusement.

"She's acting like Shira already," Zach said. "You'd never know she hadn't raised our Starship all these years instead of us."

But it was Jasper who undid her. He winked at Shira. "See, bad influence."

Shira bent over and lost it on the island counter. "I'm not sorry."

"I'd be concerned if you were," Jasper said, making her laugh harder.

However, their fun was short-lived and Shira sobered when Zach's phone rang and Alistair spoke. "It's Stacey. The call is work-related."

Zach and Jasper exchanged disgruntled glances before asking their AI to answer the call. Shira did her part by looking to Serenity and placing a finger to her lips to let her know she'd need to be quiet. The little girl smiled and nodded. She climbed back onto her stool to eat the remainder of her breakfast. Shira took the moment to feed herself as well.

"Hey, Stacey," Zach greeted, his tone flat.

"Good morning," she said in a too-chipper mood. "Jasper is with you, yes?"

"Yeah, I'm here," Jasper said. "We're having breakfast."

"Good. You'll need that energy."

The three of them exchanged glances. *What is this woman planning?*

"You haven't booked us for interviews, right?" Zach asked hesitantly.

Stacey let out a barking laugh. "Always a jokester, Zach. Of course not. I'm calling with good news, not painful ones. I've been provided information about the tournament."

The guys' backs straightened. Even Shira paused to listen. It'd only been a day and a half since the fire. The convention organizers weren't messing around.

"The convention will resume in three days," Stacey said. "There's a lot of information on what will change for online and in-person, as well as mention of the convention extending by two days. I'll forward the entire document to you both to look over. The most important part is about the tournament. That will continue to be held at the convention center. There shouldn't be any issues with the match lineups unless a team has to pull out due to the delays."

Both Jasper's and Zach's phones *pinged* with what Shira assumed was the promised information.

"I don't expect you two will need to pull out, as it's only a two-day extension to the convention, but I'm also aware of your daughter's school needs. Please look everything over and let me know immediately how you two plan to proceed. Tri-com has assured there won't be any penalization if you two do need to pull out of the tournament, given the unexpected situation."

"Thanks, Stacey," Jasper said. "We'll go over this immediately after the call."

"Good. I won't hold you up. I know you two wanted this to also be a vacation, but I expect you both to put in extra practice to make sure you're on top of your game if you do stay in the tournament."

The woman hung up without another word.

"Well, at least that wasn't too painful," Jasper muttered as he pulled up the information Stacey had sent.

"I'm surprised she hadn't made any comments about you two not practicing the last day and a half," Shira said before stuffing her face with a strip of bacon.

"That's because we've been getting in late-night practices," Zach said. "Might as well take advantage of the time-difference sleep issues."

Shira's brow rose. "What do you mean you've been staying up late? By the time we've gone to bed, it was already late your time. And you've both gotten up at half-decent times in the mornings, as if you'd gone to bed at an appropriate time."

Jasper chuckled. "Technically, we have been waking up later than we normally would our time."

Shira stared at them, now suddenly concerned. She'd always gotten on their case in the past for being awake when she was getting ready for bed, but she hadn't realized how bad it was. "Do you two ever sleep?"

"A few hours," Jasper said in a far-too-casual tone.

Shira shook her head. "Unacceptable. Not while you're under my roof."

Zach and Jasper passed an unreadable look between them, Zach speaking. "And how do you plan on doing that?"

Shira ate more of her breakfast. "I'll figure something out. But you two aren't going to like it if you decide to keep up with your stupid schedule."

The two exchanged skeptical looks, but they didn't understand what Shira would resort to in order to ensure they had a good night's sleep.

"Well, while you think about that, we should plan out today, and the next few days," Zach said. "Now that we know the status of the tournament, we will have to do

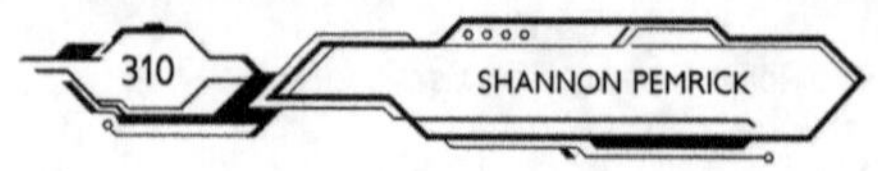

a bit more practicing than sneaking them in at night."

Shira's phone went off, and she checked the text message. It was from Kane.

> *Sorry it took me so long to get back to you. There's been some movement on my schedule, so I wasn't sure what I could tell you. I have a bit of free time after Kiara's appointment tomorrow, if that will work.*

What perfect timing. Shira looked up from her phone. "Why don't we do something fun this afternoon together, and then tomorrow I have a girls' day with Serenity? I might even give Mercedes and Narissa a call to join us. This will give you two a chance to practice for several hours without worry."

Serenity gasped, and her eyes sparkled. "I wanna do that!"

Jasper chuckled. "I have no reason to say no to that request." He looked at his phone. "My parents have been asking about spending time with Serenity, since they miss out on so much. I could talk to them about taking her for a day as well. That'll give you time to yourself too, Shira."

She shrugged. "I don't mind spending time with Serenity while you two work. But I'm also not going to stop grandparents from seeing their grandchild."

Serenity deflated on the counter. "I don't want to go. I want to spend time with She-ra…"

"Starship, you never get to see your grandparents," Zach tried to reason. "It'd just be for one day. Then you can spend all the time you want with Shira the rest of the week we're here."

"He's right," Shira said. "It would make your grandparents so happy, and I know you'd have a lot of fun with them."

The little girl huffed. "Fine… but I want to pick what we do today."

The three adults shared amused glances. If that was all it took, none of them were going to deny her.

"What do you want to do today?" Shira asked.

Serenity threw her hands into the air. "Mini golf!"

Shira nodded. She liked the idea. The guys also didn't object, making sure to tell Serenity they loved the idea, which made the girl smile brightly.

"I'm going to call my parents," Jasper said.

He slipped out of the room and Shira texted Kane back about the time he had tomorrow open for the little surprise she wanted to do for Serenity.

She also texted Narissa and Mercedes through a group chat to see if they were interested in going out. Mercedes got back to her almost immediately.

I'd love to get together. Takashi and I don't have any plans.

Narissa came in a moment later.

I'm busy in the morning, but my afternoon is free.

Shira typed back.

Great! Serenity is going to be so happy.

Mercedes replied.

Do you have a game plan yet?

> *Partially. I'll let you both know the full idea
> when I have it. I want to keep the big thing
> a secret from Serenity if I can. It'll make
> things more fun.*

Narissa responded.

So, surprise birthday excursion. I love it.

Shira hadn't thought about that, but her friend was right. With Serenity's birthday in a few days, this could be a way they could celebrate it and Shira got to spoil the girl all at the same time.

She bit her lip when she thought about the big secret she was keeping from the two of them. Not only had she not told her friends about the times she screwed Jasper and Zach in game and intentionally hid it from them when her friends made comments at the convention, she'd gone and fucked the guys again last night.

Shira had gotten on her friends' cases about their relationships when they'd been trying to figure them out, and here she was being a major hypocrite. Though, she really didn't know what to say to them, since Shira wasn't sure what to call their situation yet. And she didn't want the girls thinking too deeply about this if it didn't turn out to be more than something casual.

There was still a part of her that nagged that what she'd done was wrong. This voice said she needed to watch her rules and boundaries and that her friends were wrong to encourage this behavior. *But if it's wrong… why does it feel right?*

The guys certainly wouldn't have engaged with her like this if they didn't have some interest. Shira wasn't *that* naïve. And as much as she had reservations because of Zach, those were fading quickly.

The attention he'd paid her last night left no room to believe there was any hesitation in him. He'd been incredible. And if she looked at this objectively, it really wasn't much different from Jasper loving Zach. He'd fallen for the person, not the sex of that person.

I made rules to protect myself… but they're doing the exact opposite of that, aren't they?

"Shira, you okay?" Zach asked. "Looks like something is eating at you."

She looked up from her phone and put on a smile to hide the turmoil raging inside her. "Yeah, I'm fine. Just trying to word my next text to the girls. Don't need them misunderstanding something."

His brow rose, as if he were hoping she'd elaborate, but Shira wasn't going to. Not in front of Serenity. Though, if she were honest with herself, talking to the guys in private about what hung in the air wouldn't be easy, either.

She knew she had to—it was the adult thing to do—but that didn't make it any easier for her. This situation was something she'd tried so damned hard to avoid to begin with. But the universe was determined to keep turning her world upside down, and she ultimately failed to resist their annoying charm. *I'm just that starved for attention…*

Shira shook the negative thought from her head and typed back to her friends.

> *I also have something to talk to you two about if I can keep Serenity distracted for a moment.*

Mercedes replied at an uncomfortable speed.

> *Oh? Must be big if you don't want her to overhear.*

Shira paused and then forced herself to reply honestly.

> *Yeah, it's a pretty big deal.*

Narissa responded next.

> *Does this have anything to do with your special house guests?*

> *I'm not saying anything over text. Not even hints. You'll have to wait until tomorrow.*

Shira knew her friends would hate that response, but it was for the best. This was better done in person. Plus, it'd give her time to find the courage to talk about it with her friends.

As expected, both women responded with emojis representing their displeasure. Shira closed the conversation and responded to Kane. They set up a rough block of time based on when he thought he might be done with Kiara.

"Everything good?" Zach asked.

Shira set her phone down on the counter before grabbing a glass of orange juice one of the guys had poured for her. "Yep. They're on board for the afternoon."

Serenity cheered. "What are we gonna do, She-ra?"

Shira winked. "It's a surprise."

The young girl pursed her lips and scrunched up her nose, and Shira gave Serenity one of her pieces of bacon to placate her. It worked.

It wasn't long before Jasper returned. "All right, so my parents are insisting on having as much time as they can with Serenity, so I came up with the following game plan: they'll come by tomorrow for dinnuh and then take Serenity home with them. They'll return her to us at the convention center the day it stars back up, as they, apparently, had passes for the last few days of the convention. They're eager to watch our matches in person rather than virtually."

Shira smiled. "That's awesome. It's nice to hear they're so supportive of what you two do."

Esports had been recognized as legitimate job opportunities for decades, though VR greatly improved that standing. But even so, there were plenty out there who rejected the notion that playing video games for a living was work.

Zach laughed. "I don't think those two could ever not be supportive, even if it was something they didn't understand."

"And it helps that my mom is a retired esports coach," Jasper said.

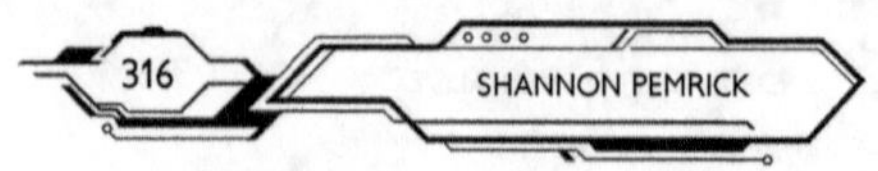

Shira blinked, her brain taking a moment to process. "Wait, what!"

Jasper laughed. "Yeah. She's into all kinds of strategy games. She was pretty bummed when it turned out I didn't like them at all and preferred MMOs, but she's supportive."

"When she's not heckling the two of us," Zach added, amusement in his voice.

Shira shook her head. She knew next to nothing about Jasper's family, so it was nice to see a bit of a glimpse. Yet, it still baffled her a bit. *Then again, people are surprised about Dad's choice in work.*

"So, since they're going to join us for dinner, we should probably plan that out, too," she said.

Jasper looked at the phone still in his hand. "Already ahead of you." He smirked. "I'm going to get some use out of that grill of yours."

Shira leaned on the counter and rested her chin on her hand. "Oh, really? Are you going to tell me you're some sort of master griller?"

"Master griller, and Zach is a master chef." He winked. "We'll back it up while we're here."

Shira pursed her lips. "Two men who will cook all my meals for me? Careful, I might not let you leave."

Zach chuckled and his eyes trailed down her body. "We do have an appointment for negotiations in the next day or two."

Heat tinged her cheeks, images flashing through her head that were of them less talking and more acting through said negotiations. *Is sending Serenity away for even a day a good idea? At this point, I can't even trust myself around them when she's sleeping in another room.*

"So, how can I help with the meal?" Shira asked Jasper, trying to distract herself.

He shook his head. "I've got it."

She gave him a long, hard look. "If you're going to do the majority of the cooking, then I want to contribute in some way. Even if it's paying for—"

Jasper held up a finger. "You're not shilling out a single cent again. We've got it."

Shira frowned. This wasn't because she didn't think they could afford it. She knew they'd budgeted for this trip, but Serenity wasn't the only one she wanted to spoil a bit. After everything they'd helped her with these last few months, it was the least she could do.

She slid her hand up his arm and leaned forward. "Please, Jasper. Allow me to help out some way. Monetarily is the easiest for me. It doesn't even have to be for the full amount."

Jasper's eyes flicked down to her lips and then lower. She knew her crop top did little to cover her at this angle. Maybe it was a little underhanded, but she knew from yesterday he enjoyed this style of shirt, and he also made it too easy to do this to him.

To add to her temptation, she circled her finger on the inner tender spot of his forearm.

Jasper let out a hard breath through his lips. "You can pay for fifteen percent." The corner of his lip twitched up. "And we get more negotiating powah during our appointment."

Shira pursed her lips and regarded him. Power against her was never a good thing to allow either of them to have. "Seventy-five percent."

His brow ticked up. "Twenty-five."

She dragged her tongue over her bottom lip, mostly thinking, but also to mess with him—which it did, from the momentary faltering of his attention. *I might kick myself later for this.* "Fifty percent, plus minor negotiating boost."

Jasper smirked. "Deal."

Shira pulled away, pushing out confidence as if she'd come out on top in this agreement, though she had a feeling her offer had just gotten her into a lot of trouble. "Orion, make sure that happens."

"Of course, Shira."

She hopped off her stool. "Now, let's go play some mini golf."

CHAPTER 17

Hot sunrays beat down on Zach while he watched Serenity attempt to "tap" her golf ball. Like usual, she hit it far too hard and missed the cup by a mile, and bounced it around the walls of the green. Serenity stomped her foot in irritation.

"It's okay, Starship," Jasper said in a gentle tone. "Just have to hit it a little softer next time."

"I did hit it softer," she grumbled.

Jasper let out a quiet breath. Zach loved his patience. It wasn't easy when she got this way.

"Serenity, would you like me to teach you a trick?" Shira offered.

His daughter perked up. "A trick?"

She smiled and handed her club and Snake's leash off to Zach. He wasn't going to refuse her. Whatever she had up her sleeve, he hoped would encourage Serenity. She loved mini golf, but also struggled to not get too

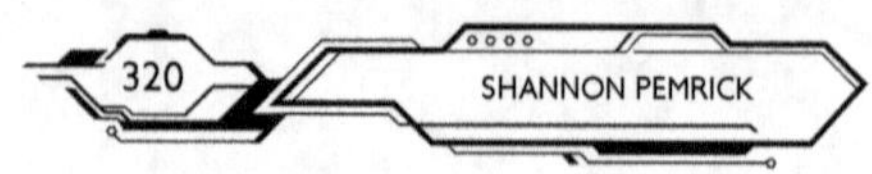

hard on herself. It was an unfortunate quality she'd picked up from both Jasper and him.

Shira ushered Serenity over to her ball and slipped behind her. She spoke quietly, showing his daughter a good way to hold her club as well as instructing her how to use her body more effectively for the swing. Her hands still on Serenity's, she swayed the two of them and hit the ball.

The pink sphere rolled down the green, smoother than he'd seen it go in the four holes they'd played so far. Serenity gasped when it barely missed the hole and rolled to a stop only a few inches away.

She gazed up at Shira with sparkling eyes. "It almost went in!"

Shira smiled. "Almost. I think we can get it in with one more swing."

His daughter practically sprang out of Shira's grasp to get into position. Shira chuckled and took her place again behind Serenity, showing her how to be gentle with the ball this time.

Zach found himself completely captivated. She'd managed to calm his daughter and bring back her fun, all without setting things up to make her feel as though she couldn't do it on her own without overbearing adults telling her how it was done. This woman was seriously too perfect.

Serenity jumped for joy when the ball rolled into the hole. "I did it!"

Zach and Jasper were quick to clap and praise her, as did Shira. The more they encouraged her, the better she'd get.

Jasper marked something down on the score device,

most likely fudging the number for their daughter's sake. Maybe it was dishonest, but Zach didn't care, as long as it didn't ruin her fun. "Next hole?"

They moved onto the next, letting Jasper go first. Shira stood beside Zach under the shade of a tree, the heat of her body teasing him. His attention flicked down to her, eyes dragging down her tight crop top and teasingly short skirt accentuating her curves. Zach struggled to focus on anything else today. Not after yesterday.

She'd been incredible. Zach hadn't thought it could have gotten any better than that day in the game, but he'd been proven wrong. The moans and sighs—her taste and smell—the way she begged and demanded more without hesitation—his pants tightened uncomfortably. There was no going back from this now. He'd never be able to forget, and Zach didn't want to.

Shira looked up at him and blinked. "You okay?"

Zach smiled and reached out, wrapping his arms around her and pulling Shira into him. Her body molded into his perfectly. "I was debating if I should do this."

Pink tinged her cheeks, and she turned her gaze back to Jasper, who was now trying to help Serenity on her swing in the same way Shira had in the previous hole. "I guess you're not immune to overthinking, either."

His brow lifted. This was a good sign. She wasn't the type to let him do this if it made her uncomfortable. And she'd made more progress opening up to them.

As much as some of it hurt her, Shira showed them more than they'd ever expected. She'd been completely and utterly vulnerable, a side of her so few were ever allowed to see, and he couldn't feel more honored to have that trust from her.

Zach would never harm her. He never saw her as the pretty broken thing she so clearly saw herself as. All he saw was a strong, irresistible woman.

Zach didn't care that she had cybernetics, or that she had lasting medical conditions. If this progressed the way he and Jasper wanted, it didn't bother him they'd never have biological children with her. None of that mattered, as long as he had her by his side.

This path was frightening in a lot of ways. It was all new, uncharted territory. But if she was willing to be patient for him, he wouldn't run from this.

Serenity's cheering pulled Zach out of his head. It appeared Jasper had gone ahead and allowed her to keep going with her turn. They did that every so often to keep her engaged. She could be patient if her turn was over, but sometimes struggled when she could still go.

He clapped and cheered, even though he had no idea how well she'd done. He felt a bit bad, but Shira was a distraction.

Serenity called for Shira to go next, and she did. Her ball curved around a barrier and just missed the cup. Her nose scrunched, making Jasper and Zach laugh.

Zach was next, and he ended up hitting Jasper's ball, sending both skittering around the green. Jasper glowered at him, and Zach shrugged. Wasn't like he did it on purpose—this time.

The three of them continued playing the hole until Jasper was the only one still having trouble. He worked his jaw and tapped his club on the ground; the wheels turning in his brain how to handle his accuracy issue. Zach almost rolled his eyes over how much his boyfriend was overthinking this.

Jasper suddenly lay out on the ground and positioned his club like a pool stick.

Shira choked on a laugh. "What are you doing? Have you forgotten what we're playing here?"

"Course not." Jasper closed one of his eyes and lined up the handle of his club to his ball. "This will just work better."

When he had the shot lined up, Jasper jabbed the golf ball like a cue ball and the green sphere shot right into the cup. He rose to his knees and held his arms up. "See?"

Shira shook her head, completely mystified. Zach laughed. *She hasn't seen nothing yet.*

With that hole finished, they moved onto the next. It was a bit more complicated than the last, located in a pirate ship and comprised of two levels. Serenity squealed and begged to go first. Multi-leveled courses were her favorite.

She framed her hands in front of her, as if she were attempting to visualize how to hit the balls into the right drop-tube out of the three options, and then she dramatically set her ball down on the tee. Shira stifled a chuckle as she leaned against Jasper.

Zach noticed how comfortably Jasper rested his hand on Shira's hip. A pang of jealousy plucked his chest. Though, it wasn't because of the contact. No, Jasper not only looked comfortable and natural next to Shira like this, he hadn't hesitated like Zach would have.

Oddly enough, that made Zach feel relieved. Working on his confidence with touching Shira would be easy enough; dealing with his past reservations over the last few months hadn't been.

Zach had come to realize his issue had been more complicated than he'd first wanted to admit. Some of it did stem from the fact that Jasper's love for him was unique. However, Shira allowed him to see that didn't make it fake.

Jasper was an incredibly honest person—sometimes a little too honest, and with no tact. And if what had happened between them that day when they'd reached their breaking point had just been them blowing off steam, Jasper would have laid that all out then. But no. He allowed them both to see how the new development would grow, and never once shied away. And as much as Jasper could appreciate a pretty woman, just as Zach could appreciate an appealing man, Jasper's affections never wavered—growing secondary attachments to Shira notwithstanding for either of them.

The other part of his issue was fear that Shira would offer something Zach couldn't give Jasper. And once Zach realized this, it was so easy for him to fix that way of thinking. Of course she'd give Jasper experiences he couldn't. She'd do the same for Zach—because the two of them weren't the same people.

When he looked at it all objectively, he could see how irrational his thoughts had been. He understood why that insecure side of him would see the situation in that way, but he was glad he could address it. And really, Shira proved just how well she fit with them. And it wasn't only their sexual chemistry.

She mothered Serenity so naturally, Narissa had to tease her about it for Shira to notice, and of course deny. And then, when it came to him and Jasper, she not only fully engaged with them in the same way he and Jasper would with each other, but she knew when to be part of things, and when to give the two of them time together. Like this morning; she'd been perfectly content to observe him and Jasper interact while making breakfast.

And even though Zach had an itch to include himself with Jasper and Shira now, he was content to watch them, too.

Serenity whiffed her first swing, and practically spun three hundred and sixty degrees from the force. Zach's back straightened, concern flooding up into him, but when Serenity laughed, he relaxed.

"That's a cool new move, Starship," he said.

She giggled. "Yeah, but I need more practice before I try again."

Zach smiled, pleased she didn't take her mess-up so hard this time. He and Jasper had missed like that many times playing these games. *Hell, who doesn't?*

Serenity tried again, and this time the pink ball shot all over the course before it found the waved dips near the three drop tunnels. The golf ball rolled over all three, hit a barrier, and rolled back.

His daughter excitedly moved in place, muttering about it needing to go into the middle hole. It didn't. The ball swirled down into the first tube closest to the tee. Serenity made a face, but soon remembered there was the second level and ran to the railing in time to watch her ball roll toward the cup.

She jumped up and down. "It almost went in! It missed, but I almost had it!"

"That's great, Starship," Jasper said with a toothy grin. "Let us get ours down there and we can all get down to the next level."

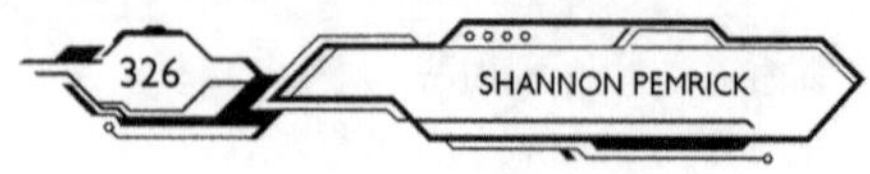

"Okay."

Zach and Jasper let Shira go first. She putted the ball, not using nearly as much force as Serenity, but she managed to get the ball into the middle hole. That proved to be a bad one, when her purple golf ball flew out of a wall hole nowhere near the cup.

"I'm glad mine didn't go in that one now," Serenity said.

Shira laughed. "Yes, I'll have to get extra crafty to keep my score low."

Zach was next, and after a little suspense from a back-and-forth roll, also ended in the middle hole. His ball bounced around the bottom in an erratic pattern like Shira's and ended up nowhere near hers. *Whatever they've got going on in that tube is some seriously crazy stuff.*

Jasper set his ball down on the tee, but barely tried, and just casually swung his club with one hand. The hit sent the ball bouncing rather than rolling, and in a strange turn of events, it jumped right into the last hole.

There was a beat of silence, and then all four of them laughed. Zach wasn't even sure how to process what he'd witnessed. And it didn't stop there. Serenity let them know the ball was rolling on the lower green, and all of them watched it go straight for the cup.

Only, it stopped just short. All their mouths fell open.

"Whoa…" Serenity whispered.

"Whoa indeed, Starship," Zach said.

She jumped up and down. "Let's get down there!"

The adults let her lead the way. They took in their positions with the new angle and found Shira's ball had actually stopped closer than Serenity's. The top-down view hadn't provided accurate angles.

"Well, I guess Jasper goes first," Shira said. "Even though that's close enough, we might not subject him to putting it."

"Who said anything about putting?" Jasper said, walking out onto the green. Like before, he lay down and popped the golf ball into the cup like he was playing pool.

Shira rolled her eyes. "What is wrong with you? Why can't you just hit the thing like a normal person?"

"This is a perfectly normal way," he defended, removing himself from the course. "And it's more accurate."

Shira gave Snake his own leash to hold before walking over to her ball. She took a moment to angle herself into the perfect position, and putted the purple sphere. It rolled into the cup without issue and she gave Jasper a smug smile. "The *real* way of playing is perfectly accurate if you're competent. Maybe you should just get good."

Jasper crossed his arms, working his jaw. Shira turned to Serenity and encouraged her to go next, though his daughter hesitated for a moment, not understanding Jasper and Shira were only ragging on each other for fun.

Serenity and Zach finished up their turns, though Zach had a bit of trouble getting his ball into the cup this time. Serenity giggled away each time he missed. He wasn't even trying to lose this badly for her sake. His aim just sucked.

Eventually he finished. He, Shira, and Serenity collected themselves to move to the next hole, when Jasper stopped them. "Wait. I want to change things up."

Zach raised an eyebrow. "Oh?"

His boyfriend still had his arms crossed and had set his full attention on Shira. "Yeah, since Shira thinks

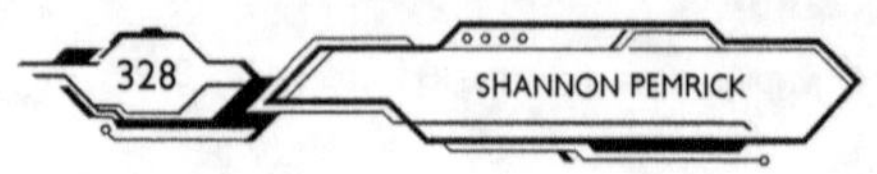

her way is so superior, I think she and I should have a little competition."

Shira stepped up to him, her hands on her hips. "Oh, do you? Let's hear your idea, then."

"It's simple, we see whose technique is better, by seeing who can score the best for all the courses going forward."

Shira cocked her head. "And the stakes?"

Jasper snickered. "The usual: winner gets to boss the loser around for the rest of the day."

"What of Serenity and Zach?" Shira asked.

Jasper shook his head. "This is between you and me. No need to drag them into this. They can keep having fun."

Shira shrugged and spun on her heels. "Fine, I'll take on your wager. May the better player prevail."

A cocky smirk slipped up his handsome face. "Oh, I will."

He watched her walk away with Serenity, as did Zach. Her hypnotic hips swayed under that teasing skirt. "That should be illegal."

Jasper chuckled. "Good thing her technique doesn't involve seduction. I'd be losing wicked hard."

Zach's eyebrows rose briefly, and he twitched his head. "Never know. That might be her secret skill. She's crafty enough to pull off something subtle that Serenity wouldn't be able to notice."

Jasper swallowed, most likely running a few tantalizing scenarios through his head already. "Whose side are you on?"

Zach shrugged and followed the girls. "Mine. I'm not caught up in your little wager. The way I see it, I win no matter which of you comes out on top."

"Oh, I'll be on top of her."

Zach rolled his eyes to convince himself to ignore his growing arousal from this conversation. "Keep it in your pants until we're at least not in public."

Jasper's muscular arm snaked around Zach's waist and he pulled Zach hard against him. He pressed his lips against Zach's ear, his hot breath traveling over his skin in a teasing caress. Zach was hard again. "You know being in public wouldn't stop me."

Zach swallowed. "You and Sara may have liked to push those boundaries, but you know that doesn't fly with me."

"As much as I think you should give it a try one of these days, I respect your decision." Jasper chuckled. "Of course, that doesn't account for Shira's position on the matter. I might luck out with her."

Zach shook his head and pulled out of his boyfriend's grip. "Why not focus on beating her at mini golf? If you win, you can have all the fun you want if she consents."

Jasper chuckled and followed. It was obvious that had been the plan when he made the wager. Not even Shira would think otherwise. Though, if she won, who knew if she would plan to do the same. She was a wild card, and Zach loved it.

The two of them caught up with Shira and Serenity. They were already waiting at the next hole.

"Slowpokes," Shira said.

"Yeah, slowpokes!" Serenity mimicked.

Jasper handed the score keeping device to Zach. "Just wanted to make sure you had time to ready yourself to lose."

Shira rolled her eyes. "We'll see about that."

It was decided Zach and Serenity would go first for the rest of the holes so Shira and Jasper could mess with each other. Might not be the most sportsman-like conduct, but there was no fun in behaving.

Course after course, they made their way through. Shira naturally went with her traditional play, taking on a more calculated approach, while Jasper stuck by his guns to treat the courses like giant billiard tables. His technique wasn't bad. He'd managed to score several pars and under par. However, Shira one-upped him with not only scoring under par but also a hole-in-one.

Now, Jasper lined up on the second-to-last hole, aiming for a par shot at the cup. Shira watched intently, knowing how important it was, given she was one over par on this hole. Jasper slid the club back to strike, when Serenity suddenly gasped loudly. Jasper twitched and then missed the golf ball.

He looked at their daughter, concerned, but the look turned to annoyance when Serenity threw her hands up to her face and giggled. "Now you won't beat She-ra."

Shira and Zach burst into the laughter. *Cheeky little thing!* It was the exact thing Zach expected from his daughter.

"You little cheater," Jasper grumbled.

Zach shook his head. "Not at all. Neither of you have any rules about Serenity and me distracting either of you."

Jasper blew out a breath and accepted his misfortune. He made his shot, and the ball rolled into the cup, giving him one over par like Shira. He rose to his feet and held out his arms. "It's working, even with your little minion helping."

Shira pulled Serenity into a quick hug. "I love my minion's help. It's going to ensure I win."

Jasper pursed his lips, then looked at Zach. "We've got the last hole left. How's the score?"

Zach was finishing his notes for this hole. "Not telling. You'll find out when we're done."

He decided this would make it more fun. If they knew the score, it could alter how they performed this last course. And really, this one was more crucial than even Zach thought it'd end up being.

"Oh, c'mon," Jasper said, reaching for the device. "Just let us see."

Zach held it out of reach. "No. You're going to be patient."

"Yeah, Daddy, be patient," Serenity mimicked in a mocking tone.

"Yeah, Daddy, you heard them, be patient," Shira said, her tone low and seductive. Her lips curled into a pleased smile when Jasper and Zach both stared at her. She then slowly turned away, her movements exaggerated as she made her way to the final course.

Zach hoped Jasper was feeling the same as him. The change in her may have been out of the blue—*But her voice…* He was definitely hard again from that. Zach would not mind if she spoke like that some more to them.

"You told me I was in trouble," Jasper murmured to him. "She'd better not keep that up, or I definitely will be."

He walked to the last hole, forcing Zach to catch up and quickly collect his thoughts. Shira's shift in demeanor was new and exciting in ways, but he wouldn't let it get him out of sorts. She'd like that too much.

Shira was encouraging Serenity with her first swing. The last hole was much different from any of the others, with multiple routes for a golf ball to take. And from the looks of it, each route had different points at the end, where the ball would automatically return to the golf house. *This is going to get interesting.*

But Zach had no idea how interesting it would get. As with the previous holes, him and Serenity scoring was fairly standard. It was Jasper and Shira who made things go off the rail.

Shira's tone from earlier was still present. In fact, her entire play changed to a dangerously flirty one. Zach had mostly been joking when he teased Jasper about her using this as a tactic. And she hadn't this whole time, so he figured Jasper was safe. He should have known better.

She swished her hips, and casually rubbed against Jasper when they were switching between turns. She used that sultry voice again as well, when saying even the most mundane things to him.

But the final nail in the coffin came after Shira got her ball into one of the score tunnels and chose to sit down on a nearby bench. She moved deliberately slowly, and by the time she was bending down, Jasper was setting up his shot. And then came her most devious tactic.

She lifted her skirt.

Not enough for any onlookers to see if they were looking her way instead of Jasper's—given that his bizarre technique had been turning a lot of heads—but Jasper did.

His eyes widened and his jaw went a little slack. Shira acted like she'd done nothing out of the ordinary, even smoothing out her skirt as if it had bunched up all on its own. It was all the right amount of tease to get Jasper to accidentally tap his golf ball—not that he even noticed.

Shira cocked her head, that tempting voice stroking even Zach's strings. "What was that, Jasper? That's one heck of a weak shot."

Jasper blinked, looked down at his now-moving ball, and swore. He didn't see the pleased, smug smile that appeared on her lips, but Zach did. She knew how to play the man, and that worried Zach about himself.

To his credit, Jasper kept his focus on his task going forward. Shira did try to distract him, and nearly succeeded, but Jasper's desire to win won out.

When his golf ball rolled into the final score tunnel, he jumped to his feet and cheered. Shira and Serenity clapped for him while Zach wrote the score. The board flashed and then added Jasper's swing count, including the distracted mess-up.

They all returned their golf clubs and Zach had a copy of their score transferred to his phone, before stepping into a shaded spot under a tree near the hedge maze. Zach worked to tally out the holes prior to Shira and Jasper's little competition.

Shira popped up and down on her toes. "Well?"

Zach lifted his brows for a second. "You're more impatient than Jasper. Hold on. I'm not the fastest at math."

"I could do it for you," Alistair offered. "It would be easy for me to tally the proper data range."

"You could, but I also enjoy making them wait," Zach said, a laugh barely concealed through his words.

Shira huffed and then tried to peer over his shoulder, but he shooed her away. She would not ruin his fun.

Though, it was the score that got the last laugh.

"That's an interesting face," Jasper said when he noticed Zach's brows arching. "Gonna share with the class?"

"Alistair, can you double-check my math?" Zach asked. He wanted to make sure he wasn't seeing things.

"I can confirm that is correct," the AI said.

Zach ran his hand over his pulled-back hair. "Well, it appears both your techniques were almost equally beneficial for you two. Shira won, by a single point."

Jasper ripped Zach's phone out of his hand, mumbling about there being no way that was right, while Shira threw a fist in the air. "Yeah! Superior skills."

Zach chuckled. He could hardly agree with that claim over a one-point win, but who was he to say anything? He had no stake in this.

Serenity cheered and clapped for Shira, clearly happy her favorite person today had won.

Jasper let out a breath. "I can't believe this is right. I was on track to win, and then those last holes…"

Shira winked. "Better luck next time."

Serenity grabbed Shira's leg. "What are we gonna do now, She-ra?"

The tempting woman in front of Zach tapped her lips. "I'm thinking we go into the maze like you wanted. After that, your dad buys us ice cream at my favorite place. How does that sound?"

Serenity jumped out in her excitement and grabbed Shira's hand so they could pay to try out the maze. Zach and Jasper watched them walk off, though Zach was also taking in Jasper's reaction.

"Are you pouting?" He could hardly contain his

amusement when he noticed the slight pucker of his boyfriend's lower lip.

"Sulking a bit," Jasper admitted. "I'll be over it in like three seconds. I really wanted to win, and I thought I'd come up with the perfect strategy to do so."

Zach cocked his head. "You're not taking it hard like you usually do."

"I know." Jasper paused and then turned to Zach. "I mean, I am wicked annoyed I lost, but I don't feel it's going to explode out of me and lash out. Maybe it's because I lost to her, and there's just no way I could act that way if she's the one who comes out the winner. Kinda like how it's not common I get upset with you when you win at something I was sure to come out on top of."

He shrugged. "Or that discussion I had with both her and Jeff the other day helped."

Zach smiled, warmth spreading through his chest. He leaned in and kissed Jasper on the temple. "I think it's a bit of both. I'm confident that issue will fade into a bad memory soon enough."

He really did believe that. They may have offered to help Shira with the trauma she needed to overcome to finally live her life to the fullest, but somehow the woman had also managed to worm her way in and heal the two of them when they hadn't thought they needed it.

Zach threaded his hand in with his boyfriend's. "Let's catch up. Otherwise, we won't hear the end of their teasing, and might land me in this loser bracket."

A devious smirk slipped up the side of Jasper's face. "Trust me. By the end of the day, it won't be much of a loser bracket."

CHAPTER 18

Jasper leaned against the warm railing with Snake lying by his feet. Both watched Shira and Serenity sprint through the maze, Zach following at a much slower pace. To most, it would appear he was taking a leisurely stroll, not caring how long it took him to figure his way through. But Jasper knew better. He was enjoying watching this game of cat-and-mouse as much as Zach was being part of it.

Jasper would be part of this little game if it weren't for the fact that he hated mazes. No matter who he was with, or which ones he tried, he could never find it in him to have fun. However, watching others stumble their way through while he got a bird's-eye view? Yeah, he very much enjoyed that.

Shira doubled back, lifting Serenity into her arms and bolting down an alternative path, narrowly missing Zach's grab for her. Her skirt swished around her legs, as if teasing Jasper's memory of the stunt she'd pulled earlier.

She hadn't lifted the article of clothing high enough for him to get a good peek, but damn, did she throw him off. Jasper's hand on the railing curled, and he dragged his tongue over his bottom lip when Shira looked behind her to gauge where Zach was, and picked up her pace.

If Serenity wasn't stuck to Shira's hip today, Jasper would have happily gone into the maze this once. He'd be fine swapping places with Zach, given Shira was a potential reward. She clearly didn't have the same reservations as his boyfriend, not that he had any issues with Zach's choice to keep most things private. It didn't matter to Jasper in the end, but a little extra thrill here and there was nice. And he'd be all too happy to catch her and see how comfortable she was.

It was the main disappointing aspect of him losing the wager. Jasper had been looking forward to seeing how much she'd allow him to ask of her. Of course, that didn't mean he couldn't still try. If he tempted her enough, she may be lured into doing what he'd hoped for anyway. *And there's still the matter of negotiations she promised.*

Jasper shook his head. He couldn't allow these thoughts into his mind. They'd drive him mad and frustrate him more than he already was. All he wanted was to be close to her. Talking to her—helping her—*teasing her.*

He took a sharp inhale of breath. When had he become so completely enthralled by her? At what point did he cross the point of no return for himself? Because he knew he was there. Jasper knew that spot well. He'd had it with Sara, and then with Zach.

Jasper's attention fell to his boyfriend, who was gaining on Shira. Watching his determination to catch the wily woman, and Jasper having the perfect view of Zach's physique, he spiraled back into those thoughts. *These two are going to be the death of me.*

Shira squealed. Zach had caught up and grabbed her around the waist, pulling her tight against him. She'd let Serenity go, and encouraged her to "keep running" while Shira tried to squirm out of Zach's grip. His daughter saw this as a game and did as encouraged, giggling all the while. Jasper chortled.

Sure, he probably should be a little concerned Serenity was tasked to go off on her own, but he could see her no matter where she went in the maze from this vantage point. And by the looks of Shira and Zach, it wouldn't have been appropriate for his daughter to stay.

From what Jasper could see, Shira had ceased squirming in Zach's arms, and he was whispering something in her ear. Jasper was too far away to get a good idea of her reaction, but it became obvious a moment later when Zach's mouth lowered to her neck and his hand migrated down her ass to the hem of her skirt.

Both of them looked up at Jasper, and Zach grinned and mouthed something like, "This is for you."

Zach's hand slipped under Shira's skirt and Jasper was sure his boyfriend had grabbed her ass, based on the way she popped on her toes and her mouth opened in a gasp.

Jasper leaned forward, his cock hardening. *I didn't just imagine that, right?* Zach pulled away from Shira, giving her rear a solid smack before heading off in the direction Serenity had run. Shira's hand flew behind her, as if protecting herself after the fact could be effective, and stared at Zach's retreating form.

Shira then looked up at him, and Jasper smirked. He very much enjoyed that.

Jasper enjoyed seeing Zach and her together. She brought out a different side in Zach, and that fascinated him to no end. Sure, a part of him was disappointed he couldn't do that for his boyfriend, and he had to fight sometimes, feeling like he'd fail Zach, but as much as Jasper hated to admit it, he wasn't superhuman. And if he couldn't give Zach everything, Jasper wanted that void to be filled by Shira.

He watched her lower lip catch on her teeth and Shira looked away, though he did catch a smile on her lips. *Oh, Shira, why are you still trying to resist us so hard?*

A frown tugged his mouth when something came to him. Was it their approach? He thought they were being fairly straightforward with their interest, especially after yesterday—a moment that still teased him—but maybe they needed to take a different approach. *I guess we could just talk it out.*

Jasper had to resist the urge to rub his neck. That was one thing he wasn't good at. Neither of his relationships with Sara and Zach had started out that way. They fit more how he was handling Shira, and it may not be doing him any favors this time.

Zach had caught up with Serenity, based on the screeching giggles that penetrated Jasper's thoughts. He peered down to find them only a little ways off from where Shira and Zach had stalled for a moment. Jasper suspected Serenity hadn't gone very far, thinking she was being crafty.

He watched them complete the maze eventually and met up with them at the exit. Serenity was beaming, and she blabbered on and on to Jasper about her fun in the maze while the lot of them made their way to the car. Joy bloomed in his chest. This is what he wanted for her.

"So, where are we going for this treat, Shira?" Zach asked.

Shira closed her door. "To see Valerie."

"Valerie?" Jasper echoed. "As in, our guildmate?"

She smirked. "Yep."

"Doesn't she run a food truck?" Zach asked.

"Yup, AFK Snacks. She offers all kinds of nerd-themed treats, but she's best known for her signature ice cream sundaes."

Serenity clapped. "I like the sound of this place."

It didn't take them long to arrive at a large, packed parking lot with trucks lined up in multiple rows. Everyone climbed out, Serenity nearly vibrating out of her booster in all her excitement. *I'm going to regret allowing her to have all this sugar.*

Shira didn't lead them right to Valerie's truck. She allowed the three of them to check out the others here to see if they interested them at all. Jasper wanted to try a few, but since they were there for the one truck, he decided to not say anything. He could always get something before they left if he was still hungry.

Eventually, they made it to a truck with an 8-bit gaming theme. The line was fairly long, but nothing that was too unreasonable to wait in. It was then that Shira allowed them to pull up the online menu on their phones to check out the food available.

The selection impressed Jasper, for a food truck. There

were things from cookies, to cakes, to scones, and ice cream. Every item had a nerdy twist, even if it was just the name, as it was clear Valerie made sure there were items available for less adventurous food connoisseurs.

Serenity gasped when Shira scrolled to a part of the ice cream list and mentioned his daughter's favorite game. "I want the Monstah Huntuh sundae!"

Shira chuckled. "I thought you might. Which one? There are three: Soul Seeker's Paradise, Nightcloak Dance, and Frostfang's Bite."

She described out the flavors for Serenity, and the little girl decided on the Soul Seeker's Paradise, a bubblegum ice cream with strawberry sauce, whipped cream, and chocolate balls.

"We'll get that to split, then."

Serenity cocked her head. "Can I have my own?"

"Well, Valerie is committed to her craft, and makes sure the portion size for the Monster-Hunter-themed items she has are oversized, just like the game. So, the sundae is so large, it's difficult for even an adult to eat on their own."

His daughter's eyes went wide as saucers. "That's amazing."

Jasper decided on a Lusara-Fates-inspired sundae, the Cloaked Dagger. It might be an obvious and basic choice for him, but it sounded delicious—dark chocolate fudge and vanilla swirl, with raspberry sauce and toffee pieces. He also spotted a banana-flavored cinnamon roll called the Barrel Bun and added that to his must-try list.

Zach mentioned he wasn't too hungry for a sundae and would instead try out the Frozen Scones—renamed iced blueberry scones—and Sweet Buns—renamed cinnamon rolls. Zach had never been a huge sweets person, so the fact he was trying even those impressed Jasper.

The line moved along until their turn was next. Inside the truck was a tall woman of dark complexion wearing stylish, yet comfortable, fast-pace working clothes over her curvy body. Carefully painted eyeliner accented her light brown eyes, and her braided black hair was pulled back in an intricate bun. Her lips, painted with purple lipstick, pulled back into a bright smile, creating dimples in her cheeks.

"Shira, you came—and brought the family this time!" she said, her voice low and rich, and sprinkled with a hint of sass.

"Hey, Valerie," Shira greeted, not correcting the way their guildmate worded the "family" title. It made Jasper's hopes jump a little higher. "Jasper lost a bet against me, so what better way to celebrate than with treats from your truck?"

Valerie clapped as she laughed. "Right you are, girl. What did he lose at this time?"

Serenity giggled. "Daddy lost at mini golf. He was playing wicked silly."

"I only lost by one point," Jasper grumbled. They made it seem like his technique was absolutely insane. *Okay, sure, it's unorthodox, but it didn't fail me like they're implying.*

Mirth shone in Valerie's eyes. "You sound desperate, as always, when you lose a bet, Jasper."

Jasper glowered. *I don't get desperate when I lose.*

Shira nudged him with her elbow. "We're teasing. We know you're not a sore loser. That's why you're paying."

Valerie laughed. "So, how much are you hurting his wallet?"

"Shira rattled off what everyone had decided while in line, and Valerie beamed. "Coming right up!"

Their guildmate turned and reached for a cup, and it was then Jasper noticed that both her arms were cybernetic. He never knew that about her.

She worked with crazy efficiency and made all three sundaes, as well as packaging the non-dairy treats, in what felt like only five minutes.

Serenity gasped when Valerie handed over her sundae to Shira. Jasper's eyes widened at the sight of the monster dish. Shira hadn't been kidding. It easily represented the comically large food in that game.

Jasper's was luckily a more manageable size, one he could easily eat himself, though he prepared to have to share some of it with not only Zach, but Shira and Serenity.

And when the non-dairy treats were offered, well, those weren't tiny, either. All in all, Valerie's prices were completely reasonable for what she gave. And Snake even got his own dog-friendly treat for free.

"Enjoy," Valerie said brightly.

"You know we will," Shira said, winking. "No better place to satisfy a sweets craving."

Valerie chuckled. "And pay off a debt."

Jasper initiated the payment transfer through his phone. "Not quite yet."

She threw her head back as she laughed. "Oh, it was one of *those* ones. Have you ever won whenever you make those challenges?"

"A few times." Jasper didn't hide his smirk. They were

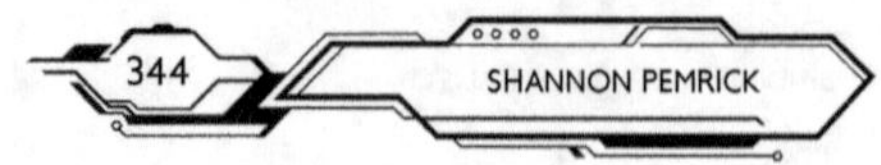

mostly against Zach, and the ones he did win against Shira, while not ending in quite the sexy results as his wins against Zach, or what he wanted today with her, they had been fun. The three of them knew the rules: Anything goes as long as the loser gives consent and doesn't feel coerced.

Valerie gave him a mocking salute. "Well, I wish you luck with whatever torture Shira decides to inflict on you."

Jasper hoped it was the fun kind, that was for sure.

"She-ra, why are you going to be torturing Daddy?" Serenity asked.

Zach coughed, and Valerie hid her mouth behind her fingers. It was easy to forget to watch what you said in a child's presence.

Shira bade farewell to Valerie, as did the rest of them, and then encouraged Serenity to follow her out of line and explained to his daughter that it wasn't torture, but "pranks" that the adults consented to. Jasper didn't mind this way of saving things. *May not be entirely accurate, but it doesn't hurt Serenity, and keeps her a bit more innocent a little longer.*

They all found a place to sit down and dig into their treats. Jasper's was fantastic. Basic compared to some of the sundaes he'd had back on the East Coast, but the quality was nothing to snuff at.

Everyone else loved their choices as well, especially Serenity. She wouldn't stop gushing about it. And, of course, there was some sharing, allowing everyone to have a larger sampling of Valerie's amazing work.

Jasper was impressed she did it all on her own. He knew she had a business partner at one time, and they'd done this out of a stationary building, but they'd had a falling out. The whole guild had been worried about her as she struggled to find the balance she needed to keep going. That was how the food truck came about.

She downsized her offerings, swapping them around every so often to keep the menu fresh, and moved around the Greater Los Angeles area. He could see why she was able to make it despite the hiccup, and he was glad it all worked out in the end for her. *We're definitely coming back the next time we visit.* Jasper didn't want to make this trip a one-time deal.

While everyone ate, and Snake happily lapped up his snack, they discussed the changes to the convention Stacey had forwarded. A lot of games panels had been moved to online, and half of the game demos were canceled by their developers. The latter was a shame to see, since that choice might impact their sales negatively, but it appeared there wouldn't be as much room as before. While the building was structurally safe, there were blocked-off areas that needed to be fixed up after the contained fire.

"So, everything ends on the seventeenth," Shira said, her words thoughtful as she took a bite of her ice cream.

"Doesn't make up for the lost days, but at least it's something," Zach said.

Jasper watched Shira. She'd come to some conclusion neither he nor Zach had. "But we're missing something based on that look she has."

Zach turned to assess her, too, and Shira blinked. "How could you two not realize?"

Serenity gasped. "That's my birthday!"

Jasper and Zach turned to look at each other. How

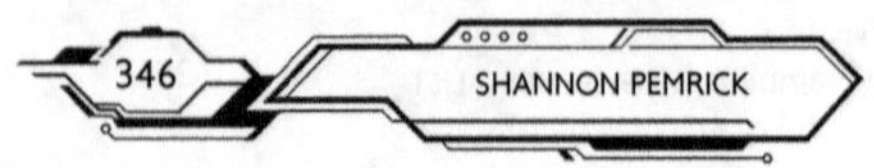

had they missed that? The convention ended two days before her birthday, that's why the trip had been presented as a gift to her. But now…

Zach let out a slow breath. "That's a lot of pressure to win the tournament."

Jasper nodded absently. It would kill Serenity to see them lose, but the idea they could do so on her birthday, if they managed to get to the finals, was a lot to worry about.

"Don't worry, I know you'll win," Serenity said before shoving a large spoonful of ice cream into her mouth.

Of course she did. Their daughter had more faith in them than anyone else in the world. Even when they did fail at things, she smiled and told them, "Next time you'll do better." And Jasper appreciated every moment of it. He'd really lucked out with her for a daughter, and Zach for helping make sure Jasper didn't screw her up.

It was the greatest fear he had as a parent. He wanted to give her the world, even if that wasn't really feasible. *Shira and Zach, too.*

"Have any teams dropped?" Shira asked, redirecting the conversation.

Jasper checked his phone. He'd assured Stacey before they left the house there was no way he and Zach were dropping out now, and she'd promised to send any tournament updates when they came. So far, she'd been silent. "Not that we've been made aware of."

Shira pursed her lips. "Means you two will be against Burnout again to settle what was started. How are you feeling about that?"

Jasper rocked his head. "Not sure. They're going to be difficult to beat, but nothing is impossible."

Zach gave her a reassuring smile. "Don't worry, we're going to practice different class combos. We know what's at stake here."

Shira's eyes narrowed. "Yeah, you promised me that before and never did."

"We've learned from that," Jasper said. Really, they had.

The qualifying tournaments had gotten them over-confident, and they didn't listen to her advice like they should have. It nearly cost them the first match. Maybe practicing this late wouldn't help them like it would have had they'd done it months ago, but it was better than not doing it at all.

And it was clear they'd have to prove it to Shira, because her skepticism didn't go away.

The four of them finished their treats, Shira and Serenity needing a bit of help due to the gargantuan size of the sundae, and then it was decided that they'd head home. Jasper would have asked to bring Serenity to a park to run off all the sugar she'd just consumed, but he did see a droop to her eyes. They'd done a lot today, so doing something chill for a bit was probably for the best. *I suppose we could use Shira's pool if the sugar hits later.*

Plus, Shira decided they were going home, and Jasper wasn't supposed to go against anything she said, according to their bet rules.

There wasn't much discussion on the way home. Everyone seemed a little worn out, and content with the silence, though Serenity ended it the moment the car pulled into the driveway. "Can I watch cahtoons?"

Shira looked to Jasper and Zach for that answer. She may be able to boss Jasper around, but she promised

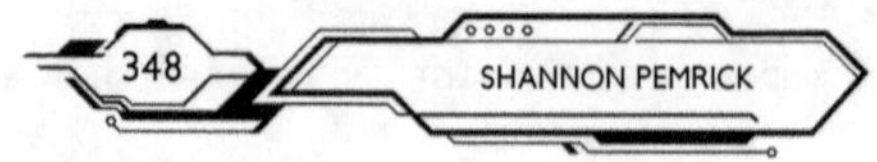

she wouldn't overstep, and he appreciated her respecting that, even with the bet.

"I don't see why not," Jasper said. "It'd be nice to chill for a bit."

"What do you want to watch, Starship?" Zach asked while he worked on getting her out.

Serenity's face scrunched as she thought. "Um, Pokémon."

Shira smiled. "Orion, can you queue up season one?"

Jasper stopped and stared at her. "What do you mean, 'queue up'? Something that old has to be interfaced from an old laptop."

"Yeah, if you don't know the right people." She shook her head and headed for the front door. "I know the right people who can save me the hassle."

"Well, don't be stingy," Jasper said, following close behind. "Share your source. I've got so many movies and shows I need to make streamable."

Shira unlocked the door, and tilted her head to glance up at him, a smug smirk on her lips. "Maybe I will. You'll have to earn that information."

His grip on the small bag in his hand tightened. *I'll earn it, all right.*

Once they were in the foyer, Shira released Snake from his vest and leash, and then kicked off her shoes. Jasper narrowed his eyes. He already knew what she was going to do to him before she casually glanced back at him and then dropped her keys on the table by the door.

"Shira…"

A mischievous smile appeared on her tempting lips, and she walked down the hall. "If you want to clean that up, you can. I'm not going to stop you."

"Are you really going to use this bet to get me to clean for you?"

"I told Camila I wouldn't need her to come in this week while you three are staying with me."

That wasn't the no he wanted.

"Besides,"—she stopped to smirk back at him, her eyes gliding over him in a way that stirred strong primal urges—"There's something sexy about a man who cleans."

And then his growing arousal was gone. Jasper rolled his eyes. "What is it with women saying that? Sara said the same thing all the time."

Shira shrugged noncommittally and continued to the kitchen. "Hurry up, I've got the perfect place for you to start."

Jasper worked his jaw, trying not to get over-annoyed. This was his fault. Had he not been overconfident about winning, he would have seen this as a high possibility.

"She could be at least a little more creative than turning me into her housekeeper," he muttered.

"Kinda hypocritical of you, don't you think?" Zach whispered behind him.

Jasper jumped and turned. His pulse raced in his ears. "Don't do that."

Zach kicked off his shoes, and that's when Jasper noticed Serenity had somehow snuck past him and was disappearing into the kitchen.

"You're avoiding my statement," Zach said.

Jasper rolled his eyes. "At least my idea is better than hers, and it's more fun for everyone involved."

"But it's not more creative, which is what you're complaining about." Zach then smirked, his eyes trailing

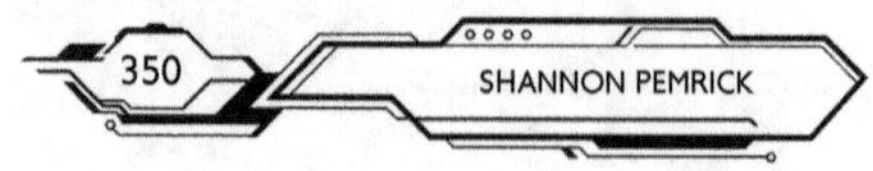

up and down Jasper's body. "And you never know, she might just be trying to get you all hot and sweaty."

Jasper leaned closer to his boyfriend. "There are more fun ways to get me to that point."

"Hey!" Shira called out. "Quit dawdling. Counters need cleaning."

Jasper threw his head back and resisted the urge to sigh. "Fine, fine."

Zach snickered and followed Jasper to the back of the house. His boyfriend was getting far too much enjoyment out of this already. *I should have wrangled him into this somehow.*

Shira was chilling on the couch with Serenity when they reached the end of the hall. Just as she promised, the cartoon was playing on the TV without the use of any computer hookups. He really needed her source. It was such a pain with the newer entertainment tech when you wanted to watch something that came out on DVDs and Blu-ray back in the day. And even though he and Zach didn't have the latest and greatest, it was new enough to also require the extra hoops—unless you had a lot of money to pay for a conversion or knew someone who could convert your media and did it for a fair price.

Without looking their way, Shira pointed to the kitchen. "Cleaning supplies are under the sink."

"And here I thought magic kept this place spotless," Zach joked before sitting down next to her.

Shira laughed. "If only."

Jasper resisted the urge to frown and tried to ignore his growing disappointment. He wanted more than ever to ignore the stupid bet and sit down with all of them like a complete family. But instead, he headed into the kitchen. The sooner he did this task, the sooner it was over with.

However, Jasper slowed his pace when he noticed how dirty the island counter was. He could have sworn they'd taken the time to clean it before leaving, but there was clear evidence of powdered sugar and even syrup that refuted his memory.

Wheels now spinning, he crouched in front of the sink and rummaged around, looking for the supplies he'd need. *Maybe I've been looking at this wrong?* Jasper had treated this like some sort of unfair punishment that also seconded as a joke for her. It wouldn't be unlike her to do it, so his gut reaction wasn't entirely in the wrong. But how he was acting was.

Jasper threw on some gloves and took in the kitchen, as if he was assessing his workspace, but he wasn't.

Shira knew about the problem he'd developed. She was understanding and supportive. And now that he looked at this situation, this was clearly her attempt at helping.

The kitchen did need to be cleaned. She could have picked any other part of the house, but she chose one that couldn't be left as it was. Because he was a bit of a neat freak, she chose a task that catered to that quirk.

Jasper sprayed down the counter.

Shira also wasn't stupid. She would have some sort of inkling what he had hoped to gain from the bet, and chose to take that away. He may not have reacted in any extreme way, but the urges to control the situation were in fact there. By her choosing an activity he found less interesting, Jasper now had to face that annoyance and disappointment without lashing out like a child.

He scrubbed the rag over a syrup spot. *Though, if I'm honest with myself, I was pretty much acting like a pouty child.* There wasn't even a guarantee Shira would go along with his plan had he won the bet. He also didn't know her plans after she had him clean the kitchen.

Jasper glanced up when he caught Shira and Zach whispering. Serenity watched the TV show with tired eyes, but Shira and Zach conversed in hushed tones, their attention on Jasper. They were smiling about something.

Jasper's eyebrow cocked. "What are you two conspiring together about?"

Clearly it had something to do with him, but it didn't seem all that mischievous, based on their light expressions.

"Nothing," Zach said, getting up and leaving the room.

That confused Jasper, for sure. His boyfriend's tone didn't seem annoyed or anything. To top it off, Shira didn't react to the sudden departure, and instead resumed watching the cartoon. *They have to be trying to mess with me.*

Unfortunately, it was kind of working.

He continued cleaning to take his mind off everything, until Zach returned, and not empty-handed.

Jasper's lips quirked up. Zach had gone to retrieve Serenity's plushie. Given she was most likely going to pass out during this TV session, it made sense. And she might fall asleep faster with it—if she didn't fight a nap. She was at the age that naps now only happened under certain conditions.

He's perfect. Jasper felt strongly about that thought— Zach was perfect. He didn't really deserve his boyfriend, but here he was, sticking it out with him through life. Jasper wouldn't let that go for anything. He loved Zach, and Jasper would do anything to keep from losing what they had.

And this arrangement to have Serenity go away for a day or two might help. Jasper didn't have any concrete plans to pull something off, and it might not happen this week, but he'd brought everything he'd need, just in case. He knew for sure he didn't want to delay it too much longer, even with him and Zach exploring the options with Shira. He could do both. Including her didn't mean he had to put a stop to his plan with Zach.

Serenity happily took her plushie from Zach and snuggled up against Shira. Jasper focused on finishing the island, then moved to the counter. There was grease everywhere from the bacon. *How the hell did we miss all this?* If he didn't know any better, he'd accuse Shira of being a time wizard and bringing all this mess back just for him to deal with.

Jasper lost track of time, and when he looked up from scrubbing a particularly tough spot on the stove, Shira and Zach were no longer lounging on the couch. Instead, they'd perched themselves at the island, watching him.

He opened his mouth to ask them what they were doing, but Zach pressed his fingers to his lips and tossed his head toward the living room. At a quick glance, Jasper noted Serenity was still on the couch. She snuggled with Snake, and her eyes gave away her zoned-out state. She was oblivious to anything but the TV, though he could understand why Zach wanted to be cautious. Serenity was fighting a nap at this point, given she hadn't already fallen asleep, but it was good practice to let her zone and relax. Everyone needed a recharge in some way, even if it wasn't a catnap.

"Do I want to know why you're just sitting here, watching me clean?" he asked in a hushed tone.

"I told you, a man cleaning is hot," Shira said before plucking a large strawberry from a plate in front of her. From the looks of it, she'd eaten three since sitting down. She smirked, her lips curving in an appealing, seductive way. "And with your impressive physique, you provide some of the best arm porn I've had the privilege of laying eyes on."

Jasper's eyebrow spiked. "Is that so?"

He wasn't quite sure what to make of her statement—or her state, for that matter. She was hard to figure out sometimes. One moment, she was shy and elusive, the next an electric temptress.

Zach tapped one of the fruits. "I agree with her. The show is quite nice."

Jasper pursed his lips and then pushed his cleaning arm across the stove, intentionally making the movement slow and elongated. Zach smirked and Shira bit into her strawberry, her eyes gleaming. The ample red juice of her fruit spilled over her lips and dribbled down her chin. Jasper's gaze followed the teasing line.

He had a sudden urge to abandon his cleaning to lick the juice off her himself. However, Zach beat him to that, in a way. His finger reached out, and in an agonizingly slow motion, he wiped the red liquid off her chin and lips. As Zach withdrew, Shira watched him with great intensity, though didn't let him get far before her head jerked. Her tongue flicked out, the overhead kitchen light catching the teasing shining silver ball in her mouth, and before either of them knew it, she'd captured his finger in her mouth.

Zach's throat bobbed in time with the hardening need forming in Jasper's pants. His hand fisted the rag tightly, every muscle in his body tight and ready to spring. He wanted to drop everything this bet was and pull her into the other room.

Shira released Zach, slowly and teasingly, a mischievous grin on her lips. "Don't take what's mine."

Jasper nearly snorted. She could say what she wanted to cover that up, but Shira knew full well what she'd just done. Jasper was used to her avoiding their advances. He could recall each time she'd pretended to not notice, or force herself to ignore them. But now, whatever switch had been flipped in her to act this way toward them—he liked it.

Zach recovered and grabbed a strawberry for himself. "Fine, I'll have my own, then."

She reached for the fruit. "This whole plate is mine. I didn't say you could have one."

Zach pulled away, grinning. "You didn't say I couldn't."

Shira pursed her lips, though she didn't voice an argument. Zach took that as permission to eat his prize. However, just before he could bite into the red flesh, Shira planted her palms on the island counter and popped up off her stool. Her mouth brushed against Zach's, and Jasper noticed her tongue dart out and slide over Zach's lower lip before wrapping around the strawberry.

She pulled away, smirking, leaving Zach open-mouthed, dazed, and with ninety percent of his stolen strawberry missing. Jasper swallowed and released the rag in his hand. He needed to be part of all this.

Before he could move away from the stove, Zach

recovered and reached out to Shira, grasping her chin with his finger and thumb. He made her look up at him, and she did, her eyes wide.

Zach leaned closer and licked a trace of sweet juice off her lips. Her eyes popped more, and he grinned. "Don't underestimate what I'd do to get a little taste of something sweet."

He rendered Shira speechless, and Jasper was harder than ever now. He wasn't sure if he'd rather be part of this, or continue to be a voyeur. There were perks to both. One thing he was sure about was his desire to whip out his cock to give himself some relief. Of course, that couldn't happen with a small human zoning out just beyond the kitchen.

This flirty game was a bit of a risk in itself. Jasper and Zach refused to hide their love in front of their daughter. They agreed they wanted her to see what love really was, so she knew how to set her own expectations as an adult. However, the situation with Shira was a bit different.

They may not have hidden their intentions regarding Shira in front of Serenity—not for a lack of trying in the beginning—but he didn't want to expose her to all the usual interactions he would between just him and Zach until Jasper knew this was going to work out with Shira. He didn't want to get his daughter's hopes up. *A little too late for that, with her already calling Shira her mom.*

He didn't mind Serenity saw Shira that way. If things didn't work out between the three of them—*It's going to work out*—then maybe they could figure out some sort of co-parenting that included her. She'd already gone above and beyond for them in the years they'd known her. It wouldn't be that long of a stretch to make something official.

Jasper's attention went back to the flirting pair when Zach pulled away from Shira. She remained where she was, however, her eyes had gone contemplative and her teeth caught her bottom lip. Jasper resisted the urge to close the distance between him and the island and lean over to help her with that problem.

Then, suddenly, Shira popped up on her toes and kissed Zach. Nothing quick or playful and teasing, but slow and inviting. Zach leaned in, sliding his fingers along her jaw until they reached her scarlet tresses. He fisted his hand in her hair, holding her captive as their kiss deepened.

Jasper bit back a groan, his pulse picking up watching the show. Damn, did he want to be part of this. He adjusted his erection through his clothes, the hard appendage too restricted now within the material confines. *I'm not going to be an idle voyeur.*

Shira broke her kiss with Zach and turned her attention to him. "I don't recall telling you to stop."

Her voice had dipped, sensual lust coating each word, calling to him. Jasper pushed away from the counter. "I discovered something that needed more pressing attention."

Shira's lips pursed, and she hummed before pulling away from Zach and the island. Her hand slid over Zach's chest as she walked around him. He turned with her, not breaking his snared attention.

Jasper watched Shira walk toward him, their eyes locked, anticipation prickling under his skin. The distance between them inched away until she was only an arm's length away.

Shira reached up, her fingers gliding over his cheek and then curling around the back of his head. She tugged him down, raising up on her toes to meet him halfway. Her hot breath puffed against his lips before their mouths locked. They both inhaled together.

Jasper snaked his arms around her waist, pulling her in tight against his hard body. Their lips parted and then connected again. Fevered need built deep within Jasper, and he kissed Shira deeper, swiping his tongue over her lips, asking for permission. It didn't come.

She pulled away all too soon and stepped around him, an alluring smirk on her lips. Shira faced him and Zach as she walked backward, toward the short hallway leading directly to the dining room.

"There's something in the pantry I want you to tackle next," she said, her tone even lower and more captivating than the last time she spoke. "Zach, I'd like you to help."

Jasper followed wordlessly, completely entangled by her spell. He didn't care what she asked of him in there, as long as it resulted in her writhing in pleasure and screaming his and Zach's names.

Shira slipped out of sight into the pantry. Jasper was hot on her heels, his simmering blood pushing him faster. The normally spacious-feeling pantry closed in around them, forcing Shira to slow, yet Jasper didn't.

Her eyes visibly widened when she realized he had no intention of stopping until there was no room left for her to go. The pent-up desire building in him all day had been called out with this pseudo-chase, and he was going to give in to it.

Shira opened her mouth to say something, but he was faster. Jasper captured her face with his hands and crashed his mouth into hers, jamming his tongue inside her warmth and devouring her with fevered need.

A startled squeak mixed with a moan in her throat. She grabbed his wrists and curved her chest into his for a moment before trying to break away. Jasper allowed the kiss to break, but held her captive.

Shira chuckled and spoke, her lips brushing against his with each word. "You seem to have forgotten who gets to tell whom what to do today."

Jasper tried to kiss her again, but she dodged somehow, with zero space between them. "Shira, don't be like this."

His cock strained hard against his pants, and every muscle in him tightened and fought against his restraint. He wanted nothing more than to push her against the cooler behind her, lift her skirt, and fuck her until she was an exhausted, pleasured mess.

Shira grinned and nipped his lower lip, teasing him further. "Don't be like what? Like I'm in the position you wanted to be in when you made this bet?"

It wasn't like he was trying to hide his intent behind the bet, besides trying to prove her wrong. He'd pushed boundaries with her when he won bets in the past, and given what the three of them had done together already, Shira would have to intentionally avoid all his and Zach's actions toward her up to this point and ignore what happened yesterday to not see Jasper's intent.

Shira forced him to release her face and dragged his hands down her delicate, soft neck. "If you wanted sex, all you had to do was ask, instead of coming up with some convoluted bet."

Jasper swallowed, his pulse pounding harder in his ears. "It worked, didn't it?"

One of her eyebrows arched, her lips curved into a devious smirk. She stopped his hands' downward descent at her collarbone. "Did it?"

He sucked in a sharp breath, concern bubbling up through his maddening desire that she was going to reject him after luring him this far. "You gave us negotiating power."

Yeah, he was going to use that now—another nonsecret. He could tell with the way she'd contemplated the compromise this morning, she knew exactly what he'd intended for it. Not that his and Zach's flirting this morning was all that subtle, either.

"I gave you *some* negotiating power. You didn't clarify how much that was, leaving it up to me."

Shit. She had him there. He'd, of course, noticed her change the wording, but he hadn't thought she'd actually use that against him.

Shira's tongue dragged across her lower lip. "But it wouldn't matter in this situation anyway, because that negotiation was used up already."

Everything in him stopped. "Used up? When?"

A hard chest pressed against Jasper's back, and Zach's hands slipped around Jasper's front and up under his shirt, the callouses of his boyfriend's hands biting into his skin.

Even though Zach was about an inch shorter than Jasper, it wasn't enough difference to stop Zach's cheek from brushing against Jasper's, the roughness of his late evening stubble scratching with his own. "When the two of us came to a fun agreement."

Jasper closed his eyes and bit back a groan when one of Zach's hands slid higher, while the other slipped down to the waistband of his pants. "So you two were conspiring against me."

"Conspiring?" Zach chuckled, his hot breath sending pleasure down Jasper's spine. "No, that would mean you get little out of this."

Shira dragged Jasper's hands down her chest again until his fingers caught the neck of her off-the shoulder crop top. "And if you ask me, you're going to get the best deal out of all this."

She then forced him to tug her top down. Her supple breasts spilled out into his hands, surprisingly no bra in the way. Jasper didn't care, immediately focusing on playing with her. Shira let out a breathy moan and then popped onto her toes to kiss him without restraint this time.

Their lips locked and his hunger from earlier resurfaced. Her hands ran over his chest on top of his shirt, while Zach kissed the back of his neck and worked the button and zipper of Jasper's pants. The sensations these two were already offering him were driving his desire into a frenzy that threatened to cloud his mind.

Jasper allowed one of his hands to release Shira and slip down her side, over her hip, and under her skirt. She moaned quietly into him as his fingers made contact with bare skin.

He traced the shape of her hip to the soft, rounded shape of her ass and halted, breaking his kiss with her, when no fabric interrupted his exploration until he touched the thin string that slid between her cheeks. "I could ignore the lack of bra, but I didn't peg you to be *that* adventurous in a skirt on a family-friendly outing."

Shira chuckled, her eyes sparkling. "As much as I'd

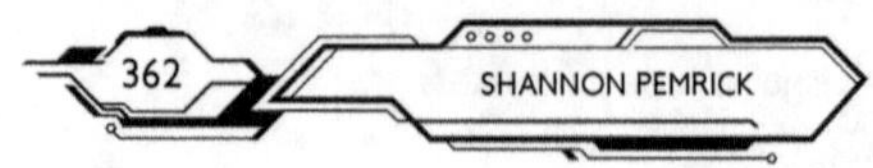

love to tell you not to underestimate what I'm willing to do, I didn't do that, this time."

He swallowed, liking how she phrased that.

"While you were distracted cleaning," she continued. "I made a small wardrobe change."

"And I made sure we had everything we'd need when we lured you in here," Zach murmured before nibbling Jasper's ear.

Jasper closed his eyes. *These two... are going to ruin me.*

Shira kissed his jaw, then lower and lower on his neck, her hands trailing down his chest. Jasper's muscles flexed and pulsed under her touch. He teased her breast for one more moment before releasing her and reaching down to caress her bottom with both hands.

Shira gasped when he gripped the back of her thighs and lifted her up. Her arms flew around his neck, her legs instinctively squeezing his sides. Jasper pressed his lips against her exposed neck while sliding his fingers along her bare inner thighs.

She let out a soft moan. "You're going off-script."

Zach chuckled. "I told you he would. But we'll lure him back."

He reached up and cupped Shira's cheek, pulling her in for a hungry kiss over Jasper's shoulder. Zach's other hand still roamed Jasper's form.

Heat simmered in Jasper's veins throughout his entire body. His fingers slid farther along her thighs, making contact with what little material made up her thong. It was already damp with Shira's arousal.

Without waiting for her to realize and react, he slid his fingers under the fabric and along her wet folds to her clit. Shira gasped, breaking her kiss with Zach.

Jasper glanced up to watch her as he teased her sensitive flesh. Eyes half-lidded, and mouth parted, she panted and moaned. The sound of her pleasure heated his desire for more.

Jasper plunged a finger inside her, and then another. Shira closed her eyes, her back arching, and a low moan rumbled through her into him. He grinned and found rhythm in slow, powerful strokes pleasuring her.

Jasper was vaguely aware of Zach's touch on him throughout all this. He was so focused on Shira that he found himself surprised when his pants loosened, then fell to his ankles. Zach's palms glided over his hips and tucked into the waistband of Jasper's boxer briefs before shoving them off, too, freeing his throbbing erection.

He bit back a groan when Zach's hand wrapped around him, rhythmically stroking in the way Jasper liked it. His pleasuring of Shira altered to match Zach's pace, and Shira practically purred her approval.

Zach's lips brushed over Jasper's shoulder, trailing up his neck and over his jaw. Jasper turned his head into his boyfriend's touch, and Zach captured his mouth with his. Hungry need drove them, their lips syncing, tongues wrestling. Desire hazed Jasper's mind, making it difficult to focus on either one of them, or remember what plan he'd intended to enact in here with Shira. He could only now think of satisfaction—for himself—for all three of them.

Shira's lips pressed against Jasper's exposed throat. Just like Zach had done, she trailed sensual kisses across his skin, up his jaw, and then to his ear.

"Set me down, Jasper," she murmured, her voice filled with pleasure. "Time to go back on script."

He refused, and instead increased his pleasuring of her. He would make her forget this *script* of hers and convince her to go along with his plan instead. His was creative and fun, if requiring a little more physically from him to achieve the end result.

As much as she groaned and writhed, she didn't relent. This time, her tongue slid over his skin. "I promise it'll be worth your while to concede this time. You're going to enjoy what we've planned."

Her sensual tones mixed with the feel of her tongue piercing gliding along with her teasing caress sent intense arousal flooding through Jasper, and his cock jerked in Zach's hand.

Zach broke their kiss, grinning. His pale blue eyes sparkled like ice after the first winter frost, yet were warm and inviting like a blanket and good book by the fire. "Oh, whatever you just did, he liked that a lot."

Shira chuckled and repeated the action. "I'm sure he did. He'll like it even better when he finally listens to me."

Jasper's gaze lingered on Zach a moment before he turned his attention to Shira. Her green eyes glimmered, a spark of summer heat, fiery passion, and spontaneous fun. Two opposites, rotating Jasper in orbit, holding him captive in a spell he willingly submitted to.

He extracted his fingers from Shira, earning one last pleasured groan, and slowly released his hold on her thighs. She slid down his front, each muscle in his body straining and responding to her touch and his forced restraint.

Shira's mouth trailed down Jasper's neck and chest, leaving a fiery trail in her wake. When her feet touched the floor, she continued to lower herself onto her knees, her lips and tongue teasing his flexing abs, anticipation sending tingles to his fingers.

Zach grinned against Jasper's ear. "You've been dying to test her piercing out since seeing it the other day. We came to the agreement, today would be that day."

Jasper opened his mouth to inquire further, since there had to be a catch. But his words came out as a hiss when Shira kissed the tender skin below his navel. She continued lower, her hands sliding down his sides and over his hips.

This forced Zach to release Jasper, though there wasn't any complaining from his boyfriend's end. No, he seemed content to watch Shira's hands skate down to the base of Jasper's hard shaft and wrap around him.

Jasper placed a hand on the cooler to steady himself. His pulse pounded in his ears, desire and anticipation burning so hot in his veins, he thought he might combust. And then, she slid her tongue along his cock.

Jasper's eyes closed, and he hissed in pleasure. Her metal piercing dragged leisurely across his engorged flesh, the right amount of pressure applied to make this extra satisfying.

Shira's eyes flicked up to him when she reached the head of his cock. Jasper sucked in a sharp breath just before she eased her lips around his thick member.

"Shit, babe," he groaned out, bracing his other hand against the cooler.

Shira slid him in and out of her mouth in a slow and controlled pace; her tongue glided over him in practiced movements.

"Feel good?" Zach asked in Jasper's ear, his strong hands sliding across Jasper's back under his shirt.

Jasper's hands curled into tight fists. "Fucking fantastic."

He knew she was good; Shira had proven that in-game when he'd seduced her on the mountain. But damn, this was so much better.

Maybe it was because she was more real—the tangible woman he and Zach could finally hold close, enjoy in so many different ways, and never let go. Or maybe it was because there was less holding them all back. Even Jasper had measured himself that first time so as not to risk running Shira off. But after taking a risk yesterday and showing her another side of them, Shira had accepted, and even enjoyed, what she'd experienced.

Zach chuckled. "If this is already fantastic, I'll be interested to hear your opinion about the rest we have in store for you."

A throaty chuckle vibrated from Shira into Jasper. He sucked in a sharp breath, which was completely stolen right after when Shira flicked her gaze up to snare him. Eyes dancing, she didn't cease her maddening attention while she reached behind herself and flipped the back of her skirt up, exposing her perfect, round ass.

With slow, sensual movements, Shira dragged her hands along the curve of her bottom, and down her thighs. One hand continued down to plant on the floor, while the other slid to her inner thigh and then disappeared under the front of her skirt.

Jasper sucked in another hard breath when she moaned, her back arching and pushing out her perky breasts. Her eyes lidded, but they never broke contact with Jasper's, allowing him to see the desire in them. It matched his own, fogging his mind—overwhelming him.

Jasper reached down and tangled his fingers in her red locks, holding her captive. Her eyes sparked, as if expecting what came next—or just enjoying the control she allowed him.

A moment of stillness passed between them before Jasper thrust his cock deeper into her throat. Shira's eyes popped, then closed when they found rhythm together. "That's it. Take it all, babe. Enjoy my cock fucking your face."

She moaned in response.

Jasper's breath came in hard, barely controlled bursts. His body hummed with pleasure, clouding his mind even further, sending him into a single-minded focus.

He barely noticed Zach's touch and warmth leave him. He didn't question what his boyfriend was up to. His mind only cared about one thing—until the unmistakable cool sensation of lube slid over his backside, bursting his haze.

Jasper sucked in a tight breath, and Zach bent closer to murmur in his ear. "Relax."

Every muscle in his body was tense. "Easier said than—"

He groaned when Shira slid her tongue around his cock in a new way, as if to remind him she was still there. Both of Jasper's eyebrows spiked to emphasize his words. "See? You two are already driving me crazy."

They both chuckled against his skin, sending all kinds of competing sensations through Jasper. Zach then kissed the back of Jasper's neck. His teeth grazed Jasper's skin, while he applied the cool lubricant over his tight hole.

Jasper leaned forward to make this easier on them

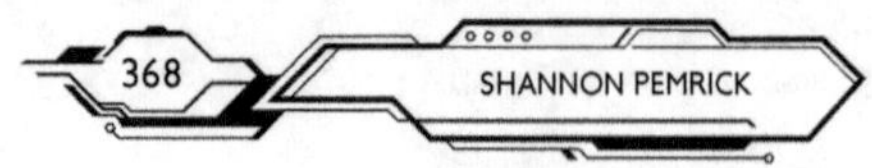

both, his tense muscles quivering with the effort to support himself. Zach worked his fingers inside him and Jasper groaned. The sensation, mixed with Shira's attention, was already overwhelming.

"Ready?" Zach murmured.

"Fuck yes," Jasper managed. If his boyfriend didn't hurry it up at this rate, he might just lose it.

Zach's hands gripped Jasper's hips. His boyfriend's hard length nudged his entrance and then thrust inside. Their groans mingled, and Shira let out a quiet, startled sound when Jasper inadvertently shoved his cock deeper down her throat in his accepting of Zach until he was buried deep.

Zach thrust hard and fast into Jasper, his hips slapping against the flesh of Jasper's ass. Wild sensations of pleasure blazed through Jasper. His breath labored and his heart hammered in his chest and ears as all sensations beyond the three of them faded away.

Shira reached out and cupped Jasper's balls with her free hand, adding another layer of powerful and overwhelming sensations through Jasper. He hissed a name out, but he wasn't sure whose.

Jasper was thrust into the crashing waves of desire, rocked back and forth between his two favorite people, unable to focus on either one for more than a second. Mind overloaded and unable to think, he could do no more than accept the tides of pleasure they fed him—coordinated in a way only he could appreciate.

Climax built in Jasper, his body tensing and feeling as though it was unraveling at the seams, unable to hold back any longer. He blanked on giving Shira any verbal warning, before he roared in an explosion of ecstasy.

His hot seed shot into the back of her throat, and Jasper was vaguely aware of her muffled scream of reached orgasm over the pulse thundering in his ears. Zach wasn't far behind them, coming hard and spilling inside Jasper.

Shira pulled away, releasing his spent flesh and resting her forehead on Jasper's leg as she gasped for air. Zach also withdrew, leaning against Jasper's back in a breathless, spent dead weight. Jasper barely supported them both with weak legs and trembling body, leaning against the cooler. The coldness seeping through the glass was a welcomed relief to his hot and sweaty skin. Jasper was vaguely aware of his hand still tangled in Shira's hair, though his grip had significantly relaxed.

The three of them remained a bizarre, tangled mess for several long moments, their heavy breathing the only sound echoing in the pantry, until feeling returned to Jasper's limbs.

He shifted, and Zach reluctantly moved, though not before he planted a kiss on Jasper's spine between his shoulder blades, eliciting a sharp hiss from Jasper.

"Told you it would be worthwhile," Zach murmured.

"Hmm…" Jasper managed, his brain still sluggish.

He helped Shira up. Her legs wobbled underneath her, and he held her close, her soft form melding into him. Jasper's brow spiked. "Your self-pleasuring that good?"

With drooping eyes, she attempted to turn her languid smile into a smirk, with little success. "Unlike you, I know all the tricks to pleasing my body perfectly."

Spent or not, Jasper's libido rose at the challenge. "Is that so?"

She snorted and leaned against the cooler, her

half-naked body on display for him. "Don't even think about it."

Though she said the words, the rosy tint to her cheeks deepened, as if she were already thinking of the ways he could please her. Before he could think of a way to convince her to allow him to try, a phone alarm went off.

"And there's the Serenity Alarm," she mumbled. "Not bad timing."

Jasper's brow arched. "The Serenity Alarm?"

Zach snickered and grabbed for his boxers and pants. "We had the AIs set up an inconspicuous alarm for when she started to stir."

Smart. No wonder the two were confident they could seduce him while his daughter chilled out on the couch.

Shira took a deep breath, straightened her skirt and shirt before attempting to fix her hair. "You two should go get some PvP practice in. I'll keep Serenity company."

Jasper reluctantly agreed. He'd rather continue to spend time with her, but they did have a tournament to win.

Zach tossed his thumb toward the door. "I'll keep her occupied real quick while you change. I'm sure you'd rather wear something less risky while lounging around with her."

Shira choked on a laugh. "Yeah, that's true. I won't take too long."

She sauntered out of the space, both Jasper and Zach watching her go. Jasper's desire to catch her pulsed deep inside him again.

"I'll meet you downstairs," he mumbled, already taking strides to follow.

Zach snorted. "Of course you can't stop yourself from wanting to get a peek at her going up the stairs."

Jasper flashed him an unapologetic grin and hurried after Shira. He knew the view would be good.

CHAPTER 19

Letting out a long, frustrated breath, Shira stared up at her ceiling, the room around her dark, save for light leaking in around her balcony curtains from a neighbor's yard spotlight. Her right arm twitched, and then her hips, as if they were trying to get away from something.

She'd really hoped she could get a break from this. With how happy she'd been these past few days, and the incredible sex, Shira had thought her body would take all the endorphins and chill out for once. But no, that apparently was too much to ask for, and here she was praying she wouldn't have a flare-up by the time the sun rose.

With another sigh, she flicked on her nightstand light and sat up. She ran her fingers roughly through her hair. At this rate, she wasn't going to be able to sleep, and she worried about the plans she'd made for tomorrow.

Shira had promised a special outing for Serenity. She'd

coordinated with Narissa and Mercedes, and even got a special gig with Kane. *And of course, this stupid, broken body of mine has to threaten to ruin all of it.*

Why couldn't she go more than a few days without everything going wrong? And why was this week so much worse than any others she had? It wasn't unusual for her to have pain flares, but it'd been a long time since she'd had so many back-to-back incidents.

She leaned against her mountain of pillows. *Don't think you're fooling yourself, you know why.* She did, and she hated it.

Movement outside her door caught Shira's attention. For a moment, she thought it was Snake. She'd allowed Serenity to have him as a bedmate, though her faithful companion always slipped away once the girl was asleep, and rejoined Shira. However, Shira soon realized the entity out in the hall was much too large to be Snake. Plus, he'd have barged in by now.

"Shira?" Jasper's hushed voice said through the crack in the door.

Her brow spiked. "Come in."

His familiar hand wrapped around the ajar door and Jasper quietly opened it further until he stood in her doorway, in nothing but his boxer briefs. Shira's brain stalled at the sight of the mouthwatering view he presented. Everywhere he could have muscle, he did. And Shira knew it; she'd felt that body of his enough times this week.

Her core pulsed at the memories. She wasn't sure what had gotten into her earlier today, except, for the first time in a long time, she stopped thinking and just did what her gut told her to do. No questions asked.

She couldn't quite remember how she'd gotten into a teasing conversation with Zach, which sparked their little plan for the pantry, but she was honestly glad she'd done it. It was spontaneous, and fun. Not something she'd done in a long time. And god, was she rewarded for her efforts. *I wouldn't mind repeating some of that right now with Jasper.*

"What are you doing up?" Jasper asked, breaking her out of her lust-turned thoughts.

"I was going to ask you that," she said.

He held up a granola bar in his hand. "Midnight snack."

Shira glanced at her digital wall clock. "It's three in the morning. Hardly a midnight snack now."

He shrugged. "Semantics. Why are you up?"

She leaned back against her pillows again. "Can't sleep."

He frowned and closed the door behind him. Still quiet, he padded across the floor until he was next to her bed. "What's wrong?"

Shira was tempted to lie and insist she was fine. She didn't want to bother him with her problems, or inconvenience him in any way. But she also knew she couldn't keep this all locked up and hidden away. It wasn't good for her. And she knew, if anything were to come of her and Jasper and Zach, she couldn't shield them from these very real situations. They'd have to see *everything* she went through, no matter how irritating it might get for them.

"My body can't get comfortable," she said. "Some aches and pains, and generally being annoying to the point sleep is impossible right now."

Jasper's frown deepened, and he set his snack on her nightstand. "Is there anything I can do to help?"

She shook her head. "I just have to wait it out, and hope it doesn't turn into a full-on pain flare."

"I know you said there wasn't a way to predict those, but did something possibly trigger this?"

Shira shrugged. "I'm pretty sure it's because of how active I've been this week. It's the most I've gotten in one go in several years. The most I get is moving around my house and walking Snake, with the occasional outing with family or friends."

Jasper went to say something, but his words halted when he attempted to sit down on the bed and fell back, sinking into her plush bed. "Whoa. This is one hell of a soft bed."

Shira pressed her hand to her mouth to suppress a laugh. "You like it?"

He thought for a moment. "Yeah. It's like a cloud. I'm glad the guest bed isn't like this. I'd be so spoiled, it'd be hard to go back to sleeping on the bed back home."

Gears started turning in her head, and Jasper caught it. He pointed at her. "Don't you dare."

She blinked and feigned innocence. "Don't dare what?"

"I know that look. I'd better not see a mattress delivery when we get home."

She huffed, the air from her breath puffing a strand of her red hair. "Fine. I just want to repay you and Zach somehow."

His brow furrowed. "Repay us for what?"

"Helping me. I'd have never gotten this far without you two." She adjusted herself to get more comfortable,

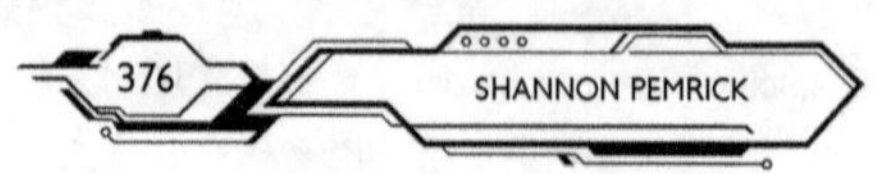

including pulling her knees up to her stomach. "And I don't know how else to repay you two."

With some slight difficulty, Jasper scooted back on the soft bed until he, too, was propped up against her pillows next to her. He then reached out with both arms and wrapped them around Shira's shoulders, pulling her into his chest. She instinctively relaxed into him, even though she was confused about what he was up to.

"You don't have to repay us," he murmured, his hot breath caressing her skin. She had to suppress a pleased shiver. "We've done all of this because we care, Shira. We don't want any compensation or for you to feel like you have to repay us."

He reached up and ran his fingers through her hair. Shira closed her eyes and bit back a moan. She loved having her hair played with.

"Though, to be honest with you, I can't say you haven't repaid us in some way already."

"How so?" Shira asked, her words coming out soft and almost dreamily.

"You've helped both me and Zach in a similar way." Jasper continued to play with her hair. "We may not have the same trauma as you, but we've got our own dark shit haunting us. You've helped us face quite a bit of it, and we're thankful for that."

Shira lazily smiled. "I'm glad. I want to be there for you both. Always."

Shit, I'm babbling. This always happened when she was in this position. And she was a little too honest when it happened as well.

He hummed thoughtfully. "Always? We'd like that."

Shira relaxed into Jasper more and glanced up at him. "Is this okay?"

The smile he flashed her, gentle and warm with a little mischief splashed in, made Shira's heart skip. "Of course it is."

His fingers slid along her scalp, drawing her deeper into her relaxed state. Shira really enjoyed his touch.

"How did practice go earlier?" She hadn't had the chance to talk to them when they'd finished, as she had been on her way to bed.

"It went all right," he said. "We really should have practiced these other combos sooner, like you said. But with more practice before the tournament starts back up, we should be able to get something more concrete worked out."

At least he can admit where they went wrong. "Are you nervous? For the tournament, I mean."

Jasper was quiet for a moment. "Yeah. I've been in a lot of tournaments, but none of them have been nearly as big as this one. It's why we couldn't get a sponsahship outside of Ajax, and really, it was luck he was willing to do it, even if we are friends. Zach and I are nobodies compared to those we're going against. The media coverage is all too eagah to point that out, and I've heard the whispering from othah teams, too."

He sighed. "It's a lot of pressure put on us to do well, and not letting that get to you is difficult. Sometimes I feel like we shouldn't even be here—that we didn't earn our way, and that'll show in these next matches."

Shira frowned, and her chest twinged. She knew that feeling all too well. "If the qualification to get here is about sponsorship, then skills to earn your way here

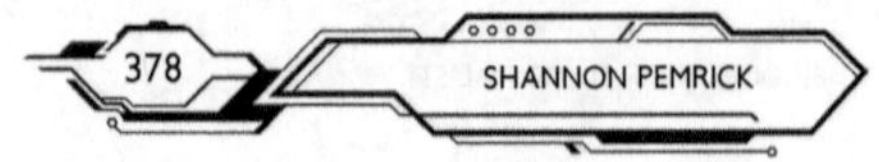

would be a farce, and all these teams putting in their all wouldn't be even half as good as they actually are."

Reaching back, Shira slid her hand across Jasper's cheek, his rough stubble biting at her skin. "You did earn your way here. You and Zach are an incredible team. Just because you've never done a tournament this large before doesn't mean you didn't work hard to get to this point."

She rubbed his cheek with her thumb. "Ajax may be our friend, but we know how he is. He wouldn't give you two a sponsorship, and then go above and beyond, acting like you're his company's permanent prize team, just because you wanted to get here. He only offered all this to you two because he knows your skill, and he knows you two deserve the chance to prove yourselves to the world."

Shira snorted ironically. "And it doesn't matter if you're well-known or not. I had a successful career where people threw my name around, hoping it'd improve their chances somewhere, even if I didn't know them. I was on so many magazines and catalogs, my gig options never ran dry. And I even was on my way to have my own clothing line. And yet, there were still plenty more people who would go, 'Shira who?'"

Jasper rested his forehead on the back of her head. "Thank you. I needed that pep talk."

A small smile spread over Shira's lips. "I'm here for you and Zach, no matter how difficult it gets."

If Jasper planned to say anything back, he didn't get a chance. An ear-piercing shriek and then crying cut through the house. Shira and Jasper bolted upright. *Serenity!*

Jasper was off the bed and running for the door before she'd thrown off her covers. *Stupid pain.* It prevented her from moving at the speed her brain wanted her to.

By the time Shira got through the door, Jasper had made it halfway down the hall and was crouched, holding onto Serenity while she sobbed into his shoulder. Zach had also woken up and made it out of the guest room quicker than Shira. He rubbed his bleary eyes, trying to wake up.

Snake ran up to Shira, whined and pawed the floor before running back to Serenity and nudging her. Unfortunately, neither Jasper nor Serenity understood what he was trying to do, and Jasper tried to stop him.

Shira moved as fast as she could, past Zach and to Jasper's side. She knelt and grabbed Jasper's hand. "He's doing his job. Let him get between her and you."

Jasper hesitated, his parental instinct screaming at him to comfort his child, then relented. Serenity blinked with confused, teary eyes.

"Give Snake a big hug," Shira whispered. "I promise it'll help."

The little girl didn't have to be told twice. She threw her arms around Snake's neck and hugged him tight. The dog wiggled as close as he could to her and patiently waited for Serenity's crying to ease into sniffles.

"Feeling better, Starship?" Jasper asked.

She mutely nodded.

Zach crouched behind Shira and Jasper, placing a hand on both their shoulders. "Did you have a bad dream?"

She nodded again. "It was... scary..."

Jasper reached out and wiped her tear-stained cheeks.

"It's okay. You're safe. Those bad dreams can't get you now."

"I don't want to sleep in my bed, Daddy."

Jasper and Zach exchanged a quick, understanding look and nodded at her. "You can sleep in—"

"She-ra, can I sleep in your bed?" she asked, her eyes wide and pleading.

The look, coupled with this situation, tugged at Shira's heart strings. She may be dealing with some pain tonight, but she couldn't possibly deny her. Even still, she looked to Jasper and Zach for permission. "I don't mind sharing my bed. Plus, Snake won't leave her side for a while after this."

The two men passed another look between them, one Shira couldn't decipher this time, and then they both nodded their approval.

Shira stood and offered her hand to Serenity. The little girl released Snake and grabbed Shira's hand with her small one, and they both headed for Shira's room, Snake padding after them. Heavy footsteps followed and Shira glanced back to see Jasper keeping pace. Zach was disappearing into Serenity's room for some reason.

Jasper helped Shira tuck in Serenity, the little girl mumbling about how soft Shira's bed was, and then Shira climbed in herself. Snake jumped up and nestled in between them. He gently licked Serenity's face, snagging a few exhausted giggles from the girl. Shira praised him with long strokes from his head down to his hips. He had done perfectly.

Zach appeared in the room, and in his hands he carried Serenity's wyvern. The little girl happily snagged her toy, thanking him for retrieving it for her.

Both her fathers took turns bending down and planting kisses on Serenity's forehead, wishing her sweet dreams. She yawned and snuggled into her pillow. Jasper flicked the light off, plunging the room into darkness.

The light seeping in through the balcony curtain outlined their retreating forms, but before they made it to the door, the two men stopped.

Shira pursed her lips. "Something the matter?"

They stood there for a moment, still as statues, and then they broke away, Jasper walking around the bed to Shira's side, while Zach headed back to Serenity's side.

Shira blinked when both climbed into the bed, the king-sized mattress barely large enough to fit all of them. *What are they doing?*

Jasper scooted in close, his hard body pressing into hers. He wrapped a tattooed arm around her middle and pressed his face into her neck and hair.

"Good night," he mumbled, his hot breath raising goosebumps all over her skin.

Shira's question died on her tongue, and she fought back the flush heating her cheeks. Her eyes flicked to Zach when Serenity giggled and mumbled something in regards to everyone sharing Shira's bed, to find him nice and comfortable.

He reached out and brushed his hand against Shira's, laying over the covers. He said nothing, just touched her in such a way that felt more intimate than she expected.

She should question them—ask what was going through their heads. But the desire to do so never came. She didn't want to break whatever spell they'd been afflicted by, or wake from what felt like the perfect dream.

The razor head glided over the last spot on Zach's face that had been slathered in shaving cream. He rinsed the blade, then his face, giving himself a once-over in the mirror. Zach had only nicked himself once this time with the new head.

Jasper's distant rummaging leaked into the bathroom, and from the sounds of it, he was muttering to himself. Either he was struggling to find something, or still disappointed they'd woken up this morning in Shira's bed, with her missing.

He'd mentioned in passing that Shira had talked last night about an increase in physical discomfort and worry that she might have a pain flare, and wondered if she'd slipped out of bed because of that. Three adults, a child, and a large dog were a tight fit, even on a king. Zach wasn't entirely convinced, however.

Shira was an early riser compared to them. And, as nice as it would have been to wake up with her still in bed with them, he and Jasper couldn't expect her to laze around until they woke, too. They were lucky she didn't kick them out immediately.

A smile tugged the corner of Zach's lips. He was glad she hadn't. It'd been nice, even if tight, everyone curling up so comfortably, as if they'd slept like that together all their lives.

Zach finished his morning routine in the bathroom and walked out. Jasper had stopped his grumbling, and from the looks of it, he'd found whatever he'd been searching for. Maybe.

In Jasper's hand, he held an envelope, but it was his boyfriend's blank stare that drew Zach's interest and concern. Taking several long strides, he pulled up next to Jasper and peered down at the envelope.

There wasn't much to it, except Jasper's name written on it in loopy handwriting Zach knew all too well. His heart lurched.

"Jasper," he said in a quiet tone. "Is that… Sara's handwriting?"

He nodded slowly in response, and tilted the envelope until a square object slipped out onto his waiting hand. It was an audio chip.

"What…" Zach's question died on his tongue when he noticed the tightness in Jasper's eyes and the flex of his clenched jaw.

"This was handed to me the day she died," Jasper murmured. "I threw it in my bag, unable to listen to it at the time. I thought I'd cleaned the bag all out and stored this away for when I was ready. I guess… I guess I didn't, and eventually I forgot all about this."

Zach rested his hand on Jasper's back. He understood. After the accident, he and Jasper stopped doing long distance tournaments. The farthest they traveled would result in only a weekend stay, and for those, they'd only needed one suitcase. They'd always chosen Zach's because it was bigger.

As a result, this audio chip remained hidden for almost six years.

"Are you ready to listen to it now?" Zach asked after a moment. As much as hearing Sara's voice might hurt Jasper, especially when he knew it'd most likely sound like she had in the hospital, Zach knew his boyfriend needed to hear her last message. And if he was ready to hear that, it meant Jasper had finally begun healing properly instead of running.

However, before Jasper could respond, Serenity burst into their room. "Daddy, something is wrong with She-ra."

All breath left Zach's lungs. Jasper straightened next to him, and they both whirled around.

"What do you mean?" Jasper asked.

She blinked with innocent, panicked eyes. "She won't wake up."

Jasper tossed the envelope and audio chip into the suitcase, and the two of them bolted out of the room. Zach barely registered his descent to the first floor, or running into the family room.

Shira lay on the couch, her eyes closed. His panicked brain ran through a million and one scenarios before it halted. Zach's eyes focused on the serene expression on her face, and the even rise and fall of her chest. A split second before Orion called out, did Zach realize there may not be anything wrong at all.

"Jasper, do not wake—" Orion didn't get to finish.

Jasper, consumed with fear, grabbed Shira's shoulders and jostled her. "Shira? Shira. Shira."

She twitched, her face skewing, and then she moaned, fighting Jasper's attempts to wake her. In his panic, he didn't recognize the signs, and he continued.

"Told you he wouldn't listen," Alistair quipped to the other AI.

Snapping out of his state, Zach grabbed Jasper's shoulders. "Jasper, stop. She's fine."

It took his boyfriend a moment to respond to his

touch, but he did halt his shaking of Shira and looked up at Zach. "Huh?"

Zach's lips thinned. It was clear Jasper wasn't in a good mindset. His eyes were wide and flicking between Zach and Shira. His grip remained tight around her shoulders.

"Jasper," Zach said again in a calm tone. "Take a deep breath. Shira was only sleeping."

"Sleeping?" Jasper blinked again and turned to gaze at Shira's stirring form.

She sucked in a deep breath through her nose, her face scrunching. One of her hands reached to rub it and she made the most adorable groaning squeak sound Zach had ever heard from her. Then her eyes fluttered open.

"Jasper?" she rasped.

He let out a staggered breath, realizing how much he'd overreacted. "Sorry. I thought…"

Shira rubbed her face with the back of her hand some more, the action so adorable Zach wasn't sure he could take it. "What's going on?"

"Serenity said there was something wrong because you wouldn't wake up," Zach offered in Jasper's stead. "We panicked and came running. We didn't realize you were dead to the world because of deep sleep."

"Hmm, oh, okay." Zach doubted she processed even half his words in her state. "Orion, time?"

"It's nine thirty-five," the AI said. "You've been asleep for about forty-five minutes."

"Okay, thanks," she mumbled as she repositioned herself and tried to wake up.

"Shira, are you okay?" Jasper asked, concern clear in his eyes. Zach was, too. This wasn't like her.

"Yeah, just tired. I didn't get much sleep because of

the pain. Came down here to get some meds and then didn't feel like walking up the stairs, so I've been trying to get sleep down here."

Zach frowned. Jasper was right about her leaving the bed early because of that. Zach really wanted his boyfriend to be wrong.

"I'm sorry I woke you," Jasper said.

Shira shook her head. "It's fine. I should get up anyway. Snake needs his walk."

The mention of "walk" got the large dog jumping up from where he lay by the back door, ears perked and tail wagging. The three of them chuckled before Shira continued.

"I also need food, and then I need to get things together for later today. I can sleep later."

"No," Jasper said, his tone firm and unwilling to budge. "You rest. We'll take care of you until you've gotten the sleep you need."

She let out an exasperated sigh. "Jasper, don't do this."

He reached out his fingers and gently caressed Shira's cheek. "We're going to do this. I'll walk Snake while Zach makes breakfast."

Zach nodded. That arrangement worked out well.

Shira blew out a resigning breath. She wasn't happy, but she clearly didn't have the energy to fight.

Jasper leaned over her and planted a kiss on her forehead before standing and walking off, calling Snake to follow. The shepherd bolted for the front door, and Serenity ran along with him, begging Jasper to go with.

Pink tinged Shira's cheeks, making Zach smirk. She couldn't hide her reactions from them anymore. With each day, they broke down more of her walls and bolting past her rules. It wouldn't be long now before he and Jasper bound her to them.

"I'll make eggs," Zach said. "Something healthy and light. You rest some more while I do."

Shira yawned and made herself more comfortable, no longer willing to resist what was best for her in this moment. "Sounds good."

Zach slipped into the kitchen. Working as quietly as possible, he made up a simple breakfast of scrambled eggs, toast, and sausage links. He'd almost been tempted to use some avocado he found in the fridge, but then thought better of it so as not to overstress Shira's stomach.

When he'd finished, Zach brought her plate and his into the family room, leaving Jasper's and Serenity's on the island for when they returned.

Shira was still awake, though her eyes drooped with her exhaustion. Zach pulled out a nearby end table, so she'd have somewhere to rest her food. The last thing Zach wanted was for Shira to feel she had to sit up and eat.

She smiled her thanks and picked at her food. Zach wasn't sure if she even had an appetite, but food would help her, regardless. The two of them ate in relative silence. He would have loved to hold a conversation with her, but he figured it was best to keep her stimuli down so she'd sleep after breakfast.

"Too quiet," Shira mumbled. "Orion, put something on the TV for noise."

The TV flickered to life and a children's station popped on. Zach choked on a laugh.

"Very funny," she muttered.

The channel switched to a home improvement channel.

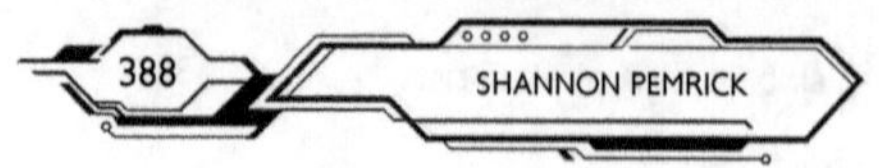

She was content with this, and Zach couldn't complain either. While he and Jasper didn't have a place they could renovate and make their own in drastic ways, Zach liked the ideas these shows generated for him in preparation for the day they'd finally have a house.

Shira turned her attention to him, scrunched her nose, and sat up more. "You shouldn't be sitting on the floor. Come sit on the couch with me."

Zach shook his head. He would not do that to her. "I'm fine. You need the space more."

She patted the cushion with more enthusiasm than necessary. "Come sit."

Zach refused to move. He wanted her to lie down after this.

"Don't make me puppy pout."

His brow arched with both interest and challenge. In her sleepy state, she was already adorable. He wanted to see how the pout would add to things.

Shira obliged without hesitation, puckering her lower lip out and tilting her head. Her beautiful green eyes sparkled in the morning sun peeking in through the patio doors, making her look a bit more desperate. *Shit, that's adorable.*

For dramatics, because after that showing he couldn't convince himself to stay on the floor, he pressed his hand to his chest while he threw his other arm out and jerked his head to the side. "No, stop. It's too cute. I can't take it."

There was a beat of silence, and then they burst into a fit of laughter.

Shira calmed herself first, her eyes sparkling with the remnants of her amusement, and then she patted the couch again. Reluctantly, he complied with her request. If she was too tired to stay awake, he'd just move.

Once he settled next to her, they resumed eating, watching the TV program. They both made a few remarks, from poking fun at the ridiculous budget-to-job-description ratio, to disagreeing with design choices and what they would have done differently.

Zach noticed the two of them had vastly different ideas, but neither were outrageous or clashing enough that it caused the other to shoot side-glances.

Their food finished, Shira leaned against Zach, her eyes drooping, but in her stubbornness she was determined to continue watching this show.

"You should lie down," he said, though he had been tempted to stay quiet. He liked this position.

"No," she mumbled. He braced to listen to her fail to explain how she wasn't actually tired, but that never left her mouth. "You're comfy."

Zach pursed his lips, a thought coming to him. "I never said I was going to move. I do have a free lap you can use."

Shira made a thoughtful sound and then slid off his shoulder and unceremoniously plopped down on his lap. Zach watched her with interest as she slipped her arms around his waist and snuggled into him. She made all manner of cute noises he really didn't expect.

The sexy, tempting vixen from yesterday who'd lured him into a pantry, and the everyday mouthy spitfire, were nowhere to be seen, completely replaced by this new side he'd never witnessed. And he liked every moment of it.

The program continued, Shira's quiet sleeping breaths mingling with the TV's sounds. Zach reclined in his

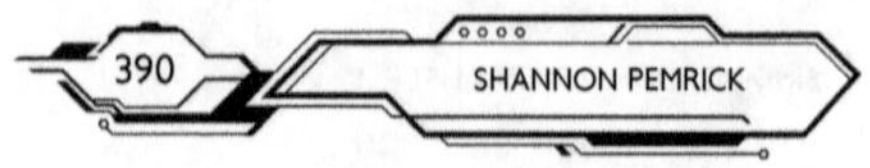

spot, grateful she'd finally conked out. She needed her rest if she wanted to feel better.

Zach understood she was frustrated and didn't want to bail on her plans today. She wanted control over her life and not be beholden to her body's demands. But taking care of herself needed to be the biggest priority. Serenity would understand; she was an aware and caring little girl. And all their friends would get it, too. He just wished she would be less hard on herself as well.

Unwilling to move or potentially disturb her, Zach settled in to watch TV. His hand rested on Shira's head, fingers sinking into her gorgeous hair. Though, over the course of… he wasn't sure how long, losing track of time, that wasn't the only part of her he touched.

Zach lay on his back, an arm propping up his head, with Shira sprawled comfortably on top of him. His other arm wrapped around her, keeping her close. He couldn't recall how this position came about, but he didn't care.

Shira's chest rose and fell against his, her quicker breaths in direct competition with his slower ones. Her nose pressed up against the crook of his neck, and her hot breath tickled his skin.

Having her this close also sent desire roaming through his body. She was so damned tempting, even in her sleep, it wasn't fair. At the same time, he also felt content to have her this way forever. It felt so natural, like when he and Jasper cuddled.

Shira twitched, and then stirred. She sucked in a deep breath, making those cute sounds again, and her bleary eyes blinked. It took her a moment to look around, eventually settling her eyes on him.

"Morning," he said, a smirk tugging his mouth.

"Morning," she croaked before yawning nice and wide. "I'm not in your lap anymore."

"Is that a problem?"

She thought for a moment, her sluggish brain booting the process slowly. "Nah." She then frowned suddenly. "Man, I missed the result for that bathroom, didn't I? Please tell me John didn't go with the piss-yellow bathroom."

Zach made a face. "Unfortunately, he did."

Shira groaned and flopped back down onto him, a bit more dramatically than needed. "What an idiot."

She then wiggled a bit to get comfortable again. "Guess I'll cheer myself up by taking comfort in my new bed."

Zach chuckled. "Do you find me comfortable enough for you to sleep again?"

She made a thoughtful noise. "Maybe. I hope not. I'm tired of drifting in and out of sleep."

"If your body says rest, then rest. I lost track of the times I missed practice because I just needed to sleep."

"It makes me useless," she muttered.

Zach frowned. "No, it doesn't. It's the sign your body is run down and needs to heal. All bodies need that."

She tipped her head to look up at him, her eyes narrowed. "This can't be healed. My body can't be healed anymore."

Jasper had mentioned a few things the two had talked about last night when he'd been distracted coming back to their room after he went to get a snack. One of those things was her theories about the increase in pain.

"That's not what I'm talking about, Shira. Your body is tired. You're using it more than you usually do." *In many ways.* "That works every muscle that hasn't felt such use in a long time, and that means they need time to heal."

Zach reached up and brushed her cheek with the back of his finger. "It'll strengthen them in time, but you can't brute-force that progress like a berserker solo-tanking a boss."

Shira's cheeks tinted a shade of pink and her tempting mouth parted, but she said nothing. Then, she suddenly smiled, her mesmerizing green eyes squinting, and she laid her head back down into the curve of his neck and shoulder. "You're right. I need to be kinder to myself."

Instead of letting his hand drop to his side, Zach threaded his fingers through her hair. She sighed and mumbled something incoherently. He took that as a sign to not stop. Zach wasn't surprised. Shira had said she liked her hair played with.

Shira snuggled into him deeper, triggering a soft heat to spread and radiate through Zach's chest. He was aware how well she fit against him, and her sweet scent wrapped around him, teasing and luring. His free hand rubbed Shira's back, earning him a pleased sigh.

He was both tingling with building desire and content with staying like this with Shira forever.

Zach's head jerked, and Shira's eyes fluttered open when the front door clacked open and voices drifted in. Small feet and tapping nails thundered down the hall, and a moment later, Serenity appeared in Zach's vision. Snake went for his water bowl, greedily lapping up the cool liquid. Jasper appeared in the room a moment later. His eyes took in the sight of the two laying across the couch, but didn't make any comments.

"She-ra?" Serenity asked in a soft voice. "You awake?"

Shira lazily smiled at her. "Yeah, I'm awake, Starship."

"How are you feeling?" Jasper asked.

"Better. Pain is down to my normal levels," she said. "I'm just tired now. I got a little sleep while you both were out. Did Snake behave?"

He smirked. "He was a little rambunctious when he saw people and dogs, but Orion warned me about that, so I was prepared. Otherwise, it was a good walk."

She smiled. "Good. And thank you for taking him. I appreciate it."

He nodded, and Serenity spoke up. "She-ra, are we still going out later?"

"Yes, Starship," Shira said. "I just need to rest a little longer, and then I'll be able to get ready for today."

Zach picked up her certainty, and it elated him. He'd really worried about her, but that put his mind at ease.

Jasper checked the time. "I should get the ribs ready, slow-cook them to perfection."

Shira mumbled about the food choice sounding good. Zach reminded Jasper and Serenity about breakfast, which they eagerly snatched up. When she was done, Serenity asked permission to play with Snake outside. Shira didn't have any issue with it, as long as she stayed away from the pool.

A good thirty minutes passed before Shira wanted to sit up. Disappointment prickled within Zach, but he didn't stop her. It had to end eventually, and if he was lucky, he'd get her back on top of him later—with fewer clothes in the way.

Besides, after Jasper finished prepping dinner, which he adamantly insisted he didn't want any help with, the two of them would have to go up and practice.

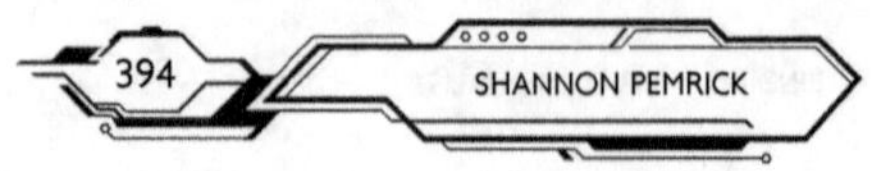

Serenity flew inside from the backyard. Her hair was a crazy mess, and her cheeks were flushed. Snake was right behind her, his tongue lolling and panting hard. She'd been chasing him all around the yard and throwing balls for him this whole time.

"She-ra, is it time to go yet?" His daughter's eyes were wide and hopeful.

Shira chuckled. "Soon. I just need to get ready. And you need to freshen up, too, wild woman."

Serenity giggled and tugged at her hair, as if that'd fix the mess. She mumbled about how much fun she had playing with Snake, and once again asked Zach if they could get a dog of their own. As much as he wanted to tell her yes, until they got out of the apartment, there was no way he could.

Instead, he distracted her with mentions of the fun secret plans with Shira and ushered her down the hall to get her all presentable again. He glanced back before the family room disappeared around the hall corner and looked at Shira. Her hair was also a bit wild, tousled from her sleep, and from his hands in her hair. Thrumming need pulsed down to his core. He really wanted to see this look on her more often—in the morning—naked with every inch of her laid bare while lying next to him and Jasper in bed.

CHAPTER 20

Shira sauntered down the hall toward her bedroom. Jasper had disappeared up here nearly ten minutes ago when Serenity almost had a meltdown that she couldn't find her Rathalos plushie—again. The little girl wasn't planning on bringing it with her, but she needed to know where it was before they left. Why this became a sudden need five minutes before the two of them headed out the door, Shira didn't know, but it made sense to her kid brain, so Jasper promised he'd help her find it.

He figured it was up in Shira's room, given that's where she slept after her nightmare, but Serenity insisted she'd taken it out of there after she'd woken up. Shira had been in the middle of finalizing things with Mercedes and Narissa, making sure they'd be waiting at Cybro Industries, Narissa's family's cybernetic company, so she'd given him quick permission to go look through her room.

She'd been confident he wouldn't do too much snooping, focusing solely on the one task. However, with the amount of time that had passed, she was now concerned. It wasn't like she had much to hide, but there were a few things she'd have liked to keep private.

Shira walked into her room, sunlight streaming in through the balcony. Jasper was easy to spot. He stood by her bed, her nightstand drawer open and a familiar journal grasped in his hands. A frown tugged his lips, and a crease had formed between his eyebrows.

Shira leaned against the doorframe. She knew she should be angry—that journal was private. And while Serenity had found it already, and it'd been by accident, Jasper was an adult. But she couldn't find it in her to be mad.

"Told you I'd gone to a dark place," she said.

Jasper's head jerked up, and his eyes went wide. "I… I…"

He struggled for words to explain himself, pointing helplessly at her nightstand. She let him flounder, finding slight amusement in his struggle, until he finally took a breath to calm himself.

Jasper rubbed the back of his neck. "I'm sorry. I wasn't intentionally snooping. I'd looked inside the drawer, hoping maybe she put her toy in there by mistake. When I was moving things around, this fell out and turned on. I didn't intend to read it, but a few things caught my eye and…"

He sighed, his words drifting off. Shira pushed off the doorframe and closed the distance between them, her pace unhurried. When she was practically standing on his toes, she reached up and rested her hands on his.

"I'm not mad," she said. "I'd have rather saved you from seeing any of that. Especially after what you've had to go through already."

Jasper closed the cover over the digital device and then pulled Shira into him. Her face smooshed against his hard chest, which vibrated with his barely contained emotions. "I'm sorry you had to go through even a fraction of that. I wished we had known each othah then. Maybe we could have each helped the other a lot sooner."

Shira breathed in deep, getting a good whiff of his hickory scent. "There's no point in wishing for things you can't change. The past is the past. It's set in stone, no matter how much we wish it wasn't. It took me a long time to come to terms with that. And even now, I can't say I don't struggle with wistful 'what if' thoughts. But they're always fleeting."

She wrapped one arm around him, still keeping her face buried in his powerful embrace. "There are a lot of things I could have done differently. I could have been a more public activist for the cybernetic community, instead of quietly donating money to activist organizations, charities, and individuals in desperate need of the tech while I hid away. I could have faced my problems instead of sticking my head in the sand and pretending I was as fixed as I could be. I didn't have to close myself off and keep people at an arm's length, even when I knew they were genuine in their offers for kinship."

Shira sucked in a steadying breath and looked up into his blazing green eyes. "I could have done a lot of things. But that doesn't mean I can't do those now. Just because I'm finally allowing myself to truly heal and grow, doesn't mean it's too late."

Jasper's fingers brushed against her cheek, and then he tucked a lock of hair behind her ear. "You are a tenacious woman. It's something I've always admired about you."

Heat pricked Shira's cheeks. She wasn't *that* amazing.

"Do you miss modeling?" he asked.

She blinked. He was gazing at her oddly, on top of that question coming out of the blue.

"I know you stopped because of how the industry treats those with cybahnetics. But you mentioned being an advocate, so I was wondering…"

Shira hesitated on the answer, Narissa's insisting offer haunting the back of her mind once again. *Should I tell him?* How much should she share about her feelings on this topic?

The choice was made for her, as Jasper noticed her conflict. Serenity got her perceptiveness from him. "What is it? You can tell me."

She let out a slow breath through her barely parted lips. "I can't give details, but… Narissa has been hounding me about a modeling opportunity with her company."

He watched her with a critical, assessing gaze. "But you've rejected her, haven't you? Why?"

Shira pulled away and plopped down on the bed. "I do miss modeling, I really do. It wasn't just a hobby for me. Even though it was a stressful job at times, I enjoyed so much of it. And I know, if it's a modeling gig with Cybro Industries, it means it'll benefit cybernetic users."

Her shoulders slumped. "But my issues with cameras…"

Jasper crouched down in front of her, one of his hands firmly grasping her thigh. "You've done really well these last few days. Hell, you even allowed a stranger to take a photo of us with you in it. I know that was difficult to do, but that's major progress compared to just the othah day, when you met us at the convention centah for the first time, and Zach started snapping photos."

He has a point.

"And if you need help overcoming that, Zach and I are more than happy to help." A heart-stopping grin spread up his handsome face. "We've seen what you used to model. We wouldn't have any issues offering assistance."

Shira's chest tightened, her lungs forgetting how to breathe. Before she'd turned eighteen, her modeling career was fairly tame, all her gigs appropriate for her age. But the moment she came of legal adult age, Shira had chosen the path of revealing-yet-functional athletic wear, swimsuits, and eventually lingerie.

Could she wear those kinds of clothes again? *In front of a camera with Jasper and Zach watching?* They'd seen her naked. That answer should have been an easy yes. But somehow, picturing herself in that situation with them felt more intimate, and had heat pulsing between her thighs.

As if some of his own thoughts mirrored hers, Jasper's eyes flicked down to her mouth, and then, after lingering there a moment, wandered lower on her body.

"I'll… consider the offer," Shira said a moment before her brain caught up to her runaway mouth.

Jasper's wicked grin deepened, the sight making her

stomach swoop and her mind run wild with all manner of tantalizing scenarios they may put her in.

"Daddy," Serenity called out in a sing-song voice. "Daddy, I found Rathalos."

The little girl appeared in Shira's doorway a moment later. "Daddy—oh, hi, She-ra. I found my Rathalos. He's tucked into bed now."

Jasper rose to his feet and smiled at his daughter as if nothing had just been happening between him and Shira. "That's great, Starship."

Serenity looked to Shira. "Are we leaving?"

Shira nodded and stood. "Go get your shoes on, and we'll head out."

The little girl didn't have to be told twice and rushed down the hall. Jasper turned and slipped the journal back into Shira's nightstand drawer. He paused and then bent down, lifting a familiar sealed white envelope with scripted handwriting up off the floor.

Jasper stared at the envelope longer than Shira expected. Her gut clenched, as if she was expecting him to turn around and grill her about it. But, after the extended moment passed, Jasper slipped the envelope into her nightstand and then slid the drawer shut.

He looked at her and smiled, nothing seeming out of the ordinary about him. "You and Serenity have fun, okay?"

Shira stuck her tongue out at him. "Of course we're going to have fun. I planned everything."

He snorted at her confidence.

"Good luck with practice today. And so you're not surprised, I called Camilla and asked her to come in and clean. Figured it would help take pressure off all of us

to make sure the house is in good order for when your parents show up."

He nodded, mumbling his appreciation for the heads-up. She could tell the idea of someone coming in to clean for them wasn't something he was used to. Shira didn't doubt it was both because of his controlling tendencies and the fact most thought a housekeeper was out of their budget.

Shira turned to head out, but then stopped and faced Jasper again. "Oh, and if you two find a good chunk of time between the end of your practice and when your parents are expected to arrive, you should take Zach out on a date of your own."

Jasper's brow scrunched and he gestured in the vague direction of where the grill was downstairs. "I've got food cooking."

"And?" she said. "We've got the most state-of-the-art smart-home system installed in this house. That tech includes appliances, and grills are considered appliances. The AIs will monitor it while we're gone."

He wasn't convinced. "Still doesn't sound safe."

Shira shrugged. She couldn't make him be comfortable with the idea, especially if he wasn't accustomed to all the safety measures that came with the tech. "It's up to you. Think of the last time you and Zach took the time to go out on a date, just the two of you."

She then left. No need to linger while he thought about her suggestion, and Serenity would be scampering upstairs any moment to find out why they hadn't left yet.

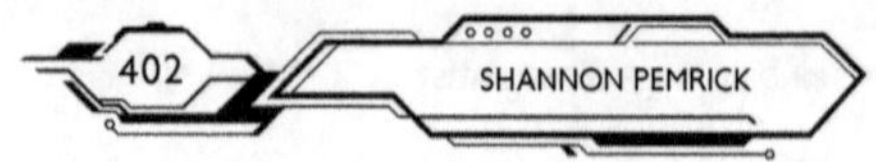

Music blasted through the speakers of Shira's car. Serenity danced in her booster in the back, enjoying the music Jasper deprived her of. Shira could roll her eyes at the memory of his attitude toward her tastes.

"You like this music, huh, Starship?" Shira said.

The young girl nodded. "Sure do. I wish Daddy and Zach listened to it."

Shira rested her chin on her palm propped up on her center console. "Well, you're in luck. I've got Orion compiling a fun playlist for you, so Alistair can play it while you're home."

Serenity's eye lit up. "You're the best! Isn't that right, Snake?"

Snake's ears perked, and his tail thumped against the seat.

Shira grinned. She loved being the best in Serenity's eyes. She didn't know why, but whenever she lost it, Shira felt the powerful need to climb back into that position again. *She's really got me wrapped around her finger…*

"Are you sure I can't sit up there with you?" Serenity asked.

"Sorry, Starship, but the law says you've got to be back there in your booster until you're a little older. Not even Snake can be up here with me. It's for both your safety."

Serenity scrunched her nose in response and Shira had to bite back a laugh. She knew the rules felt unfair to the girl, but Shira wouldn't budge on Serenity's well-being.

"Can you tell me now what we're doing?" Serenity asked. Her feet kicked in her excitement.

Shira pursed her lips. "Hmm, I think I'll wait until Narissa and Mercedes are with us."

Serenity huffed and drooped dramatically in her booster. "But I wanna know."

"But it'd ruin the surprise. And we're almost at Cybro Industries, so you won't be waiting much longer."

"Can we go inside? Daddy said that's where you got your cybahnetics."

Shira thought for a moment, then sent off a text to Narissa. A response came back almost immediately. "Narissa says she'd be happy to give you a tour."

Serenity cheered.

As Shira promised, her car rolled up to the tall building that was Cybro Industries. Narissa and Mercedes were waiting at the top of the steps, waving.

Shira, Snake, and Serenity met them up there while Orion pulled her car around into the private parking. The three adults greeted each other with a round of hugs, and Shira checking on how Narissa was feeling, before all turning to Serenity.

"Hi there, Serenity," Narissa said with a big grin. "You ready for the private tour?"

Serenity nodded, her face beaming with her excitement.

Narissa whisked them into the building, and gave the girl the tour of a lifetime, from viewing the offices to seeing a few cybernetics Narissa had pulled out to show off. And, as an added bonus, Narissa had even brought out special testing headgear and allowed Serenity to experience piloting a cybernetic arm. While the girl had some difficulties, she had a blast. It certainly wouldn't be anything she'd soon forget.

Shira was sure to snap a few photos for the memories and to share with Jasper and Zach. A prickle of regret ran through her when she did. The guys had wanted to come check the place out, too. She felt bad doing this for Serenity without them here as well. *I'll just have to make it up to them somehow.*

No sooner did the thought cross her mind, did several tantalizing options pop up. Any other situation, she might have taken a moment to indulge in the fantasies, but here, where her two best friends could see her zone out into Sexy Daydream Land, not a chance.

When Narissa officially concluded the tour, she let Serenity play with the test arm some more before asking her thoughts.

"This was a lot of fun," Serenity said, a huge smile pulling her cheeks so much it created cute dimples. "I undahstand bettah what my friend and She-ra get from the cybahnetics."

"You have a friend with cybernetics?" Narissa asked.

Serenity nodded. "Alex is my best friend. He's the best. I defend him when the othah kids are mean to him because of it."

Mercedes smiled. "He's lucky to have a great friend like you."

Her praise made Serenity even happier, if that was possible.

With the tour now over, they made their way back downstairs and outside. Serenity had changed her focus to asking Shira every two seconds if she could now know about the plans for the day, but Shira was going to make her wait until they at least made it back into the car.

Orion pulled it up and everyone climbed in, Mercedes claiming the front since she was a little taller than

Narissa. It was a tight fit for Narissa with Snake, but she wouldn't complain.

"She-ra, can I please know now?" Serenity begged, elongating the word 'please' as if to emphasize her impatience.

Shira popped the destination into her GPS and then swiveled in her seat to look at Serenity. "Okay, okay. I'll tell you some, but not all, because I want the big part to be a very special surprise."

Serenity pursed her lips in her oddly familiar way again, and then relented. "Fine."

Shira grinned. She wouldn't be upset for long. "The first thing we're going to do is go shopping. Then, we're going to go get our nails done, and then go out for a late lunch."

Serenity cheered, loving the first part of the plan. Narissa and Mercedes also loved it. Serenity deserved to be spoiled now and then, and who was more perfect to do it than Shira herself?

It wasn't long before they reached Del Amo Fashion Center and Serenity about lost her mind at the sight of the three-level shopping mall. It seemed the ones she'd been to back home weren't nearly this big. *Boy, would she die seeing the shopping centers I've been to around the world.*

Shira led the way into the mall, only needing a second to get her nerves under control. She was proud of herself. Narissa and Mercedes were also vocal with their pride and praise. All the hard work was paying off. *Maybe one of these days I will be stable enough where I can take the guys and Serenity on a trip out of the country.*

Given this excursion was for Serenity, Shira allowed her to pick which stores they went into. She didn't expect the

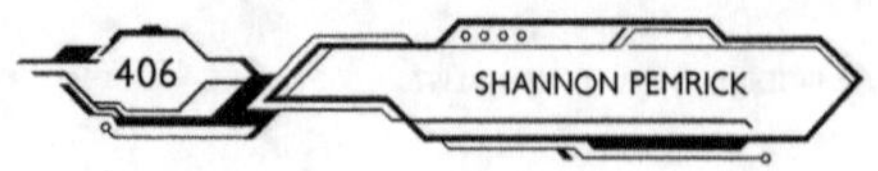

little girl would want to try to go into every single one. There was no way that would be possible, so between the three adults, they managed to wrangle Serenity into picking which types of stores she wanted to shop at, and they went from there. Clothes, toys, gaming, they shopped for it all. Serenity wanted to try on everything Shira, Narissa, or Mercedes found for her; she wanted every other toy; and there were way too many games she longed for but didn't or couldn't have.

Each time Shira agreed to buy something, Serenity had the biggest smile that made Shira's heart swell. It nearly convinced her to buy every single thing she could for the little girl, but she restrained herself. Serenity deserved to be spoiled, but even Shira knew there was a limit to that.

In the end, she bought Serenity ten outfits, two toys, and three new games for her handheld.

Serenity practically vibrated out of existence in her excitement of all the gifts she'd gotten. And the fact Shira still had more planned today kept her talking animatedly. Not that Serenity couldn't talk a mile a minute on a normal day, it just seemed to be a little worse the more excited she was.

The girl was in the midst of a confusing story when their group walked into the nail salon, *Beyond Nails*. The shop wasn't large, but Shira liked the employees. They were nice and had a lot of talent. It was also within walking distance of the small café where she planned to take everyone for lunch.

The pedicure stations were situated to one side, with shelves filled with colorful nail polish bottles lining the wall behind them. Pedicure chairs were set up on the other side, and a waiting area was next to the entrance in front of the large windows.

It wasn't busy at the moment, allowing for a technician to greet them quickly. "Good afternoon, how can we help you?"

"We need manicures for three," Shira said.

Serenity cocked her head. "She-ra, there are four of us."

Narissa smiled and flashed her immaculate French tips. "I've already gotten my nails done the other week."

"Shira, you don't have to include me," Mercedes said. She rubbed her fingers together, drawing the eye to the permanently stained skin from her job. "It'd be a waste of money for me."

Shira waved her off. "I will not exclude you. You've got the rest of the week to enjoy them. You deserve to pamper yourself every now and then."

Her friend blew out a breath. "All right, fine."

The technician smiled and led them to four pedicure stations, allowing Narissa to sit with them even though she wasn't getting work done. Two more technicians joined them, and they went over the nail application types, as well as color options. They also didn't hesitate to show examples of the designs they'd done in the past when Serenity asked.

"That one," Serenity said, pointing at the tablet. On the display were nails painted in a gradient matte magenta and violet with gloss dots of the same color strategically peppered on one side of the nail. "That looks like dragon scales. I want that, but in blue."

She turned to Shira. "She-ra, can we get the same?"

Shira smiled widely. "I'd love to do matching nails."

Mercedes went with a pink and white flower design on top of a pale peach base. Serenity kicked her feet happily and hummed while the technician painted her tiny fingers. And she found great fun and amusement in the UV nail lamp.

The women working on their nails gushed how cute Serenity was, and through some conversation, Shira learned the guys painted nails with her when she wanted, they just didn't have the money to take her out like this. Though Serenity did voice how she wished her dads could have come and gotten their nails done with them. It was cute how much she thought of the guys when they weren't around. *I hope Jasper took my advice and is planning a date for him and Zach.* That would no doubt make Serenity thrilled.

Time flew by and before Shira knew it, the four of them were sitting at the café down the street at an outdoor dining table, which Serenity loved.

She still went a mile a minute with her talking, to the point it surprised Shira the girl had a voice left. Mercedes and Narissa found it all quite amusing.

Serenity only stopped talking when she was nibbling on her sandwich. Except when she looked to Shira suddenly with big innocent eyes. "She-ra, when are you gonna marry my dads?"

Shira paused mid-bite into her piece of quiche, and Mercedes choked on her drink. Narissa's eyebrows arched high, and she looked at Shira with a clear "excuse me, what?" look.

Shira took a moment to compose herself. "I'm sorry, Starship, what did you ask?"

The girl cocked her head. "When are you gonna marry

my dads? They pay you lots of attention and make you happy, and they give you gifts when they can. You do all of that for them, and even me, too. So that means you're gonna move in with us and marry them some day."

Speechless didn't begin to describe Shira. It was such an innocent concept, a nice one if the world was that simple and easy. Not even marriage between more than two people was simple and easy. It was finally possible after decades of people fighting for that right, but the end result was by no means as easy as "traditional" marriages.

And of course, because none of this was simple or easy, Shira wasn't sure how to explain things to the girl. Not that she could explain things well even to her adult friends, listening with eager anticipation, and she had already planned to reveal her secrets to them at some point.

"Alex and I are getting married when we're adults," Serenity continued.

Shira's brow rose. "Is that so?"

She nodded and bit into her meal. "We're best friends. When we're oldah, we'll get married and live happily ever aftah."

Mercedes rested her cheek on her palm. She had a goofy grin on her face. "Do your dads know this plan?"

Serenity nodded again. "Yeah, I told them. Daddy told me I should wait on the decision until we're older, but didn't get mad, and Zach wished us luck, for some reason."

Shira suppressed a grin. It seemed her fathers, for the most part, accepted her naïve outlook and didn't see it as anything serious for now.

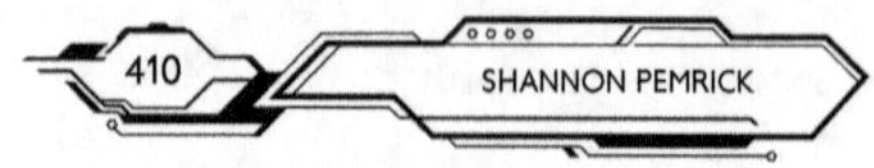

"So, when are you going to marry them?" Serenity asked again.

Damn. Shira should have known Serenity wouldn't let that go. She chewed her lip, trying to think of something. "We haven't talked about that yet."

Serenity pursed her lips. "Why not?"

"Because…" God, Shira had hoped she would have taken that simple answer. "Because there have been other things we've needed to talk about."

"Is that why you three have gone off alone a lot?"

Narissa's brow rose. Both her friends were giving her that "what aren't you telling us?" look.

"It hasn't been a lot," Shira said, trying to save herself from this situation. "But we've had a few conversations."

"When are you gonna talk about getting married?" Serenity asked, her eyes going wide and pleading.

Shira let out a quiet breath through her lips. "It won't be brought up until your dads figure out when they want to marry each other. They've been together longer."

Serenity thought about this for a moment, then went back to eating. Shira took that as her deeming Shira's responses acceptable—for now. Of course, this left Shira to deal with her friends, who were whispering between themselves, their eyes flicking to Shira a few times.

"Later," Shira mouthed. "Promise."

Shira's phone chimed, and she checked the message. It was Kane.

> *We had some equipment issues today, so*
> *I'm running late with Kiara's coloring. I*
> *hope that doesn't cause any issues.*

*We have guests coming later, so we'll prioritize
Serenity in case we have to leave early.*

If Serenity ended up being the only one done for this last part of her surprise, that wouldn't bother Shira in the slightest. This was all for her. Anything more was a bonus.

Lunch finished without any more uncomfortable conversations, though the ride to the tattoo parlor was another story. Narissa and Mercedes both weren't hiding their eagerness to pull Shira aside to grill her, and they weren't so subtle about it. Serenity was giving them funny looks.

"She-ra," Serenity said when they were nearing their destination. "Can I know now about the last part of my surprise?"

Shira's lips quirked in the corners. This was the third time while in the car she'd asked for the beans to be spilled. "Not yet. We're almost there. It'll all become clear when we arrive."

The girl huffed and kicked her legs. Shira couldn't tell whether Serenity didn't like the mystery of it all, or she was just excitedly impatient and had hoped Shira would give in to her cuteness. It'd almost happened while they were shopping.

The car pulled into a parallel parking spot in front of a small building with large glass windows. On the windows were decals saying *Tattoos* and *Piercings*. *Wicked Ink* sprawled over the entrance on the building itself in large, fancy letters.

"We're here," Shira announced.

Everyone looked out to the tattoo parlor.

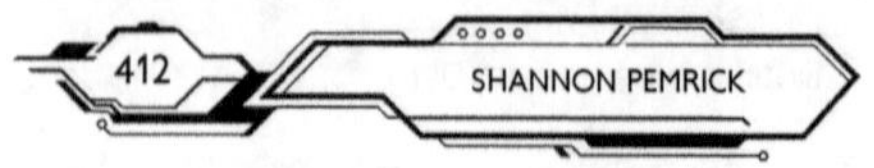

"Normally I can understand your plans, Shira," Mercedes said. "But this one is lost on me. What do you have planned with her at a tattoo shop?"

Serenity gasped, her eyes going wide. "I'm getting a tattoo?" Her face scrunched almost immediately. "But Daddy says I can't have one until I'm an adult."

Shira laughed. "That's right, you can't. Children aren't allowed to have real tattoos, but I know one of the artists here and he can make fake tattoos that look like the real thing."

Serenity squealed, and she tried to rip herself out of her booster straps in her excitement to get out. Amusement passed through the adults, and Snake happily wagged his tail against Narissa's leg.

Everyone climbed out, and Shira had to keep Serenity from running straight for the parlor door. She was happy Serenity was excited about this surprise like she'd hoped, but Shira still expected her to use her manners going into the building. A bell chimed when the door opened and cool air beckoned them inside. The inside was not what most would expect of a tattoo shop.

The area was fairly spacious, with walls covered in various paintings and framed drawings of tattoo designs. Six tattoo stations were set up in low-wall cubicle-like areas, all clean and neatly personalized to show which artists worked where. Plush couches and a coffee table furnished the waiting lounge. Several tablets lay on top of the hard surfaces. Shira assumed they were loaded with tattoo magazines and reference pictures for clients.

Three heavily tattooed and pierced people were stationed at three of the tattoo cubicles; a burly bearded man with salt and pepper hair, thick beard, and tawny skin, a petite, pale woman appearing in her mid-thirties with spiky blonde and pink hair and the most visible piercings of the three, and a lean, muscular man in his late-twenties, with gauged ears, short dark hair, and a little scruff on his chin. From the elbow down, his left arm was cybernetic. Only the younger man had a client, a short, fair-skinned woman in her mid-twenties. Her eyes were closed and she had a far too peaceful expression for someone getting her back worked on.

She had a full-sleeve tattoo covering her right arm, depicting a dice set, symbols from World of Warcraft, Dungeons and Dragons, and Lusara Fates, a Rathalos head from Monster Hunter, and other varied nerdy imagery. She laid out on her front, her long red hair cascading over her shoulders and obscuring a side view of her exposed large breasts pressed into the chair. The strings of her bikini top hung over the chair.

The artist glanced up at the sound of the bell. "Hey, Shira."

"Hey Kane," she greeted. "Kiara awake, or did she fall asleep again?"

"I'm awake," Kiara mumbled.

Shira shook her head. Last she'd heard, when Kiara got the line work done, she'd actually fallen asleep on Kane, and Shira couldn't fathom how the woman found such an ordeal so relaxing. Especially when her tattoo covered every inch of her back.

Shira couldn't see the design from here, but she knew what it was—a gorgeous and intricate design of flowers, books, mystical creatures, and magic. From all the pops of color Shira viewed, the tattoo appeared to be fully colored, or nearly there, given Kane was still working.

Kiara had posted images on social media earlier this year when she'd gotten the line work done, and then again when half of the coloring was complete. Seemed she'd finally gotten around to finishing the rest today.

Shira turned to tell Serenity they'd have to wait, but she was gone, already standing in front of a wall and staring up at the display of tattoos with wide, wonder-filled eyes.

"Looks like you've got a little fan, Abby," the burly man said to the last tattoo artist, in a deep, rumbling voice.

Abby clapped her hands excitedly. "And she's a cute fan, too."

Serenity looked at her. "You made these?"

The woman left her station and sauntered over to the lobby. "I sure did. Adrian and Kane did the ones on the other wall."

She pointed to the wall behind Shira. Serenity looked up at Abby's work again and then studied the men's work. "She-ra, who is doing mine?"

Abby blinked and then smiled. "You must be Kane's special appointment."

Serenity nodded. "She-ra says I can get a tattoo. Well, not a real one, but one that looks wicked real." She pointed to the burly man. "Is the big bear man Kane?"

Shira's hand flew up to her mouth as she tried to stifle a mixed reaction of amusement and embarrassment. She should know better than to describe someone in such a rude way.

However, instead of being insulted, the man belted out a hearty laugh. "No, little one, I'm Adrian. Kane is the one workin' on Kiara here."

Serenity blinked. "That name sounds familiar. Daddy and Dad said it before."

"Kiara is our guildmate," Shira said.

"Oh! She's the one that makes tasty cakes and writes books."

Kiara grinned. "She's a cute and a smart cookie."

"I like cookies."

Amusement rumbled through the room.

"She-ra, when is it my turn?" Serenity asked.

"When Kane is done with Kiara," Shira said. "Why don't we figure out what you want, so we're ready?"

Abby grabbed a tablet from a nearby table. "I'd be happy to help you."

"You're not getting any part of my commission," Kane said, not looking up from his work.

"I wasn't going to ask for any, dingus," she shot back. "I just want to help an adorable little girl pick out the perfect design. I'd be better at it than you."

"Yeah, sure."

Shira tittered. *Seems these two get along well.*

Narissa suddenly latched onto Shira's arm. "Mercedes, Shira, and I need to step out real quick to talk about something. Is that okay with you?"

Abby smiled. "I don't have an issue with it."

Shira looked at Serenity, trying to hide the nervous twinges rising in her. "Are you okay with that, Starship? I'll be right outside, and I'll leave Snake with you."

Shira was not looking forward to this conversation, but it needed to happen. She'd promised twice now. And leaving Snake with Serenity was for the best. It would prevent Shira from subconsciously trying to lean on his support too much during this confrontation.

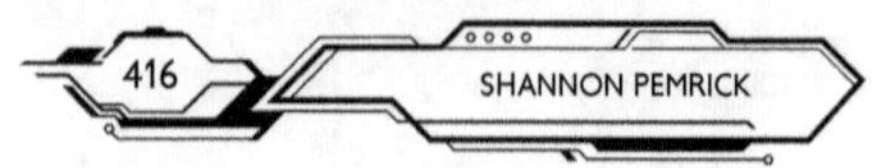

"That's fine," Serenity said, completely unfazed by the request to stay here with strangers. "Whatcha gonna talk about?"

"Just some boring adult things," Mercedes said quickly.

Kiara's eye cracked open. "Are you three keeping secrets from me?"

"Yes, but only because you're stuck in that chair," Narissa said, tugging on Shira's arm. "We'll fill you in later."

Kiara puffed out an annoyed breath, but there really wasn't anything she could do about it.

Shira gave Snake his leash to hold in his mouth and had him sit next to Serenity. Narissa and Mercedes practically dragged her out of the building before she managed to do that, and she found herself back against the wall, with her two friends a little too close for comfort with their eager stares.

"Spill," Mercedes said. "You told us yesterday you had something important to share, and it better be related to why you were evasive with Serenity, but didn't outright correct her about her assumption with you and her dads."

"And don't leave out any details," Narissa said. She paused and thought. "Okay, so some of them you can leave out. We don't need to know *everything*."

"Speak for yourself," Mercedes said, barely holding back a laugh. "She's been so nosey about our relationships she might as well give us the same courtesy."

Shira shrunk into herself, her friends' intense stares killing any sort of confidence she'd tried to work up for herself in the last twenty-four hours. She hated this feeling. Why couldn't she just spit out the truth like she could insults and information about past hookups?

Where did her backbone run off to? *Why am I so pathetic about this?*

"Can you two please be a little less intense?" she asked. "This is hard enough…"

The expressions on her friends' faces softened, and they took a half a step back to give her room to breathe.

"Just tell us what's going on," Narissa said, far more kindly this time. "We're your friends, and not only are we nosey, like you are with us, we care and want to support you."

"And it's not like you to be so nervous about telling us things," Mercedes said.

Her friends already knew what this was about. *I just need to come out and say it.* "I may have taken your advice with the guys."

The biggest smiles spread over the women's faces.

"It's nothing official!" Shira blurted. She then cringed and rubbed her neck. "I'm taking things as it goes right now and just letting things happen."

Narissa canted her head and raised an eyebrow. "You haven't talked to them about where you three stand officially?"

Shira blew out a breath, and her shoulders slumped. "This is hard for me, okay?"

Mercedes looked Shira up and down and grinned. "You got it bad, don't you?"

"Yeah… I think so…" Shira's lips twisted and she twirled a lock of hair with her finger. "This isn't like my random hookups or even my relationship with Jeremy. I don't really know how to describe how this makes me feel, but it's definitely nothing I've experienced before."

"How good are they?"

Shira blew out a breath, her body heating at the ghosting reminders still plaguing her senses. "Fucking amazing."

Mercedes chuckled. "Sounds like someone might already be addicted and she's only on the test drive phase."

Shira's lip caught between her teeth. "Yeah… about that…"

Narissa's brows spiked, a surprised, knowing look in her gaze. "You didn't."

As much as Shira didn't want to admit this, it was for the best. "I lied about not already hooking up with them before the tournament."

Mercedes' eyes popped wide and then she slapped Shira's arm. "You bitch. What the hell? Why did you lie about it?"

Narissa watched her with a more critical gaze rather than with disbelieving betrayal. "Why did you keep it a secret at all? We wouldn't have ragged on you so hard if we—"

"Because I didn't know how to process it." Shira rubbed her cybernetic arm. "Neither encounter with each of them was a planned thing—at least not on my part."

Both women in front of her snickered, knowing full well what that meant.

"I talked to my therapist about it to try and process, and then nothing really came of it after, which is why I hid it from you two. I thought that was it, just a moment of fun with each of them, get something out of our systems, and we were fine."

Mercedes' eyebrow arched high. "They dropped things after that? As in, it wasn't brought up at all?"

Shira shook her head. "No. The only thing different was that I couldn't stop thinking about what I'd done, and how much I'd liked it while also feeling fucking guilty."

"Guilty?" Narissa frowned. "No wonder you were all weird about us trying to encourage you."

"Dick move on their part, too," Mercedes said, her lip slightly curled. "At least say something rather than acting like it never happened."

Shira rubbed her neck. "Except they didn't act like that. These past few days, I've been able to look at everything, and I hadn't seen their actions correctly. They hadn't dropped it. Their antics had actually gotten worse, but they hadn't tried to outright push anything until after we met up in person."

Narissa tapped her lips. "Knowing them and how you are, it's not hard to guess they thought about waiting until that face-to-face contact was made. They weren't all that subtle at dinner, and they're not wishy-washy on what they want. Normally you're not either, but"— she winked—"I can give you a pass this time. They're something else in person."

Heat rose in Shira's face. "That's… an understatement."

Honestly, it was a wonder she could think around them. Everything they did, no matter how innocent—or not—was affecting her.

Mercedes' expression grew serious. "You are planning on talking to them to lay out expectations before they head home, right?"

Shira made a face. "Duh. This may be hard for me to navigate, but I'm not a scared teen. Serenity is going to spend time with her grandparents, starting tonight, until the restart of the tournament. I expect we'll work things out during that time."

Mercedes and Narissa passed each other a clear, knowing glance before Narissa spoke. "I don't think they're going to let you do much talking."

Shira winked, finding some of her usual confidence again. "Depends on how much begging there is."

Mercedes choked on a laugh. "Who is doing the begging?"

Shira merely smirked, making her friend burst into laughter.

"Now that we know Shira's big secret, why don't we get back inside?" Narissa suggested. "Don't need anyone asking any more questions than Kiara will."

"Nosey little hobbit," Shira muttered.

Mercedes snickered. "Your fault. You feed her so much information for her books, you know she's going to want to be in on this little secret before the three of you make any public announcements."

"Let's just try to keep it vague in front of Serenity. I don't want her coming to any more conclusions than she already has, and then have her hopes dashed if something doesn't work out."

Her friends gave a sympathetic nod. Navigating a possible new relationship was hard enough, but mix in a kid, and that added a whole new level of complicated.

When the three of them entered, Serenity was still sitting in the lobby with Abby, though Adrian had joined them. Serenity was animatedly talking about… something, completely unafraid of either tattoo artist. Snake got up from where he lay at the girl's feet and trotted over to Shira. Kiara was now sitting up in her chair, her bikini top tied and secured around her chest, while Kane cleaned up his workstation.

"So, spill," Kiara said without preamble.

"The *thing* happened," Mercedes said, winking.

"Unofficially," Shira quickly added. "The official part is being worked on."

Kiara's eyes lit up, and she cheered. "Finally!"

Shira couldn't stop the eye roll. Why did everyone have to be so dramatic about this? It was bad enough Kiara understood what happened, even with their vague wording.

Kane chuckled quietly. "This must be a long-standing situation if you four can be that cryptic and know exactly what went down."

Kiara sighed dramatically. "You've got no idea. And now it just needs to be official because this has taken too long to get to this point."

Shira shook her head and focused on Serenity rather than let this ridiculous conversation to continue. "Starship, have you figured out what you want?"

She nodded. "Rathalos!"

Of course, she wanted a Monster Hunter tattoo. Shira shouldn't have expected anything else from her.

"She's got excellent taste," Kiara said.

"She-ra, your friend has a Rathalos tattoo that's wicked cool. But it's not what I want."

"She's not sure what style to choose," Abby said. "The ones she likes, Kane can do, so that isn't an issue."

"They all look wicked pretty!" Serenity said.

Shira tapped her lips. "Hmm, Kane, would you be up for some creative freedom?"

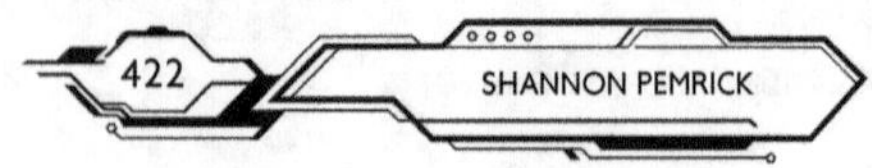

He glanced up from where he was setting out a batch of markers. "If she's okay with it."

"What do you say, Starship? Want to let him make it a surprise?"

She thought for a moment and then nodded. "That sounds fun."

"Excellent," Kane said. "I'll be ready for you two in a moment."

It didn't take him long to finish his setup and get Kiara checked out. She chose to hang around and chat, which none of the artists had issue with. From the sounds of it, they expected today to remain this slow until closing. Made sense to Shira how Kane was so easily able to get this appointment in for her.

Kane patted the tattooing chair. "Okay, kiddo, your turn."

Serenity's face lit up and Shira could see it took every inch of willpower she had to not run to the chair. It had been lowered so Serenity could climb up on her own, and once she was situated, Kane rose it to its needed height. Shira slipped into the booth and sat down on the remaining available chair.

"She-ra, what are you getting?" Serenity asked.

"Kane is going to surprise me," Shira said.

The two of them had worked that out via text. Shira had never had any overwhelming need to get any tattoos, so she hadn't thought to figure out what she'd ever get, even in a hypothetical situation. But Shira knew Serenity would want her to get one of these temporary tattoos as well, so having Kane design something for her worked in Shira's eyes. Plus, it gave him a chance to stretch his creative limits without restriction.

"What are you gonna make her, Mister Kane?" Serenity asked.

His brow rose while Abby fawned. "Aww, she's so cute with her manners."

"I'm not sure I'm old enough to be called mister," Kane said.

"Don't start sayin' you have to be my age, or I'll take you out back," Adrian warned.

The room filled with laughter.

"I won't reveal what I'm doing for Shira until it's done. The surprise is part of the fun," Kane said.

He explained to Serenity how the process will work. To make the experience as authentic as possible, he detailed the skin cleaning process, and sketching a digital design that would be projected onto her skin. He explained this would be where she'd have to be as still as possible, so he didn't mess up. Then he talked about the tattoo markers and explained to her, because they were temporary, they'd last for only a few days, but he promised the design he did for her would look real.

Serenity struggled to keep herself from squirming in her contained excitement. Shira had thought this would be a fun thing for her, but she hadn't realized just how much it may mean to Serenity.

Kane sketched out a design on a tablet, getting Serenity's input through the whole process. Shira wasn't allowed to see what they were working on, per Serenity's request, so she held up casual conversation with the others.

The snapping of gloves drew Shira's attention back. Kane was gearing himself up with proper safety gear. Serenity glowed from all the extra attention. She may have known this wasn't real, but Kane's insistence to not treat it that way made this moment extra special, and Shira really appreciated it.

Kane cleaned the girl's arm, and then used a projection device to display the design he'd worked up onto her skin. It was a cutesy, baby version of Rathalos blowing a small breath of fire. Kane grabbed the first pen and went to work.

He held casual conversation with Serenity to keep her engaged. She would giggle every now and then, mumbling about the pen tip tickling her skin, but managed to stay still for the most part, just as he'd told her. All the while, Kane's focus on his task never wavered, and his skill as an artist unfolded before Shira's very eyes.

Kane sat up when he finished, and capped his pen. "All done."

Serenity beamed, staring at the tattoo. To Shira's surprise, it did look close to a real, fresh one. *He's good, that's for sure.*

"So, Starship, what do you think?" Shira asked.

"It's amazing!" She looked at Shira with the happiest expression. "Thank you for letting me get it, Momma."

Shira smiled, the bubbling sensation matching yesterday's reaction to her using that name again. She should feel conflicted about Serenity deciding to call her mom now and then, especially in front of strangers. But after her declaration yesterday, and Jasper and Zach's lack of protests, pushed away any usual worries she would have had in the past. Shira wanted Serenity to call her mom. *I want something to come of all this…*

She refocused her mind before that thought ran away

with her in this open setting. "Your dads are going to be so surprised when we get back."

"They're gonna love it." Serenity looked at Kane. "Can I get down now?"

He smiled and lowered the chair to make it easier for her. "Shira's turn is next."

Shira checked the time. It hadn't taken him as long as she expected. If hers wasn't too complicated, they'd make it home before Jasper's parents were expected to show up.

"Your turn, your turn," Serenity said in a sing-song voice, rushing over to Shira. The little girl gave her a strong hug before letting Shira take her place in the tattoo chair.

Kane was already working on his tablet and calibrating the projector.

"So, what did you design for me?" Shira asked, settling into place.

"You don't get to see until it's done," he said, not looking up.

Shira's eyebrow arched. "And how is that going to work when it's my arm?"

"You're not going to look."

His matter-of-fact tone left her speechless. Shira flicked her gaze to her friends, who were cackling away.

Kane grabbed a pen. "Ready?"

Shira settled more and closed her eyes. "Paint away."

CHAPTER 21

Gulls cried, their calls carrying over the crashing of the ocean waves. Tangy salt clung to the air, and the warm sun sunk into Jasper's skin. Soft sand shifted under his bare feet. He and Zach walked hand-in-hand down the beach, enjoying the blissful moment between just the two of them.

Shira had been right. Going out on a brief date had been the right choice. Zach agreed to end practice early, with the promise they'd pick it back up after dinner. They'd gone out to lunch, did a little shopping at some local shops, and now were just enjoying each other's company and taking it easy. Jasper couldn't remember the last time he and Zach had a chance to do this, even though he knew Cheryl would have had no issue taking Serenity.

Thinking of Shira and Serenity, his mind wandered to wondering what those two were up to at this point. He hoped they were having all kinds of fun. Jasper wanted everything to go right with integrating Shira into their lives like they had. He didn't want to think about what would happen if it didn't work out.

Zach squeezed his hand. "You're thinking about them again, aren't you?"

A smirk tugged at Jasper's lips. "Guilty as charged."

His boyfriend chuckled. "Same. Keep wondering what they're up to right now. I know this was good for the two of us, to do something together not work-related, and don't get me wrong, I'm glad we did this, but it's also weird, you know? It feels like both Serenity and Shira should be here with us."

Jasper knew exactly what Zach meant. He loved this time with him, there was no doubt in his mind at all, but Jasper had become so used to spending all his time including Serenity, and now even Shira, it almost felt wrong to not have them there.

But, at the same time, Jasper couldn't deny he was surprised Zach had been the one to say it. He'd been doing amazingly with Shira these last few days, and that fought against Jasper's initial concerns that Zach was trying to force things, but Jasper couldn't quite shake them entirely.

A small, heavy object bounced against Jasper's leg in his pocket, its weight feeling like he was carrying the world. This date gave him the opportunity he was looking for, but before he could go any further, Jasper needed to banish these lingering doubts, and that meant he had to open the conversation one more time.

Jasper squeezed Zach's hand. "Can we talk about something?"

Zach's lips pressed into a thin line, and it took Jasper

a moment later to realize how poorly that could have been interpreted. "Of course we can."

They found a good place to sit on the beach, gazing out at the rolling water. Jasper's hand slipped into his pocket, and he twisted the box between his fingers.

"This is going to be the Shira conversation again, isn't it?" Zach said before Jasper could finish sorting out how he'd bring it up. It gave Jasper pause, and Zach nodded. "I thought as much."

Jasper swallowed. "Zach, don't be mad. I—"

His boyfriend leaned in and pressed his warm lips against Jasper's. Jasper's eyes hooded. Wherever the Zach he knew who was averse to showing public affection had gone, Jasper was all too okay with telling that old Zach not to come back. He liked this bolder person in his life.

Zach pulled away. "I'm not mad. I understand why you're concerned." His gaze turned out to the sea, and he let out a slow breath. "And you've had a right to be, at least in the beginning."

Jasper swallowed a lump forming in his throat. *Zach had been lying this whole time?*

"I know what you're thinking, and no, I'm not forcing myself to put up with this situation for you." He briefly glanced at Jasper, only to resume his watch of the crashing waves. "Since the beginning, I've been struggling to understand my feelings around Shira. Nothing made sense to me, from why her smiles sent my heart skittering, to not understanding the need to spend as much time with her as I did with you, in the same exact way."

Zach ran his fingers through his hair. "Every time

you asked me if I was okay with this, I told you I was, because I didn't want you to see how much I was trying to figure things out. I thought if I told you the truth, you'd shut this all down before I got the chance to sort out my head. And I'm sorry I did that. I shouldn't have lied."

Jasper wet his lips and grasped one of Zach's hands. "Don't be. You're right. I probably would have overreacted to your need to take things slow and figure things out. I was so gung-ho, I would have seen any hesitation as you forcing yourself into this situation for my benefit. And I'm sorry you had to be afraid of that and forced yourself into a position of lying so you could figure things out the way you needed to."

Zach squeezed his hand, but didn't say anything. The unspoken question hung in the air, and Jasper was going to have to be the one to ask, rather than Zach offering up the answer outright.

"What have you decided?" he asked.

"I couldn't stop myself from questioning the legitimacy of our relationship," Zach said. "I kept second-guessing your feelings for me because of how it all started—because I was the first guy in your life."

Jasper's heart sank. *He what?*

"But she helped me see straight. Maybe not right away, but over these last few months, and even this past week, I realized it didn't matter if I was your first. It didn't make this any less real. We fall in love with people, not just the bodies of people. And in cementing that realization, all the pieces of the puzzle fell into place with her."

Zach turned to face Jasper, his stare strong and his

eyes blazing and intense. "My feelings for her are no longer confusing—they're real and they're more sure than ever. I want this for the three of us, Jasper. I want you, and I want her."

Jasper grabbed Zach around the back of his head with a powerful grip and crashed their mouths together. The aromatic cedar scent of Zach's aftershave teased his senses.

He pulled away first and stared deep into Zach's eyes. "I'm not letting you go anywhere, and if I have to up the ante to prove I fucking love you, then this bettah do it, and you'd bettah not say no."

Zach's brows pulled together and when he opened his mouth to say something, he noticed Jasper had pulled his other hand out of his pocket. Nothing came out despite his dropped jaw. His blue eyes focused on the hinged, open box in Jasper's hand, revealing a platinum signet band with an emerald-cut blue topaz gem. Jasper swore he heard Zach quit breathing.

"You said nothing flashy, and no crazy public proposal. So, here we are, on the beach, just the two of us, with the only ring I found acceptable. Marry me, Zach."

A long silence passed between them while Zach stared at the ring. Then, he grabbed the box and turned back to Jasper. Zach's arms flew around Jasper's neck and his mouth greedily claimed Jasper's.

Jasper wrapped his arms around Zach, joy soaring in his chest. He didn't need a verbal confirmation to understand this reaction, and he couldn't be happier. Zach meant everything to him. Nothing about what he felt for this man was fake or forced. Jasper couldn't bear to lose him.

Zach pulled away first. "Yes."

Jasper smirked, and then applause surrounded them. They both jerked away from each other and looked around. A few people stood a little ways off in all directions, smiling and clapping. Zach ducked his head, pink growing on his cheeks, and Jasper chuckled.

"Not as private as I thought," Jasper mumbled. He waved his thanks to the strangers. "Sorry about that."

"It's okay," Zach said, fussing with the box in his hand. "I wouldn't think strangers would pay attention either."

Jasper kissed his *fiancé* on the cheek. A demure smile slipped up Zach's face and then he slipped the ring on. *Perfect fit.* Jasper let out a mental breath. He'd agonized over the sizing since he'd picked the ring out.

Zach pulled out his phone and snapped some photos. "I'll take some better ones later, but this will do."

Jasper snorted. He loved to hate Zach's perfectionist side when it came to photographs. "When do we want to announce it?"

"After we tell Serenity." He smiled. "And Shira."

Jasper laughed. "Yeah, she'd kill us if we pulled Serenity aside and then she found out through social." He then smirked. "Amy, too."

Zach's face paled. "Yeah, I'll tell her third."

Jasper laughed again. He liked Amy. She was a good friend, and Jasper was glad she and Zach had remained that way after everything that went down with them.

Zach leaned his head against Jasper's shoulder. "You don't think this will cause issues with Shira, right?"

Jasper snorted. "She's probably already wondering when this would happen."

"Yeah, so was I, but that's not what I mean."

Jasper pursed his lips, not sure what Zach was worried about. He slipped his arm around Zach and gave him his undivided attention so he could find out.

"How are we going to make this work?" Zach asked. "Even with VR, there's no way we can make this work long-term if it's only distance."

Jasper worked his jaw. Now he got it. "Shira mentioned she wanted to get into modeling again."

Zach's brow rose. "Yeah?"

"She just has to overcome her feahs of cameras. Which we know she is, little by little this week." Jasper paused as he tried to keep his mind from running crazy on him. Everything he and Shira talked about earlier today had already gotten his brain going about future plans. Now here he was, trying to work all that into words for Zach. "And she's considering a job here in the state once she tackles that issue."

Zach slowly nodded, as if he'd expected that bit of information to come out. "We know, even if that wasn't a factor, deciding who moves wouldn't be easy. All her family and friends are here. Our family and friends are split between here and back home. Serenity has school, and that's where all her friends are. And then there's our contract…"

Jasper ran a hand through his hair. That had been the biggest issue in his eyes. It would suck to move away from Cheryl, leaving her alone, but Jasper also knew he couldn't put his life on hold because of where his family lived. It never stopped him when his parents moved to Anaheim, or them, for that matter. And pulling Serenity from her friends would be rough, but she'd make a lot of new friends, and she could always stay in contact with her East Coast friends online. His and Zach's circle of friends was a non-issue, too. While they had friends on the East Coast, the friends they were in contact with the most often were here in California, or in another country altogether.

He pulled his phone out and stared at the dark screen. The conversation Jasper had with Shira about their tournament sponsorship sprung into his mind. "I've got an idea."

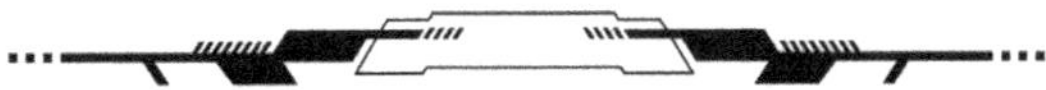

The car pulled up in front of Shira's house, the taxi AI announcing they'd arrived at their destination. Zach briefly glanced at the empty driver's seat before climbing out of the vehicle with Jasper, while Alistair paid the fare. A few months ago, the government authorized AI driving technology without driver supervision, a legislation long coming with the advancement of AI technology. Normally this would unsettle Zach, since he wasn't used to it yet, but he was… distracted.

Zach played with the ring on his finger while the taxi AI gave them the "leave a review" spiel. He couldn't help himself, nor could he be rid of the smile on his face.

Engaged. He was engaged to Jasper.

Zach had a feeling it was coming. They'd discussed it in bits and pieces of conversation during the last two years, however they'd never quite had a complete conversation on the possibility. This had left Zach wondering if Jasper wanted to go through marriage again—or marry him at all, for that matter. But here Zach was, with a ring on his finger, and he could hardly believe it.

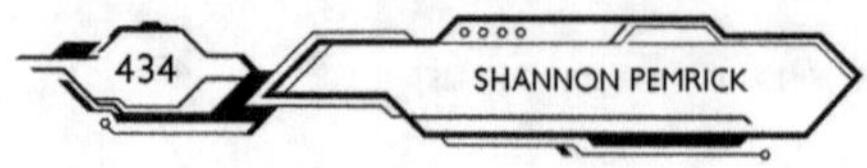

The taxi pulled away, leaving the two of them looking at the house.

"Didn't burn down," Jasper murmured.

Zach snickered. Jasper had been incredibly reluctant to leave on the date because of the grill. Alistair assured them both several times there was nothing to worry about with Shira's system, but neither of them was used to such a high-tech home. *We'll have to get used to it, though, if we're going to make this work.* Shira would never entertain the idea of downgrading. Hell, he was pretty sure that if he and Jasper owned a home, she'd make sure they had everything, even if they asked her not to go overboard.

"You think they're home?" Jasper asked.

"They are," Alistair said from Zach's phone. "You parents should be here within the hour."

The two of them had cut their date close, but even if they had been late, once Christine and Scott found out why, they wouldn't be able to be mad in the least.

Snake's barking greeted them before they'd made it halfway up the front walk. Though, to Zach's surprise, no one but the dog greeted them at the door when they entered.

"We're in the kitchen," Shira called out.

An object clattered on the counter, and Shira mumbled something before small feet thundered in the kitchen. Just as Zach and Jasper kicked off their shoes, Serenity rushed down the hall. "Daddy, Zach, you're home!"

She ran right into Jasper's outstretched arms. He lifted her up with an exaggerated grunt, and their daughter embraced him around the neck. "I had *so* much fun."

Jasper's smile practically reached his ears. "I'm not surprised. Shira is wicked awesome like that."

"Do I hear brown-nosing out there?" Shira called out. She hadn't left the kitchen, confusing Zach. What was she up to that made it so she couldn't come see them for a minute?

Jasper didn't answer, and Serenity capitalized on the moment. She leaned back, a bright smile on her face, and held up her fingers. "Look, look! We went to the nail place."

Zach leaned in to get a good look at her small nails, now painted with an intricate, blue scaled pattern. "Those are amazing, Starship. Wicked pretty."

Jasper cocked his head and reached for Serenity's arm. "Starship, what's this?"

The smile on the girl's face brightened even more, and she twisted in Jasper's arms, revealing a colorful baby Rathalos. "She-ra got me a tattoo like you, Daddy!"

Zach's heart lurched. *She did what—Idiot, Shira wouldn't actually get Serenity a tattoo.* But it sure as hell looked real. If this was a fake, it was crazy close to the real thing.

"No, it's not real," Shira said, her voice now much closer than the kitchen.

Zach looked up to see her approaching down the hall.

"No, I didn't think it was," Jasper said. "It looks wicked close, but it's definitely fake…"

Jasper trailed off when he looked up at her, seeing exactly what Zach did. Color crawled up her real arm to her neck—a tattoo. She continued toward them, a smirk on her face, and the tattoo became easier to make out.

Three dragons twisted around each other and up her arm. Two of the dragons spewed fire from their

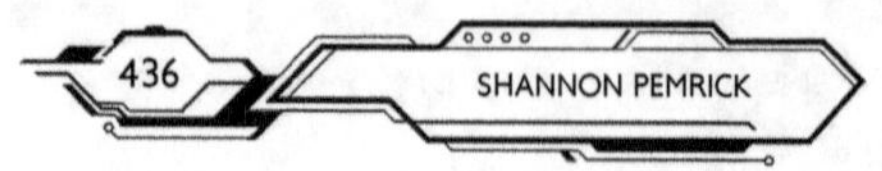

razor-sharp mouths, the flames transforming into a soaring phoenix. Large roses accompanied the mythical creatures, some even turning into flame to meld with the phoenix. They somehow didn't make the tattoo look cluttered, and filled the design out perfectly.

The color style chosen was a splashy, watercolor type.

Zach almost asked her if that was real. Then his brain caught up with him and he kept his mouth shut. There was no way it was real. That amount of work would have required a lot more time, and likely, given it was colored, wouldn't have happened in a single session.

Jasper set Serenity down on the floor and closed the distance between him and Shira, his eyes transfixed on the sight before them. He grasped her hand and lifted her arm. Jasper's fingers glided over her skin as he took in every inch of detail.

He'd mentioned on several occasions how much he'd love to see Shira all inked up. They might not be real tattoos, but it was the closest thing, and Zach had to admit, the look suited her.

Serenity grabbed onto his leg. "Mister Kane is wicked good with his special mahkuhs."

Kane? Shira went out of her way to hire a professional tattoo artist to do non-permanent tattoos? Was there nothing this woman wouldn't do to make his daughter happy? *Or Jasper and me happy?*

"No way this was done with a mahkuh," Jasper murmured. "Too clean."

Shira smirked. "She's telling the truth. Kane used a special tattooing marker to make both our pieces."

Jasper continued to trace the design, running his fingers all the way up to Shira's collarbone. He then reached out with his other hand and curled it around her waist, pulling her in close. Jasper bent her ear and whispered something Zach couldn't hear.

Shira laughed and murmured back, though she wasn't as secretive, and Zach listed. "No, I'm not going to make it permanent. It was for fun." Pause. "Yeah, I know it looks good, but I'm just not interested in something long-term."

Jasper pressed his lips into her ear more and continued to speak. Shira's eyes widened after a moment and pink flushed her cheeks. The thumb of his hand around her waist caressed her sides, as if to help emphasize whatever it was he tried to convey to her. Zach had a few guesses, like Jasper giving suggestions where she could have some "hidden" tattoos for him to find. Or even laying out what he'd do to Shira if she got a few tattoos in select areas.

Jasper's widening grin only cemented those ideas.

Shira pulled away and smacked Jasper's chest with her palm. "Absolutely not."

She was smiling, so Zach guessed she wasn't mad, and could possibly be embarrassed by whatever Jasper suggested.

Jasper's palms faced toward her and he shrugged as he stepped back. "I'm just saying, it'd be a good one for you. It'd be hot."

Small hands grabbed Zach's left hand, pulling his attention away. Serenity stared at the ring. "Zach, what's this?"

After a beat of silence, Shira let out a delighted shriek. She wrapped her arms around Jasper's neck and pulled him in for a cheek kiss. She then released him and ran over to Zach, doing the same.

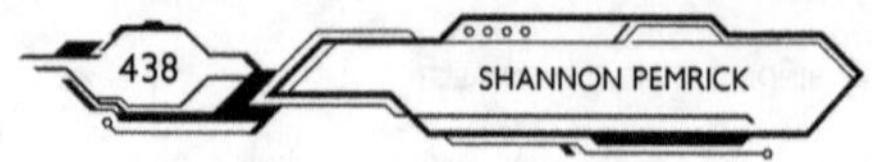

When she let him go, Shira made grabby hands. "Let me see, let me see!"

Zach laughed and lifted his hand to show off the ring. She squealed.

"Daddy, what's going on?" Serenity asked. "Why is She-ra going crazy?"

Shira immediately stopped and then backed away, acting sheepish. "Oops. Sorry."

Jasper and Zach only laughed. He was glad she was this excited.

He kneeled in front of Serenity and held her gaze. "Jasper and I are getting married."

His daughter blinked, and then a big grin pulled up to her eyes. Serenity's eyes went wide, and she giggled, dancing in place excitedly before throwing her arms around Zach's neck.

Zach pulled her into his arms and held her close. "Are you happy?"

She mutely nodded into his shoulder. Her reaction was far more subdued than he expected from her, but Zach could tell from the tightness of her grip, she was happy. *She's just overwhelmed.*

Zach held her for several moments longer, until she was ready to pull away. He kissed her on the forehead. "I love you, Serenity."

She giggled and kissed his cheek. "I love you too, Dad."

Zach's chest swelled. Hearing those words from her made him happier than he ever thought possible.

"She-ra, can we go back into the kitchen?" Serenity asked.

Shira smiled. "Of course. We still have a lot to finish before your grandparents arrive."

"What are you two up to in there?" Jasper asked.

"We're icing the cookies!" Serenity said. "She-ra is better at it than me, though."

Shira placed her hands on her hips. "Don't say that, Starship. Your cookies look creative."

Serenity's face scrunched. "That's just what adults say to not make kids feel bad."

Shira opened her mouth and then closed it. Her brow pinched together, and then she pointed at Zach and Jasper. "She's your daughter."

She headed for the kitchen. Serenity scampered after her, leaving Jasper and Zach laughing for a moment before following as well.

Shira called over her shoulder. "Tell your parents yet about the news?"

"No, we wanted to tell you two first," Jasper said. "Then we'd tell Amy, and then the whole world."

She placed a hand on her chest. "You told me before Amy? I'm touched."

Zach smiled. "I'm willing to take some heat from her for you."

Shira smirked, her eyes dancing. "You really know how to sweet-talk me."

He pulled out his phone and sent the text he'd saved in draft to Amy. Without waiting, Zach also posted on social, having already worked up the perfect draft while on the ride back. He expected his phone to blow up over the news and muted it. He could answer messages later.

Cookies, bowls, and bags were strewn about the island counter. Shira and Serenity jumped right back into decorating, and Jasper joined them after checking on the grilling food. Zach held back for now, choosing to lean against the wall and observe. He couldn't hide the smile the sight before him brought on.

Jasper didn't end up being much better than Serenity at decorating, and it brought on some good laughs. Serenity gushed about the things she and Shira did today, and as much as Zach wished he and Jasper had been there to be part of the memories, his daughter had plenty of them with him and Jasper. She needed more with Shira, and it was clear the ones Serenity made today wouldn't be soon forgotten.

Shira got some icing on her fingers, and Serenity laughed. A mischievous smirk slipped up Shira's beautiful face, and she *booped* Serenity on the nose, leaving a blot of pink icing behind. The two giggled and grinned, which turned into laughter when Jasper reached out and smeared a line of purple icing on their cheeks and Serenity retaliated with a blue icing handprint to the face.

Shira slid off her seat and jogged over to Zach. She grabbed his hand and pulled him toward all the fun, her eyes dancing with mirth. "C'mon, join us."

Zach didn't resist, feeling that magnetic pull that had only gotten stronger these last few days. He slipped onto a barstool next to her, and soon found himself sucked into the fun. It felt normal—perfect.

The doorbell rang. Snake barked and rushed for the front door. Serenity gasped, her eyes sparkling, and she scrambled off her barstool, nearly knocking her icing-covered knife onto the floor.

"That must be them," Shira said. She set her piping bag down and slipped off her stool, following Serenity.

Jasper looked at his phone. "They're early. Not bad."

Zach pursed his lips. That didn't sound right. Christine

liked to be early, however, Scott had the unbeatable record of making sure the two of them were always late. He always found something at the last minute that needed to be done right then, even if it could wait.

Jasper headed for the back door. "I'll check on the food."

This left Zach; he decided to join Shira. He reached the threshold of the hallway when Serenity opened the door, ignoring Shira's protests to wait so Snake wouldn't rush out.

"Nana, Pop-pop, you're h—" She stopped and stared at whoever was on the other side of the door. Snake stuck his nose outside between her and the doorframe, whining and wagging his tail. "You're not my Nana and Pop-pop."

A voice unfamiliar to Zach boomed in a deep chuckle. "*Ja*, she's a smart one."

Then a woman's voice followed. "She's even more adorable in person. You must be Serenity."

Snake whined more and tried to push past Serenity to get to these people. Shira's pace picked up. She grabbed the partially opened door and flung it open. On the other side stood a stocky, potbellied man with light hair and pale gray eyes, and a tall woman of lithe form, high cheekbones and dark complexion. Her long black hair cascaded and curled past her shoulders. Both wore fashionable clothing that wasn't too dissimilar to how Shira dressed.

"*Mutti? Vati?*" Shira said. "What are you doing here?"

Zach's pace slowed. *These are Shira's parents?*

Her mother smiled and reached for her daughter. "Surprise!"

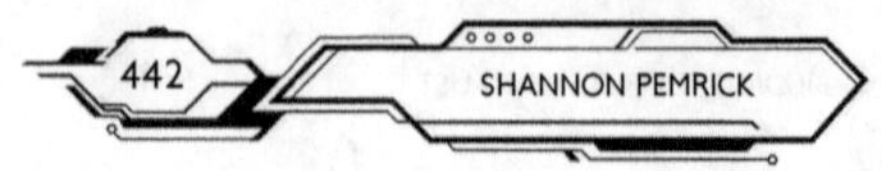

Shira chuckled and greeted her mother with a kiss on both cheeks, as well as a hug. She then turned to her father, and the two embraced in a strong hug.

"It's so good to see you, little bear," he said, his German accent not as thick as Zach expected. It was much like Shira's Uncle Luis.

Shira pulled away, though it was clearly more because Snake was trying to push his way between them, rather than Shira's father being willing to let his daughter go. The impatient dog got the attention he desired from both guests.

Shira turned to Serenity. "Starship, these are my parents, Flynn and Anita."

Serenity clasped her hands behind her back. "Hi, I'm Serenity. It's nice to meet you."

"It's a pleasure to finally meet you as well," Anita said. "Shira talks about you all the time."

A beaming smile lit up Serenity's face. "She-ra talks about you, too. She's always happy when she does."

Anita's face brightened as much as the little girl in front of her, and Zach was sure other emotions threatened to spill out. *Shira couldn't be more loved by these people.*

A twinge of jealousy flashed through Zach, and then it disappeared, smothered by disappointment with himself. Even after all these years, he couldn't quite bury those feelings his parents left him with.

Serenity pointed at Flynn's round stomach. "You got a wicked big belly."

Zach's mouth fell open. "Serenity!"

Serenity jerked her head back to him. "But he does. She-ra said he loved food like Missus Anita makes."

Anita hid her mouth behind her hand, clearly trying to

bite back laughter. Shira had a similar expression. And for some reason, Flynn had a wicked grin on his face.

He held his hand above Serenity's head. "Hmm, I thought you would be taller, tiny mouse."

Serenity's back straightened, and she stared up at Flynn. "I'm talluh than I was in the summah."

"Zat so?" Flynn bent forward and the two had a weird staring contest. Then they broke out into grins and a mixture of giggles and chuckles.

"Serenity," Zach said, his voice firm.

His daughter ripped her gaze away and cocked her head. "What?"

"What you said was rude. Apologize for your behavior."

"But he's not mad," Serenity tried to argue.

Flynn waved a dismissive hand. "*Ja*, it's fine."

"*Vati*," Shira said. "Don't undermine Zach's parenting."

Her father held up his hands, as if confused and offended Shira was scolding him. Then the German came out. Zach watched bemusedly as the two verbally sparred. He didn't understand a word of it, but that didn't make it any less entertaining.

Anita walked over to Zach, her heels clacking on the floor. He found out quickly she was taller than he expected. *I think she's as tall as Ajax, without the heels.*

"I'll apologize on my husband's behalf," she said. "For a military man, he has issues with rules and authority."

Zach cracked a smile. "Ironic."

She let out a closed-mouth chuckle and then suddenly grabbed his shoulders. "It's wonderful to finally meet you, Zach. I've been looking forward to it."

Before he could respond, she pulled him close and kissed his cheeks. Zach blinked. "Uh, great to meet you too, Anita."

She tilted her head as she smiled at him and then grasped his chin. Too startled by her behavior, he allowed her to turn his head back and forth, assessing him.

A pleased smiled spread up half her face, as if she approved with whatever assessment she made of him.

"Mom, stop that," Shira said in English.

Anita released him and stepped back. She held out a single placating hand. "Stop what?"

"He's not a model."

Ah. Shira's parents were fashion designers and Shira was a model. Made sense Anita would look for certain traits.

"Could have fooled me," Anita said, her smile not apologetic. "Perfect eyes, great cheekbones"—she lifted Zach's hand—"And we could also talk about these hands."

There was something in her tone that gave Zach the impression she was insinuating something other than modeling. And the wide-eyed stern stare Shira shot her mother only sealed that. Zach had the distinct impression Anita may have come to some conclusion about him and Jasper with Shira.

Shira continued to throw imaginary daggers at her mother. Until the back door clattered, and Jasper's voice drifted down to them. "Ribs are almost ready for—"

He stopped dead when he noticed Anita and Flynn. "You're not my parents."

Flynn laughed, holding his belly. "I see where the little mouse gets it from."

"You must be Jasper." Anita gave Jasper the same greeting she had with Zach, including the assessment. Jasper didn't understand her behavior any better than Zach had.

"Yes, the same with him," Anita said, nodding approvingly. "They both would make the perfect models."

Shira sighed and pinched the bridge of her nose. Zach jumped in and give her a hand. "I much prefer to be behind the camera lens."

The taller woman's lips curled as she gave him another assessing look. "Is that so?"

From the tone, Zach was now convinced Shira's mom was trying to imply something. How much did she know about him and Jasper from Shira? Were they aware of Shira's feelings about them? Were they supportive about where it could potentially lead?

Zach suspected she might have a small inkling, given she was acting this way, but he also didn't know the woman. She may be like this all the time.

"Hold up," Shira said. "Before we go down that rabbit hole, can we please back up to my question about why you two are here? Because 'surprise' isn't a real answer to it. You said the two of you would be in Paris until the end of the week."

Anita smiled at her daughter in a way that screamed that Shira had intentionally derailed the woman. "Yes, I did say that, but it was a fib. We had purchased a day pass for the last day of the convention."

"We wanted to surprise you," Flynn said. He then grunted. "Zen, of course, the fire happened."

A smile tugged Zach's mouth when Shira didn't even flinch at the reminder. *She's come so far.*

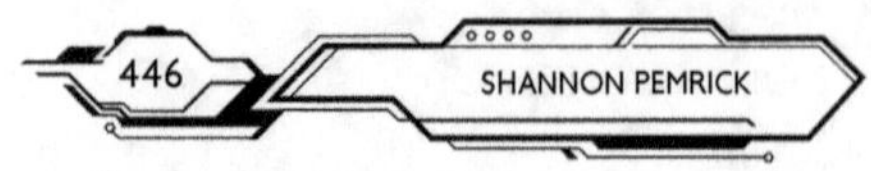

"What your father is trying to say is, we can't stay because of the delay as we have a few important meetings in the new time slots, so we thought we'd drop by for a visit instead."

"That might explain the extra food I found myself cooking," Jasper said. "I thought it was too much for six people."

Anita's lips pursed. "Were you expecting company? We don't mean to intrude on your plans."

Jasper shook his head. "You're not. It's my parents coming by. They should be here soon. Join us."

Shira looked up at the ceiling. "And, I have a feeling, someone had planned for you both to stay. Isn't that right, Orion?"

"I may have corresponded with Olivia and increased your side of the cost to compensate, Shira," the AI said.

Zach guessed Olivia was the couple's AI.

Shira smirked and shook her head, as if this behavior wasn't unusual for the AI or concerning in the least. Zach couldn't see himself being okay with such a surprise from Alistair.

"I'm gonna go decorate more cookies," Serenity announced and then ran off.

Flynn perked up. "Cookies?"

Both Anita and Shira gave him pointed looks. "After dinner."

Zach shared a look with Jasper, and Flynn let out an amused snort. "We'll see."

Shira rolled her eyes and waved everyone to head to the back of the house. "You two went to see Uncle Luis and Aunt Tiffany, right?"

"*Ja*, of course," Flynn said. "We always see zem when we're here."

Anita chuckled. "We wouldn't hear the end of it from Luis if we skipped out on a visit and he found out."

The ladies sat down at the island counter, and Shira went back to decorating with Serenity. Jasper slipped out to check on the food again, while Flynn sidled around the island to the side where Serenity decorated.

Zach leaned against the island, finding it difficult to suppress an amused smirk. He had no doubt Flynn would try to sneak a cookie, and if the older man guessed Serenity would become an accomplice in his shenanigans, then he was right. *He has troublemaker-grandpa energy.*

Anita turned to him. "So, photography?"

"It was my profession before I turned to gaming full time."

She rested her chin on her palm. "Didn't enjoy it anymore?"

He shook his head. "No, I loved it. But Jasper needed my help, so I sold my half of the studio to my partner and moved back to Boston. That's when we decided to turn it to full time."

"Do you miss it?" she asked.

He nodded. "All the time. But I have no desire to give up what I'm doing. Maybe in the future I'll go back, but for now, I'm content to have it as a hobby that I can enjoy."

She smiled, the gesture gentle and sweet. Shira may look nothing like her adopted parents, but she certainly obtained gestures and quirks, and Zach recognized that look on her mother's face. Shira got that look from her.

Zach's eyes darted to Shira when skin smacked skin.

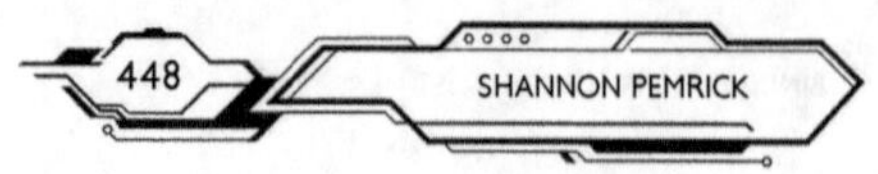

Flynn held his hand, rubbing it while pouting. Shira pointed at him, her stare a hard warning. Serenity giggled away. Even Anita laughed.

The doorbell rang for the second time today, and Snake went nuts again. Orion confirmed this time their guests were Jasper's parents. Jasper rushed to the door before Zach could think to move.

Serenity finished the cookie she worked on and offered it to Flynn. "Here, a gift."

Flynn slyly smiled and winked at her before glancing toward his daughter. "I can't say no to a gift from her."

Shira pursed her lips and this time Zach laughed. She should have expected the two would conspire against her.

Christine's voice drifted into the kitchen. "Sounds like the party is back here."

Zach turned around and barely had enough time to prepare for Christine's hug. He chuckled. "Hi, Christine."

"Oh, don't you 'Hi, Christine' me, young man." She released him and grabbed his hand. "Let me see it."

He smiled and didn't resist, allowing her to gush. Scott and Christine had seen him as part of the family long ago. Zach even called them mom and dad. And after he and Jasper had gotten together, they'd already assumed this next step would be inevitable.

The moment Christine gazed at the ring, she glowed, and then he was assaulted with motherly kisses. They lasted so long, Scott had to pry his wife off. "All right, Christine, we get it, you're happy. Let our son breathe."

A flitter of butterflies spread through Zach. He wondered how long it'd take for that to go away, even after all these years.

"I thought… uh, Zasper was ze son," Flynn said.

"Jasper, *Vati*, his name is Jasper, and he is their son," Shira said. "Zach has lived with them for a long time, though. And the two got engaged today."

Anita gasped. "Oh, how wonderful! Congratulations, you two. Let me see, let me see."

Zach refrained an eye roll and showed her as well. He understood the excitement. He hadn't stopped playing with the ring since it ended up on his finger. It was the attention that he'd have to get used to. It'd die down soon enough.

After the two women finished gushing, and Jasper got his round from them, too, both sets of parents greeted each other—Anita giving Christine and Scott the same friendly one she gave him and Jasper—and fell into conversation as if this meeting had been planned all along.

After she got her hugs in with her grandparents, and even cheekily offered Scott a cookie, Serenity challenged Shira to a decorating race.

CHAPTER 22

Shira finished her last cookie and let out a breath of relief. "All done. How about you, Starship?"

To Shira's surprise and Zach's amusement, as well as the other adults, Serenity was lounging in her seat, waiting for Shira to finish. "I finished a wicked long time ago, She-ra."

It really wasn't that long ago, maybe two or three minutes, but Zach wasn't going to tell Shira that. He was enjoying watching her inspect Serenity's work, making sure she didn't take any shortcuts by only half-decorating some of them. None were left without frosting. Most had too much, and not nearly the same finesse Shira had in hers, but Serenity's had charm all the same.

And the grandpas were all too eager to try some of her more overdone monstrosities. For "inspection purposes," they claimed. *Grandpas... Plural...* Zach could see how much Flynn already loved Serenity. He wanted things to work out between him, Jasper, and

Shira. Then he could be the big old loving bear of a second grandfather Serenity deserved. She'd already been robbed of that after his own parents abandoned him, and sadly Sara never knew her father and lost her mother shortly after high school.

"Well, looks like you won," Shira said with a breath of reluctance to admit. "Great job, Starship."

Serenity cheered and hopped down to do a victory dance. Snake absorbed her energy and practically knocked her over in his excitement. This, of course, only made Serenity laugh and run off, with the black shepherd chasing after her.

"No running in the house!" Jasper yelled after her. She ignored him.

Shira snickered and grabbed a rag to wipe down the counter. "She takes after you."

Jasper narrowed his eyes at her. "Definitely not me."

Scott threw his head back with a hard laugh. "You were worse! We thought you had hearing issues it was so bad."

Pink tinted Jasper's cheeks, and Zach joined in the laughter. Jasper really had quite the rebellious spirit as a kid.

"Jasper, the ribs are done," Alistair said.

He clapped his hands in response and ran for the back door. Jasper came to a sliding halt when they opened automatically. He stared at the folding door and then turned to Shira, who was already watching the moving barrier.

"Huh," she said. "I guess that's fixed now."

"I finished the software patch and recalibration this morning, Shira," Orion said.

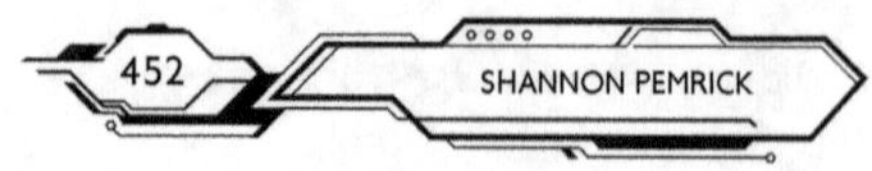

Jasper gazed up at the ceiling, holding his hands out. "And you've been allowing me to open and close the doors all day, because?"

"Timing the perfect reaction," the AI said.

Shira sputtered a laugh and went back to cleaning. Jasper shook his head and stepped outside.

Zach figured with the meat done, it would be good to pull out the rest of the food he and Jasper prepared in advance. He hadn't expected Jasper to go all-out with dinner, but Zach knew he shouldn't have been surprised, either.

Aside from the one night they'd spent with Christine and Scott when the three of them arrived, this was the first time Jasper had the chance to spend a long period of time with his parents in quite some time. They only came to visit once or twice a year, and given the costs to travel, that was a bit much even in Zach's eyes.

Plus, there was the added bonus of showing off to Shira. They'd mostly done takeout or eating out somewhere, so she hadn't gotten the chance to experience their cooking besides breakfast. This meal would also help her see what else they brought to the table, other than great company and even better sex.

Zach opened the fridge and reached for one of the covered bowls, only to notice two pitchers. One had a pale yellow bubbly liquid, and the other contained a deep red liquid. He hadn't made them, and Zach didn't recall seeing Jasper make any drinks, either.

"Jasper, did you make these drinks?" he called out.

Shira abandoned her cleaning and swooped in, grabbing both pitchers. "Nope, I did. We should all move outside to the patio. The table is a better place to eat and chat, and it's nice out."

"Did you make something when we expressly told you not to?" Jasper asked, ignoring her statement.

Zach turned to find him standing in the doorway holding a plate of steaming ribs. Snake sat at his feet, staring up at the food and licking his chops.

Shira held her head high. "I was going to contribute to all this regardless of what you told me. Deal with it."

Amused chuckles rumbled through the kitchen.

She took confident steps toward Jasper and held up the red drink first, and then the other. "I made strawberry punch and *Apfelschorle.*"

Jasper blinked and then said, *"Gesundheit."*

Flynn belted out a hearty laugh.

"It's apple soda, Daddy," Serenity said. "She-ra let me help her make it."

"Soda? You can make soda?"

Zach laughed. "Of course you can. It just requires carbonated water."

Jasper's priceless, awed expression amused Zach greatly. He really thought that was common knowledge.

"You taught her zis word, little bear?" Flynn asked.

"I've taught her many words," Shira said. "Serenity wants to learn."

The older man nodded approvingly. "Zis is good. Start her young."

"I'm learning many languages," Serenity said.

Anita leaned on the island, her interest piqued. "Really? I'd love to know all about that."

Zach immediately tuned out that conversation. He'd

heard it enough times, and knew Serenity would go onto tangents about school subjects she liked the most.

Shira slipped past Jasper to set the pitchers on the patio table. He followed with his plate of meat. Zach opened the sealed bowl; inside was his favorite recipe of potato salad.

Flynn took notice and peered into the bowl. "Why is it yellow?"

Zach's brow ticked up, and then he looked down at the dish. "It has egg in it?"

Flynn gave him the most perplexing, confused look. Had he never eaten potato salad with eggs? Zach thought it was a fairly common ingredient.

Anita turned to him. "We eat the traditional German recipe at home. There aren't any eggs or mayonnaise in that version."

Flynn's brow furrowed. "Mayonnaise? Why is zere mayonnaise in potato salad?"

"It's common for the American-style dish to have it, love," she said to her husband. "Just like egg salad and macaroni salad."

He shook his head and mumbled something to himself in German. Zach found the man interesting. And the conversation amusing, especially since Zach had made macaroni salad as well. "I'll have to get the German recipe to try out sometime."

"*Ja*, you do. Zen you will understand why it is better," Flynn said.

"Oh, stop it, *Vati*," Shira said, reentering the house. "You refuse to try any American-style potato salad, even eggless ones. You can't say it's inferior until you do."

"I know good food," her father said simply.

Shira tried to take the bowl from Zach. "Well, *I* am looking forward to variety."

Zach didn't relinquish the bowl. "You did your part. Now you get to sit back while we continue ours."

Shira tipped her head and gave him an exasperated look. "It's setting the table, not cooking. I can help with that."

"We've got it. Sit down and relax."

"Can I help?" Serenity asked.

Shira tossed her head toward the utensil drawer. "Can you get the forks and lay them out for every seat?"

His daughter scurried over to the drawer and rummaged. Shira kept her eyes fixed on Zach and tugged on the bowl. He yanked back, hard enough she took a few stumbling steps toward him. "I can be just as stubborn, Shira. Let go and take a load off your feet."

She pursed her lips, and to his surprise and suspicion, released her hold. *That was too easy.* He expected greater stubbornness from her. It didn't help he could sense all eyes on the two of them this whole time. There really wasn't much chatter going on either, as if both sets of parents were taking in their interactions with careful consideration.

Zach knew Christine and Scott's position, but he wasn't so sure about Anita and Flynn. Would they approve? Would that approval or disapproval affect any decisions Shira might have with him and Jasper?

Shira pivoted on her heels and opened the fridge, taking out another covered bowl. Zach rolled his eyes. *I should have known.* He grabbed the bowl and tried to take that from her as well. She narrowed her eyes and refused to relinquish the bowl or cease her attempts to help.

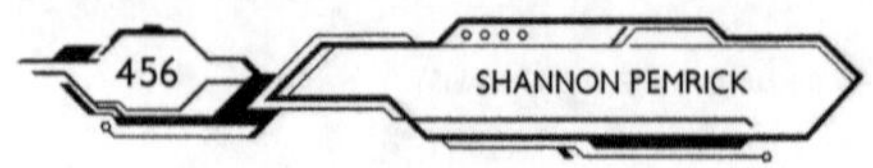

Anita's phone pinged, and that snagged Shira's attention away.

"That'd better not be work-related," Shira warned. "You can relax a few more hours."

Her mother laughed. "No, no. It's a reminder to grab a project I left here the other week."

Shira pursed her lips. "Oh, well, I'll probably need to help you find it. I moved a lot around this week since I used the room."

Anita's eyebrow rose. "You were designing? You're going to show me, of course."

Shira rolled her eyes. "It's nothing crazy, but sure."

She relinquished the bowl to Zach and grabbed her apron on the way out of the kitchen, following her mom to the stairs. Jasper shared a glance with Zach. They both knew the two women would have to be retrieved, otherwise they'd miss dinner.

Zach uncovered the second bowl, this one containing the macaroni salad he made, and carried both salads outside. Flynn, Scott, and Christine followed. Jasper was plating out another pile of ribs, and he'd also set out corn and some burgers.

"I made veggie burgers," he said. "Orion told me it was necessary to make them."

Flynn nodded. "*Danke.* Anita can't eat meat."

Mild panic and then relief flashed through Jasper's eyes. "I'm glad the AI said something. I'd hate to have made a meal she couldn't have."

The older man smiled and patted his belly. "Do not worry. We showed up unannounced. We wouldn't have been offended. And she's a resourceful woman."

Zach slipped back inside to gather plates and the rest

of the silverware for everyone. Serenity had abandoned her task and now played with Snake in the yard. He didn't mind. Zach was used to her complaining that she was bored. He hadn't heard a peep of that word from her mouth this entire week. And he'd be happy if it stayed that way the rest of their time here.

When the table had been set, minus the drinkware, which Jasper insisted he'd get, Zach volunteered to grab Shira and her mom. They hadn't been gone an unusually long time, but even Flynn had made a brief comment about the two women taking a while.

Zach assumed they'd just got to talking about designs. Shira hadn't given off any hints she was into fashion design in the same way as her parents, but it also hadn't been that long since he and Jasper found out she designed to begin with. Sure, it was cosplay, but that didn't mean she didn't dabble in casual wear or something and hadn't revealed that to him or Jasper.

He took the stairs quickly, but when Zach reached the landing, his pace slowed. Anita's and Shira's voices drifted down the hall through the partially closed door of the studio. He couldn't see them through the crack.

Zach craned his neck as he crept closer, trying to pick up on their conversation. Eavesdropping, nothing he was proud to say he was doing, but he was curious what these two could talk about for this long.

"Shira, just tell me," Anita said. "You know I'm supportive, no matter what you do. I just want you to be happy."

Shira let out an exasperated sigh. "Then why can't you drop this?"

"Because I'm your mother and I'm nosey."

Zach bit back a laugh. *She sounds like Christine.*

There was a small beat of silence, and then Anita prodded again. "Come now, Shira. Just give your mom something here before I die of old age."

Shira snorted out a half-laugh from that one. "Fine. It's nothing serious yet."

"Nothing serious?" Her mother sounded incredulous, and Zach was more curious than ever. *What the hell are they talking about?* "I know the guys just got engaged, but I can't imagine that being a deal breaker for you. Knowing you and how you talked about them before, you expected this to happen with them."

Zach's pulse slowed. They were talking about him and Jasper? *What does Shira mean by not 'serious'?*

"Yeah, I knew that was going to happen," Shira said. "It was obvious."

"Then what—oh, honey, don't tell me…"

There was a pause, as if Shira was giving her mom her iconic confused face. "Whoa, hold up. Don't you dare start thinking this is me hiding or running away, or using them as some sort of temporary coping mechanism—"

Anita calmly hushed her daughter. "Hey, stop, please. I'm sorry. I didn't mean for that to be accusatory and send you on the defensive. You've got every right to be upset with those conclusions I am worried about."

She let out a quiet breath. "Yes, I admit that was a small concern. It's a pattern we've seen from you before, and I was worried, after all the progress you've been making, you'd maybe had a bit of a backslide. It's normal when dealing with something so major."

There was another beat of silence before Shira spoke, though she let out a long sigh first. "I understand. And

I don't blame you for the conclusion. I'm sorry I got defensive. It's just hard, making all this progress and people assuming the worst of your actions, especially when that's not the case."

"I'm so very proud of you, Shira," her mother said. "Your father and I were so worried. Both the last few years and then when you told us you had a new reason to push forward again. But I couldn't be prouder of the progress you've made. And I have those two men and their little girl to thank."

A pause, and then she spoke again, this time her voice quieter, as if she were in Shira's face. "So tell me, why is this thing between the three of you not serious? I'm not judging if it isn't intended to be. You know I had quite the adventurous streak before I met your father."

Shira snorted, as if the two of them were open about such things like two gossiping friends. Zach wasn't sure how to feel about that. *Who is that friendly with their parents?*

"I just want to understand," Anita said.

Zach leaned closer to the door, trying hard not to move from his spot and alert them to his presence. He really shouldn't be doing this, but Shira's comment and her seemingly evasive behavior really bugged him now.

"I'm just… trying to sort it all out, okay?" Shira said, her voice more distressed than Zach enjoyed hearing. "I said it wasn't anything serious because we haven't discussed it in detail. That's also why I said *yet*. Doesn't mean it might not develop into something more. I'm just not getting my hopes up. So, I want to take it slow and feel out if this is just for fun, or if it's leading to something deeper. I already jumped into a deeper end of the swimming pool than I should have after not even dipping my toes into the shallow end. I don't need to toss on the diving gear before I'm ready."

Her mother laughed. "That was an oddly specific picture, but I do appreciate the attempt."

Zach didn't. His gut clenched harder than he ever recalled in his life, as if some berserker nailed him with a war hammer. Shira saw this as some stupid fling. She was open to the idea of them being more, but the fact she didn't see their attempts to be in her life as serious, permanent fixtures was a major concern.

He mentally sighed. *Can I really blame her, though?* Until recently, he had been plagued with so much doubt about his own feelings for her. And that had prevented him and Jasper from sitting down with her and talking about it.

Though, Jasper also was more of an "actions speak louder" kind of guy and would assume that'd be enough for Shira to get the hint about their seriousness about her. He and Jasper had only become a serious couple because Zach asked Jasper point-blank what they were after the fifth time they'd ended up in bed together. Jasper was stunned and had already assumed Zach understood where they stood by that point. He could roll his eyes at the absurd memory.

"So, it's not serious at the moment, but it could be." There was a mischievous tone in her mother's voice. "They must be good if you're considering it."

Zach did roll his eyes at this. *What parent had these conversations with their kid?* Christine certainly didn't with him or Jasper, and she was quite nosey sometimes. Cheryl would ask in her stead if she had such burning desires to know.

That thought gave him pause. Did Christine have

these conversations with Cheryl? Were these normal conversations for mothers and daughters to have?

"Well, duh," Shira said. "The sex is amazing."

If he had feathers, Zach would preen. An ego boost here and there didn't hurt anyone, and if Shira thought he and Jasper were that good, then the two of them had to continue to perform well to keep her.

"They're good listeners, too. Supportive…" She let out a slow breath. "Especially that."

"Have they seen some of your worst days?"

Shira didn't respond verbally, but Zach assumed she was nodding. "They've taken it so well, I honestly thought I was dreaming."

Zach's eyebrow rose. Did she really think that poorly of them, that they'd bail on her when she needed help the most?

"I know it's hard to deal with those days," Shira said. "I barely get through them myself. But they keep pushing on with me, trying to help where they can, as if it's the most natural thing in the world for them to do. They could have just walked away, but they choose not to. I couldn't be more thankful."

"They have my thanks a thousand times over," Anita said. "I'll have to make sure they're appropriately rewarded."

Shira snickered. "They hate being spoiled. They fight me all the time about it."

"Well, it's a good thing the two of us don't care and do it anyway."

Zach bit down hard on his lower lip so he wouldn't burst out into laughter. That was exactly what he and

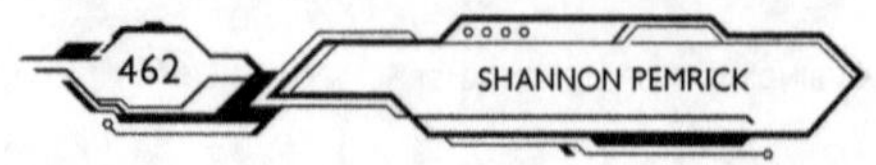

Jasper had experienced with Shira. At least he knew where she got it from now.

"What about future plans?" her mother asked. "I know you said this wasn't serious yet, but there has to have been some conversations about—"

"They know I can't have children, Mom," Shira said. Zach caught the pain in her words. "They know there won't be biological children from me, so they'd still have to adopt if they want more kids in the future."

Anita let out a slow breath. "Shira, dear, that's something I've been trying to talk to you about the last few times it's come up—"

Zach decided now was the time to cut their conversation short. Anita meant well, he had no doubts, but this was too fresh a wound for Shira. Not after all the emotions he'd witnessed from her when she explained things to them.

Zach backed up a few paces and then walked normally, not minding if he made any noise now, and knocked on the door. "Shira? Anita?"

"Come in," Shira said.

He pushed open the door and entered the studio. The two women were by one of the worktables, Shira sitting down on it. Anita had a large bag by her feet, no doubt the project she'd mentioned needing to grab. At least he knew that part wasn't a lie to get Shira alone to pester her.

"Hey," he said. "Just letting you two know, dinner is ready."

Anita smiled. "Thank you. We'll be right down."

He nodded and left, not wanting to draw any suspicion. He really shouldn't have eavesdropped, but he'd learned a lot, and needed to talk to Jasper about it.

To his surprise, his fiancé was in the kitchen still. The cups were out and organized on the counter instead of outside, and Jasper stood still in front of them, as if he were listening to something.

Before Zach could speak, Jasper noticed him and put a finger to his lips to encourage Zach to stay quiet, and then jerked his head toward the patio. Zach joined Jasper by his side and listened.

"Flynn, what are your thoughts on the three of them together?" Christine asked.

"Together?" Flynn said.

"Yes, it was quite obvious something is going on. They weren't really hiding anything in the kitchen."

Flynn made a thoughtful sound. "I do not understand it. But, if it makes my little bear happy, zen I will support her."

Zach smiled. He didn't expect everyone to understand. There were plenty of things about others Zach didn't understand. But he was grateful Flynn was honest about it and still supported his daughter nonetheless.

Jasper also seemed satisfied with the answer and resumed his current task, which looked like cutting a tomato. Shira and Anita showed up in the kitchen a moment later.

"Okay, what's left to be done?" Shira asked.

"Just finishing up the prep for these dressings for Anita's veggie burgers. Flynn told me what she liked on them."

Anita pressed her hand against her chest. "You didn't have to go through the trouble of making me something special. I would have been perfectly fine eating the other non-meat items you two prepared."

Jasper shook his head. "Not on my watch. Besides, Sara was a vegetarian. I know how to make a mean veggie burger."

Anita cocked her head. "Who is Sara?"

He gave her a bittersweet smile. "My late wife."

Anita smiled warmly in return. "I'll be sure to enjoy it for both of us, then."

She slipped outside, leaving Shira to pester them about helping in some way. Zach and Jasper managed to keep her away from the final food prep work, but instead she'd snatched some of the waiting drinkware.

Zach grabbed her wrists and stopped her from retreating. "Where do you think you're going?"

"Oh, just let me do this, Zach," she said, mixed with an exasperated sigh.

He thought for a moment and then grinned. "There's payment required."

Shira pursed her lips and regarded him for a moment before popping up on her toes and pressing her warm, soft lips against his. Zach's eyes hooded as he relished the sensation the kiss sent through him.

All too soon, she pulled away. "That enough to post bail?"

Zach pretended to think a moment released her. "This time."

She smirked, though it was interrupted by a young girl's giggling. Zach turned just in time to see Serenity withdrawing back outside. The adults out there immediately went to asking her what she found so funny, and Serenity didn't hide what she caught.

Zach's eyebrow rose toward Shira, who rolled her eyes and left. She attempted to diffuse Serenity's kissing claims by playing off the act as some sort of innocent thank you, but Serenity thwarted each attempt, and none of the parents believed a word. Zach and Jasper chuckled quietly the whole time.

Once they finished the final prep and had everything laid out, everyone settled into their seats and dug into the food. Conversation flowed easily. Banter and laughter mingled with "get-to-know-you" chats.

Shira learned about Scott's urban landscaping job and how he and Christine began traveling after Cheryl and Jasper graduated high school. Given Christine's job as an esports coach at the time allowed her to work anywhere, that wasn't a constraint for them. They'd been all over the country, but the two had stayed in California the longest so far.

Zach and Jasper learned how Anita and Flynn met by chance while he was working a security detail at a fashion show, mistaking her for the woman he was supposed to be guarding when things went south. At first, Zach couldn't believe the tale. It sounded like some fabricated story Kiara would come up with. But Shira showed them the news article of the attack.

Both sets of parents got to learn about the other's kids more. Anita and Flynn also learned a bit about Cheryl as well. And it all just felt so natural to Zach, like this was how it should be. He didn't want this to be the only moment they'd all have together. *I need to talk to Jasper about Shira's conversation with her mom and figure out our next step.*

Shira pulled out another surprise on him and Jasper. The drinks she'd made wasn't the only thing she'd snuck under their nose. Apparently, between those and the

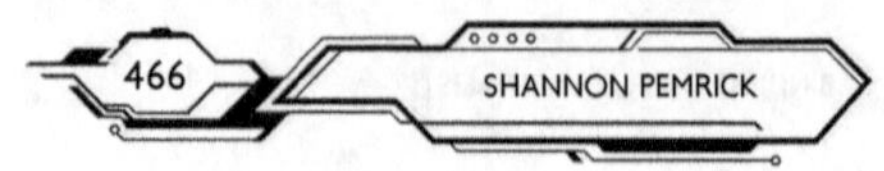

cookie decorating, she'd also made a chocolate sauer-kraut cake—one of Flynn's favorite desserts. When she first said what it was, Zach couldn't stop himself from making a face. The idea didn't sound appealing. But he'd been proven so wrong, he'd taken two slices. If she hadn't said there was sauerkraut in the cake, Zach wouldn't have known. He could have been fooled into thinking it was coconut. *It's official. Bakers are wizards and alchemists. We'll have to figure out which one Kiara is.*

Sadly, the get-together couldn't last forever. They saw their parents off, as well as Serenity, who was now eager to go spend time with her grandparents rather than disappointed, like when they first told her of the arrangement. Zach figured that would happen. In two days, she'd be gushing about all the things she did with them.

Scott honked the horn as their car pulled away, leaving the three of them standing on the walkway gazing at their vanishing vehicle.

"It's going to be quiet with her gone," Shira said. Her tone was a bit sad to Zach. Did it bother her to see Serenity leave? Would she feel the same when the three of them eventually had to return home? *How will it feel for us to leave her here?*

"We're still here to keep you entertained," Jasper said, smirking at her. Zach also grinned. With Serenity gone, they could get away with a lot more.

She pursed her lips and looked him up and down in an assessing manner. "You two need to practice for the tournament."

Zach stepped closer, his chest pressing against her back. "We will have down time. We never go more than three hours without appropriate breaks. It's not healthy otherwise."

He leaned closer to her ear. "You don't want to promote unhealthy behavior, do you?"

She leaned away while tilting her head down and looking up at him. "I don't need to promote that. You two have enough unhealthy habits already. If anything, the two of you could use some training."

Zach slipped his arm around her lower back and smirked. "Do you want to train us?"

Her brilliant eyes went thoughtful, and her teeth caught her lower lip for a moment. Zach's gaze flicked down to her tempting mouth. There was nothing stopping him from kissing her right now. Hell, there was no small person around to prevent him from dragging her inside and indulging in her addictive taste and every sweet curve.

Shira let out a quiet chuckle and pushed him back a step by his chest. "Both of you go practice."

Zach ran his tongue across his teeth behind his closed mouth and took several steps back. She was right; he and Jasper did need to practice. But that was far from his mind now, and he didn't appreciate being riled up. Though he couldn't place the blame on her. He'd let his mind run away on him.

Jasper touched her elbows. "Join us for a few games before we focus on twos? It's been a while."

Shira pursed her lips while she thought. "All right, one or two games, and then you both have to focus."

"Deal."

CHAPTER 23

Vibrant sparkles of pink and blue flew past Shira's face. She sucked in a tight breath and whirled around to face the sorcerer. He'd used his berserker and warrior teammates to distract Jasper and Zach. Unfortunately for her opponent, his attack missed and Shira was already channeling a spell.

She pivoted and thrust her hand out, the binding spell activating. Rocks and thick plant roots shot out of the ground, snagging her opponent and holding him in place. Shira made the mental gymnastics to cast another spell when Zach slammed into the sorcerer.

Shira blinked and stole a glance to where she'd last seen Zach brawling it out with the berserker. She was down and the match timer counted to the end of the match.

Jasper still clashed with his opponent, warrior to warrior. No one was going to give up until the timer stopped them.

Shira peeked at both her guy's health bars.

Health: 55%

Health: 68%

Shira's mental tracks switched her cast to two small healing spells, one for each. *That should keep them up until the timer.* She had taken her hybrid healing approach for this match, but her guys hadn't needed it as much as normal this time. They were a good team as a double-warrior combo. She made a mental note to let them know to try it more often.

Several more hits, and one lightning spell, they took down the sorcerer and almost the other warrior when the timer reached zero. Shira cheered. Not just because of the win, but also the fact she felt good playing with the guys.

Spending time with them outside the game, in person, was great. But this was what she was used to. It was a piece of familiar she hadn't had all week. And they'd played several matches last night and again this morning.

The area digitized, and the system moved the three of them into a lobby. Teams mingled about, either discussing among their own members, or with other teams. The three of them rarely used the PvP lobbies, preferring to queue in from the guild or wherever they were at the time, but today there'd been some game instability on the PvP side of the game. Most people found connecting to matches outside the lobbies difficult, if not impossible, so it was agreed they'd use the lobbies today.

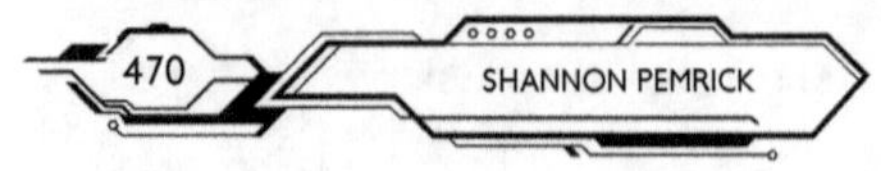

Jasper clapped his hands together. "That went great. We really killed that match."

Zach snorted, and Shira choked on a laugh. That was his third pun today after a match win.

"So, next match?" Jasper said.

Shira shook her head. "No. We have a deal."

In order to make sure the two of them practiced like they used to, Shira bargained with them. They had to do at least five twos practice matches before she would join them for threes. But, to ensure the two of them didn't get carried away playing with her, she put a hard stop at three games.

It wasn't an uncommon setup for them during the year. The guys would practice on their own, join up with her for a few rounds, and then go back to their practices. It was just less structured, and the guys today really didn't want to abide by the new structure.

Jasper blew out a breath. "Just one more game. We're doing wicked well."

Shira wasn't going to budge. The tournament was too serious. "No. Three rounds is the max. You two now need to get back to practice. Speaking of, try out the double-warrior combo again. Also, Jasper, take a look at dragoon and pugilist again. Both could be useful against Burnout."

"I think he should practice priest or druid healing," Zach said.

Shira shook her head. "No, you need to do that. There's going to be a point Jasper will need to go DPS or tank and rely on you to heal."

Zach sucked at healing. Something about it he couldn't get down right. So, practicing in the inevitable event he'd have to take up that class position was needed. Because Shira knew, no matter how much they practiced, a team could force them to try a class combo they were not as confident with.

Jasper's shoulders slumped. "All right, you win. Five matches for practice." He pointed a finger at her. "You'd better be here and ready when we're done."

Shira rolled her eyes. It was as if he expected her to run away or something. Where would she go? They were all in her house. If anything, they got the better end of the deal, as she insisted they use the gaming stations down in the entertainment room while she utilized mobile headgear.

Jasper stepped into Shira's space and wrapped his hands around her upper arms before leaning in and planting a firm kiss on her forehead. Shira's breath stalled, and it took everything in her not to allow her knees to weaken in the slightest.

She hated how much this affected her—couldn't stand how weak it made her—and yet she never wanted him to stop.

Shira didn't care who saw. The moment the three of them entered the lobby, eyes followed them everywhere. That was to be expected with Jasper and Zach in the tournament. They were supposed to be playing up a fake relationship in public because of Jeremy, but Shira didn't care to make it fake anymore.

The conversation she had with her mom yesterday still rattled around in her brain. She was truthful, for the most part. Shira was seeing where things went. But she also knew it couldn't skate by like this forever. At some point she would have to woman up and ask the guys where they'd like to stand with her. *Or better yet, I need to pull up my big girl panties and tell them what I want.*

Shira's thoughts were jarred to a stop when Jasper suddenly yanked her hard into his chest and wrapped his arms protectively around her. His armor blocked her sight, and when she tried to jerk away from the strange behavior, Jasper's grip tightened.

"Don't look," he warned. "You need to log out. Now."

"Jasper—"

"Now, Shira." He took several large steps, dragging her with him. "Please. Don't question it. Just do it now."

Shira's pulse hammered in her ears, and her breathing quickened. She didn't understand what was going on, but there was no mistaking the urgency in his voice. The urgency only compounded when Shira heard someone scream. *I can demand answers later.*

She pulled up her menu, but before she could focus on the log off button, a weightless feeling fell over her. Shira's hair flew up behind her, and an uneasy sensation of falling swooped in her gut.

Jasper's grip on her tightened. Shira's body twitched and spasmed in a sickeningly phantom-memory way. Fear kicked in to her urgency. Her breath came quicker, and her thoughts scattered.

"Shira," Jasper murmured. "We're in the game. We're in the game. Just log out. Log out."

Shira struggled to focus on her task. Were they falling? Why were they falling?

"Shira." Her name was so steady off his lips. It washed over her like a warm, protective blanket, and her skittering mind froze. "Log out."

Her eyes flicked to her menu and focused on the log

out option, which now had an "emergency" tag added to it. It glowed and then she was kicked out of the game.

Shira's eyes flew open and her senses slammed into her—the deafening sound of silence from her room, the softness of her bed cocooning her, and the cold touch of Snake's nose on her cheek. Her breathing was labored, but otherwise, she seemed okay physically.

Snake nudged her, and then again when she didn't respond, whining this time. Shira lifted a shaky hand and rested it on his head to assure him she was okay. She was okay. *I'm okay.*

"Shira," Orion said.

"I'm okay," Shira croaked, her throat dry. "Really."

"Are you sure?" he asked. "I got the emergency report from a game master that you had been ejected from the game due to a safety protocol on your account. Do I need to call Angelica?"

Shira removed the gaming helmet from her head, taking in her room as her senses continued to adjust to the jarring exit from the game. "Yeah. I'm sure."

She should be a mess right now. She should be in a panicked ball, trying to ground herself out of a PTSD panic attack. But she wasn't.

Shira didn't need to see what happened to know what Jasper tried to protect her from. She didn't know how he knew what would happen, but he'd jumped in immediately and tried to save her from experiencing a traumatic situation in the game.

She shook it out of her head. She couldn't think about it. That risked bringing on the panic attack anyway. Shira needed to distract herself. She could find out if the guys were okay when she was in a better position to text them.

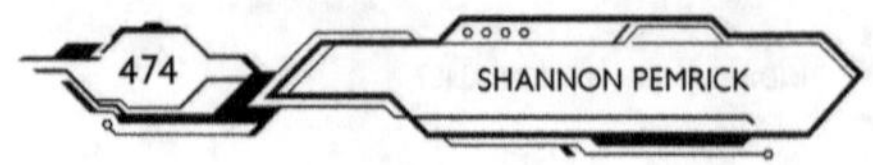

"Shira, I'm going to suggest you grab something sweet to eat, like a cookie or slice of cake, and then do some yoga, or something else calming out in the yard for a bit."

She nodded. That was a good idea.

The system released Zach's mind. He waited a few moments for his senses to adapt to the change before opening his eyes and sliding out of the gaming chair. He lifted his arms above his head for a good, spine-popping stretch.

Zach loved his job, but his body didn't. If he and Jasper didn't so desperately need this extra practice time before the tournament resumed, he'd take more breaks. But as it stood, they'd vacationed longer than they logically should have, and now they needed to take advantage of the extra time they'd been given.

He turned to Jasper's station to find him lounging and watching. "Like the view?"

Jasper smirked. "Very much. Orion, how is Shira doing?"

They hadn't spoken to her since the incident with the glitch. Zach's glut lurched at the memory. The moment she'd managed to log out, the two of them wanted to follow, but couldn't. Then, she sent them a message she was fine and that she wouldn't be hopping back on for their planned threes matches, for obvious reasons.

Shira had also insisted they use that time to get more practice in. Neither of them wanted to, but they knew she'd throw a fit if they hopped out of the game, so he and Jasper agreed they'd do a few extra practice matches before jumping off for a breather, and to check on her. Best way for everyone to get what they wanted.

"She is fine," the AI said. "You'll find her doing yoga in the backyard."

Jasper's brow rose with interest. "Yoga, huh? She's not by chance wearing leggings, is she?"

Zach snorted. "She was wearing shorts earlier. Why would you want her to put more on?"

Jasper shrugged. "Because it's Shira. I'd love to believe she's doing naked yoga up there, but I doubt she's willing to take that much of a risk with neighbors. So, leggings was my next thought."

"Shira did not change clothes," Orion confirmed. "However, if you wish to see her in tight-fitted garments, or none at all while performing several yoga stretches, you are more than welcome to make such requests to her in person."

A wicked grin spread over Jasper's handsome face. "Don't mind if I do."

He jumped out of his gaming chair and took the stairs two steps at a time. Zach shook his head. He could understand his fiancé's rush—several mental images of Shira naked and in various bent-over positions now ran through his mind—but it would be nice if Jasper chose to be calmer. Wasn't like she was going anywhere, or that they expected visitors or their daughter to show up out of the blue and get in their way.

When Zach reached the landing, he was surprised to see Jasper leaning against the hallway wall and not halfway out the back door. Zach peered down the hall, out the open nano doors, to where Shira stood on a yoga mat, her back to them. She appeared to be doing a breathing exercise while Snake sat next to her, looking up as if waiting.

However, the two of them still had a good vantage point. Especially if she bent forward in those short shorts, or backward in her white tank top. Zach was pretty sure she'd foregone a bra again today. He like that about her. She never hesitated to put her comfort first around them. Not that either of them would ever complain about that little detail.

Shira bent forward into downward dog. Snake followed her lead.

Both Jasper and Zach cocked their heads with her movement.

"If only we had another angle," Jasper murmured.

A thought popped into Zach's head. He held up a finger and slipped into the dining room, where he'd tucked his camera bag safely in a corner. This could go completely wrong, but he wanted to try. Not just because he would love to have some private photos of Shira, but because this would really push her comfort in a good way. Zach desperately wanted that camera-frightened Shira he met several days ago to become a long-forgotten memory.

When he returned to Jasper's side, Shira had changed position. She arched her back and held one hand forward while reaching behind her to hold onto her upward bent leg and balancing on the other. Zach thought the pose was called dancer, but he'd be one to admit he didn't know the names of these poses all that well. Only the more tantalizing ones.

"I'm now thinking about how well she'd do in a wet t-shirt contest," Jasper said. Zach's mind filled with the possibilities, both for her and for Jasper. "Of course, I think there needs to be a prejudging."

Zach shot him a sideways glance. "Please don't tell me you're not thinking of grabbing the hose."

Jasper snorted. "Give me some credit. I can be a little more creative than that." He grinned. "Shira looks rather thirsty. It's important she stays hydrated."

"You know I can see you two in there, right?" Shira called out as she pulled out of her pose and leaned back into a backward bend. Zach swallowed. It may not be an extreme bend with her feet and hands on the mat, but that didn't matter. Seeing how flexible she was made him hard, and rational thinking slipped away every second he continued to appreciate her. "What are you two conspiring about?"

"I'll keep her distracted," Zach murmured. It was ridiculous to encourage Jasper, but Zach didn't care now. He wanted to see just how far they could push Shira's final rule that hung on by a thread. He wanted her to see how serious they were about her. That way, when they sat her down to talk, she'd believe them without any doubts. *If you ask me, the mind-blowing sex and all the attention we pay her should speak enough for us, but this is Shira.*

Zach stepped forward, his posture casual and his camera half-poised. "I don't know a lot about yoga, but shouldn't you flex your spine the other way before torturing it further like that?"

Shira let out a light chuckle before slowly pulling out of her bend. Zach lifted his viewfinder to his face and snapped some photos. He figured they wouldn't be any good, given he hadn't gotten a chance to set up for the lighting, but an excellent shot wasn't the goal this time.

Shira pursed her lips and narrowed her eyes at him. "What are you doing?"

Zach smirked. "Making you ask questions."

She clicked her tongue. "You and Jasper are up to something."

He looked down at his camera's display. The exposure wasn't too bad—easy enough to fix up in a photo editor. "Or I thought I'd get a nice angle of you."

Her nose scrunched. "You can't be serious. It's yoga."

"And you look amazing doing it."

She rolled her eyes.

Zach took another step, though he still didn't step out of the house. "I thought it'd be beneficial for you."

Shira's brow rose. "Me? Or you?"

"Both." He grinned. "They'll stay between us."

"All right…" she said slowly, clearly skeptical. "But why while I'm doing yoga?"

"Baby steps."

Shira tilted her head, her eyes narrowing. She was so suspicious of them, not that Zach could blame her. Of course, he couldn't resist the cute face she made when doing so and snapped another photo.

She didn't even blink. "Where did Jasper go?"

"Drink of water. We need to stay hydrated, like you."

Shira pointed to a bottle of water by her yoga mat. "Why aren't you two still practicing?"

"We needed a quick break, and we wanted to check on you." *Damn, she was extra suspicious.* "Why do I feel like I've walked into an interrogation room?"

"Because the two of you came upstairs, whispered and conspired in the hallway, you got your camera, conspired some more, and then Jasper disappeared into the kitchen." She looked him up and down. "I trust you two not being up to something as far as I can throw you."

"In or out of game?" Jasper asked, appearing behind Zach with two glasses of water. He handed one off to Zach and kept the other, leaning against the doorframe and taking a nonchalant sip.

Shira narrowed her eyes further at him.

"What? We're just looking for a tall glass of water." His gaze flicked up and down, taking her in. "And we found more than one. Is it a crime to appreciate that?"

Shira pursed her lips.

Jasper waved his hand. "Don't let us get in your way. We'll just enjoy the view."

"Who says I wasn't done?"

Jasper smirked. "I'm confident you're not."

Shira watched them for a moment longer and then eased herself into warrior. "How'd practice go?"

Zach lifted his camera and snapped the shutter. "You'll be proud. We're better at our sorcerer berserker combo. Not perfect yet, but we're almost where we need to be for the tournament."

"That's good." Shira twisted her torso so her arms pointed to the ground and sky. "How about your rogue and druid combo?"

"Eh, not so great," Jasper said. "Are you going to do any more flexible positions?"

Shira snorted and twisted the other way, her back to them. "I don't know how coordinated you think I am, but don't expect any advanced yoga for you to ogle at."

Jasper stared at her ass. "Was just curious. There's plenty to ogle here to be happy with. Do you mind doing another downward dog, facing away from us?"

Shira let out an exasperated sigh and came out of her twist and wide stance. "What are you, thirteen?"

He lifted his glass to his lips while smirking. "No, just thirsty."

Shira shook her head and bent forward into downward dog, but she didn't alter her angle like Jasper had previously asked. That didn't bother either of them. Zach snapped another photo and then a second of Snake, who was still participating in his own dog way. It was cute.

Shira pulled out of her position, glanced at them, and then performed a backward bend. Jasper cocked his head and grinned while Zach pointed his lens.

Zach's gaze followed the arch of her back. Her tank top pulled tight against her stomach, pulling up just enough to tease her navel piercing. His eyes roamed up to the curve of her breasts, her piercings indenting the taut fabric covering them. The camera shutter snapped several times.

Shira raised slowly to a standing position and let out a long breath. Zach's eyes flicked to Jasper when he let out a quiet groan. His fiancé's eyes smoldered with so much contained desire, Zach was surprised he'd held himself back this long.

His restraint didn't last much longer. Jasper strode over to Shira with long, determined steps and then came to a stop in front of her. There was barely enough room between them for him to hold his glass where he did, just above her chest height.

Shira's brow rose. "Can I help you?"

Jasper's gaze didn't falter from hers. "You need water."

Her eyes flicked to her water bottle and then back up at him. "I have water. You didn't need to bring it to me."

"This is fresh."

Jasper tipped the mouth of the glass toward her and Shira touched it with her index finger, as if that would stop him. "I'm fine."

Zach took advantage of the moment to snap a photo of the two. He didn't understand Jasper's approach with this, but it was sure to play out in an interesting way.

"No, you need to be watered," Jasper said before smirking and tipping the glass. Water flooded out of the container and splashed over Shira's chest.

"Jasper!" she gasped out, her eyes going wide and body rigid. "Cold!"

Jasper merely smirked and watched her tank top soak up the liquid.

Zach snapped the shutter, capturing both their facial reactions, as well as Shira's physical. He enjoyed watching the slow process of her shirt's change from opaque to vaguely translucent and teasing what lay beneath.

Jasper's gaze roamed his handiwork. "Twenty out of ten, would do that again."

"You really are thirteen-year-old in a thirty-year-old body," Shira complained.

Jasper shook his head. "No, I told you, I'm thirsty."

Shira snorted. "More like you're hungry."

Jasper lifted his gaze back to her again, the smolder from earlier prominent. When he spoke, his voice dipped deeper, with a slight strain to it. "Yeah, I'm that too."

The sound caused Zach's pulse to spike. He liked Jasper's restrained voice of anticipation. It made it more exciting to tease him for a bit.

Shira observed Jasper. Their intentions were obvious. Ball was now in her court.

Her tongue darted out and dragged across her lower lip. Shira then grabbed the hem of her tank top and pulled the clothing tighter against her body, exposing more of her under the damp cloth. "If you wanted me in a wet t-shirt, all you had to do was ask. Now, are you going to eat me or not?"

Zach knew he should snap another photo, but instead, he peered past his viewfinder at her. Her tempting vixen side had come out to play so quickly. He was more than happy to entertain her. And so was Jasper.

Jasper reached for her and curled his fingers around her hips, pulling her hard into him. "I'm going to do more than eat. I'll class switch to priest and use my alignment rod on your cavity until you achieve resonance."

Shira snorted. "And here I expected you to tell me you were gonna Jabba all up in my hut."

Zach choked, and then the three of them burst into laughter. *Leave it to these two to cut the sexual tension like this.*

Of course, determined and one-track-minded as always, Jasper recovered as if nothing had stalled him. He dipped his head and claimed her mouth with a hunger Zach felt from a distance. Jasper's hands roamed Shira's figure, claiming everywhere he could find, while he devoured her until he left her breathless. Zach was sure to resume his shots, as difficult as it was with his growing arousal.

Jasper took a blind step toward the house, tugging Shira to follow, and murmured against her lips before kissing her again. "As much as I don't care if your neighbors see what filthy things we do to you, I'm being a little stingy today, and not willing to share the show with anyone but Zach."

Shira broke the kiss to speak, but stopped when Jasper yanked her into the house and slipped behind her. He grabbed her by the hips and pulled her hard against him, putting her on display for Zach. Yet, he didn't take another photo, as tempting as it was.

Shira had noticed the camera. Her eyes had widened a bit too much, flicking back and forth between him and Jasper.

Jasper pressed his mouth to her ear. "It's just for us. No one else will see them. But only with your consent."

She chewed her bottom lip in her contemplation. Zach dragged his tongue along his. She was a tease, even when she wasn't aiming to be one.

Shira craned her neck to look at Jasper and slid her hand up his cheek. "I consent."

Then she kissed him.

Jasper growled hungrily and kissed her back, grabbing her shirt with his free hand and pulling it tight. Heat simmered under Zach's skin as he snapped a photo. The clicking of the shutter stirred something in Shira. She moved in subtle ways that made little sense for enjoying the pleasure Jasper was promising, and more for the camera itself.

Her modeling training was rooted deep. Zach could see it in the way she moved in a regular setting. As a photographer who'd worked with models, he had a way of spotting those subtle nuances. And they were certainly coming out for this, not that Zach was complaining. It added a little extra complexity to how they were going to handle her to also maximize her fun with theirs.

Shira's lips left Jasper's, and she turned her attention to Zach. This left her neck exposed, something Jasper

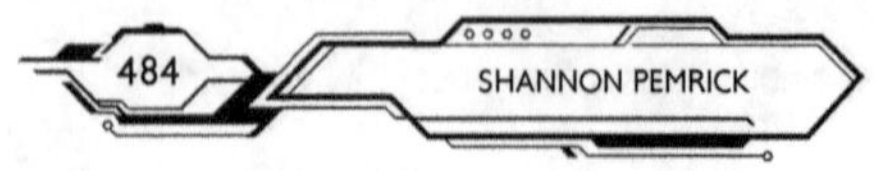

capitalized on. He pressed his mouth against her skin, kissing and nibbling. His hands roamed her curves, tugging at her clothes, digging into her exposed skin.

Her gaze never leaving Zach's direction, Shira encouraged every touch with sighs and quiet moans.

One of Jasper's hands slid up and cupped her breast, kneading and teasing. Shira's lower lip caught between her teeth and moaned. Her eyes lidded as she embraced the enticing sensations. She turned her head back to Jasper, capturing his mouth for a hungry, devouring kiss.

Zach never stopped his camera's shutter. He grabbed snaps of everything, from close up and detailed to panned out and sensual. Watching without touching, though, thrummed up a need he struggled to ignore. Zach leaned against the wall to support him, not sure how long that'd help. He'd done boudoir shoots of all types, but nothing compared to how hot this was.

Jasper lifted Shira's damp shirt over one of her breasts, exposing her taut, rosy nipple. He teased and played with the sensitive peak, going as far to tug lightly on her piercing to receive a sharp reaction from Shira. She certainly provided her own array of pleased and shocked sounds.

Shira adjusted his hand, as if the model in her knew Jasper wasn't giving Zack any good shots. Her involvement, while brief, gave Zach even more to work with, and he took the shots.

Jasper pulled up the other side of her shirt, exposing her. And he was far from done teasing both Shira and Zach. Jasper slipped his arm between her breasts and wrapped his hand firmly around Shira's throat, pinning her. His other hand trailed down her stomach, to the band of her shorts.

He slid his fingers just under the fabric. Shira moaned and squirmed from the tease, and Zach adjusted his stance. He found it hard to focus on anything but the pulsing need in his pants.

Jasper slowly pushed the front of her shorts down just enough to expose her dripping flesh and lack of panties. Their hungry kissing broke, and Jasper grinned. "Our greedy little elementalist is keeping secrets."

"I've got all kinds of naughty secrets," Shira practically purred.

"Show us." Jasper slid his fingers into the apex of her thighs. Shira's back arched, and she groaned in pleasure. Jasper held her captive at the neck, kissing her with an all-consuming hunger, and rubbed her perfect spot with rhythmic strokes.

He pushed Shira, step-by-blind-step, toward the counter until he had her pinned against it. Only then did he allow the two of them to come up for air.

Shira panted and squirmed under his touch, yet Jasper never let up. With his hand still firm against her delicate neck, he dipped his head and licked her teasingly taut nipples. Shira moaned, and then more when Jasper pulled her bud into his mouth and sucked, hard.

Jasper switched to her other breast, and then migrated down, devouring every inch of her as he pleased. "Don't hold back on me. It's just the three of us here."

Shira grinned, and Zach couldn't resist snapping a photo of that look. "I'm not. You just need to step up your game."

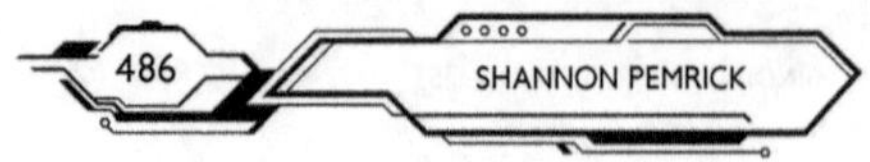

Zach licked his lower lip. She really knew how to challenge Jasper.

Jasper chuckled. "Well, it's a good thing I'm wicked hungry for this wet pussy of yours."

She sucked in a sharp breath and then corrected his wording. "Starving. The word is starving."

"Ravenous," Zach said. He knew, because that's how he felt watching this.

Both their heated gazes flicked to him. Zach swallowed. *Fuck.* If he didn't already look like a desperate mess, he was sure those looks had just done him in.

The corner of Jasper's lip twitched up and then lifted Shira up on the counter before resuming his worship of her body, kissing and licking large swaths of skin. When he scraped his teeth against her soft flesh, she and Zach both groaned. Zach wasn't sure what he wanted more at this point—to be in Jasper's place, or Shira's.

Jasper's grip around Shira's throat loosened as he migrated down. He dragged his hand down her neck and chest, adding pressure to encourage her to lie back and enjoy. Shira complied as far as bracing herself on her elbows, but no further.

She watched Jasper continue his painstaking path down her body until he came to her hips and where her waistband would be if he hadn't already been pulling it partially down with his other hands. Jasper slid his hand away from pleasuring her, eliciting a disappointed whine from Shira.

But she wouldn't be disappointed for long. Zach could tell from Jasper's movements, this slow tease was not easy on him either. He hooked his fingers into her waistband and yanked off her shorts in one hard tug.

Shira's breath caught, and she blinked. She had no idea what she was in for now that she'd challenged Jasper.

Jasper continued to lick and nibble her skin, down her hip, and along her inner thigh. He tucked his arms under her legs and propped them up on her shoulders. Shira bit her lip and practically choked back an anticipating moan.

A quick bite here, and a long, agonizing lick there, Jasper worked his way down her thigh, all the while sliding his hand back between her legs, teasing her wet folds.

Then Jasper flicked his gaze up to meet hers, and he dove in, devouring her clit with a hunger she wasn't prepared for.

Shira let out a deep moan, her head rolling back and back arching. Jasper licked and sucked in a rhythm just perfect for her. Shira threaded her fingers into his hair and rocked her hips, urging for him to give her more. Jasper did not acquiesce the request. He kept up his steady pleasuring pace, listening to her moans, until she begged.

"Jasper, please, more."

A pleased chuckle rumbled through Jasper and this time, he obliged, sliding his finger inside her and pumping her with increased pleasure. Shira's moan filled the room, louder than she'd allowed before. Jasper had won. Shira had no interest in fighting off what he offered, and Jasper was going to reward her well for that.

Of course, Jasper couldn't contain himself anymore, and tore at the button of his pants and worked himself free, his hard cock springing out. Zach swallowed, watching Jasper stroke his hard length.

Zach managed a few more photos before he couldn't

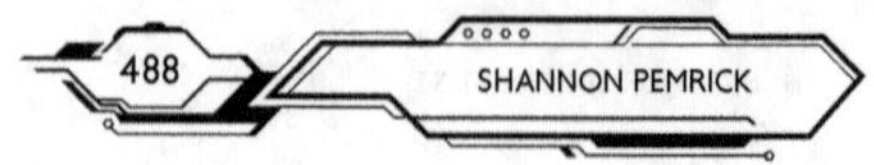

take it anymore either and tore himself free. He fisted his throbbing shaft and stroked, long and hard, in the rhythm Jasper used on himself.

Shira's breath hitched when her gaze drifted to him. She wanted it—wanted him so badly. He could see it in her eyes. Jasper was giving her a lot, but it wasn't enough. Just having Jasper wouldn't be enough for her. And Zach was perfectly okay with that.

Shira's eyes clenched shut as her pleasure nearly overwhelmed her, her moaning the most intoxicating sound. And then Jasper pulled away.

Unsurprisingly, Shira groaned in frustration, which was half-swallowed by Jasper when he straightened and claimed her mouth with his. Jasper slid his hand into her hair and gripped her tight, breaking the kiss and turning her head toward Zach.

Jasper bent close to her ear and spoke loud enough for Zach to hear. "Look at what you do to him."

He pulled her hand toward him. "Feel what you do to me? You make me want to bend you ovah this island and fuck your tight pussy until you're filled with my cum. You'd be writhing and screaming, ovah and ovah, until I gave ya to Zach to have his way with you. Then we'd both fuck ya until you were ruined for anyone but us."

His words made Zach harder and his blood simmer with hotter need. That sounded fucking amazing. Physically impossible, unless inside the game. Wouldn't be too hard to convince her to join them in there after they were done with her in reality. Or, one of them could take her in game while the other took care of her physical body's needs. *That sounds like it could be quite fun.*

"Promises, promises from that filthy mouth of yours,"

Shira crooned, her posture arching toward Jasper, as if boldly daring him. "But I don't think you can fulfill them."

Jasper dragged his teeth along her cheek in a long, exaggerated kiss. "Watch me."

He then pulled Shira off the counter and spun her toward Zach. He slapped her ass, making her gasp. "But first go walk your sexy ass ovah to Zach. He needs some attention."

Finally! Zach wasn't sure how much longer he would have lasted being the voyeur.

Shira smirked and sauntered Zach's way, swaying her delicious, hypnotic hips. Her disheveled shirt framed her bouncing breasts perfectly, and she radiated with a bold and confident, magnetic aura. Zach enjoyed the view and managed to take another photo of her, this sexy woman who was all theirs today.

Jasper clearly enjoyed the other side of the view. He leaned against the island and stroked himself before Shira had even reached Zach.

Shira gazed up at him with those lusty green eyes, her fingers sliding up his stomach over his shirt and then back down. "Looks like you need some help, Zach. Why don't I take over?"

He groaned when her fingers trailed over the base of his shaft and teased over his fisted hand. Zach released his grip. "Have all the fun you want."

A throaty chuckle came from her when she gave him an insanely seductive smile. "You both are all full of promises today. I like it."

Shira took him in her hand and stroked. Nothing crazy or that would send him over the edge, even though Zach

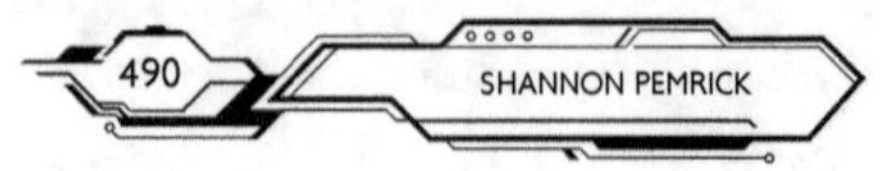

swore he was dangerously close already, but enough to send the right amount of desire and heat coursing through his body.

He swallowed when she suddenly dropped to her knees. Her tongue darted out and teased the head of his cock. Zach hissed. The underlying promises from that one tease had Zach momentarily concerned for his ability to last.

Then Shira eased her lips over his throbbing shaft, and all thoughts left. Her tongue slid along his cock, her piercing dancing and teasing with the most practiced and dirty expertise.

Zach's eyes rolled back as pleasure shot through him. "Fuck…"

Jasper was good at sucking cock, but now that Zach was experiencing this… God, did he not want to give either up. Jasper said she was amazing, but fuck if that did not accurately describe this.

"Take the picture, Zach," Jasper said, his voice low and heavy with desire.

Right… picture… Zach's overloaded brain took a minute to remember what that meant. He looked down at Shira, who flicked her gaze up to him. The view was… *Fuck.* His dick swelled even harder and a throaty, almost amused chuckle rumbled from Shira through him.

Then she released her hold with her hand and slid both of them to his hips, easing him into her more. All the while, she never broke eye contact. Zach groaned. *Feels so damned amazing.*

"Picture, Zach," Jasper growled.

Zach lifted the viewfinder to his eye and focused just long enough to snap several rapid photos of her easing his cock in and out of her mouth. He captured her lust and the power she had over him right now.

And then he lost his ability to resist.

Zach dropped his hand with the camera to his side and threaded his fingers of his free hand into her hair. Then he rocked his hips, driving himself deeper. Shira's eyes popped wide, and she squeaked in her surprise. Zach grinned and continued, easing in and out at a slow enough pace for her to handle him, and fast enough to satisfy his needs.

And adjust and accept she did. Shira's eyes hooded and her grip on his hips tightened before she picked up her own pace, taking him deeper and deeper, until he was fucking her at a frantic speed he didn't want to stop. His pulse pounded in his ears, and his body grew tense, ready for the desired release she was milking.

A calloused hand grazed Zach's cheek and then pulled his head up to meet Jasper's now-close gaze. Jasper crashed his mouth into Zach's and then yanked Shira away. "Upstairs, now."

Jasper bent and hauled a confused Shira over his shoulder, her perfect ass sticking up in the air. Shira blinked as Jasper walked away with her, and then bit her lip, stifling a moan when Jasper slid his fingers between her legs into her slick heat.

"Not fair," she complained, her voice heavy with unfulfilled desire.

"Oh, we'll be fair soon enough, babe," Jasper said, taking the stairs carefully with his precious load. "I promised to ruin you, aftah all."

She grinned, even though he couldn't see. Zach could, of course, and it wasn't an excited expression. No, it was a challenging one, as if she didn't think they would be able to ruin her. Zach was certainly up for the task. He wanted her only for him and Jasper now, and Zach would do anything to show her that.

When Jasper reached the landing, his pace quickened and the three of them were in his and Jasper's room a moment later. Jasper angled for the bed and flipped Shira down onto the mattress. She squeaked and bounced, only coming to a sudden halt because of Jasper.

He pressed his hand against her chest and pinned her against the bed. Jasper wasted no time slipping his fingers between the apex of her thighs. Shira moaned and closed her eyes, embracing the oncoming wave of promised bliss.

Zach glanced at the camera in his hand and then set it down on a nearby chair. He could get different shots of Shira another time. Zach wanted to be an active participant now.

Grabbing the hem of his shirt, Zach whipped the garment over his head and tossed it aside. This drew the attentions of Jasper and Shira. Zach then ran his fingers through the hair that had come loose from his hair tie, and worked to pull his hair tighter. He wouldn't have bothered if it weren't for the appreciative, hungry gazes eating up the sight of all the muscles of his naked upper body pulling taut.

Once Zach was satisfied with the mini-show he'd provided, he took long, prowling steps toward the bed, his attention fixed on Shira.

Jasper hadn't let up on her, and she was panting with desperate need when Zach reached the mattress. Shira reached for him, begging with her eyes and fingers, unable to form words for her desires. Zach kneeled on the bed, angling over her. Shira lifted her hands eagerly.

Zach grinned and wrapped his hands around both her delicate wrists, pinning them above her head against the mattress. Shira bit her lip and whimpered, her lower body writhing against Jasper's attentions.

With his free hand, Zach traced Shira's cheek, down to her chin, and up to her lips. His thumb glided over the soft flesh of her mouth, memorizing every detail of them.

Shira's lips parted, and her tongue slid around his thumb, drawing him inside. Her lips wrapped around him and she sucked and licked with the same skill as she'd used with him earlier. Heat thrummed through Zach's veins, desire crawling under his skin. His cock strained against his clothes, desperate to experience that sensation again. And he was tempted. Oh, was he tempted. But he wanted to hear her scream even more.

Zach withdrew his hand, earning a disappointed whimper from Shira. He bent down and kissed her, tentatively—teasingly. Shira groaned and eagerly deepened the kiss, her tongue demanding entrance. Zach obliged while sliding his hand down her neck, over her disheveled shirt, and over her aching breasts. He consumed everything that was her, searing her taste and smell into his mind.

Shira sucked in a sharp breath when Zach lightly skimmed her taut nipple. He continued, teasing her with light touches and slowly progressing to rolling her sensitive buds between his fingers until her groans sounded like pleas against his mouth.

Zach pulled his mouth away from hers, listening to

her pant for breath. He grinned, knowing just how out of breath she'd be when they were done with her. Zach then leaned over her again, but over her chest. His tongue darted out, teasing her sensitive peak, and tasting the sweetness that was her.

Shira moaned, and then again when Zach licked her again, and then again. He pulled her nipple into his mouth, sucking, flicking, and nibbling, enjoying the pleasure she vocalized as he and Jasper worked her towards climax.

Zach's hand on her other breast slid farther down, over her flat stomach, enjoying the softness of her skin. He continued to migrate lower, at a slow and agonizing pace, not just for Shira, which she made known with her whimpers of anticipation, but also himself. He wanted her thrown into the tides of bliss so badly, but Zach maintained control.

Jasper's hand grazed Zach's as he reached for Shira's free breast. The sensation of Jasper's rougher skin, contrasting against Shira's softer feel, almost derailed Zach's control, threatening to send his thoughts into other fantasies he ought to wait on.

Zach's fingers slipped into Shira's slick heat. *Fuck, she's so wet.* Shira gasped and arched her back. She writhed, fighting against his hands still pinning her down and leaving her helpless against their attentions. Zach listened to her moan and beg for more from them.

Shira's breath labored, and her movements became jerky. "Jasper… Zach…"

Her mouth fell open, and a scream tore through her with the explosion of ecstasy. She convulsed and flailed in her orgasm, her body fighting against Zach's steel hold.

Her breathing came out in punctured gasps as she came down from her high, but never settled to an even pace, as neither Zach nor Jasper were willing to ease up.

"Guys…" she moaned. "Guys, I c–can't… I need…"

A deep moan rose from within her, Jasper increasing his attentions. Zach released her nipple with a *pop* but kept his strokes against her clit steady, offering a wild variety of sensations to her now extra-sensitive body.

"F–f–fuck you both," she managed to say before moaning.

Jasper chuckled. "Soon you'll do that, too. But for now, come for us again, babe."

Shira bit her lip and rolled her head back. Her breathing labored, and then she screamed. The sound heated Zach to the core, craving more and more.

He and Jasper kept up their attention to help Shira ride out her high until she jerked away from their touch, truly unable to handle any more.

Shira panted and blinked slowly, as if dazed. Zach smiled, pleased with their work. Jasper slipped away and rummaged through the nightstand. Shira turned her attention to Zach when she recovered a little. "You can release me now, you know."

Zach chuckled and continued to hold her hands above her head. He allowed his gaze to wander over her perfect, on-display body. "No, I don't think I will."

The flush set on her cheeks deepened to a light crimson. And she was smart enough not to voice any arguments about his appreciative visual assessment.

"That's good. I'm enjoying the view too," Jasper said, returning to his previous spot. In his hand, he carried a bottle of lube and two condoms.

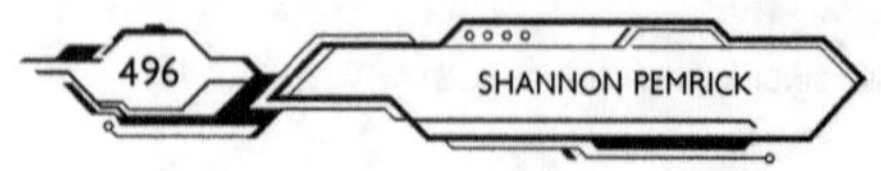

His fiancé casually set them down on the bed before leaning in and kissing Zach. Zach hummed appreciatively for the attention. He wasn't feeling left out, as his mind had been quite focused, but he didn't want to miss out on Jasper's special type of attention.

Jasper's rough hand dragged across Zach's jaw, down his neck and chest and settled on his hip. Shira whimpered and squirmed under Zach's grip.

Zach broke the kiss to glance at her, wondering if Jasper was touching her again, but no, she merely watched them with hungry eyes.

"I think she liked that," Jasper murmured.

"She wasn't the only one," Zach said.

Jasper hummed thoughtfully and then kissed Zach between his jaw and ear. His fingers dug under the band of his pants and then he yanked them down with such impressive force, he removed them even though Zach was sitting.

Shira sucked in a tight breath, and Zach sat there, a little stunned. "Did you have a hidden berserker potion hidden in that nightstand?"

Jasper chuckled and captured Zach's mouth with his, while reaching between them and wrapping a firm grip around Zach's hard length and stroking. Zach groaned. This was what he'd waited so patiently for.

"I'm undecided who I want to fuck first," Jasper murmured between kisses. "You or her."

Zach kissed him back, his mind bouncing between the tantalizing options. "You did say earlier we could both have her at the same time."

Shira inhaled a sharp breath and squirmed under Zach's unyielding grip. "Release me, Zach, please."

There was a desperation in her voice, but he could tell from the heaviness of her words, it wasn't related to him holding her. No, she had ulterior reasons for wanting to be let go.

Jasper smirked. "I think she approves."

"I think she's going to be a little impatient," Zach said.

Shira continued to struggle. "Please. Let me go."

"Why should I?" Zach asked.

"Please…"

"Please what?" Jasper asked, sliding his thumb up her inner thigh.

Shira whimpered and clamped her eyes shut.

"Tell us what you want, babe," Jasper said. He traced his thumb along her skin in an infinity shape.

"Fuck me," she pleaded. "Both of you, please."

Zach smirked. Even in such a vulnerable position, she had power over him and Jasper. And those pleas of hers couldn't be left unanswered.

Zach adjusted himself on the bed, angling to lean over her, but his grip slipped. Shira grinned, and before Zach realized what happened, she hooked her leg over his hip and he was on his back, with her straddling him. Shira's hands wrapped around his wrists, pinning his arms to the bed next to his head. She appeared quite pleased with herself, not that Zach really minded. The view from this angle was great.

Shira glanced over her shoulder when Jasper drew up behind her. He slid his fingers into her hair and pulled the long strands to drape over her left shoulder, and then leaned in to kiss her cheek, and then her jaw.

"You'd be better off paying attention to the other

side," Shira murmured, her hooding eyes betraying her enjoyment of the affection.

"No," Jasper said, kissing her neck. "This side is perfect."

Shira sucked in a tight breath when his hands slid down her sides and over her hips. Zach closed his eyes when one of Jasper's hands grazed his hard and ready cock. He needed a release, or he'd go crazy.

As if understanding Zach's need, Jasper wrapped his firm hand around Zach and stroked. Zach groaned. To further his prolonged frustrations, Shira rocked her hips, teasing Zach with images of what they could be doing if she were only seated a little lower.

Foil tore, and before Zach fully processed the cause, Jasper rolled a condom on for Zach. *Yes, finally.*

Jasper grabbed Shira by the hips and pulled her back, breaking her hold on Zach's wrists. Her hands slid down his arms, sending prickles of anticipating desire through him and down to his already straining cock.

Zach sucked in air through his teeth when Shira hovered over him.

Jasper nibbled her ear. "It's time to fuck him nice and good, babe."

Shira hummed eagerly and eased herself down on Zach. Her head and his both rolled back, and they groaned in unison as he slid inside her. When she was fully seated, Shira took several breaths before rocking her hips, using her arms planted on Zach's chest as the perfect leverage.

Heat flooded Zach's veins, the sensation of him sliding in and out of her at a slow and steady pace almost too much to handle at this point.

Jasper caressed her along her sides and up her stomach. Shira pulled herself upright, and grabbed her shirt, yanking the piece over her head and tossing it aimlessly, leaving her fully exposed and on display for them in one sexy, confident package.

She placed her hands back on Zach's chest, the angle of her arms framing her perky breasts just right, and she picked up her pace, driving him harder and harder into her. Zach's breathing hitched, and Shira's deepened, mixing with her soft moans.

Zach slid his hands up her thighs and gripped her hips. He embraced the difference of her firm and unyielding cybernetics, and soft and tender natural body—the embodiment of the two sides that made her the woman he and Jasper couldn't get enough of.

He thrusted upward. Shira gasped, her mouth parting as she embraced him filling her each time he plunged deeper.

Jasper pressed against her back and captured her breasts, playing, teasing, and tweaking her sensitive nipples in whatever way he desired. Shira moaned, closing her eyes and embracing the sensations rolling through her.

"Ready?" Jasper strained out. "I don't think I can wait much longah. I'm already jealous enough Zach gets such a fantastic view of you."

"Yes," Shira nearly begged out. "I want you both. Now."

Jasper's teeth grazed her cheek. "Bend forwahd."

Shira complied, sliding her hands up Zach's chest as she went, sending sizzling flairs through all of his extremities.

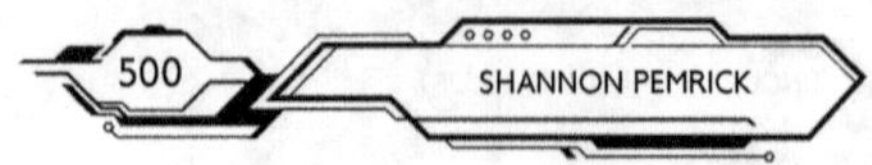

Jasper grabbed the bottle of lube and poured a generous amount onto his hands and fingers. Zach forced himself to still to make this easier on her, as difficult as it was. Then Jasper applied the lubricant over her tight hole. Shira sucked in a sharp breath through her teeth.

"Relax," Jasper whispered, slowly working his fingers inside her.

A strangled cry twisted through Shira. Her fingers dug into Zach's chest and he hissed. That had felt good.

Jasper continued to work her, grinning when she moaned and wriggled between them. "Feel good?"

"Yes…" she moaned. "Yes… more."

Shira rocked her hips, and Zach tightened his grip, holding her still. She groaned in frustration.

"Not yet," Zach murmured.

"Beg for it," Jasper said.

"Please…" she begged immediately. "Please, both of you fuck me. Right now. I need it."

Jasper climbed onto the bed and nudged her entrance with his hard cock. "As you wish."

Shira groaned, a primal sound that vibrated Zach to his core, her mouth falling open as Jasper slowly buried himself into her, inch by inch. Before he was fully seated, Zach thrust into Shira.

Zach felt Jasper as they both rocked in and out of Shira. Shira moaned and her breathing labored. With impressive balance, Jasper slid his hand through Shira's hair and grabbed a fistful, yanking her head back. She gasped and then closed her eyes, embracing every tantalizing feeling they gave her.

Everything in Zach tensed, his breathing becoming as labored as Shira's. He did what he could to hold off his orgasm, but the longer this continued, the more that grip on himself slipped.

Zach slid a hand between him and Shira, and glided two of his fingers between her dripping wet folds.

Shira writhed in a frenzy of pleasure between them, moaning and begging, until orgasm burst through her. She screamed her shattering release, drowning out Jasper and then Zach as he let go of his final strands of control and crested over the edge, convulsing and exploding within her.

Then, the room grew still, all three of their labored breathing the only sounds to fill the space.

Shira sprawled over Zach in languid bliss while Jasper barely held himself above them, his arms visibly shaking with effort.

After a few more moments passed for them to catch their breaths, Jasper and Zach gingerly extracted themselves from Shira. She lazily rolled off Zach, allowing him to remove and dispose of his condom. Jasper did the same for his before running to grab a washcloth.

Zach curled up against Shira when he returned. Jasper took his time cleaning Shira, clearly enjoying the doting task. Shira shuddered each time he brushed a sensitive spot.

When he finished, Jasper curled into Shira on her other side. Shira smiled peacefully, embracing the pleasure they'd provided her so far. Zach found himself tracing circles along her arms, over her collarbone, and down between her breasts.

"I need a moment," Shira mumbled. "Just a moment or two."

He chuckled. "That's fine. I need more than a moment."

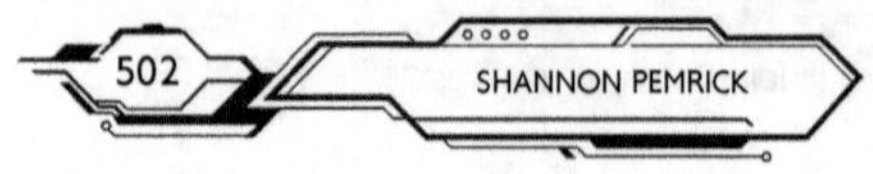

"I won't," Jasper said.

Shira cracked an eye open to glance at him in disbelief. Zach chuckled. "It might be longer than a moment, but not as long as mine. He's got an aggravatingly impressive bounce back."

"Sure…" she said, not believing them. *She'll find out soon enough.*

Zach traced his fingers along her skin, then came to a stop when his fingers grazed the uneven texture of a scar. He'd noticed it vaguely before, but wasn't in any mindset to really care to investigate. Now he was.

Zach traced the curving scar along the underside of her breast.

"Implant scars," Shira said. "From when I had them."

Jasper tilted his head and also traced her other scar. "When?"

Shira puffed out a breath. "I got them when I was eighteen. I thought it'd improve my career, and help me with some self-esteem issues I was having. But a few years after, I wanted to get rid of them. Not because I didn't like the size my tits were, but because of some other medical issues I had with them."

Zach gazed at her for a long moment. "Okay, that makes sense. Why the negative reaction to telling us? We don't care if you have implants or not."

She was quiet for a moment. "Sorry, I guess that's a holdover from what happened."

Jasper adjusted himself on the bed to see her better. "A Jeremy thing?"

Shira's nose scrunched. "Yeah. The asshole pitched a fit when he found out. Insulted me, calling me flat-chested and all these things that weren't even true. He didn't care it was a medical reason, and the dickhead wouldn't listen to me when I told him it wasn't staying that way. I had plans for more natural augmentation."

Zach's fingers lazily grazed her skin. "Did you end up doing that?"

Shira shook her head. "The day of the argument was the day of the accident. Technically, this one"—she gestured to her right breast—"was augmented to match the other, because it'd been so wrecked, but I never ended up having them enhanced like I'd originally planned."

Jasper slid his thumb over a sensitive spot of her breast, making Shira bite her lip. "Well, we knew he was a moron, but now we can call him a blind moron if he really thinks you're flat-chested."

Shira chuckled. "That's what Tanya said, along with some other choice words. She was there when I had the phone conversation with him. She took my phone and chewed him a new one."

"Damn, I would have loved to be there to witness that," Jasper said. "She sounded like a great friend."

Shira smiled. "You two would have loved—"

She bit back a moan when Jasper pinched her nipple. "Really? Already? No way have you bounced back *that* quick."

Jasper chuckled and leaned over her. "No, not quite yet, but that doesn't mean I can't get you warmed up."

He dipped his head and pulled her tight bud between his lips. Shira let out a breathy sigh, and then moaned when Zach adjusted himself to do the same for her other side.

They promised to ruin her for anyone but them. And they would.

CHAPTER 24

Shira gazed at her reflection in the mirror, for the first time in a long time unashamed of her nakedness that put her cybernetics on display. She trailed her fingers down her neck, over her collarbone, and along the phantom sensations of pleasure Zach and Jasper had left her with.

Yesterday they'd floated her into a new level of bliss that she was confident she'd never been to before. Never in her life had she ever felt ruined for anyone else, yet these two men in her life had managed to do just that. It wasn't just the incredible sex that did it, either.

It was the fun and engaging conversations and playful banter—the way they focused on her and listened with undivided attention, no matter whether the topic interested them or not—the quiet silence, enjoying each other's presence—and…

Shira's fingers slid across her prosthetic arm. She smiled.

It was their sincere and unwavering adoration for everything she was, even the broken parts.

Her fingers slid up to her false-skin-covered neck. The makeup she'd applied hadn't managed well at lasting through the night, though this didn't bother her as much as it would have in the past. Shira's fingers stopped at the edge of the artificial skin and twitched, nearly digging under as if to tell her to finally remove it.

She flicked her attention to the bathroom door. Shira had woken up in a tangled heap with the guys and slipped out of bed to use the bathroom, all without them waking up. She doubted they were awake now. But them possibly glimpsing her without the skin to clean wasn't what made her nerves tingle and muscles tighten along her back and in her gut to the point she thought she might get sick.

She had one last rule separating herself from Jasper and Zach. Shira knew she needed to talk to them about it. She had to. But the very thought of uttering the question made her throat seize.

Her hand fell away, and her shoulders drooped. She wasn't ready yet. Shira wanted to be—or she thought she wanted to. Yet something held her back…

Quiet murmuring drew her attention. Sounded like Jasper and Zach had finally woken up. *I should finish up in here.* She didn't need to be seen as some weirdo who hid in a bathroom like she was ashamed of the dirty, passionate night of sex she'd previously enjoyed with near reckless abandon.

Shira reached for the door, only to stop when Zach's words drifted in. "We need to talk to her."

"Yeah, I know," Jasper said. "We will."

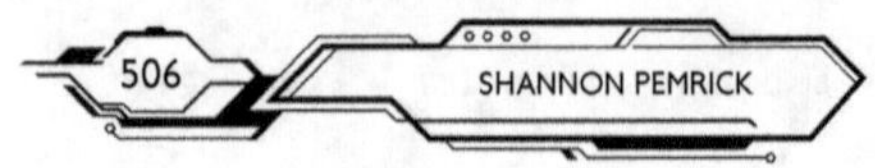

"Jasper, I'm being serious. I overheard a conversation she had with her mom the other day. She was talking about how she was treating this as a 'for-fun thing' until it might become serious. We need to sit her down and set this all straight."

Pain shot through Shira's chest like a rebounded lightning spell. She stepped back, her hand going to her chest. *They don't want to make this serious…*

Shira knew it was possible. She'd told herself not to get ahead and just take it as this went. That would make it easier to accept if it did become a "just for fun" moment with them. That should have been easy to accept because she'd prepared herself. And yet, Shira hadn't prepared for the side of her that didn't want this to end.

Her trembling bottom lip caught between her teeth. *What kind of idiotic fool am I?* Of course, this would be just for fun with them. Jasper and Zach were happy together. They were getting married, for crying out loud! That proposal should have been the flashing "turn back" sign.

Jasper let out a long breath. "Fuck. You're right. But what do we say? Communicating like this isn't my strong suit. You and Sara have both complained about it to me."

"We just gotta come out and say it. Tell her we're serious, and leave no room for her to see otherwise. It's the only way."

Everything in Shira's mind blinked out of existence. They were… serious? About her?

Shira dragged her tongue over her drying lips to wet them. She had to have misheard. She just made up what she heard to—*No.*

Shira whipped the door open. Her feet carried her

across the bedroom before she could think about what she was doing, and threw herself onto the bed. Her arms wrapped around the nearest man, burying her face into the crook of his neck. Her bare chest pressed against his warm, naked back. She didn't process who she was hugging around the neck until he spoke.

"Shira?" Zach murmured.

"I don't want this to end." The confession rang loud and strong in the quiet room.

The silence that continued for several long moments kicked up her heart rate. It beat stronger and stronger in her ears, until it was deafening. Shira's grip around Zach's neck tightened, and she wanted to scream and beg. She didn't want to hear what her doubts now whispered: she was wrong.

Strong hands gripped her arms. They weren't Zach's. No, even from touch alone, she could tell the difference between these two.

"Shira," Jasper said in a quiet and calm tone. He tugged at her arms to make her let go, and she resisted, not wanting to face her inevitable reality.

Jasper tugged harder until Shira knew she had to let go. She had to face this, even if she didn't want to face the outcome. Shira pulled away and looked at Jasper, bracing for the rejection.

Instead, his face twisted. "Why are you crying?"

Shira blinked. *Crying?* She reached up and tentatively touched her cheeks. Hot tears streamed down her face. Shira gasped and furiously rubbed her traitorous face. *How dare it make me look as weak as I feel right now?* She needed to at least look like she could handle this situation.

Jasper reached out and pulled her hands away. "Stop, you're going to rub your pretty face off, and it's my favorite feature of yours."

Shira let out a half-laugh. "I can think of several better features."

Jasper lifted her chin. His thumb traced her cheek and traveled down to her lips. His snaring green eyes followed his thumb's motion. It made her heart skip.

A frown touched the corners of his mouth. "Why were you crying, Shira?"

She went to say something, but words failed her. What could she say? "I… I don't know. I didn't even know I was until you said something."

Zach turned on the bed to better face her. "Did you think we were going to tell you no?"

Her lip quivered, and she clammed up. She couldn't admit to them what was going on in her head—the whole reason she didn't talk to them before to clarify if this was some fling or something more, when she knew she couldn't run on assumptions and a lack of clear and agreed-upon expectations. *This is so stupid!* Where did her backbone go? Why was it so hard for her to talk about these things?

Jasper's frown deepened. He dipped his head and pressed his firm lips to hers. The kiss was gentle and warm, almost apologetic.

When he pulled away, he brushed her cheek again with her thumb. "I'm sorry we had you doubting. That wasn't the intention. We want this to work. We'll fight any logistical nightmare that pops up if we have to in ordah to make the three of us work."

Zach slipped his arm around Shira and pulled her into

his chest, resting his chin in the crook of her neck. "We would have brought this up sooner so our intentions were clear, had it not been for me trying to wrestle with some personal issues."

Shira's fear and panic kicked up again. "Zach, if you don't want—"

He clamped his hand around her mouth and hushed her. "Don't you start. I'm not forcing myself to put up with anything in all this."

Shira's pulse slowed.

"Yes, I was unsure about the three of us working out," he admitted. "But that was because I was confused about how I felt. It took me a great deal of time to think and sort out my head"—Zach smiled—"and being around you, really being around you, to understand what I wanted. Then it finally clicked into place that it was okay to fall for the person I'm holding in my arms right now. I didn't come to that realization until the other day. I'm sorry it took so long to realize. I would have pushed harder for us to sit down and lay it out under better circumstances."

Shira had always worried that she was intruding—that her feelings were too much and that if she acted on them, she'd lose the two most important guys in her life. Even when their interest in her became obvious, even to her, she pretended as long as she could to not see the signs. She came up with excuse after excuse, rather than try to give all of them a better reason to face what they all had been skirting around for so long.

She swallowed and looked between the two of them before settling on Jasper. "I can't replace Sara."

Why the hell had she said that? Where had that thought

even come from? She'd never once had that concern. Right?

Jasper traced her cheek with the back of his finger. "Of course you can't. Neither can Zach. You're not a replacement for anyone, babe."

Shira's pulse ticked up once again, her breath catching for a moment. There was something in the way they called her that that hit her differently than when Jeremy used to use it. It rolled off their tongues so much better. Like it was only ever meant for Jasper and Zach to call her that.

"I know I'm still really messed up," she said. "I've got a lot more work to do on myself, but even through all this, you two have been so supportive and caring in ways I never thought possible. You two make me happier than I ever remember being, even before my accident. You've both been more than I ever thought I wanted, and I don't want to let either of you go."

Jasper tucked his index finger under her chin. "We're not going anywhere, Shira. If we letcha leave, our lives would be so much emptiah."

Zach tucked a strand of hair behind her ear. "Even if we remained *just* friends, it wouldn't feel right."

Shira's chest swelled with so much emotion. This all felt both real and a dream simultaneously.

"Now, with all this said, you're finally done with your stupid rules, right?" Jasper asked, leaning closer, his lips hovering over hers. "Did we accomplish breaking every damned one of them?"

Shira chuckled. "Until I make new ones."

Jasper made a thoughtful sound in his throat. "Well, then we're just gonna have to show our *girlfriend* what it means to be with us, so she doesn't have any reason to make new arbitrary and annoying rules."

Intense heat simmered in Shira's veins, spreading through her chest and the rest of her body. She slid both her hands into Jasper's hair, threading them tight to hold him captive. When she spoke, her voice had kicked down a lust filled notch. "Say that again."

Zach grinned into her neck, his hand gliding up her belly. "Our *girlfriend* needs some extra special attention to make up for the mistake we almost made losing her."

Shira practically purred. She crashed her mouth with Jasper's, not caring how desperate she was now. She wanted their touch, their attention, everything.

"Shira, I apologize for the interruption," Orion called out from the house infrastructure.

She didn't hold back her annoyed groan, and neither did the guys. "What? It'd better be important."

Shira knew it wasn't a reminder to let Snake out. Much like her patio doors at home, the backyard doors at the vacation home were automatic for a reason. If she was in too much pain to get out of bed, her AI could make sure Snake was taken care of in her stead.

"I wouldn't interrupt the time with your—*yes*—boyfriends, unless it was important," the AI said. "Narissa is on hold. She wishes to speak to the three of you about the tournament tomorrow."

Shira let out a slow breath. That couldn't be put on hold. The guys seemed to agree as they backed off. "Okay, answer the call."

A moment later, Narissa's voice came through the house infrastructure. "Hello?"

"Hey, Narissa," Shira greeted.

Jasper and Zach shared startled glances. "Uh, what?"

Shira's brow spiked. "You knew we were going to be talking with her."

"Yeah, but not through the house!" Jasper said.

Shira blinked, rather confused by their reaction. "Um… why wouldn't I? AI infrastructure tech has supported inline calls since… forever. I thought everyone had it."

Narissa laughed on the other end. "You'd be surprised. Some tech just gets forgotten about or doesn't have the same reach we think it should. Even my company doesn't have the latest medical equipment all the time. Remember the Holo-X that was used on you in the hospital?"

Shira thought back to the week of her accident, careful not to trigger anything for herself, and remembered some nurses and doctors using a hologram-like device to view all parts of her body, including deep tissue, blood, and even nerves. "I do. Now that I'm not dying, I can say that was some pretty cool tech."

"Cybro Industries is just getting that early next year," Narissa said. "And it'll be a slow rollout for all our specialists and technicians because of their expense."

"Much like your multi-AI network, the phone call data package is quite expensive," Alistair said.

Shira pursed her lips. She had no idea it was so out of reach for others. It gave her a bit of perspective. "So, what did you call us about, Rissa?"

"It's about the restart of the tournament tomorrow," her friend said. "Well, more specifically, your hotel accommodations. I kept them, in case there was a change in plans for Jasper and Zach. However, I got a call from the hotel inquiring if we still needed it. Looks like they're still trying to shuffle some people around who are trying to stay. Given the type of suite I booked, they wouldn't mind getting extra money from another customer who will use it."

"But you didn't want to give it up without consulting us," Zach finished for her. "We appreciate the thoughtfulness."

"What do you think?" Jasper asked. "Things are pretty good for us here."

Shira had gone to thinking the moment Narissa started explaining. It was a big thing to consider, mostly for her, but she knew what needed to be said. "We should take the room."

Jasper's and Zach's gazes snapped to her.

"I know what you two are thinking, and I know it's crazy for me to even suggest it because of that. But hear me out," she said. "It's a bit of a drive to the convention center when you factor traffic, and we've almost been late before. If we stay there instead of here, you both get more sleep and are less likely to be late."

Shira shrugged awkwardly. "And it might be difficult, but I think this would be an important next step for me."

Both guys carefully considered her, then nodded, Jasper speaking. "Okay, we'll stay there for the remaining days."

Narissa chuckled. "Well, it's a good thing I booked a luxury suite. You'll need that king-size bed and separate sleeping room for Serenity. I'll let the hotel know we will keep the room. See you three tomorrow."

The line went dead.

Zach chuckled. "Someone was eager to get off the phone."

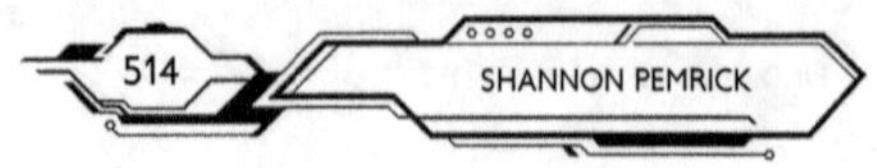

Jasper grinned at Shira and leaned closer to her again. "I'm not complaining. Where did we leave off?"

Shira rolled her eyes and pushed him back. "That's going to have to wait now. We should pack and get ready."

Jasper fought her off, and his lips brushed against hers. "We can finish what we stahted first and then pack. We've got all day."

Shira smirked. She was going to have to out-stubborn him, and given she could still think logically, she knew how to win this. "You two also need to get practice in. So, the sooner we get to the hotel and settle in, the sooner you two will get in some last-minute practice for tomorrow."

He traced her jaw with a finger and kissed her gently. "It can wait."

Shira pulled back just enough to force him to pause for a moment. "If you can, I promise I can make it worth your while. Something new I'm sure none of us have done before."

Jasper wasn't interested and tried to kiss her again. She was going to have to do something he'd really hate.

Shira slid her hand over Jasper's bare chest and kissed him back. A pleased growl rumbled through his throat, as though he'd won. Shira wouldn't fail, however, no matter how tempting it was to lose herself in all this with each touch.

She pushed against his chest to ease him back without breaking contact, as if she had the intent to straddle his lap. Predictably, he complied, while dragging his hands down the curve of her sides, as if it'd entice her more. However, as she rose, Shira swung her legs off the bed and walked away. Jasper groaned and swiped his hands after her, but she hastened out of his reach.

"C'mon, Shira," Jasper complained.

"Later." Shira stretched, which earned a frustrated growl from Jasper. Yeah, she was teasing him a bit, but she didn't feel bad.

"Fine, Zach and I can—" Shira turned to look at Jasper when he didn't continue, to find him scowling. Zach had also left the bed, and was smirking while throwing pants on.

"I agree with Shira," Zach said. "We can wait a little longer to finish what we started. And I'm interested in finding out what fun she has in mind."

Jasper flopped back on the bed and covered his face while he growled in frustration. Shira's gaze trailed down his perfectly sculpted body for a brief moment and then she tore her gaze away before she tempted herself too much.

She sashayed her way past Zach to the door. She let out a startled squeal when his hand slapped her bare ass. Heat flooded to her face, and she whirled on Zach.

He grinned and then threw a rumpled shirt over his head. "I'll take Snake for a walk, so we don't have to worry about him while we get you settled in."

Shira shook her head. "You don't have to do that, Zach. I can go on a quick walk, or even get a good play session in before we go."

Zach shook his head. "It'll be good for him to have the long walk, and Jasper took him the last few times."

A flash of guilt hit Shira's chest. She'd allowed Jasper to take Snake whenever he asked, but she should have been the one doing the walking. It wasn't like her pain was keeping her back.

Zach lifted the corner of her mouth. "Don't do that. We're not exercising like we normally do. It's been good for us to go on these walks with him." Zach tossed his head Jasper's way. "Besides, he needs to take a cold shower."

Jasper continued to sulk on the bed. "I hate you both."

Shira and Zach both chuckled. Zach refocused on Shira. "While you're packing, grab that sexy red dress."

Shira squinted, trying to think of the dress he meant.

"You did pack the dress like we asked, right?" Zach said.

"She did," Orion confirmed. "I made sure of it."

Shira snapped her fingers. "Right, that dress. Why did I need to bring that again?"

"Dinner." Zach slipped a hand around her waist. "We planned to treat you to dinner. And we're doing that. But I also think we need to combine it with telling Serenity the news about the three of us."

Shira's lip caught on her teeth. "Should we tell her so soon?"

"She's basically expecting it," Jasper mumbled. "That's why she's so comfortable calling you mom without upsetting us."

"Really, she's been asking when you'll be her actual mom for months now," Zach revealed.

Heat prickled Shira's cheeks and emotions swelled in her chest. She knew Serenity loved her, but hearing that truth was almost as overwhelming as hearing Serenity call her mom. "Okay, dinner and a conversation with her sounds like a good plan. I'll be sure to pack that dress if it means I get to see you two in a suit or tux."

"Just a suit." Zach pecked Shira on the cheek and slipped out of the room.

Jasper peeked up from his arm and beckoned her forward with a finger, his eyes gleaming and hopeful. Shira shook her head and left the room, adding a little shake to her ass, and leaving Jasper grumbling about her being a tease.

She showered and dressed, and found it easy to pack. It was only a few days, and if she forgot something, she could always slip back here really quick. Plus, Orion would know if she was forgetting anything important.

The sound of a shower running in Jasper and Zach's room echoed through the hallway when she exited. Shira went to make them all breakfast. Nothing too fancy, but bacon and eggs were more than sufficient to get them going for the day.

Zach returned home around the time she'd finished with most of the meal. The mix of smells lured him into the kitchen after Snake, who already had his breakfast waiting for him in his bowl.

Zach groaned hungrily. "I don't know if I want to eat first or shower."

Shira patted the island top. "Eat. I'm going to go check on Jasper. I would have expected him down here by now."

Zach slipped onto his stool and poured a glass of juice. "Probably trying to figure out how to pack everything just right. He's a little nutty about the suitcases."

Shira shook her head. "It's not like you have to pack everything. You both can come back here after the

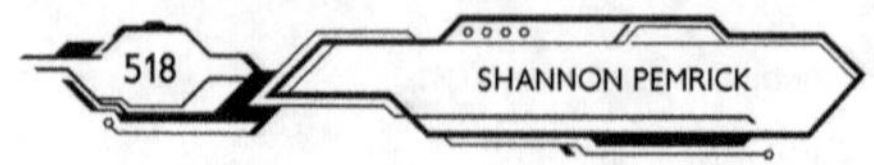

convention. Plus, it leaves room in case I go on more shopping sprees with Serenity."

Zach rolled his eyes. "Don't go overboard. We need to keep under the suitcase limits."

"Then I'll just mail it." Shira winked and walked off, canceling out any more protests.

She jogged up the stairs. When she made it to their room, she paused, listening to the stillness that was beyond the partially shut door. The water wasn't running, so she knew he was done with the shower. But if Jasper was packing, he should be making some noise. *He'd better not have laid down for a "brief moment" and fallen asleep.*

Shira pushed open the door and stepped into the room. Light streamed in from the pulled-open curtains. Jasper stood by the bed, his back to the door. His and Zach's suitcases had been laid out on the bed, several pairs of clothes already packed. There was an opened white envelope laying on the suitcase directly in front of Jasper.

Shira cautiously toed across the hardwood floor up to him, watching how little he moved. *Is he asleep standing up?*

She poked his arm. "Jasper?"

Jasper gasped and jumped. Shira jerked back, her heart kicking up to her throat. Jasper whirled around, then yanked an earbud out of his ear. "Shira."

She let out a slow breath, her heart still thundering. "Yeah, sorry, didn't mean to scare you."

He blinked slowly, as if he were still processing she was in the room. It was strange. "You okay, Jasper?"

He shook his head. "Yeah. Sorry, was just listening to something real quick. What's up?"

Shira's gaze flicked down to the tiny square device in his hand. *Looks like an audio chip.* She brought her gaze back up to him. "Um, I was just coming to let you know breakfast was ready. And to not over pack. You can come back here after the convention."

He nodded slowly. "Okay, thanks. I'll be down in a sec."

Shira watched him for a moment longer, taking in his weird state, and then excused herself. She glanced over her shoulder a few times while she walked down the hall, concerned. *I hope he's okay…*

CHAPTER 25

Soft lips pressed against Zach's neck. *Shira?* His mouth didn't move, and heaviness clung to his mind, but he was sure that was her. Her lips kissed him again, and he sighed, rolling his head back to provide better access. Zach couldn't see her. He wasn't even sure his eyes were open, but he didn't care right now.

"Zach," she murmured. "Zach."

He groaned instead of speaking.

"Zach, wake up." She kissed him again, this time lower along his collarbone, her fingers dragging down his chest.

Wake up? Was he asleep? This sure felt real.

"Wake up," Shira said again before kissing him even lower on his chest. "I want you awake for this."

Zach focused on opening his eyes. When he did, soft morning light filled the room. It took him a moment to recognize it as the hotel room and not the borrowed one of Shira's vacation home.

He wet his dry lips, trying to will himself more awake. Although, thought processes weren't easy with Shira sending bursts of exciting desire to his sleepy brain and down to his already-straining morning wood situation.

"Shira," he rasped, finding his throat rather dry.

She hummed. "Good, you're awake. Now you can enjoy this."

He opened his mouth to question her, but only a groan of pleasure came out when her tongue slid along his hard shaft. She worked her way leisurely up his length and then eased her lips around him.

Zach moaned and slid his hands into her silky, morning-mussed hair. He grabbed a fistful, but resisted the urge to take control and ram his cock into the back of her throat. He'd allow her to have her way for a moment longer.

And god, did her way feel amazing. Shira slid him in and out of her mouth in an amazing rhythm that had him rolling his head back into his pillow and closing his eyes.

She quickened her pace, as if to hasten a release from him. Zach didn't quite mind the idea of a quickie in the morning, but he wanted more from this—from her. He wanted to hear her moaning and screaming. He was so damned addicted to that sound—especially when she said his name while doing so.

Zach yanked her hair, pulling himself from her mouth, and sat up. With flushed cheeks, Shira gazed at him in confusion. Zach grinned and pulled her against him, her bare back pressing against his chest. He spread her legs around his and thrust hard into her.

Shira braced herself on his legs, managing a strangled

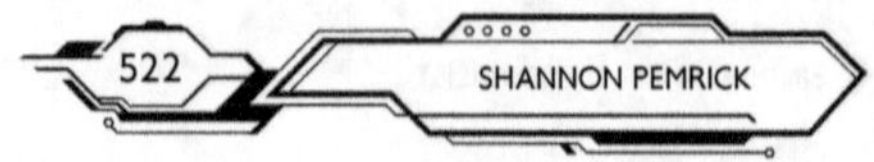

cry of surprised pleasure. Zach grabbed hold of her hips and slammed his cock into her again. And then again. And again.

His pulse thundered in his ears, and her pleasured moans only heated his veins. Shira tried to bite back her enjoyment, and Zach murmured in her ear, telling her to let their hotel neighbors know just how good she had it. Just like last night, after she'd revealed her fun surprise of giving both him and Jasper fantastic blowjobs on this bed, while the two of them fucked in game. They rewarded her outside the game until she was a puddle of pleasure and then dragged her in game to continue.

Those tantalizing memories spurred Zach on until Shira was screaming his name. His body tightened and then exploded in release.

Zach took ragged breaths, pressing his face into the back of her neck. He held her close, embracing her softness and warmth. Then it dawned on him. "Shit."

"Hmm?" she responded; the sound soft in her languid state.

"I forgot protection…"

It wasn't something he and Jasper had to think of until their decision to pursue Shira, so the habit wasn't there. Sure, they were only really needed to prevent STIs, given how much birth control had progressed and had such minimal failure rates, but most partners were more comfortable using them. At least, in the beginning of a relationship.

Shira rolled her head to the side and glance back at him. "Unless I've got to worry for health reasons, I'm not fussed. Not like I can get pregnant."

Sorrow pricked Zach's chest. She said that so flippantly, when he knew how much that still upset her.

Shira poked the corner of his mouth where he apparently showed a frown. "Don't. It's okay. I've got you, Jasper, and Serenity now. That's all I need."

Zach reached up and stroked her cheek affectionately. Shira's eyes lidded, and she leaned into the touch. "There are other options. But that's the future."

She hummed. "True. But, for now, I'm going to go jump Jasper for some one-v-one action."

It was at that moment Zach realized Jasper wasn't in bed. And instead, he caught the sound of the shower running in the ensuite bathroom. "I should feel insulted I wasn't enough for you."

"Jasper did call me greedy." She smirked. "And I've given him plenty of time to *wake up* like he asked so I can show him how greedy I am."

Zach chuckled. "You'll get used to that. It's been a long time since I've had that fun of a wake-up. But he makes up for it later."

Shira leaned in and kissed him gently on the lips. "Well, I'm here now, so you'll have more mornings like this."

Zach grinned. He looked forward to that.

Shira slipped off the bed, and he took a quick swipe at her ass. She scurried out of the way, laughing, and disappeared into the bathroom. Zach gave himself a few more moments before climbing out of bed and pulling some sweats out of his suitcase. He'd fully get ready for the day in a moment. He wanted to wake up more, and give Jasper some time with Shira.

Wandering out of the bedroom, Zach gazed around the opulent common room. He hadn't had much time to take it in yesterday, given how distracting Shira had been, plus his and Jasper's last-minute practices.

"Zach, there is fresh coffee in the pot and a breakfast sandwich on the counter for you," Alistair said through the hotel suite's infrastructure. "The fridge is also stocked with a few of your favorite additives for your coffee."

"Did Shira make it or order room service?" Zach asked.

"Yes."

Zach snorted in amusement. The exact answer he'd expect when it came to Shira's actions.

He walked into the spacious kitchen and made himself a cup of coffee and also grabbed his breakfast. While Zach wasn't exactly hungry, he knew better than to skip the meal. He'd need the energy for today.

Wandering over to the full-length windows, Zach gazed out at the sprawling city below while he sipped his coffee. Even though he should concentrate on strategizing for the matches, Zach found his mind wandering to this suite and then Shira's vacation home.

Now that the three of them were together, how much of this was he going to have to get used to? Zach and Jasper didn't come from money. Shira was aware of that, and certainly didn't care. She'd come from an even worse background than either of them, so she understood. But this was also Shira, and she liked to spoil him, Jasper, and especially Serenity. *There's no way we're not going to be living like this in the future.*

How soon into the future, that was hard for him to say. He and Jasper had a plan. They'd worked it out at the end of their date the other day. But even after that happened, it wasn't like they'd get a place with Shira right away, right?

Zach yelped when he bit his finger and then glared at his hand. Apparently, he'd absently eaten his breakfast. That was slightly disappointing, since he didn't get the chance to savor it, and it had to have been good if it was already gone.

Zach shook his head to rid himself of these thoughts. He needed to focus on today. They needed to prove themselves, otherwise their plans would fall through and it would make things harder for them. And that meant going through his usual morning routine to get himself into a better mindset.

Setting his now-empty coffee cup on the marble counter, Zach made his way into the bedroom. Jasper and Shira weren't in there yet, and one listen told him they were still in the shower—and they were definitely having fun.

Smirking, Zach laid out the clothes he wanted for the day and headed for the bathroom. Steamy heat greeted him when he opened the door, as did Shira's moaning. Zach glanced toward the shower, where he could see the outlines of Shira pressed up against the digitally frosted shower door, with Jasper pounding into her from behind.

Zach thought for a minute before walking over to the shower door. He wasn't in any position to join them after his and Shira's time in bed, but that didn't mean he couldn't enjoy this in another way.

He swiped his hand along the door and the digital frosting disappeared, revealing Shira's flushed face, parted, moaning mouth, and breast pressed up against

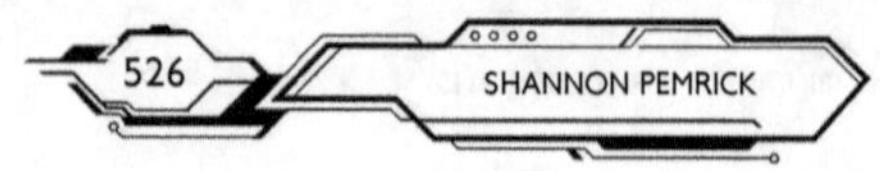

the glass. Jasper smirked at Zach and picked up his pace. Shira closed her eyes and enjoyed their "one-v-one match."

Zach's gaze dragged over the two of them, and then he turned for the sink to shave. He had quite the view while he did. "Who's winning?"

Shira groaned. "I am."

"Not for long," Jasper panted out. "You will come first."

Zach chuckled. He was quite familiar with the rules: last the longest; no one can slow down after a pace was agreed on. The only issue Jasper had with this fun game was that he usually lost. Zach suspected it wouldn't be much different here. He knew women enough to be aware how much easier they had it with delaying orgasm on purpose.

Zach had just finished smearing shaving cream on when Jasper swore. His face screwed up as ecstasy flooded through him. Shira grinned, knowing she'd won.

"Fuck…" Jasper half complained, leaning his forehead on her back.

"Better luck next time, man-slave," Shira goaded.

Zach choked on a laugh. "Is that title the result of the stakes?"

Jasper and Zach always had a stake to go along with the game.

Shira grinned. "Yup. He's now my man-slave for the day. Shira two, Jasper zero."

Jasper grumbled, and Zach laughed. "You should've known better. You can't even outlast me."

"I will one day. But until then…" Jasper flipped Shira

around and devoured her mouth while reaching between her legs to finish his task.

She reached orgasm and then the two finished their shower around the time Zach completed his shaving routine. This gave him a chance to slip into the shower, though not before stealing a kiss from both of them, and they all got ready for the day.

Much to Zach's disappointment, Shira took extra time alone to fix up her false skin over parts of her cybernetics. He'd hoped that after they'd gotten together, she'd be comfortable going without, even just around them, but so far that wasn't looking like it'd be the case for a bit.

Zach just wanted her to see how beautiful she was, cybernetics and all. *Baby steps. We can help her through that over time.*

Jasper's phone went off—it was his parents. They were making their way through security with Serenity. Jasper volunteered to bring them up, as well as taking Snake out to do his business. He let Shira know before slipping out of the room.

Zach poured himself another cup of coffee, and soon after, Shira joined him. They were in the middle of hashing out the day's plan when Serenity burst through the door.

Zach opened his mouth to greet his daughter, but she got her words out first. "She-ra!"

Zach pursed his lips and watched his daughter greet Shira first, and of course his girlfriend happily ate up her status as most important person in this moment.

"Good morning, Starship," Shira greeted in a chipper tone.

Serenity bolted into Shira's open arms for a hug. "I

missed you, She-ra. I had lots of fun, but I still missed you."

"Oh, we *all* missed you," Shira said. "But I'm so glad you had fun."

Zach glanced at Jasper, Snake, Christine, and Scott, who stood just inside the hotel room. His soon-to-be in-laws appeared amused, and Jasper was shaking his head.

"Let me guess," Zach started, "She didn't greet you first when you saw her."

Jasper chuckled. "No, she greeted Snake and then asked me where Shira was."

Christine couldn't hold back her laughter. "It was adorable."

Serenity turned his and Jasper's way. "Hi, Daddy. Hi, Dad."

That was all they got before she went to telling Shira about all the fun she had with her grandparents. That quickly changed to asking about the hotel situation, getting excited and checking out her separate room for all of two seconds, before wanting to know what they were all doing today.

It was the first time Serenity had gone through that chaotic whiplash of short attention since arriving at the start of the vacation, and it was clear Shira wasn't prepared for that. *Buckle up, Shira, it's only going to get worse.*

It honestly surprised Zach the behavior hadn't come out sooner. *Maybe because we'd managed to preoccupy her long enough.*

"Alistair, how long do we have until the matches?" Jasper asked.

"Quarterfinals will begin with Smash and Stab versus

Burnout at the top of the hour," the AI said. "Then the match with Fiery Toucans and Night Sphinxes will determine the semi-final matchup."

That soon? He thought they'd have a little more time to prepare for their match. *We had taken our time this morning.*

"There is also activity with your guild," Orion said. "It appears they're trying to organize a meetup."

Zach pulled his phone out of his pocket to look. As the AI said, Emi and Takashi were taking a tally of who was able to still come to the rescheduled dates, and organize a meetup. Naturally, Darius and Kiara had already responded.

Darius had today free, unlike tomorrow when Lion Rage, the creator of Lusara Fates and the company he worked for, did their big presentation, and Kiara, it seemed, was in the same boat. To help Darius and his team, she always volunteered to help work alongside him each year.

Of course, Mercedes was with Takashi. Both of them were nearly at the convention center. Valerie wished everyone fun. She was working, though encouraged everyone to stop by her food truck.

Ronan and Donovan chimed in saying they were around, after which Emi bantered back and forth with them, given they were standing right next to her in line for some coffee.

Narissa and Ajax were also walking about, and Rei was with Emi. Eli, who hadn't been able to afford the trip this year, wished he'd could so he could see everyone. And a few other guild members reported in, indicating they couldn't stay for the change and wished everyone

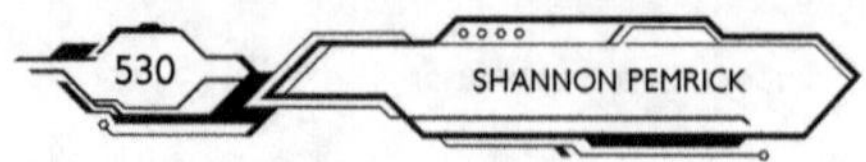

a fun time. Jasper and Zach also got a shout-out from them to kick ass in the tournament.

It was then Jasper piped in and confirmed all of them were heading down to the lobby soon. An extended meetup wouldn't be possible to swing until after today's part of the tournament, but it'd be nice to see everyone beforehand.

"Are you two prepared for your match?" Shira asked Jasper and Zach after a meeting location was decided. "Burnout is a big deal, and the two of you still refuse to tell me how your previously interrupted match went, so I've got my guesses."

Jasper waved her off. "It's fine. They may be a good team, but so are we. Zach and I have been practicing these last few days to handle each team's strongest two combos. We got this."

She pursed her lips. "Okay, if you're that confident."

Zach gave Shira a reassuring smile, though some of it felt forced. He hadn't been able to stave off all the growing discomfort twisting his gut since he crawled out of bed. Burnout wasn't just a tough team. The brother-sister duo was *the* team to beat this year, as they were last year's reigning champs. And they deserved every bit of that title.

"Let's get downstairs to see everyone," he said. "And leave Burnout to Jasper and me."

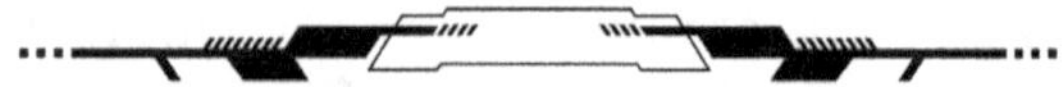

Barely twenty past nine, and the lobby was packed. Jasper made sure he had a firm grasp on Serenity's hand so as not to lose her. He would have set her on his shoulders, if it weren't for the fact that Serenity insisted she hold Zach's hand, too.

Shira stuck close to Jasper, the livelier environment making her a bit more uncomfortable than usual. He suspected it may be compounded with them coming down from the hotel part of the convention center.

Jasper was incredibly proud of how well Shira handled settling into the room and made it through the night without incident. Of course, he and Zach keeping her preoccupied didn't hurt. But that didn't mean she was in the clear, and going downstairs proved to be difficult for her this morning.

But she was here doing her best, and if she needed to slip away to calm down, he'd encourage her to look out for her well-being. Jasper didn't care if that meant she had to miss the match, as long as she was in a safe spot, both physically and mentally.

Thinking of Shira's progress, and future needs, brought his mind back to yesterday morning, and the audio chip Sara had left him. He hadn't intended to listen to it—at least not until he'd gotten back to Boston, where he could focus on whatever surprise lay in the recording.

However, when he was packing, it'd gotten jostled around, drawing his attention, and he hadn't been able to stop himself. And he definitely hadn't been prepared to hear her last words for him.

Jasper knew he should have called Jeff right then, and told him what happened and that he needed help to figure out how to process it. Then maybe he'd know how to bring it up to Zach—and Shira, too. She needed to know. *But how do I bring it up?*

Ajax was the first person Jasper spotted, taking him

out of his thoughts. He raised his hand to wave and grab their friend's attention, but Zach beat him to it. Ajax, for his part, was either six-feet plus and blind or six-plus and clueless, because he didn't see. Yet, all of Kiara's five-foot-anklebiting ass did.

The short, curvy, and busty redhead woman jumped up and down, waving a pale and heavily tattooed arm back at them. Watching Kiara appear and then disappear behind the crowd was a hilarious sight, as was the moment Ajax realized who she was waving at, after he stared at her for several long moments with a perplexed look.

Skirting around a cluster of people, their friends came into better view. Kiara stood next to Ajax, though now she had Darius, a muscular, dark-tan-skinned and dark-haired man, leaning on her head like she was an arm rest. Between her unenthused look, demands that the "frost giant" remove his unwashed, smelly arm from the "hobbit," and the fact Darius was even taller than Ajax, it was quite the comical sight.

Emi and Rei congregated with them, the former sipping on a warm cup of what Jasper assumed was coffee. Ronan, a clean-shaven, broad shouldered and muscular man of average height, and Donovan, a tall, athletically lean man with well-groomed facial hair and impeccably styled drop-fade-cut black hair, bantered with the two women.

Ronan held Rei in a headlock with a cybernetic right arm, and she tugged at his chestnut hair in an attempt to make him release her. Donovan adjusted the black-rimmed glasses perched on his nose, and appeared to be making bets with Emi, instead of helping Rei out.

Their antics froze in place upon Jasper's group's approach.

"Hey, guys," Ronan greeted, as if nothing was amiss.

Jasper chuckled, then stopped abruptly and squinted at Rei when he noticed her long raven hair. "Okay, fess up. Is the long hair or the short hair the wig?"

Emi sipped her coffee. "I'm impressed you didn't assume the long hair was the wig."

Jasper held up a hand. "Look, I've seen the magic of makeup. I'm not going to assume there isn't magic in wigs."

Ronan grabbed a lock of Rei's hair and tugged. She grunted, but her hair stayed on her head. "I'd say this is her hair."

Rei rolled her eyes. "You clearly have no idea how wigs are applied."

The two bantered back and forth for a few moments until everyone fell into a fit of laughter. Once they calmed down, guild mates who had never met in person before greeted each other with big hugs and handshakes, and then Jasper's parents and daughter were introduced to those they didn't know. There were also some congratulations and gushing about the engagement.

"Where is Narissa?" Shira asked.

"Waiting at the door for Mercedes and Takashi to get through security," Ajax said. "She figured it'd be easier for the two to find us in the crowd with a guide."

Shira nodded. "Makes sense."

Her phone buzzed, and she turned on the screen. Her eyebrow rose, piquing Jasper's interest.

"Mercedes or Narissa?" he asked.

Shira frantically looked around without answering him.

"What, did they actually get lost trying to find us?" This got a laugh from everyone but her. She wasn't even listening.

Then she gasped, her eyes widening. "Anthony!"

Jasper and Zach passed each other a confused look when she bolted. "Anthony?"

Who the hell was Anthony? She'd never mentioned someone by that name before. Or had she and he'd forgotten?

Everyone watched her rush toward a brickhouse of a man with tawny beige skin and dreadlocks pulled back into a half-ponytail. He opened his arms and lifted her into a hell of a bear hug, spinning her around. This movement exposed a curvaceous woman with umber skin, and a little girl around Serenity's age with a similar skin tone, standing behind him and watching the spectacle like the rest of Shira's friends.

This Anthony guy set Shira down, and then she greeted the woman cheerily, and the two embraced in a much calmer hug. The little girl hid behind the woman. Jasper gauged her as being shy, rather than afraid of Shira, based on the way she peeked around the woman's leg. Shira proved his theory correct when she waved her fingers at the girl, and she waved back.

Serenity slipped out of Jasper's grasp and ran for Shira, Snake going with her. Jasper's brow creased. "When did she get his leash?"

"When Shira dropped it in her excitement," Kiara said. "Your little girl was quick on the pickup."

Jasper grunted. That would figure. Serenity had gotten quite attached to Snake, and loved being his secondary leash keeper. "Anyone know who that is?"

No one did, which perplexed him even more. *Well, we won't find out standing around.* He and Zach approached, his parents opting to stick with their friends. Well, more like go over something his mother found while searching for things to do today. That didn't bother Jasper. They could run off and do whatever they wanted today.

Jasper and Zach caught up to Serenity with their longer strides, mere feet from an animated Shira caught up in conversation. When Shira noticed them, her cheeks tinted pink. "Oops. I got a little excited."

Jasper smirked. "Ya think?"

Shira clasped her hands behind her back. "This is Anthony. He's a longtime friend of mine I haven't seen in a few years. And this is Deka, his wife, and Jasmine, their daughter. Anthony, Deka, this is Jasper, Zach, and"—Shira chuckled when Serenity latched onto her leg—"Serenity."

"Hey," Anthony rumbled in a deep voice.

"It is a pleasure to meet you," Deka said, her cadence and accent foreign to Jasper.

"Great to meet you," Zach said.

Jasper agreed. "How long have you known Shira?"

Anthony smirked. "Shira and I, we go way back."

"Street days?" Jasper guessed.

Anthony chuckled. "Oh yeah. We always had each other's back."

"Anthony was the only one who didn't shun me after I went to live with Anita and Flynn," Shira said. "And I made sure to repay him by helping Anita find him the best family."

"Third best decision of my life," Anthony said with a wide grin.

Jasper's brow rose. "And the first and second?"

Anthony wrapped his arm around Deka's waist. "Marrying this amazing woman and having our little princess."

Jasper could respect that order. "So, you two haven't seen each other in a while?"

"I'm a traveling nurse," Anthony said. "I haven't been back this way for a number of years."

"Before Jasmine was born," Shira said.

Zach cocked his head. "Is that why she's being shy?"

All the adults turned their attention to Jasmine, who was still peeking around her mother's leg.

"No, I'm not shy," the girl said in a defiant tone.

Jasper took a good, assessing look at her and then smirked. He knew that look. "I think Shira might have a little star-struck fan."

Both her parents smiled, cementing the claim.

A big grin spread over Shira's face. She crouched down to be at better eye level with the girl. "Is that true?"

Jasmine played with a tablet in her hands and then showed Shira. "You and Izzy."

Shira cradled the tablet without taking it from the girl. Jasper leaned to get a quick peek. On the device was an image of two women in athletic poses. One woman was of dark complexion with high cheekbones, thick curly hair, dark compelling eyes, and lithe frame, and the other had a pale complexion with freckles, long brown hair, green eyes, and a familiar curvaceous form.

Shira's brows rose high on her forehead. "Wow, this is an old shoot. I think I was… sixteen?"

"Eighteen, two months, and three days," Orion corrected from her phone.

Shira rolled her eyes, and Jasmine giggled.

Serenity peeked around Shira's shoulder, and her brows scrunched. "Momma, that can't be you. Your hair is brown."

Jasper noticed Anthony's interest intensify with Serenity's name for Shira.

"Oh, that's right. You haven't seen me with anything but my dyed hair," Shira said. "This is my natural hair. I stopped dying it for a little while because I didn't like wigs, and my gigs needed me with brown hair."

Did that trigger the fight she had with Jeremy about her hair? Jasper wouldn't put it past the asshole.

"But your hair is red, not brown."

Shira let out a chuckle. "Starship, I've got anime-red hair. It's not possible for me to have this color naturally."

Serenity's face squinched. Jasper almost laughed. He and Zach had this same conversation with her, and she just didn't get it.

Shira patted Serenity on the head and turned her attention back to Jasmine. "I can see why you love Izzy so much. You look a lot like her."

The young girl's eyes lit up. "I really want to meet her one day. Do you still know her?"

Shira's lips twisted. "I know her. I haven't had much contact with her, though, ever since the two of us stopped modeling."

Jasmine frowned and looked at her tablet. "Are you… are either of you going to model again someday?"

Shira didn't answer right away, her expression going contemplative. Jasper wondered what made Izzy stop modeling. No sooner did the thought pop into his head, Jasmine continued to speak.

"I know you stopped because you had to get

cybernetics. But my dad says you are the most defiant person he knows."

All the surrounding adults chuckled.

"And I thought, maybe after you healed, you might think about showing everyone we are pretty, too."

Jasper looked harder at the brave girl. That's when he noticed the scars crawling along her right cheek and around her eye. And then it struck him.

He'd always seen modeling as an important job. It filled a need in advertising everyone relied on. But it wasn't until this moment he really thought about another role it filled: bringing inspiration and self-assurance to kids. They consumed everything they saw with impression-able eyes, and that contributed to who they grew up to be. So, a cybernetics user like Jasmine would see how models were treated in an industry that focused a great deal on vanity, and would internalize that within herself.

That had Jasper thinking about Zach's and his choice not to stream. If they did, even if the two of them weren't over-the-top entertaining, and just acted their usual unapologetic selves, would that have some posi-tive effect for someone who needed it?

"Do you want to be a model, Jasmine?" Shira asked, skirting the original question, but from what Jasper could tell, his girlfriend had purpose in her eyes.

The young girl nodded. "I want to be like Izzy. And you."

Shira smiled. "I don't know if I'm going to be a model again. It's been a number of years, and my life has changed a lot. I'm also still doing a lot of healing from my accident. But even if I don't, there will be people who can take up that mantle. Maybe they're someone my age. Or maybe, that mantle is meant for someone like you."

Jasmine's face lit up. "You think I can?"

"I believe that as strongly as your parents do."

Jasmine turned to her parents, who smiled and nodded encouragingly. The girl beamed and then held up her tablet to Shira again. "Will you sign this? It's my favorite picture with you and Izzy."

Shira smirked. "You bet."

A hand landed on Jasper's shoulder. He turned to look at an excited Ajax.

"It's time. You two ready?"

Jasper grinned, biting back his nerves. "Hell yeah."

Shira turned her head to the side to look up at them. "Good luck, man-slave. You too, Zach."

Jasper let out a heavy sigh. *She would call me that in front of everyone.*

Ajax's head flew back in his laughter, and the others joined in with him. "You lost a bet, didn't you?"

Jasper blew out a breath. "Yeah."

Ajax laughed some more and patted his shoulder. "Let's get you both through the match so she can get back to bossing you around."

Shira smirked, and Jasper shook his head. As they passed to head for the stairs, he planted a kiss on Serenity's head and then Shira's. She smiled sweetly at him, and he noted that she did this without recoiling or showing any signs of fighting any affection in front of the others.

Shira grabbed Zach's hand for a brief moment. "You guys got this. I've got faith in you."

Jasper's gut twisted, and he painted on a confident smile. He had told himself the same thing the last few days. They'd practiced to make up for the fumbling they had against Burnout last time. And yet, with all the practicing, he still couldn't shake the feeling it wasn't going to be enough.

We have to do it, for Shira and Serenity.

CHAPTER 26

Serenity wiggled in her seat, making it difficult for Shira to secure her spectator headgear. "Serenity, I understand you're excited, but please hold still."

The girl stopped; the only thing to continue moving were her fingers wiggling on her seat. "Sorry. I don't wanna miss Daddy and Dad's match. I promised Nana and Pop-Pop I'd tell them how it went."

After Jasper and Zach ran off, and Shira had a few more words with Anthony and his family before they went about following their own plans for the convention, Jasper's parents had let her know they were going to slip away for a bit to check out a panel. As much as they wanted to watch the guys' match, Christine had been waiting for the panel all week. Shira had no issue with that. Jasper and Zach had at least one more game after this one, whether they won or lost. Serenity had promised to pay close attention to the matches so that when they regrouped with the family, she could tell her grandparents all about how the match went.

Christine was so grateful for the girl's thoughtfulness, and so was Shira. At this point in the tournament, the next matches were too important for her to skip watching. So, if Serenity focused on fulfilling this promise, she would be less likely to grow bored and ask Shira to go do something at the convention with her.

Shira let out a quiet breath when she finally got the strap secured around Serenity's chin. "There. Ready?"

Serenity tried to nod, but the headgear was too heavy to do so without throwing her balance off. "Let's go!"

Shira smirked and pulled the earphones over the girl's ears and let Alistair draw her into the system. This allowed Shira to relax in her seat for a moment or two before Jasper and Zach's match started.

Or, at least, she would have relaxed, if it weren't for the close and intense stares burning into her. Shira let out a quiet breath and turned to face all her friends. She knew what they wanted.

Narissa, when she finally joined them with Mercedes and Takashi, immediately went to teasing Shira, from asking if she gave Jasper and Zach a goodbye kiss to spilling the beans that Shira was staying at the hotel in the same room with the guys. And her nosey friends were eager to know what was going on. Even Anthony had messaged her, asking for info, as Serenity calling her Momma didn't escape his notice.

Luckily, Shira and the guys had discussed what to tell people and when. They knew it couldn't be hidden from their friends for long, but it had to be done without Serenity knowing yet. Jasper also wanted to tell his parents in person himself, so it was a minor blessing that Christine and Scott weren't here.

Shira shook her head. "Why are all my friends so nosey?"

Ronan smirked. "Because you are, too."

Fair point. She glanced around the room to make sure no one who shouldn't would overhear this conversation. She then lowered her voice. "Yes, Jasper, Zach, and I are dating."

A mix of barely controlled squeals, cheers, and whoops surrounded her. Shira had to resist rolling her eyes.

"We haven't told Serenity yet, so if you all could keep it under wraps for a little longer, we'd appreciate it," Shira said.

Mercedes smiled. "When do you plan on looping her in?"

"Tonight. The guys want to treat me to dinner for some reason, and then we figured we'd tell her after."

Kiara chuckled. "'For some reason.' These plot ideas just write themselves thanks to you, I swear."

Shira rolled her eyes. She was sure she'd already handed Kiara enough ideas to last her three lifetimes.

"How are you going to handle the media?" Narissa asked. "After what happened with Jeremy earlier this week, and how quickly the guys' popularity is rising, I know that's been running through your mind. Can't have conflicting stories, but lying will be impossible to do in the long run."

Shira chewed her bottom lip and nodded. "That is something we're still working out the fine details on. But right now, we're going with mostly honesty. They

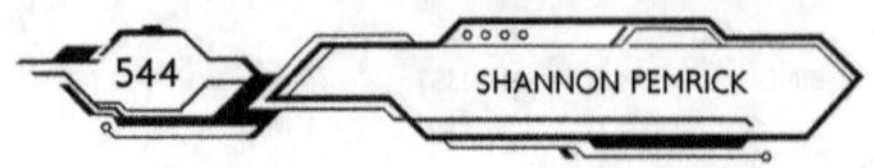

were casually seeing me, as I needed to focus on my health, and we more recently made it official."

Takashi leaned back in his seat. "I buy it."

Donovan winked at Shira. "And there were plenty of us who were convinced you three were sneaking around in the guild members' quarters."

Shira grunted. "That only happened once."

His eyebrows rose high and Donovan tilted his head to urge her to elaborate, while the rest of their friends laughed.

Serenity gasped, cutting into the mirth. That was their cue. Everyone either pulled out tablets or repositioned themselves to get a good view of the screens mounted around the room, and popped in at least one earbud to experience the gamecasters.

Shira pulled up the match on her tablet, and activated all the special stat menus she was privy to. Her pulse thrummed like moths smacking into a lightbulb. She had faith in Jasper's and Zach's skills, but she also was pragmatic.

Reigning champs and perfect streak, Burnout wasn't just any team in this tournament. And with the guys' refusal to tell her how their interrupted match had gone, she could pretty much guess how it'd really gone for them.

Jasper and Zach weren't going to have an easy time this second go-round, even with all the practice they'd done this week. *As long as they put in their all, I'll be happy whatever the outcome.*

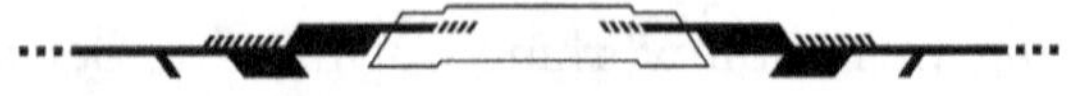

The warrior's shield slammed into Jasper, and he crashed to the ground. He choked, all the air in his virtual lungs forced out. A stun effect paralyzed Jasper in place, leaving him helpless against his opponent.

Without hesitation, she lifted her weapon and sliced it down on him, carving a huge chunk of what little remained of his health.

Health: 35%

Shit! Jasper wanted to scream. They weren't doing any better against Burnout this time around than the last. *What the hell is wrong with us?* They'd practiced all week. This shouldn't be so hard.

Blinding light slammed into the warrior, and then warmth washed over Jasper. His health jumped up ten percent.

Jasper sucked in a slow, calming breath. He couldn't lose his cool. No matter what happened, he and Zach had to just do their best. And with Zach playing a hybrid priest, going both healing and DPS, he had a good chance.

They were taking a risk with this dragoon-and-priest combo, especially since Jasper was the better healer of the two of them, but he also played dragoon better, making this combo the best they had to counter Burnout's druid-and-warrior combo. Or it would have been, had it been any other team.

This brother-sister duo was like none Jasper had ever gone up against. Their reaction times and coordination were almost inhuman.

The stun wore off of Jasper. He swung his glaive in a

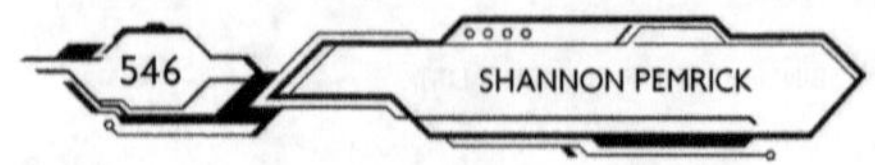

wide arching motion, clipping the warrior and shaving off a small sliver of health.

Health: 87%

He didn't hesitate and activated his jumping attack, jamming the blunt end of his polearm into the ground and launching himself high into the air.

The warrior attempted to dodge the attack, strafing to the right. Jasper grinned and came down on her, already predicting that would be the direction she'd choose.

His blade sunk into her avatar, and his attack crit carved out a chunk of her health.

Health: 71%

As a bonus, Zach shot off a heal on Jasper, bringing him up to fifty percent. *We can do this.*

Out of nowhere, a thick vine slammed into Jasper and wrapped around him. *Fuck.* He struggled against the grappling flora, to no avail.

The warrior slammed her sword into her shield, though Jasper wasn't sure why. He knew she had gone a tank specialization, and that was a clear sign she'd done a taunt, but Jasper was already focused on her. Then she activated a dash and shot past him.

Jasper's gut clenched. That taunt had been for Zach.

A fairly standard rule in PvP was to focus on the healer. However, sometimes that wasn't the best tactic. Jasper and Zach had foregone that plan, as it hadn't helped them in the last two rounds. It meant a longer potential match, but the idea was the wear down the healer's mana pool. And because Zach had a large one as a priest, it was an approach they were willing to try.

Unfortunately, that didn't help when their opponent didn't play along. And now, with Jasper immobile, Zach was easy prey to a warrior.

Zach tossed a shielding spell on himself and channeled an attacking spell, but lost it when the Warrior slammed into his shield and instantly broke through with enough damage, following up with a heavy hitting attack.

Health: 65%

Zach tossed up a quick heal and ran, attempting to keep his distance. A risky choice, since he couldn't also cast, but if the warrior continued to use cast-breaking moves, he'd be done for in a matter of seconds.

A root burst from the ground and tripped Zach. He stumbled, but the trip attack failed, allowing him to keep moving. The warrior kept pace with him, but was just out of reach for any more attacks.

Jasper struggled against the grapple holding him, but his attempts failed. This spell would hold him for another twenty seconds if he couldn't break it sooner. *Fuck druids and their mega spells.* They weren't an easy class to play, as they had long cast times and easy-to-fail spells. But when the spells held, they were some of the most powerful in the game.

Zach cast another shielding spell and came to a halt. He pivoted and cast a quick holy attack. It didn't damage the warrior all that much, but it did cause a slow debuff. Zach strafed to the side and angled toward the druid.

Once out of reach of the warrior, he cast a quick

attacking spell on the druid, disrupting his current cast, and went to channeling his own high-power spell.

The warrior ground her teeth as she desperately tried to push through the slowness plaguing her, to no better avail than Jasper's attempts to break free. *If only this grapple could be broken by my teammate. This would be a hell of a lot easier.*

Both Zach and the druid finished their spell casts at the same time. A beam of holy light burst from Zach's staff, and a fiery inferno engulfed the druid's arm like a living snake, and then shot out for Zach. The two attacked shot through each other and slammed into their targets.

Health: 45%

Health: 50%

Jasper fought against his grapple, and this time the plant matter tore. The vine ripped apart, and he was free. "Focus on the druid. I'll keep the warrior distracted as long as I can."

He caught the vaguest of nods from his partner as Zach focused on moving his arms in wide arcs and casting several small and quick spell attacks before channeling another larger one. With druids so susceptible to cast cancelation, the quicker attacks would be ideal for the whole fight, except they used up more of Zach's mana reserve.

Jasper rushed the warrior. The slowing debuff wore off, and the two charged each other head first, until Jasper launched himself into the air and came down on the warrior. She bared her teeth and took a portion of the damage, having activated a defensive skill to mitigate the blow. She swung with her weapon, slicing out a piece of his health, but nothing too worrisome.

Jasper danced around her, swinging his weapon and trying to build up his dragon-rage meter again after losing it from the grapple. *If I can just max that out, we can win this match.*

"Jasper, your feet!" Zach shouted.

Jasper snapped his attention down, but it was too late. A root shot up and grabbed his leg, immobilizing him. The warrior slashed him with her weapon one last time before charging for Zach.

She used another taunt, and the ability took hold, forcing Zach to alter his focus. *Shit!* Jasper needed to break free now, or they were definitely going to lose.

Zach attacked the warrior, and both their opponents rallied against him. Jasper swore multiple times as he struggled against this annoyance of a grapple. It only lasted a few seconds, unlike the other one, but that was all it took for Zach's health to drop to zero.

His avatar collapsed and then dematerialized. *Fuck!* They'd been so damned close.

The root holding Jasper broke, the grapple ending, and Jasper faced off against the druid and warrior. He wasn't going to win, but at least he'd go down fighting.

Taking a deep breath, he charged. The warrior ran to meet him. Jasper used his jump ability to launch over the tank, and shot right for the druid. His blade sliced into his opponent.

Health: 45%

The druid threw a heal on himself, and then another, and another. They were minor blips to his health pool, but it was an effective way to keep himself topped off as Jasper attempted to take him out, while also having to dodge and weave around the warrior.

However, one surprising offensive strike from the druid, and three powerful attacks from the warrior, and Jasper's health hit zero.

They'd lost, three to zero.

The system ejected Jasper from the game, and he took a long moment to collect himself before opening his eyes. Frustration and anger surged through him, threatening to tear him from the inside out until he exploded. Yet he took long, slow breaths until those feelings subsided. He could be upset they lost, but it wasn't going to be the end of his and Zach's careers.

They were going to the loser's bracket, sure, but that meant they weren't out of this yet. It put them in the semi-finals and gave them a chance to really prove themselves.

Jasper sucked in a strong breath. *And now that we know what we're up against, we can plan better for our rematch.*

He climbed out of his gaming chair, his senses struggling this time to orient. He paused when the room spun.

A hand touched his shoulder, and it took Jasper a moment to realize it was Zach. "You okay?"

"Yeah," Jasper said. "Dizzy for some reason."

"Maybe you didn't hydrate enough this morning," Zach said.

It was possible. He'd been a little preoccupied. He'd barely gotten some breakfast in him. "I'll be sure to grab something aftah this."

The disorientation didn't last much longer, allowing him and Zach to face the brother-sister Burnout duo. Leon was a tan, tall, and broad-shouldered man, with a wide jaw and styled brown hair. His sister, Emilia, was equally tall and tan, slim, with long brown hair with blonde highlights pulled into a side braid.

Emilia had a friendly smile while Leon's was quite cocky. The four of them shook hands.

"Great game," Jasper said. "I really thought we could pull out on top with that last one, but you two get to keep your undefeated title."

Leon grinned and spoke in a bit thicker accent than Shira's father. "*Ja*, of course we do."

Emilia narrowed her eyes and smacked her brother in the arm. Leon complained and shot her an offended look. His sister signed frantically, her glare not letting up. Instead of signing back, Leon spoke to her in German.

Jasper and Zach watched bemusedly as the two bickered.

"You getting any of this?" Jasper asked Zach. Jasper knew some sign language, but wasn't anywhere near as fluent as Zach. And nothing Emilia signed was familiar to him.

He shook his head. "There's isn't much cross over with ASL and DGS."

Emilia's hands paused, and she glanced toward them. Her cheeks tinted, and she signed "Sorry," in ASL.

Zach smiled and signed back. The two fell into a quick conversation.

"She says she enjoyed our match," Zach said to Jasper. "And she apologizes for her brother's behavior. He can—"

Zach's brow quirked up and signed something to Emilia. She smirked, and pushed her nose up with her finger, making a snorting noise. Zach burst into laughter, and then Emilia followed.

"She says he can act like an ill-mannered boar sometimes," Zach managed out.

Jasper laughed as well, and Leon crossed his arms, glaring at his sister.

Zach and Emilia signed back and forth a few more times before Emilia smirked, waved goodbye, and grabbed her brother by the front of his shirt, dragging him off with her. He complained to her the whole time.

"She hopes we do well against Fiery Toucans so we can have a rematch," Zach said. "Even though we didn't beat them, we certainly impressed her. And I told her to take a well-earned rest and prepare for us to end their streak next time."

Jasper swung his arm around Zach's shoulder. "If we survive Shira's wrath."

Zach's brow knitted. "I don't think she'll be angry. We did our best. Are you projecting your own frustration?"

Jasper's lips thinned. "Yeah, I suppose I am. I can't shake the idea we should have done bettah. We knew what we were up against, and we practiced all those combos to give us a bettah shot."

Zach slipped his arm around Jasper's waist. "And it did help us. I know it might not feel like it, but we did a hell of a lot better this time around than the other day. They trashed us before. We at least lasted a while each game this time. And we did amazing that last round. We almost had them. We can learn from this, and come back and win."

Jasper inhaled a deep breath, exhaled, and then smiled. He was right. They had done better, even if the result wasn't what they'd hoped for. They were still going to the semi-finals, and the two of them could really make their mark there.

Leaving the game competition room, Jasper expected to be greeted by their friends with pity or… well, something. Instead, most were sitting and pretending to look at their phones while covertly looking somewhere else. Narissa, Mercedes, and Ajax were the only ones to openly watch whatever had their friends' attention. And Shira was no longer with them. Serenity sat next to Mercedes, still immersed in the digital world, but with a glum droop to her body, and Snake sat at her feet. *Where is Shira?*

Jasper sidled up next to Ajax, where he leaned against the wall nearest Jasper and Zach. "What's going on?"

"Stacey just pulled Shira aside," Ajax said. "Her approach was… concerning. She's definitely up to something."

Jasper and Zach snapped their attention to where the others focused. The two women stood by the entrance of the common room. Shira's arms were crossed over her chest and she glared at Stacey. She'd gotten less and less tolerant of the woman during this event, and Jasper couldn't really blame her. His patience with his manager was hanging on by a thread—a severely frayed thread at that.

Stacey had a glare of her own for Shira as she spoke. Whatever she said made Shira scoff, but then pause when Stacey held up a tablet. Shira's hostility immediately changed to confusion and apprehension. She then reached for the device.

Jasper's gut twisted. Something wasn't right. He didn't know how he knew, but his gut said he needed to get over there—now.

Stacey spoke again to Shira, her lips curling with contempt. Shira didn't look at her. She stared at whatever was on the tablet, her eyes wide in shock.

Shira suddenly shoved the device at Stacey while the woman was in the middle of saying something and ran out of the room. Jasper's blood ran cold. That wasn't like Shira at all. And the smug look on Stacey's face didn't ease his nerves in the slightest.

Before he realized what his feet were doing, Jasper launched himself toward Stacey, and Shira's disappearing form. His pulse pounded in his ears.

Stacey turned toward his approach, the smug look not leaving her face.

"What the hell is going on?" Jasper's mouth shot off before he could think.

"I was just making sure a situation was handled," Stacey said.

"What situation?" Zach asked.

"That woman won't be using lies and deceit on either of you anymore."

Jasper's fists clenched, and his pulse sped up. "What the hell are you talking about?"

Stacey shook her head. "I took care of it. There's no need to rile you up any further and—"

"What the fuck did you do, Stacey?" Jasper shouted.

Zach snatched the tablet from her hand and looked at the screen. "What the fuck is this?"

Jasper snapped his attention to the device, and everything stopped around him. Displayed on the screen were two photos—one of mid-twenties Jasper holding a tan, brunette woman with hazel eyes. The other photo was of the same woman posing with an early-twenties Shira.

Stacey let out a controlled breath. "I didn't want to upset you with those before your next match. I needed you to focus."

Numbness fell over Jasper as realization set in. *She did not show Shira this…* "What the fuck, Stacey! What the hell is wrong with you?"

The woman stepped back, startled by his rage. "I was just acting in your best interest. I couldn't allow her to continue to deceive you after what she'd done."

Jasper saw red as his rage took over. He grabbed the tablet and chucked it at her. "We already knew, you fucking bitch!"

Stacey gasped and stumbled back, her eyes wide in fright. "But—"

"How fucking dare you drag up six years of fucking trauma and throw that at our girlfriend? After everything we've fucking been through, what goddamned right do you think you have?"

"G—girlfriend?"

Jasper bared his teeth. "Get out of my fucking sight and never come near my family again!"

Jasper sprinted out of the common room in the direction Shira had disappeared. He was vaguely aware of Zach calling out to Narissa to watch Serenity for them while they handled this emergency.

"She went to the hotel room," Alistair informed Jasper. "She's on the elevator going up now."

Jasper angled for the elevators. He shoved past anyone who got in his way, not caring how rude it was.

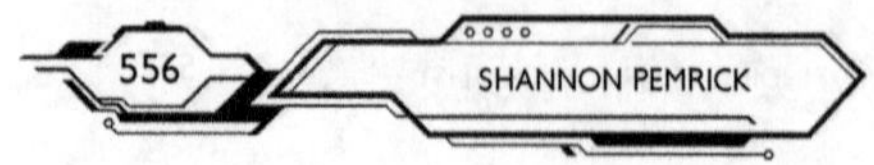

He needed to get to Shira. This was not how this was supposed to go. *Damn you, Stacey!*

He made it to the elevator and pressed the call button. His heart hammered in his chest and Jasper found it difficult to stand still and wait the painstaking seconds for an elevator to arrive.

A warm hand wrapped around his, snapping Jasper out of his single-minded focus. Zach gazed at him, his brows drawn together. It was then, Jasper realized, he'd told Stacey they'd both known the truth, when in reality, as of yesterday, only Jasper knew.

"I'll explain when we get up there, I promise," he said.

Zach squeezed his hand. "Shira first, then everything else."

CHAPTER 27

Tears streamed down Shira's face. Her back pressed against the king-size bed, where she curled up on the floor. Pain squeezed and choked her lungs. This wasn't real. None of this was real. It was a nightmare that felt like reality.

Shira's hands clenched the audio chip. It was the only piece of reality that kept her from believing that lie. She'd packed Tanya's envelope as the final trial for herself. If she could go through these last two days in this hotel room, she could face the last message her friend had left her.

But nothing could have prepared her for the reality that waited her. *What have I done?*

Shira flinched when the hotel room door flew open. Her breathing labored, and her body shook. She couldn't face them. She couldn't watch everything she'd built up crumble right before her eyes.

"Shira?"

She instinctively looked up at Jasper's calm voice. He and Zach stood in the bedroom's threshold, watching her. There was no rage, no accusation, no hatred. But how could there not be?

Shira's lower lip quivered and her tears refused to cease streaking down her cheeks. "I'm sorry. I'm sorry. I… I didn't know…"

She curled up into herself, hiding her face—her shame. How was she supposed to know Tanya and Sara had been the same person when she had run so hard from her past?

Jasper didn't have any photos of Sara on social media. She always assumed in his grief he'd deleted them all. He'd never shown her any photos of her in the time Shira knew him. And she'd never asked.

And he'd lost her because of Shira. Serenity lost her mother because of her. *Tanya—Sara—died because of me.* "I'm sorry…"

Even after Shira had heard how similar Tanya and Sara were, it was too coincidental. It wasn't possible…

Shira clicked the button on the audio chip. There was a slight pause, and then a struggling, light alto voice spoke.

"Shira, I don't have much time… to tell you everything, so I will tell you what I… can. I don't know when you'll listen to this. I know you will blame yourself for what is about to happen to me, even though you shouldn't. Maybe you'll never listen… to this, but I hope… one day you will heal enough to hear my last words to you."

There was a pause.

"My name isn't… Tanya Miller. It's Sara Quinn. Tan-ya is my middle name… and I stole Miller from my husband's best friend, Zach. I figured he wouldn't mind. My husband is… Jasper, and our daughter is Serenity."

Sara coughed.

"I wanted you to meet them. I know you would have loved them almost as much as I do. I wish now I had, so you knew who to look for after listening to this. They… they are going to need you when… I'm gone. And I pray this message doesn't find you after it's too late for you to do that."

A pause.

"I wish it didn't have to be this way. I wish I could have… told you all this in person. But I know I won't make it until after your surgery ends. I'm sorry for the grief I will cause you, Shira. But know, I don't regret… a moment of this. I am so happy, and blessed to have had you in my life as my friend, as brief of a time this was. Please, do not allow my loss to consume you. Please, don't blame yourself. Please live to the fullest, as you always have. And if this message isn't too late, please love my family as I once had. Goodbye, Shira."

The audio chip slipped from Shira's hands and clattered to the floor. A grief-stricken sob shook her body. Hearing Sara's message before had been painful. Hearing it again gutted Shira. *I don't deserve such a beautiful, kind message…*

Strong hands gripped her shoulders. "Shira. Shira, please look at me."

She didn't want to. She couldn't. Not after—

"Shira, I don't blame you."

Her heart stopped. *He doesn't…* Shira lifted her face, her gaze meeting Jasper's. He'd crouched down in front of her, his posture soft and calm instead of hard and intimidating. Zach kneeled next to her, watching with concerned eyes.

"But… it was my—"

Jasper shook his head. "It wasn't your fault, Shira. Sara wanted to go to the convention. She would have been there, with or without you, because of our tournament."

Jasper took her cybernetic hand in his and pressed her palm against his cheek. His warmth seeped into her artificial nerves. He closed his eyes and leaned into the touch. A lone tear streaked down his exposed cheek.

"You were the reason she wasn't alone when it happened. You allowed me to… say goodbye."

Jasper swallowed and controlled his breathing. "I know you didn't know. That audio chip you caught me listening to yestahday was also from her. I found it the othah day. She explained everything to me. I knew, because you nevah brought it up, it meantcha didn't listen to the message she left you."

Jasper opened his eyes and held Shira's gaze. "I wanted to bring this up aftah the convention. I knew this would be difficult on you, and I didn't want to stress ya out. I hate Stacey pulled this. I wasn't even able to bring this up to Zach before she did."

Shira's chest ached. He knew, and still he said he didn't blame her? "But, she died because of—"

Jasper cupped her face. "Because her body rejected the cybahnetics."

Shira's gut clenched. "Re—rejected?"

He nodded. "It's not common, but it can happen. Narissa did everything she could to find a workaround, but…"

Jasper squeezed his eyes shut and took a controlling

breath. He pressed his lips against Shira's forehead and then pulled her into his hard body. "I'm so happy that didn't happen to you. I can't bear the thought of not having you here, with us."

Zach leaned against Shira, wrapping an arm around her waist and resting his forehead on her shoulder. He said nothing, and yet his silence was just as powerful as Jasper's words.

Jasper released his tight hold on Shira, and tilted her face toward him. "I'll *nevah* blame ya for what happened that day. I love you, Shira. As much as I loved Sara. And as much as I love Zach. I won't letcha go for nothing."

He dipped his head and captured her lips with his. They were soft, yet demanding and possessive. Shira's heart swelled in her chest. She couldn't place her emotions, but felt his with every touch.

When he finally allowed her to come up for air, Zach tucked a finger under her chin and turned her attention to him. "*We* love you, and will not let you go."

He kissed her with the same intensity. Shira fisted their shirts, desperate to cling to them. A tear streaked down her cheek. Their love was both too much and not enough. She needed them as much as she needed air to breathe. And the very thought of losing them killed her.

Her pulse thrummed in her veins. "I love you both. I can't say that I'll ever feel like I'm enough for either of you, but neither of you are allowed to go anywhere."

She kissed Zach again, harder, more desperately. Then she turned and kissed Jasper. She took everything they offered, desperate to burn the memory of their taste and touch into her memory, just in case these two came to their senses.

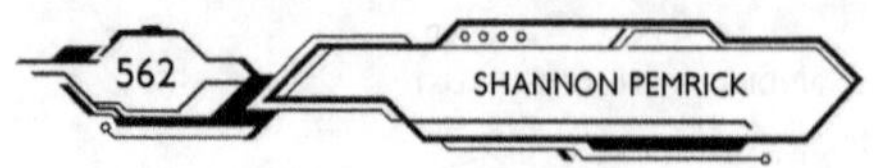

They pulled her between them, devouring everything she was—everything she gave.

She fell into their love, losing all sense of herself, where she was, and which way was up and down. Her clothes disappeared, and she was vaguely aware of theirs going missing, too, but she was too lost to care, to think and process.

Shira removed Jasper's hand from her chest and dragged it up to her neck. She dug his fingers into her artificial skin, hiding her cybernetics. Jasper responded by ripping at the material.

Her heart slammed against her ribcage, and yet she didn't want to stop. She didn't fear what they'd see. No, instead, she guided Zach to do the same at her side, exposing all she was to them.

No more walls.

No more rules.

With every mingled breath, every caressing touch, a piece of her broken self fused to another. She'd never be without cracks or small holes, but her fractures were now gilded in love and that left her more beautiful than before.

Sandwiched between them, they entered her, filled her with all they were, and gave her the pleasure she deserved. Shira moaned and begged, desperate to have more of them. She rocked between them, ardent desire flooding through her until she thought she'd burst at the seams.

She cried out, losing herself in love without pain.

When she came down, she lay in a panting, tangled heap with her two men on the bed. They held her as close as they could without smothering her. She couldn't have cared less if they did. She felt lighter and happier than she'd ever remembered herself ever feeling. Cocooned in their protective, healing love, the three of them lay there, listening to their breathing and the rhythm of their beating hearts.

"Thank you for sending those texts," Jasper murmured. "The ones you sent to Sara's phone aftah the accident. She didn't have you in there by your name, but I remembah them."

Shira traced his memorial tattoo. "You read them?"

"Every single one of them," he said. "I could tell it was your way of coping. They brought me a little comfort, knowing someone else was remembering her. It was too painful to text you back, and the day you said your final goodbye to her was even more difficult."

Shira frowned. "I'm sorry. Had I known someone was actually reading them, I would have been more mindful."

Jasper shook his head and pulled her closer. "You've got nothing to apologize for. In a way, that final goodbye helped me take the needed steps to let go myself."

His thumb stroked her shoulder. "The only thing I haven't been able to face is spreading her ashes."

Zach rested his hand on top of Jasper's. "We can do it together. All of us."

Shira's chest tightened, and tears threatened to break through. To be included in such a special moment… She appreciated the inclusion to have one final goodbye.

"What are the odds of us finding you again?" Zach mumbled, more to himself by the sounds of it.

Shira grunted. "That's a little too smart for me to math out. Astronomically not in our favor?"

"More like in our favor since it happened," Jasper said.

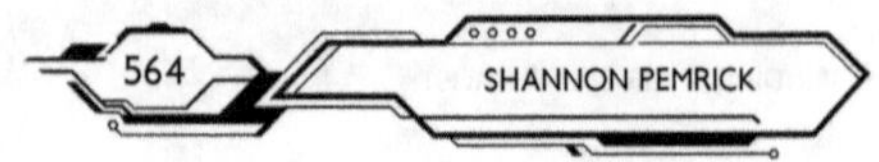

He pulled her tighter into his hard body. "And I'm so glad someone gave the three of us a second chance."

Shira chuckled quietly. "Probably Tanya—Sara. I doubt she was happy we didn't listen to her last wishes right off."

The guys rumbled with laughter.

"I can agree with that. No mattuh where she is right now, bringing us togethah through a damned game would be exactly something Sara would do," Jasper said.

"Jasper, Zach," Alistair said from the hotel infrastructure. "I found the source of those photographs."

Jasper propped himself up on one arm. "Where?"

"It appears Sara had a social media account dedicated to her modeling persona."

Jasper's eyebrows pulled together. "A secret account? You didn't even know about it?"

"We only got Alistair this year," Zach said.

Jasper pinched his nose. "Right."

Shira sat up and looked around. "Where is my phone? I know the exact account he's talking about."

Zach reached over the edge of the bed and retrieved her phone. Shira took it from him and opened her apps. Searching for Tanya Miller, Shira pulled up her friend's profile. "Here it is. And here's the photo of her and me."

That specific photo had been one of the newer ones on the account before the event of the accident.

"But where is the other one of me and her?" Jasper asked.

"Good question…" Shira scrolled through the photos. "I wasn't even aware she'd put it on here. Otherwise, I would have recognized you a long time ago."

Her phone scrolled on its own, and Orion piped in. "It appears the photo was the first ever she uploaded."

The three of them watched the wall of photos continue to scroll.

"Damn, she has a shit-ton of photos on here," Jasper said.

"Goes to show how desperate Stacey was," Shira muttered. "Annoying bitch went through all of these just to find one photo to get under my skin."

Jasper stroked her arm. "Don't worry about her. You won't have to deal with her ever again."

Shira's eyebrow spiked. "Um, have you forgotten she's your manager?"

Jasper and Zach exchanged a look. "Not for long, she isn't."

What was that supposed to mean? "What did you two do?"

"We've had something cooking for a little bit," Zach said. "Let's just say, I'm pretty sure her behavior today has made that plan even easier to enact."

"Ajax has called in the lawyer," Alistair said. "He should arrive shortly."

Shira blew out a breath. "Damn. I wanted to call a lawyer."

"Your fists aren't lawyers," Zach said.

Shira laughed. "Says who? But seriously, I have a fantastic lawyer who'd jump to help you two if I asked."

"We'll keep that in mind if Ajax fails us," Jasper said.

Shira's phone ceased scrolling. Just as Orion said, at the end of the list was the first photo Sara had ever uploaded on this account, the photo of her and Jasper. Shira had to remind herself to breathe.

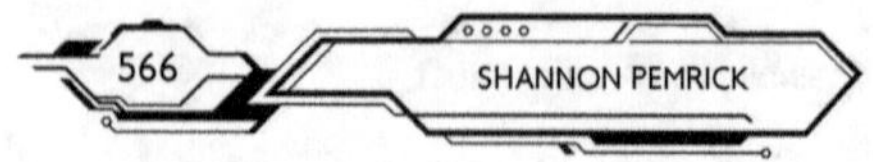

"Well, that sells it," Jasper said. "Stacey is a stalkerish, conniving bitch, and I'm going to be even happiah to watch her be thrown to the curb."

"If you wish to be present for that, I suggest you make your way downstairs and find Ajax," Alistair said. "The lawyer is here, as are Tri-com's company suits."

Zach's brow rose. "Wow. That's faster than I expected."

"I would hazard to guess it was the scene Jasper caused in public in front of a few reporters that forced their hand," Alistair said.

Jasper slid off the bed and dressed himself. Zach also left, but came back with a towel to clean Shira, before also dressing.

When he and Zach were presentable, Jasper offered his hand to Shira. "Ready for the show?"

Shira smiled. "I'll meet you down there. I need to freshen up." Her gaze dropped to her naked body. "And get clothes on."

Jasper smirked. "If we were coming right back here, I'd ask you just to wait for us like that."

Shira rolled her eyes. She slid out of the bed and shooed them. "Go on. You have a manager to dump."

They laughed, kissed her on the cheek at the same time, and left. Heat prickled her cheeks, and Shira rubbed her face. She'd done all manner of hot and dirty things with those two men, and yet it was their smaller gestures that got her out of sorts.

I don't deserve them. But she was selfish, and wasn't going to let them go at this point. She loved them with everything she was, and that was all there was to it.

Shira dressed again before slipping into the bathroom. She didn't look at herself in the mirror right away, needing a moment to prepare. When she finally did, she didn't laugh at the disheveled mess that gazed back at her.

Heat bloomed in her chest. A smile formed on her lips as pride in herself seeped into her bones. She stood in front of a mirror, with all her external cybernetics exposed. There were tiny flecks of artificial skin still attached to her from where it'd torn, but that didn't matter compared to what she'd accomplished.

Shira had exposed herself to her two guys. They'd treated her no differently than when she'd hidden behind the façade. They were true to their word.

She felt strong.

She felt powerful.

And most of all, for the first time in a long time, she felt beautiful.

And fuck you, rules.

"You can take on the world, Shira," she said to her reflection.

Sara believed in her. Jasmine believed in her. The guys, her friends, her family, they all believed in her. It was now time Shira believed in herself.

Shira leaned on the counter, her mind backtracking to Jasmine. The things that girl said to her today… Shira couldn't shake it. There were so many people out there who needed to see themselves portrayed in the media. They needed to see they were worthwhile.

Shira grabbed her phone and pulled up the modeling contract Narissa had been pestering her about for months. "I can't leave this to the next generation to fight this mess."

"Shira, are you considering Narissa's proposal?" Orion asked.

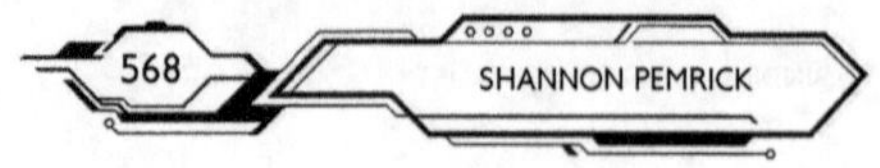

Shira stared at her phone. "Not considering. Accepting."

"This is excellent news! Do you want me to find a printer?"

Shira shook her head. "No, I'm fine with a digital signature. I need a folder, though. To conceal the tablet and make it look at least a little official when I approach her."

"I will have one ordered and delivered. When do you wish to approach her?"

Shira rubbed her face. "Tomorrow. Today has been too much for me. Plus, I also need you to track down Izzy's info if you can. It's a long shot, but maybe I can talk to her about doing this as well."

"I'd be happy to perform that task."

Shira picked off the remnants of her artificial skin and then grabbed her makeup remover. She cleaned her face and neck to give herself a fresh canvas to work with and then reapplied her makeup. She took her time, making sure to keep her now exposed cybernetics in mind as she contoured.

She let out a deep, calming breath when she finished. *That wasn't so bad.* It'd get easier with each new day.

"Are you ready to show the world your middle finger?" Orion asked.

Shira snickered. "Sure am."

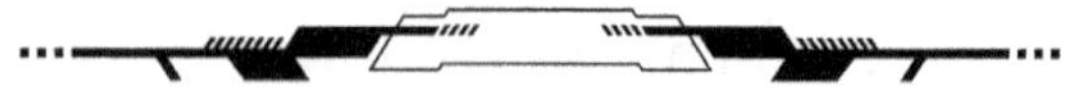

Stepping out of the elevator, Shira swung a left and slipped through the crowd, searching for the room Jasper, Zach, and Ajax were supposedly in with the lawyer.

She spotted her friends before noticing the closed door of the meeting room.

Serenity sat with Narissa and Mercedes on a bench, with several of their other friends surrounding them. She was surprised so many were there. She expected at least Rei, Emi, Donovan, and Ronan to have disappeared. They'd been discussing catching a few things today after the quarterfinal match. *They must have stuck around due to all the drama.* She'd have to make it up to them somehow.

Serenity gasped when she spotted Shira and launched off her seat. When she came in range, Shira knelt and opened her arms to receive the girl. Serenity threw her arms around Shira's neck.

"Rissa said the mean lady made you mad," Serenity murmured into her hair. "Are you feeling bettah?"

Shira rubbed her back. "Yes. I've calmed down now."

"Did Daddy and Zach help?"

Shira smiled despite herself. "They sure did."

She caught her friends snickering, and she shot a dirty look at them.

Serenity pulled away and cocked her head when she noticed the now exposed cybernetics along Shira's neck and jaw. She gently poked the acrylic surface that was Shira's neck. The artificial nerves registered as they always did, however they were more intense now that the false skin wasn't there.

A big grin spread over her face. "You look wicked badass, Momma."

Shira smirked, not caring the girl said a word she shouldn't. "Not afraid of me, Starship?"

The girl's eyes went wide. "Nevah!"

Shira kissed the girl on the forehead and then stood. Narissa walked over to her, took one look at Shira, and then threw her arms around her. "I'm so proud."

"It wasn't easy, but I got to this point eventually," Shira said.

Mercedes hugged her next. And then Ronan and Donovan heckled her, Ronan more than his brother. Shira dished it back, finding it easy to joke about her prosthetics with her friends, especially those who had them as well. It was strange for her to think that just a few months ago, none of this would have been possible for her. *I've come a long way.*

Heads turned when a tan woman with long raven hair approached. Her bright blue eyes flicked around, landing on Narissa.

"Hey, Allyson," Narissa said.

"Hey, is my baby brother still in there?"

Narissa nodded. "I don't know when they'll be done. From the look on your face, I gather things aren't looking good with the event organizers."

"Actually, it's not bad. It's been decided that if this legal meeting wasn't done by now, the semi-finals will be moved to tomorrow morning. The organizers are smart enough not to stick their fingers into a legal issue, and Fiery Toucans were more than agreeable to the schedule change. They're moving around other PvP matches to accommodate."

Narissa nodded. "It'll be a bit of a rough day for the guys if they win."

"They can handle it," Shira said.

Narissa gave her a skeptical look. "They didn't tell you about the packed schedule they already had with a signing event tomorrow morning and the finals if they made it, did they?"

Shira shrugged. "No, but that's their problem they signed up for."

Takashi chuckled. "Brutal. No remorse at all."

Narissa shook her head. "You're seeing this as punishment, aren't you?"

Shira winked. "I can't always be nice to them."

Her friends laughed.

"Can you relay this information to my brother?" Allyson asked Narissa. "I need to get back to confirm the postponement."

Narissa agreed, and Allyson ran off. It was another twenty minutes before the door opened and Ajax strolled out. Jasper and Zach followed and a well-dressed, stout man with chestnut hair and glasses exited after. Then, several more people in suits, as well as Stacey.

Shira's eyes narrowed, and she imagined she could shoot flaming daggers from them right at Stacey. The infuriating woman looked her way and pivoted her face, angling away as she hurried her steps to flee from the hostile onlookers.

Most of the people in suits left with her, but one man stayed. He scanned the gathered group, as if looking for something.

Before anyone could speak, Shira spotted a slight issue about Jasper that needed to be fixed. She strode up to him and reached for his pants without breaking eye contact. Jasper went from grinning like mad at her to casting her a concerned look.

Shira pinched the fabric of his pants in the crotch

and pulled up his zipper. "I can't believe you went into a room full of lawyers with your fly open."

Jasper blinked, mouth hanging open, and raucous laughter boomed around them. "You could have just said something. Discreetly."

Shira stepped back and shrugged, unapologetic. It was more fun embarrassing him.

Ajax shook his head and then addressed Narissa by holding up his phone. "With that addressed, no need to relay my sister's message. Her AI sent me one."

Narissa rolled her eyes. "Naturally. But it's good for the rest of us to know as well, so we can all plan accordingly."

"Speaking of planning," Shira said. "What the hell took you all so long? Were you having tea and biscuits?"

A roar of laughter erupted around her, including the stout man Shira was assuming was Ajax's lawyer, given how he stood with the three men, unlike Mystery Suit Guy.

"No, we were discussing the termination of our contract," Zach said.

Dead silence.

Shira blinked. "What?"

Jasper grinned. "You heard him."

What the fuck? She should be happy. They were out from under that awful company. But there was a problem. "I'm glad you're not with that"—she covered Serenity's ears—"shitbag company anymore, but you two need a company sponsor."

"We never said we didn't have one."

A shit-eating grin appeared on Ajax's face. "GameTech has officially taken Smash and Stab as the company's first sponsored PvP team."

Cheers erupted all around them. Shira was both happy and shocked. "This is what the two of you were planning?"

Jasper smirked. "Yup. We've been working on this for a few days now. Stacey's stunt just made it easier to execute."

Shira squinted. She didn't like the way he worded that. "That sounds like there's a catch. What's the catch?"

The mystery suit guy cleared his throat.

"Oh, right, you're here," Shira said. "Who are you?"

"My name is Ronnie. I work for the… shitbag company you so fondly insulted."

Shira crossed her arms and leaned her weight to one side. She wouldn't apologize.

"An agreement has been reached," the man said after a long, awkward pause. "Because of the egregious actions of Stacey Jane, her employment will be terminated effective immediately. We have also agreed to terminate our employment contract with Jasper Quinn and Zachariah Miller in exchange for their silence on these legal matters."

"And the fact that your contract was all kinds of illegal," Zach muttered.

Ronnie flinched, making Shira grin. Ajax's lawyer must have looked the document over and noticed that glaring error.

"So, only you two have to be silent?" Mercedes asked.

Jasper smirked. "We're the only employed members of Smash and Stab."

Shira wanted to laugh. Stacey had thrown out their request to offer Shira a coaching position on their team. And that meant only one thing.

Sketchy-suit Ronnie turned to Shira. "You're Shira Schneider, correct?"

"The one and only."

He held out a hand. "On behalf of Tri-com, I would like to—"

Shira held up a finger, silencing him, and she turned to Serenity. She hovered her hands over her ears. "Earmuffs, Starship."

Serenity giggled and covered her ears.

Shira whipped back to Ronnie and laid into him. "Don't. You can take that half-assed PR apology bullshit and shove it right up your tight fucking asshole. You even fucking try, and you'll be begging Narissa for a new one after I shove my mechanical foot right up it."

Ronnie's eyes bugged out, and her friends laughed. Her response would be no surprise to any of them. She was dubbed the "attack dog" for a reason. And Shira had found even more inner strength today, bolstering her.

"You can't buy my silence. Not after the bullshit that bitch pulled and all the shit your company has done over the years. So, I suggest you get your lawyers prepared for the shark that I'll bring to your door."

The man sucked in a tight breath through his nose and squared his shoulders, as if he had the backbone to stand up to her. "And what lawyer should I be expecting legal documents from?"

"Sophia Scarlett."

The man paled. "You're bluffing."

Shira smirked. "Am I?"

Ronnie sucked another deep breath through his nose and straightened his jacket. "Well, we'll expect her contact if you wish to proceed."

The man stalked off. Laughter erupted around Shira. Shira held her head high. *That felt good.*

"She-ra, can I take my earmuffs off?" Serenity asked.

Shira smiled and made the motion for her to remove her hands. "Yes, you can."

Serenity's hands dropped, and she gazed up at Shira. "How many bad words did you say? It sounded like you were yelling a lot at that man."

"I said quite a few," Shira admitted. "Ones you won't be allowed to repeat."

Serenity's nose scrunched. "Not fair."

"Are you actually going to do something against Stacey or Tri-com?" Ajax asked.

Shira shrugged. "I haven't decided yet. Stacey was fired for her behavior, and these guys aren't with that insane company anymore, so that's really good enough for me to let the rest go and not waste any more time and energy on them. It was just fun psyching that guy up in case I do decide to sick Sophia on them."

Ajax's lawyer sucked in a breath. "So, you weren't bluffing. That should be interesting if you pursue any legal action against them."

Jasper's brow rose. "Is this Sophia person really that big of a deal?"

The lawyer chuckled. "There are excellent lawyers, like myself, and then there are cutthroat lawyers, like Sophia Scarlett. I wouldn't want to meet her in a courtroom. I tip my hat to you, Miss Schneider, if you do pursue legal action. I will tell you, I've advised my clients of the rules of their silence, so I would counsel you to not try to get any confidential information out of them."

He smirked. "However, I can't stop them from sharing

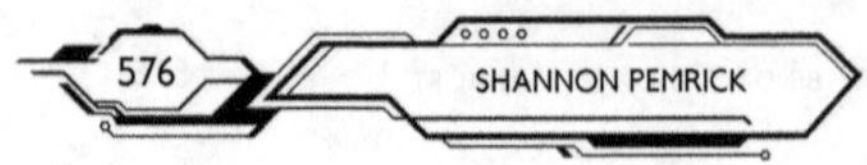

non-confidential documents or information that were not specific to our agreement met in that meeting."

Shira's eyebrow quirked. What was he getting at? She theoretically could only hit a legal battle against Stacey for what she'd done. Maybe Tri-com as a whole because they had her employed and the guys' complaints against her had gone ignored, resulting in the situation earlier.

Wait, Zach mentioned an illegal contract. Shira grinned. That wasn't something she could do anything about, legally, but socially was another matter. She'd have to "convince" her guys to tell her more about the non-confidential parts of their previous contract.

Ajax's lawyer had a few more words with Ajax, Jasper, and Zach before heading off. He had a bit of work to do to close out this issue on their end. That left them all to figure out what they were going to do for the rest of the day.

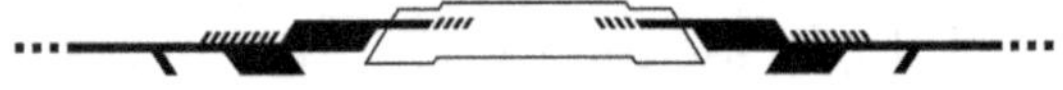

Zach finished the top button of his shirt and then straightened his sleeves, checking the cuffs. His stomach twisted, a mix of excitement and nervousness. This was their first ever dinner date with Shira. Not a date-date, since Serenity would be with them this time, but it still counted as a date of some sort.

And it shouldn't make him feel this way after everything he and Jasper had done with her, and the other family outings they'd gone on, but this dinner was different.

He and Jasper never splurged this much on a dinner. But they wanted it to be special. They wanted Shira to see how much the two of them cared, and that they were willing to go a little extra for her, even if she would have been just as happy to go to some low-scale, family-friendly eatery. *Hopefully Serenity will eat something here.*

They'd tried to pick a place that served food she'd be more likely to enjoy, but she was just a kid. He and Jasper had a contingency plan in case she decided the options weren't for her.

Jasper fussed with his tie, failing to complete a simple knot.

Zach snickered. "Need help?"

Jasper hung his head in shame. "Yes, please. You'd think I'd be able to get it right one of these days."

While his fiancé moped, Zach made quick work of the decorative cloth. He then secured his own before tucking it under his collar, all the while taking in the sight of Jasper in a suit. *He really needs to wear that more often.*

Jasper looked toward their bedroom. The door remained shut tight, and the only sounds coming from the room were muffled. Snake laid by the door, ears pricked and head turning from side to side with every sound that came from under the door.

Shira and Serenity had kicked them out, forcing Jasper and Zach to dress in the living room. Well, they could have dressed in Serenity's room, but they were confident they'd be done getting ready long before their favorite ladies were.

And the assumption wasn't wrong. Jasper and Zach lounged in the common area for twenty minutes before Snake rose into a sitting position and the bedroom door swung open. Serenity jumped out, the asymmetrical skirts of her sky blue, a-line scoop neck dress swished around her ankles. Her hair had been pulled into a side ponytail and curled into large ringlets, and she also had a light brushing of eyeshadow.

Their daughter posed dramatically. "I'm ready!"

Zach smiled. She was too cute for her own good.

"And so am I," Shira said, sashaying out of the room.

Zach's mouth fell open. His eyes trailed down her body, taking in how the red bodycon dress with an asymmetrical hem hugged her curves. The tight, off-the-shoulder sleeves and sweetheart neckline accentuated her breasts, and her black heels emphasized the shape of her legs. Large hoop earrings and a light dusting of makeup completed her stunning visage.

Zach was all too aware of how instantly hard he was. He'd imagined so many times how sexy she'd look in this dress, but holy fuck had his mind not done her justice. And seeing her so confidently show off every surface cybernetic she had didn't hurt her one bit.

Shira's red lips curved into a dangerously tempting smile. "You two are drooling."

Zach snapped his mouth shut. Jasper actually checked for drool, making Shira laugh. The sound sent a flutter through Zach's stomach.

Jasper ran his hand through his hair. "You look… stunning."

"Even better than we imagined," Zach added.

Shira twirled a lock of her beautiful hair. Her lower lip caught in her teeth while she looked away, a slight flush to her cheeks. "Thank you. Not too much?"

"Definitely not," they both said in unison.

She returned her gaze to them, the red on her face deepening. Zach's pulse skipped. Getting through dinner would be the most difficult thing he'd done this week.

"You two clean up nice," Shira said as she gave them a long appraising assessment.

Zach tugged on his sleeve while Jasper confidently pulled back his shoulders. "We had to attempt to compete with you."

Shira rolled her eyes.

"What about me?" Serenity asked. She still stood by Shira, her hands clasped behind her back and looking even more adorable.

"You"—Jasper quickly closed the distance and pulled her into a hug, kissing their daughter on the cheek— "look wicked beautiful."

Serenity giggled. "Thanks, Daddy."

She then glanced Zach's way. He smiled. "You look a little older. You're growing up fast on us."

Serenity grinned. "That's cause I'm gonna be seven tomorrow."

Zach released a quiet breath. That she was. *Where did the time go?* It didn't feel that long ago he'd driven up to Boston to visit after Sara had come home from the hospital with Serenity.

"We ready to head out?" Shira asked.

Jasper snatched the car keys from the counter. "We just have to pull up the cah."

Orion called the car while Shira dressed Snake in his service vest. She also had a bow tie for him for the formal occasion, which Serenity gushed over. Zach had to admit, as a little ridiculous as it was, it was a snazzy look for her faithful companion.

They made their way to the elevators.

"Where we goin', Daddy?" Serenity asked.

Jasper pressed the call button. "Pesce Luna. It's an Italian restaurant."

Serenity squinted. "So… pasta?"

Zach bent down and kissed her perfect head. "All kinds of pastas."

Serenity cheered. Hopefully, this was a sign that she would like something on the menu.

Shira's car waited out front for them. It certainly turned heads, as did Shira. Maybe he and Jasper did, too, but Zach would be lying if he noticed. He had enough eye candy between Shira and Jasper to keep his attention occupied all night.

Jasper opened the driver's door for Shira while Zach had Snake jump into the back and then situated Serenity in her booster. Her dress made it a little annoying, but they managed.

The drive to the restaurant took a little longer than it should have, thanks to traffic, but they'd left early in case that happened. Losing their reservation would not be ideal after all the trouble they went through securing it.

Their car pulled up, and they climbed out. The host greeted them, checked their reservation, and had them wait for their table to be ready. They didn't have to wait long, and the host showed them to their table.

The night went by in a delightful blur. The drink choices and food were amazing; even Serenity had no trouble at all eating her dish, and the company was even better. Conversation flowed as easily as it always did, and he and Jasper openly flirted with Shira. They already had her, but it warmed things up for when they broke the news to Serenity. Plus, Zach enjoyed seeing Shira also flustered in reaction to some of the things they said.

All too soon, dinner ended and they were back in their hotel. Serenity was wired from all the excitement of a fancy dinner and the dessert—mostly the dessert. However, they really wanted her to get ready for bed. Not because it was all that late—it was quite early— but they knew it'd take a while for her to calm down if she didn't focus on something, and Zach and Jasper had other plans with Shira after they revealed to their daughter the new change in their lives.

"I don't wanna go to bed," Serenity complained.

"You don't have to sleep yet, Starship," Jasper said. "Just get ready for bed and settle down. We'll read a little, and then the three of us have something important to tell ya."

Serenity blinked up at her dad. "Whatcha gotta tell me?"

"You have to get ready for bed first."

Their daughter looked between the three adults and then scampered off to her room, calling for Snake to get ready for bed with her.

"I should also change," Shira said, turning for their bedroom.

Jasper reached out and pulled her close to him, sliding his hand down the curve of her hip. "No."

Shira raised an eyebrow at him. "And why not?"

He pressed his lips against her ear and spoke just loud enough for Zach to "overhear." "Because if anyone is gonna strip you out of that dress, it's gonna be us."

Shira turned her head a bit and smirked. "Can I at least take these shoes off?"

Zach stepped up behind her and stroked the back of her shoulder with his finger. "Those stay on longer."

Shira sucked in a sharp inhale. And then the three of them were cooled down when Serenity called out, "She-ra, how do I get this makeup off?"

"I'll be right there, sweetie." Shira slipped away and headed for their room.

"Don't change," Jasper reminded her as he removed his suit jacket.

"Says the guy disrobing," Shira muttered.

"Just the jacket." Jasper draped the jacket over a chair. "And my shoes."

Shira rolled her eyes and disappeared. Jasper removed his shoes, as did Zach. He was in the midst of pulling off his jacket when Shira breezed through the common area to Serenity's room. Zach's eyes followed the sway of her hips, and he appreciated her coordination in those heels. Jasper stood next to him and let out a slow breath as he rolled up the sleeve of his dress shirt.

Zach chewed his bottom lip, which didn't go unnoticed by Jasper, who smirked. Getting past this talk with Serenity, with the two people he loved the most being major distractions, was not going to be easy for him.

Shira poked her head out of Serenity's room. "She's ready for bed."

Zach's eyebrows rose high on his forehead. *That fast?*

Jasper also didn't hide his shock. "Really? Serenity is nevah ready that quick for bed."

Shira winked and pulled back into the room without revealing her secret.

"We have to negotiate that info from her," Jasper mumbled before heading into the room. Zach followed.

Serenity sat in her giant hotel bed with Snake sprawled out with her. Shira sat on the edge of the bed, tucking Serenity in under her covers.

Zach sat down next to Shira, sliding his hand along her thigh. She gave him a playful, warning look.

Jasper grabbed their current read off the nightstand, one of the Magic Treehouse books they'd gotten Serenity earlier this week, and he sat down on the bed next to their daughter. However, he didn't start reading to her like he normally would.

Serenity gazed up at them with slow, blinking eyes. "You wanna tell me something?"

"We do," Jasper said. "But first, I have a question. What do you want the most for your birthday?"

"Um…" Serenity played with her fingers, as if reluctant to give an answer. "If I tell ya… it might not come true. That's how wishes work."

Zach smiled sympathetically. She was so innocent. But what she didn't know was they already knew her biggest wish. Narissa had mentioned she'd spilled her wish beans while he and Jasper were helping Shira through the issue Stacey had caused. Of course, she didn't have to tell them, as they already knew. Serenity had been quite vocal about it before they'd arrived in California.

Shira rested her hand on Serenity's lap over the blanket. "I promise, you telling us won't ruin your wish."

Serenity gazed at her with uncertain eyes. "Are ya sure?"

"Cross my heart."

Serenity pressed her lips together and thought some more, staring at her twisting fingers. "My wish… is that

She-ra becomes my momma for real, and she lives with us, and we're one big, happy family."

She continued to stare at her hands for a few more moments before hesitantly looking up. Her eyes were wide and fearful, as if she already thought Shira was wrong about her promise.

Zach understood. While Serenity had a rather innocent view of relationships, she was smart enough to understand things were sometimes complicated, and they didn't always work out like we wished.

Luckily for her, everything had worked out, and the three of them could smile at her.

"What if we told you that was happening?" Zach said.

Serenity's eyes widened more, and she looked between the three of them. "Really? No pulling my leg?"

Zach reached over Shira's shoulder and she grasped it with her hand, entwining their fingers, while Jasper reached out and rested his hand over hers on Serenity's lap.

"We're not pulling your leg, Starship," Jasper said. "The three of us love each other something wicked fierce, and we're gonna try to make this work."

Their daughter's eyes sparkled. "She-ra, you're gonna come live with us? And talk like us? And, and, and…"

They laughed as her excitement overwhelmed her, and she squealed.

"We haven't talked about living situations yet," Shira told her honestly. She glanced toward Zach and then Jasper. "I'm not sure when we will, but we're going to work on dating each other first. Moving in is a big step."

She was right, but it was tempting to jump straight into such conversations. They'd known each other so long, the idea of living separately didn't make a whole lot of sense anymore. And then there was the recent development of being GameTech's official team. He and Jasper hadn't quite ironed out all the logistics for that with Ajax. It may not be Shira going to Boston to live with them, and instead them going to live with her. *She does have a house with a yard.*

"And I don't think I'll be talking like you three all that much," Shira continued. "Maybe a few words here and there, but nowhere near you or Jasper."

"I dunno," Jasper mused. "We might be able to get you to talk like a Southie."

Zach laughed. "Yeah, no. No way she'd talk like them."

Shira stared at them with wide eyes. "What do you mean by talk like them? Are you saying you all talk differently?"

The two of them grinned, and she paled.

"Depending on what area of Boston or surrounding burbs and towns, you'll find there's a bit of variety in the way we speak," Zach said.

She pointed at him. "But… but… I thought you were a special case because you left for a while."

Zach chuckled. "I am a special case, but not for that reason. Remember, I came from Vermont. Even as a kid, I retained a lot from that area because of my parents. Those of us from Vermont and New Hampshire have a New England accent. It's not like those from Mass, let alone the Boston area. Though, to be fair, even mine is light compared to others I know."

Shira's head tipped back, and she stared at the ceiling as if she were praying or something, making him and Jasper laugh. Serenity also giggled.

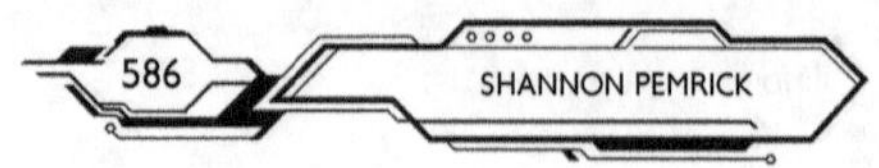

Shira sucked in a long breath and then looked at Serenity again. "Is this all okay, Starship?"

Their daughter nodded enthusiastically. "Best birthday present, evah!"

The adults smiled. There'd probably be amazing ones after this, but it'd be hard to top this particular present.

Jasper cracked open the book and read a chapter to Serenity, allowing her to try and read sections as well. Shira and Zach relaxed and listened, enjoying the family story time.

When the chapter ended, they each kissed Serenity goodnight. She complained she wasn't tired and wanted to stay up, but they reminded her they had to be up early, and the adults had some… "boring" adult things to talk about. Unsurprisingly, Serenity pouted.

They let her sulk, leaving the door cracked in case Snake decided to leave. He wouldn't fit on the bed with Jasper, Shira, and Zach taking up all the room, but he'd probably try again, like last night.

"What is the plan?" Shira asked as they walked into their room. Jasper shut the door behind them. "That big reveal with you becoming Ajax's official team is still hard for me to wrap my head around."

Jasper ran his fingers through his hair. "We haven't finished talking to Ajax about that. We're not one hundred puhcent sure what he's going to require of us. Like we said earlier, Stacey's stunt fast-tracked the contract buyout plan."

Shira sat down on the bed, nodding. "That makes sense."

Zach cocked his head, noticing the way her lower lip

caught in her teeth, and she tapped her fingers on her other hand. "What is it?"

"Well…" She bit her lip and glanced up at them. "I decided to sign on to model for Narissa's secret project."

Zach and Jasper stared at her. Then big grins spread up their faces, and they bent down to kiss her, Jasper's mouth meeting hers first, then Zach. Shira squeaked in surprise.

"This is amazing news," Zach said, warmth blooming in his chest. He could hardly believe she'd even said those words. Just this morning, she'd been afraid to be seen by even them without her artificial skin. Zach couldn't be more proud to see how far she'd come.

"I know this might put a wrench in the plans," Shira said, shrugging awkwardly. "But after really thinking about the opportunity, I couldn't let myself keep saying no. I have to do this."

Jasper shook his head. "Don't worry about it. This is important, on so many levels. I don't want you to evah let go of an amazing opportunity like this because of us. We'll talk about it, so we're all on the same page, but that final decision is always up to you. We'll support you."

Zach agreed.

"And speaking of surprises, Narissa pulled me aside to let me know of one she has for Serenity. I guess that headgear she gets to use for the tournaments isn't the only tech getting an upgrade for kids this year."

Zach's back straightened, and Shira's eyes widened. "They're doing it for the gaming chairs?"

Jasper nodded. "I didn't get the details on this new tech Ajax made, just that Narissa and him want to offah

Serenity the chance to try it out on stage. She thought it'd be a great surprise present for her."

"You said yes, of course, right?" Zach said. He didn't want to think about Serenity's reaction if she found out they'd denied her this opportunity.

Jasper's face scrunched. "Duh. Even if these are prototypes, I trust Narissa and Ajax to put our daughtah's safety first. And I'd get worst father of the year awahd if she found out I said no."

Zach smirked. "Who will go on stage with her?"

Serenity could be a social butterfly, but she could also be shy. And she'd never been in front of a crowd.

Shira sucked in a breath. "Would you two mind if I did it?"

They looked at her, their interest piqued.

"I haven't told Narissa about my decision. I planned to tell her tomorrow," she said. "So, I'm thinking this might be a good way to hint it, while also testing my resolve?"

Jasper smiled. "If you think you're up for it, I don't mind."

Zach had no qualms against it either.

"Good." She grinned and grabbed both their ties, yanking them forward. "Now, I'm tired of talking."

Jasper smirked against her ear. "That desperate for us, babe?"

Her grip on them tightened. "I only get you for a few more days before you two have to go back. I'm getting what I can."

Zach kissed her neck. "We have VR, which arguably handles our insatiable appetites a lot better."

Shira groaned. "Not the same."

Jasper grabbed her by the elbows and tugged her onto her feet. Zach stepped up behind her, reaching for the zipper of her dress. "Then, let's not waste any more time with getting you out of this dress."

Shira tipped her head back. "Shoes stay on?"

"Definitely."

Another booth girl pressed up against Zach, while three more almost fought to have their chance to pose with Jasper. Both he and Jasper couldn't help but be amused. This hadn't been the first time during these photo ops with GameTech investors that the ladies had acted like this. Their line of fans watched on, waiting for the fan autographs and photos to begin. *Our fans…*

Zach was having a hard time wrapping his head around that reality. They'd gone from nobodies who'd managed to score a position in this tournament, to having fans. *Maybe we really should consider streaming.* Ajax had brought it up during the initial proposal call, and now Zach was actually considering the idea.

The photographer took a few more photos before he finished. The girls clung to Jasper and Zach, as if hoping they could get more, but Zach had had about enough. "I need to get something to drink before we continue with the signing."

The women complained, begging for a little more time, but Zach wasn't about to give in, and Jasper was right with him. Ajax gave them a hand, using his authority to usher the workers back to their vendor booths.

They stepped away, turning to where Shira and Serenity sat nearby with Mercedes and Narissa. Serenity took a water bottle from Shira and ran toward them. She had the biggest smile on her face. Jasper and Zach met her halfway.

"Wotta for you!" Serenity announced.

They knelt, and Jasper accepted the bottle. "Thanks, pumpkin. Are ya having fun? Not too bored?"

Serenity shook her head. "No. Momma's friends are fun."

Jasper sipped the drink and then passed it to Zach. "That's good to heah."

Zach relished the cool liquid when it hit his throat. It was nice being able to hear Serenity call Shira her mom without a pang of worry. They knew with all the media attention, their relationship wouldn't stay low on the radar like they'd pretended to be doing when Shira had her altercation with Jeremy, so they all agreed they wouldn't try to keep it quiet anymore. And that included allowing Serenity to be vocal about Shira's place in her life. It may confuse some, but that wasn't their problem. They were going to be a happy family, regardless of what others thought.

Serenity pressed her finger against her lips and did a poor job of whispering. "Don't tell Momma I told you, but she was saying some mean things about those

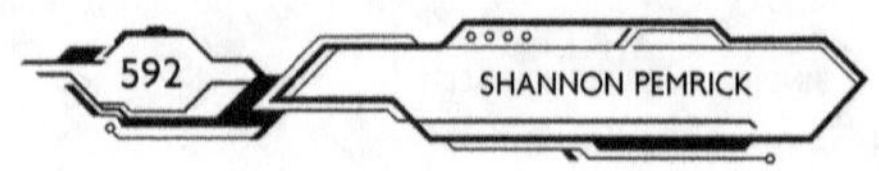

girls you were posing with for pick-chahs. Rissa and Mercedes poked fun of her because of it, too."

Zach and Jasper passed an amused look. Seemed someone was getting a little territorial.

"Don't worry, Starship," Zach assured her. "We'll talk to her about it without mentioning your name and get to the bottom of the problem."

Serenity pressed her lips together. "Is she in trouble?"

Not in the way you think. Zach bit his cheek, his pulse kicking up. He struggled to keep tantalizing ideas at bay of punishing—or rewarding—Shira for her behavior. Not something he should think about while talking to his daughter.

Jasper grinned. "Nah. We just want to make sure something isn't wrong. Communication is important in a relationship."

Their daughter nodded, taking in the bit of advice. Hopefully, reinforcing that idea would help her when she was older.

Zach's attention drifted when one of the booth workers walked past them. Zach's jaw set. Britney strode up to Shira with purpose. *What the hell does she want?* She hadn't joined in for the photo op like they'd expected, after her comments in their first meeting. If she was going to cause another scene, she was in for a rude awakening. Neither he nor Jasper would allow her to stress Shira out again.

His eyes flicked around, searching for Jeremy, but the douche-canoe was nowhere in sight. That confused him. If he and Britney were together, he would know about the photo op, right? With the way he'd acted on day one of the convention, Zach would have guessed the waste of space would want a second chance to dig under Shira's skin.

Britney sat down next to Shira but didn't look at her. Instead, she stared at her feet, twisting her fingers together. Narissa and Mercedes turned toward each other, to give Shira the space to deal with this, but they were definitely watching with disdain.

"What do you want?" Shira asked, not even attempting niceties.

"Were you genuine with your reaction when you found out I was engaged to Jeremy?" Britney asked.

"Yeah. It's your life, and if you were happy with him, then more power to you."

Britney pressed her lips together and then stopped wringing her fingers. She flashed a now-ringless finger. "I dumped him."

Shira's brow rose. "Oh?"

"I didn't know the true reason you two broke up. He had claimed in the past you dumped him during some mental breakdown in the hospital, and after he gave you a few weeks to heal, the two of you talked and decided to split mutually. Since you hadn't come back into the public eye to say otherwise, I had no reason to think he might be lying."

Shira grunted. "I always wondered how he saved his ass after that."

"It was his insult that gave me pause. I'd never heard him call someone with cybernetics that. I tried to brush it off as him being a jerk to you, for whatever reason he decided that day, but then your comment before you left got me thinking." Britney finally lifted her gaze to meet Shira's. "I confronted him and made him tell the truth."

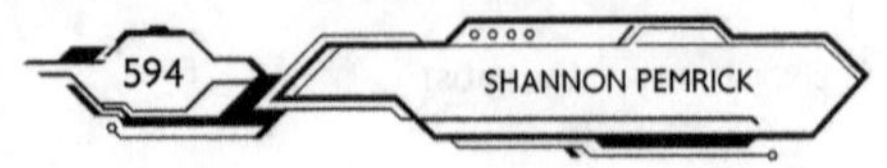

Her gaze fell for a brief moment, and she took a deep breath. "I don't like you, Shira, but not even you deserved that. I don't hate people with cybernetics, and I'm absolutely disgusted with him. We had our issues, but that was not something I'd ever be willing to overlook."

Shira shifted in her seat to move into a more comfortable position. "I think that's the closest you've ever come to apologizing to me."

Britney snorted. "Don't get used to it."

The two women chuckled. Zach squinted. Were they actually getting along? He didn't understand this situation at all.

Britney's gaze turned toward him and Jasper—or more specifically, Serenity. "More out of curiosity than anything, is she really yours?"

"She's my daughter, yes," Shira said without missing a beat. "But Tanya was her first mom."

Britney froze, the color draining from her face. She slowly looked at Shira. "She…"

Shira nodded somberly. "She didn't make it."

The blonde woman's shoulders sagged, and her head dipped. "I'm sorry to hear that."

Her eyes flicked toward him and Jasper again, and then back to Shira. "You three are really together?"

Shira grinned. "Yup."

Butterflies fluttered in Zach's stomach, and warmth as intense as a priest's holy magic bloomed in his chest. The pride in the way she admitted that out loud… Zach didn't quite have adequate words to describe how that made him feel.

Britney's eyebrows rose briefly. "You know how to upgrade, that's for sure."

Shira's grin remained. "You can only go up after Jeremy."

Britney grunted in agreement. She then stood. "Well, good luck with whatever you decide to do with your life."

"Same."

Britney walked away. Shira looked Zach and Jasper's way, smiled, and then resumed conversing with her friends, who politely asked for more information about "Tanya." Zach hoped she'd be able to handle talking about it. It was all so fresh, and even Zach still struggled to believe the coincidence.

"That was wicked weird," Jasper said.

Zach nodded. He still wasn't sure what to make of the situation.

"Daddy, are She-ra and that lady friends now?" Serenity asked.

"Hmm, I wouldn't say they're friends," Jasper said, his nose wrinkling. "But I don't think they're enemies anymore."

"Oh, okay." She took the water bottle from Jasper's hands and ran back to Shira.

"I guess that's our cue to get back to work," Zach said, biting back a laugh.

The rest of the hour went by in a blur. Zach lost track of how many people he spoke to, photos he took, and times he signed his name on something. The feeling of surreality didn't disappear throughout the entire event.

When things ended, a little later than planned because Zach and Jasper felt bad for leaving before the whole line had been seen, they regrouped with their friends, as well as Jasper's parents, who'd rejoined them after going off to check out some demos.

Christine was fussing over Shira—again. They'd broken the news of their relationship to Jasper's parents this morning, and she wouldn't stop showing her excitement.

Ajax's hands landed on Zach's and Jasper's shoulders. "Letting you two know, I'm going to have to slip out during your match to get ready for GameTech's presentation."

Jasper nodded. "No problem."

They'd already figured that'd be the case, given their tighter scheduling this morning.

"I also had Shira added on the tournament roster as your coach," Ajax said. "So, she'll take my place."

Shira grinned wickedly, and Zach and Jasper passed uncertain glances. Maybe trying to make her their official coach wasn't such a good idea.

"Just do well, and I won't have to use my disappointed-mom voice in front of everyone," Shira said, making their friends laugh.

Zach grimaced. She'd never used a voice like that on them before, but there was always a first time for everything.

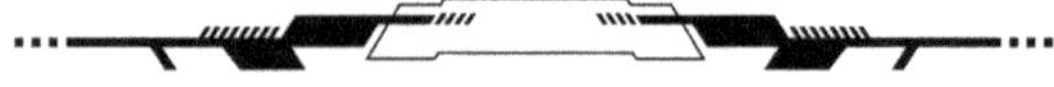

Serenity tugged on Shira's hand, urging her to walk faster to catch up with her dads, and yet the girl was not willing to let go. She'd been on-and-off clingy this morning, not that Shira minded.

Christine went on and on about the panel she and Scott had sat in on the day before. Shira didn't really understand much of it, as it was all about the technical aspect of esports and where predictions lay for the future, but she did her best to follow along. It was something the older woman was passionate about, and Shira would be dammed if she was going to be rude and brush that off just because she didn't comprehend.

Their group walked into the tournament lounge, to find it a little more crowded than expected. Shira figured it was due to the new scheduling, creating a bit more overlap in the different tournaments going on. Lusara Fates wasn't the only big game making buzz here.

Serenity stopped dead in her tracks, her eyes going wide. Shira cocked her head. "Starship?"

The little girl didn't respond right away. When she did, she shook Shira's hand back and forth. "Momma. Momma, it's them!"

She looked up at Shira, her eyes shining. "Momma, it's Grannie!"

Serenity practically vibrated. When she'd learned her dads were up against Fiery Toucans in the semi-finals, Serenity couldn't contain her excitement. She wanted to meet the elderly couple so much and get their autographs.

"Momma, can I meet them?" Serenity asked as she tugged Shira's hand and bounced in place without letting her feet leave the ground.

Shira smoothed out the girl's hair. "After the match, remember? We don't want to distract anyone."

"Who are we distracting?" a shaky woman's voice asked.

Shira looked up to see Abigail and Everett approaching, Abigail relying on a cane to get around. After Serenity showed interest in the pair, Shira did some digging the other day, and learned Abigail had experienced several

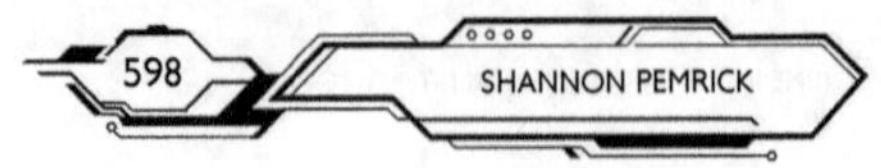

health issues early in her life. Modern medicine and cybernetics assisted her with ensuring she maintained a fulfilling life, but she was still left fairly frail from it all.

Serenity gasped, and Abigail grinned, her eyes squinting. "Do my old eyes spy a little fan?"

Serenity tucked her arms behind her back and toed the ground, acting shy all of a sudden. "Hi, Grannie. Can… can I have your autograph? Grandpa Ev, too?"

Everett placed his hands on his wife's shoulders. "For an adorable young lady like yourself, how could we say no?"

Serenity beamed and dug out her tablet from the satchel Shira bought her yesterday. She pulled up her autographing app and held it out to the older couple.

Everett took the device and signed with a loopy signature, and then held it for Abigail to sign. The gentleness in the way he helped his wife brought a smile to Shira's face.

When they handed the device back to Serenity, she barely looked at the screen before holding it close to her chest. She had a face of utter joy and bliss. Shira hadn't realized how much this would have meant to Serenity.

The girl had talked about how she wanted to get their autographs, but this week was the first time she'd ever heard of Serenity's love for the PvP couple. *How many other teams is she a fan of that we could have gotten autographs for, had we known?* Shira made a mental note to dive into understanding Serenity's interests to help herself understand them, as well as assisting Serenity in cultivating them further.

"How about a photo as well, dear?" Everett said to

Abigail. "I think our little fan would appreciate something like that."

Serenity's eyes lit up, and she turned to Shira, who was already pulling out her phone. Of course she'd allow that.

Her daughter, struggling to stand still and reign in her excitement, posed with the elderly couple. After a few snaps on her phone, Shira gave them the all clear she'd captured enough.

"Thank you," Serenity said. "Sorry that my daddies are going to have to kick your butts today."

Shira's hand flew up to her mouth and Christine and Scott barked out boisterous laughs. Everett had a look of surprise and Abigail squinted while grinning.

"So, it's your dads who are matched against us today? Well, we'll have to see if those two young men can keep up with us. We're not called Fiery Toucans for nothing!"

Serenity grinned, enjoying the spirit of this old woman. It was then Jasper and Zach reappeared.

"We're heading in," Jasper said, kissing Shira on the cheek.

Zach kissed Shira's temple and then rubbed Serenity's head. "Be good."

"I will. Go kick butt!" Serenity said.

"Just don't choke," Shira said, smirking.

Jasper threw his hands up, offended, and then the two ran off. Abigail chuckled quietly and winked at Shira before shuffling away, Everett close behind.

"Let's go find a place to sit," Christine said.

They did, though it didn't feel that long before the match not only started, but ended. Jasper and Zach swiftly and mercilessly handed Fiery Toucans their asses and ended with a three-to-zero-win. Shira was actually impressed. They'd had an impressive match against Drunken Dwarves earlier this week, but that paled compared to this match.

Shira plugged her ears as Christine shrieked. She launched to her feet and danced around without a care who watched. And Scott… he laughed instead of trying to calm his wife down. *Yep, Jasper is definitely their son.*

Jasper and Zach exited the tournament room, ushering their two elder competitors ahead of them like the gentlemen they were.

"No hard feelings," Shira caught Jasper saying to them.

Abigail had the biggest smile on her face. "Absolutely not! That was invigorating, young man. I haven't felt so alive in a tournament in years!"

Shira's eyebrows raised. That was an impressive compliment. During Shira's search on the couple, she had learned the two had made it to the finals last year, only to be slaughtered by Burnout.

"Does that mean you're gonna finally retire, Abby, and let the youngah generation handle these games?" Christine said, turning many heads.

Abigail snorted. "Of course not, Chrissy. It means I'll have a lot more fun in the years to come."

The two women laughed.

"Nana, you *know* her?" Serenity said, her mouth agape.

"Christine and I go way back," Abigail said. "Those were the days. And then she had to switch genres and become a coach instead."

The way the older woman said those words with exasperation and a hint of contempt, it got Shira and a few others laughing.

"Why didn't you say anything?" Jasper asked.

His mother shrugged. "I thought I had at some point. Guess not."

Everett smiled. "You should be proud of your son. He's got our vote for the semi-finals."

"We're always proud of him," Scott said, an enormous smile curling up his face. "Both of them."

Jasper's cheeks tinged pink, and he rubbed the back of his neck. "Jeez, no pressure or anything."

Everett laughed and patted Jasper's shoulder. "No, none whatsoever. Good luck, you two."

"And wipe that cocky smirk off that Burnout boy's face," Abigail said, raising her cane into the air. "Lord knows he needs a good slice of humble pie."

Laughter rumbled through the room. The older couple left after sharing a few more words with Christine, and giving a few bits of encouragement to Serenity if she ever decided to follow in her dads' footsteps.

Jasper looked around. "Guess we should head ovah to the GameTech reveal if we're not too late."

Shira shook her head. "You guys didn't take all that long winning. Ajax only left ten minutes ago."

He scratched his head. "Felt wicked long. Those two may be old, but they didn't make it easy."

"Could have fooled us," Scott said. "I thought those two were losing their edge."

Christine snorted. "Not to me."

"Well, of course not," Scott said, his tone a bit mocking. "You're a coach and you see everything."

Shira pressed her lips together as the two playfully bickered. It really was rarely a dull moment with this family. *What have I gotten myself into?*

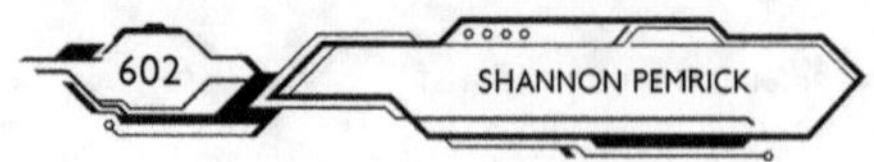

When the two had finally called it quits ragging on each other, they announced they'd be going off to catch the end of a panel that overlapped with the semi-finals. The two planned to slip over to the GameTech reveal after, if it hadn't ended. Shira and the guys wouldn't be able to get them backstage, so to speak, if they did this, but she doubted the two minded mingling with the rest of the con-goers.

"They're about to start the presentation," Orion said after Jasper's parents split off from them at the elevator.

Shira pursed her lips. "We won't be late, right?"

"As long as you don't dawdle, you might catch Narissa and Ajax before they go on stage."

Jasper threaded his fingers with Shira's. "Then, let's make sure we're there to support our friends through this mega reveal."

Serenity looked up at her parental figures. "What is the reveal? What does Mister Ajax do?"

Zach patted Serenity on the head. "Ajax is the one who made the gaming pods we use."

Serenity's eyes went wide. "That's wicked cool! What is he gonna talk about today?"

Zach shrugged. "We don't know. Ajax and Narissa have both been keeping it a secret until they go on stage."

"Then let's go and see!" Serenity said. She attempted to scamper off, but Zach caught her by the back of the shirt to keep their daughter close. He then rested his hand on Shira's lower back, since her other arm carried her folder with her tablet. Shira had planned to have Serenity carry it for her in her satchel, but then thought better of it. *Maybe I should have bought a satchel at one of the booths while the guys were doing their signing.*

Making it to the backstage of GameTech's presentation wasn't too difficult. They were almost refused by security, but luckily, Allyson was nearby.

Narissa and Ajax stood together near the entrance to the stage. Mercedes and Takashi were also with them; they appeared to be talking. Kiara and Darius were nowhere in sight, though they'd run off before the semi-final match because of some Lion Rage thing. Shira suspected they were still tangled up in that, so they probably would miss the reveal.

Shira's brow rose when someone from the stage on the other side of the wall began the GameTech intro spiel. "Looks like we made it just in time."

Serenity gasped and tugged against her father's grip. She really wanted to get there quick.

Zach released her, and they watched her run straight for Narissa and Ajax. "Wait, Rissa!"

Shira, Jasper, and Zach passed perplexed looks between them. Apparently, their daughter wanted to do more than just watch from the very start.

Their friends turned their way, and Narissa waved to Serenity. "Hey, Serenity."

Serenity called out again as if she didn't hear, or realize Narissa didn't go anywhere. "Rissa, wait!"

She ran up to Narissa and latched onto the woman's leg. "I have something to tell ya before you go out there."

Narissa looked to Ajax and nodded. He smirked and ran out onto the stage, hyping up the crowd. Narissa focused on Serenity. "Now, what did you want to tell me?"

Serenity beckoned her closer. Narissa crouched down and the little girl kissed her on the nose. "Good luck."

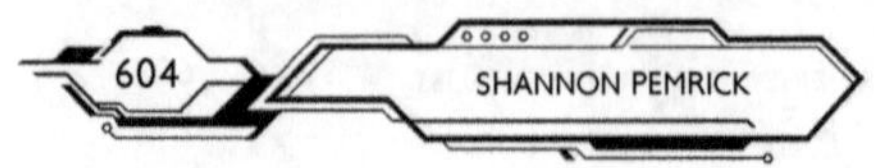

Shira pressed a hand to her chest. A unison of "awws" sounded around them. *She's too precious.*

Narissa kissed Serenity back. "Thank you, birthday girl. You're going to like what we reveal. And the gift I have for you."

Serenity's eyes lit up. "You remembered!"

Narissa laughed. "Of course I did." She stood. "I can't give it to you right now, though. I have this presentation to get through."

Serenity nodded several times. "I'll wait!"

Shira left Jasper and Zach's side and approached Narissa, whispering in her ear. "We'll be sure she's ready."

Narissa nodded. As she turned away, her eyes flicked down to the folder in Shira's arm. Her friend didn't say anything, but her piqued interest didn't escape Shira's notice. Narissa sauntered over to the offstage entrance, waiting for Ajax to call her out. He was eager to do so, and she received a loud reception walking out.

Shira pulled Serenity in front of her, and positioned them to get a great view of the stage. She also had Snake lie behind her to make sure the three of them weren't in the way of crew members. She wanted to be sure she and Serenity were in a good spot when Narissa and Ajax needed them.

"Look at this beautiful woman, huh?" Ajax said.

"Just a reminder, we're not talking about you here," Narissa said.

The crowd laughed, as did everyone backstage. Ajax placed his hand on his chest. "Well, thank you for the compliment, but I'm not talking about myself."

She crossed her arms. "For once."

Shira shook her head. Her friends were something

else. But the energy they had on stage was exactly what Shira needed to feed off of.

Her fingers tingled, and Shira worked on her breathing. This was one hell of a huge step for her. And she wasn't backing down.

Ajax shook his finger at Narissa. "Careful, now. Or I won't let you do the slides."

Narissa held up a remote and smirked. "I don't need permission."

Ajax searched his person, his expression one of shock. Seemed Narissa had snatched it when he wasn't looking.

Ajax shook his head. "Sneaky little thief. And here I thought you were a good little priestess."

"That's not what you said last night!" Shira yelled out. She should have bitten her tongue—she really should have. This was a family-friendly event. But these were her friends, and Shira was known for acting without thinking a lot of the time.

Narissa's mom, Ayana, stared at Shira with wide eyes and a hand on her chest. That was the cause for the tiny twinge of regret Shira had for letting her mouth run wild. That, of course, was drowned out quickly by the heavy roaring laughter from the audience. Even Narissa and Ajax were amused.

"She's talking about the guild raid last night," Ajax said, trying to ensure it was disguised as a "family-friendly" event.

"No, I'm not!" Shira called out. *Shit.*

Ajax pinched his nose and Narissa covered her mouth as she tried to control her laughter. "Careful, Shira, our intellectually-challenged berserker is going to go into a rage at this rate 'cause his head hurts."

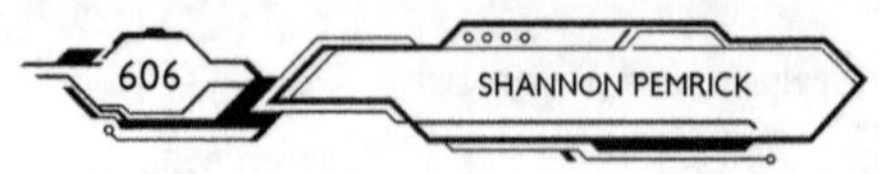

Shira belted out a hearty laugh.

Ajax pointed at Narissa. "Watch it. Or I'll make you do this presentation on your own."

Narissa shrugged and turned. "Or I could go play with the new toy instead."

She clicked the remote, the screen behind them displaying the first slide of the presentation. Cheers and shouts of excitement echoed through the room. Ajax shook his head and started up the presentation. While he did, Narissa motioned for some GameTech employees to roll something covered out onto the stage.

Shira's brow spiked. She could not for the life of her figure out what that thing was. She knew it was some sort of tech reveal, that much they'd told Jasper so he was informed enough to consent to Serenity trying it out. But this thing being wheeled out had no shape she'd ever seen before. And it definitely didn't look like a chair. *Unless the two dressed it up so no one could guess what it was.* She wouldn't put it past her friends to do that.

Shira pursed her lips. It dawned on her that it was also strange Narissa was on stage with Ajax. She hadn't questioned it at first, since the two were dating. But Narissa wasn't a GameTech employee. And it was clear she was part of all this.

Shira didn't have to wait long for the answer. Ajax finished his spiel and he and Narissa each took an end of the covering.

"GameTech would like to announce its newest virtual-reality gaming model."

The two pulled off the cover, revealing a long machine with a hinged, open lid. Computer paneling stretched along the sides of the pod, and comfortable padding lined the interior.

The crowd went wild, and Ajax made a few Vanna White poses to add to it all.

Shira's mouth fell open. *This* was the new stage of VR gaming?

Never in her lifetime did Shira think VR would go this way. She still remembered the days before Ajax created the chairs—uncomfortable headgear for visual and audio sensation only, and weird glove controllers that poorly simulated physical touch.

Jasper and Zach leaned closer in their attempt to get a good look at the new machine, and listened harder as Ajax and Narissa went into a deep explanation behind the chair-to-pod change and how Narissa's involvement was needed.

It seemed, because of the new design, which was created for better inclusion and just overall health of gamers, Cybro Industries needed to help because of cybernetics. And then there was an added benefit.

"Age limitations are mostly a thing of the past now," Narissa said. She paused to let everyone absorb the shocking news. "Children, who all love games, can now get a taste of this world as young as five."

Five? Shira couldn't believe her ears. That was a huge jump from the minimum age of ten for the current VR machines. And from what she knew through conversations with parents, most of those kids had to use the portable headgear until they were tall enough for the chairs.

Serenity tugged at Shira's hands. "She-ra? Is it true? Can I play games like you and Dad and Daddy?"

Shira licked her lips, her brain still trying to catch up. "Yeah, it looks like it is, Starship."

Her daughter squealed. This was one thing she'd always wanted.

Allyson walked past them, a gaming headset in her hands. She oozed confidence and her eyes screamed mischief as she strode out onto the stage. "Hold up, Narissa. We all know I can't let my baby brother have all the fun today."

Shira choked on a laugh. There it was. She always had to kick Ajax down a peg. Of course, it was always in good fun.

Ajax threw his hands up. "Why are you two so mean to me?"

His sister winked, and held up a newly designed portable gaming helmet. "The stationary designs aren't the only ones to get an upgrade."

Loud cheers erupted.

Allyson smirked. "I couldn't let you traveling gamers be left out in all this. The new designs will feature upgraded hardware, greater stability, and also the same approved age range, thanks to Narissa's involvement."

She turned things back over to Narissa. It looked like she had only planned to do that little reveal, which made sense to Shira. Yes, the new age limit was amazing, but the new pod design was a huge deal.

"All right, now back to what I was about to say," Narissa said, the crowd quieting down. "To show off this new age range, I've got a very special birthday girl here waiting offstage."

Shira sucked in a quiet breath. *Here we go.*

Serenity gasped, and looked up at her. "She-ra, does she mean me?"

Accepting a headset from a nearby crewmember, Shira geared up and held out her hand to Serenity. "Yes, she does. Let's go out there."

Her daughter stared at her offered hand for a moment and then took it. Shoulders back, Shira confidently strolled out onto the stage. Snake followed on Shira's other side, and Shira did everything in her power not to clutch his leash like her life depended on it. *I can do this.*

Serenity tried to emulate Shira's bravado as the crowd gushed over how cute she was. However, Shira noticed her frantically darting eyes, and how much she struggled not to shrink into herself. Even Snake sensed it. He slipped behind Shira and padded on Serenity's other side, as if to shield her from the crowd. The young girl placed a hand on his vest for added support.

She lasted the entire walk on her own. However, when they reached Narissa, Ajax, and Allyson, she pressed into Shira and asked to be held. Shira didn't refuse, and Serenity curled into Shira's neck. Shira's friends gazed at the girl sympathetically.

"Honey, can you tell everyone your name?" It was a safe ice breaker for Serenity.

It took the girl a moment to respond. "Serenity."

The crowd melted. Shira smiled and rotated so that Serenity could see them. This also exposed all of her surface cybernetic prosthetics. And yet, Shira didn't fight any need to flee. *I've got this.*

"And can you tell everyone how old you are?" Shira said.

Serenity played with her fingers. "Seven. Today's my birthday."

She received a huge happy birthday, triggering her to hide her face, but she managed to muffle out a "thank you."

"And is that younger or older than the virtual reality minimum age?" Shira asked her.

"Daddy says I can't play his game until I'm ten yeahs old."

Ajax placed his hands on Narissa's shoulders. "And what if we told you, someone your age can now play?"

A big, goofy grin spread across her face. "I want to kick his butt like She-ra can."

Laughter boomed through the room, everyone unable to contain themselves.

Narissa smiled. "Well, a friend at Lion Rage helped us out and set up a demo just for you to try and show off to everyone. Do you want to do that?"

Serenity's eyes popped open. "Can She-ra play with me?"

Shira kissed her on the forehead. "Of course. That's why I'm here with you."

A lie. She didn't know anything about this demo present. But no way in hell would she let that slip in front of Serenity.

Ajax patted the gaming pod. "You can either use this, Serenity, or you can use the portable device my sister holds."

Serenity hesitated, scared about making the wrong choice. "The pod looks scary."

Ajax hung his head while she received some sympathy from the surrounding attendees. It didn't surprise Shira.

Serenity was hit-or-miss with her bravery, and being on this stage had shaken a lot of her confidence.

"I'll be more than happy to use it, Ajax," Shira said. "As a cybernetics user, I'd like to give it a safety test."

Ajax grinned.

People scrambled around to set up the devices. Serenity sat in Narissa's lap while Shira climbed into the virtual pod. She had Snake stay with Serenity.

Serenity giggled as Allyson strapped the portable helmet to her head and made the correct size-related safety adjustments. Then, she was given a countdown and sucked into the game.

Ajax gave Shira similar treatment, making sure everything worked just right.

Her heart pounded against her rib cage. Just laying here was such a different experience from being in a chair. And it was in this moment, as the lid closed over her, she was glad Serenity chose the headgear. This would have terrified her. Even Shira had to work on her breathing, and she wasn't claustrophobic.

She closed her eyes to block it all out. It was just like the gaming chair. Only comfier. *Damn, this padding is great.* It was like laying on a cloud.

The sensation of VR immersion fell over her, and soon, Shira found herself in a virtual forest. Tree leaves rustled in the breeze, casting dapples of sunlight on the ground, and birds flitted overhead through the canopy.

Shira took some time to feel out her connection between the world and her avatar. Shira had been assigned a rogue class for her avatar. The armor weighed on her body as she expected, and the sensations of the forest, even down to the taste in the air, all registered like it should. *I'm not sure if it feels more real or not, but in the very least, it's not worse than the current models.*

Shira wouldn't be surprised if Ajax hadn't done any upgrades to the senses simulation and focused on the new overall design instead. She could only imagine how difficult it had been for him to convert the machine from the chair style. Shira knew, at the very least, it had caused issues with cybernetics.

Ajax had been blowing up his cybernetics on some super-secret project a few months ago, which had caused him and Narissa some tension. And the fact Narissa had specified she'd been involved for the health of cybernetic users; it didn't take a rocket scientist to put two and two together.

Serenity appeared a moment later, garbed in leather armor and a bow and quiver. Her daughter squealed and then took to the new experience faster than Shira had ever witnessed someone take to VR or a virtual game.

She ran around like a bat out of hell, wanting to see everything in this small demo scenario. Shira chased after her, desperately trying to get Serenity to focus. The girl's excitement warmed Shira's heart, however, Darius had put in some effort for this demo, and there was still so much for Serenity to experience beyond surface visuals.

It took a while, nearly all their demo time, but Serenity did stop to look at her. "What's up, Momma?"

Shira blew out a breath. "Starship, I know you're excited, but we have quests to do before our time runs out."

Her daughter's eyes popped wide. "Quests? We get to do quests?"

"Sure do. Let me show you how to activate your quest log."

It took a little bit for Serenity to get the hang of the mental processes to activate her log, but warmth bloomed in Shira's chest when she did. Serenity then tried to read out the quest, Shira helping when a word stumped her.

They were to follow some unusual tracks, using an ability only Serenity had for her ranger class. Shira had a feeling what this quest had been designed as, but she wouldn't give any hints to Serenity.

She taught Serenity how to activate her skills, and this time, her daughter caught on a bit quicker. Shira followed Serenity through the underbrush. The girl's face scrunched with all the concentration she could put into this task.

They came out into a small clearing. On the other side, a dire wolf snoozed in the shade. Its ears pricked when Serenity gasped.

"Okay, Starship, what does the quest tell us to do now?" Shira prompted. She wanted to make sure Serenity finished the quest before their time was up.

"Um…" Serenity read the prompt. "Capture or befriend… the choice is yours." She gasped. "I want to be friends with a wolfie!"

Shira smirked. She had a feeling that'd be the answer. It was almost as if Darius knew little girls loved animals and would do anything to have a beast such as this for a pet.

"It's a good thing you're a ranger. You have a skill that allows you to tame a beast and make it your companion."

Serenity pursed her lips and her eyes glazed over as she

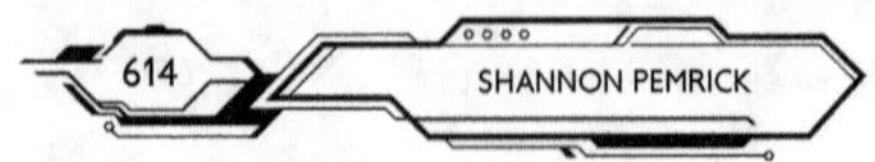

focused on checking her skills. Shira knew she found it when the girl squealed. A chunk of meat appeared in her hand a moment later. "Okay, wolfie, you're gonna be mine."

And after throwing some meat to the wolf, Serenity in fact did tame it. A big heart appeared over the beast's head when the taming completed, and then vanished.

Serenity's eyes went wide when the towering canine walked up to her. She tentatively reached out a hand and touched its muzzle. The wolf nuzzled her, and Serenity giggled. Serenity thew her arms around the neck of the beast and pressed her face into its plush fur and inhaled its musky scent. She murmured something, and it sounded as if she were about to cry.

Shira's chest swelled. This couldn't have gone any better for her first time in VR. It was everything she ever wanted Serenity to experience.

Something flashed in Shira's peripheral. The time had reached zero. "Okay, Starship, demo is over."

"What, no!" she whined. "I wanna keep playing."

Shira smiled. "I know you're having fun. But this is a demo. We can look into playing later, okay?"

Serenity frowned, and her shoulders sagged. "Okay…"

Shira pat her on the head to comfort her and then taught her how to log out. Once her daughter disappeared from the system, Shira logged out as well.

She took a moment to allow the transition sensation to fade from her body before opening her eyes. The lid of the pod greeted her, though not for long when Ajax opened the machine. He offered his hand, and she accepted his assistance, finding it not all that necessary with how easy she found it to climb out.

Shira stretched and got a sense of how her body felt after all that time, and she was seriously impressed by the lack of tension in her neck and spine. It'd only been a fifteen-minute demo, but even by that point a chair design would have caused stiffness to set in.

Allyson removed the helmet from Serenity, and before Narissa could speak to the girl, Serenity wrapped her arms around Narissa's neck. "Thank you, Rissa! Best birthday, evah!"

Narissa hugged her back. "You're welcome, sweetie. I'm glad you liked the surprise."

The little girl hopped off her lap and ran over to Shira. "Momma, I want to go tell Daddy and Dad about the fun I had."

Shira smiled down at her. "We'll do that after I say one thing."

A grin spread across Ajax's face. "What do you have to say about the new machine, Shira?"

"Yeah. Goodbye gamer neck."

The three of them laughed, as did the crowd, as Shira walked off with Serenity, Snake close behind.

Serenity bolted for her dads, latching onto Zach's leg. She spoke a mile a minute, gushing about her experience.

Jasper pulled Shira close and handed her folder back before he kissed her on the forehead. "I'm wicked proud of you."

Mercedes popped up behind Shira and threw her arms around Shira's neck. "Same here! You surprised all of us."

A demure smile crept onto Shira's face. "Thanks. That was easier to do than I expected, but I still had my difficulties."

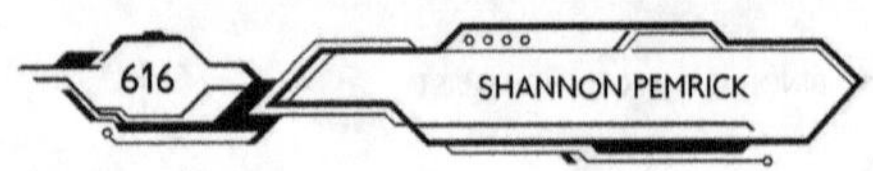

She kissed Jasper on the cheek. "Sorry for stealing that first moment with Serenity experiencing VR. I know that was a big milestone."

Jasper squeezed her. "If I had an issue with it, I would have said something last night. It was just as amazing to experience from here."

"Especially since we got to watch you strut out on stage," Zach added.

"Why is no one listening to me?" Serenity complained.

Her dads apologized and gave her their full attention. They also had to let Serenity down gently when she begged for a VR headset of her own, seeing as they weren't out on the market yet.

Shira turned back to the presentation, figuring the Q&A would start soon, and everything in her stopped. Narissa stared up at the display screen, which read:

Hold on.

"What on earth?" Narissa said, before jumping to the next slide.

One more thing before questions happen.

"Guys…" Shira said. Everyone looked at her and she pointed when she noticed Ajax reached for something in his back pocket. "Guys… Guys, something is happening."

Narissa continued to stare up at the screen, confused by the next slide that had just her name displayed.

"Oh, my Lawd," Ayana shrieked. "Benjamin! Benjamin! It's happenin'. It's happenin'!"

Narissa's father, who was off a little way speaking with Ajax's mom, rushed over to his wife. "What is it, dear?"

Ayana's eyes glowed. "It's finally happenin'!"

Narissa didn't see Ajax pull a small box out of his back pocket. Nor did she immediately see him lower himself down on one knee. Only when she read the next slide, telling her Ajax had an important question for her and everyone watching gasped, did she turn.

The display remote clattered to the ground and her hands flew up to her face.

"Narissa, will you make me the happiest man alive, and stay my player number two, until game over?"

Mercedes and Shira clung to each other, a squeal threatening to shriek out of Shira. It was happening!

Narissa struggled with words, and instead answered Ajax with a nod. An enormous smile spread up Ajax's handsome face, and within seconds he was on his feet, lifting Narissa in the air, and spinning them around. She dipped her head and kissed him.

Shira and Mercedes couldn't hold back anymore. They screamed.

As did the crowd and everyone around them.

Ajax eventually set Narissa back down and planted a kiss on her forehead before slipping the ring on her finger.

"Hallelujah, about time! Now give me lots'o grandbabies!" Ayana called out.

Shira and her friends roared with laughter while Benjamin practically facepalmed.

Narissa also found her mother amusing. "My mother, everyone."

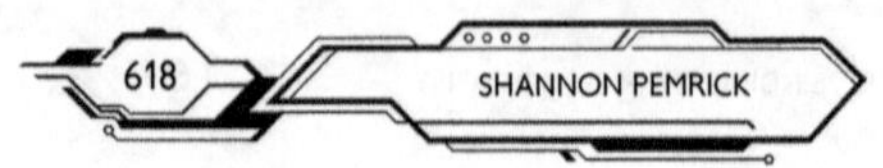

She then refocused and addressed the audience on how to submit their questions for the Q&A.

Twenty minutes later, Narissa and Ajax had covered the questions they could. Ajax informed the crowd that limited demos would happen at the GameTech booth shortly, and the championships for Lusara Fates would be using the approved prototypes. Jasper and Zach gave each other high-fives.

The pair exited the stage, and Narissa wasn't given any time before Shira and the others swarmed her. She had to show off her ring several times before things calmed down.

"Rissa, does this mean you're getting married at the same time as my dads?" Serenity asked.

Narissa laughed. "No, sweety, we'll have different dates."

"Ok, good." Serenity turned to her fathers. "When are ya gonna marry She-ra?"

Shira choked, and Zach blinked. Jasper stood there for a moment, then cleared his throat. "It's a bit too soon to talk about that, Starship."

"But you and Zach are gonna get married."

"We've been dating longah."

"Rissa, how long have you and Mister Ajax been… dating?" Serenity asked.

Narissa pursed her lips, eyes darting frantically between Serenity's parental figures, desperately screaming for help. If she said the truth, that'd throw Jasper's argument out the window.

"Jasper," Alistair said from his phone. "Your parents are waiting for you and Zach. Your mother seems to have come up with some sort of strategy for you to possibly try in the finals."

"Sick," Jasper said. "Tell her we'll be right there."

"Oh, and they have a gift for Serenity."

Serenity's eyes lit up, and her need for wedding answers vanished. "I want presents!"

The adults around her laughed. What kid didn't?

Ajax also had to run to his company's booth to handle the flood of people expected to be there, wanting their turn with the prototypes. He promised the guys he'd make it for the finals. No one wanted to miss that big moment.

Narissa wished him luck, and Shira did the same for the guys, promising she'd catch up with them before the finals started. They knew her plan, so it wasn't difficult for them to go find Jasper's parents without her.

Shira's gut clenched. This was it. This was the moment she'd prove to herself that she'd grown from the scared woman she'd become, and showed the world her middle finger again.

Narissa was already looking at her, unspoken curiosity clear in her eyes.

Shira held out her folder containing the tablet with her signed contract. "I'd like to talk to you about something before I join them, Doctor."

A massive grin spread over Narissa's lovely face. She knew exactly what this was about. "Step into my office, Ms. Schneider. I'd love to go over the documents you've brought me."

CHAPTER 29

Roots shot out of the ground and wrapped around Jasper's leg, pinning him in place. *Shit!* He desperately carved at the plant, but his attacks couldn't prematurely break the hold before Emilia took advantage of her brother's grapple and sliced her sword down on him.

Health: 35%

Jasper gritted his teeth and retaliated with his daggers. It did little to her health, but he had no other abilities to help him. He'd blown all of his good evasion skills a bit ago, and all of his good attacks came from being stealthed, which he couldn't do with this root holding him.

Zach came to Jasper's aid, but Leon kept his sister's health up, allowing her to focus on Jasper.

Health: 27%
Health: 15%
Health: 9%

There wasn't any getting out of this mess. None of Jasper's abilities were coming back in time. So, he made his stand there until his health reached zero.

The system shoved Jasper's presence out of his avatar body. The body disappeared from the game, and a sense of weightlessness fell over his mind. He could still see the one-sided match in front of him, but Zach wouldn't be able to see him. They could communicate still, though Jasper didn't see the point.

This would be their third loss in a row in the finals. If it were any other game, that would be it, they'd be out. But the finals were a best of nine. Of course, with how badly they were getting their asses handed to them, Jasper was starting to think forfeiting the remaining matches was a better idea. No one wanted to see such a terrible team pairing. *We don't deserve all the attention we've received, and we certainly didn't deserve to get this far.*

Zach's health reached zero before the death timer called the match. The arena disappeared and Jasper found himself in their team lobby with his avatar restored. The five-minute interval between match time started, giving each team a chance to strategize and change classes if needed.

The two of them sighed in unison.

"What should we do?" Zach asked.

"We can't keep going if we're gonna lose like this every match," Jasper said.

"Hey."

Jasper's spine went rigid at the sound of Shira's voice coming into the team chat through a headset. Her tone wasn't harsh or filled with venom, like he'd expected after their poor display. And honestly, that unsettled him.

"What the fuck, you two?" Again, she said words they expected, but not in the tone they expected.

Zach passed him a perturbed glance. "Aren't you going to yell?"

"Please yell," Jasper said. "It's a lot easier when you're kicking our asses verbally after we've screwed up."

"No, I don't think I will," she said. "I think you two need to stop acting like fools and actually put some effort into this."

Jasper's hands clenched into fists, but he couldn't summon the anger to fight the accusation the way he could have if she'd raised her voice. "We are trying."

"Are you? Or are you letting your last match with them and all their hype get into your head?"

Jasper's fist laxed and he and Zach looked at each other. *Is she right?*

"Think about it," Shira said. "You know how to deal with a druid-and-warrior combo. You practiced your own combos to figure out what would combat that."

"It's not just about the combo," Jasper said. *Player skill makes a tremendous difference.*

"And that's why you two have spent hours studying Burnout's playstyle. You know this."

Shit, she's right. Jasper ran his hand through his hair. After getting their asses handed to them by Burnout the first time, he and Zach had dedicated their practice to defeating them in the rematch. They'd been confident about winning against Fiery Toucans. Sure, Everette was one hell of a pugilist PvPer, which was a rare class in the PvP scene, but Jasper hadn't been worried about defeating them.

As a result, he and Zach practiced combos they'd never thought of before. Including—Jasper took a deep breath and brought up his class list. He had particular classes he played all the time, and ones that were main backups. However, Jasper prided himself on being ready for anything, and worked on gearing all classes in the event he needed one in an emergency.

Scrolling through the list, Jasper selected the pugilist class. His leather armor swapped out for cloth, and his weapons became hand-wrapped fists.

Zach changed his class to priest and nodded. They both knew what had to be done. This wasn't a conventional pairing of classes, but that's also what made it work for them. Jasper just needed to hit hard and fast to outdo Emilia the super warrior.

"Thanks for the pep talk, Shira," Jasper said. "We'll take it from here."

"Don't disappoint me." Her tone was still soft, but the thinly veiled threat didn't go unnoticed and spiked Jasper's heart rate for a minute.

The timer ticked down to the last thirty seconds. Jasper and Zach talked strategy while working out their nerves. They could do this. *We will win this.*

Time hit zero, and the system ported them back into the arena.

Jasper took no time to break out into a sprint down the middle of the area toward where Burnout spawned in. Zach threw on a protective shield and took off after him, but he wouldn't be able to keep up with the pugilist speed.

Hit them hard and fast. Screw what anyone thought about this strategy. No one was prepared for this. Especially not Burnout.

They barely had time to notice Jasper charging before he slammed into Leon. Jasper activated his strongest stun, and it took hold. He then activated a rapid-punch attack, pummeling the defenseless druid.

Emilia recovered from her shock, and drew her weapon. Light slammed into her and she stumbled back. Zach stood at a distance, ready to defend Jasper as best he could.

This whole plan hinged on Jasper utilizing the most difficult part of his class that made it a major reason so few played it for PvP: glass cannon.

Pugilist hit hard and fast, but couldn't take much in the way of hits. That's what made things difficult against Everette. He knew that class inside and out, and hit hard. And now Jasper would do the same. All he needed was Zach to keep him healed and Jasper had to down Leon. Without him, Emilia wouldn't do as well against him and Zach.

Jasper activated skill after skill, burning through all his cooldowns and combos. Emilia attacked Jasper, trying to save her brother, but her damage couldn't outpace Zach's healing. And then he blinded her.

Leon's health plummeted, and there was nothing he could do to defend himself.

Health: 75%
Health: 64%
Health: 50%
Health: 37%

The second stun Jasper landed on Leon ended, but Jasper was ready. He may not have had a standard stun at the ready; however, he did have his executing ability.

Leon's health wasn't at an ideal percentage to guarantee the kill, but with the ability's stun effect, Jasper could cover the minimal distance should the attack fail to finish his opponent.

Inhaling deeply, Jasper activated his dragon soul ability, and his body filled with intense energy. He slammed his fists into the druid's chest. Leon choked and his health plummeted.

Health: 2%

Emilia sliced into Jasper, dropping his health.

Health: 89%

Jasper ignored her, slamming his foot down on her brother's chest.

Health: 0%

Leon stared up at him, his eyes wide, and then his avatar disappeared from the playing field.

Zach protected Jasper in another shield, coming in clutch when Emilia swung at Jasper. Her nostrils flared and eyes widened to where the whites overpowered her pupils. She swung furiously, her teeth bared and eyes silently demanding Jasper's head for his audacity with taking out her brother.

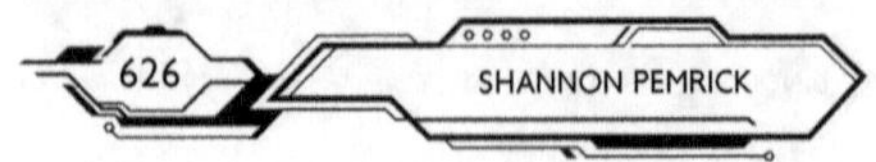

Jasper stumbled back, the light-footed nature of his class keeping him from toppling over. Zach attacked her with some weaker light spells, since he hadn't gone the hybrid route, but it did nothing to draw her attention. She had picked her target. *So be it.*

Feigning left, he jumped right, dodging an attack, and slammed his fists into her side. They did little to her health, but that wasn't the point.

Jasper was out of high-damaging abilities. He only had to waste enough time for the timer to hit zero.

And waste time he did. With him right up in Emilia's face, she focused on him, allowing Zach to use all his mana on healing and shields. When the ability came available again, Zach blinded their opponent. Jasper took advantage of this and used a tripping attack he didn't need against Leon.

Emilia crashed to the ground; Jasper followed up with an axe kick. She grunted, her body flattening against the ground. But before she could throw him off, the timer ran out.

The timer… it ended… Jasper stared down at Emilia, who looked up at him, smirking. Numbness blanketed his mind and body. They'd… won?

Jasper and Zach were teleported to the lobby where they stood side by side, staring at each other. Energy broke through the numbness and the two of them whooped. Jasper grabbed Zach around the waist and hauled him up, spinning the two of them.

It was just one win, but it was a win. They'd broken Burnout's perfect streak, and even if the two of them failed to beat the brother-sister duo any other time in the finals, they'd made their mark.

Jasper heard Shira smile into the mic. "See? Now, go kick some more ass."

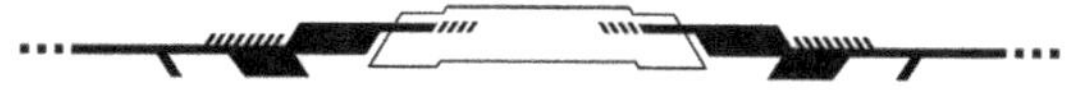

Pain pulsed through Zach's head. The arena spun, his eyes struggling to focus, and his stomach lurched, threatening to expel his non-existent virtual stomach. *Fuck poison.* And fuck druids at that. And screw Burnout for being the only team Zach had ever seen master a double-druid team.

He and Jasper had been doing amazing after their first win. They'd really shaken their opponents' confidence and, as a result, started an intense come-from-behind victory.

Now they were tied up at four wins each. This was the crucial match that decided it all. All their hard work came down to this.

And the brother-sister team had to throw a wrench in his and Jasper's plan by choosing a combo they'd never seen them play before. Hell, it wasn't even a common choice in the PvP scene.

But with Leon's insane healing skill and Emilia's strategic DPS plays, they were proving to be one hell of a problem to beat, even though Zach had chosen his priest healing spec and Jasper went DPS elementalist—a nod to Shira and all the help she'd given teaching them just how that class worked inside and out, as well as all her support through everything.

Lightning shot through Zach's blurry sight. From the shriek, Zach guessed his spell had hit Emilia fairly hard. Zach wanted to help Jasper, but this poison prevented him from casting spells. And his instant cast-cleansing skill wasn't available from the last time he needed it because of Emilia's poison spells.

Zach lurched back when something sharp whipped him and his health dropped.

Health: 58%

As a healer, he was a prime target, so it didn't surprise him. What did was the effect it had on his sight. He could see a little better. The pounding and nausea had eased a bit, and a quick, squinting glance at his debuff told him that attack had damaged the effect's hold on him.

Focusing on his spells and pushing past the disorientation, Zach managed to throw up a shield on himself. That'd only stall a little bit, but it was something.

The vine that'd attacked him before tried again, and then again. It bounced off the protective shield, but sapped the protective barrier's strength each time.

Emilia raised her hand to cast another spell to cause him grief, when Jasper shot a scorching ball of molten fire and rock at her face. The attack exploded on impact on her body and she stumbled back, her spell canceled.

Health: 71%

Zach's dispel returned, yet he didn't use it. The poison had almost ended, and, while a bit of a risk, it was better he held off for a different time.

That time came when Emilia cast another poison spell, but this time on Jasper. At the same time, Zach's wore off. He grinned and dispelled the poison. Emilia bared her teeth and began casting another spell.

But Zach was quicker.

He focused on his blinding spell and aimed it at her. The spell made contact before she could finish her cast, and she flailed around. With her distracted, Zach switched his mental processes to healing up Jasper before slamming Leon with an attacking spell. Those were risky, as they sucked up more mana than his healing spells in this spec, but the less mana Leon had at his disposal, the more of a sitting duck the brother-sister duo would be.

Molten fire struck Leon, and then Jasper followed up with three lightning attacks, the last one arching and tagging Emilia. This forced Leon to split his healing attempts between the two of them. The typical focus-healer strategy was always a good one, but adding extra damage to their teammate now and then never hurt.

Zach gasped when a large vine sprung out of the ground and wrapped around him, applying a binding effect. He whipped his head toward Emilia, who had her arm out in his general direction. She was still blinded, but she'd managed to push through that and get that spell off. *I should have moved.*

The blinding spell was one of his best disabling offensive spells, but was also one that any opponent could overcome if they were aware enough of their surroundings.

Leon threw healings spells at himself, all the while Jasper continued to pound the healing druid with elemental attacks. But his freedom to attack uncontested didn't last long.

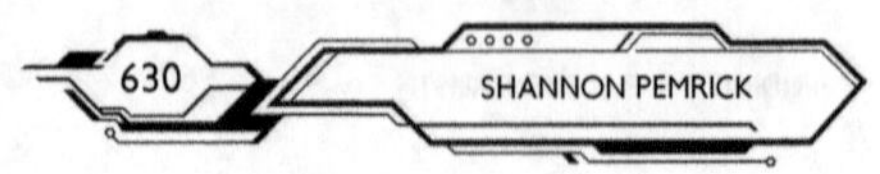

Emilia broke free of the blind spell and assaulted Zach with all manner of spells.

> Health: 65%
> Health: 63%
> Health: 58%
> Health: 50%

It unsettled Zach how quick she was suddenly. And then Zach realized, a little too late, she had activated a haste ability.

His health continued to plummet as she used harder and harder spells against him he couldn't out-heal her. And he was running out of mana.

"Stay focused?" Jasper asked.

"Yes." It might be stupid, but Zach would try to out-heal this as much as he could while Jasper hammered away on Leon. It kept Emilia focused, and between druids and priests, priests had the better burst heals.

Multiple vines shot out of the ground and whipped Zack, shaving off smaller amounts of health, but sometimes interrupted his spell casting. Zach gritted his teeth and threw another shield over him. It didn't last long under the assault, but it was enough for Zach to cast a stronger heal.

Zach stole a glance at Jasper and Leon. Jasper had the druid in a slight panic with all the elements Jasper threw at him. Zach grinned. Emilia wasn't the only one with a haste ability.

Zach's heart leapt into his throat when another grappling root grabbed him. *Shit.* Emilia still hammered away on him, his health dropping dangerously.

Health: 48%
Health: 32%
Health: 29%

Zach quickly took in his spells, but nothing would break him free of this. Jasper tried to split his attention between Leon and the root, attempting to break its hold prematurely, but that only drew Emilia's attention. Without a dedicated healer, Jasper was forced to waste mana and heal himself.

Fuck. Zach did his best to stay calm. He couldn't panic. They could come back from this.

But Emilia was determined to not make that happen. She focused again on Zach, and by the time he broke free of her grapple, his health was dangerously low.

Health: 19%

His pulse beat heavily in his ears and he started the metal gymnastics for a strong healing spell, when the wind picked up around him. Zach's breath caught. He knew this execute spell all too well.

Zach now had a choice to make.

His eyes flicked from his own mana pool to Jasper and Leon's stats. The Burnout brother wasn't holding up well. His mana had just about been depleted, and his healing spells available weren't matching Jasper's attack.

Zach might be able to out-heal Emilia's attack, but he'd be out of mana, and he'd foolishly used his one allowed mana potion much earlier in the match.

The wind screamed, and slicing blades cut into Zach.

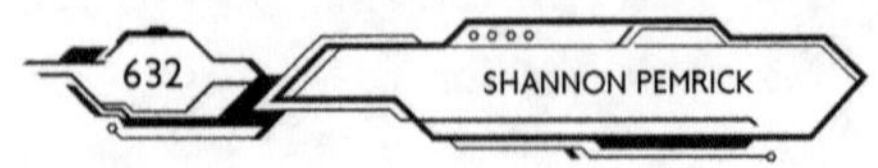

He threw a strong heal onto Jasper, ignoring his own depleting health.

> Health: 18%
> Health: 16%
> Health: 12%

Zach attacked Leon with his strongest available offensive spell, managing a nicely timed crit.

> Health: 9%
> Health: 8%

Zach threw a shield on Jasper, who shot him a concerned look. Zach grinned. "I'm counting on you, Jasper."

He then slammed Emilia with a blinding spell.

> Health: 5%

Her spell wouldn't be canceled with that debuff, but that wasn't his goal. The furious gale sliced one last strong blade into Zach, and his health dropped to zero.

The game ejected Zach from his avatar body into an invisible spectator form. Jasper didn't react to the teammate loss. Like the pro he was, he took advantage of Zach's risky sacrifice and summoned lightning and continued his assault on Leon.

The druid healed himself until his mana ran out. His eyes darted to his sister, who struggled against the blind spell. Leon made a desperate but futile effort to run out of Jasper's range. Jasper summoned a blade of water and sliced the remaining health from the fleeing Burnout member.

Jasper didn't stop to celebrate the small victory. He pivoted and threw lightning at Emilia. Emilia gritted her teeth and made an attack with whipping vines. The blinding spell had half worn off by now, allowing her a minute amount of accuracy, though the attack's damage was reduced.

Zach's pulse pounded in his mind, drowning his scrambled thoughts. This was it. It all came down to this caster-versus-caster showdown.

With the way deaths were calculated to favor the team with the most recent kill, Jasper only had to hold out for the three-minute death timer, and their team would win. *Three minutes. Who ever thought a three-minute timer for the finals was a fantastic idea needs a good slap.*

The blinding effect faded, and Emilia attacked Jasper with ferocity. The two battled it out back and forth with damage spells, self-healing, and debuffs. Every time Jasper made some ground, Emilia would knock him down.

Zach wanted to help, come up with something to say, but without knowing Jasper's available spells, he couldn't give any suggestions to kick her down harder.

And then the inevitable came—out of mana.

The two circled each other, gauging both their opponent and their mana bars for when their small amounts of natural regen would give them a chance to cast. They could go for melee attacks, which were terrible for casters, but still effective enough in this situation. But it also meant their opponent could do the same to them.

Jasper benefited from the stalemate more, but Zach knew Emilia wouldn't let the timer run out.

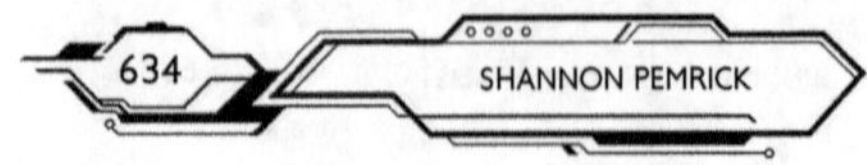

Zach's attention slipped to the countdown in the corner of his vision.

Sixty seconds.

That's all Jasper needed to hold out on.

Emilia launched herself at Jasper, swinging her decorated staff. Jasper took the hit and retaliated with his mace. Blow for blow, they matched each other, only shooting off a spell on the rare occasion.

Zach's eyes flicked back and forth between the match and the timer.

Forty-five seconds.

Health: 37%
Health: 38%

Thirty-two seconds.

Health: 27%
Health: 28%

Twenty-six seconds.

Health: 25%
Health: 24%

Nineteen seconds.

His breathing labored. This was too close. And with both health pools nearly identical and dangerously low, it was now anyone's guess who would pull this off.

Then Emilia grinned. Zach's gut clenched. *No…*

She threw out her hand and a root shot out of the ground, grabbing Jasper by the leg. It wasn't the bigger, mana-draining one she had, but that didn't matter. This allowed her to get out of Jasper's range and pull a potion bottle.

No! She hadn't taken her one allotted mana potion yet.

Right in front of Jasper, she popped the bottle into her mouth and her mana pool ticked up. Dramatically dropping it on the ground, Emilia made a showing of her casting a heavier spell and slamming Jasper.

Health: 13%

Jasper tugged at the root, but it wouldn't matter here. So, he gave up on that and stood his ground with dignity. Emilia hit him again and then readied for the finishing blow.

Jasper chuckled and struck her with a large crackle of lightning when his mana pool ticked up.

Health: 17%

It wouldn't save him, but from the smirk on Emilia's face, she appreciated his ballsy defiance.

Health: 0%

Zach's eyes flicked to the timer.

Ten seconds.

Furious denial roiled in him. They'd only needed ten more seconds and they would have won this!

The arena disappeared, and soon after, the system ejected Zach.

He lay still on the padding cocooning him, allowing

his senses to adjust and his emotions to equalize. The disappointment of getting so far only to trip at the finish line wasn't an easy pill to swallow, even for Zach.

But he did. He'd climb out of this gaming pod and hold his head high, accepting his defeat with dignity and humility. *We made it farther than most ever thought we would, even ourselves. And we put on a good show for it.*

When he was ready, Zach pushed the release button on the inside. The locking mechanism clicked and pistons hissed, allowing the lid to lift. The dim lights of the room were harsh against the darkness of the pod. Zach squinted and took another moment to adjust before attempting to get out. That proved easier said than done. The padding was so form-fitting, he wasn't sure his body wanted to leave.

A GameTech employee ended up having to give him a hand. Zach resisted the urge to rub the back of his neck in his embarrassment. Everyone knew there would be a learning curve to these. And given they were only prototypes, Ajax may make some changes by the time he was ready to release the retail version.

Jasper sat on the edge of his pod, rapping his fingers against it while he stared at the ground. He looked up when Zach approached. He smiled, though it took a moment for it to reach up his face, and the two embraced.

"We did good," Zach murmured, trying hard to see the positive, even though the disappointment stung.

"No, we did great." Jasper pulled away and held Zach by the shoulders. His eyes sparkled. "We did great. We gave them a good run for their money, and I sure as hell can't complain about that exciting finish."

The two of them turned when they heard Leon's

voice moving closer. He argued with his sister in German while she emphatically gestured. At times, those gestures were in Jasper and Zach's direction. *I hope they're not going to act like poor sportsmen with us ruining their streak.*

Emilia didn't come off as the type, given how kind she was when they'd beaten their ass the first time. But Zach wasn't as sure about Leon. He had an ego.

The siblings turned to Jasper and Zach. However, when they were only a few feet away, and before either party could say anything, Ajax hissed Shira's name.

Jasper and Zach turned just in time to see her rushing toward them, breaking a number of rules everyone was told about before the start of the finals—namely, the one where only techs and players were allowed in this room. Everyone else was supposed to remain outside, especially after the finals ended.

They did not anticipate Shira the rule-breaker.

Jasper, being the closest to her, swept Shira into his arms, lifting her up off the ground. She framed his face with her hands and their lips locked.

The kiss didn't last long, and soon Zach found himself with Shira in his arms, also kissing her.

"I am so proud of you both!" Shira beamed. "You did so amazing."

Zach smiled—really smiled. Her praise banished the lingering disappointment Jasper's own words had weakened. The two of them really made him feel like the real winner here.

Leon grumbled something in German, drawing their attention back to the brother-sister team.

Shira snickered. "He's upset you two get such special treatment when they were the ones who won."

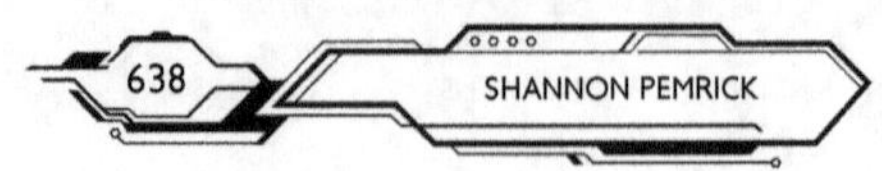

Leon's eyebrows shot up, and his sister laughed. Zach suspected he didn't expect her to be capable of translating.

Jasper tossed his head toward Leon, giving her the silent okay to give him something if she wanted. Zach didn't feel a need to say no. He felt possessive of Shira in certain ways, but not *that* possessive. And he trusted she'd do something appropriate.

Shira sashayed up to Leon and cupped his face, pulling him down for a kiss on the cheek. "*Herzlichen Glückwunsch.*"

A goofy grin spread over Leon's face. Shira looked at his sister, who held up a hand and shook her head.

"Shira," Ajax hissed. "Get back here. You're going to get us in trouble."

Shira rolled her eyes and waved to them before strolling away to rejoin Ajax. Her pace really showed she didn't care what anyone thought of her behavior. Zach loved it.

"Isn't zat your coach?" Leon asked.

"Coach, girlfriend, and certified personal ass-kicker. Yeah, that's her," Jasper said.

Leon rubbed his cheek where Shira kissed him. "Lucky you."

Didn't they both know it.

Emilia rolled her eyes, clearly not impressed with her brother. She then held out her hand to Zach for a handshake.

Zach smiled and happily grabbed her hand. "You two are something else."

"Of course we are," Leon said. Winning, even with a broken streak, did nothing to humble him. "But you are not so bad."

It was probably going to be the best compliment they'd get out of him.

Jasper shook hands with Emilia next. "I thought I had you until you pulled that potion. That was a wicked play."

The woman smiled brightly and tried to sign something in ASL for Zach to understand, but she struggled, so turned to her brother to translate. Unfortunately, she seemed to go a little too fast for him, and she stomped her foot with impatience.

"Hold on," her brother complained. "I need to translate twice."

She rolled her eyes so hard, one might have thought they'd pop out of her head.

Zach pressed his lips together so he wouldn't laugh. The two's antics were amusing. Yet, he sympathized with Leon. Translating one language for a conversation was hard enough.

Leon opened his mouth to translate when he caught up, only to pause. His brow furrowed, and he spoke to his sister in German. From the tone, Zach guessed he was asking for clarification.

Of course, Emilia just gave him an exasperated look only a sibling could give.

Leon sighed. "Emilia says she enjoyed ze match. And she wants to…" He squinted as he searched for the right word. "Rematch?"

Jasper grinned. "I'm down for practice and rematches."

A bright smile pulled up Emilia's face to her ears, and she threw a fist in the air. She then whipped out her phone, and they shared contacts.

The four of them left the room together, holding relatively easy conversation. Leon warmed up to them as

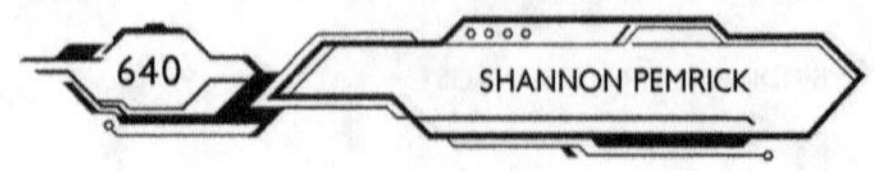

they went, but Zach had a feeling his attitude wouldn't change a whole lot.

They split their separate ways when friends and family swarmed Jasper and Zach. Serenity was sad they didn't win, but happy they almost won. The praise, even when losing, did wonders for Zach. They really had done well.

"No regrets?" Jasper said to Ajax.

Their friend laughed. "Not at all! You two really know how to put on a good show, even if you don't win."

"We all know it was Shira's magic pep talk that did all the work," Mercedes teased.

Shira rolled her eyes while the guys laughed. She wasn't entirely wrong. Without Shira there to give them the kick in the ass they needed in the gentlest way possible for her, the two of them would have given up after that third loss. They needed her more than she probably realized.

Narissa checked her phone. "We're not all that late for the Lion Rage presentation. We could make it to most of it if we all hurry."

That would be the last one before the trophy ceremony for all the tournaments, and then the closing ceremony. And it would be good to support Darius if they could.

Shira turned away from them to speak with someone Zach couldn't see around their friends.

"Oh, right, that," Ajax mumbled, as if he knew what was going on.

Jasper and Zach passed each other a look.

Shira whipped back around. "Alex is here for the interview."

"I can regroup if you want to hold off until after the convention. I'm easy to work with," the disembodied voice said.

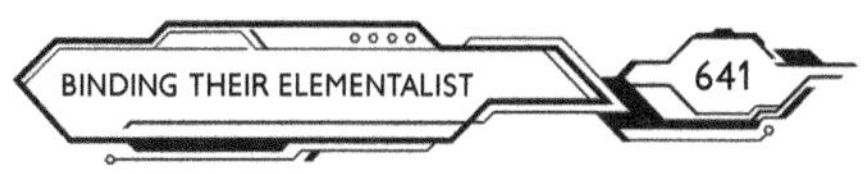

Jasper's brow rose. "Interview?"

Shira smirked. "Yeah, while you were getting your rears kicked, Alex approached us about an interview."

"I couldn't see the harm in you two doing one," Ajax said.

Zach tipped sideways to peer around their friends. Alex waved. "You sure you don't want to interview the actual winners?"

Alex's eyes widened. "Are you kidding? After that performance, I want to hear it all from you two. And the fact I scored a one-month exclusive while others were so focused on securing their interviews with Burnout, I'm not giving up that chance for anything."

His gaze flicked to Shira. "Plus, I also get my interview with Shira."

Zach and Jasper passed her an impressed look. She shrugged. "It's not that big a deal."

Both he and Jasper tipped their heads at her. *Not a big deal, my ass.*

Their spitfire of an elementalist had really grown into the raging inferno they always believed she was. He couldn't wait to grow with her, for as long as she wanted them around.

Laughter burst from Shira's lips, and she held her sides. Her friends laughed around her at Ajax's stupid joke. They all lounged outside on her patio. After the closing ceremony, no one wanted to part ways. It was one of the few times so many of them were in the same place. So, Shira recommended they all head back here

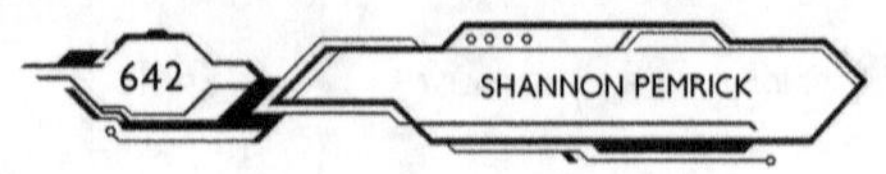

to hang out, and extended the invite to any of their other guild mates in town.

Jasper and Ajax happily took on the grilling duties while Shira and a few others whipped up some sides and drinks.

Serenity happily splashed in the pool, playing with Snake, which was a good distraction for her. Shira's eyes glanced at the mound of wrapped gifts set up on a side table. This get-together had also turned into a mini birthday party and Serenity wanted desperately to open all the generous gifts immediately. But Christine wanted to bake her a special cake, so she was forced to wait.

Zach lifted his head from her shoulder, having finally gotten himself under control. Shira sat comfortably on his lap after he'd pulled her there. Her friends made a few teasing comments, but this time Shira didn't have to fight any urge to deny and hide away. Embracing these deep emotions she'd bottled up and denied for so long was an incredibly freeing sensation.

Scott ran into the kitchen when Christine called for him, and then a moment later, Christine stepped out onto the patio. "Time for cake!"

Serenity screeched and launched out of the pool faster than Shira thought possible. Jasper intercepted her with a towel, and Shira threw one over Snake before he had the chance to shake all over everyone.

Once both were sufficiently dried, Serenity climbed up onto her chair and squirmed, waiting for her grandfather to bring the cake out. When he did, Shira's mouth fell open.

Scott carried a sizable red and black frosted cake with several burning candles and an enormous Rathalos figurine on top. Everyone sang happy birthday to Serenity. Her eyes glowed watching her grandfather carry the impressive cake over.

Serenity gasped and then squealed when the cake was set in front of her. "This is amazing, Nana!"

Christine soaked up the praise from her granddaughter. In Shira's eyes, she deserved it. This was an impressive cake. The longer she gazed at it, the more little details she found.

Kiara, the resident pastry chef in their group of friends, also gushed over the delicious piece of art.

Serenity made a wish and then blew out her candles, only to find one of them a trick candle. Instead of being irritated, Serenity laughed and blew on the candle a few times before it finally went out for good. Jasper helped Serenity cut the first piece, since she insisted she wanted to make her slice, revealing the two-tier chocolate layers.

Christine also brought out some ice cream for those who didn't want cake, or wanted to overload themselves with sugar—like Serenity.

Shira struggled not to scarf down her incredibly moist and tasty piece. *Christine should have sold cakes for a living.* She wasn't the only one who thought that. Kiara continued to gush and begged to know her secret. Given how delicious Kiara's treats were, that was some heavy praise.

Naturally, Serenity was ready to open all her gifts before she even finished her cake and ice cream. Shira convinced her to at least clean her plate before they went to the gifts. Even if the surrounding adults hadn't finished, she'd been patient long enough to be rewarded.

Jasper and Zach grabbed some gifts at random. To Shira's surprise, Serenity didn't tear into her gifts the

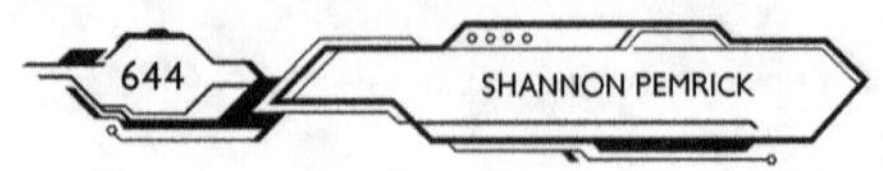

moment they were set in front of her. She took the time to appreciate the wrapping and read out all the tags before tearing the paper.

Kiara and Valerie had given her various baking and cooking goodies. Takashi and Mercedes gifted her a fascinating origami-like light she could build herself into three different animals. Her grandparents gave her some science kits that looked like they'd make the perfect amount of mess she'd love—and her parents would hate the cleanup for.

The gifts continued, though Shira noted Jasper and Zach were particular about skipping a select group of gifts. She knew one of them was the gift from the three of them, but she wasn't quite sure about the other three, especially the really large one. It had to be the biggest box in the pile.

Then it finally came time for those gifts. Jasper first gave her two thin rectangular boxes of similar sizes.

Serenity cocked her head when she read one of them coming from Shira and her dads. "I gots a gift? Daddy, you said the co-vention was my gift."

Jasper kissed her on the head. "We thought you deserved anothah gift."

Serenity grinned and ripped into the wrapping paper. Contained underneath was a hand-crafted box Shira made in her craft room. Serenity turned it in different ways, taking in the fun little details Shira had stuck on them that gave hints of what lay inside. Serenity then shook the box, like she did a lot of her gifts, only to hear nothing.

Serenity pursed her lips. "Is it empty?"

The adults laughed, and Shira assured her there was

something inside. So, her daughter opened the box. She gasped and squealed.

Inside was a printed paper with the cover of the Monster Hunter ranching game she had wanted but forgotten her dads were going to look into getting her. Since game downloads were all digital, they'd come up with a creative way to surprise her, without having to use her handheld, which was currently still downloading the insanely large game.

"I wanna play this right now!" Serenity announced as she bounced in her seat.

"But, Starship, you've still got some gifts left," Shira said.

Serenity's eyes rounded. "But… but it's the game I wanted!"

Zach kissed her on the head. "The game is still downloading. You'll have to wait either way."

Serenity pouted. Zach nudged the other wrapped box. "Open this one. You're going to love it."

Shira's brow rose. What did he know about it? Serenity read off Darius' name, so it wasn't some secret gift from Jasper and Zach that Shira didn't know about, but it was clear they knew something about this gift.

Serenity tore open the wrapping, revealing another handmade box. This one wasn't as neatly created as Shira's, but the thought was there. Serenity then blinked when she opened the box, which revealed a cover of Lusara Fates.

She looked up at her dads and then Darius. "But I can't play dis game yet."

"Sure you can," Ajax said, grabbing the obscenely large box waiting to be opened, and plunking it down in front of Serenity. "Happy birthday, kiddo."

Serenity stared at the wrapped box for a moment before screeching and flinging Darius' gift toward Kiara by accident. Everyone laughed as she tore open the wrapping to reveal the new portable gaming headset that would be age-approved for her.

The girl wrapped her arms around the box and hugged her now-favorite gift. "Thank you, thank you, thank you! Now I can play with Daddy, Dad, and She-ra! I wanna play right now!"

"Later," Jasper said, causing their daughter to pout.

"Ajax, I thought those were still just prototypes," Shira said. She didn't remember his talking about this going to market during the reveal. Though maybe she'd missed some information while playing the demo.

He shook his head. "The pods are still in the prototyping stage, but this new portable design is already up for preorder. My sister was working on the new age-tech upgrade long before I got to working on the new pod designs this past summer."

That made sense.

"Is that all the gifts, then?" Scott asked, looking at the table where the gifts had been.

"No, there's one more," Zach said, grabbing the last remaining small box. "It's from Narissa."

Serenity gratefully accepted the gift and gave the amazing wrapping job a good, appreciative once-over. Narissa really knew how to wrap a gift, that was for sure. But, the hands of a seven-year-old could not be stopped from destroying all the meticulous work.

Beneath the wrapping was a sleek black box with no identifiable print. Serenity cocked her head and then opened the hinged lid. Inside, nestled in black satin, was a sleek watch. Serenity gasped and pulled the timepiece. "She-ra, this is the thing you won today!"

As if reacting to her voice, the screen of the watch lit up, and then a beam of light burst out into a spherical force field. A small, doll-like figure with pale skin, black and red spellcaster robes, and red dragon scale crest with horns materialized in front of Serenity. A spiky red tail swished behind him.

"Hello, Serenity," Alistair said, the AI's green eyes blinking slowly at her. "I hope this form is acceptable to you. If not, we can use the app on one of your parents' phones to go through the customization options. I can also have more than one saved appearance to appeal to each of you, since I have been registered to three owners."

Serenity stared at the AI projection, tears brimming her eyes. She reached out to touch it, only for her fingers to phase through the pseudo-physical form. "You get to be with me all the time?"

"All the time, Starship," the AI confirmed.

She held the watch close to her chest. Shira's throat tightened. It was clear in the way she always talked to the AI she loved it like her best friend. This was such a thoughtful gift.

"Narissa," Kiara said quietly, so as not to ruin the girl's moment. "How did you get one? The company said they were only available for preorder, beyond the few lucky people who won them."

Tarvos, the leading company for AI technology, and the creators of the AI tech everyone here used, was one of the few non-game-related companies to hype up a new release, given AI tech was becoming so integrated in gamer life. They'd announced the new watch tech, which created a holographic avatar of the AI companion. To hype up the new tech up for preorder, with a release shortly before Christmas, they gave away one hundred of their watches to convention attendees.

Shira glanced down at the watch on her wrist. She, Narissa, and Takashi ended up being lucky winners.

"No, I didn't get my hands on another one," Narissa said, smiling. "That's the one I won. I thought Serenity would love to have it instead."

Serenity gasped. "But this one is yours!"

Narissa shook her head. "Not anymore. I permanently registered your AI onto the device."

At present, the company had only gotten a single AI to work on a device at a time. AIs could be swapped out in homes that had multiple AIs owned by single users if they did a temporary registry, but until the technology improved, they couldn't be used at the same time.

Serenity held the timepiece against her chest. "Thank you."

She then turned to Shira. "Momma, is Orion done installing on yours?"

"I am," Orion said from the house. "As are all the other AIs."

It'd been decided, since so few had gotten their hands on the giveaway units, they'd all temporarily register their AIs to the won units to see what their AIs might look like. It'd create hype for those who had to wait until next month, as Narissa had gone ahead and preordered all their friends one. It was all too generous of her, but she wouldn't listen to anyone who insisted she didn't need to go that far.

Serenity held her watch out to Narissa. "Rissa, I want to see your AI, too."

Narissa smiled and nodded, taking the timepiece from her.

Shira played with her watch, checking out the various settings not related to the AI program, and then opened the app. She scrolled through the various customizable pieces to Orion's avatar, and scrolled through the options until she was happy. She saved the avatar and then Orion took over the rest.

The hologram projection activated and created the technological field needed for the AI's form to move about freely around her. Orion appeared as a semi-robotic bard doll with a blue lute. Shira had given him a big puffy purple hat with a blue translucent ribbon attached on the top. Puffy purple sleeves covered his small arms, and matching purple pants billowed around his legs. His body comprised of two blue and orange metal spheres that hovered close together but never touched, as if held together by magnets or some other invisible force.

Shira gazed at her AI's avatar, smiling at this very real moment of her artificial companion that'd been with her through her worst days, having a pseudo-form.

Takashi handed his watch over to Mercedes to try first. She eagerly had Tasha boot up into the watch. Tasha took the form of a tan-skinned woman with red and orange hair pulled up into two side buns by wide metal bands. She wore a blue skirt, and over that a pale orange long shirt with a dark orange pattern that looked a lot like a waveform. A blue scarf was wrapped around her neck, and Tasha's eyes matched her shirt, her pupils

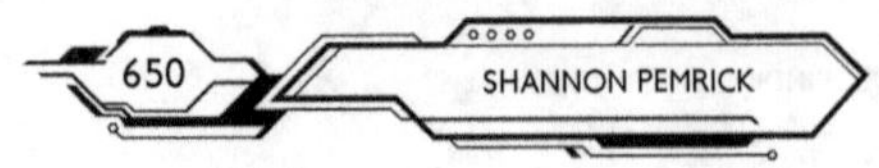

even having a waveform that actually moved, as if she were monitoring Mercedes' heart rate.

Tasha hovered by Mercedes, her arms crossed and a disapproving frown on her cute face. Mercedes squealed, loving her AI's form.

Shira turned toward Narissa when she had Picard temporarily registered with Serenity's device. The AI projected as a dark-skinned gentleman with slicked back black hair and thick moustache. He was dressed in a fine tuxedo, and had metal earmuffs on his ears that made them look like elf ears. Attached to the left one was a digital, square monocle, which hovered in front of his eye.

Picard hovered next to Narissa with his eyes closed and arms behind his back.

Narissa giggled. "Is that what you want to look like, Picard?"

"I find it quite dignified, Doctor Narissa," her AI said.

Shira noticed, with the extra digital fields overlapping, Orion could move about more, as if the fields synced up. *This is so amazing.*

Digital flower petals flowed through the patio. Takashi had taken over the watch, and now Ochi hovered around him as a pale man with short gray hair. He had on a green jacket with long sleeves that hung longer than his body, and green pants. An open gray vest was pulled over the jacket, and tucked in his hair on the top of his head, he had two speakers that looked a bit like frog eyes to Shira. He also had some spheres attached to the back of his head in a cascading line, like a braid of hair. These spheres lit up with a green light, but as the AI looked Takashi's way, who was looking at his girlfriend, the lights turned red, like the AI was monitoring Takashi's emotions, and the AI tossed out rose petals around the couple. Takashi and Mercedes laughed.

Ajax was next when Narissa handed him the timepiece, after Serenity's approval. The girl was really into seeing everyone's AIs that this point. Ajax's AI, Kirk, came out as a burly, blue-skinned orc with red eyes. He had some sort of black and white training gear that clung to his muscular form, and a red sash cinching his waist. Bulky metal bands that Shira suspected were supposed to look like weights clamped Kirk's wrists, and black and red headphones were perched on the AI's head.

Both Ajax and Kirk flexed with each other, making Narissa laugh and Serenity cheer and clap.

And the fun didn't stop there. Kiara desperately wanted her turn, and the more AIs were shown off, the more excited everyone was to have their own.

Shira reclined in her seat, smiling and watching all these important people in her life enjoying their time together. Her heart swelled with how amazing it was to surround herself with all these people and it feel normal to her.

Long gone was the scared woman who struggled to leave her house to be seen by other humans. Gone was the frightened woman who struggled to see her self-worth. Absent was the lonely person, afraid to give her heart to someone else.

Shira pulled out her phone and pulled up an image Zach had shared with her earlier. It was from their time on the beach when Zach took those photos of her in her sun hat. She smiled at the life in her own eyes looking back at her.

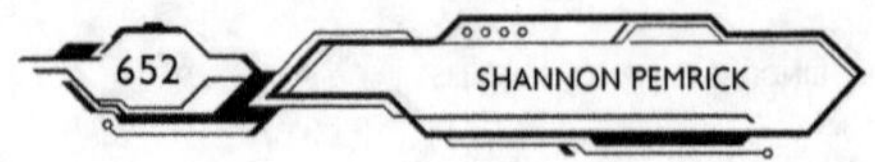

Her fingers tapped the screen, setting that image as her profile picture on her social media. And then, she changed her relationship status.

Shira set her phone face-down on the table and smiled and laughed along with her friends. She hugged her daughter and stole kisses from her boyfriends.

Mercedes came up behind her and pulled her into a hug and Kiara lifted her phone to snap a photo. Shira smiled, without flinching away or faking her joy.

She might still be a little broken, but she was healing. And she had everything she'd ever wanted right here.

EPILOGUE

The BMW pulled into the driveway and cut into park. Shira adjusted her sunglasses before slipping out and taking in a deep breath of the warm spring morning air. She shut the car door and turned, taking in the sight of Jasper and Zach climbing out of the vehicle as well and gazing at her house.

Serenity's giggling caught Shira's attention, and she looked down, finding both her and Snake standing next to her. The young girl practically bounced in her giddiness.

"I see someone has mastered her booster buckle," Shira said.

A wide, pleased grin spread over Serenity's face. "Of course I did! I'm seven now, and I can do things on my own without help."

Oh boy. Little Miss Independent was getting even more so, and quickly. Shira had a good idea how insane this was making Jasper.

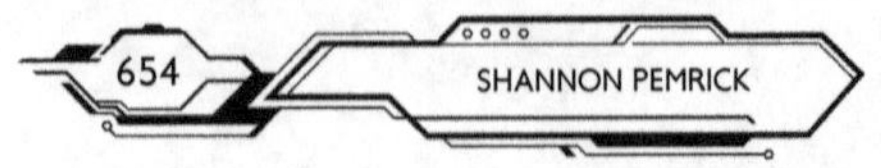

"Can we go inside now?" Serenity asked.

Shira glanced at her two *boyfriends* to find them still gawking at the house. She thought their reaction to the Los Angeles vacation home was interesting. Today would be even more so. *I wonder how they'll react to some of the other vacation homes we've got.*

She dropped the thought. One step at a time. "Yeah, we can go in now."

They could grab the luggage later.

Serenity squealed and ran off for the front door with Snake. Shira grabbed Jasper's hand, giving him a firm tug to follow, snapping him out of his daze, and the two of them walked around the car to grab Zach.

"Ready?" Shira asked them.

"Honestly, no," Jasper admitted. "But it's not like we have any other choice."

"Well, you do," Shira said, leading the way up the walk. "It's just not the option any of us want."

"And that makes it a non-option," Zach said.

Shira rolled her eyes.

Serenity bounced in place, too eager to stand still or even to peer into the windows around the door to get a good peek inside, and then practically begged Shira to unlock the door quicker. Sure, Shira could have Orion do it, but making the three of them wait just a little longer was more fun.

When the door swung open, Serenity burst inside, though surprisingly, she didn't go running around like crazy. She stopped inside the small foyer and removed her shoes before gazing around in a far calmer manner than Shira thought would be possible with all her excitement a moment ago.

Even Snake poked the little girl with his nose, as if her sudden energy drop concerned him.

Shira led the guys inside, and slipped off her shoes while they took in everything in visible sight, from the open living room to the spacious kitchen, and then the elegant dining room.

Serenity turned back to Shira and gazed up with big, pleading eyes. "Can I go exploring now?"

Shira placed her hands on her hips. "Well, duh. But is it really exploring when I've shown you every room like a million times over video chat?"

"Of course!" Serenity's back straightened. "In person and on a video are much different. Like you're much prettier in person, Momma."

Shira choked up as emotions flared instantly at that name. She wasn't sure when she'd stop reacting like that, but Shira hoped it wasn't anytime soon. "Well, with that logic, then have at it, Starship. This is your new port. You need to know how to navigate around it."

Serenity giggled and unhooked Snake from his leash. Snake bolted into the kitchen for a drink of water, and his faithful companion followed.

This allowed Shira to take in Zach and Jasper's states. As she expected, they weren't able to hide their awe. "Well, what do you think?"

Jasper made an attempt to speak, failed and blinked, then tried again, but failed again, making Shira laugh. "Elementalist got your tongue?"

That seemed to help snap him out of his daze, though instead of the house, he focused on her. His eyes trailed down her body, taking Shira in inch by inch. "Not yet, but maybe soon."

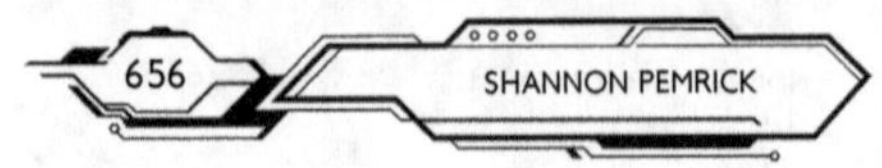

Heat bloomed in her chest and spread south between her legs the longer he gazed at her. It'd been months since she'd been with them in person. Sure, she was with them every day technically in game, but this was different. Their presence was just that much more real here. It made her ache for their touch.

Serenity came barreling back into the foyer. "Can I go check out my room now?"

Her room. Shira had to swallow a forming lump to speak. "This is your home too, now. You don't have to ask permission."

The biggest smile Shira had ever seen on Serenity—since the three of them sat her down to tell her the news about the development of their relationship—bloomed on her adorable face. And then she was gone, taking the stairs as if it were an Olympic sport she'd been preparing for her whole life.

Shira couldn't take her eyes off the retreating girl, emotions swimming in her chest. After Ajax made his announcement to take Jasper and Zach on as Game-Tech's official first esports team, the planning had begun.

The guys decided they'd move to California. It made sense to them, given they'd need to meet with Ajax several times a year in person, and do far more public events than what their past company had. There was also the added factor of dating Shira.

Sure, they could have sat down to figure out living situations after they'd dated a while, but this was a no-brainer in their minds.

And Jasper's parents didn't complain either when they heard the news. Even Cheryl took the news well. Hell, Shira was pretty sure Jasper's sister wanted them gone by how she offered to help them pack immediately. It took her a little while to learn that was just how Jasper and his sister were with each other.

It made Shira feel a little guilty, since, even if their job wasn't the ultimate reason for the move and Shira herself had been, she'd be forcing them to leave Jasper's sister behind. Jasper had caught onto the guilt fairly early and did his best to reassure her.

It also helped her through their next decision: the three of them moving in with her.

It might have been fast for many, but it came from a logical standpoint in her mind. Apartment costs in Los Angeles were crazy high. Not that San Francisco was much better, but L.A. had been the primary focus at first for their move.

Shira had offered them the Manhattan Beach house to rent, with her parents' approval, of course, but the guys didn't feel right doing that.

And that left them with one last choice.

"Are you guys sure you want to move in?" Shira asked. "I know it was a bit crazy for me to offer so soon. I could have helped you find a nice apartment to live in first."

Jasper and Zach had made it clear that if they were moving, they'd move to be close to her. At first, they rationalized the choice to not ask her to move to Los Angeles with them was because Shira already had a house she loved and a mortgage that only had a few years left to go, as well as her own family and friends. But then things started to rapidly expand with Narissa's cybernetic modeling agency idea, and they were going to need to cover more than the one city.

This gave Shira a life path she never thought about:

running a modeling agency herself. She and Narissa agreed Shira would take on ownership of a branch of the agency to help get things going in San Francisco, and she would do so in partnership with her parents' business, offering both companies a great advantage.

Jasper stepped into her personal bubble and cupped her face. "How many times are we gonna have to tell you, we're glad ya offered to let us move in wicked quickly, so we didn't have to be the ones to impose the question?"

Heat seared Shira's cheeks. She'd made the proposal rather hastily, but it was her guys who'd jumped on the offer even quicker. She swore she didn't even have the whole suggestion out before they were nodding and accepting.

"And don't you dare bring up the commute again for when we need to meet up with Ajax, or do some mandatory company PR thing. You're worth that extra time."

Shira pressed her lips together. She had been about to mention it.

Zach slid his arm around her waist. "We've known each other long enough, this makes sense. Now we can discover each other's living habits and learn to adapt. It's really the only thing missing, and we can't learn that if we don't live together."

Jasper planted a tender kiss on Shira's forehead, and her stomach did its stupid swoop thing. *Damn these men…*

"We're in this together, no mattuh what happens going forwahd," he said.

Zach pressed his mouth against the cybernetics on her neck. "We love you, remember?"

Shira's lower lip caught between her teeth, heat

spreading from her face, down her body and to her extremities. They hadn't touched her *real* body in so long, this was slowly blooming into torture. "I love you both as well."

Jasper tipped her head up and bent his down, his lips brushing against hers. "God, we've missed you."

He kissed her, slow and soft, savoring her as if she was the first drink of water after being lost in a desert. Or maybe that was her, because, hell, did she feel thirsty now.

Shira ran her palms up Jasper's stomach, feeling the flexing hard muscles of his abs under his shirt. She didn't care they were still in the foyer. She wanted to take advantage of every moment she had with her two guys, because she only had a week with them.

As eager as the three were to move in with Shira, Jasper and Zach agreed they wouldn't pull Serenity from school early. She was already going to say goodbye to a lot of her friends. They wanted to make the transition easier over a summer break. It also gave them time to coordinate ways for Serenity to stay in contact with her closer friends, like Alex.

So, this week, they took advantage of a vacation of hers to fly out and visit Shira, as well as bring along some things to leave here before the major move.

Quiet giggling interrupted them. All three adults looked up the stairs at Serenity.

"Yes, Starship?" Jasper asked slowly.

"Which room is gonna be the baby's room?" she asked.

Shira's mind blanked. *What did she ask?*

Jasper sighed. "Serenity, we already told you, there's no baby."

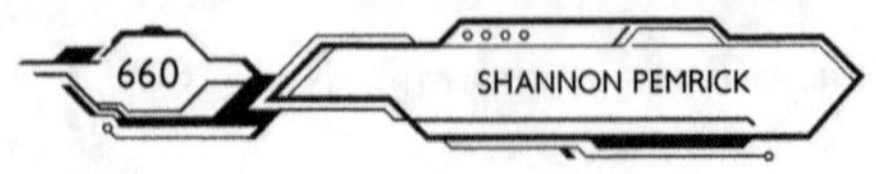

"But you said you and dad were gonna have a baby with Shira soon."

Shira's brain finally caught up, and she stared at her two guys in disbelief. "You told her? I told you not to get excited about this!"

Zach held up his hands. "We didn't tell her anything specific. She overheard us talking about it after you told us the news. We were a little too excited, we didn't think to make sure a little mouse wasn't eavesdropping." He glanced up to Serenity and projected his voice. "But we made it wicked clear there was no plan for any siblings anytime soon."

Ever since the accident, Shira had struggled with the idea she'd never have the family she'd dreamed of. Any mention of it messed her up, and because of that, she'd avoided the topic whenever her mom brought it up.

But her mother knew something important regarding this, and wouldn't allow Shira to avoid the conversation anymore after her parents found out about her official relationship with Jasper and Zach. Anita sat Shira down and revealed to her that when Shira had been going through surgery, Anita and Flynn had been given a huge medical choice.

Shira's uterus couldn't be saved in full, but, if allowed, what could be would be harvested and preserved until medical technology had advanced where it could be regrown or recreated. Because her parents knew Shira had wanted a family, they made the choice to go ahead with that plan. If Shira hadn't wanted to continue the preservation later, once she was in the right presence of mind to make such decisions, it could be disposed of at that point.

Her mother then proceeded to remind Shira of the eggs she'd frozen when she was twenty. Shira hadn't been sure how long she'd focus on her modeling career for, so it'd been a choice she made, as a just-in-case.

The news had shocked Shira, as well as given her new hope. But it hadn't prepared her for the breaking medical news announced two months ago. A medical lab had successfully created an organic lung using donated tissue. Furthermore, they planned to create several more organs, to be sure they could replicate their results, and if they could, they would start opening up trials.

Shira had been so excited, she immediately told the guys. She knew she should have been more controlled, especially since she needed to make sure she didn't get her hopes up, but the reality was just too much for her to handle alone.

Serenity stared down at Shira with a confused expression. "You're not having a baby, She-ra?"

Shira sat down on the stairs and beckoned Serenity to come down and sit with her. She did, gazing up at Shira with intense interest.

"No, I'm not having a baby. There's been some medical advancement that may allow me to have a baby of my own someday, but there are no guarantees."

"If you can't have a baby, then what?"

"Then, if your dads and I are up for it, we will look into something called surrogacy, or we will adopt."

"Like you were?"

"Yes, like I was."

Adoption had always been on the table. Shira had just been so relationship-adverse, she never thought about adoption because of the unlikely chance agencies would approve of her single status.

Serenity pursed her lips. "So, what room will be the baby's if I get a little baby brother or sister?"

Shira couldn't stop the amused chuckle. *Determined as always.* "We'll figure that out when the time comes. In the meantime, you have to focus on your own room plans."

Serenity's eyes lit up. "My room is wicked big! So much bigguh than my room back home. I'm gonna need more stuff."

Jasper and Zach both choked.

"Why don't we focus on making sure all your stuff will fit in this room first, then we can discuss the prospect of filling it more," Jasper said.

Zach opened the door. "We can start with what we packed in your suitcase."

Serenity cheered and ran back up to her room while Zach retrieved the bag.

Shira's phone double *pinged*, and she pulled it out of her pocket.

"Whatcha got?" Jasper asked.

"Oh, just a reminder about Narissa's baby shower on Thursday." Shira squinted at her phone to make sure she was reading this text right. "And it looks like Kiara is planning a last-minute surprise birthday party for Darius. She wants to capitalize on everyone being in L.A. and wanted to throw it for Friday."

Jasper shrugged. "I don't see why not. Would your parents be up to watching Serenity for an extra day?"

Shira snorted. "Are you kidding? They'd take her for the next three months if we asked. My mom seriously told me they need to make up for 'seven years of lost time' with their grandbaby."

The biggest and brightest smile spread over Jasper's face. Shira knew her parents' acceptance of them meant a lot to Jasper. Though, she had to privately admit it didn't quite compare to Zach's reaction the last time it'd come up around him.

Zach returned with Serenity's suitcase and hauled it upstairs. It was then that Jasper noticed the digital photo frames on the wall angling up to the next floor. He took them in, one by one, each photograph depicting unique moments of Jasper, Zach, Serenity, and Shira.

One of the digital frames swapped out a photo for one that made Jasper pause. Shira swallowed. She hadn't told Jasper or Zach about this little wall decoration she worked up, especially not some of the particular photos she added. She hoped Jasper wouldn't be upset.

Jasper reached out and touched the wedding photo of him and Sara. After a moment, it phased out to one of Sara holding Serenity as an infant. Another photo in the next frame over changed to of the three of them, happy and smiling.

"I had the AIs get those to me in secret," Shira admitted quietly. "I wanted to surprise you. She's part of this family, and I thought it would be best to show that with these photos."

Jasper stared for a moment longer, the photo of Shira and Sara popping up, and then in a blink, he descended on her. His mouth captured hers. Shira squeaked, not expecting this reaction.

He pulled away and smiled at her, tears brimming in his eyes. "Thank you."

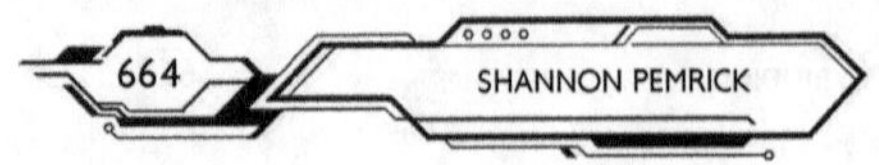

Shira smiled. She still struggled with the guilt, knowing she was a big reason he lost Sara. Jasper had reassured her over and over that he didn't blame her, and tried to remind Shira that Sara had gone to the convention of her own free will, and none of them could have ever predicted what would happen that day.

Therapy had also helped Shira process it all. Sometimes she found herself still shocked that Tanya and Sara were the same person. And yet, it also made so much sense that she wasn't sure why she hadn't realized the connection sooner.

Jasper pulled away and gazed deep into her eyes. "Come back to Boston with us until we move."

Shira blinked. "W—what?"

"Come live with us in Boston for a bit."

She opened her mouth, but words failed her. *Spend the next two months on the East Coast with them?*

"That would mean you'd have to fly back with us, but I thought maybe it'd be possible now? And then we can all fly cross-country togethah for the move out here."

Shira let out a slow breath. She'd done well with the whole buildings issue, working so damned hard to overcome it. But was she up for flying? "Can I think about it?"

"Yeah, of course," Jasper said, his voice sincere. "There's no pressure. We'd just like for you to see Boston with us, meet Cheryl and Ray, and honestly, we really just don't wanna be apaht from you for that damned long again."

Her heart lurched. He made it hard to say no.

"No pressure, but we are hoping you say yes, because

we already bought your ticket," Zach said from the landing above.

Shira's eyes popped wide. "You two did not prepay a flight for me."

Jasper shrugged, unapologetic. "Cheapuh and easiuh to coordinate with our return flight than a last-minute booking."

Shira puffed out her cheeks. Now there was a greater weight of obligation to say yes. Flights weren't cheap. "I'll say yes right now if you guarantee you've got a buyer for your beat-up car."

Jasper let out an exasperated sigh. "Why are you so insistent I sell the Subie?"

"Because it's a piece of junk?" Zach teased.

"She's not! She might need a bit of a tune-up, and maybe a paht or two replaced, but she's a good cah. Sure, maybe she can't do the cross-country trip herself. We can tow her."

Shira chuckled, and a wicked grin pulled her lips. Jasper stepped back with unease, but she jumped to her feet and grabbed his hand. "I'll show you why."

Jasper resisted, clearly not trusting her, but one glance back at him, and he was putty in her hands. Shira led them both to the door of the attached garage.

She grabbed the handle but didn't open the door, glancing back at her boyfriends. "Ready?"

They exchanged bewildered looks and then nodded.

Shira swung open the door and stepped into the spacious three-car garage. "Tah-dah!"

She gestured to the brand new 2108 Subaru Crosstrek with horizon-blue pearl paint, then turned back to Jasper

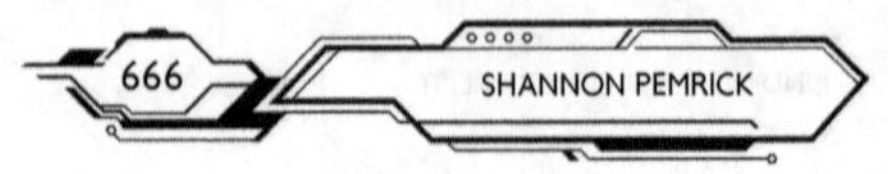

and Zach. Their expressions were as priceless as she'd hoped. Jasper's mouth literally hung open.

"Shira… What did you do?" Jasper asked slowly. "You did not buy me a cah."

She smiled, pleased with herself. "I present to you, your new *cah*. Now you can get rid of your beater because you don't need it."

Jasper took several steps forward, gazing in awe at his new vehicle.

Zach slipped in behind Shira and bent close to her ear. "You're going to tell us how much that cost you, so we can pay you back, right?"

Shira pressed her lips together. She refused to give that up so easily.

"Shira," Alistair said through the house infrastructure, the AI's voice much different now. "I am reporting in, so you're aware most of my upgrades are complete. There are some upgrades I will have to hold off on until the move-in, as they are incompatible with the Boston apartment."

Jasper whipped around to face her, his eyes wide. "You bought him upgrades, too?"

"Jasper and Zach will need newer phones when those final upgrades are made," Alistair said.

"Make sure replacements are on order by the time we're all packed up and heading cross-country," Shira said.

"No," Jasper said. He took a step toward her. "You're not paying for our new phones. And you sure as hell are telling us how much ya paid for this cah so we can pay you back."

Shira stiffened her spine and held her head high. "You

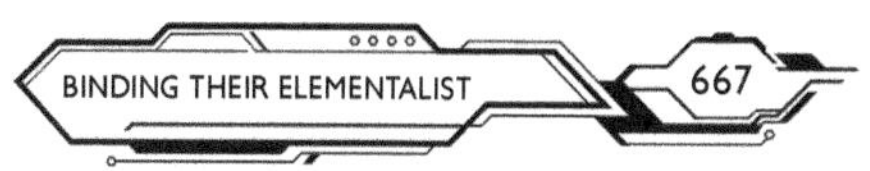

both decided you wanted me in your life, so you're just going to have to get used to this."

Jasper sucked in a deep breath through his nose. The blue in his eyes deepened, and his gaze flicked down to her mouth. "Fine. Then we'll have to pay you back in other ways. Right now, we're going to test out how roomy that back is."

He grabbed her by the hips and yanked her into his hard body, crashing his mouth into her. Shira groaned, heat instantly pooling between her thighs. She wasn't going to say no to this kind of repayment, because it was the only way she'd allow it at this point.

They were in this for the long haul. She was getting everything she wanted in life, and more. Nothing would stand in her way of keeping these two men in her life and making them happy. And nothing would impede the love and happiness she deserved.

ABOUT THE AUTHOR

Shannon Pemrick is a full-time USA Today best-selling author of slow-burn romantic fantasy, fuller-time geek, and dragon obsessed. She also has too many novelty mugs, not enough chocolate, and a forbidden love-affair with all things shiny. When she's not burning her fingers across a keyboard handing out adventures and HEAs, she's rolling dice and getting lost in RPGs or searching for brides for her dragon overlords.

You can learn more about Shannon by visiting her website at:
Shannonpemrick.com

www.ingramcontent.com/pod-product-compliance
Lightning Source LLC
Chambersburg PA
CBHW060740210726
48292CB00012B/23